The Empire Of Fire

Copyright © 2023 Matt Waterhouse
All rights reserved.

Also by the author

The Four Guardians series:
Out Of The Ashes (2016)
The Burning Plains (2018)
In The Serpent's Lair (2020)
The Empire Of Fire (2023)

<u>Other Works</u>
Red Saints (2017)
The Eye Of The Universe (2020)
The Kodiak Novella Series

Well, this one took even longer than *Serpents* did. Of the third instalment in the series, I said: *"I expect it will be my longest."*

Oh, Matt, you sweet summer child.

Of course, *Empire* being the longest is somewhat fitting, as it is the finale, the culmination of a decade of time spent working out what the heck is going on in Planar.

Lee and Karl, thank you once again for everything.

Thank you family, thank you tutors and teachers and thank you Lou, once again, for the front cover.

Thank you to Leslee Sheu, who has been a great help and guiding light for the Four Guardians. Check out *Kumasagi* when you've finished this one.

Artists before ideologues, always and forever.

The Empire Of Fire

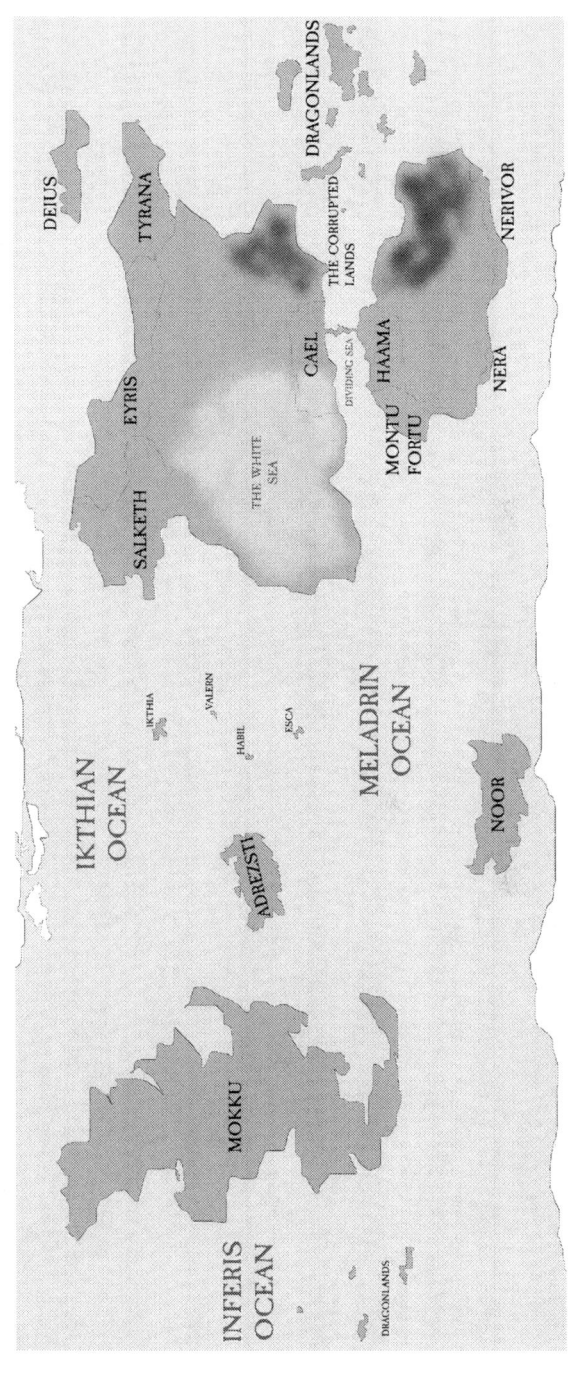

Matt Waterhouse

The Empire Of Fire

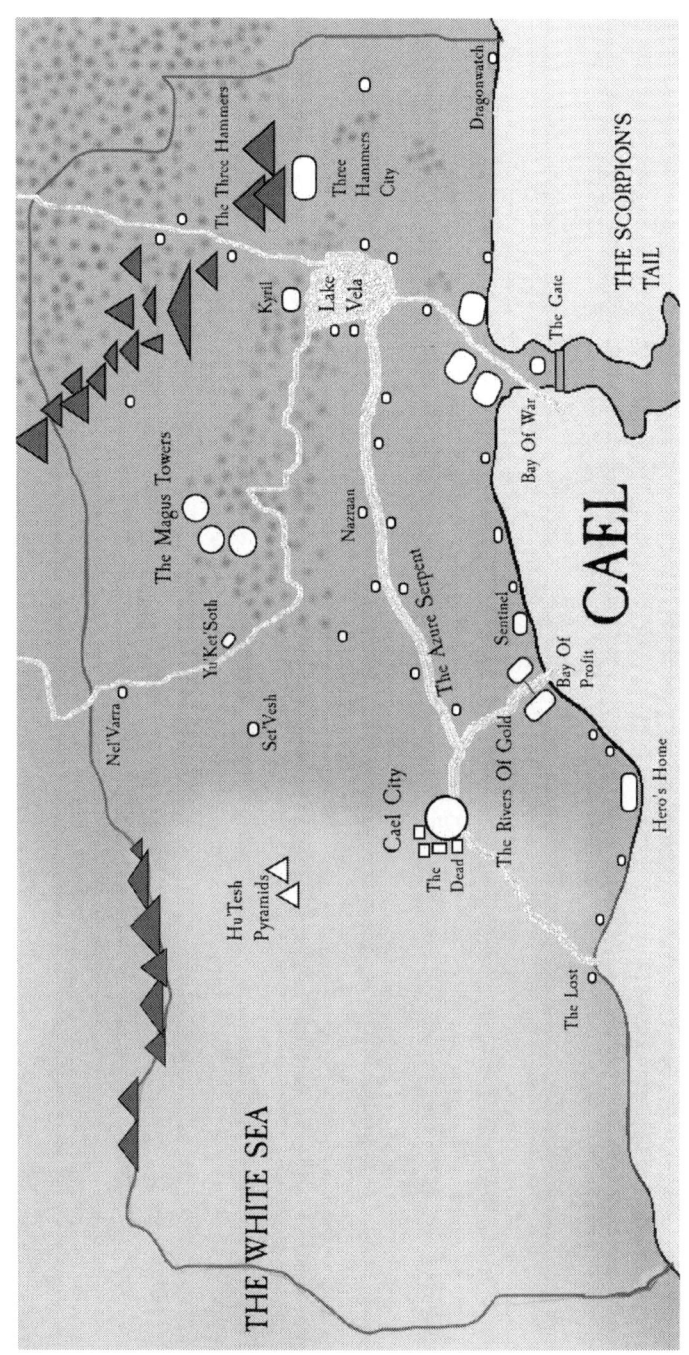

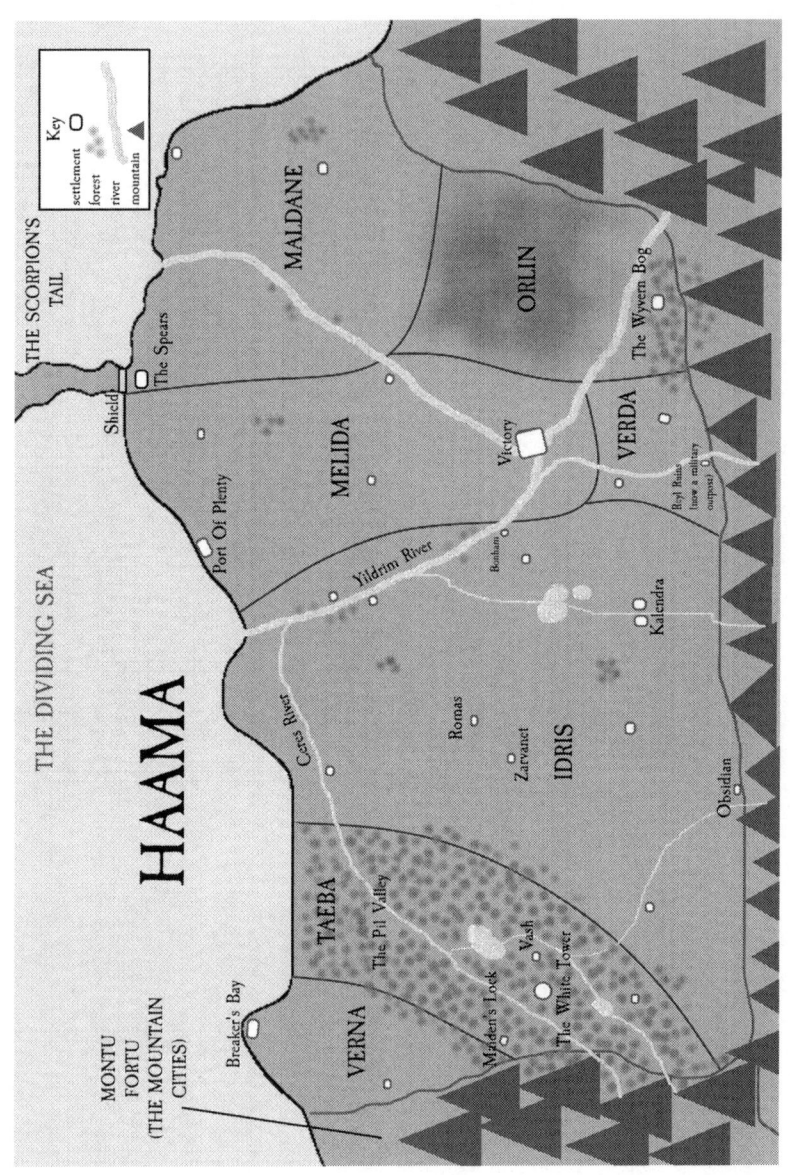

The Empire Of Fire

Matt Waterhouse

"They're watching...
They've always been watching us, they always will watch.

I've seen them ... heard them whispering in my dreams
so often that I can hear them when I'm awake.

Am I even awake? Have I ever been? Is this the dream, this world we think we know? I can't tell any more. It's all a never ending twilight, and none of you who walk in it have any idea.

I've seen what lurks in the dark between the stars
... and it has seen me..."

(The last reported words of former Arch Mage Horus,
interned as a patient at the Cael City Asylum.
He was killed in an attempted escape, during which
six nurses and doctors were murdered.)

The Empire Of Fire

1

The sounds of steel-booted feet hammering against the marble floor filled Princess Allessandra's dreams, so much so that when her eyes opened, she wasn't entirely sure that she was awake. It wasn't a surprise. She had known that she would be found quickly.

Eluco, her most trusted guardsman, and one of the golden-armoured soldiers her parents had insisted upon her, were kneeling beside her. Their faces were concerned, although Eluco's seemed to be directed at not only her, but the soldiers of the Black Fleet that were all over the room.

Eluco gave her a nod, so subtle it seemed involuntary.

He had succeeded. Their plan had worked. The prisoners had been sprung from their cells, and they had escaped the city on her airship.

Allessandra blinked, and looked around at her bedchamber. She was laying on the floor, polished so thoroughly she could see the orange light of the dawn reflected in it. She made a show of confusion, looking around drowsily.

"*What happened?*" she said weakly.

"*Tomek was a traitor,*" Eluco said gently. "*He is a Mage, and a powerful one. He knocked you out, and Jenifer.*"

Allessandra looked around for Jenifer, her handmaiden, but she was nowhere to be seen. "*Where is she?*"

"*The soldiers took her away while she was still unconscious. They claim they were going to the palace doctor.*"

Allessandra felt ice spread through her body. She reached out and took his hand, lingering for just a moment. She could see the worry on his face. "*Help me up, please.*"

Eluco reached around and placed a hand on the small of her back, lifting

The Empire Of Fire

her with ease. The scar on her stomach reminded her of its presence angrily, despite the care Eluco took, and she held back a hiss. She steeled herself as best she could before looking out at Victory.

The city before her was dying a violent, brutal death.

She had been mistaken. It wasn't dawn, not yet. The orange light she had seen reflected in the polished marble was from the fire, the fierce blaze chewing its way through the buildings and people below. It illuminated the smoke it was belching into the air. Beneath the roar of the flames she could hear shouts and screams, could smell the wood and stone burning.

Above the city, the military airships of the Black Fleet hovered menacingly, their cannons occasionally blasting a projectile of energy at a target below.

She turned to the rest of the room's occupants. There were a dozen Black Fleet soldiers in the room, and half that many of the palace guard. All were examining her chambers: her washroom, her desk, her study, her balcony, even her bed. There was an officer among them, her uniform pressed, rank and medals pinned to her chest and well maintained.

Allessandra's cabinet had so far remained untouched, or so it seemed. She crossed the room to it, and opened the drawer. The communication stone that linked her to her ship sat in the secret compartment in which it was stowed. She palmed it swiftly.

"*What are you doing, Your Grace?*" The officer asked sharply.

"*Getting a drink, while you invade my privacy and burn down my city,*" Allessandra snapped. She pulled a glass from the same drawer as the stone and filled it with brandy. "*What the hell are you doing in here, and where is my handmaiden?*"

"*She is being attended to by the palace doctor, Your Grace,*" the officer said smoothly. "*I am afraid she hit her head quite badly when she fell. We are tracking the movements of the Resistance member who attacked you, nothing more.*"

The officer took a step towards her, and bowed low. "*In aid of that investigation, I must ask you a few questions, Your Grace. Please, have a seat."*

Allessandra looked at Eluco, who nodded again. What the officer had said about Jenifer had been a lie. Both she and Allessandra had lain down on the floor voluntarily to *avoid* striking their heads, when Thomas had taken the necessary measure of rendering them both unconscious.

Allessandra crossed the room to her desk and sat down. The officer approached with a notebook, but did not sit down herself. She stood, pacing slowly, trying to hide how closely she was watching the princess's face, reading her body language. Likely a tactic of intimidation, looming over the person who was being questioned.

Allessandra made no attempt to hide her fury. She clasped her hands in front of her, and glared at the officer. *"Well?"*

"You requested that this 'Tomek' was to join you in the palace this evening, according to Guardsman Eluco."

"I did."

"For what purpose?"

"He was a soldier who came from western Haama, who had seen extensive combat. He was to give us information on what was happening in the west ... western Idris and Taeba, and so on."

The officer peered at her. *"It never occurred to you that he could be a member of the Resistance?"*

"Why would it have? He passed the scrutiny of the army, of the ministers. He was awarded one of our highest medals for valour, a well deserved medal given what he did to earn it."

"We have his recent record, we know what he has done. For a Resistance spy, he has been quite the thorn in their side."

Allessandra snorted. *"Then it appears he was a very committed spy."*

"What happened in this room, before he attacked you?"

"We were conversing about the situation in the west, the Taeba clans and their destruction. Since the fleet left for Taeba to engage the undead threat, I have been concerned for their safety. When your ... bombardment of Victory

began, he struck."

The officer checked her notebook. "*You guardsman has said as much. Tomek was alone?*"

"In here, yes."

The officer nodded. "*You should know that the terrorist was not alone when he was spotted. The men were wearing armour of the palace guard. Your personal guard, to be precise.*"

Allessandra swallowed, and turned to Eluco. He sighed, and sagged. "*I'm sorry, Your Grace ... they're dead. He attacked us after you fell ... he killed them. I only survived his attack because I caught him off-guard, but he still knocked me senseless.*"

Allessandra caught his lie, and ran with it. "*What? Dead? They ... they can't be ...*"

"*They ... he blew them apart, reduced their bodies to dust with fire and lightning.*"

The officer frowned as she noted something down. "*We have found no 'dust', guardsman.*"

"*Tomek must have disposed of ... of them. The armour is what he needed, for the accomplices your witnesses saw.*"

"*Other agents in the palace?*" The officer said incredulously. "*The palace has rigorous security ...*"

"*Not rigorous enough!*" Allessandra snapped, letting some of her outrage slip through. It was enough to make the officer falter a little.

"*I am sorry for the loss, Your Grace.*"

"*They were old ... friends.*" Allessandra wiped her eyes. "*For a long time they were part of my personal guard.*"

"*Indeed.*" The officer looked into the notebook once more. "*One of the prisoners who was released is Helen, your former steward.*"

"*Her ties to the Resistance were suspected, I'm told they led to her arrest.*"

"*Ties that you vehemently denied and protested, through official and* unofficial means."

"Well clearly I was wrong," Allessandra snapped. "Guardsman Eluco."

"Yes, Your Grace."

"Go to the palace doctor, ascertain Jenifer's safety. If she is not there, tell me immediately."

The officer straightened up. "*I'm not prepared to let him go unescorted, Your Grace, with all due respect.*"

"*I'm not prepared to have him go alone, if you insist any of your men upon him,*" Allessandra countered. She nodded to the nearest pair of palace guardsmen, who stood to attention and bowed. "*Go with guardsmen Eluco, ensure his safety.*"

The soldiers seemed hesitant. One of them stepped forwards, coming as close to her as he dared, which was still several feet away. Allessandra beckoned him closer. He approached slowly, until he was only a few inches from her. He spoke in a whisper. "In Haaman, if it pleases, Your Grace."

"Go on."

"We will obey, as is our duty ... but I don't want to leave you here with them."

Allessandra nodded. "You suspect they will kill me in my own bedchamber?"

"If ordered to, yes."

Allessandra found herself unable to smile reassuringly. It died in her heart when she saw the sincerity in the guardsman's eyes, and given the screams on the night wind, she couldn't disagree with him.

"Your colleagues will still be here. Eluco will be alone without you. I understand your worry, but I can take care of myself, if I have to."

The guardsman opened his mouth to protest, but she stopped him with a hand. "This is my command, and my decision. Responsibility for my safety lays with me alone."

The guardsman closed his eyes and nodded. "As you command, Your Grace."

The Empire Of Fire

He backed away, and signaled to another soldier. Both stood to attention in front of Eluco.

Eluco looked at Allessandra, and nodded to her. "*We'll make sure she's safe, Your Grace.*"

The officer pointed at two of the Black Fleet troops. "*Go with them. Bring four of the guards outside with you.*"

The pair saluted and left the bedchamber, the cacophony of their heavy boots receding beneath the chaos outside.

"*I didn't know women in your position had phalluses they liked to measure,*" Allessandra muttered.

"*I don't consider anyone above suspicion, Your Grace,*" the officer replied smugly. "*Not even you.*"

Allessandra noticed the palace guardsmen exchange a few looks of anger. "*Is there a reason for the tension between our respective soldiers, officer?*"

"*Perhaps it is the possibility that yours are traitors,*" the officer snapped.

"*Perhaps it is the fact that yours have set fire to their homes. The Black Fleet is not above the law, no matter the strings Lord Marshal Vehnek pulls with the Royal family. What he has done here constitutes an act of war, and both sides of that conflict are represented in this room.*"

The officer stood straight. "*An act of war? Putting down dissidents is no act of war, unless you sympathise with them.*"

Allessandra gestured to the chaos outside. "*If a foreign power had done that, you would be mobilising for a counter attack right now. However, it wasn't a foreign power, it was you. The only reason I haven't had you executed is that your death would be used as an excuse to incriminate me, and allow the Lord Marshal to grab for more power.*"

The officer opened her mouth to speak, but the door interrupted her. Minister Evandro walked into the chamber, his robes haphazardly put on, his eyes red with tiredness, smoke, grief, and fury. At his back were palace and city guardsmen, more than twenty, with more in the corridor behind him.

"*You are dismissed,*" Evandro said to the officer curtly.

"*First Minister, I must insist ...*"

"*You are dismissed! Take it up with Vehnek if you must. Take your soldiers with you, or you and they will be removed.*"

"*I* will *take it up with the Lord Marshal,*" the officer sneered, as she gestured for her soldiers to leave. "*Remember your place, old man. You'll find the number of friends you have is getting smaller and smaller, and no-one can survive alone, no matter how long they've licked the boot.*"

She pushed past him to leave, and one of Evandro's soldiers closed the door behind her.

For a long time, neither of them said a word. The new contingent of guards spread out and began searching the room. Evandro's face was illuminated in red and orange light, his gaze fixed on the city.

"*What are your men doing, First Minister?*"

He blinked and shifted his focus to her. "*No doubt that ... sycophant and her cronies planted evidence in your bedchamber, or a device or incantation to spy on you. It is better for everyone if they are found and disposed of.*"

"*I appreciate that.*"

"*I heard that you had been attacked only minutes ago. Are you alright?*"

"*Don't worry about me, First Minister. Worry about the city.*"

He gave no response. His voice had been choked, his eyes glistening. Allessandra had, in that moment, never seen an older man than Evandro appeared to be, crooked and broken, sagging in the face, hair thin and wiry.

"*How bad is it, First Minister?*"

He swallowed. "*Old Town is in ruins. The fires have spread to the Fisheries and The Overlook. The Temple Square is all but gone, the Old Town Market is gone. They haven't stopped.*" Evandro's hands began to shake. "*That bastard, Vehnek ... he hasn't stopped. He won't stop. Who in all the hells could be left for him to kill?*"

Allessandra found herself stepping forwards, and enclosing his wrinkled, bony hands in hers.

"*What are the casualties?*"

The Empire Of Fire

"*We don't know. There's no way we can know. People had no warning, some would never have had the chance to get out of their beds.*" He shook his head at the blaze. "*The minimum projection is ... thousands.*"

She could scarcely believe the number. "*The ... minimum?*"

"*There have been a steady stream of people fleeing the violence. The injured are being treated in the streets while Vehnek's troops are busy elsewhere, but we don't have enough doctors to help them. The worst injuries ... they'll lead to more death.*"

Allessandra let his hand go and pressed her hand to her forehead. "*What are we doing about it?*"

Evandro shook his head. "*Levez mobilised the City Guard, and took control directly. She was helping coordinate an evacuation, but she reported direct military action against civilians by the Black Fleet. She was moving into Temple Square ...*"

He leaned on the window sill. "*No word since. Not a word from her, or any of her men. Just ... silence.*"

Allessandra thought back to her work with Levez, about her no-nonsense attitude, seemingly harsh at first. She had little time for bureaucracy, and absolutely none for the glitterati, like Allessandra had been. The working relationship between them had only begun since Allessandra's own awakening, and had only heightened the respect the princess had for her.

The first woman to rise to the rank of General, the first of many. Written in the annals of history.

She had seemed invincible.

"*She might be alive,*" Allessandra whispered, her voice hollow. "*It's Levez.*"

"*She might. We'll see when we see.*" He sighed. "*What happened in here, Allessandra?*"

"*There was a Resistance member planted in the Standing Army. He earned honours with them, he earned an audience with me.*"

Evandro raised an eyebrow. "*Personally, in here, in the hours before* dawn?"

"Yes. We were suspicious of him ... just not suspicious enough. Members of my guard paid with their lives."

"Many of them. There are reports of an escape from the palace dungeons."

Allessandra sighed. "*Several, apparently, according to the officer.*"

"*Very specific escapes, Your Grace. Helen among them.*"

Allessandra sighed again, making a show of frustration. "*And as such, suspicious eyes have fallen upon me. The presence of half the Black Fleet infantry in here isn't so surprising anymore.*"

"*If you were involved, Your Grace ... I cannot protect you. None of us on the Council can, and I don't know if many of them would want to. Not after tonight.*"

Allessandra nodded. "*I understand, but First Minister, we have to do something about what has occurred tonight. I will support a full investigation into the prison break, of course, but we must prioritise. What the Black Fleet have done in the city is unacceptable, and leaning into these lost prisoners instead of doing something about the damage done would be a mistake that would lead to all of our heads rolling.*"

"*What are we supposed to do about them, Allessandra?*" Evandro snapped, frustrated. "*Now that the Standing Army have gone, our people are outnumbered, and the casualty list among the City Guard is growing fast. Communications from here are likely being monitored: we cannot call for help, even from Cael.*"

"*You know exactly what Vehnek's doing, Evandro. Anyone could. This is a coup. A military coup.*"

He nodded, pale. "*That is certainly how it seems.*"

"*Then we have a duty to fight it, do we not?*"

"*Careful!*" he hissed. "*Remember what I said: the walls have ears here.*"

Allessandra cursed herself silently. "*My parents will no doubt arrange a visit once word reaches them of this destruction. When they come, they must be protected. Vehnek is not above moving against them, I know it."*

Evandro gazed at the city. *"I agree. I will chair a meeting of the council immediately. I would like you to be present, if you are up to it."*

"I am."

***

Not a soul spoke in the Council Chamber.

It was emptier than it had ever been. Aside from Allessandra and Evandro only Brynden, the Minister for Haaman Cultural Affairs, and Carrasco, the Minister Of Foreign Affairs, were present. Allessandra wondered where the rest of them were, and with everything going on in the city, she at least hoped some of them were safe.

"Simply put," Allessandra said, *"the actions of the Black Fleet tonight must not be tolerated."*

"This night?" Brynden squawked in broken Caelish, the fat in his face jiggling. *"The Black Fleet have been too bad since they come here!"*

"The Black Fleet have taken action against dissident elements that have been hiding in Victory for decades," Carrasco said. *"Those terrorists have been allowed to roam freely for far too long."*

"Not even!" Brynden yelled. *"Can you excuse tonight with the same excuse?"*

"Tonight ... tonight was problematic," Carrasco allowed. *"It will have repercussions abroad, that will reach far. Effective certainly, but careless."*

Evandro shook his head angrily. *"Allowing this, making allowances for it, no matter how small, guarantees that it will happen again. This kind of violence should not be added to the lexicon of Cael and Haama relations."*

"It is how relations began, in their current form," Allessandra said quietly. *"We have a chance to repair damage past and present, and it is not one I am prepared to waste."*

She stood and grimaced at the pain in her stomach. It was getting worse.

Perhaps she had torn a stitch when she fell. "*I am tired of being reactive. We are always playing catch-up to evil people like Vehnek and The Ghosts, who are trying to destroy every bridge we try to build. We must try harder, and give no quarter.*"

"Vehnek has his supporters abroad, in Mokku particularly," Carrasco said. "*In moving against him, you could incur the wrath of the largest military force in the world. They are not above interventionism, regardless of Cael's relationship with them.*"

"They need us for that military force," Evandro said. "*They need Cael.*"

"And if Vehnek can take Cael for them, so much the better," Carrasco countered. "*Doubtless deals have been made behind closed doors. In the destruction of the Resistance, thorns are being removed from Mokku's side as well as Vehnek's.*"

"Are you listen to you self?" Brynden bellowed. "*The city is on fire as we talk! What do we do?*"

"Minister Brynden is right," Allessandra said. "*We must secure the safety of the people, before anything else, but we will still have to be careful. Mobilise what remains of the City Guard, and as many of the palace guardsmen as we can spare. Mages as well. Get the fires under control, get to work on shelters for those without homes, and watch the Black Fleet. I will tell them to cease their attack.*"

"Vehnek doesn't answer to you, Your Grace," Carrasco said darkly.

"He will this time. Contact General Kelad, Breaker's Bay, Kalendra, The Port Of Plenty, and the Royal Family. Request humanitarian assistance. Explicitly state that we want no military aid whatsoever. We will need building materials, food and water, doctors, medicines."

"The other cities in Haama present a security risk that Vehnek will not allow," Carrasco said.

"Contact them anyway, Minister. If there will be an issue, let there be one. Let him protest the arrival of supplies that will help the people. I will make sure the people know exactly who blocks them."

Carrasco grinned. "*I understand, Your Grace. I'll contact them immediately.*"

"Public relations," Brynden spat in Haaman. Allessandra raised an eyebrow at him.

"Minister?"

"You're concerned about the perception of him among the people of Victory, when I can assure you that he is utterly despised."

Allessandra smiled tightly. "This isn't about public relations. It's about the truth, and about the end of this ... reign of terror before it begins."

Brynden sighed. "I hope so, Your Grace."

Evandro held up a hand. "*We are all but defenseless here without air support. There isn't any way we can stop him engaging in further violence.*"

Allessandra pursed her lips. "*First Minister, deploy all of the cannons on the palace roof, and point them at his ships.*"

Evandro's mouth dropped open. Brynden and Carrasco exchanged a glance. "*Your Grace ...*"

"*Prepare the palace's barriers, I want them at full strength.*"

"*We have never had to use the Silver Throne's siege defenses,*" Evandro said urgently. "*We don't know if they even work!*"

"*I doubt that the palace Mages would allow them to remain untested,*" Allessandra said.

"*But he could level the palace in moments!*"

Allessandra shook her head. "*That would be overplaying his hand, don't you think? A direct attack on a member of the Royal Family would turn enough of Cael against him to scupper his plans. His ships may be powerful, they may be advanced, but they are few. The Standing Army's fleet outnumber them.*"

"Let us not forget the deep ties the Caelish Royal Family have to the governments of Salketh, Mokku, Noor, Adrezsti ..." Carrasco said thoughtfully. "*Among others. Attacking the Palace would rally the most powerful people in the world against him.*"

Evandro wrung his hands. "*It could backfire. He may know that the* world would turn against him, and simply not care. I doubt he plans to stop here."

"He doesn't have the numbers yet," Allessandra said. "He can't afford to strike now."

"He will call your bluff," Carrasco muttered.

Allessandra eyed him stonily. "*Bluff? Who said anything about a bluff? Evandro, deploy the men, deploy the cannons, raise the barrier. I will be on the roof.*"

***

Eluco was waiting for Allessandra outside the council chamber, his face stony. There were a number of Black Fleet soldiers around him, and as many of the palace guard. Evandro was close behind her, speaking urgently, but as quietly as he could.

"*Your Grace, you should be in bed. You have been through an ordeal tonight!*"

"*I won't hide in my bedchamber like an heirloom you keep away from prying eyes,*" she snapped. "*Not while Victory burns. Not while people are dying, and you can't convince me otherwise.*"

"*Part of my role on the Council Of Ministers is to advise you,*" he replied. "*That includes pointing out alternatives, and potential difficulties. I'm well aware that you are impossible to convince once you have your mind set on something.*"

She turned to him and frowned, but she could feel her mouth turn up in a grin. "*Am I really that impossible?*"

"*Worse. Be careful, Your Grace.*"

"*I will.*"

Evandro smiled at her, before his face hardened. His attention fixed upon the soldiers in front of him. "*Palace Guard, present arms.*"

Eluco and the rest drew their blades.

The Empire Of Fire

"*Take the Black Fleet troops here to the dungeons,*" he said.

Half of the Black Fleet soldiers had their swords half drawn, but even the ones that had realised what had been about to happen were heavily outnumbered.

"*Drop your swords, ladies and gentlemen,*" Evandro said calmly. "*You are to be detained for your own safety. I hope you understand.*"

"*Understand?*" one of the officers thundered. "*Are you mad? You know what Vehnek will do to you. To all of you!*"

Evandro nodded solemnly. "*Take them away.*"

"*Not you, Eluco,*" Allessandra said. "*Come with me. First Minister, you know what to do.*"

Evandro nodded. "*Yes, I do. Good luck, Your Grace.*"

Allessandra strode away, towards the stairwell that led up to the roof. Eluco walked close beside her.

"*Jenifer was not taken to the palace doctor,*" he said quietly. "*I don't know if she was even taken in that direction.*"

Allessandra felt a wave of sickness wash over her. It went far beyond worry. Her steward had been brutally beaten, and Jenifer was just a handmaiden.

"*The dungeons, maybe?*"

"*Possibly. I hope she's alright ... but there's a good chance ...*"

"*I know,*" she said. Her voice cracked. "*I shouldn't have mixed her up in this. I shouldn't have mixed you up in this, or Berek and Orso, or Helen, or Seret, or any of the people in Victory.*"

"*You might be the only thing protecting them,*" Eluco said quietly. He took her hand and squeezed it. Her eyes widened in surprise, and he smiled grimly. "*I don't regret a thing, and neither does Jenifer.*"

Allessandra exhaled. He had stopped her hand shaking, at least. "*I hope you're not wrong. I think we might be about to find out.*"

Eluco stepped ahead of her to open the doors, into the scarlet night air. Allessandra's eyes began watering, and she coughed into the smoke, seeing the tendrils of it shift and swirl around her. She let out a cry of pain through gritted teeth as her stomach muscles contracted around her scar. Eluco moved beside her, holding her close to him.

"*Mage! Over here!*" he bellowed. Allessandra heard footsteps approaching quickly, and heard them falter.

"*Oh! Uhm ... Your Grace ...*" the Mage stammered.

"*Protect her, now,*" Eluco ordered.

"*Y-yes, of course.*" The Mage spoke an incantation, and Allessandra felt the air around her beginning to clear. She straightened her posture, and wiped her eyes.

"*Thank you,*" Allessandra said, still a little breathlessly. The young Mage smiled shyly.

"*You're welcome, Your Grace. The incantation will last for twenty minutes, so I'll stay close, if you'll permit me.*"

"*Please do,*" she said. "*Walk with us. What is the status of the palace defenses?*"

"*The generators are spinning, Your Grace. The barrier can be raised at your command. The cannons are deployed, their crews are ready.*"

Allessandra nodded. "*Is there a way I can speak to the Black Fleet ships?*"

"*They have refused requests at communication, Your Grace.*"

Allessandra frowned. Their colours had been well and truly nailed to the mast.

The cannon crews were running back and forth, heading towards each emplacement. The runes woven into their robes glowed bright red and green through the smoke. The ones that spotted Allessandra and Eluco paused and offered a quick bow, before moving on. She could see anger written on every face, tears tracing lines through soot-stained cheeks.

The Mage gestured to their right, at what looked like the trunk of an oak tree, fixed in an iron frame. The metal tube was pointed at the city skyline, cloaked in thick smoke.

The Empire Of Fire

"*One of our larger emplacements, Your Grace,*" the Mage said. "*I had hoped it would never be used in anger.*"

Allessandra nodded. "*As did I. Is there a way to clear the smoke?*"

"*There are incantations that can be used.*"

Allessandra took a deep breath, steadying her nerves. Was this a point of no return?

No. That had passed when the Black Fleet had deployed.

"*Raise the barrier, and clear the smoke.*"

The Mage nodded.

Allessandra felt the air around her swell and spark. The hair on her arms stood on end, and powerful white light blasted through the smoke in all directions. The light merged together and shone brighter, pulsing rhythmically. It became a vast bubble of energy, protecting the palace in all directions. Warmth spread through Allessandra's body, and it seemed to bolster her confidence, steady her, banish her fear away.

The smoke began to quickly dissipate, revealing the extent of the fire's damage to Victory. Old Town was a ruin. People were streaming through the streets frantically, thick throngs of them, chased by flames and black-clad soldiers. The smaller warships hovering above were circling, the larger simply observing the carnage below. The largest pair, the twin-hulled *Annihilator* and Vehnek's *Inquisitor*, were lower than the rest, the dragon-heads on the prows sweeping back and forth, hungrily scanning the burning city below.

Upon the roof, every cannon was pointed towards the fleet. Allessandra examined the firing lines to her left and right as she approached the edge of the roof. The smallest were in the front row, right at the edge, and were mostly unmanned. They were six feet long, meant for closer range.

"*Why are they ...*"

"*We are expecting the smaller ships to get in close, Your Grace,*" the Mage said.

"*And you are expecting that they will open fire.*"

The Mage paused at that, then nodded. "*Yes, we are.*"

She looked to the second row. These cannons were all manned, twelve feet long, set on springs to cushion the recoil. The third row were the largest, long range and powerful. They were arrayed along the roof in every direction, although as far as she could see, all of them were pointed at the fleet.

"They are awaiting orders, Your Grace."

Allessandra met the Mage's gaze. He was looking pointedly at her.

"My orders?"

"Yes, Your Grace. You mobilised this defense. You gave the word."

Allessandra blinked at him. *"I'm not a tactician, I'm ... a princess."*

Eluco stepped forwards and placed a hand on her shoulder. *"Tell the cannon crews to prepare for volley-fire, all three rows. Prepare the long range guns to fire first, they'll make the point loudest."*

Allessandra stared at him. He glanced at her and shrugged. *"You need a sword arm, you've got one."*

Allessandra's mouth turned up in a grin, then turned to the fleet and gritted her teeth. *"Can you amplify my voice so those ships can hear me?"*

"Yes, Your Grace, but I doubt they will respond."

"Make it loud enough so they can't avoid it."

The Mage grinned, and placed a hand on her back. Warmth spread through her nerves, and collected in her throat. The Mage nodded.

"Black Fleet ..."

Allessandra's voice boomed out across the city, echoing between the buildings. She heard windows in the palace below shatter. It seemed that the chaos of battle and slaughter fell silent for a split second. Her eyes widened in surprise. Eluco nodded in encouragement. She took a breath, and her jaw clenched.

"This is Princess Allessandra, Regent of Haama. You will receive no second warning. You have ten seconds to cease your hostility against the people of this city, or you will be fired upon."

Eluco's breath caught beside her, and she took his hand quickly and tightly.

The Empire Of Fire

She counted them down under her breath. After two seconds, the barrage from every ship above resumed, unyielding.

She nodded to Eluco, who nodded. "*Ready the heavy cannons. Target the largest ships and prepare to fire.*"

The eighth, ninth and tenth seconds passed all too slowly, as conjured fire on top of conjured fire blasted buildings apart, engulfing people as they tried to flee. Allessandra's grip tightened around Eluco's hand, her teeth began to hurt from how hard she had clenched her jaw. Her vision blurred with tears.

The Black Fleet didn't stop.

Before Eluco could give the order, she screamed in fury.

"FIRE!"

The single word pierced the night, and was swiftly followed by rolling thunder.

Her ears began to ring fiercely as the heavy cannons blasted into life, bolts of lightning, flame and force streamed across the city and smashed against the barriers of the flotilla. The dragon-heads mounted on all of them howled in pain and rage.

Immediately, all of them ceased firing, and slowly began to rise. They turned towards the palace, and began to advance.

"*Well, at least they stopped firing,*" Eluco muttered. "*Your Grace, you give the order. That way, the fleet will hear it as well. Say 'ready volley-fire.'*"

Allessandra grinned. **"*Ready volley-fire!*"**

Above them, the fleet began to slow. The *Inquisitor* pushed forwards until it had taken point.

The Mage nudged Allessandra, and held out a communication stone to her. "*Lord Marshal Vehnek is requesting a parley, Your Grace. Allow me to lift the incantation on your voice.*"

She nodded, and felt the heat around her neck ebb away. The Mage handed the stone to her, and she held it in front of her mouth.

"*Lord Marshal.*"

"*Allessandra,*" Vehnek said smoothly. "*I gather our operation has caused you some alarm."

"Your operation is somewhere between an act of insurrection and an act of war. Cease your hostilities immediately, and leave Victory airspace."

Vehnek chuckled. "*I'm afraid I cannot do that. To leave Victory entirely would contravene a Royal Decree, and I would like my head to stay on my shoulders.*"

"Your skiffs can stay, if you wish. Anything larger must depart, and keep a distance of at least five miles from the city wall. This is non-negotiable, Lord Marshal."

Vehnek paused, seeming to consider the order. "*I will agree to the departure of my fleet, per your demands, as long as the Inquisitor remains. I have a lot of important work aboard, you understand, and given the number of cannons you seem to have at your disposal, you would still have me considerably outgunned.*"

Allessandra glanced at Eluco, who pursed his lips.

"*If you are to remain, you may only keep two of your skiffs as escort.*" Allessandra said firmly.

Vehnek paused again. "*I accept your terms.*"

Above, segments of the fleet began to slowly turn away. Most of the skiffs swept over the palace and kept flying, with the larger battleships banking to the north and south. The *Inquisitor* remained, hovering on the other side of the barrier. Two skiffs slowly pulled alongside it, and waited.

"*That was too easy,*" Eluco muttered.

Allessandra watched the *Inquisitor* closely. The dragon head on the prow locked eyes with her and growled.

"*I'm inclined to agree,*" she said. "*I want that fleet watched at every hour of the day. Every movement.*"

The Mage bowed. "*As you command, Your Grace.*"

"*Eluco ...*" a wave of nausea swept through her, and she swayed on her feet. Eluco placed a hand on her back, and kept her upright.

"*Are you alright?*" he murmured.

The Empire Of Fire

She took a deep breath, and nodded her head. "*Eluco, dispatch a contingent of the palace guard, and a contingent of the workers. See what we can spare from the food stores and send it down into the city. Fight the fires, assist the doctors, make sure people are fed and sheltered as best you can.*"

"*I will,*" he said. "*You should lay down for a while. You haven't slept for more than a day.*"

"*I probably should, but I won't. We don't get to sleep, Eluco. Not now. Not until those fires are out.*"

2

Lord Marshal Vehnek stood on the prow of the *Inquisitor,* listening to the growls and grunts of the dragon-head directly below him. He smiled to himself, eyes closed. It really was almost alive. Without looking at it, he was very nearly able to fool himself.

The dragon-heads had fooled many people before. That was part of the point. The first battle was fought with the eyes, with the mind. Fear was a greater weapon than any sword, cannon, or incantation.

He opened his eyes and gazed down at Victory, glowing in the light of the dawn. Most of the fires had been put out. The soldiers and workers Princess Allessandra had deployed had been working through the night. The damage would be repaired in time, but the fear would last far longer.

Cael's enemies were trembling, and as bitter as the thought was, that was worth the unfortunate amount of collateral damage.

Even without Mora's transformation, it would have been worth it.

Trade had just resumed from the Fisheries. Vehnek watched carts of food trundle up the canal street, turning to different parts of the city and depositing their wares, like beetles in a hive, going about their business.

City-folk had filled the streets, either forced there or going voluntarily to help. Several lines had formed before the carts that had stopped, waiting for food as patiently as they could. In other places, those lines were crowds, pressed against city guardsmen who were trying to keep order.

"How many minutes before they get violent?" Vehnek mused to himself. The dragon-head below him growled, and he smiled down at it. It seemed to respond to him sometimes, and it always amused him.

He listened as heavy footsteps approached, with the clack of a walking cane on the deck punctuating them, rhythmic, almost musical.

"*Good morning, Miranda.*"

The Arch Mage stopped beside him, and leaned on the railings. Her breathing slowly went from pained and laboured to more relaxed. "*The Princess works fast, doesn't she.*"

"*She has a lot of supporters who are willing to follow her commands,*" Vehnek muttered. "*More than I thought she had.*"

"*She will be a thorn in our side. We should remove her.*"

"*The Royal Family will remove her when the time comes. The King will not stand in the way. The Queen is making sure of that.*" He shifted his posture, giving Miranda his full attention. "*How is our guest?*"

"*Taking hold. Luckily, at least for the moment, It is as restricted as we are in a human body. We are using ether to keep Mora's body unconscious.*"

"*Is that necessary?*"

"*We would use magic, but we can't take the chance that the entity will use the energy to charge itself. According to the material we have, the control process can be somewhat violent. When It takes a host, It tends to test their capabilities and limits. Given Mora's power and potential, It could destroy the Inquisitor.*"

"*I see.*"

Miranda reached out and touched his arm. "*Are you alright? The two of you were ... involved.*"

"*It was a means to an end, and that end has come. How long before It is ready?*"

Miranda withdrew her hand. "*I don't know. We will stop administering the ether soon. Tomorrow perhaps. It depends when the chamber in the palace is ready. I would prefer it to awaken in a safe location.*"

"*I agree.*"

Miranda lingered, shifting her weight. Vehnek noticed the whiteness of her knuckles on the hand gripping her cane.

"*Go on.*"

Miranda bit her lip. "*I'm told that there has been an escape from the palace dungeons ... several prisoners have been released.*"

Vehnek focused on her. She didn't meet his gaze, purposefully looking at the city.

"*Seraphine was one of them,*" he said quietly. "*The Construct as well, I would guess. Why spring one, and not the other?*"

Miranda nodded, and said nothing.

"*Unfortunate. The Construct would have been a great help for the Colonel's research. Its dissection would have allowed us to see its inner workings in even more detail. Seraphine would have given us no information, but her capture was symbolic. Who else escaped?*"

"*A former member of the palace staff, and one of the Colonel's scientists. The staff member was the Princess's former steward.*"

Vehnek grinned. "*That's certainly interesting. The scientist?*"

"*Jack Kilborn. Very experienced. He has worked on many projects for the Colonel and the Arch Mages.*"

"*Kilborn ... that's a Haaman name.*"

Miranda nodded.

"*Immediately evaluate the Colonel's staff. All of them. Question them, dig through their backgrounds. Any dissident elements, eliminate them. The Princess is another matter ...*"

"*You think she had a hand in the escapes?*"

Vehnek's smile grew. "*I'm almost certain of it.*"

Miranda shifted uncomfortably. "*That's treason. Removing her is one thing ... but treason is a capital offense.*"

"*Indeed.*"

Miranda turned to him, not hiding her worry. "*I have no love for her, but killing her would be a mistake. She has too much popular support.*"

"*If we can tie her to treason directly, she will lose it. I want to know exactly how those prisoners escaped. Every step, every collaborator. They have surely left the city, there was enough chaos last night to cover their movements,*

The Empire Of Fire

so I want your best people working on it, no less."

Miranda bowed. *"I understand, Lord Marshal."*

"Straighten up, Miranda, I'm not royalty. Bowing is reserved for useless people."

She stood straight. *"I have better news. The black dragon has reached the Magus Towers."*

Vehnek smiled. *"Was there any damage to the bones in transit?"*

"No. My people took every precaution."

"Good. Is the expedition prepared?"

"Yes ..." Miranda scowled. *"I'm not sure about this."*

"I know."

"You're chasing a hunch."

"A hunch with historical and geographical backing. We've scouted the area in question, and initial reports say that there are a number of structures spread across the canyons and mountains."

"Ruins?"

Vehnek shook his head. *"It does not seem so, not all of them, at least."*

Miranda folded her arms. *"Buildings in a desert don't prove that this ... metal warlord exists."*

"We'll find out. The alternative is intolerable." Vehnek's fingers tightened around the ramparts on the prow. *"The eternal pariahs. The world uses our research, our technology, our genius, while they bat away our seat at the table. They sit back while our people starve to death, while the desert swallows our land whole. Without that warlord, our plan will take centuries to come to fruition. Perhaps millennia. There won't be a Cael left by then."*

Miranda touched his arm again, more hesitantly. *"But if Mora was wrong ..."*

"Then she was wrong. We owe Cael to explore the possibility, and it is a very strong possibility."

Miranda gazed out at the city. *"Do we owe them, too?"*

Vehnek glanced at her, and sighed. *"Perhaps. For getting rid of the* terrorists in their midst, maybe they owe us."

"At a high cost. There are many who will have been rendered homeless by the fires, many who will have died. A lot of the city guard are dead, including Defense Minister Levez."

"Your doubts are growing."

"I have lived in this city for a long time. Places I visited, ate, laughed in ... a lot of them have been destroyed at your order." She looked down at the city, a look of nausea on her face. "Was it worth it?"

"Yes." Vehnek said sharply. "Yes, it was. We removed the wolves hiding among the sheep, threats to us and the populace both. We will take over the security of the city, and ensure they do not step here again."

He looked back towards the hatch that led below decks, where his former lover's body lay unconscious. "Unlocking the chains on our new friend ... freeing It ... It will bring us greatness. It will allow us to thrive. It will allow our people to thrive. Everything we have done was worth the price, even if the price was high."

"If you say so," Miranda muttered.

Her doubt sent a flash of anger through Vehnek. "It's a little late to back out now, Arch Mage."

"I'm aware of that, Lord Marshal."

"Have you been outside the walls of Cael City recently?" he said quietly. "Have you seen the lost souls who can't afford to live inside? The ones who can't find a home because there aren't any homes left, who have to dig holes in the sand to stay alive?"

Miranda bristled. "I know what they're going through."

"You've heard what they're going through, but you haven't seen it. Starving children, people blasted to bones by the sandstorms, the dead left in their holes to rot because no-one is left to check on them."

"Do you care more about them, or your own legacy?" she muttered. "Cael's prosperity is your victory, isn't it."

Vehnek studied her for a moment. It would be so easy to simply push her over the rampart. With her leg in the condition it was, accidents would surely happen. Her doubts could lead to betrayal, and if that was the case, her silence was more valuable to him than her voice.

No. Not yet.

"*I suppose. We don't get to control our legacy, Miranda. My father and grandfather are considered heroes and monsters both, depending on who you ask. I haven't given much consideration to my own future. Cael's future, however ... that's worth my concern. Never forget it.*"

Miranda said nothing. She simply limped back towards the ship's hold with a sigh.

"*Miranda.*"

She stopped.

"*The bones of the Black Dragon mean we have accounted for four of the dragons we used in the war. Do we have a lead on the fifth?*"

"*The records are spotty. We suspect it was used in conjunction with our army, in the burning of the Orlin Forest.*"

"*Indeed ...*" Vehnek mused. "*It was brought down in that attack, was it not?*"

"*So Kelad's reports say, although it isn't clear how. We haven't had much of a chance to scout the area successfully. The wyvernborn are fiercely territorial.*"

Vehnek nodded. "*You have eliminated certain areas in the searches you have conducted, I would guess.*"

"*Much of what used to be the forest is clear. The mountains too. At this point our chief area of interest is the Wyvern Bog itself.*"

"*Hmm ...*" Vehnek said. "*Conceivably, the wyvernborn could have killed it. Both the Standing Army and the Black Fleet have lost airships in the area, for the most part we have left them alone. Perhaps it is time to re-evaluate that position.*"

"*There aren't enough of them to resist us,*" Miranda said quietly. "*They will have almost died out by now anyway.*"

"*Then we should speed that process along,*" Vehnek said. "*The Bog is lush, prime for farming. We will provide more work, more food for Cael, we will eliminate another threat ... and find that dragon.*"

Miranda said nothing for a moment. "*A military solution did nothing for Taeba.*"

Vehnek smiled to himself. "*The situation there will work itself into our advantage. Initially we didn't take certain variables into account in Taeba. We won't make that mistake twice. We will need to thoroughly, and very quietly, observe the Wyvern Bog. Only when we know what we're fighting will we deploy.*"

"*I agree,*" Miranda said.

"*Good. Now, you have a patient to tend to.*"

Vehnek sensed she had more to say, but she seemed to decide that silence was more profitable. She limped away.

Vehnek looked down at the *Inquisitor's* dragon figurehead. One of its ruby-red eyes was regarding him coldly, the facsimile of life and emotion almost real. He smiled down at it in return.

He wondered how it would react to the bones of its forebears. Perhaps it would understand what they were, what they meant. Perhaps Vehnek was letting his imagination run wild.

In many ways, it was immaterial. The final bricks of the road to Cael's future were being laid, and the days of their opposition were numbered.

The Empire Of Fire

3

Deep within the mountains of the Wyvern Bog, Bassai slowly strode down a familiar rocky tunnel, past store-rooms, laboratories, and the cells where he had been imprisoned only hours before.

Despite the change in that circumstance, he wasn't free of escort. Likely because of his destination, he had a retinue of warriors walking with him, seven in total, along with one shaman, shuffling along slowly behind them. Zeta led the procession, both as the Alpha's most trusted warrior, and as the only one brave enough to present Bassai with her back.

"I cannot believe Barada agreed to this," she muttered. "The impertinence of it ... no good will come of it."

Bassai said nothing. He focused on putting one foot in front of the other, running over the questions that he wanted to ask. He still had no idea how he was going to word them. In many ways, they were questions he had always wanted to ask, questions he had always wondered. Now that he had a chance to get the answers, they had all but escaped his mind.

The pathway split ahead of them, and the procession took the path that led upwards, into a wall of searing heat. It was manageable, but the further upward they traveled, the more uncomfortable Bassai became.

The procession halted at at the point the passageway turned sharply upwards. It had practically become a wall of jagged rock. Above them were the tunnels that led to the dragon's lair, and apparently his laboratory.

Bassai stared at the rippling air above. The heat of the tunnels wrapped around his body like a thick blanket, uncomfortable for now, but he knew it would be stifling, and even lethal above. He gave a sidelong look to the shaman who would shield him. It would be a difficult enough climb without helping get it up there as well.

He looked at the creature's eyes, barely any flicker of emotion passing over them. It was a sad sight, like the ghouls raised by Ydra, but alive and feeling, living in pain. When he was young, they had terrified him, but now he had grown older and wiser, that emotion made no more sense.

Zeta folded her arms beside him. "Are you just going to stand there?"

Bassai turned to her. He could tell by her face that her bravado was false. Of course it was. Above them was the abode of a god.

She narrowed her eyes at him. "What?"

"You've never been up there to see him."

She shook her head. "Only the Alpha goes up there. No other is allowed."

"Until now."

Zeta eyed him. "You made yourself a nuisance, far too much of a nuisance, for far too long. All for a few words with him."

Bassai looked up again. "I have to know. I must. This is an opportunity that will never come again, perhaps."

"But why *must* you know?" Zeta pressed. "And *you,* of all wyvernborn. It's the height of hubris."

Bassai eyed her with a glare. "You have never questioned why? Never, even in your own mind, alone?"

"What does *why* matter? What matters is action, not flowery words."

"Actions do not happen without reason, people do not change without reason to."

Zeta snorted. "You cannot compare Father to us."

"It seems I just did. I suppose we shall see if I am wrong."

Bassai guided the shaman to the wall ahead of them, and along with Zeta, began to climb. They fitted the shaman into a harness to help hold it steady, and took the ascent in stages, careful to stay inside the shield the misshapen magic user cast against the heat. The rock was coming close to scalding Bassai's hands and feet, but the shield was taking the edge off.

He glanced down. None of the other escorts had joined them.

"Only us?" he said to Zeta.

"They will not come. They consider themselves unworthy to see Father."

The climb took almost half an hour. Once they scrabbled over the lip of the incline they were hit by a wave of searing heat, and the shaman increased the strength of its shield with a pained grunt.

"Thank you," Bassai said to it, laying a hand gently on its forearm.

"Get on with it," Zeta muttered, gesturing down the tunnel ahead. The opening on the other side of it was glowing with intense flame.

They began to walk towards the glow, Bassai glancing around at the tunnel walls. The runes etched into them were all glowing with a scarlet light, pulsing like blood vessels. The floor seemed to recede away from them, the tunnel stretching longer and longer.

"When He looks upon you, kneel and bow your head," Zeta murmured.

"I understand."

At the end of the tunnel, the dragon descended, pressing its head close to the tunnel mouth. Its great blue eye filled the space, and focused on them.

Zeta knelt immediately, and Bassai followed her cue. She bowed her head, and extended her wings to their fullest, angling them downward.

There was a rumbling sound that rolled over them. Bassai could see the azure glow of the eye illuminating the tunnel floor.

"An exile."

The words blasted down the tunnel, and made Bassai's ears ring. Pure dragontongue, perfect pronunciation and inflection. There was an inhalation, moving the air around them, and a growl so deep it shook their bones.

"You are of the Alpha's line."

"Yes, Father," Zeta replied. Her voice was mumbled, reverent, but the language still held the same power, booming from her throat.

The huge slitted pupil twitched over to Bassai. *"Reeva. An old clan, proud, a scent I had thought lost. You are one of mine."*

"One of yours?" Bassai said. His voice was weak and pathetic against the dragon's. The great beast snorted.

"He knows little of our ways. Ignorant child."

Zeta turned her head to Bassai. She had tensed up, he could see the fear she was holding back. "You are of his brood. It was his magic that birthed you."

Bassai looked up into the dragon's eye, which narrowed at him.

"Cast your eyes down," Zeta hissed.

Bassai fixed his eyes on the floor.

"No. Look at me, exile."

Bassai looked up slowly.

"You have travelled far. I smell the trees of the west on you, the open grasses. I smell the great grey and brown blocks, coated in smog, that the humans seem to enjoy living in. I smell the mountains, the Bog waters ... and something else. You have travelled further than most ... to the realm of death. Usually, one does not return from that place."

"I was pulled from there," Bassai said. *"I returned to fight the Caelish, but my task has changed. Peace is our goal, now."*

"A noble goal. Perhaps an idealistic one. That does not explain why you are speaking to me now, why you have been deemed worthy of an audience."

Slowly, Bassai stood. *"I have questions ... and news from the outside. Important news, that you may not hear otherwise."*

"Questions. Every wyvernborn has questions. Most do not have the impertinence to ask."

"Perhaps I do."

There was a deafening boom of laughter. *"You take after me more than you realise. Enter, all three of you."*

Bassai caught Zeta's stare as the shaman shuffled past them. The dragon pulled away from the tunnel.

Bassai marvelled at it. The creature's scaly hide was a record of war. Scars and pockmarks criss-crossed its body and wings, along its muscles as it stretched. Its scales were the colour of rust, bony spikes ran along its spine, down its tail.

The wings remained folded back as it curled around the fire pit in the centre of the chamber. Bassai stood at the mouth of the tunnel, and padded down the stone stairs leading down to the chamber floor. Zeta stayed a foot behind him, and he could feel her eyes on him. He glanced around at her. While she was closely watching Bassai, Zeta's hands were trembling, her breathing fast, her muscles tense and stiff.

The chamber was vast, stretching up further than he could see. The walls were covered in so many runes that the stone was glowing red. The fire pit was making the air dance and thrash. The dragon settled on the other side of the blaze, watching the pair.

"Speak, then, exile. What is your purpose for being here?"

Bassai took a deep breath of the smoky air. *"For a long time, I have been separated from the wyvernborn, and from the dragons. Belief has been a significant part of my life while I have been away. I have prayed to the human Gods, in human temples."*

Zeta growled behind him. The dragon huffed, and she fell silent. *"The human Gods do not just govern the humans. I am aware of them."*

"They offer comfort, but they do not answer questions ... the most important questions. One cannot look the human Gods in the eye."

"You believe I can answer your questions."

"Indeed, should you choose to. I cannot compel a being of your stature to answer anything ... but I must ask. I am compelled to ask ... and now more than any other time in our history, they must be asked."

The dragon huffed again. *"Speak, then."*

"Barada has told me what you are doing in this chamber, how you have adapted blood magic to birth wyvernborn without killing the human they grow inside. No other dragon ever cared about human life. Why do you?"

The dragon curled its body around the fire, snaking its head around. Those fierce blue eyes narrowed at Bassai. *"The lives of the Orlin humans are necessary for the wyvernborn to exist."*

"No other dragon gave much care for the wyvernborn either."

Zeta snarled, but the dragon silenced her with a look. *"The exile is right. The wyvernborn were never what the dragons wanted. We used our blood magic to try and make more of us, not more of you ... but things have changed. There are no more dragons. The last of us were twisted into weapons of war ... myself included. Soon, the wyvernborn will be all that remain of us. You are our legacy. You are our children ... but you and the Orlin humans are inescapably bound together. The Orlin were an enemy for a long time, but a valiant one, unworthy of the fate the former Alpha would have given them. Perhaps your binding to them will make you better than we were."*

"Better than you?" Zeta exclaimed. Her mouth closed quickly once she realised that she had spoken in the manner she had, and her eyes turned downwards.

"Speak, warrior. Such opportunities have not come before, and may never come again."

Zeta looked up slowly. *"How could we be better than you? The dragons were the greatest creatures to roam this world. You ... created us. You gave us life."*

"We forsook you."

Zeta frowned, and looked at Bassai, searching his eyes for an answer.

"You were never taught this by the Alpha, or by the elders."

"She never had to learn," Bassai muttered. *"The Wyvern Bog has changed since my time. Your presence here is new to me."*

The dragon stretched and lowered itself, until its head was resting on its front claws. *"In a way, it is a comfort to know that the lesson is no longer needed ... yet it is still an important one to learn. One that should not be forgotten, or ignored. Do you both know why you exist?"*

Zeta moved close to Bassai. She swallowed, her eyes fixed on the dragon. *"You just said ... you wanted to make more dragons."*

The Empire Of Fire

"You weren't able to do it naturally," Bassai grunted.

The dragon snorted. *"We became obsessed with purity of the blood, of our descendants. For millenia we shifted away from our vast clans, and shrank in our scope. We divided for the smallest and most irrelevant of reasons, the most insignificant slight or crossed word. Our clans were drawn along bloodlines first, then bloodline and belief, then bloodline, belief and opinion, then further and further. Once we divided, we warred. We massacred old friends, extended members of the old broods, even siblings. Young in their nests were put to flame, freshly sired eggs were boiled until they burst. Only when no more blood could be shed did we realise our folly ... but then we found more folly. The wars ended, but the division remained ... and the inbreeding began."*

Both Zeta and Bassai watched as the dragon closed its eyes in contemplation and mourning. Neither of them dared to speak, careful to not even make a sound. Only the roar of the fire pit, and the wheezing of the shaman behind them, could be heard.

"As the centuries passed, fewer dragons were born. We attempted to solve the problem any way we could ... magic, alchemy, pleas to whichever gods we thought would listen ... until we discovered Meutalos. While the dragons died, the humans rose and multiplied. No-one would miss a few of them here and there, on the more remote island settlements."

"But it didn't work," Bassai said, keeping his voice as level as he could.

"It worked as we intended sometimes ... but not often enough to bring our people back to the fore. Many were weak, sickly things that only lived for a matter of days. Some were incapable of flight, and starved. The wyvernborn were the run off, you were ... too human. We did not see you as creatures with your own thoughts and souls. We did not see you for what you are ... our children. Our arrogance, our stupidity, did not allow it."

The dragon huffed a jet of searing hot smoke, *"When the humans finally came for us, there were eighteen left. The sand-walkers took to the seas in a vast fleet of ships, and hunted us down one by one. Twelve dragons died resisting capture. Another took her own life when they captured her. The rest of us were held, and tortured, broken, twisted to their will."*

Two blasts of flame suddenly flashed from the dragon's nostrils. *"It was an affront to everything we were ... driven by desperation and idiocy, until we were dominated by inferior beings."*

Bassai grunted. *"They aren't so inferior."*

"They only dominated us because we had weakened ourselves. The fact remains. The dragons are superior in power and intellect, as are the wyvernborn. There is a debt of blood that humanity will pay for their crimes against us."

"Most of those crimes were committed by the dragons against themselves."

Father's azure eyes narrowed as they focused on Bassai, seeming to glow brighter. *"And what of their crimes against you?"*

Bassai didn't even think about looking away, but his mind betrayed him. Old rage boiled within him at his treatment, at the treatment of old friends who had left the Bog, and been hunted like animals, skinned as trophies, held in pits and left to starve.

"As I thought ... you have not escaped the great pain either. The agony of the wyvernborn is written into your history, over and over again across the centuries. Our sons and daughters have been slaughtered without mercy, tortured and maimed."

"Your sons and daughters have slaughtered, tortured and maimed as well," Bassai countered. *"Rezara would have agreed with you and enacted your retribution ... yet she died in disgrace."*

"Rezara wanted the Orlin to be nothing more than breeding stock."

"An unworthy fate."

"An unworthy fate for a valiant foe, as I said ... and what they have become proved that Rezara was short sighted and maniacal, and more than deserving of her fate ... but make no mistake, the Orlin of the present day are an exception to the humans at large. The debt remains. When the inferno is

rained upon them, the balance will be restored, and it will be paid."

Bassai shook his head. *"You must not."*

Zeta growled at him again. The dragon leaned forwards, the eyes and snout only a foot or so from Bassai, peering at him, taking in his scent. *"I truly have the most disobedient, impetuous children. You bear the scent of pain, the scars of human cruelty, yet you beg me to show mercy."*

"Without your mercy, your children will never have a chance to flourish. We will have to live with the humans eventually, when there are too many of us to remain in the Bog. Attempting to dominate them will only lead to war, and the deaths of more of your sons and daughters, and my siblings."

"We will annihilate them."

"Perhaps. Perhaps not. The humans are more determined and resourceful than you realise ... Father. They have conquered the oceans and the skies, they utilise magic to conquer death itself."

The dragon growled softly. *"What would you have me do?"*

"Sheath the sword, for now. Should the humans raise theirs against us, the time for the rain will be at hand, but until then, we must try to live beside them."

"Why should we?" The dragon settled its head on its front claws. *"I am well aware of your mission for the so-called Resistance. Barada has consulted with me about your little war, asked for my counsel, even though I can give none. My work is far too important ... and I keep out of the politics of this place. My word sways them too easily, and in here, I do not see enough of their world to advise them on the matters that trouble them."*

"What do you think?"

"I am concerned about the sand-walkers, about their sky-ships. The wyvernborn and Orlin have been able to repel their scout groups and raiding parties, even expeditionary forces that have attempted to gain a foothold through the mountains. We have repelled the ships, although they have been limited to smaller ones mostly."

"They have fleets of larger ships, capable of the destruction you have *wrought in days gone."*

"*Barada has told me your stories. They worry me. Enough of my children have been killed by the humans. I have wondered if it is past time that I take a more active role in this place, more even than bringing the young to life. Whether we join your cause or not, our lives hang in the balance. Eventually, regardless, it will no longer matter. I am in the twilight of my life. Without me, there will be no more wyvernborn."*

Bassai felt the grief of inevitability, but opened his body with a step forwards. *"What if the humans could assist you? Aid in your research?"*

The dragon gave Bassai a quizzical look, and raised its head in surprise. Its snout turned up, and it bellowed a laugh that shook the chamber. *"You really have been among them for too long. The idea of trusting the humans with our future children ... our very existence ..."*

"You already are, Father," Bassai said. *"Like it or not, we are at their mercy. There is an army at our doorstep."*

The dragon grunted. *"You are not wrong."*

"Father ..." Bassai breathed in the smoke, deeply. An ancestral fragment of his mind had longed for the scent, for the warmth in his lungs. His experience ran counter to his blood. *"It is true I have lived among the humans for a long time, and become invested in their conflicts, their problems, their Gods. I know the humans. I know their potential. They can be good, they can keep their word, they can help you. I know many who would help you on principle. If they could see the Wyvern Bog today, they would work to preserve it. They would work to preserve you."*

"I wish I had the faith in them that you do." The dragon exhaled and stood up to its full height. He towered above them, taller than the building that had housed the Haaman Government. *"If there were a guarantee ... if the future of my children could be assured ... I would consider joining you. But that guarantee does not exist, and getting it would be impossible."*

"*You have been working for a century, and you have made progress. The mothers live. The wyvernborn ... we are strong. Formidable, when we used to be runts, unwanted."* Bassai bowed his head in deference. *"You have changed as well. You protect us, help us grow."*

"You could be stronger than us, one day. Time is required. You know my terms."

Bassai nodded, and met Father's eyes with his own. *"Provided you keep the sword sheathed ... I agree to them."*

The dragon leaned close to Bassai, closer than it had before. Its pupil narrowed to a fine slit, focusing on him. *"What I have seen the wyvernborn achieve is wonderful. Violence all but ended the dragons' reign. Strength, but with calm, is how you will grow, on that we agree."* The eye turned cold. *"Make sure you remember, and tell those who consider themselves your masters: when the time comes to wield that sword, it will be wielded without hesitation or mercy. The rage of the dragon will be sated, or it will infect and rot my children, as it rotted Rezara. I will not allow it. Should my children be threatened, all those who threaten them will burn."*

4

Ember listened to the chorus of the morning birds in the canopy around her. She watched them flit from branch to branch, gathering loose twigs and leaves to build their nests. Below them, the wyvernborn and Orlin were doing the same.

The new births were a cause for celebration. One of the new fathers sat below, welcoming well-wishers who were bringing bundles of food, skins of fresh milk, fresh herbs that tingled Ember's nostrils even from this high up. She recognised it, a faint, old memory, as Eyhr, said to help a new mother with her sleep and recovery after birthing.

The new wyvernborn baby was in the arms of a young girl, rocking him gently. Ember watched the man as he turned to look at them, smiling warmly and ruffling her hair.

She looked away. Despite the new life in the settlement, the day felt more bitter than sweet. Perhaps the wyvernborn would join them, perhaps not, but the decision hadn't been reached ... and they were running out of time. Sooner or later, she would have to depart, and continue the fight.

This was the closest thing Ember had to a home. It broke her heart to leave it behind, and it wasn't a guarantee that she would ever return.

The man she loved was gone, perhaps dead. Thomas, one of her closest friends, could be in the same state behind enemy lines. She had found a home, but she was turning her back on it, to fight against an empire, for a group that sanctioned murder.

Part of her wanted to abandon that war and remain here. She had never been one to run from a fight, but still ... it was intoxicating to be among her own people.

The Empire Of Fire

"Oh ... hello."

The confusion in the man's voice below made Ember look down. Kira was standing in front of him, smiling awkwardly.

"Hello," Kira said. "Congratulations on the newest member of your family."

The man nodded. "Thank you."

"How's your wife?"

"The shamen are taking good care of her. She'll come home tomorrow."

Kira smiled tightly. "Have you decided on a name?"

The man chuckled to himself. "Not yet. We'll decide when Erin comes home, and we'll need to get a list of wyvernborn names together. It's difficult to choose when the name's in another language."

"I can imagine." Kira took a pouch from her belt. "I asked around ... I heard that part of a new birth is that the community bring gifts to help you take care of the baby ... I brought you this. It's not much, but we travelled light."

She handed the small pouch to the father. "What is it?" he asked.

"It's salt, for preserving. Just in case. We have a saying in Mokku: sometimes it rains."

The father nodded and bowed his head. "Thank you, and ... well ... just thank you."

Kira smiled, and began to turn away.

"Kira!" Ember called.

She looked around, and then up into the tree. She waved. Ember beckoned her over, and her face fell a little bit.

Kira trudged over. "You don't want me to go up there with you, do you?" she called up.

"Absolutely I do. I can talk you through the climb, don't worry."

Kira grunted. "I ... fine."

Ember grinned down at her as she examined the tree trunk, circling it, then circling it again. "It won't bite you, Kira."

"Where am I supposed to start?"

Ember rolled her eyes. "Run your hand over the bark. At the roughest point, look for a knot, and use it as a foothold, then find the next one for your hand and foot, and so on."

"I'll fall!"

Ember glanced around and grabbed onto one of her guide ropes. She made sure it was secured to the branch above her, before tossing the end of it down. "There, use that. Then, if you fall, it won't matter."

"If I fall, I'll probably end up throttling myself," Kira grumbled, as she tied the rope around her waist, feeding her arms through each of the loops. Taking a deep breath, she began her ascent.

"Oh, one more thing. This is important: don't look down."

Kira glared up at Ember's grin, and started climbing.

Ember watched her as she lifted herself three feet off the forest floor, then six feet, then ten feet. Kira's hands found easy purchase on the old bark, the grip of her boots sticking to it like they were lined with tar.

"You see?" Ember called to her, feeding the rope through her hands. "You're doing fine. Keep it up, you're almost halfway."

Kira responded with a strangled grunt, before her foot slid away beneath her. She cried out, and flung herself against the trunk, clinging to it like a passionate lover. Her feet scrabbled against the bark below her, before her toes dug in. She panted, forehead leaving a growing patch of damp on the tree.

"You alright?" Ember called down.

"No." Kira's voice was muffled by the tree. "I looked down."

"Told you. Don't worry, you won't fall. That's what the rope's for."

"Ungh…"

"Good core strength, by the way. A lot of people wouldn't have been able to hold on as well as you did."

"Ungh…"

Ember gave a gentle tug on the rope, just to let Kira know she was still there. "Carry on whenever you're ready. Remember, I've got you."

She saw Kira nod, taking a few deep breath.

The Empire Of Fire

"Fu ... Ember, I can't do it."

"Sure you can, you're more than halfway."

"I'm terrified of heights, always have been. I'm going to throw up."

Ember raised an eyebrow. "Don't think about it. Look up. Focus on what's ahead, not what's behind you. Remember, I've got you."

Kira's breathing slowed and steadied. She stayed there for a moment, gathering her strength.

"Don't take all bloody day, though."

Kira glared up at Ember, and began climbing again. She pushed higher and higher, until she reached the branch that Ember was sitting on.

"Good job. Now, this is the tricky part."

Kira sighed. "*This* is the tricky part, huh?"

"Yep, but I've still got you, and you can do it. You need to shimmy this way. The footholds get a little slippery, but you'll be within reach of the branch."

Kira moved to her left slowly, inching closer to Ember. Her nostrils flared to take in as much air as possible, her eyes bulged out of her head. Ember could see the pupils dancing lower, wanting to check her feet.

"Don't look down."

"I'm trying," Kira muttered through gritted teeth.

"Focus on feeling your way with your feet, use all your senses. Eyes for your hands, touch for your feet."

Kira exhaled and nodded. She inched closer and closer, grimacing as she probed the bark with her feet. Before too long, she was within reach of the branch.

"Right, now work those abs. Keep your balance, reach out for the branch and grab it."

Kira let go of the trunk and grabbed the branch, swinging herself onto it. She exhaled, and grinned at Ember, who nodded with a smile. "Nicely done. Took me ages to learn how to climb like that. Tie yourself to the branch above us, then relax."

Kira did so, and tried to settle herself. "Up this high, I probably won't be relaxing too much."

"I get you."

Kira looked around. The Orlin and wyvernborn below them were moving back and forth with bags of corn and vegetables, running between the trees in some cases. A group of the younger ones were having a race, and it was close. The Orlin were smaller and more nimble, whereas the wyvernborn were more powerful, their long strides covering distances like a sprinter.

"Nice view up here, I can see why you like to climb."

Ember smiled. "You get a different perspective, a bigger picture all at once. It really shows what they've become ... both of them, not just the wyvernborn."

"Hmm ..." Kira murmured. "It makes you think, doesn't it? They've achieved so much, considering where they started. What they haven't developed technologically, they've made up for in the peace between them."

"Don't be so sure about their technology," Ember said. "Wyvernborn are able to have children, and they've held out so far."

"The second part of that is tactics, not technology," Kira said. "Waging warfare when you're this outnumbered requires thinking in creative ways. The Orlin and wyvernborn coming together was probably the best thing to facilitate that thinking. They're different in a lot of ways, and similar in a lot of ways. I won't argue with that first point though, about the children. No-one should be robbed of the joy of bringing new life into the world."

Ember nodded. "I imagine you have plenty of experience, fighting against the odds with the Resistance."

"Yeah, a little. Mainly in the hills. Line of sight can be the difference between life and death, you stay high when they're low down, you use divots and ditches to get the advantage of terrain, herding the enemy where you want them with misdirection. When you don't have the lives to waste, you have to pick your battles."

Ember turned to her. "Well, you seemed to do alright. You stayed alive."

The Empire Of Fire

Kira sighed. "I suppose. What we did, what we had to do ... there was no room for ... decency, or mercy ... it was awful."

"But you still held. You led them well." Ember sighed. "I wish I was half the leader you are."

Kira turned to her with wide eyes. "You're doing well."

"No, I'm not. I haven't really achieved anything apart from put us in a cell. I haven't secured the wyvernborn or Orlin support, all I did was make them maybe think twice about turfing us out."

"They said they were considering joining us."

Ember grunted. "Feels more like lip service."

"It's not a rejection outright."

Ember sighed and looked around at her. "How did you stay strong on the plains, under fire for all that time?"

Kira went silent for a moment. "I'm not sure I did. I think it chipped a lot of the old me away. You didn't see me before I arrived here with my parents. Dresses, the shorter the better ... flitting between friends and partners, bullying my little brother ... I don't recognise myself now. Losing them, and losing the friends I made in Zarvanet ..."

Ember nodded. "I've always been stubborn, but since I joined the Rangers I've gotten worse. Actually ... since I left Orlin, all those years ago. Dragging my brother through the mud to get somewhere we could eat, get some shelter. It hardened me up ... but it made me a real bitch at times too. Unpleasant, my own worst enemy. Put me in charge, and it all gets worse. When things start to go badly, I can't cope with it, and I find it really hard to forgive mistakes. I wish I was more like you, whether or not it has changed you."

"I think you're selling yourself short ... or you're selling me too high." Kira sighed. "I'm no angel. Zeta's right about me. I'm ignorant of people who aren't Mokkan ... who don't look like me. You should see Mokku, Ember ... it's wonderous. Flying ships, floating palaces above lakes full of fish. Long carts on metal rails that rush between cities in hours ... gardens that stretch for miles ... but it's all built on the backs of millions of slaves. Slaves in Cael and Mokku both. We like to think we're the enlightened ones on this world, but we're far from it. Being here, where people could be free, where we can make change ... it was intoxicating, for someone like me. Orphaned, angry ... feeling like I was better than the poor pale people under Cael's boot. Thinking I could be their glorious revolutionary, their saviour ... their messiah. It was a fantasy. It was all a fantasy, and I got lost in it."

Kira's voice was wavering, barely above a whisper. "People died because of my fantasy ... and what right did I have to push it on them? The right of an arrogant little girl with a grudge, and a chip on her shoulder."

"You gave some hope to people who needed it, I suppose."

"I gave them false hope. What was I going to do in Zarvanet? What kind of a base would that have been for my revolution? One filled with the burned bones of the children who lived there. Maybe with you ... I can atone for them. Find that freedom for the rest of the people here who need it."

Kira looked down and wrung her hands. "The wyvernborn that killed my parents are here, in the Bog."

Ember looked at her. "Have you seen them?"

"I've spoken to them."

Ember exhaled a breath. "That must have been a lot."

"They recognised me straight away. I didn't even have to say anything. They looked like they were staring at a poltergeist."

"I can imagine."

Kira stared out at the people below, running and working and eating together. Her voice cracked. "They apologised to me. We spoke for a long time ... they told me how desperate they were when Rezara was in charge of the Bog, how little food they had, how brutal her leadership was. They had to bring back pillage, a certain amount, or they would be starved or sent to their deaths in a raid against a fortress or a battalion. They fled her regime, and roamed around Idris and the mountains for decades, living off scraps of what they could steal. They were just trying to survive, and they had to do horrible things."

Ember sighed. "I don't want us to be driven to that."

"We're closer to it than you think," Kira muttered. "You saw what those creatures I left in Zarvanet could do ... what they did to those soldiers."

Ember had nothing to say to that for a moment. "We have to get out of desperation then, don't we."

Kira nodded, but her breaths remained ragged and pained. "Ember ... I'm sorry. At the outpost ... I'm sorry I was so careless ... that he had to come in ... that he was caught."

A lump formed in Ember's throat. "There's nothing to forgive."

She reached out and squeezed Kira's shoulder. "All we can do is try and be better. Both of us. What happened ... it wouldn't be fair to ..."

A bell sounded, then another, then another. Bells drew closer and closer, before the wave of sound passed them. Ember followed it with narrowed eyes.

Kira wiped her tears away with her sleeve. "What the hell is that about?"

"I'm not sure ..." A new wave approached them, rustling of leaves, and the beating of leathery wings against the air. "Can you climb down a rope alright?"

Kira nodded.

"Come on, let's get down, quickly."

Kira and Ember threw the end of their safety ropes down, and started descending. The ropes stopped about six feet above the ground, and they dropped the rest of the distance. Ember landed in a crouch, and Kira landed with a grunt.

Above them, close to fifty Orlin fighters swung and leaped between the trees, moving swiftly. They were all armed with blades and bows, and all of them were armoured in reinforced leather. Above the canopy, Ember could see wyvernborn swooping above the treetops.

"You mentioned they ran drills," Kira muttered.

"This isn't one of them," Ember said. "The wyvernborn weren't mobilised above the treetops before."

The people around them were looking up at the procession, and were quickly moving into shelter, packing up their wares, or sprinting into burrows dug around the roots of the tallest trees. The wide eyed expressions, and well drilled precision of their movements, told Ember that their fear was absolutely real.

"Come on," she said, unslinging her bow. "We should follow them. They might need our help."

Kira and Ember took off at a run, following the trail of sound that the Orlin were leaving, even though they were completely out of sight. They seemed to be moving in a straight line, towards the edge of the Wyvern Bog.

They passed a group of wyvernborn who were uncovering a huge, four-limbed, harpoon-throwing crossbow from under a canvas sheet. They picked it up and shifted it over to a large wooden platform, tied by rope to a tree with thick, sturdy branches. They were beginning to hoist it upwards as Ember and Kira passed out of sight.

"A ship," Ember grunted as they ran. "There's a ship coming. Those are anti-air defenses."

"Caelish?" Kira muttered.

"Must be."

A third figure joined them in their sprint, coming at them from their right hand side. It was Astrid, cloak billowing, sweat beading on her forehead. She pointed to the right.

"Over there," she gasped. "Barada is there with Sandra …"

The three of them changed direction, weaving between the trees, until they came to a small clearing. Barada and Sandra were in leather armour, and were both heavily armed. Sandra had a long knife on each hip, along with a quiver of arrows on her back. Her bow was long and heavy, held in one hand. Ember had to do a double-take at the musculature of her shoulders and arms, that had been concealed by the gowns she had been wearing before.

Barada's huge greataxe was strapped to his back, with long scimitars on each hip. He turned his draconic head towards them as they sprinted into the clearing, narrowing his slitted eyes.

The Empire Of Fire

"You should leave, humans. I cannot guarantee your safety here."

"What's going on?" Ember panted.

"My scouts have spotted an airship on our perimeter. It is of Caelish design."

Ember exchanged an exhausted glance with the others. "Only one?"

"They often lead with a scout ship, a skiff or frigate, that observes the defenses we have set up to counter them," Sandra said. "Usually they see nothing, they are too far out and our fortifications too concealed, but this one has passed the point they usually turn back."

Ember peered up through the canopy. "Where is it coming from? Due North?"

"West-northwest," Barada said. "Not the usual vector, but still one that is well defended."

There was a swoosh of air as Zeta and another wyvernborn landed beside them. She gave Ember and the rest a brief nod.

"Report," Sandra said, her tone clipped.

"The ship is ... unusual," Zeta growled. "It is small, barely half the size of a standard skiff, and it is ... colourful."

Barada frowned. "What do you mean?"

"The hull is painted blue and purple, the sails are pink. It is not a military craft ... more a courier ... or a yacht."

Barada and Sandra exchanged a glance.

"Could be a change in tactics," Kira muttered. "They're distracting you with something brash and brightly coloured. They could be flanking you."

"Or counting your fortifications," Astrid added. "If you bring the ship down, you will give a position of one of your anti-air defenses away."

"Or more, if it's a small ship it could be quick, nimble ..." Ember muttered.

"There is nothing in any other direction," Zeta growled. "It is alone."

Barada folded his arms and looked at Sandra. She shook her head tightly, her face grim. Barada nodded. "Stay down, wait until it is close ... then try and herd it this way. We will bring it down with a harpoon barrage. Three projectiles should be sufficient."

Zeta nodded, and took off again, beating her wings aggressively. The gusts of wind they kicked up threatened to knock Ember and Astrid over, but Kira held them upright.

"Limit what's revealed …" Kira said quietly. "Yes, that's the best option."

Beside Barada, harpoon teams began loading projectiles into their huge emplacements. They cranked the four arms back into position, harpoons in the breach. The heads of each projectile were large and heavy, barbed and serrated at the edges.

"Fire on my command," Barada bellowed.

They waited, and after a minute, the airship appeared. It was a few hundred feet up, as garishly painted as Zeta had described.

"Ready!" Barada commanded.

Beside Ember, Astrid suddenly wavered, swaying on her feet. Kira turned in alarm, and grabbed onto her. Her eyes had rolled back into her head, as if she was in the midst of fainting.

Sandra glanced at her, eyes widening. "What's wrong with her?"

Barada looked around, and frowned. "Take aim! Track target!"

The emplacements angled upwards, leading the small craft's course.

Astrid blinked, and tensed. Her eyes returned to normal, and widened. "Barada, wait! Hold your fire!"

Barada's head snapped around. "What?"

"They're allies!"

"On a Caelish airship?" Sandra said.

Astrid stood up. "Trust me. They have two of our leaders aboard. Our people are in control of the craft."

Barada snarled. He turned up to the airship again, and waved a hand to the weapon crews. They dismounted, unloading and de-priming the crossbows.

"I suppose they will want to land somewhere," he grunted. He pointed at one of his nearby wyvernborn. "You! Send that ship towards the swamp for a

The Empire Of Fire

water landing. Sandra, send your archers. Watch them on the way in and keep them under close guard. I will take no chances."

Sandra signaled the trees on either side, and they erupted into life, with Orlin warriors dropping and swinging towards southern sides of the Bog. The wyvernborn warrior took off and swooped up to intercept the ship.

Barada focused on Ember, Kira and Astrid. "If they are with you, you meet them, and bring them to the Alpha dwelling. Sandra and I will meet them there."

He took off.

Ember turned to Astrid. She was panting, electric. "Thomas is on that ship, Ember. I spoke to him, and to Seraphine!"

Ember gaped, and grabbed her shoulders. "You're certain?"

Astrid leaped on her, hugging her tightly. "No doubt."

Ember felt a tidal wave of joy rise up and wash over her. "What the hell are we waiting for, then?"

Kira smiled. "Thomas is one of the leaders now? That's impressive."

Astrid took hold of both of Ember's hands, tightly. Ember raised an eyebrow.

"He's not the other leader."

"Then who ..." Ember's throat caught. Her eyes filled with tears immediately. "... Is it ...?"

Astrid nodded, smiling from ear to ear. "Ironclad's here."

***

Thomas rubbed the scar on his neck with the tip of his finger, deep in thought. The damn thing had started itching as they had pulled away from Victory, and he was perplexed as to why. Seraphine had all but purged the corruption from his body.

He was standing on the prow of the *Sand Dancer*, watching the retinue of wyvernborn on either side of them, guiding them downwards. He marvelled at their prowess in flight, gliding with ease, changing their direction with minute movements of their tails or the muscles in their wings. As brutal and fearsome as they were on the ground, it looked like they had been born to take to the air.

He stepped back away from the edge of the ship, and moved to the helm. Captain Seret was exchanging clipped words in Caelish with Berek and Orso, who were strapping their armour on.

"I wouldn't do that if I were you."

The two soldiers glared up at him.

"You'd like that, wouldn't you," Orso growled. "You'd like us to be vulnerable in this stinking swamp full of monsters, at your mercy."

"I'd like you to calm down and not do anything rash, to be frank," Thomas replied evenly. "These are people who you've been trying to wipe out, remember? Caelish armour won't play too well here, I'll have enough trouble explaining your presence here in the first place."

"The princess trusted you with our lives, and maybe the lives of everyone Victory and beyond," Seret muttered. "That trust had better not have been misplaced, for all our sake."

"Placing her trust in a traitor," Berek scowled. "What has it all come to?"

Thomas fixed him with a glare. "Be careful who you call a traitor, Berek. Save it for those who want Cael to be a terror, not a nation. We want the same thing, we want the same people to live, on both sides of the Dividing Sea."

The *Sand Dancer* dropped below the tree line, the sunlight mottling among the leaves. The smell of water teeming with life tingled Thomas's nostrils. The air grew thick as treacle, and warmth wove its way between his clothes and coated his skin in sweat.

"This ship has only ever done one water landing before," Seret grumbled. "It ruined the paint ..."

Orso gave her a look. "That's what you're worried about? The paint?"

"The ship belongs to a princess, of course I'm worried about the paint. You think I picked out these colours?"

The Empire Of Fire

Thomas narrowed his eyes at the canopy surrounding them. There were human faces up there, perched on the branches, carrying bows, keeping a close eye on the ship. He raised a hand and waved, only to be met with scowls. In a twist and whoosh of smoke, Kassaeos popped into being directly behind Berek and Orso, who leaped a foot into the air in shock. He grinned at them as they glared at him.

Thomas gave him a frown and a shake of the head, and Kassaeos raised an eyebrow. "What?"

"Now isn't the time for that nonsense. We're surrounded ... completely surrounded."

Kassaeos folded his arms. "Fine."

"How's Seraphine?"

"Awake, talking plenty. She's not eating much, water's all she can keep down, but it's better than last night. Helen's tending to her while I get a look around."

"There are humans here," Thomas muttered, nodding to the trees. "Up high. You know about that?"

Kassaeos shook his head. "We give the Wyvern Bog the widest berth we can. Descendants of the Orlin, maybe?"

"They must be. That must have been really something for Ember ... she's been away from home for so long ... she thought they were all gone."

Kassaeos chuckled. "We should've guessed some of them would have made it."

"That's not the surprising thing. The surprising thing is that the Wyvernborn let them stay."

"Is it really that hard to believe? Their common enemy gave them a common ground. They were both victimised almost to extinction by the same army."

Thomas raised an eyebrow. "Then why won't they help you, I wonder?"

The wyvernborn escorting them landed in the soft ground, and watched the *Sand Dancer* settle in the swamp water. Seret spoke to the engineer below decks, and the ship's generator spun down, leaving them to gently bob in the water.

"*Let me talk to them first*," Thomas muttered to the Caelish crew. "*I have more experience with wyvernborn than any of you do.*"

He nodded to Seret, who gritted her teeth, and moved to the port side. She extended the ship's ramp. It touched the bank of the pool, and Thomas moved over.

"*Don't draw any weapons, don't make any sudden moves.*"

Seret nodded, and backed away. Thomas took a deep breath, and stepped onto the ramp.

It creaked under his weight as he slowly padded towards the shore. On either side of the wood and iron was a seemingly bottomless pool of murky water. He could see movement beneath the surface, gently waving, brushing against the *Sand Dancer's* hull.

One of the wyvernborn waited a few yards from the bottom of the ramp, arms loose, stance rooted. It was a female, tall and powerful, wings folded at her back.

Thomas stepped onto the sodden ground, and stopped. "I am Thomas. I represent the Haaman Resistance, and the Silver Throne of Cael."

"We recognise neither authority. However, the Alpha has permitted your landing, on the advice of your fellows. Do not violate that allowance."

Thomas bowed his head. "I understand, and I offer what assurances I can that we will not."

The wyvernborn frowned at him. "You are more deferential than the others were."

"I have asked many questions about your people to those who know you well ... although my information is out of date by more than a century."

The female nodded. "That wyvernborn you asked is Bassai, I would assume."

Thomas nodded. "Is he well?"

"He is ... in contemplation."

"I will not pretend to understand," Thomas said with a half smile.

The female looked at him quizzically. "You are a curious human."

Thomas bowed his head again. "There are Caelish soldiers aboard the ship. They are not a threat to you, they are allied to our cause. We have a situation that threatens all of Haama, one that supersedes all other concerns."

"We are deliberating your conflict with the Caelish currently," the female grumbled, eyeing the people on the *Sand Dancer's* deck. "Against our better judgement, I would add."

"I am not talking about the conflict with the Caelish."

She peered at him with a puzzled frown as three figures erupted from the tree line behind her. One of them was running towards the *Sand Dancer* far more quickly than the other two were, her scarlet hair flying out behind her.

Thomas laughed as Ember leaped into his arms, holding him tightly.

"You smell like a bonfire," she said, her voice muffled against his shoulder.

Thomas's throat caught at the memory of the burning city from which he had fled. "Yeah? Well, you smell like a swamp."

She caught his tone and pulled back, gripping his upper arms tightly. "What happened?"

"Victory ... Vehnek attacked Victory. It was still burning when we left."

Ember gritted her teeth. "He ... why would he ... how did you get away?"

"Long story, I'll tell you all of it ... but we have bigger problems ... and we have an opportunity, Ember. We could end all this ... all this fighting. We could end it."

Astrid and Kira caught the end of what he said as they slowed beside him.

The wyvernborn took a step forwards, her eyes wide. "What did you say?"

He met her gaze as he put his arms around Kira and Astrid both. "Peace. We have a chance at peace."

***

Ember descended down to the *Sand Dancer's* sub-deck, followed by Thomas. The scent of medicinal incense and oil filled her nostrils. There were only three doors down here, all on their left, and the nearest one was wide open.

The corridor was brightly decorated and wide, with portholes on on side that were shuttered closed. The wooden bulkheads were lined with gold paint along the edges, with the panels alternating shades of pink, purple, and sky-blue. The floor was carpeted in deep red.

Ember peered into the first room, and met the weak gaze of Seraphine, laying on one of the bunks. Kassaeos was sitting beside her, and smiled up at her under the brim of his hat. Another woman was there too, middle aged, with light olive skin and steady hands as she redressed the bandages around Seraphine's ankles.

Similar bandages were around her wrists. She was thinner, more withered than Ember remembered. She was pale and her eyes sunken, but the gaze emerging from them was bright, full of joy at her presence.

"Ember …" she murmured. "You look like you've been busy."

Ember sat at the foot of the bed. "We thought … when we heard about the clans, we feared the worst."

Seraphine looked at the bulkhead, a cloud passing over her. "You feared correctly. I am trying to … look forwards … see a path for us to follow … but I can't …" She glanced at Thomas. "Although apparently you can."

"He thinks he can," Kassaeos muttered.

Seraphine slapped his arm weakly. "If the stories of The Mage are even half true, he'll be on to something. It'll need to be something big, though. What they sent against us in the Pil Valley … they showed us no mercy. The battle was all but over in minutes."

Thomas shook his head. "It's for everyone to hear, not just some of us … and I'm still formulating the ins and outs of it."

Seraphine nodded, and looked to Ember. "He's next door."

Ember's fists tightened, and she nodded. "How bad?"

Seraphine exchanged a glance with Kassaeos, and Ember's jaw clenched. "I'd rather know before I go in there."

Both of them looked up at Thomas.

"They were examining him, closely and intrusively," Thomas said quietly. "We don't know what they were looking for, but based on his condition ... they were taking him apart, opening him up ... and according to the scientist we brought with us, they did it while he was awake."

Ember stared at him, and jumped off the bed. "Take me to see him."

Thomas led her from the room, and took her next door. As the double doors opened, the smell of incense and oil hit her in the face like a handful of pepper. She coughed, her eyes watering, and squinted into the dark room.

The shutter over the viewport had been lowered, the room lit with lanterns turned as low as they could go. Once, this had been a luxurious bed chamber, if a little small. The bed and both of the wardrobes had been pushed together to form a kind of half-cushioned slab. To keep it level, the legs of the bed had been removed, and repurposed into a makeshift frame that held a few tools and flasks on the table in the corner.

Upon the slab lay Ironclad, groaning weakly, unmoving. His armour was open, but beneath a blanket that was quickly being put in place by a middle aged Haaman man.

There were fresh welds in the armour on Ironclad's arms and legs. His knees were supported by more slats of wood to hold them still, almost like splints.

"You have visitors," the Haaman man said gently.

"I know ... thank you, Jack."

Ironclad's voice was haggard, like the creaking of metal plates and rivets under too much strain. Ember felt herself trembling, and Thomas's hand linked with hers.

"How do you feel?" Thomas asked him.

"I imagine slightly worse than I look," Ironclad replied. "You're not alone, I can hear more breathing from the doorway."

Ember blinked, and walked forwards. She wove her fingers gently around his hand, and looked down at his face.

There were more welds on the armour on his head, especially around his eyes, which were ... gone. Empty voids into his head, with no sign of the blue light that had been there before. The two jewelled orbs that had been there before were entirely gone.

"Em ..." he groaned.

She covered her mouth to stop the sob, and leaned down, planting a soft kiss on his metal cheek. It was warm beneath her lips, and she felt as if his energy was bleeding away into the air.

"I'm here," she whispered. "I'm here, and I'm not going anywhere."

She heard the Haaman man take a step forwards. "I'm sorry, but ... I don't think that's a good idea right now, given what repairs I have to make ..."

Ember looked up at him sharply. "I'm not leaving him."

The man looked up at Thomas, who stepped in. "You don't know what's underneath the armour, do you?"

She frowned around at him. "What does that matter? Thomas, I'm not leaving him, not now. He's been ... I can't even imagine what's happened to him. Being here ... it'll help him."

Thomas held her free hand tightly, and she frowned at him. "What's under the armour..."

"I don't care what's under the fucking armour! I told you I'm not leaving him, I'm *not* leaving him!"

Thomas gritted his teeth.

"Thomas... let her stay."

Thomas looked down at Ironclad, the down at the floor. "Are you sure?"

"She's all I thought about."

Thomas swallowed and took a step back with a nod.

Ember felt Ironclad's fingers brush against hers. "I am beneath the

The Empire Of Fire

armour, Ember. What I was before the armour ... but ..."

She frowned. "You? What do you mean, 'you're under...'"

The realisation made her mouth close by itself. She looked down at the blanket covering his chest, and tears filled her eyes. "They put you in here... all of you..."

"It's not ... a pleasant sight," Ironclad groaned.

Ember moved the blanket aside, away from his chest. Steam rose and filled her eyes, and she blinked it away.

Between the two segments of Ironclad's breastplate was a mess of clockwork gears, between tiny pipes that pumped oil all around the vast body. She could see the fluid rushing from one limb to another.

All of this machinery surrounded the skeleton, curled up like a foetus, in the centre of the body. The bones were cracked and charred, there were tiny rivulets of melted iron and steel still stuck to the shin bones where his armour plating had been.

Ember reached out a trembling hand to Ironclad's cheek, and held his hand tightly with the other. "I'm still here," she murmured. "I'm not going anywhere. You can't scare me off that easily."

His fingers curled around hers. "You can continue your work, Jack. We'll be alright."

Jack exchanged another reluctant glance with Thomas, before he sighed to himself, and picked his tools up once again. "I'll try not too make it too painful ..."

"You always try, and that's all I can ask," Ironclad groaned, although his voice had taken on a warmth through the pain.

Jack glanced at Ember. "Yes well, I'm telling her more than I'm telling you. It will be a difficult few days, although a lot of the most vital work is done."

"Just make sure I can be at the meeting with the Alpha ..." Ironclad croaked. "I don't have to fight, just talk."

Jack swallowed and wiped his brow. "Yes, well ... I'll try."

Ember nodded to him in thanks. "There's a lot of time it seems … which might be a good thing in a way. Ironclad … there's a lot to catch you up on …"

The Empire Of Fire

5

Kelad shifted between clumps of dirt and outcroppings of rock, dematerialising and rematerialising above the ghouls standing below and around him. There were hundreds of them standing on the slopes outside the Pil Valley, staring out at the rest of the district, likely an early warning system of some kind. All were the rotting bodies of Taeba clansmen.

Kelad was careful not to attract any of their attention, shifting as silently as he could, shimmying along the thickest branches, sticking to the early morning shadows. The climb was easy when augmented by his abilities, but he was still careful. He was a valuable asset, particularly with a battle on the horizon.

Despite that, he was still the most logical choice to scout the battlefield. He had decades of experience, even without the powers granted by his status as an Aether.

He materialised in the shadow of a cluster of rocks around a twist of tree roots. A pair of ghouls caught his eye.

They were clad in buckled and breached Caelish armour, with brown dried blood caked around their underclothes. Their jaws were slack, their faces gaunt and lifeless. The remainder of the defense and occupation forces would probably be in the same sorry state.

His men would have to know exactly what they would face. They could not be allowed to waver in their duty, not even for a second, and pitting themselves against their own countrymen, even dead countrymen …

Kelad resumed the climb, popping through the canopy of the trees, atop rocks, and clinging to tree trunks. The incline was steep, and quickly becoming sheer. Twenty or more yards above him, the trees all but disappeared and became clumps of mud and jagged rock.

He had been careful to pick out the valley wall that was the least hospitable, the most difficult to climb, on the logic that it would be the least closely watched. Only here did he seem to be right.

He reached the end of the vegetation swiftly, shifting from tree to tree. Looking up, he gritted his teeth. The nearest platform for him to use was out of the range of his shifting ability by a few feet, a rock covered in muck and rotten wood, perhaps five feet across.

Kelad crouched on the tree trunk, wincing at the creak of the wood. Below him, the ghouls groaned and hissed at the sound. He held still, held his breath even to limit his movement, until the dead began to calm.

Once the sounds had reduced to the background growls of before, Kelad took a deep inward breath. He looked up once again, judging the distance in his mind, estimating the height of the jump required, the power his legs would have to exude to make it. Once his own breathing was level, he began to slowly crouch, bouncing as gently as he could.

Completely focused, he sprang up, and at the apex of his jump, he shifted upwards as far as he could.

He stretched out an arm in front of him as he rematerialized, and felt his fingertips brush against crumbling crumbs of mud, that fell away into his own face.

He was short by a full yard.

He began to fall back, drifting like a feather, as if the world around him had slowed. He gritted his teeth to keep from crying out in alarm as the platform fell away from him, knowing there was a full second before he could shift again.

That second passed, and he shifted upwards again.

When he rematerialized this time, for a moment he thought he might have misjudged the shift. The platform was nowhere to be seen, but after a few feet of descent it slammed into his back. He let out the air in his lungs through gritted teeth, suppressing the grunt of pain.

The Empire Of Fire

"*You're getting too old for this,*" he muttered to himself. He didn't look anywhere near a hundred and forty five, but in that moment he felt it as surely as if he were on his deathbed.

He listened closely to the ghouls, who were snarling once more. Once they were silent, he pushed himself to his feet.

The ascent was much smoother. The jagged rock walls provided plenty of handholds, and he found he didn't need to shift at all after a certain point. It certainly made his climb much quieter, and that in turn meant he could hear some of what was happening in the Pil Valley itself.

It sounded as if a furious crowd of people were inside, roiling and roaring in madness with wild animals and demons of the night wind. Their stampeding footsteps were clear as a thousand military drums beating in a synchronous pulse.

Still fighting, perhaps. Kelad dared to hope for a moment that someone had managed to hold out. He knew Commander Moran well, he had trusted him implicitly to hold the Valley against counter-attack, should it come. Unfortunately it had come in overwhelming force.

The incline began to become a slope, a hillside, levelling off, and Kelad slowed his pace. On level ground there would be ghouls, no doubt, standing silent sentry between the trees.

There was a glow in the air now, reaching up over the valley walls, up to the stars. The unmistakable glow of fire.

Kelad crawled forwards, his belly brushing the ground. He spotted the silhouettes of the dead, facing outwards, ever vigilant.

They would spot the fleet when they went on the offensive, he had no doubt. There would be no element of surprise, but the Caelish would have the advantage of terrain. The abominations could swarm a ground force, perhaps, but they couldn't fly.

He would potentially have to wait to deploy the ground forces until a good number of the dead had been retired permanently. Despite the size of the force coming to liberate the valley, he had less men at his command than

Moran had in defending it in the first place.

He shifted past the first line of ghouls, once more taking up residence in the treetops. He shifted along them, until he had a good view of the Pil Valley itself.

The valley floor had been churned into mud by thousands of feet. There were only a few copses of trees remaining, the majority had been felled for the structures that the army had begun to build. The lake was still, strangely serene in the chaos and death.

The Caelish fortifications had been ransacked, scattered across the trampled grass, dried blood smeared across the debris. There was no sign of any corpses, at least ones that were inert.

Ghouls swarmed by the tens of thousands, smashing against one of the buildings, what would have been the town hall according to the plans for the Pil Valley settlement. The dead threw themselves against the walls, cracking them. Shouts and screams came from inside, arrows and blasts of magic came from the upper floors, but did little or nothing to halt the mass.

Kelad frowned at that. Conventional methods ineffective, at least from the ground. Hand to hand combat would be disastrous, given the numbers at play.

He watched the bursts of magic as they battered the ghouls, setting some alight, stripping flesh from their bones, freezing them ... but most kept coming. Intensity of energy, he couldn't tell from the ridge. The best plan remained the fleet, attacking from above.

A flash of flame appeared among the swarm, raised up high. It pointed at the building slowly, and the ghouls moved as one, a tidal wave that smashed against the wall and crumbled it. The screams grew louder. The second floor buckled, the dead flooded through the gap they had made ... and the screams were silenced.

Kelad's gaze shifted across to the lake, where a series of row boats and cargo barges were floating at the centre. People were in them, laying low, peering over the side at the dead watching them on the shoreline.

The Empire Of Fire

***

Delik ducked back down, his eyes closed tightly. He hugged the bottom of the boat, and trembled.

"*Delik, stop looking at them! They'll see you!*"

Usma gritted her teeth. "*They already know we're here, Bojan ... they're watching us. They're waiting for something.*"

"*We should have brought more weapons ...*" Bojan hissed. "*We're vulnerable out here ...*"

"*Va'Kael ...*" Zahna whispered. "*They just pulled down the town hall ... the whole thing ... they just pulled it down.*"

The rest of the people in the boat whimpered, whispering prayers to each other, holding each other against the chill in the air.

"*Oh no ...*" Usma whispered. "*Bojan ...*"

Bojan closed his eyes tightly, steadying himself, and looked up at the shoreline.

The dead were moving closer, packing in and pressing themselves together, right up against the edge of the lake. All of them were looking right at the boats, right at Bojan, some eyes rotten, some eye sockets completely empty. They made no sound at all, which was more unnerving than if they were hissing and snarling like rabid dogs.

The stink of them had grown stronger. Now they were so close, Bojan could practically see the maggots crawling on their skin. Soldiers he knew were among the crowd, staring at him, through him, without any expression or recognition.

"*Start rowing,*" Bojan hissed.

Usma tugged on his sleeve frantically.

"*I said ...*"

"*There's no point, Bo'.*"

Bojan looked around. The dead were on the far bank, now, on every bank. *"You know I love you, right?"*

Usma stared at him. *"Well ... I do now."*

"Just ... wanted to say it, while I still can."

Usma barked a laugh. *"So you're telling me now ... when we're ..."*

She trailed off as her eyes fell on the bank of the lake. Bojan turned around.

The dead were beginning to part, leaving a pathway, perfectly straight. A lone figure was walking steadily towards them. Row by row, the dead bowed their heads in reverence, until the figure had reached the water's edge.

She had been a clanswoman, a warrior. She held a thin rapier at her side in a loose grip. Her face was gaunt, her hair white, her eyes pale, her bone white skin contrasting the black arteries and veins that criss-crossed her arms, neck, and face. She had been dead for days, as dead as the rest of them ... and yet there was an intelligence behind her.

Her rapier ignited into a brilliant jet of flame. Usma flinched beside Bojan, and he took her hand tightly. *"Bo'..."*

The dead woman raised her flaming blade, and pointed it at the boats. The front row of the walking dead stepped into the lake.

They strode in on all sides, the water rising up to their waists, their chests, until they were fully submerged. Still they kept coming.

Zahna shook her head. *"The water's too deep ... they can't reach us."*

Bojan looked into the water. Dust from the footsteps below was turning the clear surface murky and brown. The movements of the dead were clouded. *"Don't be so sure."*

A pale face appeared in the water faintly, perhaps ten feet below the surface. A second appeared behind it, then a third, clearer and closer, eyes staring up at the boat.

"Pick up your blades!" Bojan yelled. *"Oars, sticks, whatever you have!"*

Usma stared at him with wide eyes and scrambled to the oars,

The Empire Of Fire

grabbing one and readying it above her head.

They heard Zahna scream, and turned to see the dead hands pawing at her. Others were grasping at the side of the rowboat, all of the rowboats in their little flotilla. Bojan almost lost his footing, helping Usma stay on her feet.

Before either of them could reach Zahna, she was pulled into the water. The boat rocked again, throwing Usma and Bojan to the deck. When Bojan looked up again, a tidal wave of the dead was washing over the side.

***

Kelad watched as the boats were overturned and swamped, and slipped the communication stone from the pouch on his belt.

"Razorback, this is General Kelad. Keep your voice down in response."

Ketesh, his helmsman, answered with a whisper. "*I am here, General. What are your orders?*"

"*Send one of the skiffs to pick me up from the established point. I'll be there in two hours. Split the fleet. Keep the Razorback at the head of the second, third and fifth squadrons, send the fourth and sixth in a wide course around to the west. Prepare the cannons for bombardment.*"

6

In the Alpha's burrow, Thomas walked back and forth, recounting the events of the previous days and weeks: the engagements with the Ghosts and Black fleet on the journey through Idris, the state of Victory before and after the riots, Princess Allessandra, and finally the crisis unfolding in the Pil Valley. Barada and Sandra sat quietly and listened to him, while Zeta barked the occasional question for him to navigate. Ironclad leaned forwards, grunting in occasional spurts of pain, but paying attention to every word the Mage uttered. Ember and Bassai listened too, but Ember's attention kept being pulled towards Ironclad, every time he made a sound, eyes tracing the burns, buckles and hasty welds in his armour plating.

Kassaeos held Seraphine close as she quietly wept.

"It can only be Ydra's power," Thomas murmured as he paced. "Reports from the Caelish scouts indicated thousands of ghouls in the Pil Valley, that cannot be killed conventionally."

"Which means that any engagement with them on the ground will simply end with even more ghouls in the host," Ironclad muttered. His voice had the quality of a rusted iron hinge on a heavy door, pained creaking under its own weight. "They don't know what they're walking into."

"Well, that may not be entirely accurate," Thomas said quietly. The rest of the council waited as he readied himself. "I ... informed my commander in the Caelish infantry."

Barada and Zeta growled, almost in furious harmony. Sandra's hand closed over two of Barada's large fingers.

"An interesting decision," Bassai said. "The correct one, in my opinion. The ghouls, when augmented by Ydra's abilities, are a greater threat than the

Caelish."

"They are not a threat you spoke of before," Barada snarled.

"We didn't know about this," Ember insisted. "If we had, we would have told you."

"I had no choice," Thomas said. "These ghouls cannot be killed with blades and bolts ... without forewarning, all the Caelish would be doing in an engagement is adding to their ranks."

"How many ships were sent?" Ironclad grunted.

"Seven at least, led by General Kelad's *Razorback*."

Ember's lip curled. "Kelad, eh?"

Thomas nodded with a grunt. "I know ... the point is that each carrier is capable of carrying five hundred soldiers, the battleships two hundred. No doubt the fleet would have been bolstered by more airships on the way."

"If they stay airborne, these ghouls surely won't stand a chance," Sandra said.

"I would agree ... but Ydra knows ... knew about those ships just as well as we do. She knows how to take them down, and I wouldn't bet on her not pressing that advantage."

Seraphine looked up, and wiped the tears from her eyes. "Thomas is right. If there are as many ghouls as the Caelish army suggest, that means ... that the dark power, the necromancy, has consumed Ydra fully. It knows what she knows. It will be well aware of the threat."

"Then the Caelish fools are walking into a trap," Zeta growled with a grin. "Good. Let them fight it out. That means there are less for us, and your Resistance, to deal with when the time comes."

Thomas paced once more, shaking his head in frustration. "In a way, but there are two things to consider. The ships engaging in the Pil Valley belong to the Standing Army, not the Black Fleet. That force is the only thing standing between Vehnek and unilateral control of the Caelish armed forces, Kelad's ships were defending the people on the farms and in the city. They are good men and women, potential allies in our bid to get the tyranny out of Haama. If they go in there alone, they'll be slaughtered, and Ydra's army grows larger. That dead force will spread across the country, and keep growing exponentially, and you won't be spared here in the Wyvern Bog."

Bassai smiled. "Then it appears we have a common enemy."

"Exactly." Thomas stopped and clasped his hands behind his back. "We have an opportunity here, if you are willing to hear me."

The council watched him, as he took a breath.

"We mobilise a force of warriors, and assist the Caelish."

Ironclad leaned back with a groan. Ember narrowed her eyes at him.

"You really did go native in that city, didn't you," Kassaeos hissed. His black eyes were locked on to him, sharp as razors.

"We're all native to Haama," Thomas said quietly.

Barada stood up from his wide chair with a snarl. "You come here on an enemy ship, you bring the enemy here, and demand we follow you into battle, on a fools mission against thousands of the dead … and fight by the enemy's side, no less."

"I know," Thomas said, holding out a hand. "I know how much it is to ask … and if I had seen this place before, seen that the Orlin were alive and that you were living in peace … I might have tried to think of another path. You will be able to turn the tide in our favour, however, and this is a problem you share with everyone in the country, friend and foe alike."

Sandra stood as well. "What could a handful of our people possibly add, if the Caelish fleet wouldn't succeed?"

Thomas looked down for a moment, and his jaw set. "Two things. The first is protection for Seraphine, Astrid and myself. We deploy in, get to Ydra … and try get her to regain some control of herself."

"At this point … there may be nothing to regain," Seraphine muttered, fresh tears running down her cheeks.

"Then we … deal with her. Help her find some peace."

"Kill her, in other words," Zeta grunted.

Thomas sighed with a sad nod of his head. "Ydra's power is the key.

The Empire Of Fire

Without that, the ghouls will be vulnerable to our blades and arrows."

"It's not just a power, Thomas, it's *alive*. It's aware." Seraphine leaned against Kassaeos, overcome for a moment. "With what happened in the Valley, so much death at once, it would have overfed that thing inside her."

"Which fully emphasises the need to end this, before her power is bolstered even further," Ironclad said. "She would recognise us, we could get through to her … and again, if it doesn't work, we can end it."

"Dragon fire would be able to destroy them if they get close to the Wyvern Bog," Barada growled in a low, deep voice. "This is not our problem."

Thomas straightened his back and glared at Barada. He shook his head, and his voice became a snap. "Unacceptable."

Barada reared up to his full, eight and a half feet of height, and flared his wings at the challenge. Bassai let out a short grunt. Zeta took a step forwards.

Thomas held his ground. "The second reason you have to be there … and we have to be there … is a little dirtier, but no less important: optics. Political optics. We all rise up with the good, honourable people of Cael and Haama … that are present in the Standing Army, I promise you … and defend this country and its people. It couldn't be denied. Stand with them, stand on common ground."

Sandra's eyes widened. "You're talking about the grounds for peace."

Thomas nodded. "An end to a hundred and two years of bloody conflict that will be the end of all involved."

Kassaeos gritted his teeth. "There can be no peace with them. They are bleeding us, burning us, you've seen it."

"Vehnek is, yes … and the army opposes him. We unite, and we make his tactic of violence unsustainable. He relies on our division. We take his power away … and we take the power of the Ghosts away too. Understand, the current tactic of violence, against both hard and soft targets, isn't working. All we've done since the occupation is repeat the same stupidity, expecting that this time, the result will be different. *This time,* they'll give us what we want. Have they, ever?"

"Thomas ... you saw ... you felt what they did to Melida City, what they did to all of us, all of our friends," Ironclad muttered. "The deaths of farmers since then ... I agree that the violence needs to end, but I don't think it can while the Caelish are here in Haama, lording over us all."

Ember frowned, and shook her head. "The Orlin and wyvernborn were at loggerheads for decades ... Ironclad, look at them. They live together, lead together, they fall in love and have children. They make sacrifices for each other. They found peace ... and if the Alpha before Barada had her way, it would be the opposite."

Ironclad was silent for a moment. "I can't look at them. The enemy took my eyes."

Ember exhaled, and her head hung low, her shoulders sagging.

"The situation has some parallels, but they are not completely analogous," Bassai grunted.

Ember straightened up, jaw set. "But the principle is there. Haama and Cael are joined together now, they have been for decades. Ripping them apart will cause too much damage to both countries."

"They need us, need our help as much as we need theirs. Ironclad ..." Thomas began, and paused, facing him. "Tobias ... there's a reason why Rowan allowed us to become The Four Guardians, those warriors of legend. It was so people would listen to us when we came back. People like Donnal may have corrupted it, but Rowan didn't bring the Four Guardians back to fight a whole new war, have people die in our name. He brought us back to end it ... and we *can* end it. It's right there in front of us." He looked at Barada. "For you as well, Alpha. The executioner's blade will always be above your heads if you don't act."

There was silence as the room considered Thomas's words.

"Do you know how many people in Donnal's Resistance have come to us, demanding, begging us to join them?" Sandra said to him, stroking her chin.

Thomas shook his head.

"I couldn't begin to count. We have denied them every time."

The Empire Of Fire

Barada's wings lowered, his chin raised. "But not this time."

Zeta's eyes widened, and she stood up straight.

"You are the first to truly prove that you want peace. More than that, your peace may actually be possible ... and we cannot turn our backs."

Sandra took his hand in both of hers, squeezing it. "Zeta, we'll need your best. Wyvernborn and Orlin, archers, harpoonists, and close-in fighters. Make sure at least half are flyers."

Barada looked down at her, and his mouth turned up in a toothy grin. "My love ... it has been a while since you and I have fought side by side."

Sandra smiled. "I never stopped practicing with the bow."

The Alpha's draconic eyes danced over her figure for a moment. "I can tell." He looked up at Bassai and Ember. "You were right ... both of you. We will have to fight for our future, and fight for the final peace."

Thomas's and Ember's eyes turned to Ironclad. Barada followed their gaze to the crippled Construct, sitting in the chair that he'd had to use to be dragged into the burrow. He was still, like a sculpture dedicated to war.

"All of us," Ironclad stood with a groan. "All of us will fight."

Seraphine shook her head. "You seem unaware of the odds. Tens of thousands of ghouls, bolstered by an army of Caelish soldiers if we're too late. Even if we're not, we only have Thomas's word that those soldiers won't attack us ... we'll be outnumbered."

"If you can't trust them, trust me," Thomas said. "I know those soldiers ... I know they're honourable."

Everyone turned to Bassai as a low, rumbling growl escaped his throat. Zeta and Barada frowned at him.

"No, Seraphine. *We* will have the advantage," Bassai said. Then he made another sound, a fierce set of snarls, deep enough to shake the ground beneath them. Zeta's eyes widened, and she looked at Barada sharply. The Alpha straightened up and extended his wings again, this time more slowly, stretching them out so far they almost reached from wall to wall.

"Leave us," Barada said softly. "We must confer, Bassai and I, Sandra and Zeta."

***

Ironclad peeled off from the group with Jack, grunting and groaning in pain. Ember watched him go, not bothering to hide the worry in her soul. Thomas squeezed her hand gently.

"He'll be alright. He's been though a lot more than we could've imagined."

Ember nodded to him, and strode into the trees to find the rest of their party.

Kira listened to Ember as she recapped the meeting, and shrugged. "War it is, then. Didn't expect to be going in side by side with the Caelish."

"Or the wyvernborn, for that matter, after how long it took to get them to even consider taking up arms," Ember said.

"If you hadn't, my pleas might have fallen on deaf ears," Thomas said with a smile. "You've done well here … you know how stubborn a wyvernborn can be."

"Or an Orlin," Ember said with a grin. "Kira, where's Astrid?"

"Talking to Donnal. There's a chance we'll get more support. Apparently, Resistance fighters captured three squadrons of airships, and one or two of them could be helpful in this escapade."

Thomas nodded. "The more the merrier."

"How does she know about that?" Ember asked.

"She's been in contact with him since we left Obsidian," Kira said. "He asked her to update him every step of the way."

"Nice of you to let us know that was happening," Ember replied flatly.

Kira shrugged. "What did you expect? With the amount that was at stake with these negotiations …"

"It does make sense," Thomas said quickly, before Ember could cut in. "His lack of trust is a little disconcerting, but it makes sense. I should like to have a word with Donnal, when we next cross paths with him."

Ember glanced at him, at the hardened look his eyes. Before she could ask him anything more, her attention was drawn to Seraphine. Kassaeos was helping her along the forest paths, with an arm around her waist. One of the wyvernborn was walking beside her at a politely slow pace.

"Your shamen will need ice magic ... nothing else I've seen is as effective. Holding them in place is second best to putting them down permanently."

"With the recent births, not many shamen can be spared, Lady Seraphine," the wyvernborn grunted.

"Even as few as four would make a difference."

"The Caelish will have Mages with them," Thomas called over to them. "I made sure to tell my commander that they would be needed."

Seraphine peered at him with a dark look in her eyes. "Your commander? Just how far undercover did you go?"

"As far as I felt I was required. A little further than I originally thought, truthfully. So far, in fact, that the princess presented me with one of the Caelish military's highest honours."

Seraphine's lip curled. "You were receiving awards, and doing their bidding, while I was being tortured."

Ember glanced at Thomas, who seemed unperturbed by Seraphine's words. "I was given the award for defending farmers that the Black Fleet, and your terrorists, were murdering in their beds."

"Thomas, not now!" Kassaeos hissed.

"Terrorists?" Ember said incredulously. "That's a little ..."

"No, it's entirely appropriate," Thomas cut in. "Donnal will be made to answer for it, as will you, Seraphine, if you knew what he knew."

"Can you stand?" Kassaeos said to Seraphine, his tone on the edge of a knife. His left hand had closed around the hilt of his rapier.

"Don't," she said, taking on an air of calm.

Astrid slowly walked through the trees, coming towards them. She looked between the two groups that were beginning to form, and glanced questioningly at Kira, who shook her head quickly.

"Is ... I hope I'm not interrupting."

"No, please, interrupt away," Ember said, the tension in her shoulders growing.

"I have just been in counsel with Donnal. I informed him of the situation, and asked him if he could spare a ship or any warriors." Astrid pursed her lips. "I'm ... afraid he won't be able to spare anyone."

"Of course he won't," Thomas muttered.

Astrid looked at the forest floor. "He is also ... he's telling us to return to Obsidian, and not go anywhere near Taeba. He's happy to let the Caelish army engage the ghouls alone."

Seraphine frowned. "What do you mean? Is he aware of the full scale of this threat?"

"He ... is confident that Obsidian can hold against the ghouls. They have a highly fortified choke point ... he's confident they could hold out against them. He may have a point."

"He doesn't," Thomas said flatly. "He hasn't engaged these things before, and typical of him, he is absolutely fine to watch in his kingdom while the innocent in Idris are swept away by the tide."

Ember grimaced. "Yeah, we can't ignore this."

"Absolutely not," Seraphine grunted. "Do not bother contacting him again, more than likely the conversation will be circular. He likes getting his own way ... and this is bigger than him and the Resistance."

"Not only that, but his choke point is useless, if what you're saying about these things is true," Kira muttered. "They'll just keep coming until they break through."

"Well, the most important thing for us is that our numbers will be far fewer than they could be," Ember said. "We'd have to use that ship you brought ... which means convincing the captain to send it and her crew into hell."

"I can convince her," Thomas said. "Her, and the soldiers too. We can just tell them they'll be able to rejoin their ranks, no questions asked."

"That's irresponsible," Seraphine argued. "They all know too much."

"They all helped you and Ironclad escape. Treason is a capital offense. They're in it now, regardless of whether or not they want to be ... and they saw that city burn, the same as I did."

"They're loyal to Cael," Kassaeos snapped.

"They're loyal to Allessandra. That's the choice, Allessandra or Vehnek, and the princess is a far better bet than the Lord Marshal. A cursory look at the political situation here should tell you that."

"Better we take the ship for ourselves, and put the Caelish in the cells here," Kassaeos said.

Ember watched Thomas narrow his eyes, and put a hand on his chest. "If you can't convince them to come, it's the best option."

***

Thomas meditated on the deck of the *Sand Dancer,* preparing himself for the fray. The warriors of the Bog had readied themselves for a day and a night, and now the time for their march to war had drawn near.

The Caelish allies that he had brought with them had reacted to the coming fight as businesslike as ever.

Captain Seret had folded her arms. "*To maintain combat speed, we'll need to strip a few things out. Most of the furniture, some of the supplies ... and we can't take that many people. Thirty at most, and that's thirty Orlin. The wyvernborn are too heavy.*"

Thomas had stared at her for a moment. "*You understand what I'm asking of you ... and you understand that I'm asking, not demanding.*"

At that, she had quirked a bemused eyebrow. "*Yes.*"

"Good. Is that thirty Orlin once we're there? I'd imagine the Wyvernborn will need to land on the ship to rest while we're on our way ... and a few of us will be there too. Ironclad, Ember, Seraphine, myself ..."

"*Yes, yes, but we'll be dropping you in early on and quickly. We'd be too vulnerable hovering in one place.*"

"*I agree. We haven't seen any ranged ability from the ghouls yet, but better not take the risk.*" He had then looked at Berek and Orso. "*What about you two?*"

"*What about us?*" Berek had said. "*Don't have much of a choice, do we?*" Thomas had sighed. "*Of course you do.*"

"*We can't get off the ship, Tomek ... Thomas,*" Orso had grunted. "*We stay here, we'll probably be thrown in a dungeon, and that's not why Allessandra sent us with you. She sent us with you to help.*"

"*I promise both of you ... we want peace. Nothing else. What we're walking into is going to be brutal ... and there are no guarantees that our plan will work, or that we won't be fired upon by the Caelish Fleet.*"

Berek had snorted. "*But if it works ... it'll definitely get us all somewhere.*"

"*Definitely. Somewhere far better than where we are now.*"

Berek and Orso had looked at each other. "*We have to, then,*" Orso grunted.

Presently, Thomas opened his eyes as the bustle of a crowd drew near. He looked over at the warriors that were beginning to form up on the solid ground beside the marsh. Orlin and wyvernborn, strapping on armour, checking the tension in bows and the fletching of arrows, the sharpness of blades and axe heads. He recognised the same determination he had seen every day in Bassai and Ember. The stoic confidence of the wyvernborn was bolstering the Orlin, their nerves being dampened down. Young warriors were being given a talking-to by the older ones. Pacts were being made, jokes were being told, but not too many.

This was big, and they all knew it. They had been told exactly what they would be facing, and therefore were under no delusions. They knew what was at stake, and even in the veterans, the tension was clear.

"*When are we going?*" Berek grunted, leaning on the railing to watch them.

"*As soon as we can,*" Thomas muttered. "*The fleet will be engaging the ghouls soon ... we can't afford to wait.*"

The trees parted, and Barada walked into the clearing, followed closely by Sandra, Zeta, and Bassai. The warriors all cheered for a moment at their presence, their eyes following Barada to the centre of their midst. Bassai walked past them all, directly to the *Sand Dancer*.

"Warriors! Hear me!" Barada bellowed. "We are mighty! We are what the world sees when the word *strength* crosses their minds, let alone their lips. The wyvernborn bested foe after foe, unchallenged ... until we met the Orlin. Quick, well trained, intelligent ... a might of a different kind. For decades we warred, until we were brought together by the fires that burned away the old world. For decades, we have learned together, lived together, built together. For years we have waited for our time ... a time when we can live without fear of the outside world."

He growled, from deep in his chest. "Yes, friends, *fear*. We turn our backs on it, snarl at it, but it remains, so now we confront it. We nod to it, in the knowledge that it is there, and it will not go anywhere. We use it as fuel for our strength, fuel for our future, the fuel for a lasting peace."

There were murmurs from the crowd, nodding of heads, growls of affirmation.

"The wyvernborn have not taken to the air in force for three hundred years. We do so today, so that one day soon, we will not have to. Our sword will be sharp, but sheathed, but not today. Today we wield the sword. Today we stand shoulder to shoulder with our Orlin brothers and sisters. Today we fight!"

The warriors raised their blades and bellowed. Barada spread his arms wide, a five foot long greatsword in each hand. His wings spread to their full span, angled upwards, and the warriors roared as one.

"Today we fly!"

7

Kelad listened to the ghouls moaning, his eyes closed. The sound of them carried on the wind, even from the distance the fleet was holding position. There was palpable silence aboard the *Razorback,* and the other ships in the squadrons nearby, the anticipation of conflict, and the quiet dread from the horror they were about to face.

Kelad had fought in more engagements than he could count, and his crew were the best in the fleet, yet their nerves were obvious. He was glad he had no heart, otherwise it would have been hammering. He could feel the same nausea, the same tingle that would have come from blood rushing around his body.

The living dead, augmented by a dark power of an unknowable magnitude and capability. None of them had faced such a bastardisation of nature before now.

Kelad sighed, opening his eyes. He glanced over at the other ships nearby. Two other battleships, four skiffs, and three carriers, all at full readiness, their cannons in place, their hatches open. The dragon-heads on each prow of the larger vessels snorted, as tense as the crews.

This group, and the others to the west, represented two fifths of the Aerial Navy assigned to Haama ... with the exception of the Black Fleet, conspicuous in their absence. Kelad allowed himself a bitter smile. Lord Marshal Vehnek had a guile far more pronounced than his father and grandfather, a social tactician. Three outcomes were possible from this engagement: a victory, which could be spun into Vehnek's victory, a defeat, which Vehnek could use to expand his and the Black Fleet's influence and lessen Kelad's, or a slaughter, in which case the Black Fleet would be nearly unopposed in the air.

He watched as the *Razorback's* ground commander, Codesh Ulan, stepped up onto the bridge platform. His light olive skin and permanent frown greeted Kelad like an old friend. That frown never left his face, either on duty or on leave, even when he and his squad had received the Silver Wreath.

"The men are ready for the drop, General."

Kelad nodded. *"Good. The other platoon commanders on the Razorback have their orders?"*

"Yes, sir."

"Join me for a moment."

Ulan nodded, walking beside Kelad as he stepped to the very rear of the bridge, out of earshot of everyone.

Kelad lowered his voice. *"You have yet to tell me the source of your intelligence regarding these ghouls, Commander."*

Ulan gritted his teeth, staring out at the Pil Valley. *"General ... I know we are going out on a limb ... but there can be no other explanation for the ease of the army's defeat here."*

"Indeed. My reconnaissance confirmed some of it, certainly the rumour of a necromancer at the head of the horde ... which came from you directly, not from the scouts."

"Yes, sir."

"So ... where did the intelligence come from? Do you have a reason to keep this from your superior officer?"

Ulan sighed. *"The source ... was a soldier. One who had been stationed in the west, and been into Taeba District. Apparently he had encountered this necromancer before."*

"His name, Commander."

"General, please understand ... I, and the army at large, owe this man. I wouldn't want there to be adverse consequences for him. His name is Tomek. He was attached to my squad for a brief time, he received the Silver Wreath with us. Believe me, he earned it."

Kelad nodded. *"I see. Tomek ... interesting that you weren't immediately willing to tell me who he is."*

"*Some would consider that he knows too much, and make certain arrangements accordingly.*"

Kelad's eyebrow twitched. "*Am I such a man, Commander?*"

"*With all due respect, you have been.*"

Kelad frowned around at him, a concerned grin crossing his lips. "*You wound me, Commander, and I don't think you're being entirely honest with me. You have your own doubts about this Tomek.*"

"*At first, perhaps. Not any more. Especially as he was telling the truth.*"

Kelad allowed himself to nod. "*Perhaps I agree. We will speak on it no more.*"

Ulan saluted.

Kelad pushed past him, to the helm. "*Ketesh, open communications to all ships in the fleet.*"

"*Aye, General.*" The helmsman cranked four levers, and touched every communication stone on the plinth beside her. She nodded to him.

"*All squadrons, all troops, this is General Kelad. Proceed with phase one on my mark. Ground troops, remember, fight to dismember. All Mages, all cannons, prepare ice magic. Groups one and two, signal readiness.*"

One by one, all the airships in both groups signalled. Kelad nodded. "*Group one, begin.*"

The ships around the *Razorback* surged forwards. The sound of the ghouls started getting louder as the Pil Valley drew closer. Kelad folded his arms.

"*Ketesh, let the carriers pull ahead. Move us into broadside position alongside them, and prepare the starboard cannons.*"

"*Aye, sir.*"

The wind roared in the *Razorback's* sails. Kelad could see the valley in full now, the glint of the water within, the dark clusters of thousands of bodies surging across the dead grass.

"*Commander, what do you make of that?*"

Ulan narrowed his eyes, and looked into the telescope mounted on the bridge railing. "*They are all ghouls? There are tens of thousands!*"

"*Indeed. Air support will be essential.*"

Ulan looked in again. "*The settlement is all but destroyed. I can only see a few scattered beams ... piles of wreckage. General ... are you sure that there are even survivors?*"

"*We cannot be sure of anything, Commander, nor can we abandon our people.*"

The groan of the dead grew in volume, a sudden increase that furrowed Kelad's brow. "*We've been spotted.*"

Ulan looked around at him, and peered back into the telescope. "*There, atop the valley walls. There are figures on the treeline.*"

Kelad scratched his cheek. He stepped forwards to the communication stones, and touched the ones corresponding to Group One. "*This is General Kelad. Trim sails, cut speed to one third and pull south. Carriers, prepare for drop.*"

He switched stones. "*Group Two, reposition to the north, and stay low. Keep your distance until the word is given.*"

All ships in both groups acknowledged. The groan of the dead became a roar, but no hostile action was taken towards them.

So far, everything was going to plan.

"*General, permission to speak candidly,*" Ulan muttered.

Kelad nodded.

"*We can drop thirty six hundred troops to engage in the southern pass. We could be outnumbered six, seven, maybe as much as ten to one. It might not be enough of a diversion.*"

"*She sent a number of ghouls after survivors that numbered in the hundreds, not the thousands. There is a good chance that they will come out to meet us in force.*"

The southern edge of the Pil Valley came into view. The walls of it rose like a small circular mountain range, before the ground dipped down into the bowl of vegetation and water, that the clans, their own settlers, and now the dead had turned into a dustbowl. A cleft sat at the southern edge, bordering a vast field of black ash and blood.

Kelad regarded the battlefield silently, the remains of two pitched battles, two massacres, one a massacre of clansmen, the other of Caelish soldiers and settlers. There was no indication that there was ever any life, any grass or creatures grazing. Trees were blackened stumps, flowers were stomped into the mud.

Footprints had churned the blackened dirt, leading into the valley, straight through the passageway between the rock faces.

"*If I may, sir, I don't like those valley walls,*" Ulan muttered. "*If we go between them we'll be ripe for ambush.*"

"That bottleneck can be used against us just as well as we can use it ourselves," Kelad agreed. "However ... we may not have much of a choice in the matter."

Ulan wheeled around, teeth gritted. "*General...!*"

"This necromancer defeated the defenses here, defeated this bottleneck once already. She's not stupid, these ghouls are being directed. They'll never ride out to meet us in the field. We have to spring her trap."

"*We'll lose most of our force!*"

"No, Commander. All they have to do is draw enough ire for us to extract survivors, then they fall back. We hit the necromancer from the air, we deal with the ghouls permanently. Our reserve will step in if things get desperate."

Ulan grimaced and let out a ragged sigh. "*As you say, General.*"

Kelad clapped a hand on his shoulder. "*I'm not in the business of throwing lives away ... especially now. It pains me that such tactics appear necessary, I would never have considered them until I saw the threat first hand.*"

Ulan nodded tightly. Kelad looked around at the fleet as the *Razorback* swung around, its cannons pointing at the valley passage. The three carriers were in position, the other two battleships in the fleet hovered over them.

He opened communications with Group One. "*All ground forces: deploy.*

The Empire Of Fire

Air support, watch the valley walls and the passage. Check your targets, fire on hostiles only if there are large groups on the attack, let's not play our hand too early."

Kelad watched as the carriers settled onto the ground, landing on their flat bellies. The bay doors at the rear opened, pulled open by crewmen turning cranks attached to chains on both sides of the behemoth ships. Ramps extended, and the army began to disembark.

The siege engines came first, in lines of three at a time. The hexagonal vehicles were all fully manned, both of their front-mounted cannons set in their ball turrets swinging to the left and right, testing their mobility. The five soldiers on top of them, behind the ramparts put there to protect them, were making sure they had plenty of ammunition for their crossbows. On each one, another light portable cannon was being fixed onto the front rampart, for maximum field of fire.

There were twenty seven of the siege engines in total, nine to a carrier, at the sight of their first engagement, their first victory. The battle of the Pil Valley had been a resounding success ... that had become an unmitigated disaster in the aftermath.

The infantry followed, hulking heavy troops with greatswords and thick armour, standard footsoldiers armed with crossbows and longswords, hundreds of Mages in light armour. They arranged themselves into square groups of thirty six, falling in behind the siege engines. The small groups had been instituted for maximum mobility, so they were more easily able to reinforce each other.

Kelad glanced up at the valley. The roar of the dead stayed as loud as before, but there seemed to be no activity. He thought he could see figures in the treeline, but he couldn't be sure. There were too few, and they were too far away to strike with anything but the cannons.

"We're being watched ..." he muttered.

Ulan grimaced. *"But this is the force they're supposed to watch, isn't it ... so that's fine."*

Kelad nodded. "*Go below, Commander. Prepare your troops.*"

Ulan saluted and jogged across the deck.

"*Carriers signalling, all troops deployed,*" Ketesh said.

"*Good. Have them lift off. Begin Phase Two.*"

The carriers took to the skies again. The *Reverence* and the *Valkyr* held position above the ground forces on either side, while the third carrier, the *Majestic*, pulled alongside the *Razorback*. The skiffs rose slowly until they were flying above them.

The *Kallus* and the *Spearhead*, the other two battleships in the group, pulled ahead of the carriers, and once the formation was complete, the army moved forwards. Three siege engines led the way in a triangle formation, followed by a mixed company of infantry, pulled tight to conceal their numbers from the front. More siege engines followed, then more infantry, and so on, layers of death, some of the finest in the Caelish Standing Army.

How many would be lost for this gambit?

"*All battleships, watch those valley walls closely,*" Kelad ordered. "*They may try to flank us and hit us from above. Reserve, fall back a hundred yards, prepare to cover or reinforce.*"

The passageway was almost a kilometre in length. The armed force took the pathway slowly, the reserve pulling back away from the entrance as the last of the infantry moved in. The three siege engines at the point of the army were two hundred and fifty yards in. Kelad took a breath and looked up.

The dead were massing. Most of them were drawing close to the mouth of the pass, as if they were grains of sand beginning to pour through a timer. The trickle of them became a stream, without any need for haste, a steady, unrelenting march towards the Caelish.

"*Siege engines, prepare to fire at five hundred yards. Fire blasts first, then hit them with ice at one hundred.*" He turned to the helm. "*Ketesh, trim sails, keep our speed low. Ready all cannons, including the dragon-head.*"

He sent the same order to the other battleships and skiffs. The siege weapon mounted inside the dragon-head at the front of every ship was very effective, but was easily burned out after three or four sustained shots. They would have to be used sparingly ... but one would be needed soon, especially considering the numbers coming right at them.

Below, the front three siege engines opened fire. Blasts of flame flashed forwards, and engulfed half of the first row of ghouls. They continued walking for a few steps, and Kelad felt a short stab of fear like a serrated knife. However, one by one, they crumpled to the ground.

The dead army doubled their pace.

The siege engines fired again, including the crew mounted light cannons on top. More conjured blasts of flame, and more ghouls fell. Their pace increased again.

"*Ketesh, nose down. Dragon-head, fire on my order.*"

The crew grasped a hold of the ramparts and guide ropes around them as the *Razorback* pointed downwards at an angle, trying to lead the advance of the dead. Kelad heard the dragon-head roar and snarl, as if it knew exactly the kind of nightmare it was looking at.

"*Fire!*"

The ship trembled as the dragon-head's mouth opened, and a long, intense stream of focused fire and lightning blasted out with a thunderclap. The light it gave off was so bright that Kelad had to look away, and the boom of the impact was deafening.

The beam dragged along the ground, straight through the ghouls. The weapon was like an extension of a monstrous creature, snarling and grinding as it chewed through the rocky ground and walking corpses. There was a blast of heat from below that hit the *Razorback* in the belly, and Kelad checked in with the advancing troops for any signs of trouble.

The beam extinguished as the power reserves depleted. "*Recharge,*" Kelad barked, and checked the damage below.

A line of blackened earth was drawn from the impact point to a hundred yards back. It had gone from flat ground to a divot in the ground a foot and a half deep at least. There was no sign of the legion of ghouls that had been there, likely they were little more than ash and vapour now.

The rest of the ghouls surged forwards, stomping through the ruins of their comrades without a care in the world.

At just over a hundred yards before the two armies would clash, the siege engines opened fire with blasts of ice magic. Clumps of the front row of ghouls froze solid, and the rest surged around and through them, snapping parts of them off, crunching the parts to nothing as the advance became a stampede.

"*Va'Kael above us,*" Kelad whispered to himself. He picked out the communication stones linked to the other two battleships in Group One. "*Kallus, move into the centre and ready your dragon-head, we'll rotate with you and cover the flank. Skiffs, make ready to charge.*"

He sent a hand signal to Ketesh, and she nodded, sweeping the *Razorback* to port. Kelad kept his eyes down at the front line as more frozen ghouls were trampled underfoot. The last fifty yards disappeared between the siege engines and the dead. He heard the impact of hundreds of bodies against the armour plating of each one, surging between them to try and get at the footsoldiers.

As the *Razorback* pulled towards the valley wall, there was a shout from the sentries on the port side. Kelad tore his eyes away from the frontline and looked down as bolts of lightning and flame erupted from the treeline. They smashed into the port side of the *Kallus,* setting the wooden slats on fire and melting the iron armour. The battleship's innards spilled out of the side, and the dragon-head on the prow roared in pain.

"*All ships, raise barriers!*" Kelad ordered.

There was an explosion deep inside the *Kallus's* hull, blasting crew off the deck. It was little more than a floating wreck now, rapidly descending as the generator inside failed. The helmsman aboard aimed the dying ship at the dead ranks, and it smashed against the valley wall, shattering like a vase. Debris, large and small pieces, showered the ghouls, crushing some.

They kept coming though, undeterred by the piles and fragments of ship and dead Caelish airmen. With a sinking feeling in his gut, Kelad watched as

The Empire Of Fire

the burning and broken bodies of the *Kallus's* crew hauled themselves up, and joined the ranks of the necromancer.

He snatched up the communication stone to the fleet. "*Group One skiffs, the necromancer is close. Keep an eye out for her on the valley walls and use your spyglasses to check the back ranks. All cannons, all ships, target the treelines on either side of us and fire at will!*"

The thunderous volley of cannonfire smashed against the trees, shattering the trunks into splinters and felling them swiftly. Shards of wood and sawdust blasted outwards, and quickly, the cannons were revealed.

They were of Caelish design, the defensive cannons that Kelad had deployed to the Pil Valley after it was occupied. Now that they were closer, he recognised the walking corpse of Arch Mage Velen, body riddled with splinters the size of broadswords.

Their eyes seemed to meet across the expanse of air. There was no recognition in the man's eyes, even though he had been a colleague for decades. There was nothing of him left, not even an echo of a whisper.

Then he was gone, incinerated by a cannon blast from the *Razorback's* broadside.

The battle churned below them. The siege engines were trying to roll forwards, crushing some of the ghouls under their large wheels. Still, the dead were climbing on top of each other, swarming over the ramparts and onto the top of them to get to the infantry, who were locked in battle. The small platoons were making micro adjustments to their positions, pulling back and pushing forwards, striking and retreating to regroup, before striking again. For the moment they were deadlocked, and the siege engines were still firing their cannons, but there was no forward movement even possible.

From the other side of the pass, cannon shots blazed out at the airships, absorbed by the magical barriers protecting the hull. There was more movement on the top of the valley walls, more ghouls, thousands of them. They were surging up from the valley itself, thousands more, covering the beaten grass and the shattered tree trunks. As soon as they appeared, Kelad signalled the commanders in the infantry. *"Incoming from above. Reserve, prepare to fire."*

They were moving exactly the way Kelad though they might. Some began pouring over the side of the pass, down onto the army. The infantry repositioned away from the walls, and engaged all along the line. More ghouls surged back over the wall and dropped onto the hard ground outside the valley, met with volleys of cannonfire from the siege engines at the rear even as they lay broken and flailing at the bottom.

"All ships, prepare for Phase Three," Kelad snapped. *"Commander Ulan, prepare for drop."*

The orders were acknowledged. The ghouls at the bottom of the valley walls engaging the reserve were breaking the fall of the ones behind them, and they were beginning to encircle the army in the pass. Some were charging the reserve, trying to get around behind them. Two of the skiffs hovered above, attempting to thin the herd.

The time had come.

"Begin Phase Three," Kelad barked. *"Ketesh, full ahead, get the Majestic on our wing."*

"Aye!"

The *Razorback's* sails billowed, and they pushed forwards swiftly.

"Group Two, move in, cover the rescue party. Group One, reinforce the ground troops. Ketesh, time to the settlement?"

"Sixty seconds, General."

He nodded. *"You have command of the ship."*

The helmsman gave a quick nod, and Kelad shifted, sending himself down two decks, into his quarters.

He had no magic to speak of, aside from his innate ability to smoke-shift from one place to another through the Aetherial Plane. This engagement would doubtless require it, however, and he had just the thing. Aside from his longsword, always attached to his hip, he had something else he had only used at practice ranges, a gift Lord Marshal Vehnek had given him.

The Empire Of Fire

It was a device from Mokku, a weapon they had developed using Cael's research. The handle was curved for the purpose of ergonomics, with a small lever for the wielder's forefinger to manipulate. The barrel was similar to that of a portable cannon, light enough for the device to be pointed and fired with one hand. At the back, the lever was connected to an assembly that was shaped to hold small, spherical magic stones, which the lever mechanism touched to an amplifier at the back end of the barrel.

Touch the stone to the amplifier, and bang. The device fired any spell stored in the stone.

Kelad grabbed a bag of stones containing ice magic, and each one held enough charge for three shots at best. He quickly attached the pistol's holster and the bag to the harness around his waist, and took a quick moment to steady his breath.

The fear remained a constant, no matter how many battles he fought. He, after all, had seen the end of his own life first hand. He had felt the pain of burning to death, and even now his nerves hadn't entirely recovered. Perhaps that's why he flaunted himself around so much, quaffing brandy by the bottle, bedding socialites and royals, leaping into the fire.

Maybe he just wanted to feel something. Anything, any feeling that matched up to the simple pleasures of being alive.

Before there could be any more useless introspection, he pushed himself from the room and slid down the deck traversal ladder to the bottom. He threw open the door into the hold, where Commander Ulan and his soldiers stood immediately to attention.

He regarded the faces of the finest under his command, perhaps the finest in the entire Caelish army. Almost all had received honours, some even from royalty. Medium infantry, well armed and armoured, a mix of range, magic, and blade.

Commander Ulan saluted Kelad, and everyone else in the bay followed suit. Ulan fixed his helmet on.

"*You know your jobs, you know our goal,*" Kelad said. "*Ten seconds to drop."*

Kelad shifted, and materialised at the bay doors. He glanced back. *"First squad, on me."*

A dozen soldiers took their place beside him, grasping onto the rappel ropes and harnesses. The bay doors opened, the rear of the *Razorback* facing the entrance to the Pil Valley. The battle raged on, but their flight had not gone unnoticed.

The dead were coming.

"Drop!"

The first squad rappelled to the Valley floor, and Kelad jumped after them, shifting to a point close to the ground so he could land safely. Ulan's second squad followed immediately.

The troops began fanning out as the *Majestic* slowly settled to the ground. Kelad took in the surroundings. Despite the absence of bodies, there was obvious carnage all around them. The ground was churned and beaten by the stamping of feet, the soil was blackened by flame and blood. The choking stink of smoke and burned flesh filled the air.

The settlement that had been in the process of construction was mostly reduced to blackened skeletons and torn down wooden logs and planks. Kelad pointed, and the squads pressed forward into the ruins, searching for survivors.

The main force of ghouls were four or five minutes away, if they charged at full pelt. The stragglers though, they were much closer, clusters of thirty to forty staggering towards the rescue party. Kelad whipped the communication stone from his belt, and unclasped the buckle holding the pistol in its holster on his hip. *"Squads eleven to twenty five, establish a defense perimeter. Two squads to a group, keep the dead away from the Majestic and the settlement. Ketesh, signal the skiffs in Group Two to move in and harass the groups closing in on us."*

He drew his pistol, and joined up with the defense force as they began to mobilise.

The Empire Of Fire

***

Elizia suppressed the shaking in her hand as she combed quickly through the debris of the iron smith's forge. A phantom itch plagued her, where her left wrist used to be. She absent-mindedly rubbed the prosthesis that had replaced it against the top of her greaves, to no avail.

Sweat was pouring from her brow. The last time she had picked through debris like this had been in Victory after the riots, the time before that: Bonham.

The time before that, though, had been Zarvanet, and the terror of that fateful night lanced through her now like a dagger coated in frostbite.

Her arm: gone. Her friends: murdered in an unspeakable way, by creatures born from a nightmare. Here she was now, thrust into more nightmares.

Ulan pointed her, Yaro and Lazar to the left, to a long building that had been gutted, torn open like the remains of an animal that had fallen victim to a predator. They jogged up to it and peered into the breaches in the walls.

Nausea made Elizia's heart twist. This had been a barracks, probably for workers. The beds were tussled and upturned, covered in dried blood and viscera. The tables were on their side, with rotting food all over the floor, drawing flies. It was completely deserted.

"Elizia, check around on the north side of the building, and make it quick," Yaro hissed. *"Some of these buildings have cellars, could be survivors sheltered inside. Lazar, watch the exit."*

"Yes, sir," Lazar grunted.

Elizia held her breath and nodded. She edged inside, Yaro behind her. The floorboards creaked beneath her feet, and she gritted her teeth, all too aware that she was giving away her position with every step. However, that also meant empty space below her, perhaps a basement, perhaps just storage beneath the floor.

She edged around the debris, keeping an eye on every shadow, jumping at every sound that could betray an enemy or reveal a survivor. As she approached the corner of the room, she spotted a hatch on the floor. It was wide enough to fit a person easily, and she turned back.

"*Yaro, hatch!*"

He jogged over to her, and helped her heft the heavy wood and iron door open. The space below was no more than three or four feet high, nothing more than a storage space. The floor was compacted dirt, and there seemed to be nothing down there but empty space. However, there were also whimpers, whispers, the plaintive cries of fear.

"*Caelish army,*" Yaro barked. "*Come out, we have a ship ready to get you away from here!*"

A thin face appeared from the darkness, eyes pleading, covered in grime. The figure was so grimy and starved that Elizia couldn't tell if they were young or old, man or woman. "*You're ... here ... to ...*"

"*Yes! Come, come quickly!*"

He extended a hand to the survivor, and lifted her out of the cellar. Another two faces replaced her, staring up at their saviours.

"*You're alright, we'll get you out of here in no time,*" Elizia said gently, steadying her voice. "*How many of you are there?*"

"*Thirty one,*" the survivor stammered. "*We've been there since it started ... how long has it been ... I ...?*"

"*It doesn't matter now. What matters is, it's over.*" She looked up at Yaro, who was helping the thirteenth and fourteenth people out of the cellar. They were trembling, listening to the distant sounds of cannonfire, and airships sweeping overhead.

"*Lazar, are we still clear?*" Yaro called back.

"*Still clear, sir. Looks like a good number of survivors are coming out.*"

The last survivors came up, and Yaro swept an arm towards the breach. "*Let's go. Lazar, take the lead, Elizia, cover the rear.*"

They emerged out into the smoky air, and the refugees began to cough and splutter. Lazar and Yaro guided them towards the *Majestic,* Elizia made sure they all kept pace as best she could, but she couldn't keep them from looking around.

"*Oh Va'Kael, they're coming! They're coming!*"

"*They're our problem, not yours,*" Elizia barked, "*keep moving, we've got you.*"

Two skiffs swept down from above, and fired their broadside cannons at the stream of walking corpses coming at them. Some of the survivors wanted to watch, wanted some catharsis for their terror, but Elizia hurried them on, not only because they were slowing everyone down, but because the sight of the ghouls getting back up again would have sent them into a blind panic.

Their group reached the *Majestic*, and Yaro and Lazar halted, waving the survivors aboard. Medics and crew members carrying hot food and water were waiting for them. Elizia looked back at the ruin.

There were gaggles of thin, bedraggled people being guided out of the broken buildings. They were stumbling and staggering, falling over debris, being manhandled along by the soldiers. Two more skiffs swept overhead, their cannons raining ice down on the dead.

The last of the refugees they had picked up stumbled aboard the *Majestic*. Elizia turned to Commander Ulan, who had joined them with Pardek and Mule, and more survivors. "*Commander, is this everyone?*"

"*I don't know.*" He looked around. There was a definite end to the incoming survivors, and he glanced over at the advancing enemy. The swooping skiffs were certainly closer than they had been. The perimeter forces were readying their weapons, signalling that the dead were within two hundred yards. "*We can't afford to wait, or no-one leaves.*"

He collared one of the crewmen. "*Get to the bridge, tell them to take off when the last of this group are aboard. Begin Phase four.*"

"*Aye, Commander ... but what about the soldiers ... General Kelad ...*"

"*We'll get out on the Razorback when the time comes.*"

The crewman bolted back into the ship. Everyone turned around to face the perimeter. Most of the squads who had gone into the settlement were now at the ship, the others were moving in at the end of the stream of settlers. Elizia glanced back into the bay. There seemed so few of them, so few survivors from the thousand or so builders, cutters and workers that had been sent to the Pil Valley. They now numbered less than two hundred, probably.

The last of them entered the bay, and Ulan nodded. *"Get those bay doors closed, and get out of here."*

There was a nod from the crewmen within earshot, and Ulan turned. *"Squads one to ten, form up on me!"*

They moved back, and even before the bay doors were fully closed, the *Majestic* lifted from the ground, reaching up towards to the altitude for fast flight. The *Razorback* ceased fire and rose as well, pulling two of the attacking skiffs into formation beside it. Phase four was simple: for the *Majestic*, run like hell. For everyone else, cover them while they ran like hell.

Kelad's flagship followed the carrier's escape course, overtaking and sending cannonfire into the valley walls, clearing them as best they could from any potential enemy fire.

"Commander, if the Razorback's leaving ... how are we getting out?" Elizia muttered.

"They'll be back," Ulan said quietly, before his voice raised to a firm, barked order. *"Move up and reinforce the flanks! We get encircled, we're dead!"*

***

At a hundred yards, Kelad took a breath, and levelled his pistol at the ghoul directly in front of him, a large man dragging an axe along the ground. *"Mages ... open fire!"*

He squeezed the lever, and the pistol jumped in his hand. The bolt of ice magic struck the ghoul next to his target in the chest and froze it solid. The rest of the Mages levelled their gauntlet amplifiers forwards, and let loose bursts of frost and shards of thick ice. More were frozen, a whole group of them in fact,

The Empire Of Fire

over to the battalion's right hand side.

Kelad fired again, and again, hitting two more ghouls, the Mages sent more shots forwards, but the frozen ghouls were quickly overtaken by more.

Fifty yards.

As Kelad quickly replaced the expended stone in his pistol with a fresh one, he glanced around. The *Majestic* was almost level with the edge of the Pil Valley, the *Razorback* and other skiffs were ahead of it, bombarding a gap in the dead army's defenses.

He drew his sword. "*All ranged troops, fire at will! Blades to the frontline!*"

Three more shots from the pistol joined the volley of crossbow bolts and blasts of ice energy slamming and tearing into the onrushing horde. A few were stopped, but the horde was not.

There was no time to load the pistol again, and no point in doing so either. The front line of soldiers engaged, little more than small rocks jutting into an onrushing river. The ghouls washed over and around their tight ranks, thrusting claw-like hands, blood caked weapons, and their own bodies as a whole at them.

The two skiffs above slowed to a hover and bombarded the ghouls with cannon fire from above. The dead ranks were thinned a little, but they were just as unerringly relentless, as if the airships weren't even there.

Kelad stabbed forwards with his longsword, slicing off an arm from a dead clansmen, and another from a Caelish settler whose throat had been torn out. His soldiers were doing similar, but the dismembered were replaced by two more ghouls who were undamaged and ferocious.

Even worse, those among his ranks that dropped to the ground from fatal wounds were granted no peace in death. He watched a woman beside him nearly beheaded by axe blow, her blood spraying across the rest of the walking dead. No sooner had she fallen, she shuddered and stood again, blood leaking through her helmet, thrusting her blade into the ribs of the man beside her.

Kelad snicked off her arms, whirling to engage another group closing on him. With the confines of bodies pressed around him so tightly, there was nowhere to shift, no escape or respite. He was relying purely on his bladesmanship.

Unsustainable. They would be dead in moments.

He clasped the communication stone on his belt, continuing to fight as it was clutched in his grip. *"Razorback, the moment that the Majestic is away, swing around to pick us up. Signal the main force to fall back!"*

***

"Understood, General," Ketesh barked. The *Razorback* was beginning to pass over the valley walls, cannons on both sides peppering the top of them. The pair of skiffs with them were close on either side, keeping up a constant field of fire.

Ketesh's executive officer sent the signals to the rest of the fleet and the armed forces. She glanced up at the *Majestic,* five hundred yards above them. Their sails had caught a north westerly wind, and the lumbering leviathan of a ship was moving at a fair speed. It had cleared the Pil Valley entirely. Two more skiffs from fleet group two were flying beside it as escorts.

Ketesh took a breath. Phase four was complete. Now came the hard part, the part that would claim the most lives.

Phase five: eradication.

Given the General's last order, it seemed that they would have to do it from the air.

Ketesh spun the steering wheel, and the *Razorback* began to slowly turn. The skiffs were more swift in the turn, pointing back the way they had come before the battleship was halfway there.

A series of thundering booms made Ketesh's head whip around. Cannonfire was erupting from the trees, slamming into the barriers protecting the skiff which was now behind them.

The smaller craft's generator was overwhelmed quickly, and a dark cloud suddenly burst from the canopy below them. As it arced towards the stricken skiff, Ketesh realised that they were arrows, wincing at the hundreds of rippling thudding sounds as they impacted the hull, as well as the screams of the crew on deck. Ahead, the other skiff was listing, leaning like a drunk.

"*Increase speed, full sail!*" Ketesh barked. "*I want those barriers as strong as they can be, pull Mages from the cannons if you have to!*"

She squinted at the skiff behind them. The crew on deck were picking themselves up, and she realised with horror that all of them were riddled with arrows. Most stood still, then turned as one, staring at the *Razorback,* staring at her. The craft began to turn towards them.

"*Va'Kael ... belay that order! Man the cannons!*"

The skiff's sails were billowing, and it moved swiftly, before the *Razorback* could bring its weapons to bear.

"*Brace for impact!*"

The skiff struck the *Razorback* like the fist of a prizefighter. The barrier around them flared. There was a thudding sound from below the deck and black smoke poured from the open hatchway.

Ketesh held on to the wheel madly as the *Razorback* listed and began to tip, creaking under its own weight. She looked up at the skiff that had hit them. Parts of it were jutting through the barriers, it had been reduced to little more than a jumble of iron and wooden debris. The sails were torn and limp. As she watched, the barrier faded and disappeared.

"*Full sail, full sail!*" Ketesh shrieked, grasping the wheel tightly and swinging it. "*All cannons target the valley walls, target the skiff, target everything!*"

She heard the thrum of bow strings and the deafening claps of lightning magic, and looked up over the deck. Soldiers and Mages were firing everything they had at the other skiff, that was falling towards them like a meteorite.

"*Oh Va'Kael ...*" Ketesh mumbled.

***

The splintering boom of the impact echoed across the valley. Kelad caught a glimpse of his flagship as he spun away from a ghoul and removed its arm. With a flourish he drew his pistol and froze three more with it, using them as a barrier so some of his wounded could be pulled back.

When he looked around again, the front half of the *Razorback* was smashing into the valley wall. The back half was still floating in mid air, spinning slowly, engulfed by a fire that had started somewhere below decks.

His dead heart broke at the sight of it, and he leapt back alongside Commander Ulan and some off his men.

"*Seems like Phase five just jumped out of the window,*" Ulan grunted.

"*Not yet it hasn't. Close ranks, tight as you can. Get those arms off and get them frozen! Commander, cover me.*"

"*Aye. Elizia, Yaro, on me and stay tight!*"

Kelad stepped back and pulled a communication stone off his belt. "*Ketesh, can you hear me?*"

There was no sound, only dead air from the ruins of his ship. "*Spearhead, Valkyr, Reverence, this is General Kelad.*"

"*General!*" Captain Obrek, commanding officer of the *Spearhead* shouted. "*What are your orders sir?*"

"*We just lost the ...*" Kelad gritted his teeth. "*We just lost two skiffs and the Razorback. Rescue team's surrounded, we need a ship to get over here and pick us up. The other skiffs are occupied by aerial bombardment.*"

"*Understood ... but General ... if we or any of the skiffs leave now ...*"

"*What's your status, Captain?*"

"*We're looking at twenty five percent casualties in the ground forces. The only reason it isn't more is the cover we're providing from above. If we, or either of the carriers leave, they'll probably be overwhelmed.*"

Kelad's fingers tightened around the stone. "*Then hold position. Try and open up an escape route, and regroup. When I fall, you have command of the fleet.*"

The Empire Of Fire

Obrek paused, taking in his words. "*Understood, sir. I'm ... I'm sorry, sir.*"

"*Don't be. Get as many of our boys home as you can.*"

"*Aye.*"

Kelad replaced the stone and reloaded his pistol, steadying his breathing. He pushed the grief out of his head, shoved it aside as if it were a loud, belligerent drunk, and prepared to die with a little dignity.

Death had been a cold mistress the first time, one he had been in no rush to run back to.

He raised his pistol, and froze three more ghouls. He popped a new stone into the breach. Three more were frozen.

The soldiers were tightly packed in around him, a whirling dervish of blade and magical bolt. One would be engulfed and overwhelmed by the dead every twenty seconds or so, a slow whittling of his forces. He began to notice more and more Caelish infantry, his own men, in among the crush of walking corpses pressing in on them, and gave them no more quarter than the others.

If only that necromancer were nearby, he could at least try and end her. There was absolutely nothing to see aside from the thousands upon thousands of bodies around them.

"*Lazar!*" he heard someone cry, as a soldier in front of them fell back, choking on his own blood, trying to rip off his helmet to get at the cut across his throat. Kelad looked down at him while he popped another stone into the pistol, at the medic that was struggling to put pressure on the wound. He watched the light leave the young man's eyes, and as soon as the medic leaned back, he froze the body.

The medic jumped and looked up at him in horror.

"*Better that, than what's surrounding us,*" Kelad snapped. He sent the next two shots into the enemy.

The rescue squads numbered less than a hundred now, but fought on regardless, covered in gore, swords flying. More ghouls immediately around them were frozen than unfrozen, but it didn't seem to deter the enemy in the slightest.

"Don't let them scare you! Show them your hearts!" Kelad roared like a creature from the deep recesses of the Hells, and fired again. The rest of the troops joined him in the war cry, drowning out the cries of pain from their fellows, bolstering them against the fear that could wrap around them.

Kelad could see the remainder of his fleet, firing their cannons down at the dead. The remainder of the group two skiffs circled overhead, their small-arms doing what damage they could.

It wasn't enough to save him and the others, but maybe in their courage, they could buy the main force a few seconds, minutes even, if they stood firm.

They continued to roar like the monsters that had razed Haama in years past, like the facsimiles of them on the front of the battleships, like crazed barbarians. They kept fighting as their numbers dropped to less than seventy, then less than sixty, then less than fifty.

Then, as if it were responding to their own cries of rage and valour, came another roar, echoing across Taeba.

It was a phantom sound, a sound ripped from the past, an impossible sound that froze Kelad's cold heart and cracked it. It split the ears, shook the bones, and even made the ghouls on all sides pause for a moment, as if they could no more believe what they were hearing than the living.

He thought for a moment that it was a figment of his imagination, that death's approach was making him relive the circumstances of the last time he had become acquainted with it. In his final moments, perhaps old ghosts and memories were coming to the forefront of his mind. Old battles he had fought, old foes he had slain, old flames he had lain with. This was a memory he had no desire to relive, and yet, here it was, swooping towards him.

But, no. It came again, much closer, much louder, and there was no mistaking it.

The fearsome, bellowing roar was that of a dragon. Death coming not in cold, but in searing heat, borne on wings of terror.

One dragon was a scant possibility, but this was not a random winged beast. This was a specific dragon, whose roar of fury and triumph had been seared into his memory. This dragon was supposed to be dead, far far to the east, its bones reduced to dust by the dragonfire it had expelled all over the Orlin Forest.

Kelad tightened his grip on his weaponry. Of all the manners of death that could have descended upon him, this was the most poetic.

He had watched that dragon burn the Orlin Forest, commanded the slaughter himself.

Death to its claws, or its hellfire, would be what he deserved.

8

Ironclad slowly moved back and forth across the *Sand Dancer's* cargo hold, feeling the weight of the huge greataxe the wyvernborn had given him to wield. His body felt heavy and sluggish, but he was re-familiarising the flow of his movements and the limits of his reach, which had changed despite Jack's best efforts.

"It's too soon for you …" Jack muttered, pacing alongside him, wringing his hands. "Combat on this scale …"

"Like it or not, I am one of our best weapons against the dead," Ironclad grunted. "Shield and armour are a natural part of me. The others will need me to get in the ghouls' way."

Jack shook his head. "It's irresponsible."

"You haven't treated many soldiers before, have you," Ironclad chuckled. "The worst thing for people like me is waiting on the sidelines while our friends fight on our behalf. Every body on the line makes a difference."

Jack looked up at him sharply. "I didn't help get you out of that dungeon so you could throw yourself into certain doom."

If Ironclad could have smiled, he would have. "I don't intend for it to be a doom, certain or otherwise."

Jack grumbled to himself for a moment. "How are the eyes working out?"

"Well enough." Most of what Ironclad could see around him was shades of light and dark. People were represented by columns of shadow, with a curious glow around them that separated them from the background. What that glow represented, he couldn't say, but it was consistent in every person he had met so far on the *Sand Dancer*. The soul, perhaps, whatever energy the body displaced and produced.

The Empire Of Fire

"I worked on those eyes ... I know they're not a shadow on your blue ones."

"What colour are they?"

"Purple. The wyvernborn shamans work with amethysts, they work well as a platform for magical lenses. Luckily for you I ..."

Ironclad turned towards him, blocking an imaginary foe with his shield in a sweeping motion, and swinging a low parry. "Go on."

Jack cleared his throat. "I took your old eyes out in the first place. I documented every connection I needed to make."

Ironclad grunted. "Well ... at least you remembered to bring your notes with you. Would have been a little awkward if you'd left them behind."

He heard the door open and turned. He recognised Ember immediately, her aura was bright, and for the first time, he recognised it as bright green, green as the leaves in the Orlin Forest.

He moved out of his fighting stance and drew towards her, transfixed by the glow of her.

"Fighting fit?" she said, her voice tense as the fabric of a full sail.

"You're beautiful," he murmured.

Ember paused. "Is that a yes or a no?"

"I'm as ready as I'll ever be, and you're not talking me out of it."

"What makes you think I'll try and talk you out of it?"

"My ears are as sharp as ever ... even if that dragon out there grunts and roars so loudly it shakes the hull."

He heard her sigh. "I reserve the right to be worried about you ... and with a battle on the horizon, that goes double. The Pil Valley's in sight. It's not good."

She gestured to the door, and he followed her, using the cargo lift to get up onto the deck.

***

Ember joined Thomas and Bassai at the prow of their small airship. The wyvernborn and Orlin on deck were leaning around to look ahead as well, at the black smoke billowing from the Pil Valley. Zeta and Sandra were leading the detachment of warriors, frowning at the carnage waiting for them.

There were shapes floating above the valley entrance, flashes of energy passing from them to the ground. Thunderclaps were audible even from this many miles away, blasting through the air to their ears, and as they drew closer, came the echoes of screams.

Thomas was rubbing the thin line of discoloured skin across his throat, all that remained of the scar Mora had left. He was frowning to himself. Ember nudged him, raising an eyebrow.

"It's probably nothing ... just nerves," he muttered.

"Hmm ..." Ember looked ahead at the valley again. "Looks like we're right on time."

"Or too late," Bassai grunted. "Their numbers will be even higher now."

"We can deal with them, so long as we get to Ydra," Thomas said. He turned to the other warriors on deck, now including Ironclad. "Look for the flaming sword! We find that, we find the necromancer."

Zeta roared, and the warriors behind her and flying alongside the ship echoed the war cry. Sandra's Orlin bowmen shouted in the old Orlin tongue, and Ember found herself shouting it as well.

"Blood for the forest, blood for our kin!"

She looked across to the dragon soaring above them, leathery wings spread wide, tail out straight for aerodynamics. It had been keeping purposefully slow in order for the *Sand Dancer* to keep up, but now it was starting to pull ahead. Its eyes were fixed on the Pil Valley, as if it could smell the dead on the wind.

It began to descend, and Ember caught sight of the wyvernborn on its back. Barada was at the fore, clutching onto the spikes and spines at the base of the dragon's neck. He had fifty more with him, preparing for the coming engagement.

The Empire Of Fire

Ironclad stepped behind them, shield strapped in place, heavy greataxe held loosely in his right hand. "We have to stop meeting like this."

"I didn't pick the place," Ember muttered. "Blame the Mage."

"It came highly recommended," Thomas said drily. "Although I'd expect crowd trouble."

"Did they finish the tavern at least?" Ember asked.

Bassai grunted. "They would have kept the stores of alcohol underground."

"Wine?"

"Must you all do this before we are about to give our lives to change the course of this country?"

Ironclad chuckled. "Definitely."

"Wait until the smell hits *you*. You will not be laughing any more."

"I can't smell."

Bassai snorted, his expression dark. "I envy you."

The three airships above the valley entrance were firing towards the writhing mass below them, and on the walls on either side of the pass. It was impossible to tell who was still alive and who was a ghoul at this distance. The violent surges and waves of bodies crashed against siege engines and infantry, and before long, the battlefield became clearer.

There were two groups of Caelish military: one in the pass, one at the mouth of the pass. Both were surrounded, being slowly whittled down. Hundreds of magical bolts flew from behind the front lines, hitting ghouls and freezing them, as both groups drew slowly towards each other.

Seraphine pushed her way through the bellowing warriors, leading Kassaeos, Astrid, Kira, Berek and Orso. She leaned over them, a rueful smile on her face. "The fools. They put so much stock in their weaponry, their siege engines, their terror, and now they're being slaughtered by their own victims."

"Can you sense Ydra?" Ironclad grunted.

"She isn't close … but I can feel the power moving and surging through every ghoul. She's deeper in, in the valley itself. You'll see her before I can sense her."

Ironclad nodded, watching the dragon as it accelerated. "Here we go. Captain!"

Ember watched Seret tear her eyes from the carnage below towards him. She was a pleasure pilot, and now she was going to war. Her jaw was set, her cheeks damp.

"Stay at this altitude, and take us over the valley."

Thomas translated the order, and she nodded.

The dragon dived down like an arrow. When it was four or five hundred yards above the ground, the wyvernborn on its back released their hold and opened their wings, gliding around in a spiralling downward course.

At three hundred yards, the dragon pointed its nose upwards and it began to level out. At a hundred yards its wings flared, and its jaws opened.

The blast of flame streamed down into the walking dead, and Ironclad couldn't help but wince. Ember glanced up at him and took his hand tightly.

The great beast of legend, that had brought Haama to its knees a century before, flapped its wings and swept back up into the air. All it left in its wake was dust and charred bones, some of which were still attempting to stumble onwards towards the Caelish lines. The dragon banked around and breathed another inferno down on the ghouls.

When it pulled up again, the sound of cheering and whooping reached Ember's ears. She snorted. "Of course they're cheering."

"They worship the dragons, or the idea of them," Kassaeos grunted. "They probably think the damned thing was sent by Va'Kael himself."

"I wonder what they'll make of us, then," Bassai growled.

As it banked up again, there was a flurry of cannonfire from the top of the valley wall. The first was a near-miss, the next went well wide as the dragon dived and pivoted to the side. Airships were much slower, much less manoeuvrable than something born to take to the skies.

Barada's wyvernborn banked in formation towards the cannons, scattering outwards like the ripples displaced in a pond as a cloud of arrows

The Empire Of Fire

erupted from the trees. They closed in again as they drew close to the wall, dropping firebombs in among the treeline. Ember watched them land with a lump in her throat, knowing the butchery they had flown into.

She looked up into the valley, at the growing lump of ghouls in the centre. Two skiffs were turning above them slowly, cannons hitting the mass over and over.

The dragon began to climb again, and strafed the ghouls below once more, roaring in the purest, hottest fury that Ember had ever heard.

Astrid scanned the valley with a telescope, checking every group of ghouls within sight for Ydra. The wyvernborn on the walls ran and leapt off, wings opening immediately. They swept low, dropping more firebombs, some moving even lower to swipe at the dead with their axes and swords. The Caelish forces rallied at the sight of them along with the dragon.

"More are turning towards the pass," Astrid muttered. "Still no necromancer."

"She's here," Seraphine said. "I can feel her."

"This power ..." Ironclad said thoughtfully "... how does it work? Does she have to see the ghouls to direct them?"

"Maybe," Seraphine said.

"Not to raise them ... but it might fit with what I saw when I was scouting her," Kassaeos said. "If the dead are close enough to her she can do it at will. Unless it has gotten stronger ... she didn't have this many dead to control before."

"Let's assume that's the case, it gives us something to go on, right now we've got nothing," Ironclad muttered. "If she's the commander, the general, she'll be looking over the battlefield, directing her army. Where's the highest point in the valley?"

"Somewhere on the walls ... and it'll have to be on the opposite side of the valley to the pass, otherwise she couldn't see ..." Astrid muttered. She swept the telescope around slowly. "There! Looks like a rise, opposite the pass here."

"Then she'll see us coming," Thomas muttered. "She probably already has."

Ironclad nodded. "Zeta, your warriors are going to have to engage the mass at the centre of the valley, Sandra, your archers too. Once we're dropped off on the ridge, leave Ydra to us."

Zeta nodded, but Sandra narrowed her eyes. "There's no telling how many she'll have covering her. Take the shamen with you."

"Good idea." Ironclad looked past them at Captain Seret. "Forwards, but keep us at this altitude!"

The *Sand Dancer* picked up speed, moving over the walls and into the valley. Astrid kept her eyes forward, but Ember looked over the side, glaring down at the battlefield.

At the centre of a ring of frozen ghouls, a few dozen Caelish soldiers fought furiously, thrusting forwards with swords, sending pulses of magical energy into the enemy. The skiffs assisting them were having almost no visible effect, blowing some of the dead away certainly, but not affecting the mass entity that the individual corpses had become.

They were fighting in the bones of a settlement, one that the dead had torn to pieces. Chapels, barracks, settlements, stores, they were all gutted and even burned. Ydra had been here, attacking the settlers herself.

Zeta roared on the deck, and her wyvernborn, ten on the ship and forty in the air, dived. Their wings flared, and they began dropping firebombs on the ghouls close to the Caelish, their agility allowing them to be more precise than the skiffs in their assault.

"Do they have a chance?" Kira murmured.

"That depends on us," Ironclad replied.

Ember watched the wyvernborn twisting and turning in the air, engaging physically, casting their bombs from above. The ghouls carried on as if they weren't even there, as if the knowledge was at the front of their maggot-eaten brains that the wyvernborn would tire eventually, have to land, and be swarmed. She looked over at Seraphine, who was watching the battle as closely

The Empire Of Fire

as she was.

"You talk about this power in Ydra like it's alive, like it thinks."

Seraphine nodded. "Power, at a certain level of strength and intensity, takes on a mind of its own."

"What does it even want? What does it gain by holding the Pil Valley?"

Seraphine looked at her with eyes as dark as an eclipse. "More bodies. Thousands more. Death makes it grow. Soon, there will be so many of them that they will be able to march across Haama unopposed."

Ember shook her head. "How could Vehnek allow something like this to happen?"

"It helps him achieve his own goals," Kassaeos chuckled. "Without the air force of the Caelish Standing Army, the Black Fleet will step in and expand. Vehnek's influence grows. He clearly thinks he can deal with the problem when it stops being useful."

"Foolish," Bassai grunted.

"Not in his mind," Thomas said, "but he doesn't know what he's dealing with."

"Don't be so sure," Ironclad muttered. Seraphine looked up at him, and Ember could read the silent message passing between them as if they were screaming it. They knew something, or suspected it.

"What's going on?"

Ironclad fixed his amethyst eyes on the distant knoll ahead, getting gradually closer. "I suspect, in fact, that Vehnek knows the scale of the ghoul threat, knows the origin of it, and has the power to deal with it ... and that makes this even more important. We have to end this here ... at all costs."

Thomas and Bassai looked around at him, and nodded their agreement, not because they knew what he was talking about, but because they knew he wasn't saying it lightly. Another silent message passed between Seraphine and Kassaeos, and they nodded.

"We'll do what we can," Kira said. "If it's all the same, I'd rather not die today."

"Sometimes men plan, and Va'Kael laughs," Thomas muttered.

Kira swallowed, and Astrid nudged her. "This is why we fight, isn't it? For a better future. A better future we might never see."

Seraphine turned to her sadly, and looked back at the knoll with an intensity. "She's there."

Thomas nodded stiffly as well. "Something's there … but it's not her. It's … darker than her. Black as tar … and it's looking right at us."

"Does this ship have barriers?" Bassai grunted.

"I don't know …"

Ironclad grunted. "Ember, check with the Captain."

She nodded, and wove back through the Orlin archers. She cast a glance at Sandra, who muttered an order to the rest of the warriors. All of them nocked an arrow, and moved to both edges of the ship, getting into a shooting stance. As she went, she caught the eye of Andrei, who offered her a short, warm, smile. She nodded to him, but didn't return it, moving on before she could feel any guilt over the response.

At the helm, Captain Seret's knuckles were white. She was gripping the wheel tightly, breathing heavily. Helen, the former steward of the Regent, was standing beside her, flanked by the two Caelish guards that Thomas had dragged with him in his escape from Victory.

"Does the ship have any defenses?"

Helen translated the question to Seret, who shook her head, gripping the wheel tighter.

Ember exhaled. "Then I suppose we're relying on manoeuvrability."

Helen translated again, and the response from Seret was a short laugh, a slightly mad, slightly shrill bark of a sound. She spoke quickly and bitterly, spittle flying from her lips.

Helen winced, and turned to Ember with gritted teeth. "She said that with the number of people they have aboard, that won't be easy. The ship is a pleasure yacht first, not a warship."

Ember glanced at Seret. "Tell her we'll do what we can with the Mages and shamen."

The response was a snort and a roll of the eyes. Ember didn't take it personally, instead she turned to the two soldiers. "We'll need them down there with us."

Helen translated, and the pair looked at each other. After a pause, they both nodded. They grunted a couple of words, and Helen jumped forward to hug them both individually. The soldiers closed their eyes and squeezed her tightly.

Ember watched them and waited. Helen pulled back. "They're fighting for the princess, and for Cael. They're with you."

Ember nodded, and looked at each soldier in turn. "Thank you."

Both nodded before Helen could translate. Ember turned back to the front of the ship, and they followed her. Some of the shamen were coming up on deck through the cargo lift, and were enchanting the arrows of the archers. One held out a shaking, malformed hand to Ember as she passed, and stopped her. Its milky eyes glowed as it fumbled with the quiver of her arrows, and a short pulse transferred from its twisted fingers and into the ammunition.

"Thank you," she said gently.

She began to move away, but the shaman stopped her. It raised a hand to her cheek, trembling with the effort, grunted at it did so. Ember resisted the involuntary urge to recoil, holding herself steady. The crooked-fingered claw was rough but warm, the scales flaking.

The creature's useless eyes locked onto hers, white pupils and irises barely distinguishable. It opened its drooping mouth, and let out a choking, stammering set of sounds. Ember could say nothing in response.

"It's dragontongue," Sandra said, appearing beside her. "Before we fight, the shamen sometimes come to us, enchant our arrows, give us a few words."

"What did it say?"

"'Be brave.'"

Ember looked back at the shaman, and reached up, touching the hand on her face. "Thank you."

The shaman grunted, and patted her cheek gently before shuffling away.

"It's the only time we ever hear them speak, aside from when we give birth," Sandra said quietly. "Then, they bless new life, encourage our strength in recovery."

"They really care about us, don't they …" Ember murmured.

"Yes, they do." Sandra smiled at her. "I forget sometimes that you used to fight the wyvernborn."

"The wyvernborn burned our family home," Ember said. "I hadn't thought about it, but I guess the warriors that did it are probably still alive. They might be fighting with us here."

"Can you find it in your heart to forgive them?"

Ember shook her head. "No need: I let it go long ago. Now, it will never happen again."

Sandra hugged her with one arm. "Good luck down there. Do your best to come back."

Ember grinned. "I always do my best."

Sandra glanced at the pair of Caelish, and nodded to them. Ember led them alongside Ironclad, and they both couldn't help but gawk up at him.

The knoll was approaching fast. The top contained sparse vegetation, the odd skeletal tree, devoid of bird, leaf or tuft of moss. The patches of grass were brown, the rocks grey.

Figures stood still as statues, watching the *Sand Dancer* as it flew closer. There were cannons up there, pointing right at them.

Even though there were tens of thousands of ghouls already engaged in the valley below, hundreds remained on and around the knoll, surrounding a single figure standing at the highest point.

She was thinner than Ember remembered, than she had been when she was alive. Ydra's short, limp hair fluttered in the breeze. Her armour was mismatched, with scraps of leather and Caelish steel plate, her skin was bone white.

The woman she had fought beside, who had saved her life and likewise,

The Empire Of Fire

was all but gone. The figure atop the knoll had a different gait, a different energy even. Ember didn't need magic to feel it. A frighteningly calm fury, the steely gaze of a gambler who was sure she held all the cards.

As Ember watched, the long, thin blade in her hand ignited in a jet of light green flame.

Ironclad looked around at Sandra, giving her a nod. Ember saw him steady his stance, and raise his head.

"FOR HAAMA!"

9

Thomas gritted his teeth as the *Sand Dancer* accelerated, and ahead of them, Ydra pointed at the four cannons on either side of her, then the small airship. Bright blasts of fiery energy burst from the cannons and rushed to meet them in their charge.

"Barriers!" Seraphine yelled, and extended her hands forwards. Thomas joined her with his hands, and Astrid's gauntlet amplifier glowed as she pointed her open palm at the projectiles. Thomas called upon the reserves of power within him, granted by the Gods, and felt it bleed and spread from his hands, joining the energy of Seraphine and Astrid, weaving together like layers of armour. At the prow of the ship a curved wall of blue light bloomed into existence, and the cannon shots crashed against it, exploding in a quartet of fireballs that went off like booms of thunder.

Seraphine, Astrid and Thomas all took a step back with the force of the impact. It was like being punched, shots to the body that jarred their bones. Behind Thomas, Seraphine grunted in pain.

"Are you three alright?" Ironclad said.

"Those are fully amplified shots," Seraphine gasped. "If we're going to get through to Ydra, we can't protect the ship like this, the barriers are sapping our energy too much."

Bassai wheeled around and roared back to the shamen in dragontongue. They shuffled forwards together, wheezing, as four more shots of flame struck the barrier. This time the punches were hot, like the knuckles had been replaced by burning embers from a bonfire.

"Bassai, we're going to need that little surprise a little quicker than we thought," Ironclad grunted.

The Empire Of Fire

Bassai nodded and took a gentle hold of one of the shamen, grunting to it in their language again. The rest of the twisted wyvernborn extended clawed hands, and Thomas felt their energy joining his own, bolstering it with an old magic, like a deep, low voice singing in a foreign tongue. The voice amplified his own bravery, lit a flame within him.

"Archers ... loose!" Sandra cried, and every bowstring behind Thomas thrummed. Beside him, Ember drew an arrow back and sent it ahead, hitting one of the ghouls operating a cannon. It was forced back by the impact, and burst into flames. Thomas dared to hope it would fall, but it lurched back to the cannon, sending another blast towards them, before it finally crumpled.

"We can't afford to keep this up, even with the shamen," Thomas shouted.

"One minute!" Bassai said. "They're coming now."

"Not a moment too soon," Kassaeos said drily.

Thomas kept his barrier raised with one hand, turning to the helm. *"Captain Seret! Be ready to slow sharply!"*

Her eyes were wild, but she nodded. The moment he had his reply, he turned back to the prow. Keeping his barrier high against the rain of fire, both of his hands were glowing with radiant light.

At the corner of his eye, a new set of shapes appeared above the treeline, rising from the edge of the valley and diving, skimming the treetops of the knoll. Five hundred wyvernborn warriors, the bulk of their forces, kept in reserve until the last moment.

The ghouls never knew what hit them. The five hundred rose a few yards, and all dropped firebombs in a strafing run, right on the dead army. The top of the knoll erupted in flame and smoke, splintering cracking booms rippled across the valley.

"Now!" Thomas yelled back to Seret. The *Sand Dancer* slowed so suddenly that Thomas had to grip the railing. Behind him, Orlin warriors leapt forwards to keep the shamen on their unsteady feet.

The cannonfire ceased immediately. Ydra disappeared from view behind the blast, but Thomas could still feel the dark thing she had become, surging and roiling, reaching out to every ghoul.

"Ready yourselves!" Ironclad bellowed. "Ground force, follow me!"

The *Sand Dancer* pulled low, fifteen feet above the top of the knoll. Ironclad swung himself over the side, and dropped.

Thomas, Ember and Bassai were hot on his heels. Thomas sent a blast of air upwards from below them, slowing their fall. Behind and above them, Astrid and Seraphine did the same, allowing them, Kira, Berek, Orso, and four of the shamen to hit the ground safely. Kassaeos appeared beside them on the ground in a whirl of smoke.

The wyvernborn above banked and made their way into the valley, preparing to engage the main force of the dead. The *Sand Dancer* rose, Sandra's Orlin archers watching the smoke from their vantage point on the deck.

The knoll before them was more black and grey now than green. The sparse trees had splintered. Ash and smoke filled the air in a thick cloak, and Thomas felt it stinging his lungs. He nodded to Seraphine and Astrid, who began tearing strips of cloth from their cloaks to cover the mouths of those that needed it. One of the shamen drew close and waved a claw at them. It gestured to the cloths, and grasped a hold of them, muttering to itself. The cloths shone once it had completed its incantation, and it handed them back, gesturing for them to tie it around their faces.

Astrid offered one. "Do you..."

The shaman grunted and waved its hand dismissively. As the three Mages began distributing them to those that needed the protection, Bassai, Ironclad and Kassaeos kept watch ahead, immune to the smoke's effects.

"Low visibility ... I don't like it," Bassai grunted.

"Protect the shamen, and the Mages," Ironclad ordered in a low voice.

"How much can you even see?" Kassaeos muttered.

"More than you can, I'd wager," Ironclad replied. "She's about a hundred yards ahead of us, marshalling the ghouls that are still intact. We have to move now. Heavy hitters in the front row, Mages second. Ember, you and our Caelish friends cover the shamen."

He set off, with Bassai and Kira either side of him. Thomas and the Mages followed. They kept their pace as steady as they could, so they didn't leave the shamen behind, and merged with the smoke.

Thomas could feel the cold, damp feeling growing closer and closer, like the smell of mouldy and rotting wood, writhing maggots, the soil of a graveyard. He tried not to focus his vision at all, to keep his peripherals clear.

"Ironclad ... she'll feel if we use magic," Seraphine whispered. "If we see ghouls, we'll have to engage them hand to hand."

Ahead, he nodded, and turned them a few degrees to the left, then to the right. "She'll feel it if we engage them in any way," he murmured. "Follow my steps precisely, and close ranks. They're in the smoke, all around us."

Thomas held himself back from forming incantations in his hands, naked without his magic at the ready. Listening closely, around the sounds of war bouncing around the valley, he could pick out footsteps and dragging sounds on either side of them, and behind them.

How many had the firebombs dealt with? The enchantments on the fire made it far hotter, and far easier to spread. Every so often, a scrap of blackened bone crunched under one of their feet, proof that it had worked to an extent.

"How close are we?" Ember whispered from the rear.

"Fifty yards," Ironclad replied. "Bassai, drop back. Tell the shamen to get rid of this fog when I signal. That'll be the ten yard mark. The second they do so, we charge."

Bassai slowed, letting everyone past, and began growling to the shamen in dragontongue, a hoarse whisper that made sweat pool at the back of Thomas's neck. Despite it being the voice of an ally, the language was too old for his ears, for anyone's ears.

Bassai rejoined the front rank, and it was almost as soon as he did that Ironclad signalled them all to halt. Forty yards of traversal had disappeared into the smoke.

Ironclad set himself. Kira cracked her neck, Bassai readied his sabres, tightening the strap that kept the off-hand blade in his mutilated hand. Beside Thomas, Seraphine and Astrid were as focused as a pair of gladiators on the verge of a deathmatch.

He glanced back at Berek and Orso as Ember kept an eye on the fog around her. Both of them were in full armour, helmets and all, and were tense as a garotte.

"*Have courage, my friends,*" Thomas whispered. "*We fight for life itself.*"

Ironclad raised his arm. Behind Thomas, the shamen hissed. The front two ranks prepared to charge, their weapons ready.

Ironclad's hand dropped. The shamen chanted in unison, and a bubble of air extended from them, pushing smoke away. The moment it passed them, Ironclad charged. Kira and Bassai followed right behind him. Seraphine, Thomas and Astrid took off after them.

The bubble passed over Ydra, and her retinue of corpses. When she turned to face them, five yards away, her dead face was turned up in surprise.

Ironclad blasted through three of the ghouls around her, letting out a cry of pain as Ydra's burning blade plunged into his side. Kira leaped through the gap and impaled her in the chest with her spear.

Ydra's head snapped around and she swept the blade from Ironclad's flank, sweeping it through the wooden shaft of Kira's weapon. The speartip remained buried in her chest, but no blood leaked from the tear in her skin.

Bassai bent low and slammed into her, lifting her and throwing her to the ground. She caught him with a wild slash of the rapier, passing through his chest. He roared in pain and fell back, putting pressure on the wound that was leaking dark red blood. Thomas wanted to stop, but he knew he couldn't, even as the groan of pain became a choking sound. Bassai had given them an opening that they couldn't pass up, and before Ydra could haul herself to her feet, the three Mages jumped on her, restraining her arms.

Seraphine grabbed the sides of her head, holding it tightly as she attempted to thrash from side to side. "Take hold of my arms, but keep her still!"

The Empire Of Fire

Thomas and Astrid struggled to keep Ydra still with one arm, whilst grabbing onto Seraphine with the other. Thomas focused in on Seraphine, joining his energy with hers, focusing it to a fine point that buried into what remained of Ydra's mind.

***

"Cover them!" Ironclad bellowed. "At all costs, let nothing through!"

He could see the thing that had taken Ydra's body and her mind, the vast web of death it had become. Its tendrils were attached to every ghoul atop the knoll and in the valley. They had wavered for the barest fraction of a second when Ydra was hit, before increasing in strength, growing ragged and spiky like they had picked up needles. The ghouls were glowing with an aura that was sickly and pale green, and they were coming.

One bore down on him at a sprint, and he smashed his greataxe into its chest, burying the blade into flesh and bone, sending it flying away almost split in half.

Bassai's blooded breathing was ringing in his ears. He didn't dare turn to him ... he couldn't lose focus. The wave of the dead was bolting through the fog, surging towards them.

More came into view, and Ironclad struck the first. The fog swirled and shifted into the figure of Kassaeos, who stabbed one and knocked it away. Ember sent an arrow that pierced another, and it burst into flames as the enchantment on it triggered.

The Caelish soldiers, Berek and Orso, were close together, swinging their blades into ghouls that tried to flank and engage the Mages. Ironclad saw the magic attached to some of the ghouls snap away as they fell under the force of blade and bow. Those ones remained still on the ground, finally at peace. The rest were more ferocious, faster, black foam bursting from their mouths. Ironclad's enhanced hearing could pick out the each individual breaking bone in the monstrous corpses, pushing their bodies past the limit and not caring in the least.

"Ironclad!" Ember shouted. "We'll have a barrier around us in a few seconds!"

Arrows flew from above them on the *Sand Dancer,* and ignited ghouls into columns of flame in the fog. Ironclad and Kassaeos began mopping up the stragglers, Kira joining them with a war axe. She was bloodied across her face, a huge gash in her cheek. Blood was streaming down her arms, she was panting and letting out whines of pain.

The shamen began chanting behind them, and warm energy began bleeding around the fighters. The number of ghouls grew and grew, surging around them, trying to encircle them, but Ironclad's reach and Kassaeos's speed were holding them off. Any that escaped them were hit by one of Ember's arrows. Even then, the numbers were growing exponentially. No matter how many fell, permanently, still more were getting up again, even if they were in pieces, crawling or dragging themselves towards the living.

All the while, Bassai's breathing was getting faster and more ragged, shallower and bubbling more. Ironclad kept swinging, faster and faster, praying to the Gods that the shamen would speed up.

"Now!" Ember shouted. "Back up!"

Ironclad stepped back, dragging Kira back with him. Kassaeos shifted back, the Caelish soldiers jumped backwards, and a bubble of bright white light formed around them.

Ironclad wheeled around. Bassai was still, blood running from his jaws. "Get one of the shamen to help him, now!"

"We could lose the barrier ..." Ember said, her voice thick.

"Then we hit whatever comes at us *hard!*" Ironclad growled. He pointed at one of the shamen, glowing with energy. "You! Help him!"

The shaman shuffled over to Bassai, and the barrier glowed a little more dimly. Ironclad turned to the rest of the fighters, paying especially close attention to Kira, who was panting and groaning in pain. "Cover every gap around every shaman. The Mages need time, we're the ones who give it to

The Empire Of Fire

them!"

***

Thomas's footsteps clicked against the smooth stone ground. It was like tile, but without any seams, jet black. He could barely see his feet, or the bottom of Seraphine's robes. It was as if the two of them and Astrid were floating along the alien landscape that Ydra's dead mind had made for them.

It was impossible to tell where the ground ended and the star-filled sky began. Billions upon billions of bright points of light were all around them, clustering together in great masses of colour, clouds and swirls of purples, reds, golds, greens, blues, vibrant and alive out in the blackness. All of it was swallowed by the unblemished floor under their feet.

There was only one place for them to go, only one landmark. A pyramid dominated the landscape, barely visible against the darkness. It seemed to grow out of the ground, the top flat, the structure impossible to discern from where they were, about a mile away.

"Gods ... look at that ..." Astrid whispered.

Her eyes were fixed upon a ring of blazing orange flame, vast and distant, off to their left, opposite the starfield. It spun in a spiralling pattern, reaching out into the stars with its fiery fingers, yet ever contracting towards its middle. The space at the centre of the ring was featureless, a great black hole in the stars, like the soulless eye of a gargantuan spider.

When Thomas's eyes found it, the feeling of cold was immediate, the chilling, bone piercing cold of doom, ancient and unknowing, a power his mortal being couldn't comprehend.

"What is it?" he whispered, as if the thing could somehow hear him.

Seraphine stared at the void, trying to comprehend it, and slowly shook her head. "I have no idea ... it must be enormous ... millions of miles across."

Astrid pointed. "The ring around it is being drawn inwards, look."

A sphere, distant to their eyes, was slowly moving inwards, towards the maw. It silently cracked in half and began to crumble, the chunks moving inwards.

"Is that ... was that a world?" Thomas said.

Seraphine glanced at him, and Astrid, both transfixed. "We don't have time to stare. We have to find what's left of Ydra. Our friends are out there right now."

Thomas tore his eyes away from the vortex, and back to the pyramid. "Only one obvious place to check. What are we looking for, exactly?"

"We're looking for her," Seraphine said tightly, setting off towards the structure with the pair in tow.

"Her as in Ydra herself?"

"What's left of her, yes. She will be here, somewhere in that pyramid."

They began moving across the ground as quickly as they could, watching the pyramid drawing closer and closer. It seemed to have three sides, equilateral aside from the flat top. There was no gate or entranceway in sight, and no guards.

"Seraphine ..." Thomas muttered. "You said Ydra's been taken over by an incantation ... or at least her body has."

"A powerful one, yes."

"Then what in the name of the Gods is all this? Where are we?"

"We're inside her mind," Seraphine muttered.

"Inside her mind? This is her *mind*? Is this meant to be somewhere she's seen, somewhere she's been?"

Astrid looked around, shaking her head. "I ... don't think anyone's been here."

"So ... this *isn't* her mind. This is something else."

Seraphine glanced at him and gritted her teeth. "It looks as if the incantation itself has re-shaped her mind as it has seen fit. It already exerts influence over her body."

"It did that with aid of Tobias's old axe, infused with dragonfire ... but it's an incantation ... a spell. You're ... you keep making it sound as if it's intelligent, thinking..."

Seraphine nodded. "Yes, I am. I cannot explain it any other way."

Thomas's eyes widened. "Wait ... it *is*? How?"

"Thomas ... I don't know."

"Thomas. Ah, yes. I remember Thomas."

The three Mages stopped, and Thomas winced at a sudden burning pain at his throat. The voice had come from all around them, echoing and bouncing around the stars. The runes on Asrid's gauntlets began to glow, and balls of fire formed in Thomas and Seraphine's hands.

"Can you see it?" Thomas rasped.

Seraphine shook her head.

"Do you even know what you're looking for?" Astrid murmured.

Seraphine shook her head again.

"How would it know me?" Thomas whispered.

"I have ... touched you before. Prized open the jaws of death that had clamped themselves around you."

Thomas narrowed his eyes. "What does that mean?"

"That I gave you back your life, Thomas. And I gave Emeora her life. And I gave Bassai his life. Your friend took liberties with my power ... broke the rules ... and now I can rectify that hubris."

***

The dead threw themselves against the barrier on all sides, howling and screeching. Arms phased through the energy wall, only to be shoved away again.

A ghoul stumbled through, only to be met with a blow from Ironclad with the force of a guillotine, sending it flying back into the barrier. Another popped through behind him, felled by Ember.

Two more shoved their way in, engaging Berek and Orso. As they chopped them down, even more burst through and leaped on them. Orso cried out as blades fell upon him.

Kira moved across to engage, Kassaeos shifted into place with her. Ironclad bent down near one of the shamen.

"Open the barrier beside me, strengthen the rest of it."

The shaman hissed. Beside Ironclad, the barrier began to dim, fading away into the fog. A gap began opening, about eight feet across.

"Form on me," Ironclad bellowed. "Em' stay back. Let nothing through."

As soon as the gap was open, Ironclad swung his axe, crushing a ghoul's head. Immediately after, the ghoul swung its blade around, glancing off Ironclad's shield. The dead surged around the barrier towards the gap, finding it as Kira and Berek joined him.

The *Sand Dancer* swung around above them, drifting sideways as if it were skidding on ice. Arrows came down and froze ghouls with ice enchantments.

Ironclad could see the energy bleeding from Ydra intensifying in strength, the needles becoming sharper, finding the ghouls, trying to find the wounded warriors inside the barricade. The energy wall around the gap brightened and thickened.

***

The three Mages reached the pyramid, the entity's gargantuan voice bouncing around Thomas's head.

"You understand the laws that govern your existence, and you know that your continued presence is an affront to it. You know that you cannot halt what has begun."

"Did you know this?" Thomas grunted to Seraphine. "Did Rowan make some kind of deal with this thing?"

"I wouldn't trust this thing, Thomas," she hissed. "It's trying to delay us. It knows what we're doing."

They were approaching the edge of the pyramid, with a view of two of its three sides. The sides were unblemished, without a sign of brickwork or erosion. There were no signs of a foundation either, it was as if the pyramid had grown up out of the ground. The lines from the ground to the sides of the pyramid were completely unbroken, curved like the base of a hill.

Astrid frowned. "I don't see a way in. Maybe on the other side?"

"Maybe," Thomas muttered. "Seraphine ... the White Tower ... a magical amplifier of that size ... it wouldn't go unnoticed."

There was a chuckle from all around them.

"You think the Caelish did something to bring this ... thing here?" Seraphine said, although she was distracted by the structure.

"No ... not them ... although this is familiar. A familiar feeling, something ..." He shook his head, banishing the thought. "It could be that there's a way into this pyramid on the other side ..."

They began moving along the wall at a jog. "There's nowhere like this place in any land I know of," Thomas muttered as they ran. "There must be some frame of reference for all this."

"When I entered Ydra's mind before, it took the form of tunnels," Seraphine said. "A long labyrinth of tunnels leading to a central point. It was nothing like this. I think ... there may be nothing of her left."

"What if we destroyed her body?" Astrid asked.

"The incantation is connected to thousands of vessels just like Ydra, some of them magical. It would simply jump into one of them. We must do this from here."

They reached the edge of the wall, with a view on the third side of the pyramid. Just like the others, it was completely smooth.

"**The way is shut,**" the voice rumbled. "**You cannot get rid of me so easily. More powerful forces than you have tried, and failed.**"

"What do we do now?" Astrid said.

Seraphine shook her head. "This thing is toying with us."

Thomas shook his head. "Maybe ... but it's governed by laws too. Maybe not the same ones we are, but there are constants of existence. Energy isn't infinite, it has limits."

"Right," Astrid exclaimed, clicking her fingers. "It maintains the ghouls, allows Ydra to control and direct them, allows the former Mages to use their magic. There are tens of thousands of them."

"And that number grows every time one of our warriors dies," Seraphine added. "The power it's exerting outside of Ydra must be enormous."

"Correct," Thomas said. "For all intents and purposes, this is its realm: inside what's left of Ydra. It has the most influence here, but there's something else shaping the environment."

Astrid shook her head. "What d'you mean?"

Thomas pointed at the pyramid beside them. "Why is this here? Why does it need to be here? It's a landmark in a featureless landscape, next to that … maw out there. What would be more demoralising to us than an infinite waste, no indication of direction, with something completely unknown and destructive so close?"

"I enjoy watching you waste time … while your friends join my legion. Bassai is close. The one you call Orso is closer. Kira, too."

Astrid ran a hand through her short hair. "Thomas …"

Thomas nodded, keeping the ache in his heart under control. "I know … but why say that? It's trying to distract us from the pyramid. It didn't make the pyramid … Ydra did. She isn't completely gone, she knows we're here, she's pointing the way."

Seraphine looked up at the structure. "If there's no way in … we have to go up."

"The top was flat," Astrid agreed. "But this is an entirely smooth surface. No grip. How do we get up there?"

Thomas formed a ball of ice in his hand, and grinned. "However we can."

***

Ember picked her shots carefully, waiting until a ghoul attempted to flank

The Empire Of Fire

the group defending the gap in the barrier. Others were still attempting to burst through the energy wall on all sides, and she was keeping as vigilant as she could.

Orso was dying, his wounds too severe to be treated with healing magic. He was gritting his blood-stained teeth, holding on so he wouldn't join Ydra's army.

The three Mages were kneeling around Ydra, frowns of concentration on their faces, eyes closed tightly. A ghoul forced itself through the barrier, bearing down on them, and Ember took her shot, felling it. It smouldered and crumbled like it was made of ashes.

The shouts and groans of exertion and pain in front of her were a distraction she didn't need. She wanted to jump in, help her friends, help Tobias, but she had to stay where she was. She was the last line of defense, the extra dimension to their force.

Kira was flagging, covered in blood, running on rage alone. Kassaeos was shifting every five or six seconds, covering every gap he could, stabbing and slashing, putting crossbow bolts into heads from close range. Berek was sticking close to Kira, both protecting her when she overstepped and swinging his sword to keep the dead back.

The focal point was Tobias ... Ironclad. His feet were dug in, shield high, jabbing and chopping with the axe. No matter how many ghouls piled up in front of them, he seemed immovable, like a mountain.

A ghoul threw itself against the barrier again and again. Ember kept an eye on it, and as it shoved itself through, bit by bit, recognition dawned on her.

The ghoul was a woman, slim, skin drawn back and thinning, pale. Her eyes were sunken, her hair limp, her teeth stained and gums drawn back. A deep cut on her head had festered.

Ember had fought beside Rihd in Taeba, at the White Tower and against more ghouls that Ydra had raised. She watched the dead woman struggling through the barricade, ignoring the searing burns it left on her skin.

Ember drew an arrow back, waiting until Rihd was through the barrier completely. She said a quick prayer under her breath, and as Rihd's foot cleared the energy barrier, the arrow flew.

Rihd had time to bare her teeth, before the arrow set her alight, incinerating her as she reached towards the Mages.

***

Thomas gasped as he hauled himself higher and higher, forming ice in each hand that stuck him to the pyramid's wall. Seraphine floated up on a cushion of air, but in the world that the entity had created, there was almost no wind at all. She had to re-cast the incantation every few seconds to stay up, ascending slowly. Claws had grown from Astrid's gauntlets, digging into the walls, her boots giving her traction on the smooth surface.

Progress wasn't fast, but it was consistent. They climbed higher and higher, getting closer to the flat summit.

"The inhabitants of your world are more impressive than most," the entity murmured. **"Your connection to energies that remain a mystery or a myth to many is rare. Yet, you are still oblivious to the building blocks of your world, of the universe, of the very air you breathe."**

Thomas ignored the voice as best he could, continuing the ascent, but it was impossible. The pyramid seemed to buzz and vibrate with every word it said.

"You are stumbling around in the dark, limited by your frail bodies and primitive minds. Your conflicts among yourselves are inevitable, never ending. They will lead to your oblivion."

The summit was a few yards away … but then it seemed farther again. Hundreds of feet farther. Thomas groaned.

"Did it just …?" Astrid grunted.

"Yep."

"Keep going!" Seraphine said, her eyes focused. "We're going the right way, it's trying to delay us."

The Empire Of Fire

"It's working," Thomas muttered, but he gathered his strength regardless, forcing himself to put one hand in front of the other again, and climb.

"Is there anything we can do?" Astrid said, clawing her way upwards. "What's to stop it doing that again, and again?"

"Nothing, unless its power diminishes," Seraphine said, staring up at the summit. "If I can contact Ydra ... she may be able to help. She has the power to shape this world, we've seen that with the pyramid."

She reached a hand upwards, and closed her eyes. "Ydra, can you hear me? It's Seraphine. We're here to help you."

She began to descend, and grunted in frustration. "I can't reach her, and stay up at the same time. Can you hold me?"

Thomas nodded. Seraphine floated closer and reached out a hand. Thomas spread more ice on the side of the pyramid, making sure he was rooted at hand and foot, before taking Seraphine's hand and pulling her in, using the arm to wrap around her waist. Astrid edged across to help as well, holding the sorceress's knees.

"Ydra," Seraphine said. "We can help you, but we need you to help us. We have to find you. We're close, but the darkness is blocking our path." She took a few breaths, and Thomas heard her voice crack. "I want to make it right. I want to be there for you the way I should have been. Please, Ydra. Help us."

Thomas waited, looking upwards. The pyramid continued to tower above them, nearly invisible against the stars.

Seraphine closed her eyes tightly. "Ydra ... if we can't stop it, it will swallow Haama. It will end all the life we know, all the life to come."

"Life is a gift wasted on the likes of your primitive races. There are too many of you already. Too many for your world."

"Where there's life, there's a chance for things to be better, a chance for us to innovate, to create ..." Seraphine urged.

"To maim, to destroy, to waste the years you are given. Better you be controlled, directed in a better way. Better those who drag you backwards be prevented. When controlled, all will be equal. All parts of one great

being, everlasting, undying."

"We can be more than we are," Seraphine countered. "More than this thing could ever dream. We have the potential to be greater, and we can't do that without life, without that element of chance, without learning from those around us. All that future, all that potential, hangs in the balance … it's up to us. We need your help, Ydra."

The pyramid grew no taller, but the base expanded at an alarming rate. The slope lessened beneath them, until they could stand.

"We'd better run for it," Astrid muttered, picking herself up.

Thomas nodded, and the three of them bolted. It took little time before their legs began to ache with the strain of the uphill climb, but they carried on regardless, lungs burning.

***

As one, the ghouls surrounding Kelad and his men halted their attack. Axes paused mid-swing, swords mid-thrust, snarls upon faces froze.

The Caelish paused as well. Kelad glanced around at them and bared his teeth. *"Don't let up!"*

A few more of the dead were cut down, before all of them disengaged, sprinting off towards the valley wall. Kelad narrowed his eyes at their path. They were heading for a rise, a knoll atop the rim of the Pil dustbowl.

"General!" Ulan grunted, holding his side. He nodded his head towards the entrance to the valley.

The ghouls had disengaged from their forces completely, and were sprinting across the blood-soaked ground towards them. The dragon strafed above them, breathing blasts of infernal flame onto them. Wyvernborn strafed the flank, throwing firebombs down, but no matter how many fell, the dead wave continued to wash across the Pil Valley.

"Get out of their way!" Kelad shouted. *"Anyone with a ranged weapon, engage, everyone else, pull the wounded out with you!"*

The Empire Of Fire

He slipped the last stone into his pistol, standing with eight other soldiers readying their crossbows. Ulan was staggering, marshalling their dwindling forces, dragging away or carrying those that were wounded but still alive.

"Start moving out of their path, aim for their legs," Kelad ordered. *"We might not be able to put them down, but we can slow them down, and wherever they're going, it's better they don't get there."*

There were murmured confirmations from around him. They jogged across as quickly as they could, but the thousands strong army were spread wide, and were at full sprint.

They had minutes.

"Head for the buildings, one that's still intact!" Kelad bellowed. He ran with the archers, helping the injured along with everyone else, picking up their speed. The nearest intact building was a one or two room shack, barely big enough to fit the surviving troops: four or five dozen perhaps. Of those, there was no telling how many were originally assigned to the *Razorback*.

It wasn't often that a pang of pain shot through Kelad in the way it did then, a fresh hopelessness even more sour than his already tart brand of cynicism.

The roar of the great, leather-winged beast that twisted and turned above them was a sound that had plagued his nightmares, even in his solitary hour of sleep, for a hundred years. The pain of that searing flame coloured his every waking moment too. Cael had forced them to be allies in the conquest of Haama, and this particular dragon was very familiar. The blue-eyed terror, one of the five that they had used for their own gain.

Commander Ulan burst through the front door and moved aside, helping the injured in. Kelad reformed his archers at the corner of the building, and spread them out in a line. *"Shoot your bolts at will, aim for the leading ghouls."*

The crossbow bolts flew towards the army, with little noticeable effect. The ghouls were still at long range. The next few bolts may have hit, Kelad saw some of the ghouls tumble to the ground, only to be trampled under the feet of those following them. The horde were not slowed.

Kelad levelled his pistol as they closed into range. Narrowed his eyes. Picked a target.

The first shot snap-froze a ghoul, which shattered under the force of those following it slamming into its body. Kelad bared his teeth and fired again, and again, to similar effect.

The dead were fifty yards away and closing fast. *"Pull back behind the structure,"* Kelad ordered. *"Keep them away from the injured."*

The soldiers waited at the wall for the swarm to overwhelm them. The footsteps drew closer until they were a thunder that drowned out every other sound in the valley.

The army sprinted past without so much as a glance in their direction. Kelad remained still, watching them closely. They didn't seem to care about the Caelish in the least. They were moving in the same direction as the others, towards the knoll.

***

The ghouls around the barrier were thickening. Their hisses had become roars. Hands that beat on the energy wall were breaking, weapons chipping, bending and splintering. Ironclad was aware of all of them, he could feel the arms of the dark force inside Ydra directing them, intensifying.

"Keep it up!" he bellowed. "The Mages must be getting through!"

The hollow boom of cannonfire bounced across the valley, coming closer and closer. The *Sand Dancer* was still sweeping overhead, but sounded further away.

A message rang through his head, a hissing, snarling voice that was incomprehensible to his mind. It was followed by the tense voice of Sandra.

"Ironclad, all of the dead are converging on you. The remainder of the Caelish army are rallying for pursuit. Father and the wyvernborn are attacking from above, but they aren't slowing. You have minutes before they are upon you."

The Empire Of Fire

"I understand," Ironclad snapped. He crushed a ghoul with the force of his axe blow and stamped on another.

Beside him, Kira fell, blood bursting from her mouth. Ironclad caught her with one hand and spun, laying her down on the dusty ground beside Bassai. He heard Ember's arrows whiz past his head, saw the majestic, emerald glow of her energy standing bolt upright, back arched.

The shaman tending to the wounded grunted and shuffled across to Kira. Bassai gritted his teeth and reached across weakly, taking her hand.

Ironclad had no time to give the injured any more thought than that. He spun and barrelled back to the front line. Shoulder out, shield high, he felt the wet impact of skulls and torsos against it. His axe swung down, wrenched out, sliced across again and again, chewing up ghouls as if he was a serrated tooth in a predator's mouth.

***

Thomas planted his foot on the flat summit of the pyramid, and readied incantations in both hands. Astrid and Seraphine were close behind, panting.

The three moved inwards slowly, hands high. The summit was flat, black, featureless save for one thing in the centre of it. A solitary figure, thin and drawn, on her knees.

Thomas signalled, and the Mages spread out, moving to surround her. As they got close, she looked up at them.

Ydra was skeletal. Her eyes were dark hollows, her nose little more than a hole in her face. What remained of her skin was pale white, tinted with greens and greys, thin and stretched, drawn away from her mouth so her teeth were always slightly bared. The hair on her head was patchy and limp, her body was crooked and bend out of shape.

"There's nothing I can do," she croaked. Her voice sounded as if her throat was being sawed into by a razor blade. "I tried ... tried to get away ... but it followed me ... overwhelmed me. When the clansmen died ... it tethered them to my heart and ripped it out."

Seraphine knelt beside her and took her hand. "Can you stop it?"

"I don't know. I ... am trying ... but I don't have enough ... in me."

"A dispelling incantation could solve it ..." Thomas looked around at the spiral, at the desolate landscape, at the stars. "Or perhaps not. Ydra ... what can you tell us about this thing?"

"It is no ordinary incantation ... as we know it," she rasped. "It has ... a mind of its own ..."

"We've noticed," Thomas muttered.

"It ... hungers ... consumes. It has ... consumed me ..."

Seraphine lay a hand on Ydra's gaunt cheek. "Not completely, not yet. You're still here, with us. You can fight it, you can beat it."

"I am all that keeps her alive," the voice boomed. **"I sustain her. Get rid of me ... and she dies."**

Ydra's head turned up to Seraphine. The empty sockets, the holes in her head, seemed to lock onto her eyes. "Seraphine ... I'm dead already. You can't save me in that way. It killed me ... I'm rotting. I can smell the decaying of my own body."

Seraphine closed her eyes and bowed her head.

"There must be a way," Astrid insisted, crouching beside her.

"We would need more Mages, more power, more time," Thomas said. "Putting a stopper in death, or bringing someone back from the Astral Plain, is as close to impossible as you can get at the best of times."

"Let me go," Ydra whispered. "Let me go, and make it count for something."

"I wish ..." Seraphine began. Tears shot from her eyes, and froze in mid-air, tinkling to the flat surface of the pyramid's summit.

"I wish it hadn't come to this. I wish I had been a better teacher. I wish I hadn't pushed you into the darkness."

"Pushed? You *shoved* her into the darkness. She turned her back on you, Ydra. Limited you, didn't give you the strength you could have had to

The Empire Of Fire

control the impulses that were a part of you. I give you that strength. I will never abandon you."

"It will never let you go," Thomas said. "Its hold will always remain, and it will always use your body and your strength for its own gain."

"I will not remain in its grasp," Ydra growled weakly. "I refuse ... I would rather be nothing than a puppet."

"Rather be nothing ... and nothing is what she would be. The Astral Plain you worship is out of her reach, and it always will be."

Astrid gasped. "No ... if she can't ascend ..."

"Seraphine ... it doesn't matter," Ydra rasped. "Just ... deal with it, whatever the cost. The clans don't believe in what you believe in. I'm a clanswoman ... I didn't belong in your tower."

Seraphine leaped forward and took what remained of Ydra into her arms, holding her tightly. "We can make it stop ... we can make the pain go away."

"Bury me in the trees," Ydra whispered. "Bury me with Vargas, and Rihd, and Boras, as many of the Dead Men as you can find. We will nourish the land."

"I'm so sorry," Seraphine sobbed.

"Don't be sorry. We all made our choices, we all paid for them. We did the best we could, and if it wasn't enough ... I forgave you long ago."

Thomas and Astrid knelt on either side of Ydra's corpse-like body, and leaned forward to embrace her.

"It was an honour and a pleasure to fight beside you," Thomas murmured. "Find peace in the forest. I'll pray for you."

As one, the Mages' hands began to glow, like they were holding suns at the height of noon. The freezing world around them began to radiate with warmth, and the smell of decay slowly began to freshen into the scent of a woodland clearing, teeming with wildflowers.

***

The ghouls' faces twisted from emotionless to furious. The hisses and moans became roars of rage. Their numbers around the barrier were increasing between blinks, crushing inwards, cracking the bones of those at the front without a care. Ember heard the skulls of the front ranks crack, and saw the faces distort, skin warping and tearing.

One broke through the barrier to her right, and she felled it with a swift arrow. Her fingers brushed against only four more arrows as she nocked another.

"Ironclad, I'm running low!"

"I hear you! Kassaeos, move back!"

The assassin formed beside her in a whirl of black smoke. The crossbow attached to his wrist was loaded with a barbed bolt. He shot Ember a wink. "I hope for your sake that you're carrying more than that bow."

"For your sake, I hope you've got more than that mouth."

Kassaeos barked a laugh, then his head snapped up. He raised his arm, and sent the bolt into another ghoul that shoved through the barrier.

There were so many ghouls around them that it seemed they were in a pit. They were piling on top of each other, higher and higher, pressing inwards. The barrier was warping under the pressure of them.

Three more breached the shield in one go. Two fell to arrow and bolt, and Kassaeos shifted in to slice the third down with his rapier.

As it fell, more burst through, bearing down on Thomas, Astrid and Seraphine. Too many.

Ember sent an arrow into one. Kassaeos sent a bolt into another. Five remained.

Ember drew another arrow in a blink. Kassaeos shifted forwards and engaged with his blade, taking one down. The remaining four snarled at the Mages, entranced in their task with Ydra.

Ember loosed the arrow, catching one as they charged. She nocked another as Kassaeos shifted again, cutting a fifth ghoul down, leaving two. They raised their blades, preparing to strike.

The Empire Of Fire

One of them burst into flame and fell back, arrow sticking from its chest. Ember's hand was already back behind her, reaching for another, but all it found was an empty quiver.

The last ghoul's blade swung down.

***

Astrid let out a grunt, and shuddered. A hint of rot crept into the air around them. Thomas felt a stab of pain at his throat. Seraphine looked up in concern.

"Astrid?"

"It's nothing," she muttered. "Don't stop."

Ydra's skeletal face turned to her, and she leaned forwards. Thomas could feel the entity leaning in towards them. It was creeping towards Astrid, wrapping thin tendrils around her shoulders.

"Astrid..." he started.

"Thomas, I'm fine!" she snapped.

"Don't allow it to take you," Ydra rasped. "It will try and bargain with you, try and have its way with you by brute force."

"Not with us here, it won't," Thomas growled.

"Your words are empty. Only I have dominion over the dead," it boomed.

"Dead?" Seraphine cried out. Astrid shook her head.

"Keep it up. I still have time."

"Focus, Seraphine," Thomas shouted. "Look!"

Ydra's shrivelled hands began glowing, gentle starlight coming through her necrotic flesh. Her power entwined with the three of theirs, forming a bright beacon in the void.

***

Ember hacked at the ghouls coming through the barrier with her shortsword. Kassaeos was dashing between them as they pushed themselves inside, slashing with his blade, shifting back to the middle to pick a shot with his crossbow.

The wyvernborn shamen had closed inwards, shrinking the barrier's surface to consolidate their power. Still, the army outside grew, almost covering the entirety of the dome, blocking out the sunlight.

Ironclad and Berek continued fighting at the gap in the barrier, covered in brown blood. Ironclad wasn't tiring, but Berek was flagging noticeably, panting, grunting in pain and crying out in anger.

"Fall back, Berek," Ironclad snapped. "Shamen! Close this gap by two yards!"

The soldier snapped something in Caelish, and Ironclad shoved him backwards into the centre with Ember and Kassaeos. The gap narrowed until there was barely an inch on either side of the Construct's body. He continued to strike, and Ember could hear impacts against his metal body, and his shield.

The barrier bent inwards beside one of the shamen, and blades crashed through, slicing into its scaly hide. It hissed with pain, and as Ember moved over to assist, the ghouls broke the barrier, flooding in and overwhelming the wounded wyvernborn.

The barrier flashed, and like a sheet of ice under boiling water, began to disappear.

***

The glow in Ydra's hands spread throughout her body, and she seemed to burn with a light that could only have been present in the highest realms of the Gods. The three Mages basked in the warmth of it, adding every scrap of their power to hers. The darkness backed away, farther and farther until it was drowning in the glow.

The pyramid was gone in an instant. The night above turned to day. A

The Empire Of Fire

sweet breeze flowed across them, the ground softened and sprouted with grass.

They were in a meadow, surrounded by trees in full spring bloom, with wildflowers in chaotic sprouts and flares of bright colour.

Ydra looked alive again, as she had appeared when they had parted ways at the White Tower. Her pallor had become tan again, her skin was smooth once more. She took a deep breath in, and smiled, her eyes closed. "As it should be."

She turned to Seraphine, Astrid and Thomas. "You've done so much for me ... I ... I'm so sorry. I wasn't strong enough."

"No ... you held on, and held off a being with more power then an army," Thomas said, taking her hand. "We find strength together. In battle, in peace, in life and death. You aren't alone. You never will be again."

Ydra's eyes glistened, and she took their hands in hers. "Just one last thing left to do..."

***

All across the Pil Valley, at the same moment, the ghouls fell.

Mid-stride, mid claw or strike, the hold on them released, and they became corpses once more, sprawling on the ground. Finally, they were at peace.

Every body that had been hastily buried in the forest, or left for the crows without respect, dropped to the ground. Every member of every clan that had gathered in the valley for their final charge, or who had fallen on the way, returned to eternal rest. Every Caelish soldier that had slaughtered them in their own hubris, or those who had come with Kelad to protect the innocent whom the dead would have swallowed, were let go to begin a hero's rest. The small number of wyvernborn, Orlin, and Haaman Resistance that had fallen, were embraced by the arms of the Gods.

Ironclad 'watched' it all through the veil of blindness, 'watched' the energy from the entity inhabiting Ydra vanish into the air. He saw a torrent of souls rise into the sky, joining the wide field of energy high above. Ironclad stood slowly, staring at it.

It covered the entire sky, like a vast, dense starfield in daylight, lined with auroras and sparkling twists of cloud. As he watched, it all drifted together and became clear to his new eyes. He could see continents, oceans, rolling hills and beaches. Lakes glittered, forests and jungles stretched across valleys and plains. No cities blotted the landscape, although there were villages, integrated seamlessly with everything around them. Boats bobbed around on the seas, huge fleets of them, sails unfurled and billowing. Airships sailed through the sky.

He viewed it all as if he was looking down at Haama or another land from high above, with awe. It all glowed with the light of the souls rushing towards it, weaving between the trees, dancing with the clouds, diving in and out of the clear water with joy.

Then it all faded away. The last of the souls found peace, and the Astral Plain became sky once again.

Behind him, there was wail of anguish. He turned. Seraphine reached out as Astrid tipped sideways, blood soaking through her robes from the wound in her neck. He approached as Seraphine tried to heal her, the magic flickering in her hands, her reserves depleted from her efforts with Ydra.

Ironclad put an arm on her shoulder gently, and shook his head. "She's gone, Seraphine. I saw her soul go. She's at peace."

The magic dispelled from Seraphine's hands. She sagged into Kassaeos's arms.

Ironclad looked down at Ydra. She lay on her back, her eyes closed, the flame in her rapier extinguished. Grief lanced through him at the sight of her, his former comrade in arms, a woman they had tried to save from herself. Now they had, but she would not live in the peace they had made, that she had contributed to.

Sending her and the Dead Men off alone … what a mistake it had been. They had all been sent into hell, and had created their own, falling under the influence of the power that had long tried to grip Ydra permanently.

Across the battlefield, the dragon roared in triumph. The wyvernborn flew in formation on its wing, dropping and landing among the dead. Above them, the *Sand Dancer* lowered, into a spot where there were almost no trees.

Thomas patted him on the forearm. "We should make contact with the Caelish forces, before anything can be spun. The sooner and more firmly we make our case, the better."

Ironclad sighed. "Tell Captain Seret. How are Bassai and Kira?"

"The shamen are tending to them. They should live ... but it might not be pretty."

"Talk to Berek."

Thomas raised an eyebrow. "Berek?"

"Orso fell."

Thomas's eyes widened, and he wheeled around. Berek was kneeling beside his comrade, helmet off and beside him, openly weeping. The Mage took off at a run, skidding to a halt beside him, dropping to his knees. Words passed between them in Caelish, in anger, in bitterness, in sadness. They fell silent, before Thomas untied a bottle from a pouch in his robe. He uncorked it, and took a sip, then held it out to Berek.

The soldier hesitated for a moment, but took it and drank. He gazed down at his friend's body, then reached out, taking hold of Thomas's shoulder.

"We did it ..." Ember muttered, drawing Ironclad's attention.

"We did, but we're not quite finished yet. We need to have a conversation with ... our allies. Then, we need to bury all of these people ... and that will take time. Ydra deserves a burial at least."

"Rihd is ..." Ember's voice cracked. "Rihd ... was up here too. We should be able to find some more of the Dead Men."

Ironclad nodded, and squeezed her hand. "Let's get everyone on the *Sand Dancer* ... everyone that can be moved. Astrid, Orso and Ydra as well ... Rihd too, if you can find her. Get word to Sandra and her archers to assist."

Ember nodded, and jogged towards the small airship. Ironclad turned to the injured, surrounded by shamen. Bassai's eyes were half open, locked onto Ironclad, only wavering at the dragon's roar. Kira was still, being closely tended to. Ironclad nodded to the wyvernborn, before turning back to the Valley.

The remnants of the Caelish army were filing in through the entrance, reduced in number considerably. The remaining airships in their fleet were floating above, drawing in but keeping their distance from the dragon. Two carriers, three skiffs and a single, damaged battleship. The losses had been staggering ... but they had prevailed. A victory ... one that they would have to build on quickly.

Every point he needed to make ran though his head, every argument, every appeal, but it was sluggish, tired, bitter.

Why ally themselves with torturers and slavers? The ones that murdered Melida City and paraded its corpse, spitting on it by calling it Victory of all things, who hunted innocent people on the plains, who had all but erased the clans from existence.

How many friends had died because of the Caelish people? How many had been been tortured, like he had been?

The dragon's roar pulled him from his thoughts. Soaring, swooping and diving, relishing the spreading of its wings again after a century under the mountains. As he turned again, towards his friends, he caught Sandra's eye. She smiled at him tightly, giving him a nod. The Orlin bride of a wyvernborn, part of a union unheard of in his day.

It was his own bias, his own trauma, holding him back. He had to give them a chance. The Caelish who had wronged him, most of them, had died decades ago.

He strode back towards Thomas and Berek, and knelt before them. "It's time."

Thomas nodded solemnly.

"Berek and Orso should come with us. Orso should be buried with his people, as a hero. He will not be forgotten."

The Empire Of Fire

Thomas nodded, and repeated the words to Berek in Caelish. Berek grunted something in response, and Thomas sighed raggedly. "He says it's a high price, and he hopes it buys something real. I'm forced to agree," he shook his head. "I knew there could be losses ... Gods above ... but Ydra, Orso, Astrid ... Bassai and Kira could never recover from this. Astrid ... she knew she was dying, and she held on. She held on to finish it, she didn't tell us how bad it was. She was so brave, Tobias ... and Orso ..."

His voice became thick. "I've not known many better than him. This could be more difficult than I thought ... I have to clear my mind ..."

"A Caelish soldier ... a man of his own god, a man we would have faced in yesteryear ... and he died for peace between our nations," Ironclad said. "Ydra and Astrid died for the same reason ... to save both our nations ... possibly the world itself. Their deaths will not go to waste."

10

The *Sand Dancer* lifted from the knoll, and drifted down into the valley. Thomas stood on the prow, going over his ideas, making sure they were all in order. Berek stood beside him silently, still locked in the cage of grief, all too soon thrust into a new challenge.

Thomas was only a little way behind him in that regard. The purpose of all this was the only thing keeping him from breaking, and the valley's activity was a welcome distraction.

The two remaining Caelish carrier ships had settled onto the valley floor at different points: one at the entrance, one at the centre next to the ruins of the settlement. Every spare deckhand and every soldier was acting as a corpsman, either providing medical attention to the wounded or carrying the dead soldiers into the ships. The wyvernborn were assisting, carrying two bodies at a time, and even managing to do it in a way that seemed respectful. Barada was directing them, bellowing at the top of his voice, swooping over their heads.

The dragon was regal and serene now that the battle was over, settling down some distance away, drawing stares of wonder and fear from the Caelish soldiers. It was using its wings and claws to smother the dragonfire that still smouldered on what remained of the grass. Tendrils of thick black smoke rose into the sky from the patches.

One of the shamen hissed behind Thomas, and he turned around. Sandra nodded and jogged back to Captain Seret at the helm. Thomas frowned at her as she walked back, and the *Sand Dancer* changed course to land beside the dragon.

Sandra stood beside Thomas and Berek at the prow. "Father needs the shamen to assist him. Without them, the valley will be damaged beyond repair."

"Like in the Maldane Reach," Thomas muttered.

"And what's left of the Orlin Forest. They have shielded the Bog, but if we can't remove the corruption in the Orlin soil, it could spread in eventually."

"But they can do something here?"

"They say it's early enough that the corruption hasn't fully spread into the ground yet."

Thomas stroked his chin. "Something else that Father can help with, perhaps, and the shamen. If the Maldane Reach can be repopulated, and Orlin, perhaps there really can be peace. They invaded Taeba out of desperation, because they needed food for Cael and Haama both."

Sandra grunted. "People don't fight so much when their bellies are full."

"Precisely."

The dragon watched the shamen shuffle from the ship, down the boarding ramp. It extended claws, picking them up and putting them down gently on the ground. Thomas gaped at it. When the last one was down, the dragon seemed to meet his gaze. It grunted at him, a short, deep sound that shuddered the air around him.

Thomas bowed his head, eliciting another series of grunts. Thomas looked up with a start. It couldn't have been ... but it had almost sounded like a chuckle.

The dragon's head craned around and looked up at the battleship slowly drifting above them. It focused in on the mechanical facsimile of a dragon-head on the prow. Thomas had no idea how conscious or alive those moving ornaments were, but this one was very aware of Father. It made no sound whatsoever, gazing down at its forebear in what looked to be wonder.

Father snorted, and went back to its business. The shamen shuffled around it, glowing with arcane light. The *Sand Dancer* lifted off, and drifted slowly towards the largest cluster of Caelish troops.

Ember and Ironclad joined them at the front of the ship, looking down at the remains of the day.

"We need to speak to someone in charge," Ironclad muttered. "Who did you say was leading the forces here?"

Thomas grinned tightly. "An old ... acquaintance. General Kelad."

Ironclad let out a growling, groaning sound, that could have been a sigh. Ember's jaw clenched.

"I know. It won't exactly be a happy reunion ... but he's our man. We're in too deep to blow it all now."

"I hate it when you're right," Ember muttered.

"*You* hate it?" someone growled behind them.

Bassai was barely standing, supported by Seraphine and Kassaeos. There was a bandage wrapped around his chest that stank of a number of different salves. His scales were dull in colour, his knees were weak, but he was alive.

"How are you, my friend?" Thomas said with a smile.

"Not dead," Bassai grunted. "Well enough to stand with you."

"You put a lot on the line to give us our chance with Ydra," Thomas said, stepping forwards, readying an incantation to ease his pain.

"And paid well for it, although not as much as I could have. Save your spells, I will be fine."

"I see him," Ember muttered. "In the ruins."

Thomas turned back to the prow. Kelad was standing beside a battered dwelling, ground strewn with debris, surrounded by a gaggle of Caelish soldiers. Thomas didn't recognise any of them at a distance, all were wearing full armour and helmets.

There would be questions, if Ulan's soldiers were among them. There would be heartache if any had fallen. Good people, who cared, who fought for what was right.

"*They would have been on the front line,*" Berek muttered, as if he had been reading his mind.

"*I know.*"

"*None of us asked for this,*" he said. "*Our job was to patrol, to keep the peace. Orso and me ... we were just supposed to guard the princess. Nothing ever happened to her, except once, in the palace gardens. Keeping people away from her was never any bother, really. Never thought I'd see a war ... a battle like this."*

"*You were lucky to live in peaceful times ... and you're lucky you kept up with your training and didn't get soft.*"

"*Not enough,*" Berek muttered bitterly.

Thomas looked at him and shook his head. "*No, Orso fought well. He kept us alive, gave us our chance.*"

Berek said nothing. Thomas sighed to himself, observing the General once more, feeling himself incapable of any words of comfort that would have been effective in the moment. Kelad was watching the ship closely, his face betraying nothing. If he recognised them at all, he had no reaction to their presence.

Behind them, Seret's crewman lowered the boarding ramp. Thomas took a breath, and looked back at his friends. "Onward."

Ironclad nodded, and they moved back to the ramp and disembarked. Sandra, Seraphine and Kassaeos joined them, and as their feet touched the ground, there was a swooping of wings above them. Barada landed heavily beside the *Sand Dancer,* with Zeta close behind. Both had cuts riddling and criss-crossing their scales, black blood staining their armour. Sandra stepped over to the Alpha and Beta, examining their wounds, holding on to Barada's clawed hand tightly for a moment.

More of the soldiers on the ground were beginning to converge on them, and the ship. They formed into several units, spread around thirty yards apart, posting up on several sides. A clear warning.

Kelad strode forwards to meet them, followed by the rest of the soldiers with him. They met in the middle, but remained perhaps fifteen feet apart. Thomas saw a few of the armoured soldiers react to his and Berek's presence, in confusion, in disbelief. One even seemed to move for a lunge, but was stopped by another. Berek's eyes were locked on the ground.

"There's been enough death today, don't you think, Kelad?" Ironclad said stonily, breaking the silence.

Kelad didn't answer. Instead he took each of them in, one by one, offering a deferential nod to Barada and Zeta in particular. He focused in on Thomas, Ember, Ironclad, and Bassai. "You know, since the engagement at the White Tower, I have been curious about you. Reports of an Orlin archer, a wyvernborn without wings, a robed Caelish man using magic ... and a Construct, a dead warrior, resurrected inside a body built for war. A unique group, one I would never have expected to encounter twice, years apart. Yet, it appears I have. In the same country. In the same conflict. I suspected, due to the fate of the first group and the following around them, that they had become icons, and that another group had simply taken up their mantle ... but now ... looking you all in the eye ..."

He looked at the four in turn again. "Bassai. Thomas. Emeora Vonn. Presumably, Tobias Calver. We, of course, have already met while you have been in this form."

Ironclad grunted. "I take it you visited me during my stay in the Colonel's dungeon."

"He was keen to show you off. I hope there have been no ill effects, to you or Seraphine."

Seraphine's lip curled, but Thomas shook his head to silence her. Ironclad grunted again.

"Eyes aside, no."

"Indeed. I would ask how that scar I gave you all those years ago healed up ... but having seen what's under that shell of yours, it seems to no longer be a problem."

"You mind telling us how *you're* still alive?" Ember growled.

Kelad grinned and spread his hands. He became an entity of swirling smoke before their eyes, before reforming as himself. Thomas glanced at Kassaeos with a raised eyebrow.

"I see you're familiar with Aethers, given your companion," Kelad said smoothly. "It wouldn't surprise me if we were turned after the same engagement, although I managed to keep my hair."

Kassaeos was very still, his face stony.

"I thought so. The hostility among you is interesting, I must say. It leaves me wondering whose idea this was, coming to our aid in this engagement."

"Mine, General," Thomas said, taking a step forwards.

Some of the soldiers nearby shifted, and stepped forwards as well. One held the rest back, and stood beside Kelad. He removed his helmet, revealing the sweat-soaked face of Commander Ulan. He was holding himself upright, although a hand was at his side, red with blood.

Thomas felt himself straighten to attention, wounded by the grim look of betrayal on a good man's face.

"This ... is Tomek, General. The other soldier is Berek."

Kelad nodded. "You provided Commander Ulan with the intelligence concerning these ghouls we fought."

"I did."

"Without that intelligence, the army would have been slaughtered."

"Worse, General. You would have added to their numbers."

"I noticed ... and I am grateful." Kelad's mouth turned up in a narrow grin. "I must admit, I find this very quaint. We're speaking to each other with such respect, something that is unheard of between blood enemies."

"We don't have to be blood enemies, Kelad," Ironclad muttered.

"Tell that to your terrorists."

"They aren't *our* terrorists. We haven't been present for a century."

"Please, General, let us not disappear into the weeds of time and bitterness," Thomas urged. "We want peace. Look what we just accomplished together: we just saved this nation. We can help you now: with your wounded, with the dead ... and more, so much more."

"Oh?"

"The dragonfire corruption. The advancing sands in Cael. The bitterness that has infected Haama and Cael for a century. We used to work together, we were allies, not a vassal and master. We can't change the past hundred years.

We don't want to break our two nations apart ... it could only be done with a sharp knife and a river of blood."

"Neither of which are especially constructive." Kelad glanced at Ulan. "Your help with the wounded would be appreciated. I will guarantee, on my honour, that no arms will be raised against you. I would promise that ... even if there wasn't a dragon in our midst." He switched tongues to Caelish. "*Give the order to the men. Accommodate our ... allies ... within as much reason as etiquette allows. I gather you and your two former comrades will have some things to say to each other.*"

Ulan broke from Thomas's gaze. "*It will be done, General.*"

"On your honour?" Ember said stonily.

Kelad turned back to the alliance, and pressed his hands together. "Believe it or not, miss Vonn, there is some honour present within the empty cavity that once held my heart. I'm sure you have your own business to attend to here. Once it is complete, we will perhaps have some things to discuss, will we not? I will be the last to leave this Valley. You will find me here, when you're ready."

***

It took the remainder of the daylight to load the dead Caelish soldiers onto one of the carriers, and the clansmen onto the other. Once loaded, the clansmen's carrier lifted off and made the short journey to the mouth of the valley, where the crew began bearing them into the forest. With the addition of the shamen's magic, the wounded were all stabilised, ready to be healed and rehabilitated at Breaker's Bay.

The *Sand Dancer* took a short journey as well, to bury Ydra, Vargas, and the other Dead Men beneath the trees. Reluctantly, Thomas hadn't gone with them. He had to prioritise peace making.

"*Orso too?*" Yaro grunted, covering his eyes. "*Va'Kael above us ...*"

"*Who else did we lose?*" Thomas asked, dreading the answer.

The Empire Of Fire

"*Pardek, Ilian, Virs, Aket, Ori and Lazar.*"

Thomas bowed his head. "*I'm sorry, Yaro. Is Elizia...?*"

Yaro snorted. "*Come on now, you've seen that girl fight. She's fine, few cuts and bruises. Commander Ulan said that you gave him the intelligence that the necromancer was here ... and it seems you dealt with her. If you hadn't done those things, we'd have all died.*"

"*So did Orso, and Berek.*"

Yaro leaned back on the ruined hut and shook his head. "*What were the three of you even doing on that ship ... with the enemy? You know there are going to be questions asked when we get back to Victory.*"

"*I'm a member of the Resistance.*"

"*I know that, that's clear as daylight,*" Yaro snapped.

Thomas took a deep breath. "*I was meant to gather information on the Caelish. I did. I gathered that you were no different than us. You want people to be safe, your families, your friends. You want the bloodshed to end.*"

Yaro folded his arms. "*Is Berek with you and your friends too? Was Orso?*"

"*No, they're men of Cael. Their loyalty can never be questioned: they were ordered to come with me.*"

"*By who?*"

Thomas almost blurted Allessandra's name out. "*I can't say ... but it was someone who was just as loyal to Cael.*"

"*Then why give that order?*"

Thomas hesitated, thinking immediately of Yaro's wife and children, but the man had to know. "*The Black Fleet hit Victory. They set it on fire, it was burning when we left. We heard cannonfire on the wind.*"

Yaro stared at him, a cloud descending over his face. "*If you're lying to me, you piece of ...*"

"*What would be the point? You'd find out the moment you got back.*"

His expression softened, and desperate lines creased his brow. "*My family ...*"

"*Where do they live?*"

"*South west, next to the Fisheries.*"

Thomas nodded. "*Old Town was the focus, but the fire was spreading.*"

Yaro paced, head in his hands, as Berek and Mule approached. The latter embraced Thomas tightly, while Berek stood still, eyes far off.

"*Mule, it's good to see you.*"

"*You too, sir.*"

"*You don't have to call him 'sir', Mule. He's not one of us,*" Berek muttered.

"*But we just fought together, sir,*" Mule insisted. "*We fought on the same side, and we won!*"

"*Some of us won.*"

"*The ones who died won too, Berek,*" Yaro said quietly. "*They died protecting Haama. People on the Idris Plains, in Victory, in the Bays, in the lands where those wyvernborn come from, were defended. They get to sleep one more day ... in peace.*"

"*You're more ready than some for that peace,*" Berek replied, voice tight. "*There are some that would rather set the land on fire than join hands with an old foe.*"

Mule straightened up. "*Not me, sirs. I think ... I think this could be a beginning. A real chance.*"

"*I hope so,*" Thomas said. "*Those bridges remain to be crossed. We're still apart, in some ways.*"

Yaro nodded over to the ruins, where a wyvernborn shaman knelt, pressing healing hands over a man's chest, stemming the tide of blood leaking from him, before a Caelish medic applied a salve and bandages to the wound. Other wyvernborn were lifting debris from a group of civilians that the initial rescue team had missed, picking them up and flying them over to the field hospital deploying from the nearby carrier. Sandra and Barada were deep in discussion with two official looking military men, perhaps commanding officers.

The Empire Of Fire

"*Those bridges are being crossed as we speak,*" Yaro said. "*We're looking at a new Haama and Cael taking shape before our eyes.*"

"*We just might be ...*" Thomas turned to look at Berek, who was watching the old enemies mix together with his arms folded. "*Do you know where I can find Commander Ulan? I ... owe him an explanation.*"

"*He's by the lake,*" Mule said. "*To be honest, Tomek, I'd be more worried about Elizia.*"

"*His name isn't Tomek,*" Berek muttered.

"*It doesn't matter,*" Mule replied. "*He never did wrong by any of us. I'll go with you.*"

As they set off across the dustbowl, Thomas glanced over at the slave. "*You think this will be enough to break those chains of yours, Mule?*"

"*I don't know. Maybe. The Silver Wreath wasn't.*"

"*We got those for saving a village. What we just did saved a nation ... and together we might save its soul.*"

Mule shrugged. "*I don't think that's how it works.*"

"*It's Thomas, by the way. My real name.*"

Mule gave him a smile. "*I'm afraid I don't know mine. It's still just Mule ... for now anyway.*"

***

Ironclad stepped from the grave with a groan and a grinding of metal. Jack eyed him with a look of understandable concern. His chassis was dented in so many places that he couldn't individually pick them out. He was being subjected to waves of pain, constant and unrelenting. Difficult to ignore, but a pain that he would persevere through, particularly now.

Seraphine, Bassai, Ember and Kassaeos lowered Ydra into the grave slowly, as they had for the rest of the Dead Men they had found among the ghouls. All were covered already, Ydra was the last.

Once she too had been laid to rest and buried, the others stood around the graves. Seraphine waved a hand, and the graves bloomed with flowers, a tribute of life that they had all helped to strengthen.

"Does anyone have anything to say?" Ironclad grunted.

"She fought until the end," Seraphine whispered. "Even after most of her had been consumed, a little spark of light remained, and she fought. When Astrid fell, Ydra joined that spark with ours."

Her watering eyes turned to the *Sand Dancer,* where Astrid lay in state, ready to go home to Obsidian where she would be buried. "They were both so brave ... and I failed them."

"You never failed Astrid," Kassaeos muttered. "As for Ydra ... you did as right by her as you could. Alone, against that thing inside her, there was nothing either of you could have done."

"There are few who could look a devil in the eye and not fall," Bassai muttered. "There are even fewer who would have the strength to stand up again. She was a soul in torment. May that torment be at an end."

Ironclad would have smiled if he could. He had come to deal with an unspeakable threat ... and had done so while saving a friend, in a way. It had been the only way she could have been saved, a mercy, but more than that. She had died as herself ... and that was a gift, in a way.

Many died in fear, or died unaware of what had taken their lives away. Some died after their minds had eroded away slowly. Ydra had found a way back.

He unwrapped his fingers from Ydra's rapier, and gazed down at it. Without the flames, it appeared almost harmless. It was an old weapon, beginning to rust in places, yet the runes on the hilt were as sharply etched as when it had been forged. It had seen plenty of blood, her own friends' blood. "Do we bury this with her?"

"We should," Seraphine said, wiping her eyes. "But we can't, not yet. A weapon of that nature will be an ... asset."

"We can bury it with her when it's over," Ember murmured solemnly, hands clasped behind her back. "Is that what she would even want?"

The Empire Of Fire

"She was a warrior," Bassai grunted.

"And a leader," Ironclad said. "Let her lay in peace, without weapons of war."

His giant hand found Ember's waist, and they stood beside the graves in silence. He said a prayer in his mind to the Gods, to the wide expanse of heavens above him, and a sudden warmth enveloped him. Not the intense, deadly heat of dragonfire, but something more gentle, a summer sunlight. His vision shifted, the forest melted away, and a field appeared. Long green grass, ears of golden corn and wildflowers in a thousand shades of colour sprang up around him. His vision returned to him, he could no longer see energy and aura, but like he had when he had been Tobias Calver.

He strode forwards, brushing the grass aside with hands of flesh and blood, relishing the cool feeling of it, the smells of the lush plantlife, the way the air tickled his skin. Goosebumps raised along his arms, drawing a laugh from his heart.

The laugh was echoed by another belly-laugh ahead of him. A joyful sound, lively. He pushed through the grass and corn into a clearing, where a number of people turned towards him.

They were dressed in simple clothes, still the garb of clansmen, but devoid of armour and war paint. No weapons were strapped to their hips or backs.

Ydra smiled at him as she caught his eye. "So that's what you look like under all that armour."

"In a way."

She was as alive as she had been at the White Tower, the last time he had seen her, but it was as if a great weight had been lifted from her shoulders. Her back was straight, she wasn't as gaunt, but lean and graceful.

She was standing apart from a number of other figures. Vargas nodded to Tobias with a smile, as Rihd put her arms around his shoulders. He recognised Kolnil, the man who had lost everyone he loved, playing with his children, embracing his wife.

"It's not exactly what I believed awaited me after death," Ydra chuckled, raising an eyebrow at him, "but I could get used to it. You're not meant to be here yet, though, I can feel it."

Tobias ran a hand through his hair. "I think I'm just ... being allowed to visit. I was praying for you, and for them."

"Ah. Why were you praying?"

Tobias stepped forwards, and took her hands in his. "I was asking the Gods to take care of you ... look out for you and your people. I wanted ... I wanted to know that you would be alright, that your soul would ..."

Ydra squeezed his hands to stop him. "I'm fine ... I'll be fine. I ..."

She sighed, and laughed to herself. Her eyes glistened. "I wish I'd had your strength, your will. You were one of the only people who could ever set me straight."

"I have it on good authority that you were strong enough to stare death in the eye, and beat it."

"Not death," she muttered. "Not exactly, but I appreciate you saying so."

She held him tightly, and it was a feeling that struck him with a longing. The warmth of another person against him, the feel of them breathing, reacting to him.

"I hope it's a long time before I see you up here, or wherever we are," Ydra murmured. "All of you."

Tobias smiled. "Don't worry about us. You earned this place, you earned this peace. Treasure it ... I imagine you'll have plenty of adventures."

She looked around. A new figure had appeared, and was greeting the Dead Men warmly. His hair was greying, he was about Ydra's height, broad shouldered and powerful. His face seemed familiar, but Tobias couldn't place it.

"I'll have a few, no doubt," she murmured, as her eyes met the man's. She turned back to Tobias. "Good luck. Take good care of those friends of ours."

"I will ... and when the time comes that we see each other again, I'll see if I can bring a barrel of mead."

And then it was all gone, as if a candle had been blown out. Pain returned to his gargantuan body. Ember seemed so small as she looked up at him.

"You okay, big guy?"

Ironclad grunted. "Just saying a prayer."

"Any news from on high?"

Ironclad nodded. "Of a sort."

***

Commander Ulan barely acknowledged Thomas's presence at first, directing those under his command. He was sending rowboats out over the glassy lake, salvaging derelict barges and debris. How they had gotten in there, Thomas could only speculate. Fishermen, or settlers who had sought futile refuge from the dead.

He waited patiently. Ulan glanced up at him occasionally, regarding Mule with a scowl as fierce as the one he was giving Thomas.

Finally, he had no more orders to give, and he turned to them slowly. *"What do you want?"*

"To see you, sir. To speak, to explain, if I can. To mourn."

Ulan shook his head. *"There isn't anything you could say to explain. I know full well. You deceived me, and the squad, and the Admiralty, and the Regent."* He pointed bitterly to the rest of the Resistance. *"They trust you too much to be someone who recently turned his coat. More likely, you were a mole, chosen because you spoke Caelish, walking among us in a dead man's armour."*

Thomas held his gaze as best he could, despite how intimidated he felt around his former commander. *"I don't know who the armour belonged to, Commander. Whoever they were, they didn't die by my hand. It's true I was a mole, a spy, but my intentions were not to make things worse. If it were, I would never have warned you about Ydra."*

"Ah, so you were sent to be peacemaker? A spy-come-mediator?"

Thomas clenched his jaw. *"No ... I was sent to gather military* intelligence. The plan changed ... and it changed quickly."

Ulan nodded. "Well, I can only hope your intelligence won't result in too much more of our blood."

"Commander Ulan, you must believe me..."

Ulan rounded on Thomas furiously, and Mule took a step back, his eyes glued to the dirt. "Believe you? Seven of my men are dead, including Orso! You warned me about a necromancer, not cannons! You put my command in jeopardy, you could make a laughing stock of the Standing Army when we need it the least!"

"I didn't know about the cannons, sir..."

"STOP CALLING ME 'SIR'!" Ulan roared. "You're not under my command, you never were."

"No ... I was. I was loyal to you, and to the squad. The plan changed because YOU changed it, Commander. You and the squad changed it. You are a good man. The squad were all good men. We're fighting the same people ... we're fighting those who waited until you left Victory to strike at the citizenry. We're fighting the people who sent you all here to die. The people who we stopped from murdering civilians in their homes, in the streets."

Ulan folded his arms. "You're saying the Black Fleet attacked Victory?"

"My cover was blown, but the ships bombarded the city while I was in the palace. I was sent, with Berek and Orso, to gather a force to assist you."

Ulan raised an eyebrow. "By the Regent?"

Thomas opened his mouth, almost cursing himself. He lowered his voice. "You didn't hear it from me, Commander."

"Then I owe her my life, as much as I owe ... others."

Thomas spread his hands. "I ... don't know what I can do to change things, to give us somewhere to begin properly, to start again. I proved to you that I was trustworthy."

"You gained my trust, yes, for your own benefit."

"For all our benefit."

Ulan snorted. "That remains to be seen. That's what all this probably is:

another way to gain our trust, gain access to our underbelly."

Thomas sagged. *"That isn't so."*

"On your word?"

"On my word as a man of Cael."

Ulan shook his head. *"You haven't been a man of Cael for a long time."*

As Thomas wracked his brain for something to say, anything to say, another soldier approached.

It was Elizia. She carried her helmet under one arm, and she didn't even look at Thomas as she approached. *"Commander, you're needed aboard the Spearhead."*

Ulan nodded, casting a single glare back at Thomas. He began to walk, and Elizia turned without a word.

Thomas opened his mouth, but Mule quickly nudged his arm and shook his head.

***

As the sun set, the remaining Caelish survivors and casualties filed onto the two remaining carriers. Two of the skiffs slowly pulled alongside them as they drifted towards Breaker's Bay. They picked up speed, and disappeared out of sight, leaving the final skiff to hover at the Pil Valley's perimeter as the battleship remained hovering just above the compacted ground.

Kelad waited alone on the battlefield, watching the dragon swoop and soar high above. Ironclad wondered what the man was thinking as he approached with the rest of his companions. His face was passive, he regarded the dragon without fear or reverence, simply with neutrality. When his face turned to the approaching allies, he straightened up, his arms clasped behind his back.

The rest of the Four Guardians were beside Ironclad, along with Sandra, Barada and Seraphine. Kassaeos was aboard the *Sand Dancer*, preparing it for its journey to Obsidian. Kelad had requested no retinue for himself, an interesting show of good faith on his part.

I suppose the battleships count, Ironclad thought. *Then again, we have a dragon.*

They stopped, barely three feet apart, closer than they had ever been with or without weapons drawn.

"Well then, Calver and company ... where do we go from here?"

"Our separate ways, to begin with," Ironclad said. "After that ... it will depend, perhaps on our superiors, but we can certainly have some influence over those matters."

Kelad raised his eyebrows with a little 'hmm!' sound. "Easier said than done, wouldn't you agree?"

"That is going to depend on who your superiors are."

"I have many, mister Calver, from military to royalty. Doubtless they will all have their own opinions, as is standard for these types of things."

He sighed to himself, gazing around at the derelict settlement, at the lake, at the blood staining the ground. "A dark day. A bloody day. Many good men and women died, ours and yours."

"They're one and the same, General," Thomas said, stepping directly beside Ironclad.

"Today, they were, yes. Some might call it the one ray of blessed sunlight bursting through storm clouds. Some will call it an elaborate ploy to throw us off balance, curry favour so a knife can be plunged in the neck. Others will say it's an undiscovered country on the horizon, which could hold treasures or horrors. Do we land, or carry on as we were? The latter is certainly a safer option, but is it a wiser one?"

"That island has something we need," Ironclad muttered.

"Yes, yes." Kelad paced. "Can you believe it? We are all, in our own way, some of the oldest warriors in this ... conflict. Here we all stand. I watched four of you die."

His eyes flicked from Ember, to Thomas, to Bassai. "I gave the order to loose the arrows that put you three to death. I told Kallus Vehnek that I wanted to hang your bodies from the walls of Victory and leave them to rot, and I would have. If you had told me then that I would be standing beside you, fighting beside you ... I would never have believed it, and not just because of the obvious. You four and your Rangers were an annoyance for years, the revolutionaries you spawned: for decades. Here we stand, looking at that mysterious nation, together. Is it that easy, do you think?"

"No-one said anything about it being easy," Bassai grunted.

Kelad laughed. "I suppose not."

"It wasn't when we did it," Sandra added, holding Barada's arm. "In your day, the Orlin and wyverborn were worse than blood enemies."

"And look at you now," Kelad muttered.

"Bassai and I proved we could work together," Ember said. "Thomas proves that Caelish and Haamans could work together. We proved it today."

"We proved it for *decades,* General," Thomas insisted. "We were allies, strong allies."

"A century and a half ago," Kelad said with a wave of his hand.

"This morning," Ironclad grunted.

Kelad laughed out loud and shook his head. "You're all bloody stubborn, which I suspect is what made you such a pain in the arse. You don't seem to be fools, though, and you've gone to great pains to come here. Helping us can't have been easy." He eyed them. "You know, if you'd let us die, the Caelish fleet would have been crippled. Might have given you an easier fight later on down the line."

"We know, General," Thomas said smoothly. "So does Lord Marshal Vehnek, and I imagine he was counting on it."

Kelad narrowed his eyes. "I've heard the rumours spreading among the men."

"You'll see it in person soon enough."

"Hmm. Well, until we meet again. For now ... you can expect no hostility from the Caelish Armed Forces under my command, orders or no orders."

Ironclad nodded, and extended a hand. Kelad looked at it with a smirk, and took hold of his index and middle finger.

"We will contact you when we have a delegation together, and join you in Victory," Thomas said, his back straight, a smile of relief unable to conceal itself behind the wall of stoicism needed for negotiations. He swapped to Caelish. *"Go safely, General."*

Kelad bowed his head. *"You and yours as well."*

The General shifted away, and Thomas patted Ironclad on the shoulder. "Let's go."

***

Kelad listened as the *Spearhead's* crew prepared the battleship for full liftoff, and fast travel. They were busy, moving heavy machinery, chaining the cannons securely to the deck. The generator was spinning, whumping rhythmically, the quickening heartbeat of a predator preparing for the prowl.

Above it all were the sweeping whoosh of the dragon's wings. He heard it roar, and the crew around him paused for a moment, only resuming under his glare.

He made his way onto the top deck as the *Spearhead* took to the air. The dragon, wyvernborn and *Sand Dancer* had cleared the Pil Valley already, speeding in a south-easterly direction.

Kelad padded to the helm, where Commander Ulan was waiting. Captain Obrek stood beside his helmsman, looking at him stonily.

"Cheer up, Captain. We won."

Obrek shifted his weight onto his other foot. *"At what cost, General?"*

"Many lives. My ship and crew. Thousands of civilians. Thousands of good soldiers. We bought victory against a formidable enemy ... and we may have bought something else. Something unexpected."

Obrek's eyes focused forwards. *"Yes, sir. I have a communication from the Vjadra."*

The Empire Of Fire

One of the skiffs that had flown cover, and the only other vessel in formation with them now. *"Don't leave me in suspense, Captain."*

"They want to know if they should pursue the rebels."

"Tell them: no. Nothing will be served by following them: we know where they're going. Obsidian, the old mine to the south, or the Wyvern Bog, or both."

"Yes, sir."

Kelad straightened. *"Send to all remaining ships in the squadron, to be immediately relayed to all captains in the Aerial Navy: As of this moment, all anti-rebel operations from our ships are to cease. Extend to ground operations as well. All units are to stand ready for further orders."*

Obrek hesitated. *"General ... are we operating on orders from the Lord Marshal, or the Defense Ministers of Cael or Haama?"*

"If they order me to resume operations, I will do so. Inform any and all commanding officers who have any reservations about the orders I just gave to speak with me directly for clarification."

"Yes General."

Kelad almost turned away, but instead he faced Obrek. *"You should require none, Captain, having seen the battle first-hand. You're alive because they assisted us."*

Obrek grunted. *"As you say, General."*

Kelad walked away from the helm to the rear of the ship, looking at the Valley as they slowly departed. So much blood over this one area of Taeba, tens of thousands of lives. A needless loss, probably. Who knew what other horrors lay in the undergrowth, ready to emerge when the loggers came in to clear the trees to make room for farmland?

Commander Ulan joined him silently. Kelad waited for him to speak patiently, content to let him ponder the consequences of the day.

Finally he spoke. *"You do realise, of course, General ... that with a dragon, the Resistance are a tangible threat to every settlement in the country, including Victory. They could even cause considerable damage to Cael City."*

"Indeed. However, Cael City could withstand worse, and I doubt they

would be stupid enough to waste an asset of that magnitude on such a futile attack. Calver and his compatriots are not stupid, and they are not butchers. Provided they can rein in the more extreme elements of their forces, they will not attack a city or town or village in Haama. A tactical waste, given the reprisal that would ensure from Cael, and even further abroad."

"They used it here."

"Of course they did. They needed the dragonfire to beat that necromancer, and project power to us. They have a sword, but it is a sword they know when to wield and when not to."

Ulan nodded, but his concern remained etched across his brow. "*They are in possession of a catastrophic weapon, along with the military secrets Tom... Thomas ... no doubt imparted. There are many who won't be comfortable with the situation.*"

"*I understand your concerns fully, as I will understand theirs. However, consider the alternative. An undead menace, unstoppable, rending its way across Haama. New potential farmland unusable, the blood to win it wasted. Idris overrun. Haama a land ruled by walking corpses, and Cael cut off from its primary source of food, left to starve. An end to two nations, millions of lives. Which do you prefer, Commander? That, or a powerful force on our doorstep that came to our aid, and that seems to want peace?*"

"*The latter, of course.*"

Kelad nodded. "*Considering what may be waiting for us when we return to Victory, we may need them.*"

"*You've heard the rumours.*"

"*I have, and they are most disquieting. You and I both know that The Black Fleet will never agree with what occurred here today. This is counter to every plan Vehnek has made to consolidate power in the region. We will need friends.*"

Footsteps approached, and both military men turned. Captain Obrek clasped his hands behind his back. "*Your orders have been confirmed, sir. Some captains have requested to speak to you personally. Also, we have

The Empire Of Fire

received word from the Port Of Plenty that the royal barge is on approach."

"Scramble four battleships and ten skiffs. Of that force, send two of them and eight of the skiffs to Victory immediately. The rest are to escort the King and Queen to the city."

"Aye, sir. Our course?"

"Continue on, Captain."

Obrek nodded, and gave a salute before returning to the helm. Ulan cleared his throat. *"Are we going to war, sir?"*

"That depends on what we find in that city."

Ulan nodded. *"Agreed."*

"Good man. Your soldier, Berek, debrief him. I will be present. I want to know everything he knows ... absolutely everything."

11

Jack had spent almost the entire flight patching the breaches in Ironclad's armour, heat-treating the dents that blunt instruments had left in his chest. The *Sand Dancer's* hold was full of smoke and vapour from the oil that ran through his body, and every hatch that could be opened was open to let the thick, choking smell out. His shield was in worse shape than he was, but he could deal with that himself at a forge. As Jack worked, he listened, muttering to himself as Ironclad told him about what he had seen with his limited vision. Ember sat beside him quietly, her hands on his.

"I can't explain it," Jack sighed. "Perhaps your other senses have compensated for your sight, much as ours do if a sense is lost."

"It's quite the compensation. I think I'm starting to see light, though … light and shadow."

"Does that mean it's coming back fully?" Ember asked. Ironclad could hear the hope in her voice.

"It might be, although I'd have to do some further examinations. Do they have equipment I could use in Obsidian?"

Ironclad shrugged. "I would have to ask Seraphine about that, or Thomas."

Jack moved to the door. "I can do that now. Will you be alright here?"

"Yes. Jack, before you go … thank you for everything you've done for me. You could have been killed for it."

"I still could be," he muttered. "Or not, if you're successful in your endeavours. I'll be back soon."

He left the room, and Ember squeezed Ironclad's hand, leaving a trace of the bright green aura only visible to him on his armoured gauntlet. "Could be close to the end."

"Could be. It's strange, isn't it?"

"Strange, yeah. Strange in a good way. Looking forward to a little peace."

"Hmm." He had to change the subject away from the future. His own future held too many unknowns that he had no desire to think about. "I think we might be in for a lot of difficult, awkward conversations. It's like stepping out of a volcano straight into a rockslide."

Ember snorted. "With a dragon around, yeah."

"Not just the dragon. We're looking at six distinct groups, six distinct cultures. What are we supposed to do with all of them? We have to move forwards, while keeping everyone happy."

"Uniting while keeping everyone's cultures as intact as possible."

"Exactly. I think we can do that now, but when they don't have a larger threat to fight? We beat the dead ... what happens now?"

"The Orlin and wyvernborn don't have a larger enemy any more, do they? I mean, Caelish patrols ... but it didn't seem like there was a massive existential threat to them, not even extinction. They solved that problem together, with Father's help."

"Father?"

"The dragon. My point is, their bigger problems went away, and the old divisions didn't return."

"They continued to help each other with their problems. To make it work with the Caelish, we'll have to do the same."

"Thomas has an idea about that, so he tells me." Ember smirked. "We're on the verge of something tangible. The Regent in Haama seems like she's on our side in terms of wanting peace, she's obviously connected to the Royals. Kelad ... bloody Kelad of all people ... seems to be on our side. Have we actually won?"

"There's still plenty in our way, but we're walking the right path."

"Once we've walked it, what then?"

Ironclad looked around at her. "Cottage in the countryside? Few acres of land to plough, in walking distance of the Wyvern Bog?"

"Do we have to have a room for Thomas and Bassai?"

"Not to live in, no. A spare room."

Her hand tightened around his. "I'm not joking with you. I really want to know."

The aura around her was almost blinding. "It's been so long since peace was even an option, I couldn't tell you. I don't think I want to be in a city ... living near the Bog would mean being close to the Orlin and wyvernborn, where Bassai would be. We're owed a little peace."

"Peace to do what, exactly? Settle down?"

Ironclad shrugged. "It's one choice. We could travel, see the world, find new people and new places to get to know. Explore, like the first sailors."

She nodded once. "So ... play it by ear?"

"I suppose."

She smiled sadly, her aura changing to a deeper cyan colour. "I can't help thinking they'll never let us leave. That there'll always be a battle to fight, a city to guard, an enemy to pursue."

"If it comes to that, I'll be by your side."

The aura returned to its emerald colour, before the doors swung open once again. Ironclad could tell it was Thomas even before he turned to examine him and his energy.

"Sorry, am I interrupting?"

"Never stopped you any other time," Ember grumbled, but with a smile on her lips.

Thomas chuckled. "We're descending over Obsidian. Thought you'd want to know."

"Hmm." Ironclad stood slowly. "Yes, thank you. You have all your arguments in order, I hope."

"I suppose. I'll want to have a word with Donnal in private first. I think you should be there too, and Seraphine."

The Empire Of Fire

"Our new friends as well?"

Thomas thought for a moment and shook his head. "No, later. The Black Fleet aren't our only remaining enemies. We have to get to grips with the Ghosts first."

***

Donnal sat at the head of the table, his eyes hard as chunks of iron. Seraphine and Kassaeos were to his left, Ironclad and Thomas to his right. Every map, plan and piece of intelligence that had been unfurled and displayed before had been rolled up and stacked neatly away from them, on a desk pressed against the wall.

Ironclad could hear the sounds of immense hustle and bustle through the doorway and beyond it. Quick footsteps darted back and forth through the tunnel network, equipment jostled and jangled as it was moved out into the main chamber. Echoing through from the dwellings beneath the overhang were the sounds of chattering and cheering, even the odd swooping of wyvernborn wings.

"So, if I'm understanding you correctly, you engaged in battle alongside a force of Caelish warships, led by General Sel Kelad, no less. You did so against my order and judgement. Astrid, who I couldn't even begin to replace, is dead." Donnal glared at them from beneath his brow. "You committed forces, sided with the enemy, and got our best Mage (present company excepted) killed. My right hand, dead, laying in state in a Caelish airship's cargo bay. Have I missed anything?"

"The outcome," Ironclad said, turning from the noises outside. "A threat to Haama was removed. We have a force of wyvernborn and Orlin, and even a dragon on-side. We have taken the first steps to a negotiated ceasefire with the Caelish military."

"A ceasefire they will not keep, any more than they could grow gills and kiss the ocean floor. It is against their nature. They live to control."

"I have yet to see much evidence of that."

"Neither have I," Thomas muttered. "You wanted an intelligence report, I take it, on the capital city."

Donnal exchanged a look with Seraphine, then glanced at Kassaeos. The assassin's mouth turned upwards in a tart leer, and he folded his arms.

"Go on, although after the purge, all of this will have changed, and be near useless."

"Don't be so sure of that. From what I saw, the city is made up of roughly two thirds Haaman, to one third Caelish residents. For the most part their interactions are civil. With a few exceptions they are even friendly. They are colleagues, friends, family ..."

"Collaborators," Donnal grunted. "They sell out their own people, people who are fighting for them."

"Perhaps your people should try not murdering them," Thomas snapped. "You're well aware of the Ghosts, I imagine."

Donnal's eyes slipped over to Kassaeos and Seraphine again. "We have contact with them from time to time. They are in deep cover."

"So you're aware of their tactics."

"They do what they have to."

Thomas cast his eyes over to Kassaoes, who looked away. Ironclad leaned forwards. "What are their tactics, exactly? I would like to hear from both of you, and you, Seraphine, if you're aware of this as well."

Donnal clasped his hands together. "The Ghosts are ... *were* a group of infiltration based Resistance fighters. Their priority was disruption of infrastructure, intelligence gathering, destruction of property, agitation ... assassination if needs be."

"Trained here?" Ironclad asked.

"Some of them. The Mages were trained at the White Tower. Others came from outposts in the farmlands."

Ironclad nodded. "Two questions spring immediately to mind. First of all, assassinations of whom?"

The Empire Of Fire

"Caelish military officials, or members of government. Some of the more wealthy beneficiaries of the occupation."

Kassaeos leaned back, his arms folded, listening closely. Thomas's jaw tightened.

Ironclad caught the reactions in the change in their auras. "Exclusively?"

Donnal's eyes met Seraphine's for a split second. The aura around him flickered. "That's my understanding, although collateral damage is expected."

"Given their manner, collateral damage would be guaranteed," Thomas muttered.

Ironclad turned to him. "Speak."

"Donnal left out a considerably large group of people the Ghosts kill, indeed the most common group: the civilian population, and not in instances of collateral damage. Those victims were and are neither wealthy, nor are they beneficiaries."

Donnal remained stony-faced. "The definition of beneficiary is subjective. They benefit from the safety provided to the city, from the rape of the farmland, from the taxes."

"Children as well?" Thomas asked quietly.

Donnal flexed his shoulders. "I can only imagine they were caught in the middle, at the wrong time."

Kassaeos snorted, half to himself. Seraphine looked at him sharply, but the glare seemed to bounce off him. He directed his response at both of them. "So it's their own fault, hmm? They should have been more careful?"

"Their parents should have been."

Thomas pursed his lips. "What of the Haaman children? More collateral damage?"

"There are no angels in war."

"Ah," Thomas leaned back. "No angels in war ... except we're not at war, are we, Donnal? We lost the war a hundred years ago. When your people storm into school houses and butcher the students, setting the building on fire when they're still alive and unable to escape, they are not fighting on a battlefield against an enemy, they are committing an act of mass murder. An act of terrorism."

"One man's terrorist is-"

"Don't even bother," Thomas snapped. "What about the people they capture and beat and force to serve them?"

"*They* have done that to us for decades," Seraphine countered.

"Which makes it acceptable when your side does the same thing?" Ironclad asked.

"The Caelish set the rules of engagement."

Ironclad saw the aura around her brightening in rage, and held her gaze. "Are you happy that Mages you and your grandfather trained are being used to kill children?"

"How many children died in Melida City, when the dragons came?"

"That's not what I asked."

Donnal folded his arms. "All of this is immaterial. They've gone silent, our more subtle eyes in the city have confirmed the destruction of every hideout, every safehouse. The Ghosts are dead. All of them, give or take a prisoner or two."

Thomas clasped his hands together. "The Black Fleet killed them?"

"A massacre. A purge."

"Then they've saved us the trouble."

Donnal bared his teeth. "So much for the deaths of the innocent."

"The Ghosts have been a bane to every man, woman and child in Haama. They have actively stopped any progress at all towards any kind of peace. They have never cared who they killed. The bloodbath, had they ever been in charge of anything, would pale in comparison to that purge, and I don't doubt that without us, you would have found some way to replace them with worse."

"That purge is proof that their actions, and actions like them, are justified," Seraphine said hotly.

Thomas shook his head, his voice staying perfectly level. "Their actions have only solidified the control the Black Fleet can exert over this country. All you did with those Ghosts was create a brigade of useful idiots, as good as doing Vehnek's bidding."

Ironclad held up a hand. "That's as good a place as any to address my second question. If their job was to provide intelligence to you, why did you need Thomas to go in? You hadn't been getting the information you wanted."

Seraphine pursed her lips. "The information had … dried up."

"Not completely," Donnal said quickly. "But someone who speaks fluent Caelish could go further, with Kassaeos's assistance."

Thomas looked at them both with incredulity. "Your spy network couldn't speak fluent Caelish? After a century of that city and the nation being bilingual?"

"Of course they could speak … that's not the issue." Seraphine sighed to herself. "They simply … dropped out of contact, and they have spoken less and less to Obsidian over the years. They aren't spying for us anymore … they're fighting for us. They're our first line of defense … and offense."

"Your first line of murderers," Thomas snapped.

"We don't need or want your approval or your permission to fight for our rights, or our freedom," Seraphine shot back. "You have no idea."

"You have no idea how alone you are." Thomas shook his head with a grimace. "You know how much support you have in Victory, from the Haaman population? None."

Donnal snorted.

"Oh, of course there's the odd outlier, here or there, but your Ghosts have cost you more than lives. They're your monsters … and they're your face in the east. They have nothing but disregard and contempt for innocent lives, and it is arrogant presumption … and downright idiotic to think that people don't notice. It's their friends you kill. Their family members and children. They *hate* you, and they should. You assume they're stupid enough to look only at skin, they look at more than that, they look at what you're doing. You claim you're fighting for freedom, but you're either lying or blind. You're fighting for fighting's sake. For hatred."

"What would you have us do?" Donnal exploded, throwing his chair aside. "Let them take our culture and destroy it? Let them glorify the destruction of our language and our people?"

"Kassaeos?" Seraphine hissed. "You, of all people, can't let this pass unchallenged."

The assassin sighed heavily, but the sound was nearly invisible to the ears. "I *can't* challenge it, I don't think. I wish I could. You're right, of course. We can't allow Haama to be erased and become just a ... collective farm for Cael. We can't just roll over and show our bellies ... but Thomas isn't wrong either. The Ghosts tried to kill us, both of us. They're not in their right minds."

Seraphine's eyes widened at him in horror, then in fury. "How could you..."

"Go there yourself, then!" he hissed. "No, I don't like that they have sandball stadiums in every town in Haama. No, I don't like that the farms are taxed to oblivion. I don't like that we're ruled by a council of Caelish ministers and a Caelish princess. I don't like that you can't get proper beef and potato stew in the city ... but the Ghosts can't change these things! We can't change them by doing what we do now! We've gained no ground for a hundred years, all we've done is get people killed."

"All it takes to stop it is people who recognise the madness, and that it has to end," Ironclad muttered. "Thomas ... this princess you've spoken about ..."

"She's impressive. She's well-read, and I think she has support. With her and Kelad ..."

"Alongside the wyvernborn and Orlin, we represent everyone in Haama, except the Black Fleet." Ironclad nodded. "It's the best chance we have ever had to end this."

"You want to *negotiate* with *them*?" Donnal hissed. "After everything they've done?"

"What did the dead fight for, except an end to the conflict? For the chance for our children's children to flourish." Ironclad shook his head. "We don't have a choice. If we carry on marching, we simply march into our own graves, and everyone else's."

"You'll never get anyone here to go along with that."

Thomas fixed Donnal with the coldest glare Ironclad had ever seen. "They will with your support."

"Why would I give it?"

Thomas didn't waver. "You sanctioned and supported a band of murderers. You won't do it for something that will actually get you what you want?"

"I want the Caelish kicked into the sea!" Donnal roared. "No less!"

"Which will stop the fighting?" Ironclad said calmly. "The Caelish army won't let Haama be if you actually succeed in kicking them into the sea. They'll be back in force, and everything is going to be worse. Peace, however ... you make that work, you'll never need to fight again."

"We have more to offer each other than violence," Thomas urged.

"You have no ... you haven't seen ..." Donnal's hands tightened so hard that the table creaked.

"I'll put this bluntly," Thomas said. "If you sanction the Ghosts, sanction their murdering rampages of our own people, you shouldn't be in charge."

Donnal and Seraphine stared at Thomas. Even Ironclad was a little taken aback.

"You ... you can't be serious," Seraphine exclaimed. "After everything Donnal's done for us ..."

"Get you killed?" Thomas snapped.

"Kept us alive!"

Ironclad held up a hand. "I don't think we would dispute that. The problem is, we will soon come to a time when you don't need to keep them alive. The problem is, Thomas is correct. You don't see the people in Victory as Haaman, even, at least that's how it seems."

Donnal sat back. "How could I? They live in comfort and warmth, with roofs over their heads, behind thick walls."

"They're attacked by the Black Fleet just as you are, and they're attacked by you and your Ghosts too." Thomas leaned forwards, fingertips tapping on the table. "Your operations cut off their food and starve them, their children are put to the sword, their homes are burned ... just as yours are."

Donnal narrowed his eyes. "It wasn't just me who sanctioned the Ghosts."

His gaze swung to Seraphine. She pursed her lips, but nodded. "It's true."

"Did Rowan know?" Ironclad muttered.

"Rowan didn't know about them at first. You must understand ... and explaining this is no substitute for being there first hand ... so many were dying because of Ulan Vehnek's policy. Iron fist and slaughter were his bread and butter. We needed to fight back."

Thomas nodded. "And those who did were seen as heroes."

"*You* were our heroes of legend. Fighters who fought for years, and gave their lives for us. Our children grew up hearing about you and your stories. You were emulated."

"We know. We were the model for your bloodshed," Ironclad growled. "We've seen the statues. After Ulan Vehnek died, however, and the situation calmed, you carried on."

"In fact, they got worse," Thomas muttered.

Seraphine bit her lip. "I ... might agree that it went on for too long ... but we never had a choice."

"When did Rowan find out about the Ghosts?"

"He ..." Seraphine's throat caught, and she took a breath to gather herself.

Kassaeos took her hand, and continued for her. "When Rowan found out, he was upset, horrified, and he refused to train more Mages. This wasn't that long ago, in the scheme of things. Perhaps twelve or thirteen years."

"He was isolated in Taeba, there wasn't much way for him to know," Donnal said.

"In other words, your left hand didn't know what your right hand was doing," Thomas said.

The Empire Of Fire

"He left the military matters to me and my predecessors. You were his prime focus, and it was for that reason he continued his ties to us."

Thomas raised an eyebrow. "He agreed to continue with the process to bring the Guardians back, but refused to train Mages?"

Seraphine nodded.

"Why?"

There was a moment of silence. The question hung in the air. "What do you mean, 'why'?" Seraphine asked.

"Why did he continue with that? We're good, but we're not other-worldly beings, we're not indestructible. Four more warriors wouldn't help you win a ground war, which he didn't seem to approve of. Moreover, why bring us back, if we're the symbol you line up behind, and use to justify your people's actions, bloody or otherwise? He knew you would do that, so why? Why would he encourage you?"

"Because he knew us," Ironclad said. "Because he knew the people behind the story."

Thomas smiled with a sad shake of his head. "He knew that we would reject your Ghosts idea of justice, and yours. He knew what we were, and he knew what you are, Donnal. A good warrior, in many ways a fine man ... but driven to the brink. Covered in scars. Blood in your eyes. It says a lot that you refuse to change in the face of both your mentor, a father figure for many who started your Resistance ... and the Four Guardians you worship, who gave you bravery and hope when the nights were darkest."

Seraphine and Donnal watched the Mage as he spoke. Kassaeos's eyes remained fixed to the table.

"With the wyvernborn here, and willing to help us get to peace, you'll have to change," Ironclad said flatly. "They are only here because they believe in *us*, in *our* word. *Our* capability to bring us all to peace. Peace that Astrid died for."

Donnal looked away. Seraphine blinked and fixed her gaze to the table. Thomas even closed his eyes.

"She believed in us, in the wyvernborn, and in your ability to listen. Was she wrong?"

"Maybe she was," Donnal muttered.

Thomas looked up sharply. "Or maybe she saw things *you* haven't seen. Maybe she has seen Orlin and wyvernborn ... and a *dragon* working and living together in peace, and beginning to flourish. I could scarcely believe it myself, but they're here, now, in Obsidian. They're here to talk. Do you want to find out what happens when you betray a wyvernborn?"

Donnal glared at him. "What about betraying us? Consorting with the enemy won't be taken lightly."

"Betraying you?" Ironclad roared. He stood so fast his chair was propelled backwards by his heel, splintering into the wall. Donnal and Seraphine recoiled. Kassaeos's hand grasped the hilt of his rapier, perhaps an instinctive movement.

"Betraying you, Donnal? You've been lying from the moment we arrived. You betrayed everything Rowan stood for, for the sake of your blood lust. You're in no place to talk about betrayal."

Thomas raised a hand and placed it on Ironclad's forearm. "All we're asking is: give this a chance. Look at what Astrid saw, what Seraphine and Kassaeos have seen with their own eyes. Hear and see how they lived, what they did, and understand that what we're saying *is* possible. Not easy, no-one is claiming that it'll be in any way easy, but possible."

Donnal shook his head. "Hearing and seeing them won't change my mind."

"Then it won't, and we'll be in the same position. Which means that you'll continue with your glorious war alone. You might even win, against all the odds. However, what are you going to do afterwards? What happens when you overthrow the Caelish and their fleets fill the skies over Haama all over again? Let's say you win again, against even greater odds. What happens when those Haaman people, whose lives the Resistance made more difficult for decades, decide that you shouldn't be in charge? What happens when it's you and your

The Empire Of Fire

children that are murdered from the shadows? What happens when the next Donnal rises up to challenge you?"

Thomas stood. "I won't tell you to get in line, but it would be much better for all of us if you did. If you won't, please get out of our way."

12

Bassai strode along Obsidian's stone pathways, between the tiny carved huts. Heads peered out at him with narrowed eyes or smiles of recognition, and he simply bowed his head in their direction whenever he saw them. Until he recognised specific faces, his walk would continue.

The scope of Obsidian was surprising, considering it was confined to the cavern. The passageways twisted and turned, perhaps giving the illusion of scale, the small huts pressed in together tightly. Tactically, attempting to take this place with infantry would be a chaotic nightmare of ambushes and knives in the dark. The stones were beaten smooth and slippery, and only the most elite troops would be able to stay upright, as well as wyvernborn.

It wouldn't come to that, he was sure, now. Peace would be upon them soon, if Thomas was correct. With General Kelad standing beside them as well … unusual as the thought was … they might stand a chance against the Black Fleet. They may even have the numbers to make them back down from a fight, which was the ideal situation. The fewer innocent people died, the better the outcome would be.

A small voice cried out in surprise to his left, and an even smaller figure flew from a doorway, bolting towards him. Her blonde hair flew wildly around her beaming face. She jumped and clamped to Bassai's leg like a limpet.

Usually such an action would have made him growl, but given who the figure was, he gave a single snort instead. "Hello, Pia."

The little girl said nothing, but tightened her vice-like grip on him. He thought for a moment about what humans found comforting and bent down to gently ruffle her hair. It seemed to work, Pia beamed up at him.

"Have you been taking care of your brothers?"

She wrinkled her nose. "I don't see Lance, ever. Rory's better."

"Hmm. Is your mother home?"

Pia nodded.

"Do you want to stay on my leg, or come up higher?"

"Higher."

Bassai reached down, and Pia grabbed his arm. He lifted her with a grunt as his chest reminded him of the deep cut that was still healing. Pia sat up on his shoulder and held the side of his head.

"Hang on tightly now."

"'Kay," Pia chirped, beaming.

Bassai strode to the small home, and knocked on the door. His knuckles left dents in the soft wood, which smelled of damp and the musty smell of insect musk.

The door opened, and Kaitlyn's face lit up at the sight of the little girl practically attached to Bassai's head. Radiant as she was, he could see the fatigue pulling at her face, and the dark circles under her eyes.

"The children told me that a ship had come in ... told me they saw your friends, and a lot of wyvernborn."

He nodded, ducking through the doorway, covering Pia's head so she didn't bump it. Rory was sitting in the corner, playing with a pair of soldier figurines. He waved at Bassai shyly.

Kaitlyn leaned around and kissed him on the side of his snout, her strong arms moving around his waist and shoulders. "I heard there was a battle in Taeba."

"There was, and we won."

Kaitlyn smiled tiredly. "Good ... good. Pia, go and play with your brother for a bit."

Bassai put her down, and she scurried over to Rory, jumping on him with a tiny war-cry. Kaitlyn turned his bemused face away from them and took his hand, leading him outside.

"I hate being in that hovel," she murmured. "There are bed bugs in every sheet, and roaches in every wall. It's cold, and damp, and grey ... and all I'm doing is complaining." She rubbed her head. "Sorry."

"Don't be. You are used to the open air, a sky above you, not a rock ceiling. I am not sure I could live in Obsidian either."

She smiled sadly, and kissed him again, closer to the edge of his mouth. He leaned his head towards her, resting his forehead against hers. She stroked the side of his neck.

"You've done more for us than you had to," she murmured. "I have ... I'm responsible for those children ... it's a strange time for them. I have to think about them ... the young ones haven't realised yet that their father ..."

Bassai held her tightly. "I expected nothing from you, Kaitlyn. All I want is for you to find peace for them, and for you. There will come a time when it will be easier to move on for all of us ... it will be a welcome day."

She tightened her grip on him, and he allowed it, even though the fresh wound on his chest stung.

"When that time comes ... I hope I won't be in this place," said with a sniff. "It's not just the bugs and the stone ... every face here is angry, and every whisper promises bloodshed. Even the farmers want things to erupt. I don't like it. I don't like what they say to Lance, especially."

Bassai fixed his intense eyes on hers. "You don't have to live here. There is somewhere else you can go, somewhere where you can see the sky, peaceful and protected, and where you would be welcome."

Kaitlyn almost smiled, but it wouldn't take hold. "Lance wouldn't want to leave."

"He's made friends here?"

Kaitlyn shook her head. "No. Not friends."

***

The wooden sword clashed against Lance's ribs, and he crumpled, breathless. The older boy sneered at him and offered a hand mockingly, taking

The Empire Of Fire

it away as Lance reached for it.

"Caelish soldiers aren't going to show you mercy!" The teenager crowed.

"Let him up," the trainer bellowed, striding over. The older boy stepped back.

The trainer leaned down and prodded Lance with a club. "We've talked about your lower block, boy. You want a broken rib?"

"No."

"You want to be bisected, leaving nothing but your legs and your tiny balls?"

Lance's eyes were blank. "No."

"Get to your feet. Krast, Tella, go at him again."

A stocky girl with a club stepped forwards with the older boy, and both strode towards Lance with their wooden weapons swinging in his direction.

The thud of Bassai's feet into the dirt circle stopped them all for a moment. The trainer narrowed his eyes at him. Lance looked around with a squint, but couldn't muster any expression.

"Get out of here, lizard," the trained growled. "You're not welcome here."

Bassai snorted, maintaining his stride. The trainer scowled and nodded another of his lackeys over, a squat pink man with a puggish, pinched face.

"You hear me, scaley? Interrupt my training sessions and you'll get in trouble."

Bassai sized both men up for a moment, halting in the centre of the ring. "Training, eh? Why don't you demonstrate your training for all your child soldiers? You and your pet pig. I promise not to rip out your innards with my *lizard* claws. Not while you have clubs, and not anything meaningful to hit with."

The two men glanced at each other with a sneer. "Why not? Pay attention, you lot!"

The lackey swung his club towards Bassai, who used the portly man's momentum to sweep him out of the way, trip him, and break his arm in two places with a twist.

The trainer charged right into Bassai's other fist, and his nose dissolved with a crunch. The man's orbital bone caved in, and he crumpled, his bellow abruptly silenced.

Every trainee, including Lance, took a step back in shock. The fight, if it could be called that, had lasted a hair shy of a second.

Bassai grunted and unclasped his armour, eyeing the goggle-eyed trainees with a growl. He revealed the thick, medicine-soaked bandage across his chest. "That's right. I am injured, and yet your trainer will never look quite the same shade of ugly ever again."

He strode up to Krast, towering over him. The boy swallowed, his knuckles going white as his grip on the training sword hilt tightened.

"You, boy, are worthless. If all you want to fight are those younger and smaller than you, none of these other trainees will ever be able to rely on you in battle." Bassai's head turned to the stocky girl. "You, girl, are just as worthless. You follow this idiot in his endeavours. You follow those you consider your superiors blindly. You might be even more stupid than all of them."

He reared up to his full height. "Attempt to hit me, if you wish."

The girl backed away immediately. The boy hesitated, but pulled back as well. Bassai went with them.

"As I thought. You realise that you are a smaller force? That you will never be in a position of strength against the Caelish? Worthless." He shook his head. "You are lucky. You are training in an age where soon, there may be peace. Five years ago, you would have been just as likely to be killed by your own mates as the enemy. That's what happens to useless soldiers who are so pathetic they are more likely to be a detriment."

The recruits backed away even further at that. Bassai leaned forwards, his eyes aflame. He let out a short roar, like the angry bark of a hell hound, and the children scattered like pigeons.

He reached out a hand and collared Lance before he could follow suit. The boy swallowed and turned his eyes slowly up to the wyvernborn's face.

The Empire Of Fire

"I'm sorry I couldn't beat them ..." he stammered. "I ..."

"Walk with me."

Lance trudged after Bassai. They walked through the mouth of the Obsidian cavern, past carts and crates, past the *Sand Dancer* in its berth. The wyvernborn nodded up to Captain Seret, who was watching the surrounding people for threats. She returned the nod, her face breaking into a grim smile.

The open air was a stark, beautiful contrast to the oppressive, dank, darkness of the cavern. The sunset bled bright orange and scarlet across the sky, the smell of grass filled Bassai's nostrils. Some of the tension left Lance's shoulders as the roof disappeared from above them. It was still warm enough out to enjoy the evening, and the night choir of insects were testing their voices, beginning to hum and chirp before the moons rose.

Bassai stopped, and planted himself on the grass, tail curving around him. His eyes turned to Lance. "Sit."

Lance sat beside him.

"You showed some courage, standing against those two without backing down."

"I had to," Lance muttered.

"What if you didn't have to?"

Lance frowned. "What do you mean?"

"What if you did not have to fight?"

Lance shook his head, turning as red as the sunset. "You sound like mum."

"Is she wrong?"

"They killed my father!" Lance shouted. "And my sisters! Killed them, and burned down our house!"

"The people who live here turned your family into targets."

"They told me you would say that."

Bassai growled. "If Donnal and his people had their way, you would all drown in blood. You know his people have murdered their own share of farmers?"

"They do what they have to."

Bassai growled. "The age old excuse of the oppressor, and the terrorist. What will they do when the fighting stops?"

Lance shook his head. "It won't stop."

"I imagine they told you that as well."

"The ..." Lance screwed up his face. "We will always struggle. The revolution never ends."

The words were said without emotion, as if he was reciting them from a script.

"The revolution is probably going to end before the day is out."

Lance shook his head. "No ... you're lying."

"You have certainly been lied to, but not by me, or your mother."

Lance shook his head.

Bassai grabbed the shoulder pad of his training armour. "You know where we just were? Why we were there?"

"You were fighting."

"And we won ... with the Caelish. Together. Allied against a great evil that would have swept across the nation. It would have consumed everyone here. You, your mother, your brother and sister. We, and the Caelish, saved your lives."

"We would've won. Nothing can get in Obsidian if we don't want it to."

Bassai grunted around at the canyon walls. It would be a difficult siege for an invading army, even one attacking from above. "An army tens of thousands strong that couldn't die? Could you have beaten that?"

Lance hesitated. "*You* did."

"We knew something you didn't." Bassai leaned forwards. "You have a choice over which side you pick. You have chosen endless war when you could choose peace."

"There is no peace with the Caelish."

"There is a ceasefire right now. No hostilities. We can make that permanent. There will be no need to fight. Fighting will not bring anyone back

The Empire Of Fire

to life."

"If we don't fight ... then my father's just ... dead. Just murdered ... it doesn't mean anything."

"Would he have wanted you to be a child soldier?"

Lance's eyes lit with fire, running with furious tears. "I'm not a child."

"You're thirteen. Training with a weapon is a good idea, learning to fight ... but war is no place for someone your age." Bassai leaned in closely, taking in the boys muddy, bruised face. "Answer my question. Would your father have wanted you to be a killer? That's the best case scenario, if you were to live and thrive as a warrior. Worst case, you would be left face down in the mud and your own blood, with these other children who delight in beating you. Your mother loses another child. Pia and Rory lose their brother. Would he have wanted that? Do you want that?"

"He wouldn't want to be dead," Lance mumbled.

"No ... but joining the cause of the people here will not bring him back, or your sisters, or the farmhands, or any of my friends that have perished in all this. There has been much suffering ... too much to add more."

Lance stared around at him. "You've been fighting them *forever*, why can't I? Why is it only you and your friends that get to fight?"

"Believe me, I wish we did not have to. Perhaps we have fought so hard because we know what was lost, what was taken away from Haama. We remember when Cael was not an enemy, we remember Haama at its most lively, at its most independent. We lived it. They accepted me after my exile, despite what I had done." Bassai fixed one eye on Lance. "It was a place like that that made men like Tobias Calver, trained him and honed him, gave him something to protect, but it did not make enough men like him. You never know what you have until it is gone ... long gone, and you cannot bring it back."

"We can't let them get away with it ..." Lance growled.

Bassai leaned forwards, placing his hands on both the boys shoulders. "Fighting for anger's sake will do no favours for anyone. It will only fuel the fire that burns a hole in your heart, burning away the edges, making it larger, until you have no heart at all. Do you know how many scars I have?"

Lance shook his head.

"Ninety one. My body is a map of the pain that has been inflicted upon me, and that I have inflicted in return. Look at me, really look at me."

Lance did, and Bassai knew what he saw. The slices and burns across his shoulders and chest, his neck and face. The deep gouges on his stomach and arms where axes and swords had bitten into him. The burns, the scrapes, and his missing fingers, lost saving Lance's youngest siblings.

Horror crossed the boy's face, and he turned his eyes down.

Bassai patted his shoulder. "I learned the lesson too late that anger served no-one, not even me. It seemed to, for a short time, a time that gradually grew shorter and shorter."

"So ... I shouldn't fight?"

"You should know how to fight, and be ready to fight. You should learn how, and you show courage, show an inner strength that counts for far more than muscle. Strength will help you, you will be able to protect your family, but you must keep your sword sheathed until you need it. A good man with a sheathed sword can do more for those he loves than a dozen sycophants in a cave. When that man draws his blade, you know he means it."

Lance nodded, quiet. "The other recruits are still going to ... hit me."

"Then move, run rings around them. If there are two of them, make sure one is always behind the other, then you only have to deal with one. Parry strikes to knock your opponents off balance, and press your advantage. Don't let them push you around."

Lance nodded again. He looked at the sunset with a sigh. He looked older than thirteen to Bassai's eyes. He had been forced to become a young man, and he would be pulled now between being a good man and being a man that could be used.

For his sake, and the sake of all the children in Obsidian, even across Idris, this had to work. Peace was their best chance ... everyone's best chance to move forwards, to finally move on.

***

At the same table that had held the tense conversation prior, every space was now filled. Barada and Sandra were at one end, Seraphine and Donnal at the other. Ironclad, Ember, Bassai and Thomas lined up on one side between the two parties. Opposite them were Kassaeos, arms folded, with two figures that Ironclad hadn't expected.

One was Kira, her coffee-coloured skin waxen and almost grey, looking exhausted, covered in bandages, garbed in a loose robe. She smelled of musty medicine, but had insisted on being present. Seraphine had an eye on her, as did Thomas.

The other figure was Helen, the Regent's former steward. Thomas had thought it appropriate to have a representative from Victory, and one who in a way represented the Caelish at the table.

"We weren't aware any Orlin survived the war," Donnal said, with considerable warmth in his voice. It even seemed genuine, to Ironclad's ear and what he could make out with his new eyes. "I wish we'd known before, but I'm sure you had your reasons for keeping it a secret."

Barada and Sandra glanced at each other. She spoke: "It was necessary to keep as many eyes away from the Wyvern Bog as a possible ... the Caelish of the time may have considered us a threat."

"No doubt they would have, especially considering Father," Barada grunted. "The less people that knew, the better."

"We could have used your help before now," Seraphine muttered.

"To be frank, before now, there was nothing in it for us." Sandra folded her arms. "You would have used the Orlin and wyvernborn both in your war, drawn eyes to our families, and gotten them wiped out."

"There's not much difference now," Donnal said. "Here you are ... because they convinced you."

He gestured to the Guardians. "They got you here, with us, and I want to know what they said to get you here."

"They have the capacity for peace," Barada grunted. "They are the first of you that have shown it. He has put plans into motion that will achieve it." The Alpha pointed at Thomas, who smiled tightly.

Donnal nodded. "And the desire for peace, and the capacity for peace, are conditions of you allying with us permanently?"

"The necromancer and her army were a threat to the nation, and in dealing with her we provided an outstretched hand to the Caelish, which they seem to have taken."

Sandra clasped Barada's hand. "You are in a position, thanks to the combined efforts of your people, ours and the Caelish, to end all hostilities and get the best possible terms."

Donnal's face set, and his hands clasped together. "Terms of our surrender."

"Terms of a permanent ceasefire," Thomas urged. "Look … we're in a ceasefire now, because we proved that we are stronger together than we are apart. Ydra, Gods grant her peace, was a threat that Obisidian and Victory might not have weathered even with our walls and defenses. It won't take much to make the ceasefire permanent. Kelad is on our side, Princess Allessandra is on our side. A lot of Victory wants an end to all this. When we say favourable terms, we don't mean surrender."

"Then what do you mean?" asked Seraphine.

"A relationship. Perhaps even an alliance. Favourable trade, independent protection, better representation of Haamans in this country. Our own government, without interference from Cael. Reduction of taxes, lessening the burden on the Idris farmers. The re-establishment of our army, an improvement in trade with other nations, raising the standard at which every citizen in Haama lives."

"And that all sounds wonderful … on paper." Donnal leaned back in his chair.

The Empire Of Fire

"Independence will be non-negotiable, and I assure you we'll get it," Thomas countered. "Independence means we get the rest of it too, we'd just get it slower. Think of it." Thomas counted the points off on his fingers. "The Caelish remove a thorn from their side, you all but rid Haama of the majority of Caelish influence from on high, the fighting stops ... or at least reduces a great deal. We co-operate, like we used to."

"With my grandfather's work," Seraphine muttered.

"Yes. The man of peace can augment it even beyond death. His work to make the desert sands recede before they swallow Cael, building on decades of research before him ... in principle it will work. I know that research, I worked on the preliminaries, I saw the progress he had made at the White Tower. With the resources of a strong Haama, and a strong Cael, it will work. They won't need our farmers after that. They won't need our food."

Seraphine and Donnal looked at each other.

"I believe Thomas is correct," Helen said, speaking for the first time. "I don't think much of a stomach for war exists in the general populace, or in the Standing Army. The Black Fleet is another matter ... but they will be outnumbered." She turned to Barada and Sandra slowly. "The dragon may present a problem, though. The Caelish know how devastating they can be, if weaponised. They may feel a knife is being held to their throats."

"Father is not a threat to Cael, unless they make it so," Barada growled.

"A concession can be made to restrict his movements, perhaps," Thomas muttered.

Bassai growled, but bobbed his head. "Father is more concerned for the wyvernborn than war. More likely than not, he would agree, but not for free."

Barada grinned toothily. "Spoken like a true wyvernborn, with true words. We will need more land, more room to plant trees. There will be more of us than the Bog can support soon enough, and the mountains will not do for the Orlin. Too arid, too remote, sparse vegetation."

Ironclad stood and moved to the cabinet, picking up and then unfurling the huge map of Haama on the table. The Wyvern Bog ended up right under

Barada's nose.

He and Sandra peered at it, and Sandra's fingers brushed against the land adjacent to the Bog to the north and east, a segment of Verda District, and a little of Melida.

"You think you'll need that much?" Ironclad asked.

"Eventually," Sandra said. "The land here isn't populated, aside from a farm or two, and while they are a little wary of the wyvernborn, there haven't been any incidents between us or them. In fact there have have been times when we have traded, and offered protection to them."

"Still, they will have to agree to your terms," Ironclad said. "They will be directly affected, although it may not come to that."

Barada growled. "Why?"

Ironclad pointed at the wasteland that used to be the Orlin Forest.

Barada shook his head. "The soil is corrupted by dragonfire."

"Who knows dragonfire better than a dragon?"

Seraphine folded her arms. "You cannot be serious. That amount of Verda and Melida..."

"May not be needed," Ironclad interrupted.

"But how long is the dragon going to take to remove the corruption from the land? Is it even possible?"

Ironclad looked to Barada, who shook his head. "Don't know. The shamen would know better, they're the ones that deal with Father and his magics the most."

"In other words, you're relying on hope," Donnal grunted.

"Educated hope," Thomas said, leaning forwards. "Logically, the dragons would have to be able to cure the corruption of their dragonfire. They're carnivores, they consume wildlife, that wildlife would have to eat vegetation at some point in the food chain. Corrupted soil kills the vegetation, the dragons would eventually starve. The natural world doesn't work counter to itself."

"There's only one dragon left," Donnal pointed out.

"That is not because they ran out of food," Bassai grunted.

The Empire Of Fire

"Either way, it's going to take time, right?" Ember said. "Especially with only one dragon."

Helen bobbed her head. "But not limited resources. Haama has Mages, Cael has the Magus Towers."

"Why would they help?" Sandra asked with a frown.

"Because we're forgetting the obvious: if the corruption can be cured from what remains of the Orlin Forest, it can be cured from the Maldane Reach. If it can be cured from the Reach, Haama will have access to more farmland, which would lower the burden on Idris even further."

Thomas nodded, smiling broadly at Helen. "Another road that leads us to peace."

"In which case, land would be small price to pay," Ember muttered. "The trees of Orlin could live again ... truly."

"That's not all that's ... in it for the wyvernborn," Kira croaked, speaking up weakly for the first time. "With help ... more could be born. Even if it was just ... only a few Mages helping the dragon ... more minds on a problem brings the ... solution closer."

Ironclad chuckled to himself, and shook his head. "Never thought I'd see the day."

"Day?" Barada grunted.

"Where any of this was possible ... any of it ... and a bigger day is still to come. There could come a time when all our people will live together without any animosity, perhaps in the cities."

Barada and Donnal snorted at the exact same moment, and the Alpha bellowed a laugh. "Some might. There are a couple of examples of Orlin and wyvernborn that lived in cities ... and they did not come out of it too badly."

He looked pointedly at Bassai and Ember, the latter of whom raised an eyebrow. "Well, we did die ..."

Barada threw back his head and laughed again. "But it did not stop you."

"Victory could do with more trees," Helen said with a smile.

Barada grunted at that, and Sandra took his hand. "The reason we are all together in this room isn't that we share a common enemy, it's that we share a common value: a desire for peace. You never know what the future will bring."

"The wisdom of my wife has no limit that I have seen … but I am more concerned with the here and now, and the figurative serpent in the room." Barada sat up straight, the chair creaking beneath him. "The Caelish will have to be persuaded, negotiated with … However, I agree to an alliance, as long as peace remains a priority. With this … Allessandra sympathetic, even a potential ally, there is more of a chance for it than I have seen in centuries."

The eyes of the room turned to Donnal and Seraphine. He nodded to her, and she clasped her hands together tightly. "We are … in agreement."

"Yes, we are," Donnal muttered. "Difficult as it may be for some of us to accept … the future depends on what we decide today, in this room." His eyes turned up to Barada. "Your people, and the Orlin too … you do not keep to the Gods, do you?"

Barada shook his head. "We do not have a belief in the powers in which you speak of."

"Our beliefs are a version of yours, I think," Sandra said. "A different interpretation."

Donnal shook his head. "Our belief in them receded over the years … as the temples fell. We found new belief … in the Four Guardians."

His eyes turned up to Ironclad, Ember, Thomas as Bassai. "Our faith in you … what you represented to us: bravery, defiance, sacrifice … friendship and camaraderie. You kept us going, you kept us alive, and in my eyes, you haven't steered us wrong. I know you don't like some of what we've done, that you don't approve that it was done in your name … but without you, we wouldn't even be alive. We owe you that … and ignoring you now wouldn't be right."

Seraphine nodded. "There are elements of the Resistance that will … will resist this peace. But … neither Donnal and I will."

"Neither will I," Kira croaked.

Kassaeos nodded, his black eyes alight with something close to hope.

The Empire Of Fire

Ironclad, in that moment, wished more than anything else that he could smile. His hand gently gripped Ember's.

"Then, our Alliance is formed."

13

For the first time in Allessandra's memory, Victory was silent.

The Silver Throne Palace's cannons were all still poised and ready. She had kept them constantly crewed, and as a result, the remainder of the Black Fleet had not acted up.

At this point, Vehnek's forces were beyond outnumbered. A fleet of airships had appeared from the north, flying the colours of the Standing Army. They were keeping a very close watch over the city, and the ships that until recently had been explicit allies.

The bottom floors of the Palace, including the throne room itself, were currently accommodating as many of the citizenry that had been rendered homeless as they could. Blankets and food had been distributed, and the palace doctors were doing what they could for the injured. Bringing them in had lifted some of the burden on Victory's remaining hospitals. One had been destroyed in the attack, two others had been damaged.

Smoke drifted about the city in thick white wisps of cloud, spectres of the now-extinguished fires. The ships above were half-concealed in them, as if they were using them as cover to pounce on more prey. As the Mages that remained in the city guard cleared the smoke with gusts of conjured wind, it returned and filled the skies again.

She was terrified, despite the brave face and straight back, the arsenal at her command that was poised to defend the city. While the *Inquisitor* was here, while Vehnek was here, the rest of his fleet could be anywhere in Haama, wreaking havoc. She had cannons, but the City Guard was heavily depleted. Defence Minister Levez had been missing for four days, and at this point, was presumed dead. Minister Janek too was nowhere to be found. His estate in the Fisheries had caught fire, and he was presumed to have perished or fled. With

The Empire Of Fire

no Defence Minister, a reduction in numbers, and a low number of palace guard compared to an army, Allessandra was more vulnerable than she had ever been before. Only her status as Regent protected her, her royal blood.

No-one else in the palace had that. No-one else in Victory had it either. None of the charred bodies in burned buildings had been heirs to a nation. The power of government wouldn't save the Council of Ministers, old men and women that would be overthrown at knifepoint at a moment's notice. Her handmaids, her protectors ... the people in this city and nation she was responsible for.

She even feared for the Resistance, who had at this point been all but rooted out of the city and set aflame. How could they be brought to the table after all that? How would they trust her after such slaughter?

Booted footfalls on the stone roof drew close to her. Eluco, alongside forty of the palace guard, were surrounding the remaining Council Of Ministers. All of them had been perfumed and put into their finest clothes, as would befit a Royal visit.

First Minister Evandro drew close to Allessandra, with Eluco at his back. They both stood beside her, on either side.

"*I have news of the engagement in the Pil Valley, Your Grace,*" Evandro murmured. "*It seems we were victorious.*"

She grunted. "*General Kelad?*"

"*He is at the head of the escort bringing your parents to the city.*"

Allessandra nodded. "*And the purpose of their visit? They seemingly ignored the summons, and have not spoken to me on the matter.*"

"*Humanitarian.*"

"*Public relations,*" Allessandra spat. "*Never waste a crisis, so they say.*"

"*Considering the battle, they will likely honour General Kelad as well.*"

"*And Vehnek, don't you think? For ridding Victory of the Resistance scourge that has been causing so much trouble?*" Allessandra shook her head. "*Probably not Levez, though, who died protecting this city.*"

Evandro shifted his weight onto his other foot. "*I know. On that, Your*

Grace ... I would anticipate that the King and Queen will likely name Vehnek as Defence Minister, on a temporary basis. It will be the in-road he needs to permanently dissolve the Council."

"And the Black Fleet will be dug in, taking up the slack with Victory's defense, as well as Haama's. How many of Kelad's task force survived the battle?"

"All the carriers, but two battleships were lost, as well as at least two skiffs. The rest of the aerial navy in Haama are split between Kalendra, Breaker's Bay and the Port Of Plenty."

Allessandra shook her head. "*Far enough away to not reach us in time. They were conspicuous in their absence during the attack, weren't they?*"

"No-one was able to send a message to them. Long-distance communications were cut."

Allessandra turned to him in surprise. "*Cut?*"

"Equipment destroyed, operators and guards slaughtered. The Black Fleet's representative told us that it was the trigger-point for a coup attempt, and thus was what prompted their attack ... or rather, their response."

Allessandra narrowed her eyes. "*A dog that wasn't barking until after the murderer left the house. Eluco?*"

He stood to attention. "*Your Grace.*"

"*Use what resources you can and investigate this attack, this 'coup attempt'. I suspect it isn't what it seems.*"

"So do I, but it has been two days. If it was the Black Fleet, they will no doubt have covered their tracks by now."

"If they missed anything, I want you to find it. While that equipment is being rebuilt I want you and you men to guard the workers and Mages rebuilding it. That's your pretext. While you're in there, search."

Eluco nodded. "*I can try.*"

"It is our only lead. The bodies of those killed will no doubt have been disposed of. The room will have been thoroughly cleansed, but not without scrutiny from our people. They may have missed something."

The Empire Of Fire

Minister Evandro shuddered. *"How did it come to this? A city in flames. A power grab. Killing our own to frame an enemy. How could it happen?"*

"History tells us it happens slowly," Allessandra muttered. *"Then quickly. We have been frogs swimming in a pot, while the water comes to the boil. Vehnek's hand is on the burner ... if we don't act soon ..."*

From the blanket of smoke hanging above Victory, a number of dark shapes appeared. They emerged suddenly, a pair of battleships with the Standing Army, a skiff in between them, leading the fleet like the point of an arrow. Behind them were two more, and four more skiffs, spread out to cover the flanks.

At the centre of the fleet was the royal barge. The *Sovereign's* bulk was not blocked by any of the other ships, vast sails fluttering, cannons retracted behind hatches. The golden trimmings on the hull were dulled by the smoke surrounding it. The prow, shaped like the head of a snake, approached like a predator, but Allessandra stood firm. For the first time in her life, she didn't fear the approach of her parents. She was instead enraged by it.

Two of the battleships moved either side of Vehnek's flagship, the *Inquisitor*. Allessandra noted that both had brought their cannons to bear, but no shots were fired. News had clearly spread, news of the perpetrators most importantly of all.

Five hundred feet from the roof of the palace, the fleet halted, and began to reposition to allow the *Sovereign* room to descend. The skiff at the front of the procession drifted downwards slowly, floating closer to the edge of the roof. When the top deck was in line with the princess and Ministers, a figure beside the helm vanished in a whirl of smoke, and reappeared in front of Allessandra and Evandro.

Kelad bowed reverently to her, nodded to the Ministers, and saluted the palace guard. Allessandra squinted at him. He was holding himself as he always had, didn't seem injured in any way, but some of the cockiness had disappeared from his bearing. He was tense, more tense than she had seen.

"Are you alright, General?" Allessandra asked.

"There is much to go over, Your Grace. I expect this to be a very thorough debriefing, with many questions." He smiled at her tightly, then looked to the Ministers, switching languages to Caelish. "*First Minister Evandro ... I seem to have missed quite a lot. What is the death toll?*"

"*We're still counting, Sel. Including the missing, we could have lost between three and seven thousand. Many of the City Guard are among them, including Levez.*"

Kelad showed no emotion at that. "*Has Morad explained himself?*"

"*I doubt we're even on his mind.*"

Kelad bobbed his head. "*I would agree, knowing him. What of Miranda and Mora?*"

"*As far as I'm aware, they haven't been seen.*"

"*What is so significant about Mora?*" Alessandra asked.

Kelad turned to her. "*I wish I knew. Perhaps nothing, but perhaps everything. This is a delicate situation ... which is about to get even more delicate. Vehnek may be forced to accelerate his plans. Without a doubt, she is a part of them.*"

Allessandra glanced up at the fleet. The *Sovereign* was closing in, and the fanfare was being blown by the palace's standard bearer. She glanced around at the battleships. "*Where is your ship, General?*"

Kelad stiffened. He raised his chin to stretch his neck. "*The Razorback was lost, I'm afraid, Your Grace.*"

Allessandra nodded slowly, and held his wrist gently. "*I'm sorry. Survivors?*"

Kelad shook his head. "*Aside from some of the soldiers she carried into battle ... no. I do not weep for them, Your Grace. They died for Haama, and for Cael. Because of them, we will see a new dawn. I only wish that dawn wasn't cloaked with the smoke that came from senseless death.*"

He glanced around at the cannons that she had deployed across the palace roof, and a smile tugged at the corner of his mouth.

"*General Kelad, in light of recent events, and while you are here, I would*

The Empire Of Fire

like to offer you the temporary position of Defence Minister," Evandro said. *"I would rather fill the position before the Royal Family land and appoint someone of their own, someone who would more likely be an informant or ... worse. Also, if you are to be used as a scapegoat, you will have some administrative protection."*

Kelad raised an eyebrow. *"I accept, thank you. Once you have a better candidate, please let me know so I can resign. Desks are very unbecoming of a General worth his salt."*

Evandro smiled, and shook his hand, not seeming to take the remark as a slight. *"I've found that most decent military men feel the same."*

Allessandra looked up as the *Sovereign* settled level with the roof, as the skiff had. The debarkation ramp extended and locked into place in a slot at the edge. It was wide, with guard rails on either side, and lush, grippy carpeting to walk on.

"I hope he's as accommodating after I tell him how we won," Kelad muttered in Haaman. Allessandra frowned at him, but her attention was pulled to the top of the ramp as King Alesio and Queen Mirell began to stride down, escorts in front, beside and behind them.

It had only been weeks since they had last visited. They looked the same as they had then, but in dark coloured clothes, just as beautiful and tailored, but intended for mourning more than for celebration. Her father's paunch seemed a little more pronounced, her mother's features seemed more angular than before. They wore expressions just as lavish as their clothing, brows high, foreheads wrinkled in grief. They reached the bottom of the ramp, and Allessandra noticed the Mages following them closely, projecting protective bubbles around their heads to filter the smoke away from their eyes, noses and mouths.

Around Allessandra, everyone knelt and bowed, and she herself half-bowed, her fury growing.

"Rise," King Alesio commanded, but his voice fell at the end of the word, to indicate he was troubled.

Queen Mirell stepped forwards. *"Allessandra, I am glad to see you well.*

We have been worried for you since the news reached us."

Allessandra said nothing in response, tensing as Mirell moved forwards to hold her demurely. Her hands made contact with her, but nothing else did. It was all for show.

Her father's hands were the opposite, warm against her cheek and her back as he took her into his arms. She forced herself to remain cold to him, bringing up her hands to gently push him away.

The Queen had already moved on, turning to the others on the roof. *"Minister Evandro, General Kelad. I am glad to see you both well."* She looked past them and smiled. *"Ministers, it warms my heart to see you also."*

"We should get right to it," The King said, stepping away from Allessandra. *"The rest of the formalities and procedure can wait, we are anxious to hear the report of our victory at the Second Battle Of The Pil Valley."*

Allessandra raised her eyebrows at hearing that the engagement already had a name for the historical record.

"I will, of course, be at your service, and at your convenience," Kelad said with a bow. *"I am happy to begin as soon as you are ready."*

"In which case, we shall meet you in the Council Chamber once we have had a private word with our daughter."

"Of course, Your Majesty." Evandro motioned to the guards, and the procession turned around, escorting the Ministers and Kelad back from the roof and into the palace. The 'private' word her parents wanted to have was hardly private. They were still surrounded by guards and attendants.

Allessandra waited for one of them or the other to speak. Her eyes flitted from the King to the Queen. *"Well?"*

They looked at each other. The Queen shook her head. *"We warned you that this would happen."*

Allessandra stared at her, then stepped back. *"We have nothing to discuss. The Ministers will be waiting for you."*

"Allessandra!" Alesio stepped forwards, glaring at Mirell for a moment.

The Empire Of Fire

"*All that concerns us is your safety and wellbeing. I cannot imagine how horrible it was to witness what happened here, and neither can your mother. We know you were personally attacked by an infiltrator.*"

"*And my handmaiden, Jenifer, who remains unaccounted for.*"

"*Lord Marshal Vehnek took action to protect you and this city,*" Mirell said, forcing gentleness in her voice. "*That action was certainly brutal, and ruthless, but that threat has been drastically reduced, if not exterminated ... and you turned the Silver Throne palace into a fortress in response. You fired upon his ship! If you were not Regent, you would be in the stockade.*"

Allessandra nodded, saying nothing for a moment. "*Lord Marshal Vehnek ... is a criminal. He has been tearing through Idris like a child tearing through scraps of paper, slaughtering innocent people. He was doing the same here, before I stopped him. Continue to rationalise it all you want, mother, I will not make you see sense. You have both turned a blind eye to the social problems, tyranny, and suffering in this country for far too long. If you won't defend it, and its people, I will.*"

She turned on her heel, ignoring the King and Queen as they called her name, trying to make her stay, or argue her into submission.

***

The Council of Ministers sat in silence as Kelad recounted the battle to them, every event of it. The initial stages, the insertion of his soldiers, the rescue of the civilians, the gruelling engagement with the dead, the arrival of the Resistance and wyvernborn, the death of the necromancer Ydra, and finally the verbal agreement of a ceasefire between him and the Resistance leadership.

Kelad watched his audience closely as he spoke. The King and Queen listened with gradually widening eyes, surprise and horror written into their expressions. Evandro stroked his chin, intently hanging on every word. Carrasco was as unflappable as ever, probably weighing up the amount of coin various possible events in the city to celebrate a treaty or parade for war would cost them, such was his new duty as Minister of the Treasury as well as Foreign Affairs. Brynden was agitated, drumming his fingers irritatingly on the table in front of him.

Allessandra could barely keep the smile from her face, which wouldn't do for her at all. She at least kept her biggest and most obvious smile for the finale, where he spoke of the ceasefire.

Those he was most interested in were Vehnek, Mora, and Miranda, who sat in a row of three chairs on the King's side of the table. Miranda was the easiest to read, she was bright red with fury, tapping her cane on the floor. Vehnek had the face of an experienced military man, the serenity under fire that Kelad had taught him to wear. He was hanging on every word, his mind working through solutions. Mora said and did nothing at all, seeming to watch the proceedings with quiet amusement.

"*Given your numbers, it is disappointing that you did not attempt to apprehend the Resistance leaders,*" Queen Mirell stated calmly.

"*I have had too much experience with dragons to attempt such a suicidal action, Your Majesty,*" Kelad replied coolly.

Evandro nodded. "*I would agree, knowing the history of this city in particular. However, this is more than concerning. Given recent events here, terrorists having access to a dragon ...*"

"*It doesn't seem appropriate to label these particular Resistance fighters terrorists, First Minister,*" Allessandra admonished. "*Their actions may well have saved the country.*"

Miranda let out a short, annoyed laugh. "*Victory could stand against an army wielding cannons and armoured airships, let alone a mindless horde of walking corpses.*"

"*That horde would have been a million strong or more by the time they got here,*" Kelad said with a raised eyebrow.

"*I must speak, me share the First Ministers worry,*" Brynden managed in his limited Caelish. "*Dragons am a bad. Many deads because of their use against Haama ... many Haamans dead. It could be saw as poetry justice to* attack Caelish in the same way."

Evandro cleared his throat. "*I hadn't considered that.*"

"*All they want is revenge, First Minister,*" Vehnek calmly stated. "*I suspect Brynden is correct.*"

Evandro looked up, to see who among the Ministers had yet to speak. His eyes lingered on Mora, then he looked away. "*Minister Carrasco, your thoughts please.*"

Carrasco smiled tightly. "*We might be missing a key element, here. The dragons are supposed to be dead. We had assurance from the Lord Marshal's father and grandfather that those they had used had been euthanised. Were they lying, or wrong?*"

Kelad watched as Vehnek twitched, his eyes tracking over to the multi-tasking Minister dangerously. "*Neither, Minister. They were all dead.*"

"*I concur, to a point,*" Kelad cut in. "*Our understanding was that they were all dead, although we didn't see one of the bodies. That particular dragon was part of the force that burned the Orlin Forest. Our force there was repelled, and reports stated that the dragon was brought down and assumed dead. Ergo, the answer is that Kallus and Ulan Vehnek were simply wrong.*"

"*Wrong, and careless,*" King Alesio growled.

"*And now that carelessness threatens us all,*" the Queen added. "*It seems a pre-emptive strike will be necessary.*"

"*During a ceasefire?*" Allessandra snapped. "*Really, mother, you're a better diplomat than that.*"

"*And you are no tactician, with all due respect, Your Grace,*" Vehnek said smoothly. "*It is likely in the care of the wyvernborn, and they are very impressive warriors. The most impressive among the Resistance, now that they have joined them in their cause. With a decisive enough strike, we can eliminate them and the dragon.*"

Mirell nodded with eyes gleaming. "*Which will force them to the table, in surrender.*"

Kelad wasn't surprised by any of this, so he pushed his point further.

"You both speak of them like they are nothing more than bloodthirsty terrorists. Bloodthirsty terrorists would not have helped us bear our injured and dead to the ships, or helped tend to the wounded. They would have certainly attempted to finish our forces off, especially with a dragon on their side."

"What better way to lull you into a sense of false security, Sel?" Vehnek said with a tight lipped smirk.

"Remember who you're speaking to, boy." Kelad kept his voice calm, resisting the snap.

"They have increased their military capability past the point of acceptability," Vehnek countered, eyes gleaming beneath a frown at Kelad's slight. "The wyvernborn alone would do that, regardless of their low numbers, but a dragon? They are a direct threat to Victory, and even to Cael City."

Allessandra scoffed at him. "*Absurd.*"

"The impertinence of youth knows few bounds," The Queen snapped. "No, the Lord Marshal is correct. They are too much of a threat now to be left alive."

Kelad folded his arms. "With all due respect, Your Majesty, Lord Marshal, that is the exact opposite of their intentions. They have no intention of assaulting Cael, in fact they spoke of assisting us in halting the advance of the desert. They spoke of our pre-war relationship, one of cordiality and even friendship. I would have agreed that they might be trying to pull the wool over my eyes, if the people who spoke to me hadn't been The Four Guardians, among others."

"The Four Guardians?" King Alesio grunted, leaning forwards.

"Four figures who have been effectively deified by the Resistance forces. Four real people, who were killed in the Battle Of Melida City. They are alive, likely due to magical interference."

"After a century?" The Queen scoffed.

"I fought against them many times, face to face. I as good as killed three of them. I promise you, it was them. The Lord Marshal is well aware that it is *possible, although whether or not he will admit it here and now is a matter of debate. Tobias Calver, Emeora Vonn, Thomas, and Bassai. Where they lead, many of the Resistance will follow, I suspect."*

Kelad fixed Vehnek with a stare. The Lord Marshal raised an eyebrow, but made no immediate move of denial. Mora was a far more curious anomaly. At the mention of the four, Vonn in particular, she had absolutely no reaction.

The woman who had killed her son. Not even a blink, or an acknowledgment of the name.

"*Regardless, they are honourable people. They aren't the sort to betray, they have proven that before this particular battle. One of them, in fact, provided the intelligence that saved those of my men that survived. Betraying us after the battle would have been easy, and perhaps it would have been advisable, given our current conversation. They didn't. Their actions in allying with us in that battle have immense weight, although it perhaps takes an old soldier like me to see it. As it stands, the ceasefire between us is informal, pending meetings such as this one. As Defense Minister, I hereby recommend that it be formalised immediately."*

Vehnek straightened. "*As Defense Minister, you're going soft, old friend.*"

"Hardly, Lord Marshal," Allessandra said calmly. "*I second the motion, and move for a Council vote. The matter: maintaining the ceasefire until we reach a negotiated settlement."*

Queen Mirell glared at her. "*You cannot be serious."*

"*You have not been here to see how the people of Victory, and the people of Haama, have suffered under the current paradigm. Citizens are hungry and scared. Entire cultures have been excised from the country, as one might excise a tumour. These were not a cancer, they were people. Living and breathing. Add to that the desolation of the Maldane Reach and the beginnings of desolation in Idris, coming from tyranny over the farmers, through taxation and the sword of the Black Fleet hanging above their heads. Their grievances are legitimate, and have not been addressed."*

"*We rebuilt them from the ground up,*" Miranda spat.

"*We destroyed them first, did we not?*"

"*We had to!*" The Queen snapped. "*But Miranda is correct. We did not only build them back, we built them back better than before. Those 'people' that were removed from this country were savages.*"

Kelad's back straightened and he tried to keep the venom out of his face and voice. "*With all due respect, Your Majesty, the murder of those 'savages' would have turned this entire country, and Cael, into a realm ruled by the walking dead. If it were not for my men, and those you claim to be enemies-*"

"*You forget your place, General,*" Queen Mirell hissed, but beside her, the King raised a hand.

"*General, I do not need you reinstate your testimony of the battle, but are you absolutely certain that the scale of the undead threat was as grand as you say?*"

"*Yes, Your Majesty. The ghouls could not be killed by conventional means, and were capable of using our weapon emplacements, possibly due to the incantation that kept them alive, or some remaining vestige of magic in the body. Their numbers would have been difficult to thin ... and in fact would have grown exponentially. We had difficulty dealing with them ... I cannot imagine the slaughter had they reached Idris. By the time they would have reached Victory, as I said previously, they would have numbered close to a million. Victory may be formidable, but an army of that nature could easily have found a way inside the walls: through the sewers, through tunnels, even over the walls themselves. Assuming a siege, the dead do not tire, or hunger, or fear. They could easily have waited you out, Ministers, until the people of this city, starved, rioted in desperation, or made a mad rush for death or glory.*"

Kelad clasped his hands behind his back. "*For clarity, may I have access to a map?*"

Allessandra looked around. "*Eluco.*"

Her lead guard nodded, and disappeared down the stairs for a moment. Barely a minute later he had returned with two attendants, carrying a map of

The Empire Of Fire

Cael and Haama together, separated by the Dividing Sea. They arranged it on a large, easel-like stand, pinning it so it remained flat.

"*Thank you,*" Kelad muttered. He cleared his throat and gestured to the only land connection between Cael and Haama: the thin strip of land to the west known colloquially as the Scorpion's Tail. It was the subject of a number of tales to frighten children and adults alike, being completely uninhabitable and arid, although with signs that it once had been lush and populated. In the here and now it was fortified on both sides with segments of the Standing Army.

"*How many live in Victory? Three quarters of a million, give or take those that the Lord Marshal sees fit to incinerate. Two to three million ghouls could overwhelm the walls on either side of the Scorpion's Tail in minutes, adding to their numbers. A defensible bottleneck? Perhaps ... however ...*"

His finger moved from the northern point of the Scorpion's Tail to the ocean on either side of it. "*The dead do not breathe. Walking along the ocean floor would be little more hassle for them than walking in a field, albeit slower. From there, a more than two million-strong, unkillable army could surround and engage our military forces at the Bay Of War and Three Hammers. The same variables apply with the hypothetical engagement at Victory. Eventually our troops would have broken. Again, every settlement between there and Cael City would be swept away by the tide. The Magus Towers could perhaps mount an effective defense, but how long would that last? Against likely three and a half to five million dead at this point? The Arch Mages are most talented, but every Mage has a limit to their power. Sooner or later they would break as well.*"

Finally, his finger traced across to the sprawling metropolis of Cael City. "*How many people are stuck outside Cael City's walls, forced to live in the desert? A hundred thousand, give or take? A hundred thousand more footsoldiers in the dead army. At this point, we could be looking at numbers reaching over five million ... swallowing our nation whole. Again ... they would find some way in. How many live in Cael City?*"

Kelad shook his head. "*At a certain time, Your Majesty, both you and Her Majesty The Queen would have been awoken by the roar of seven to eight million dead voices, screaming across the city that your balconies in the Golden Throne Palace look out over.*"

The King had grown whiter and whiter over the course of Kelad's testimony, but the Queen snorted. "*Speculation.*"

"*Coming from intelligence and direct engagement in combat.*"

Minister Carrasco tapped his fingertips on the table, staring at the map. "*I vote in favour of ceasefire.*"

Vehnek snorted. "*That was quick, for you.*"

Carrasco shrugged. "*I don't see any optimistic alternative to the General's projection. It seems we were saved from a very unpleasant fate, as was Salketh, most likely. If an ocean would not have stopped the dead, a desert would not have stopped them either.*" He smiled his familiar contemplative smile. "*If Princess Allessandra is correct about the motivations of our opposite numbers, both nations will certainly prosper far beyond our current status. From a coin perspective, the decision makes itself. Optimism, Ministers. Optimism means that people spend their coin. We have had precious little true optimism in our lands in recent years.*"

"*I concur,*" Evandro murmured after a moment. "*This is not a matter of past crime. It can no longer be. We must consider the future. This platform upon which we stand, with potential peace before us, has been built by Cael and Haama, represented by most or all of our citizens. It has also been built in blood. The blood of patriots, the blood of the innocent, the blood of those that have opposed Caelish rule for a century, all united in a common cause: rescuing us from our own folly. I also vote in favour of ceasefire.*"

Kelad glanced at the Royal Family. The Queen was looking at the four who had cast their votes in disbelief and fury. Her hands were trembling on the armrests of her chair. The King was very still, focusing on the map, and on Vehnek's party.

The Lord Marshal simply watched with a raised eyebrow. Mora seemed as she had at the beginning of the meeting, quietly amused at the proceedings, lounging in her seat. Miranda was the opposite.

"No. No. No. You have lost your collective minds. You, princess ... they broke into your gardens and tried to kill you! They have slaughtered innocent Caelish and Haaman civilians for decades! If it wasn't for The Black Fleet they would have rioted through Victory until they sacked the palace ... and you're damned lucky they were eradicated ... all of you! This ceasefire is an affront to the dead, including Defense Minister Levez. Would she approve of this?"

"You dare speak her name?" Evandro shot at her, with a fury so sudden that Kelad had to suppress a shocked smile. *"An honoured member of the Council, decorated by the Standing Army with every medal we have, caught in your crossfire like so many other of those same innocent Caelish and Haaman civilians whose deaths you exploit for your own ends."*

"All for nothing, if you move ahead with this madness," she hissed in response. *"I vote against."*

Four to one. Brynden had yet to speak, as well as Mora and Vehnek. Mora had no vote, but the makeweights would be King and Queen. With their power of veto, they could simply overrule the Council's vote.

Brynden cleared his throat, and spoke: not in Caelish, but in Haaman.

"I will not use your tongue for what I have to say here." His head shook, his jowls quivering. "You've lived here long enough, you know the language of this country, although precious few of you choose to speak it. No, instead you make *us* speak Caelish. I am the only Haaman Councilman, even though we are *in* Haama. It is offensive, ladies and gentlemen, Your Majesties, that Haama has barely any say over itself. It breeds the resentment that makes blades and clubs sprout out of bare hands that could be held out in friendship, or allegiance. However, it has never been. Those like myself that are chosen to represent Haama have barely any say in matters of state, seen as apologists for men and women that brutalise and take their rights and culture away."

His forehead was damp as he looked around at Kelad and Vehnek. "Your militaries are wielded against the populace like a pair of hungry serpents, always watching. That must end, and only one of you has the wisdom enough to end it. After the slaughter of the Black Fleet's assault on Old Town, this Council can no longer turn a blind eye, nor see and refuse to act. Sheathe the blades, I say! Tie up the sails of the flotilla! Make the effort to find something we can share, so the blood of our nations is spilled no more."

The Queen snorted. "*Even with five votes in favour of ceasefire, we will tie the vote, and The King and I can overrule you. There will be no resolution while a dragon hangs in threat above Haama.*"

Kelad shook his head. "*There is no threat from the dragon, Your Majesty. This has been proven.*"

"*Because they stayed their hands against you? Do not make me laugh, General. There is no point continuing with this charade, the decision is made.*"

Allessandra leaned across the table. "*We have only heard six of the ten votes, mother, even if Vehnek's woman is to be considered, which she should not be.*"

Kelad glanced at Mora, but again, the former clanswoman did not react.

"*Then, hear mine and The King's votes. We reject this notion of ceasefire outright.*"

"*I vote in favour,*" King Alesio calmly stated.

Even Kelad was taken aback. Allessandra gaped at her father in shock. Queen Mirell began to redden, turning slowly to him. Carrasco raised a curious eyebrow, Brynden sagged in relief, Evandro clasped his hands together on the table before him.

Vehnek smiled narrowly, giving a barely noticeable shake of the head. Miranda dropped her cane, and Mora ...

Mora sat still, and observed.

"*Alesio, you cannot-*" The Queen began.

"*You do not speak for me,*" The King snapped. "*The Council will not be overruled by any Royal decree. This is not a matter for Cael alone. After the obscenity of a city in flames, the stink of the dead ... it would be madness to continue on that pathway. Sheer madness.*"

The Empire Of Fire

Mirell's eyes turned ice-cold. *"You will be the death of Cael."*

"Our own stubbornness would easily have been the death of Cael, as we have seen and heard from General Kelad. Our daughter is among those who know Haama far better than you or I. Reports tell a fragment of the tale of this nation, a tale of old wounds and woe. One can only know what information is placed before them. My decision is final. As for the 'death of Cael' ... change is a sort of death. If one is lucky, it is the death of yesterday's folly. Change is not always good, regression and progression sometimes borrow the other's cloak. If Haama is to stand on its own, as an ally and not a vassal, it must forge that path with as little interference from the crown as possible."

Eyes turned to Vehnek and Mora. The Lord Marshal smiled to himself, and shrugged. *"I abstain. With six for, including His Majesty The King, there is no point in casting a vote either way."*

Mora watched his mouth as he spoke. She slowly turned back to the rest of the Ministers. "I abstain."

"Then the motion is passed." First Minister Evandro nodded to himself. *"We will have to arrange a communication with these ... Four Guardians of yours, General. Your recommendation?"*

"I may have to ponder on that, First Minister. Perhaps an envoy, to arrange a face to face meeting. A neutral location may be difficult to find ... it will have to be discussed with our opposite numbers."

Evandro nodded. His eyes moved from Kelad to Allessandra. *"With the permission of Your Majesties ... Princess Allessandra has been instrumental in peace efforts in the city. She may be our best choice to accompany the General in this matter."*

"Allessandra is not a girl any more. She is a woman. She does not need our permission," The King murmured. Mirell gaped at him, shaking with fury.

Allessandra bit her lip. Her eyes fell from her parents to Evandro, who nodded to her deferentially.

"I will ... though I will need others to advise and negotiate alongside us ... should the General agree to join me."

Kelad smiled. *"That ... will also require pondering, Your Grace."*

His eyes fixed on Vehnek, who was looking at him with the same passiveness he had throughout the meeting. However, beneath the surface lurked a predator, studying a meal from the shadows.

The Empire Of Fire

14

The walk to Vehnek's lodgings in the palace was longer than Kelad expected, not in distance, but in trudge.

He had no men with him, but he was armed. His sword was on his hip, as was his pistol, loaded with a fire stone. A sensible precaution, although one that was far from welcome.

He had known Morad Vehnek since he was born. He had known his father from birth to death. He had promised Kallus Vehnek, Morad's grandfather, that he would watch over his descendants for as long as he lived, advise them, give them support. For the first time, he was violating his old friend's wishes.

The fleets remained above Victory, with no problems between them. Detachments of his men had dropped into the city to provide support to the populace. The cannons on the palace roof remained crewed. The optimism he had hoped would descend over him in the wake of the Council's decision had yet to do so. With the beginning of evening, he knew that there would be some form of hell to pay, although the manner of that hell wasn't immediately clear to him.

The doors to the lounge were heavily guarded with Black Fleet heavy troops. The dragon head helms they wore seemed to snarl at him as he approached. The light troops reinforcing them stepped forwards, parting to let Kelad through slightly too late for decorum. The General gave them a wry smile as he passed, ready to engage them if he had to. They already saw him as a traitor, an enemy. Hopefully Vehnek had more sense.

One of them opened the doors into the bedchambers. Kelad stepped inside with a minor flourish.

"No shifting in, my old friend?" Vehnek muttered. He was settled in a large chair, with a small table by his right hand. He closed the report on top of it, bound in a flat leather cover.

"Using the door keeps your guards busy, gives them something to do. We're speaking Haaman today, are we?"

Vehnek smiled. "For Mora's sake. Her Caelish is still limited."

Kelad followed his eyes to the bed, where Mora lay sprawled on the sheets. Her eyes were open, looking straight up, her mouth turned up in a smile. Above her, a number of bunches of black silk spun in a twisting spiral, right out to the edges of the ceiling.

"Good evening, Mora."

She didn't reply. Her eyes remained fixed on the spiral.

It occurred to Kelad that during the meeting, where all except Brynden had spoken exclusively in Caelish, she had shown no signs that she had misunderstood, or been trying to understand any of it.

"Ah, well ... we all must find our own ways to decompress," Kelad muttered. "Should we speak elsewhere, so we don't disturb her?"

Vehnek shook his head. "No, no need. She is quite capable of maintaining her focus. You'll be pleased to know that she's close to finding what she needs to focus the power we took from The Watchtower."

"Ah ... most impressive. She has grown in power considerably in a short time." Kelad glanced at her. "Forgive me for speaking of you in the third person, my dear."

She did not reply.

"Mora is in deep meditation, I wouldn't expect her to say much." Vehnek leaned back in the chair. "Sel ... you never cease to surprise me, for good and for ill."

Kelad shrugged. "If I were predictable it would make me a far less effective tactician."

Vehnek chuckled, keeping his eyes on him. "Where are the Resistance based?"

The Empire Of Fire

"Surely you should know that, given that the Black Fleet have been engaging in operations in Idris for decades."

Vehnek held his unwavering gaze. "Where are they, Sel?"

"I don't know. I didn't have anyone follow them. It seemed an exercise in bad faith, considering the circumstances. Besides, the safety of the Royal Family took priority." Kelad's black eyes bored into Vehnek's. "Not to mention the safety of the city where I live."

Vehnek raised an eyebrow. "I shouldn't have to explain it to you. You're well aware of the military chain of command. You're a General, I'm the Lord Marshal."

"I've seen you shit in your swaddling clothes, Morad, don't pull rank with me. I've read every report I can get a hold of concerning that night. It was a slaughter."

"You expect me to blow the fanfares to signal a fair fight against terrorists?"

"I expect you to be more careful with overwhelming force, when there are civilians in play. Burning down homes and temples, arresting citizens by the hundred, murdering city guards?"

"They were in our way. Their mistake. We ordered them to stand down."

"So it is their own fault?"

Vehnek spread his hands.

Kelad grunted. "I see."

"Come now, Sel. Look at the achievement. We have eliminated the Ghosts, perhaps the most brutal terrorist force in the country ... aside from the wyvernborn."

"The wyvernborn?"

"Indeed. The Wyvern Bog is now a place of interest, considering that they have decided to enter the fray. Especially with the knowledge that they have a dragon to wield against us."

Kelad shrugged. "Perhaps so. Va'Kael only knows where they're keeping it."

"The mountains, of course. Deep inside, beneath the rock. We will find them." Vehnek stroked his chin. "During the council meeting, you spoke of the Four Guardians."

Kelad glanced at Mora, who slowly sat up, rising from the bed and drifting across the room to the window overlooking the city. "I did, at least that's how they're known among the common folk. Your grandfather would have known them by the same monikers that I do. Tobias Calver, Bassai, Thomas, and Emeora Vonn."

"Indeed," Vehnek said distantly.

"Once again, you are completely unmoved by the mention of their names, Mora."

The sorceress seemed to ignore him.

"Even after Thomas escaped your clutches. Even after Emeora Vonn killed your son."

"Fury towards them was no longer useful to me," Mora said, almost to herself.

"Hmm." Kelad watched her closely, until Vehnek spoke again.

"What are they like?"

Kelad raised an eyebrow. "The four? They're a curious bunch. Calver himself has undergone some changes, which would make him rather more problematic to engage in combat."

"Yes, I'm aware of that particular change," Vehnek said with a grin.

"The others are as I remember them. It is as if no time has passed at all."

"Incredible ..." Vehnek murmured. "It worked. The incantation was merely theoretical, but it truly worked. You're certain they aren't doubles, or people who have simply taken up the mantle."

"It was them." Kelad sat opposite Vehnek, holding his arms loosely on the armrests. "Just a guess ... this incantation is what you were going to the Watchtower for?"

Vehnek nodded. "Think of it, Kelad. An army so formidable none could stand against us. Finally seen as equals by those princelings across the sea."

"Hmm." Kelad's fingers drummed against the armrests. "The army's for use against them, then, and not against Haama."

"Apparently we're about to get in bed with Haama and make sweet, peaceful little cherubs with them." Vehnek snorted. "Then what will our strength be, in the eyes of the world? Backwards, reactionary, the tool of a blowhard. Gathering dust until our enemies decide we're not as useful as they thought."

"Who said anything about getting rid of the army, Morad?"

"It's only a matter of time. Bleeding hearts lead to blood everywhere."

Kelad smiled. "So do indiscriminate bombardments."

Vehnek angled up his head, looking at Kelad over the bridge of his nose. "It sounds as if some of your loyalty has been shaken, my old friend."

"Shaken? I couldn't say. If it seems I have changed, keep in mind that I am one of few survivors of a battle that was only won because our so-called enemies rode to our aid. I certainly remain loyal to Cael."

Vehnek tilted his head. *"But are you loyal to me, old friend?"*

The tone of the Lord Marshal's voice as he spoke in Caelish had been light, but dangerous. Kelad chuckled. *"Why, are you conspiring with Mokku? Unless your priorities have changed, I don't see how I wouldn't be loyal to you. You've hardly shaken my loyalty."*

"Glad to hear it." Vehnek leaned back. He stroked his chin. *"Because I'll need you."*

***

The gentle knock at her chamber door roused Allessandra from sleep. She sat up slowly and stretched.

She found that she needed more sleep lately, or perhaps the recent days had caught up with her. She rubbed her eyes and sighed at the early evening. *"Come in."*

The door opened, and King Alesio strode into the room. Behind him, a smaller figure came in.

Allessandra didn't recognise her handmaiden for a moment. Jenifer's face was bruised, her eye and lip swollen. She was wearing the ragged clothes of a prisoner.

Allessandra stared at her as she tumbled forwards into her arms. They held each other tightly, until the princess touched her cheek. *"The bath has been drawn, go and get clean. There will be a dress ready for you, and I'll have some salve brought up to the chamber."*

Jenifer nodded tearfully, and padded into the washroom.

"She was in the dungeons, in Vehnek's custody," The King murmured. *"I had her released, against his objection ... as well as the Queen's."*

Allessandra paced for a moment, concerned for what Jenifer may have revealed to the Lord Marshal's interrogators. She walked over to the windows, and steadied her breathing.

The King joined her. *"How are you feeling, love?"*

"Tired."

"That doesn't surprise me, considering. There aren't many in Royal history who have faced down a fleet and made that fleet blink."

Allessandra smiled, and closed her eyes as he wrapped a tender arm around her.

"You truly care about the people of this city, this country ... as every Regent should, but few have. I am ashamed to say ... I never did, when I was Regent of Haama. The Regency was merely a means to an end, an experience that would lead to the Golden Throne. My heart remained with Cael, with no room for any other." He squeezed her arm gently. *"It seems that Haama has grown to care for you, too, in its own way."*

"I have tried to do right by them, when I am able," Allessandra muttered. *"I failed them for too long. I was just an ... empty dress. I would have failed Cael as much as Haama as Queen, when my time came."*

"You realise that should this ceasefire become a treaty, and Haama goes

its own way, you will no longer hold a position of power."

Allessandra sighed. *"Actually ... it hadn't crossed my mind. I will have to get to know Cael as intimately as I have Haama, in that case, as preparation."*

"You will be a wonderful Queen, if this is anything to go by," Alesio said with a smile.

Allessandra turned her face away, hiding some of the turmoil his words had caused. She may not even live to become Queen of Cael.

"What's wrong?"

"How is mother?"

"Let me worry about your mother, Allessandra. Her anger will subside sooner or later, when she realises she's wrong. It does happen from time to time, believe it or not."

She smiled to herself. *"Father ... thank you for what you did for Jenifer."*

"She was being held without charge, and without trial. I was not prepared to allow it. Besides, they had gotten nothing out of her of any use with their questioning ... and worse methods."

Allessandra's heart leaped with relief. *"It isn't surprising. She hadn't done anything wrong."*

"When did that ever stop a Vehnek from doing something like that?" He held her shoulders. *"I'm very proud of you, you know. Your mother will be as well, when she has time to simmer down."*

"She seems to have become rather attached to the Lord Marshal and his agenda," Allessandra muttered.

"She will learn. I suspect her distaste for your friend, General Kelad, has put her in a certain mindset."

"What about you?"

"The man saved Haama and Cael, with the help of our ... and what may no longer be ... our enemies."

"Yes ... he did."

The King held her warmly. *"We will be departing in the early morning. I trust you and the others to conduct the negotiations, you don't need Mirell and*

I for that. Better she in particular not disrupt things. I hope we can have dinner later on."

"*After I bathe.*"

He smiled, and departed.

Once Jenifer had washed herself, and dressed, Allessandra sent for Eluco to escort her to the palace doctor for better care. She then bathed, gazing down at the scar across her stomach and side as she washed it carefully. The skin had knitted together, more or less, still scabbed over. It needed more salve.

Once she was done, she wrapped herself in a towelled robe, and moved back through to the bedroom, where General Kelad was waiting for her.

She raised an eyebrow at him. "Really, General, you should learn to knock."

There was no amusement or mirth on his face. "Are we alone?"

"I tend not to bathe in a group."

He strode up to her, stopping only when he was a foot away. "Care to explain why your personal airship was fighting at the Pil Valley? Why it was bearing members of the Resistance to war?"

Allessandra stared at him, and felt sweat forming on her brow. Luckily she could maybe pass it off as water from her bath. "What do you mean?"

"Your ship, and your crew, were engaged in military action. Don't bother denying it, you had the damn thing painted like a bouquet of flowers."

"I don't command Captain Seret," Allessandra lied. "I have no way of doing so. If she wanted to fight ... that was her decision alone."

Kelad gave her a look. "Perhaps ... however, there are a few sentries that spotted the ship leaving the city on the night of the fire. A night which coincided with a breakout from the dungeons beneath the palace. Two prisoners escaped, one of which I captured, and both of whom assisted in that same battle at the Pil Valley."

Allessandra reared up and folded her arms. "Are you accusing me of something, General?"

"Stupid girl, don't play your games with me. I told you to be careful. Is

The Empire Of Fire

enlisting your own ship to act against Cael being careful?"

She snorted. "And here I was, thinking you were committed to peace."

"Peace is very far from guaranteed in our current times, even though we made strides towards it. Your mother doesn't want peace. Vehnek doesn't want it. Both are more than powerful enough to divert or disrupt any attempt at a treaty ... so now, more than ever, we need to be smart and not impulsive."

"It seems, without that ship and those prisoners, we wouldn't even be in a position for any kind of treaty."

"No, and bold moves like yours can pay off, but the idea that fortune favours the bold is one of the biggest lies we tell to the young."

Allessandra shook her head. "I'll tell you exactly what I have told everyone else: the truth. A member of the Resistance infiltrated the palace, and tricked his way into a meeting with me. Infiltrated via your Standing Army, I might add. I was threatened, made to call for the *Sand Dancer*, and Jenifer and I were knocked out."

"The ship you just said you had no way to call for?"

Alessandra opened her mouth to retort, before realising the mistake she had made.

"And I imagine that this Resistance member was called Thomas, or something like that? I know he took your two former guards with him. They fought beside the Resistance members. One of them ..."

He paused, his voice softened. "One of them died, Allessandra. Orso. We brought his body home."

She rocked back against the window, gaping at him. She had sent them out with Thomas, it was her fault. "B-Berek?"

"Alive, although he was wounded. He's here as well."

"*Va'Kael protect him,*" she prayed in Caelish. Tears were flowing over her cheeks, dripping onto the floor. Kelad padded forwards and held her for a moment.

"*When will this stop? When will bloodshed ... for the sake of a century-old war ... finally end?*"

"If you aren't careful, it may never end," Kelad muttered in Caelish. He pulled back. *"I need you to listen to me very carefully, Allessandra. Helen will have taught you, many a time, that history is written by the victor. All of these coincidences: your ship, your former guards, your steward escaping from the dungeons; they won't go unnoticed. They will inevitably be spun by those who don't want your peace, and you will become the scapegoat if they prevail. They will make you a traitor, a villainous conspirator. Do you understand?"*

Allessandra wiped her eyes and nodded.

"I can have Berek brought here, if you wish."

"I'll go to him." She looked Kelad in his black, spider-like eyes. *"What do* you *want? Is it peace, or something else?"*

Kelad raised an eyebrow, and smiled to himself. *"I don't really know, in truth. I had never thought it was possible to achieve, until now, until I saw it could be done for myself. I wonder ... if Vehnek had been in my place on that battlefield, would he have voted differently in the Council? Would I have been in his position had I remained here? I cannot say, but I am a man of honour. I won't turn against those I have fought beside, not when they saved my life and the lives of my men. Not when we saved our nation."*

15

Ember awoke nestled in the crook of a large, iron arm, warm to the touch. She lay there for a moment, becoming aware of the soft purple glow in the small bedroom. Ironclad was, of course, awake.

Most of the room was taken up by the bed, big and reinforced enough to accommodate a gargantuan metal man. It seemed comfortable enough ... at least he had never complained about it.

She wondered to herself if he had been awake all night. She knew that he didn't sleep, that he couldn't. That was the point of the Construct, probably. Fight without tiring, endlessly, all day and all night. Relentless, unbreakable.

Did he just lay there, staring at the ceiling? Did he think back to the days before he was locked into a metal shell? Maybe he watched her as she slept, watched over her for any threat that could descend upon them in the night. Maybe his new eyes were searching the heavens, trying to bore through the ceiling and the rocky caves above.

His head turned slightly towards her. "Did you sleep well?"

"How did you know I was awake?"

"I always wake up before you."

He rolled over carefully until he was facing her. She leaned up and kissed him. "Do we have some time for ourselves today?"

"We should have a little while. The meeting's this afternoon."

"Good. We haven't had much of a chance to have a proper look around the area. It might be nice to hike up around the mountains and hills to the south ... without danger of an attack."

Ironclad chuckled. "We can take some lunch up there."

"We could." She nestled down again, resting her head against his chest, listening to the movement of his inner workings. "I'll probably still take the bow ... just in case."

"Makes sense."

"Bring that tasty axe of yours too."

"Will do."

She looked up at his violet eyes, shining in the low, cozy light. "To think ... we're probably going to go back to ... what used to be Melida City soon."

"I didn't see much of it myself ... and considering what was being done to it when we escaped ... I'm not sure I want to."

She held him closer. "They'll have plenty of people rebuilding, if that princess of Thomas's is anything to go by." She patted his chest. "Come on, big guy, let's get the sun on our faces."

She pulled on her clothes, simple cotton trousers and a plain light shirt that laced up at the neck. As she tied her boots, she brushed a hand over her leather armour. She considered it for a moment, before Ironclad's hand wrapped around her waist.

"No fights today," she muttered. "We're not doing anything crazy, just walking in the hills ..."

"Worst comes to worst ... I'm armoured. Get behind me."

She grinned. "Good idea, I can use you as cover."

"That's what I'm here for."

She chuckled as they left their small abode in the Obsidian cavern, and made their way down to the market, tucked away at the edge of the bowl where the carts and cargo sat in the staging area. Ember bought a few strips of grilled chicken and bacon, along with a sour peach. The seller waved off any attempt at payment with a warm smile, no matter the insistence.

Once they had bought some fresh juice as well, in a jar, they strode out through the staging area and the training yard. Bassai gave them a wave as he watched over the young fighters sparring. Thomas stood beside him, chatting idly, and Bassai barked a laugh that they heard echo around the rocky cave and out into the world.

The Empire Of Fire

The pre-noon sun was gentle on their faces as they emerged from the cavern. Even though peace seemed to be cresting the horizon, the defenses in the canyon leading to Idris were still fully manned and ready. Ironclad and Ember bypassed it entirely, climbing up the side of the rocky hillock. Ember hopped between the rocks and swung herself up, while Ironclad strode up, digging his feet into the dirt.

They passed by a series of small caves, with tiny paintings and etchings on the walls. Perhaps old homes, dug from the rock. Perhaps places for the young of Obsidian to conceal themselves away, sneaking a drink with their friends or a kiss in the shadows.

At the top of the hill they strode south towards the mountains, across rolling fields of wheat and wild corn. They walked until the grass started to become compacted soil and rock, looping around until they were moving back towards the plains.

Ember settled at the top of a hill covered in long, green grass. Insects bounced between the wide blades, almost as if they were half-asleep. Ironclad handed her the food they had brought.

He sat as she munched on the chicken and bacon, waving some of the insects away as they bumped against his chest. They seemed as curious about him as they did the grass.

"Mmm ... you can't beat this kind of food," Ember muttered, wiping her mouth. "Fresh, proper food, you know?"

"I do."

She stretched back on the grass, leaving the peach for now. "Have you ever left Haama?"

He lay down with her, ears still trained on their surroundings. "No. Well ... I don't know if the Mountain Cities count. If they do, yes."

"They'd say they count."

"Then yes I have."

Ember grunted thoughtfully. "I never have. Furthest north I've been is the Port Of Plenty, furthest east the Orlin Forest, furthest west Breaker's Bay, furthest south the mountains."

Ironclad shrugged a shoulder. "In our day it wasn't common. There were no airships, no wide travel across the world."

"Now it is, though … and we're about to have a lot more time on our hands." Ember glanced over at him to gauge his reaction. He didn't seem to have much of one, except for the brighter glow of his eyes. "You ever thought about getting out there? Seeing what it's all about?"

"Out where?"

"Anywhere. Over the White Sea to Salketh, over the Meladrin to Noor or Adrezsti or the ruins of Esca. Cael isn't far, and all we know about the place is what we were told. Barely anyone goes east these days, even though the dragons are all but gone."

"Mokku?"

Ember snorted. "Even with you around they'd probably try and enslave me."

He chuckled. "We'd have to take Kira, just to be sure."

"A little time alone with you doesn't involve Kira, my love," she murmured. "How's she doing?"

"Kira? Recovering, but she might be laid up for a little while. Infections in some of her deeper wounds. She probably won't see the peace treaty signed."

"Shame. She worked hard for it, you know."

The clouds twirled gently above them. He let out a rusty sigh. "I can't help but think we're fools to think this is about to end."

"When did you get so pessimistic?"

"Caution more than pessimism. I want the prosperity Thomas talks about to become a reality, I want to believe he isn't just that same dreamer, selling the right people on the dream."

"I suppose we'll find out." She rolled over to face him. "Airship or boat?"

"Hmm?"

"When we travel. Airship or boat?"

He turned his head towards her. "Aren't airships both?"

The Empire Of Fire

"I asked around. Boats are cheaper. We're not exactly rich."

"Hmm..." Ironclad murmured. "Have we been paid at all since we came back to life?"

"Not a penny, although we haven't spent any either, aside from on booze."

"An airship can be our payment, then. Decent sized. Green sails. A couple of cannons, just in case."

"As if either of us could fire them. We can rely on the bow for a bit ... or get one or two of those scorpion harpoon throwers that they have in the canyon..."

"Might be pushing it a bit. To afford those we might need to make a whole other peace treaty with someone."

Ember grinned, closing her eyes, letting the sunlight bathe her eyelids, giving her vision a blue hue. "Adrezsti first ..."

"She has spoken."

She slapped his iron thigh playfully. "Adrezsti, then Noor. Humid, then cold."

"Northward after that. See if we can find and chart any new islands. Visit Ancient Esca, Habil, any other we can find."

"Then swing east to Salketh. Fly over the White Sea, visit Cael maybe, then home."

Ironclad's head slowly turned to her. "Not further east, hmm?"

"There be dragons, love. Besides, I'd want to take Bassai with us if we were headed that way."

Ironclad hummed to himself. "Think about it, Em'. We'd leave ... and come home to a brand new Haama, or thereabouts."

"For the better, hopefully," Ember sighed.

"An independent nation is better than a vassal."

"An independent nation with a friend in Cael. Maybe with a friend in the Mountain Cities ... as long as there are still people there."

Ember tried to push the sour thought from her mind, but it lingered stubbornly. The meeting would allay that concern, or distract her from it. She wasn't entirely sure why it had even been called, only that Ironclad and Donnal had jointly called it.

Her eyes moved over to the west, past Ironclad, to the black and grey cloud billowing from Montu Fortu, where the great city of Uncur used to be. A still-burning fire, the effect of which filled the sky decades after the city had been razed. It was what Haama could have been … could still be if it all went wrong, and here she was, talking about sojourning away with her lover on a pleasure voyage across the world.

"How much higher d'you think we can go?" Ironclad was looking right at her, purple eyes shining.

"Higher?"

"Up into the mountains. We've got time."

Ember stretched and looked around. The mountains themselves were a little far away, but rocky hillocks rose directly behind them.

"We can probably climb that hill closest to us. Better view, maybe."

"Let's go."

***

When they arrived back, the only people in the meeting room were Seraphine and Donnal. Ember tapped Ironclad's chest.

"I need to have a quick word with Seraphine."

Ironclad hummed and strode over to Donnal, where the two began conferring as well.

Seraphine smiled up at Ember tiredly. "Ah … Ember."

"You alright?"

"Busy times, with no chance for rest, unfortunately."

By Ember's reckoning, the aging sorceress had not properly rested and recuperated since her interrogation and torture at the hands of Mora and the Black Fleet. She reached out a hand and entwined her fingers with Seraphine's.

"Try and take a little time for yourself. Just an afternoon. We can survive a few hours without you ... probably."

"I'll believe it when I see it," Seraphine muttered wryly. "What about you? Are you well?"

"Mostly." Ember took a breath. "In the Mountain Cities ... do you know if there's anyone left?"

"There are pockets of habitation. Umber is still populated, but most of the people live below ground or in the mountain caverns. We hear from them on occasion, but they have never shown any desire to involve themselves in the war. They seem to just be trying to survive."

"I can understand that."

"Many of us can."

Ember nodded. "Do you think anything can be done? That the dragon could help them?"

Seraphine spread her hands. "I wish I knew. The wyvernborn's magic is a mystery to me. I don't know how that creature could have done any of the things it has done ... yet it has." She shook her head. "Perhaps it is possible, but only time and research will tell."

The others began filing into the room, in various degrees of mirth. Thomas and Bassai were laughing as they had been before. Helen, the former royal steward, joined them quietly, and sat down without a word. Shortly after that Jack came in, not wasting the opportunity to give Ironclad a quick glance-over. Ember nodded to him with a smile when he turned to her.

Kassaeos shifted into being beside Seraphine, making her jump. He grinned over her scowl. "Shall we begin with our iron companion telling us what this is all about?"

Ironclad turned to him and gestured to the table. All sat and waited for him to speak.

"As we are all well aware, the path to peace is rocky, full of pitfalls and snakes in the grass. It is the path we are currently walking, and there is one particular serpent I am keen to avoid, or behead if it attempts to strike. Lord

Marshal Vehnek has been attempting to hunt Donnal and Seraphine's people for many years, following in the footsteps of his father, and his father's father. I have called this meeting so that the threat he presents can be correctly gauged."

Thomas nodded his head and leaned forwards. "I don't think there can be any question that the man presents a serious threat. In terms of his motivation, you said it yourself: this is the work of his father and grandfather. He will not want to be the Vehnek who surrendered."

"But he isn't being asked to surrender," Helen sighed. "We're asking him to negotiate, to come to the table and talk. It has nothing to do with his failure."

Bassai growled. "In war, victory is your gauge of honour. You typically force a surrender, force your enemy to the table to avoid their destruction. The terms are yours to control, and work in your favour. This is different. It is intended to benefit both Haama and Cael. It is not a Caelish victory."

"Nor is it a Caelish defeat," Helen returned.

"We are at the mercy of perspective," Ironclad rumbled from the head of the table. "This is the reason for our meeting now. There will be ill-feeling from many, I suspect. There will be those who want nothing to do with Cael or Haama. There are even more that will harbour some level of grief for the many crimes that have been perpetrated over the decades. However, not all of them command a fleet of elite, well-equipped soldiers. Vehnek has the means to violently act upon his discontent."

"Especially since he already has," Jack added. "He burned Victory almost to the ground; a city under Caelish control. What would he be capable of if faced with the Wyvern Bog, or Obsidian?"

Helen sighed. "He had me imprisoned for suspected Resistance ties. I agree he is dangerous … but to break a potential peace, break the first ceasefire in decades … it would be madness. The man is certainly a potential threat, but he isn't mad, isn't illogical."

Jack nodded. "On that we agree."

"Burning farms and villages isn't logical," Donnal growled.

"It is if they're your enemy. If you want control of their land to feed your people. The famine in Cael grows more dire every year."

"Spoken like the indoctrinated," Donnal retorted.

Jack bristled at that. "I dislike suffering. I have seen many Caelish people on the streets of Cael City who are so thin you can see their bones. I have seen people who have to live outside the walls and beg. If I had the power to change that, I would try to. Is that not why you fought? To ease the suffering of your people?"

"Some of us," Ember muttered.

"This is the point of getting to the bottom of it," Thomas urged. "We cannot assume the man is mad, fighting for the sake of the fight. We have to assume that Vehnek's motivations are noble, at least to his own mind."

Ironclad folded his arms and turned his violet eyes to each of them in turn. "What do we know, then?"

Jack glanced around and cleared his throat. "We know that his plans seemed to involve you ... or involve Constructs like you. The ... work ... he had the Colonel conducting ... was a thorough examination of your inner workings. Your eyes, movements, consciousness ..." he trailed off.

"Go on," Ironclad grunted.

"Your ... tolerance for pain. Your survival instincts, survivability. How much damage could be done before ..."

As he met Ember's gaze, he trailed off entirely, and fixed his eyes on the table.

"In order to build more," Thomas mused.

Jack nodded.

"It's not surprising," Thomas continued. "Ironclad has, in effect, been the perfect prototype and example of what a Construct is capable of. The White Tower alone would have seen to that."

"I had the impression that whatever Vehnek was planning began before I appeared," Ironclad muttered.

"But you accelerated it, more likely than not." Kassaoes leaned back in his chair and clasped his fingers together. "Black Fleet airship movements have increased by half since before Thomas and I had our trip to Victory. Their operations have gone a little farther afield than before, focused on the north and east."

"The White Sea?" Seraphine asked.

Kassaeos nodded. "Don't ask me why. There's nought there but sand."

Ember caught Seraphine's expression, and leaned forwards herself. "Is that true?"

The sorceress glanced up at her, then around at everyone else. "Now, I couldn't say for sure ... but there was something there, a hundred years ago. I imagine it's still there."

The rest waited quietly as she gathered her thoughts. "Many centuries ago, Salketh was the primary power on the continent. They faded over time, but one general of their army remained. Legend tells that he was the finest military mind who ever lived, commanding absolute loyalty from his soldiers, through admiration rather than through the sword. When Salketh's power waned, through events and struggles beyond the general's control, he took his armies and marched into the desert."

"A fine mind indeed," Kassaeos said with a quizzical eyebrow.

"You joke, but he flourished. He established a stronghold that lasted long after Salketh shrank to the shadow it is today. It was called the K'thann Ma'zhuur ... The Undying Citadel. During the Cael-Salketh wars, the Citadel was sieged repeatedly, without success."

Bassai snorted smoke from his nostrils. "Impossible. In the desert, nothing grows. They should have starved."

"The General and his army did not eat."

Ironclad leaned forwards, arms falling to his sides.

"They were undead?" Donnal asked.

"They were Constructs," Ironclad said slowly, before Seraphine could finish the thought. She nodded to him.

"That General would have been invincible," Ember muttered. "An army that doesn't need to eat, drink, sleep ... made of armour, capable of wielding

The Empire Of Fire

heavy weapons with the kind of strength you couldn't get out of ten soldiers..."

Ironclad's voice was quiet, but the words still vibrated through them all.

"And he's still there."

Everyone around the table looked up at him again. He was standing still as a statue in a ruin.

"That's where I came from, isn't it. You took ... me into the White Sea. You found this general, and he built this body."

Seraphine swallowed. "That's what my grandfather did, yes. At least, that's the story he told me. But ... he would never go into detail. Others told me that he went into the desert with a hundred men and women ... and fewer than a dozen returned."

"So Vehnek's gone there as well?" Bassai snarled. "Or he plans to?"

"Likely he plans to," Jack cut in. "He has construction information, plans for the inner workings of Ironclad, but the spark of life is what eluded the Colonel. Constructs are a marriage of armour, sophisticated engineering, and magic. It was the magic that proved to be the barrier."

"Magic that this general has ..." Ironclad murmured, beginning to pace.

Thomas sighed and shook his head. "There's more to all this. It's not just about increasing his military might, or about feeding the hungry. In order to do that you wouldn't need to exert so much control over Haama the way he has, particularly its government. The Council Of Ministers didn't seem to know the extent of his operations. We heard that he had essentially seized control of them, and limited the powers of the Regent. He couldn't have done so without the backing of the King and Queen."

"They would approve of a plan to empower Cael, surely," Ember muttered. "Feed those that need feeding, strengthen the army, remove problems like us in Haama..."

Kassaeos grinned. "All of that makes Vehnek look good ... what's in it for them?"

"Exactly." Thomas focused on Donnal, Seraphine, Helen, Kassaeos and Jack. "You know more about the current situation between Cael and the rest of the world than we do. You know more of its history in the last century."

It was Helen who spoke up, sharply. "Cael is hated."

Donnal snorted. "I wonder why."

"Believe me, I understand why, and I understand your pain, being half-Haaman myself. The reasons are many, and some are even fair. The occupation of this country is seen as an act of barbarism and tyranny. Cael is one of only two nations remaining that continues the institution of indentured servitude."

"Slavery," Thomas said stonily. "Call it by its name."

Helen pursed her lips and bowed her head. "Cael and Mokku are the only nations that still practice slavery. Part of the negotiated settlement that ended the last war was the explicit term that no Haaman would be enslaved. None were ... formally. The farmers in Idris and the Maldane Reach were very much under the thumb of the military."

Helen paused, and looked to Jack for assistance. "You will know more than I, at least in differing detail."

Jack bobbed his head. "I know what my former colleagues told me: that despite the distaste towards Cael, almost every nation around the world benefits from their advances in magic and technology. The first airships were built in Cael, the first siege engines, the first magical amplifiers, even many of the first incantations were discovered by the Caelish Magus towers. In Cael itself, there has started to be a considerable feeling of resentment, especially among academics, business owners and arcane scientists."

"Not among the commonfolk, but I'd guess they have bigger problems," Donnal muttered.

Ember frowned. "Resentment?"

"The hypocrisy of it," Kassaeos chuckled. "The exploitation of Cael's resources and advancements, while they are demonised by the rest of the world. Whether or not you think they deserve that reputation, Mokku are given far more leeway."

"Because they were once enslaved as well, and they overthrew their oppressors," Thomas added. "They were treated brutally, according to their own history."

Kassaeos barked a laugh. "You should see how they treat their slaves now, Thomas. Brutality barely smudges the polish."

"That's my point. They have leveraged their victimhood. Cael doesn't have that luxury."

"Their armies and fleets don't hurt either," Donnal snorted.

"So it is not just about the technology," Bassai mused. His claws drummed on the table. "It is about the threat. Should Cael stop supplying Mokku with these advancements, there is every chance of a war that would lead to Cael's destruction."

"And Haama's," Ember muttered.

Seraphine nodded. "It is doubtful they would stop at Cael. They would encounter the same problems that Cael have now: a lack of food."

The idea of Haamans enslaved en-masse seemed to pass through the minds of everyone at the table.

"Historically speaking … Haama would be culturally destroyed," Helen said after taking a breath. "What we now know of as Mokku used to be six separate nations. All were conquered and subjugated after the uprising."

"They would call it a liberation," Thomas muttered. "But as Ironclad said, we're at the mercy of perspective."

"Precisely." Ironclad clenched his fists. "Vehnek will also know all of this … and he will want to protect Cael. Perhaps part of him would want to protect Haama as well, but only once we're brought to heel." He began pacing. "An army of Constructs would be formidable on the ground, but modern warfare is not fought only on the ground. The navies, the airships, the arcane …"

Seraphine shuddered. "Perhaps the arcane accounts for Mora's presence. The energies within her are old and powerful … more so than in any Mage I have encountered … apart from Ydra." She swallowed at their late friend's memory. "I could feel the energy in Mora even when I was imprisoned and isolated, through layer upon layer of insulated rock."

"She is a talented Mage ..." Thomas muttered, rubbing the faint burn Mora's torture had left on his throat.

"No, not her," Seraphine shook her head. "Inside her, at her core. The power that rests within her is like a pyre in pitch blackness. It ..."

She fell silent, her eyes falling to the table. Instinctively, Kassaeos's hand joined hers.

"Go on," Ember urged.

"It ... felt as if it was aware of me," Seraphine said quietly. "As if it recognised that I was a Mage, that it was getting a measure of me."

Donnal frowned, and Bassai folded his arms.

"Aware?" Thomas was frowning as well, but in concern more than skepticism.

"Is that possible?" Donnal said, with a hint of incredulity.

"It sounds exactly like what we encountered inside Ydra." Thomas looked at Seraphine, his concern growing. He touched his throat again. "That thing wasn't an incantation, it spoke, thought, recognised us as a threat and reacted to us."

Jack and Helen looked at each other and conferred for a brief moment.

"If it wasn't an incantation, what was it?" Bassai growled.

Thomas shook his head. "I have no idea."

"Dark magic, dark energy," Seraphine muttered. She shook her head. "But like nothing that walks this world. What it was transforming Ydra's mind into wasn't a place I recognised ... it was more like a ... platform among the stars."

"The ring, you remember that?"

Seraphine nodded with a shiver.

"What ring?" Ember demanded.

"It was ... well, two rings, actually. The structure it built seemed to be a part of one, but there was a larger, fiery ring, surrounding ..." Thomas's mouth closed, and he had to steady his breathing before he could speak again. "A ring of fire around a void. A deep blackness that swallowed the light of the stars

The Empire Of Fire

themselves. Sucking, drawing in rocks and worlds and clouds of colour to be crushed to nothing, in an unending spiral."

Ember exhaled a breath. "At least you got rid of it."

Thomas, staring into space, slowly shook his head. "I don't think we did."

The eyes of the table focused on him again.

"But it released Ydra," Ember said quietly.

"Released her, yes ... but the thing itself ... it could be anywhere."

Ironclad looked quickly and sharply to Seraphine. "In Mora?"

"I don't know. The entity inside Mora didn't have control of her ... yet."

Jack and Helen fell silent, and Jack nodded for her to speak. "I'm afraid there's more. In the palace, the Silver Throne Palace ... leading to the gardens ... there were dragon bones. A whole skeleton."

Thomas thought for a moment, and frowned. "I don't remember seeing that."

Helen shook her head. "Now it's gone. It was removed after I was imprisoned."

"The Colonel took the skeleton," Jack added, leaning forwards. "I believe it was transported to Cael, to the Magus Towers. After that ... I don't know. But this Mora ... She came to the laboratory. After she left ... I overheard mention of a watchtower. Not said in the mundane way such a structure would be described, but with more reverence, more importance."

Kassaeos became very still, his black eyes widening slowly.

"I remember," Ironclad muttered. "I overheard that conversation as well."

Seraphine sat bolt upright. "The Watchtower? In Uncur?"

"What was there?" Bassai snapped.

"An ... incantation."

Thomas noted her pause and leaned forwards. "What do you mean 'an incantation'? Like a fireball, or like the thing that raised the dead?"

Seraphine hesitated. "More like the latter ... more than you think, actually, but not quite. It was ... what we used to bring you back to life."

She looked at Thomas, Ember and Bassai in turn. Ember felt a chill come over her, confronted by her own mortality so explicitly. Bassai snapped her out of it immediately.

"Vehnek now has that incantation. What can he do with it?"

Ironclad paced. "Bring someone back ... but who? We need more."

Kassaeos blinked and his focus seemed to return to the room. "That's the problem ... there isn't much more than that. While we were in Victory I infiltrated the offices of some of the highest officials in the city. There was nothing in any of them, any of their safes, their secret compartments. The Council Of Ministers knew nothing. Kelad knew little. The Regent knew nothing."

"Vehnek can't be acting independently," Thomas muttered. "Politically speaking, his power is limited, it's all concentrated with the Royal family. Like we said, I would bet that one of or both the King and Queen are backing him."

"An Arch Mage went with them to the Watchtower," Jack said. "A man named Lucian, one of the more powerful and notable of them. Another, Miranda, is part of his inner circle. The Magus Towers must support him as well."

"Acting in the shadows ... because there would be push-back otherwise," Ironclad murmured.

"Vehnek seized control of the Haaman Council Of Ministers with Royal Decree," Jack nodded. "I don't think they factored in the crisis with Ydra ... certainly not our support of the Caelish Standing Army."

Ember snorted. "Aye ... well, things fell into place for us, didn't they. We knew Ydra ... and we had a dragon helping us, from our negotiations with the wyvernborn."

"Hmm ..." Bassai growled. "Without us a dragon would have been the only thing that would have stopped her, perhaps. Kelad's forces would have been annihilated."

Ironclad stopped walking. "Leaving the Black Fleet unopposed. The dead army would certainly have dealt with us as well, had we not gone."

The Empire Of Fire

Seraphine nodded slowly. "It's quite the risk to take, though, isn't it? Just to get a better foothold?"

"No, it wasn't a risk at all," Ember muttered. Her mind was spinning. "It's exactly what Vehnek wanted. A crisis that would reduce or even wipe out his enemies at home ... and one that he could solve." She looked up at Seraphine and Ironclad. "The dragons. He wants the dragons. Could he bring them back to life with that incantation from the Watchtower?"

Seraphine thought for a moment, brow furrowed in the same way Rowan's did when he was deep in thought. "Maybe. He would need their remains."

"Which he must have. The black dragon's bones, and the ones that attacked Uncur, at least. He's had decades to explore the Eastern regions and find more." Ember had to stand up as nervous energy filled her. "Gods above, the dead wouldn't have had a chance against four dragons, let alone however many he found ... and it would have been *his* victory!"

Bassai snorted. "Vehnek the hero, the defender of a land his grandfather conquered and his father subjugated. With them and the Black Fleet in the air, and Constructs on the ground, he could challenge Mokku, and he would have gained the political influence and capital to do so."

"Wait a moment ..." Thomas muttered. "It's even worse than that."

His eyes fell on Ironclad, who grunted. "Dragon Constructs? Is it possible?"

"Airships that can float are commonplace, Ironclad. They weigh thousands of tons. Think about the Annihilator, how big that thing is. With a powerful enough generator you could lift an even greater mass." He shook his head. "It's not a matter of if it's possible, it's a matter of when ... and this peace we want is a direct threat."

"And now that we've taken his victory away from him ... he'll be moving faster," Donnal grunted.

He stood. "Seraphine, send word to the Wyvern Bog, tell them what we know. Thomas, do the same with Kelad. It's not a simple treaty any more ...

it's an arms race."

The Empire Of Fire

16

The machinery that made it possible for the people of Planar to communicate over vast distances was known to few, and accessible to fewer. The complex array of dishes and focusing lenses were attached together by a web of fine metal tubing, brass and silver and steel. Each dish sat on a mount in front of a round window facing outwards, encircling a round map of the continents with Victory at the centre. The windows and dishes lined up with their corresponding dishes in other cities across the world.

Eluco strode around it all slowly and carefully, his eyes focused on anything that could have been an irregularity in the chamber. The vast windows were all shuttered and bolted, and had been since the murders. Arcane engineers were working on the destroyed dishes, and Royal Guards were standing close to them. They seemed to be in no hurry, though, going about their business with the speed of someone striking for more pay.

The damage wasn't as extensive as Eluco had considered it might be. In fact, the dishes and lenses were completely intact. It was the tubes that had been severed, the fine woven wiring that had borne the brunt of the brutality. Whoever had cut the communications of the Silver Throne Palace had been no ruffian. They had known what they were doing.

He looked around, towards the palace guardsman he had taken on as an assistant for this matter, and gave him a nod. Vakesh had a sharp eye, and had proven trustworthy during the events of the fateful night.

Some were calling it the Night Of Terror. Others, more aligned to the Black Fleet, were calling it the Night Of Cleansing Flame. The news pamphlets and town criers were giving both stories, depending on area and allegiance, and there had been a number of unfortunate incidents where printers had been ransacked and set on fire, and town criers had been beaten or even murdered. Those pushing the latter narrative seemed to be the ones on the end of the worst violence, and it was one more headache for the city guard to massage away while they were picking up the pieces that Vehnek had left in their lap.

Vakesh strode over to Eluco, around the map. Instinctively, both lowered their voices.

"*Anything?*"

Vakesh shook his head. "*It's as we thought. The Black Fleet have been very thorough. There's not much left ... but now that we're here, there are a few questions that need answering.*"

"*Aye ... actually seeing the room itself ... more questions than answers. How the Ghosts got in, for example ...*" Eluco looked around at the windows. "*The room is closely guarded, they would have been cut to pieces if they'd have tried to come in through the door.*"

"*A door which wasn't forced or broken, as well.*" Vakesh frowned. "*Disguises, perhaps. They've been known to employ them before in attacks of this nature.*"

"*But what kind of disguise would be inconspicuous? Palace guards have no reason to come in here. Arcane engineers come in if something's broken. Operators work in shifts, so if they came in early, and they weren't the usual workers, that would arouse suspicion.*"

Vakesh nodded thoughtfully. "*All I can think of is a group of nobility, coming in to arrange a conference with someone far away ... perhaps in Mokku or Noor, where it would have been daylight.*"

"*Possible ...*" Eluco scratched his chin. "*In order to execute this kind of operation successfully, you'd need speed and silence. The guards outside were killed, weren't they?*"

"*Yes.*"

"*People you knew?*"

"*That's the strange thing: no. At least I don't think so. I can't account for any missing palace guardsmen. If we could get a look at the bodies ... but all of* them are gone too. Burned, I believe."

Eluco snorted and shook his head. "*Very inconvenient, isn't it.*"

"*For us. If they didn't come through the door, they must have come through the windows.*"

"*Which means climbing up a closely guarded tower unnoticed.*"

Vakesh shook his head. "*Without leaving a mark on any of the walls, arcane or otherwise. They could have roped in, but to do that you'd have to hook in with a grapple. No marks for that either. Those aren't tracks you can cover without a stonemason.*"

Eluco paced. "*And that's just getting in. Getting out after is an entirely different matter ... covered in blood, making noise, even with the bombardment outside.*"

He gazed around. It was as if none of it had even happened, now. The attack hadn't been communicated to the palace guards until long after the evidence had been washed away.

"*Think, Vakesh ...*" Eluco murmured, lowering his voice again. "*You're Black Fleet men. You've just committed murder ... committed treason against the crown, even. You cannot be caught ... because what your end goal is is far bigger than you. What do you do?*"

Vakesh stared at him. "*Is that what you think happened here?*"

"*I'm almost certain. Put yourself in their shoes. The Ghosts are the perfect scapegoat, and the attack justifies your move against them in the city. Add to that the confusion of it, and the palace can't contact an ally in Cael or otherwise. Note now that the engineers aren't in any hurry.*"

Vakesh glanced around. "*I did notice that ... but this is all conjecture unless it can be proven.*"

"*Correct, so follow the logic. What do you do?*"

Vakesh stroked his chin, and glanced around uneasily. "*Replace the guards at the door, first. Reassign them in the shake-up, and have my men take up their roles in the palace guard. Put them on the shift that coincides with our attack on the city. Then I'd probably strike at the same time. Have the men at* the door let the killers in, and wait outside so everything appears normal to passers-by."

He looked around again. "*In here ... strike hard and fast, kill the operators, and start breaking things. Trouble is, the damage looks finely done. They would have brought in a specialist or a Mage to cut the amplifiers off.*"

"And leave the way they came in, through the front door," Eluco muttered.

"Deploying into the city to cover your tracks. No, probably leaving on a skiff bound for Cael, limiting the chances of being caught." Vakesh cursed. "We'll never catch them."

"Catching them is beyond the point. We just have to prove it was the Black Fleet who did it. Now, where's the point in all that where the mistake is made?"

"Probably in the fight."

Eluco nodded. "*Check the floor. Scuffs, blood, tread marks, anything that could have been missed.*"

The pair split again, and patrolled around the space, one step at a time. Eluco scanned over every inch that seemed irregular or discoloured. The floor around the map was smooth and polished, his steel boots almost skidded across it. Difficult to fight on such a surface, unless you had the right footwear. He looked at the engineers again with a scowl. He had seen workers like them smash through repair work of that nature dozens of times in the city. This lot were either rookies, or incompetents.

After one circuit of the room, his eyes shifted to the map. It was giant and beautifully carved from wood and metal, painstakingly painted by hand, marking every island, river and mountain range over their vast world. Even the known forests and jungles were marked. An unnecessary expense, but then again this was a palace. Royalty had to have constant exposure to extravagance, lest they forget how high above the common folk they were.

Eluco grunted to himself. Allessandra wasn't of that sort, it seemed, despite the stories of her he had heard from the criers and in the taverns.

The Empire Of Fire

Perhaps apart from her taste in exotic, figure-hugging dresses.

It was upon the map that he noticed the smudge. It was black and grey, grainy, across the corner of the depiction of Mokku's Udo Jungle. He looked up at Vakesh and stopped walking.

Once the man had caught up to him, Eluco lowered his voice. *"Fetch the Royal Guards. Tell them to relieve those engineers and fetch new ones, preferably from the Standing Army. Then I want them guarding the door and the room."*

Vakesh nodded. A moment later the gilded soldiers clanked into the room, their heavy plate armour gleaming. They immediately approached the engineers, who were both puzzled and protesting their dismissal. A few glances were thrown Eluco's way, especially from the loudest amongst them. Vakesh swiped a pouch of their tools before it could be picked up, and shot Eluco a wink.

Once the protesting charlatans had been ejected, the pair were alone in the chamber. They crossed the map and knelt beside the smudge.

"Any tweezers in there?" Eluco muttered.

"Aye ... hang on."

Vakesh leaned down and started gently probing the grains of the smudge. He picked up one of the larger fragments and held it to his nose. *"Hmmn ... smells a little oily, almost. It's not blood."*

Eluco sniffed it, and nodded. *"They use this stuff on Black Fleet boots, on the soles. Standard issue. It's meant to give them better grip on stone."*

"Right. Another clue."

"We need to start limiting the movements of Vehnek's men, and quickly. Grains of dried gripping oil aren't enough to kick him into a cell, but they're enough to make the Ministers treat him with a little more concern than they have been. Vakesh, you stay in charge here, supervise the repairs with the gold boys. Don't let anyone in that isn't the princess or me ... and check every soldier that's on duty. No infiltrators."

***

Tyranian port was a sweet, yet tart delicacy to the tongue, and Vehnek had developed a taste for the foreign drink. He would have preferred a Caelish fire-whiskey or a jar of dalivetra, but many of the fields that grew the embral barley and even common zhernoth wheat were barren, and covered in sand. Neither plant would grow in Haama, the rebel infested bane of his life.

"*It's more simple a mechanism than we ever realised.*" The Colonel mused, swirling the purple liquid around in his wide-bottomed glass. "*We assumed, given the complexity of the soul, that it would require a complex cage.*"

Vehnek nodded, barely paying attention. "*And?*"

"*The complexity is not in the cage, but in the mechanisms that protect that cage and its contents from harm. Our ribs protect the heart and lungs, etcetera. This is similar, but more ... elaborate.*"

Vehnek put his glass down, and glanced at the bottle. Half-full. He popped the cork and topped up his glass. "*Another?*"

"*Please.*"

Vehnek poured, and studied the Colonel for a moment. The man seemed supremely confident, and full of that hair-brained excitement that came from men in his field. As such, he needed focusing. "*The key question, Colonel, is: can you replicate it?*"

The Colonel smiled. "*Of course! Getting a soul into it is a matter for Mora, perhaps.*"

"*And the rest of it?*"

The Colonel leaned back, his eyes casting out across the city, at the ships above the skyline. "*My engineers and arcane engineers are confident that the armour they have created will offer protection and intimidation, although it may require a little creative thinking in later sets when it comes to the materials. After all, they will have to be able to fly.*"

"*Airships can fly.*"

The Empire Of Fire

The Colonel smiled. *"Not like a dragon."*

Vehnek grunted. *"Yes, yes ... those 'air dynamics' you told me about ..."*

"Airships are meant to be siege engines, battleships, even fortresses in the air. They are meant to strike fear in the enemy, move slowly and hover if they have to. Dragons are fast, and devastating, unmatched in flight. Even on the ground they can be formidable."

"Yes, yes, I'm aware of the accounts from Kelad and his troops, I heard the stories from my grandfather."

The Colonel peered at him. *"You are also aware, therefore, that they are difficult beasts to control."*

"It won't be a problem, I assure you. They will defer to power."

The Colonel's eyes narrowed. *"I hope you're right. You have a lot of faith in your paramour."*

Vehnek smiled. *"Indeed, now that she has been improved."*

The door slowly opened, and Mora drifted into the room, as if she had been summoned. A long roll of thick paper was tucked under her arm, tied by a pair of silk bows. Her face broke into an amused smirk at the sight of Vehnek and the Colonel in their armchairs, and she seemed to study them for a moment.

Vehnek met her gaze, trying to get a measure of the darkness within her. That seemed to amuse her even more.

"How are you, my dear?"

Mora's smile grew, and she laughed out loud. "I'm well, Vehnek. Very well," she replied in Haaman.

The Colonel raised an eyebrow. "Would you prefer we spoke in Haaman?"

"It makes no difference." She peered at him for a moment. "Colonel. That's right, isn't it?"

He glanced at Vehnek with a frown of confusion. "I ... yes. You don't remember me?"

"Of course I do," Mora chuckled. "I am experiencing many new things of late, gaining a ... new perspective. It is quite a lot to process."

She wandered over to them, and Vehnek felt the hairs on the back of his neck stand up. His warrior's instinct recognised the entity as a threat as it drew close, sending a tingle down his arms and to his fingertips.

Mora leaned down and picked up the port bottle. She studied the dark-green glass, swirled the liquid around, sniffed the lip.

"Would you like a glass?" Vehnek asked with a steady voice.

Mora upended the bottle into her mouth, and swallowed enough of a mouthful for almost a measure and a half. Her eyes flitted around as she considered the sensation. The Colonel gaped at her.

"What an interesting ... drink. Like honey and lemons and summer fruits ... and fire." She smiled at Vehnek. "Like that ... wine we tried, but more."

"Much more." Vehnek gestured to a seat, but she ignored it and simply brushed her fingertips against the fruit in the bowl on the table, grapes and apples from the Idris plains.

"Oh ... I came in for a reason, didn't I," she muttered to herself. She unwrapped the silk bows around the parchment roll, and Vehnek cleared the table.

"This is dress-silk," the Colonel muttered, picking up one of the discarded bows.

"I ... enjoy the ... feel of it," Mora said as she unfurled the huge document on the table.

The map showed the edges of Cael and Salketh, but was dominated by the White Sea between them. The sands and arid mountains, the cracked canyons and dead plains stretched for nearly twelve hundred miles north to south. The Gravestone mountain dominated the landscape, almost five hundred miles north-northwest of Cael City. A lonely mountain, part of no range, taller than any other peak on the continent.

Mora's finger touched a point south west of the Gravestone, in and beside a long canyon that sliced through the desert.

"The Desert King's realm lies there," she said calmly. Her finger glowed for a moment, marking the point with a perfect, singed circle.

The Empire Of Fire

The Colonel grunted and shook his head. "There? That's closer to us than Salketh, that makes no-"

"The canyon was a river," Mora cut in, just as calmly. "He travelled down it with a fleet, until he reached a defensible point, where he stopped and built his kingdom."

"Lord Marshal ..." The Colonel began.

Vehnek held up a hand. "*You're certain?*"

Mora looked up at him in surprise and laughed in his face. "Feel free to deploy your silly, floating wooden barges to search elsewhere."

Vehnek flashed a scowl. "*I'm merely making sure. We've come far, and now we're on the brink.*"

"He is there, Vehnek."

He sat back with a smile. "*Pack what you need, Colonel. We leave as soon as all are prepared. On your way out, send in Uvenk.*"

The Colonel looked from Mora to Vehnek with a frown. "*Are you certain about this?*"

"*Our time is shortening quickly, too quickly. We go now, or things will progress too far in the wrong direction.*"

The Colonel grunted and grumbled as he went to the door. Vehnek smiled and kissed Mora's hand, making her raise an eyebrow.

"What a strange gesture."

Vehnek snorted, leaned back with his glass of port, sipping the warm liquid and holding it in his mouth.

Uvenk strode in and crossed the room as if he were marching to war. Vehnek smiled to himself. The man was a seasoned, loyal aide, and he had been waiting for the order that was about to be given.

He stopped in front of the chairs and saluted.

Vehnek put down his glass. "Mobilise my ships from the Bay Of War. Squadrons one through nine are to rendezvous with the *Inquisitor* and our escorts above Cael City. Squadron ten are to pull south over the Scorpion's Tail with the *Annihilator*."

He stood. "Ten's orders are to burn the Wyvern Bog to a cinder, and eliminate that dragon. Leave none alive."

The Empire Of Fire

17

...following the incursion into the Old Town district, Black Fleet soldiers were confronted by a force of Victory City Guards at the temple to the Haaman Gods, commanded directly by Defense Minister Levez. Once informed of the order to eliminate the terrorist forces using the temple as a stronghold and hiding place, Levez's men engaged ours, and were beaten back. Information was subsequently recovered in the remains of the terrorist stronghold that the Defense Minister had been a long-term informant for the terrorists, which is to bolster further investigations into the City Guard's inability to apprehend the criminal leaders.

Motions have been set forth to posthumously strip Defense Minster Levez of her honours and titles, with all property and land passing into possession of Black Fleet administrative services until agreement is reached over the...

Allessandra slammed the report down on her desk and glared up at First Minister Evandro and General Kelad. Evandro had turned an angry shade of light purple, while Kelad was silently looking down at the desk.

"*This is an utter travesty,*" Allessandra spat.

"*I'm afraid that there is very little we can do on an official basis to deny or block this report, Your Grace,*" Evandro grunted. "*As you can see on the final pages, there are a number of eyewitnesses to this, many of them in the Black Fleet. Even members of the citizenry are named.*"

Allessandra rubbed her head, knocking her hand on the table to punctuate her words. "*But is there any concrete proof? What about this so-called 'evidence'? Has it been verified as legitimate?"*

"*Not by us,*" Kelad muttered. "*They have yet to release it or even a copy of it.*"

Evandro smiled tightly. "*Other witnesses are another matter entirely. There have been a few that have approached us, they're currently in the palace.*"

Allessandra looked up at him in surprise. "*When did this happen?*"

"*A little under a day before this report was even published, Your Grace.*"

Kelad patted the older man on the chest with the most genuine smile he had ever given to a politician. "*Well played.*"

"*People have been very quick to come forwards. The Temple To The Gods was in a very public square, almost as large as the Old Town Markets. There was no way they could have conducted their attack cleanly. Many civilians were killed that night, in the square and the temple.*" Evandro looked up. "*Allegedly.*"

Allessandra smiled at him, and nodded. "*We need to get our hands on that evidence.*"

Kelad shook his head. "*There's no point, Your Grace. It doesn't exist.*"

"*How can you be sure?*"

"*While I am no expert in the arcane, I have had more experience than anyone within a hundred miles when it comes to conjured fire. That temple wasn't set ablaze with oil and pitch. Conjured fire doesn't leave much, it melts stone. Any paper or parchment would combust within a fraction of a second.*"

Allessandra folded her arms. "*So this is?*"

Evandro nodded his head. "*Misdirection. Perhaps the architect of this report knows that our first instinct would be to defend Levez's name. It seems to have been specifically curated for the Council of Ministers and the higher ups in the Standing Army.*"

Kelad nodded. "*In a game of cards, you don't play the cards, you play the player. Something big is about to happen.*"

Allessandra rubbed her head. "*On the verge of peace. Vehnek seems to be making his move.*" She rested a hand on the piles of paper on the desk, dozens of reports and census documents, territorial maps and scouting records. It was all part of the recipe that was meant to create a beautiful meal that everyone could eat and not spit out in disgust.

"*Are you both ready for our preliminary discussions with the Alliance?*"

Kelad shifted his weight. "*I'm afraid my reading has been a little limited, Your Grace. I have been somewhat preoccupied, and I wouldn't count on my presence at the negotiations.*"

Allessandra's heart sank. "*I ... see.*"

"*Yourself and The First Minister are more than well-equipped. I have every faith in you both.*"

"*They know you, Kelad ... they trust you ...*"

Kelad grinned. "*Well ... I wouldn't go that far.*"

"*You fought beside them, they don't know me or Evandro.*"

"*Thomas does.*"

"*We will be fine, Your Grace,*" Evandro reassured. "*We are all in the same situation. Peace has never been considered before. No-one seems to know how to move forwards.*"

Kelad smiled at her. "*Project strength and honesty. Assure them that you believe what you believe. You are a symbol of peace, at least that's how people in this city consider you. The First Minister has the experience of negotiations with foreign powers. I would wager there are few better than the two of you together for this particular task.*"

Allessandra blinked at him and exhaled slowly. His words were kind, they seemed genuine, but she felt the pressure on her increase.

"*Has your envoy returned?*" Evandro asked.

"*The skiff returned this morning. There has been an agreement on what would constitute neutral territory.*" Kelad unfurled one of the maps and pointed to an area in the Dividing Sea. It was off the north-western coastline of Haama, midway between Haama and Cael, at the mouth of the Meladrin Ocean.

Allessandra nodded. "*Well, we'll have some striking scenery. Perhaps a little perspective, both nations should be visible if the weather is clement."*

"*And if the ocean is clement,*" Evandro said with a smile.

"*I don't think it would be a good idea to go there on a battleship.*"

Kelad nodded. "*Agreed. Alternate transport has been arranged by Carrasco.*"

She leaned back in her chair. "*Well then ... I suppose all I have to do now is keep reading, and hope that our good friend Vehnek decides not to ruin everything.*"

There was a sharp knock at the door.

"*Enter.*"

Eluco came in and marched to the desk. He saluted Kelad, and bowed to Allessandra and Evandro. "*Pardon the interruption, Your Grace. There are two matters that require your attention. Long-distance communication has been restored.*"

She exchanged a look with Kelad. "*That was fast work.*"

"*Well, when you have arcane engineers that are pulling their weight ...*" Eluco muttered. "*The ones Vehnek assigned were taking their time.*"

Kelad chuckled. Eluco bobbed his head. "*I agree, General. However there is more. There is evidence that Black Fleet troops were-*"

"*Present at the massacre,*" the General finished, his voice deliberately monotonous.

"*Give the General and First Minister all of your evidence, Eluco,*" Allessandra commanded. "*This is more their area than mine, and they will be the first response to him in the coming days.*"

"*Of course, Your Grace.*"

She looked at everyone present. "*I think we adjourn there for the moment. Is there anything else?*"

Evandro and Kelad shook their heads, but Eluco remained hovering. "*Yes, Your Grace. The palace doctor is here to see you.*"

Kelad raised an eyebrow and glanced at the princess.

"*Thank you, Eluco. A simple check-up, General. No need to be concerned."*

The General bowed with a grin. *"When it comes to you, Your Grace, asking me to be unconcerned is akin to asking a boulder to weep."*

Once they had departed, Eluco led Doctor Tevos into the chamber. The Caelish physician had been in service to Allessandra and the Council Of Ministers for six years. She was a tall woman, who had gradually become more plump as the summers had passed. Her manner had always been kindly and professional, endlessly patient when dealing with difficult politicians or stubborn teenage girls.

Eluco bowed and left them to their privacy.

"How are you feeling, Your Grace?"

Allessandra smiled and shrugged with a quiet breath. *"I'm well, thank you. There has been some pain in my stomach, and I admit I am exhausted, although given recent events..."*

Tevos smiled. *"I understand that the Black Fleet and the Royal Family have been keeping you busy."*

"Oh, not just them ... history is in the making, right now, as we speak. The pressure is somewhat ... firm."

"Indeed. Unprecedented peace in our time, potentially. Please disrobe, Your Grace."

Allessandra complied, shrugging off her dress but holding it around her waist with the decorative silk band that wove around her hips. Doctor Tevos unfastened and then removed the bandage that covered the slash wound across her belly. She hummed to herself thoughtfully.

"The inflammation has gotten more severe. Have you been applying the ointment?"

"I have ... although I may have missed one application the night of the fire. I'm not sure."

"Possibly due to stress ... but you must apply the ointment twice a day to keep it down. Has there been any pain?"

"When I bend, sometimes when I sleep in an awkward position on my

side. Getting in and out of the bath."

"Itching?"

"Oh, yes," Allessandra said emphatically.

"Weeping from the wound?"

"After I bathe, sometimes."

Tevos stood again. *"The skin seems to have almost healed over beneath the scab, finally. You should really have a trained attendant bathe you for the moment."*

"I ..." She held her tongue from the admission that she did not know who she could trust in these matters, with Vehnek's influence. *"If you have a recommendation for a specific attendant, I would be grateful. Someone who you have worked with for a long time."*

Tevos nodded. *"I have someone in mind. Does it hurt when you sit down?"*

"Not any more."

"Good. Let's sit."

Allessandra frowned. This was a new stage in Tevos's visits to her chambers. She nodded, and both of them sat on the couches placed by the window.

The doctor settled and drummed her fingers on the armrest. Allessandra peered at her as she gazed out of the window.

"I have spent the last two days examining your phial of blood. It shows signs that your body is fighting an infection."

Allessandra swallowed. *"I ... see. Is there medicine that would assist?"*

"To a degree. However, there is a chemical in your blood that should not be there ... and I cannot remove or nullify it with any of my equipment in the palace."

"Meaning?"

"There is a foreign presence in your body. It shows signs of infection, as I said, but it seems to be more resilient. It seems largely benign, but the swelling and inflammation around the scar suggests that it is becoming more

malignant."

"Doctor, I am not a professional. Please speak plainly."

Tevos leaned forwards, and took her hand. *"You are ill, Your Grace, and you will become progressively more ill if something is not done. Unfortunately ... there is nothing I can do. I can slow the progression of the illness ... but I cannot cure it."*

The confirmation of her fears was not as brutal an impact as she had feared it would be. The moment she had decided to venture into the city and put herself in danger, she had accepted the consequences. *"How long?"*

"I must run more tests, draw more blood to be sure. You are not in immediate danger ... as long as you keep rested and regulate your diet. Green vegetables, some red meat, water. Only very pure alcohol, no wine."

Allessandra smiled. *"Thank you, doctor. Please send the message to my cooks, and to the caterers. I need a stiff drink, I'm afraid, and I only have wine and port in the cabinet."*

Doctor Tevos squeezed her hand and smiled sadly. From her medicine pouch she withdrew a small bottle. It was a third the size of a wine flask, filled with a clear liquid, like the purest water from an untouched mountain stream.

Tevos took two small glasses from the cabinet and filled them. *"Have you tried this before?"*

"No."

"It is Noorani ice wine, although it isn't actually wine ... or made of ice for that matter. It is made with potatoes, I believe."

Allessandra wrinkled her nose. *"Potatoes?"*

Tevos raised her glass and smiled. *"To your health, Your Grace. May you remain strong."*

"To your expertise, doctor."

The moment the liquid touched her tongue, it felt like she had put a snowflake in her mouth. It tasted like water mixed with salt and sugar, sharp yet sweet. It should have burned when she swallowed it, but instead it tingled gently.

"I could quickly get used to this."

"No more than three glasses a day, Your Grace," Tevos murmured. *"It is stronger than it appears ... much like yourself."*

A smile died on Allessandra's lips as quickly as it was born. *"Just not in body."*

Tevos looked away. *"I promise you ... I will leave no stone unturned. I will raise this with the Magus Towers, with doctors across the world if I have to."*

Allessandra finished the glass. *"Be careful what you say if you do, doctor. Especially now ... there are important days ahead. Do not mention my name."* She put the glass down. *"In fact ... it might be better if you do nothing at all. Continue to work on it yourself."*

Doctor Tevos said nothing for a moment, before draining her own glass. She swallowed, breathing slowly, before looking up at her.

"Your Grace ..." she began. She put the glass down on the table and began wringing her hands. *"If you are not treated ... it may not matter how well you regulate your diet, or what medicine I give you. If it progresses and spreads faster than the treatment ... it will kill you."*

Allessandra nodded. *"I understand. However ... there are more important things than my life. Far more. My duty is one of them."*

Tevos opened her mouth to speak, perhaps as a counter, but the words died quickly. She pursed her lips, perhaps in disapproval, perhaps holding back an emotion. *"As you say, Your Grace."*

***

Vehnek's uniform was pressed and devoid of creases. Spotless, every button polished. The thin layer of armour beneath it was barely noticeable; his second skin. His sword was sheathed and ready, fixed to his back with a harness of black studded leather.

He studied himself in the dress-mirror in his chamber. Almost

The Empire Of Fire

immaculate. He straightened his collar, and watched Mora as she watched him, her eyes quietly amused.

"Why bother with the fancy clothing?" she wondered. "Why so clean and formal? It will only become dirty, won't it?"

"Appearances," he muttered. "I'm the Lord Marshal of the Caelish Armed forces. I have to look like this."

Mora snorted. "You have strange priorities."

In truth, polishing his uniform had given him something to do, something to busy his hands with while he considered what was coming. Part of him was excited at the coming of a new dawn, another terrified of the implications of that breaking sunshine.

Cael would never be the same. They would be a power unlike any other time in history, at least militarily. Haama would be folded into the new, invincible nation, allowing the starving to migrate and farm the lands. The Magus Towers and Haama's magic resources would be dedicated to the problems of the desert and the dragonfire corrupted land ... and they would have a fresh dragon corpse to study. The country would heal, eventually, and in the meantime, they would be strong enough to dissuade any threats.

Mokku would react as poorly as ever to the threat. The swallowing of Haama would certainly cause a ripple in the other nations. Public opinion would turn against them, but it was already against them, it always had been. This would be different ... it would be borne of terror, the terror of winged oblivion swooping down on them from above the clouds. He was confident he could easily turn Salketh against the Mokkan dark-skins, Tyrana as well. Both were too close to Cael for their own comfort. Noor would remain as neutral as they always had, stubbornly fortified in the snow and ice. Adrezsti would likely join with Mokku, they would have little choice. They were right in arms reach of the hungry, grasping, black hands of the Mokkan military.

Perhaps the threat to their power would force the Mokkan Ruling Elders to give Cael better trade terms. Maybe a grudging peace treaty would force respect, a few favourable marriages would solidify somewhat of a partnership, but it would certainly not last. Mokku's spies and stolen riches bought off many people in power, and a peace would give them time to quietly buy off the nations around Cael, buy off Ministers, insist that they want a seat at every table they could sit at.

Then Cael would be all but lost. No ... better to strike first.

The dragons would sweep down from above the clouds and smoke, incinerate the elite before they could scramble a defense. Mokku would be leaderless and rudderless, and would fall into chaos. Perhaps another attack to destroy military strongholds. Destroy trade. Destroy farmland. Let the darkskins eat each other in the chaos.

He smiled to himself and stood up straight. That would be his legacy, one that would dwarf those of his forebears.

"You will have a visitor," Mora muttered. Her eyes were closed, a smile was tugging at her lips. A moment later, there was a swirl of smoke beside the door, and Kelad gave a half bow.

"*Good day, Lord Marshal.*"

"*Ah, Sel. I trust you are well.*"

"*I am, especially now my suspicions have been confirmed.*" He grinned at Vehnek's uniform, striding across the room, circling Mora. Her eyes followed him with a raised eyebrow and smile that was almost sultry.

"*If I may say so, you look like a couple preparing to be married. You are a picture of beauty, Mora.*"

"I ... appreciate the compliment ... General," she said, her eyes locked on his.

"*Unfortunately, I know Morad very well, and I know he isn't the marrying type.*" Kelad focused on Vehnek. "*Very well presented. Your medals?*"

"*They'll stay un-pinned.*"

"*Ah ...*" Kelad's black eyes seemed to shine. "*When are the fleet deploying?*"

"*Tomorrow at dawn.*"

The Empire Of Fire

Kelad chuckled. "*I see ... that would mean ... before sunset today. Perhaps within the hour.*"

Vehnek glared at him, but ended up returning the grin. "*Here to see me off, old man?*"

"*Here to join you, actually.*"

Mora snorted. Kelad turned his head towards her slightly. "*You are an intelligent, beautiful woman, Mora, but you are not practiced in politics.*" His eyes refocused on Vehnek.

"*I told you, I'm loyal to you. That loyalty is not shaken.*"

"*I bet.*" Vehnek muttered. "*You're too slippery for your own good, Sel. You're like oil.*"

"*Full of energy? Vital for the operation of complex machinery?*"

Vehnek turned from the mirror. "*Like I said: slippery.*"

"*I have a fleet ready to join you.*"

Vehnek snorted. "*I wouldn't call your meagre forces a fleet. Certainly not the ones here.*"

Kelad raised an eyebrow and cocked his head. One battleship and seven skiffs were under his immediate command. There were far more in the Standing Aerial Navy across the sea at the Bay Of War, but they would take time to deploy.

"*Well, more fast support wouldn't be a detriment, would it? Certainly not another battleship. You forget your enemy, Morad, but then again, you haven't faced them.*"

"*And who would my enemy be?*"

"*The wyvernborn, of course. They are certainly your most immediate threat. Them, and their dragon. You'll need my forces, because they've seen what you'll be up against. They'll be far better when it comes to fighting them, and consider this: wyvernborn are very swift in the air. More skiffs will, in fact, be an asset ...*" Kelad shrugged. "*But I can stay here if you wish. You'll lose a lot of your force without me, more than half for sure. Perhaps you'll still prevail.*"

Vehnek searched him for a lie. Mora was watching them both with that same, quizzical smile. Kelad spread his hands. *"When have I ever steered you wrong, Morad?"*

"Your song and dance with the princess and the Council Of Ministers is more than a bane."

"Oh come now, you're smarter than that. Those terrorists have a dragon, *for Va'Kael's sake. They have the wyvernborn on their side, very impressive warriors. They have stolen airships. Do you think I am stupid enough to not recognise a clear threat?"*

Vehnek held his old friend's gaze. *"Hmm... very good. This peace treaty is a ruse, then. Is that right?"*

"Lull them into a false sense of security. Tame the lamb, feed it, nurture it, then cut its throat as it cuddles up to you with love. But these aren't lambs. They're wyvernborn. They're a menace. They've been a menace since their strange, twisted creation, however it came to pass. They can't be controlled, by force or by allegiance ... and that silly, perfumed girl wants to negotiate with them." Kelad snorted and shook his head. *"There is so much blood between us and those terrorists, and those wyvernborn, there won't be any successful treaties. Even if Allessandra manages to come to some kind of agreement, the wyvernborn won't honour it. They believe they're better than us."*

"The fabled Dragon's Arrogance, hmm?"

"We'd be opening ourselves to complacency, that they would use to harass and reave, take inch by inch. They're not unlike the Mokkans in that regard. Shadow-walkers."

Vehnek glanced at Mora, who was brushing her fingertips over the map that remained unfurled on the table. Without looking up, she spoke. "If he wishes to join the attack on the Wyvern Bog, let him. You will have a greater force than his, so any treachery will be very short-lived. Besides ... he will certainly not be leading the attack."

Kelad bobbed his head. *"A sensible precaution."*

Vehnek stared at him coldly. *"Betrayal would be very unwise. Now more than ever. I promise you, it won't be forgotten."*

Kelad bowed his head. *"On his deathbed, I promised your father that I would watch over you. I promised your grandfather the same, before every battle he and I fought in side by side. That promise binds me to your safety and well-being. It binds me to your side. Promises to two men, two good friends, before witnessing their last breath of this mortal existence."*

His eyes were wide, intense, and furious as he locked his gaze with Vehnek's. *"You question my loyalty to you and our nation far too often. Never do it again."*

***

Allessandra watched as every airship gradually disappeared from Victory's skyline, leaving the ruin they had wrought in their wake.

The Black Fleet and Kelad's ships had left together, side by side as allies. Had the General betrayed her? She didn't know, but she suspected she would find out fairly quickly.

She held the communication stone close to her chest. It wasn't as warm as it had been when she used it before, the magic held within it was close to running out.

"Captain Seret, are you there?"

After a moment, the captain's relieved voice practically screamed at her from the stone. *"Allessandra! Are you alright?"*

The princess smiled to herself, and put a hand on her chest. *"I'm fine, Seret, I'm fine. Are you and your crew? I heard that you put the Sand Dancer through her paces, somewhat."*

There was a short pause. *"Yes ... well it was quite the surprise for me as well."*

"Are you all in one piece?"

"Yes, we're fine. We're all fine ... we were well protected by the warriors on board. Your Grace ..."

Allessandra bit her lip. "*Seret ... listen. This isn't a social call, and I don't think this stone has much left in it. Vehnek's ships left the city, heading north. Kelad's with him. I don't know where they're going but I doubt it's anywhere good.*"

"*I understand,*" Seret said, her tone immediately businesslike. "*I'll let them know here ... but the negotiations ...*"

"*I'm not planning to cancel them. Are our friends?*"

"*No. Allessandra, watch yourself. This could get nasty ... apologies in advance if the Sand Dancer gets any scratches.*"

The stone's glow ebbed away, and Allessandra put it back in its hiding place, secreted away in the drinks cabinet. She rubbed her face and sighed. As she padded across the room, the door to her chamber opened. Eluco strode in, taking two steps, his eyes scanning around, hand on the hilt of his sword.

Allessandra cocked her head at him. "*Since when did you stop knocking?*"

"*I heard voices,*" he said, slowly relaxing his posture.

"*You heard my voice. Come in, close the door.*"

Eluco shut the door behind him. She gestured for him to lock it, and he did so with a raised eyebrow. She lowered her voice. "*I was talking to Seret, letting her know about ...*" she gestured to the empty sky.

"*How is she?*"

"*Well, it seems. Drink?*"

"*I'm on duty ... but only for the next two minutes.*" He grinned, and she realised how much she had wanted to see that smile. It had been a rough day, a bleak day, although perhaps it was the final day of rain before the spring bloom.

Allessandra moved across to the cabinet again and took out the Noorani liquor that the doctor had prescribed to her. Eluco frowned. "*No port?*"

She hesitated before pouring. "*I've gone off the port, I'm afraid. Would you prefer it?*"

"*Most drink of any nature suits me, it comes with the soldiery. I was just *under the impression that it was your favourite, Tyranian especially."*

"Well ... I suppose it was, for a time."

She poured the clear liquid into a pair of small, narrow stem glasses. Eluco sniffed it. *"Is this ice wine?"*

"Yes. Have you had it before?"

"A few times, when I was stationed at the ports. Traders from Noor used to bring a few cases for the taverns and eateries. It's been a while."

"I didn't realise you'd been out there."

"Hmm, a year in each. It was good work, mostly standing close to trade disputes and looking like we'd intervene. Barely any trouble at the ports, I suppose because everyone's on their best behaviour."

Allessandra rubbed her hands together. *"It must have been fascinating, being around so many different kinds of people."*

"I suppose," he shrugged. *"I doubt it's much different to being here when foreign dignitaries visit."*

She snorted and waved her hand. *"They're politicians, all only slight variations on a theme. They're after their own interest, hiding knives behind smiles, maddeningly and falsely polite, and so on. They're ... we're not normal people ... we're very specifically worse."*

Eluco chuckled. *"I don't know ... some of you don't seem so bad."*

"You didn't know me a year ago."

"Well ... it was interesting, yeah. Taverns are the best place to people-watch and meet, I don't suppose you go to many."

"No, not so many," she replied wryly. *"Perhaps we should go to one. There must be a few lively places in the city."*

Eluco laughed. *"There are a few, although they'd probably start behaving themselves if you came in."*

"A disguise, then."

"Last time you disguised yourself and went on an adventure in the city I had to rescue you."

Allessandra turned away, her smile faltering. *"So you did."*

"*I'm sorry, Your Grace. I didn't mean to drag it up ...*"

"*No, it's ... it's alright.*"

She listened to his footsteps as he drew closer to her, until he was half a foot away. She could see him in the corner of her eye.

"*If you're serious about heading to a tavern, there is one that you might enjoy in Breaker's Bay.*"

She forced herself to smile. "*Oh?*"

"*Hmm, it's on the north-west coast, right on the edge of town on a rise. It's a lighthouse, really, but the bottom floors were built out into a public house. It overlooks the repair stations and the standard docks, people like to go up there to watch the ships come and go, sea and air both.*"

"*What's it called?*" she murmured, her voice seeming far away to her ears. *What's it called, this place I probably won't live to see?*

"*The Lighthouse, for obvious reasons. They have drinks from all over the world, and food too. The crews tend to go there all the time, probably to get a taste of home. So many of them have been away for months, even years. Here.*"

She looked around at him. Eluco was holding one of the small glasses out to her. She took it, and clinked it gently against his. He drank all of his in one go, but she sipped. The taste had been pleasant before, but now it was bitter in her mouth, burning in her throat.

"*Are you sure you've got a taste for this stuff?*"

She didn't answer, but finished it in a single, acrid gulp.

"*Allessandra, are you alright?*"

She must have taken too long to answer, because one of his hands rested between her shoulder blades. It was warm against her bare skin, and it seemed to rouse her.

"*Many things hang on the next few days,*" she murmured. "*Maybe our very survival, and even if we are successful, the Lord Marshal might take actions that render our peacemaking moot.*"

"*We can try, I don't think there's much more than that.*" He was quiet for a moment, perhaps considering that he was touching her in a manner that would have ensured the removal of his hand, had the wrong people seen him. "*The General left with him.*"

"*I know. Did he say anything to you?*"

"*No. What would he say to me? I'm a glorified City guardsman in his eyes.*"

Allessandra closed her eyes with a sigh. His hand stroked upwards to her shoulder and held her there gently. She turned to him with the words caught in her throat.

Eluco's brow furrowed. "*There's more to it, though, isn't there.*"

"*It's ... with everything going on, it's selfish. There are bigger things to worry about than me.*"

"*Not to me.*"

Her eyes met his. A smile sprouted on his lips. "*I am charged with your safety, after all.*"

Allessandra couldn't return the expression. "*Doctor Tevos visited.*"

He nodded. "*I know.*"

"*I am ... ill.*"

Eluco's smile vanished. "*The scar?*"

She nodded. "*The doctor who treated me, the one you took me to, warned me it could happen. It was the medication he used. Doctor Tevos told me that it has begun to have a more pronounced effect on me.*"

"*How bad is it?*"

She attempted to keep herself together, and mostly succeeded. "*I may well be dying.*"

Now that the words had been said, it was as if they energised her every muscle, every nerve. She reared up, and turned to face him.

Eluco was staring at her in disbelief. "*You can't be.*"

"*Two doctors have presented me with the same probability. I could doubt one, maybe. I can't doubt two.*"

"*But ...*" His expression changed as his mind seemed to sift through the possibilities open to her. She reached out and held his hands.

"There's no getting around it."

He sighed angrily, and his jaw set. "*So ... what are you going to do?*"

She actually laughed out loud at the question, taking herself by surprise. "*Carry on. What else can I do? What else matters, except them?*" Allessandra gestured at the ruined city below them.

"*What about you?*"

"*I'm not important.*"

"*Yes, you are.*"

"*Eluco ...*" She let go of him and stepped away, leaning on the windowsill. "*I'm not important. I'm not anything, really, just a person with a fortunate birthright. There are no children I'll leave without a mother. Very few friends who I can trust any more, now that I know how many of them were only here for my influence, for my status, or my favour. My family are across the sea, and they may be no better than the false friends. My mother is explicitly against me, I doubt she will have any inclination to weep over my coffin. I'm alone, in a hostile land, on the verge of a conflict that will destroy it or leave it a slave. Even if things go right ... go the way I hope in my dreams ... I won't see the fruits of it. I won't see this place become what it could ... I may not even see the city rebuilt.*"

Her eyes were streaming, but her voice never wavered. "*There have been hundreds of things, thousands even, that I have taken for granted. Things I've wanted to do, places I've wanted to go, that I will never see. And I wonder if ...*" She gritted her teeth. "*I've known that this was a possibility since I got that scar in the first place, and I wonder if that's why I'm so quick to believe that Thomas and his friends are genuine, why I've been so quick to trust Kelad. I've committed treason twice in a very short time. I can't help but wonder if I'm still that same young fool, that same stupid girl I used to be.*"

"*No, you're not. You've been far from a fool in the time I've known you, except in the way we met, maybe. You've been strong enough to do what you have to do, and smart enough to not make things worse.*"

"*Look at that city, Eluco,*" she whispered. "*It got so much worse.*"

The Empire Of Fire

"*It didn't get worse because of you. You actually care about people, and not because it's easy, or because it makes you look good. Lesser people would only care about how seeming to care might benefit themselves. Faced with this news, lesser people would think they had nothing to lose. They would think about the short term, paper solutions to cover problems the size of canyons. They would think about their legacy, perhaps, with the ruling classes. You're only thinking about how to make things better for the people who matter, the people who look to you.*" Eluco walked forwards and stood beside her. "*You asked questions that no other Regent or Minister asked, because the answers would put them in the eyeline of dangerous people. You took actions that no-one else tried. You took the initiative to see uncomfortable truths ... no matter the cost.*"

He took her hand tightly. "*Allessandra, you have no idea how much that means to people like me. I didn't think I'd see it in my lifetime.*"

"See what?"

"*Someone in your position that ... cares. That listens. That doesn't turn a blind eye to the wrongs that people commit, that aren't intimidated by Lord Marshal Vehnek, or anyone else.*"

She looked at him with a sad smile. "*You're wrong about that, Eluco ... I'm terrified of him, of what he could do.*"

"*He won't get anywhere near you. Not while I breathe.*"

She took him in, the earnestness of his words, the strength and warmth of his hand, the falling sunlight turning him a purer gold than the Royal Guards.

"*Take off your armour.*"

Eluco raised one eyebrow, then both of them. "*What?*"

"*You heard me.*"

"*Are you...*"

She stood on her tiptoes and grabbed hold of his neck, pressing her lips against his. Eluco needed no more than that. He swept her into his arms immediately, and carried her to the bed.

18

At the break of dawn, Eluco kissed Allessandra awake, and the pair got ready for the most important day of their lives.

Allessandra chose a dress of simple elegance for the negotiations themselves, hem an inch above her ankles, the colours white with golden weaving. Her shoulders remained bare, but she chose a light blue sash to wrap around herself for a little warmth. The sea breezes would be brisk. Eluco donned his armour once more, and left to return to his own chamber in the palace barracks. When he returned, he had his helm with him, as well as a golden cloak, the same weaving as the Royal Guards.

"*Are you ready?*"

She took a deep breath, and nodded.

A contingent of Royal Guardsmen met them on the palace roof, along with First Minister Eluco, as well as Carrasco and Brynden. As Ministers for both Foreign and Haaman Cultural Affairs, the negotiations concerned them as much as they concerned Allessandra.

"Good morning, gentlemen," she said in Haaman, her tone formal.

All three of the Ministers bowed. "*It is an exciting day, for sure,*" Evandro said warmly. "*I am looking forward to getting started.*"

Allessandra smiled at him. "In Haaman, First Minister. Likely our negotiations will not be in Caelish."

She looked pointedly at Carrasco, and shot a clandestine wink at the beaming Brynden.

"I couldn't agree more," the rotund Haaman Minister chuckled, jowls jiggling with mirth. "The noun to verb forms in Caelish are a nightmare, I've never been able to get my head around them."

The Empire Of Fire

"Conjugating verbs in Haaman is impossible, Bryn'," Carrasco muttered.

"I am forced to agreement," Evandro said with a nod, then thought for a moment. "Force to agreed?"

"Forced to agree," Allessandra stage-whispered. "This is why you need the practice."

Evandro coughed and straightened up. "As you spea ... say, Your Grace."

She smiled at him, then cast her eyes around at the skyline. A dot was approaching from the west. She squinted at it, unable to make it out. "Is that our transport?"

"Yes, Your Grace." Carrasco's voice was smooth as he stepped forwards. "One of mine, from the trading fleet: *Mira's Favour*. You'll find her most agreeable."

"She certainly has an agreeable name." Queen Mira was one of the most accomplished rulers of Cael, presiding over a golden age of the nation. She had been the first queen, in the days when there had only been kings.

"I must admit ... there are days where you make me think of her, Your Grace," Carrasco murmured.

"Flattery will not get you as far as you think, Carrasco."

"It may seem like flattery, I assure you it's simply the truth. The people seem to love you, in their vast majority, and history hasn't given that same favour to many rulers in the past. Your father, perhaps."

"We'll see."

The airship was pulling closer to them. It was a wide, long vessel, almost as large as the *Sovereign*. There were four banks of sails on the top and on the sides of the hull, moving more quickly than any ship its size should have been able to. The largest sails were at the front, getting smaller the further back they went. As it got closer, its shape became more defined, wider at the front and narrowing the further back it went.

"Built for speed in strong winds," Carrasco muttered. "Experimental design. Needs refinement, but when it isn't fully laden it goes at quite the clip."

"Clip?"

"A Haaman idiom. It's fast, Your Grace."

The airship slowed as the crew trimmed its sails and it dropped lower, hanging at the edge of the roof. There were shouted orders on the deck, and a wide boarding ramp was slung out. Flags were raised on the masts, the symbol of the diplomatic core: two joined hands in gold on a white background, and the symbol of the Caelish Royal Family: the serpent wrapped around the pyramid, with a golden crown on its head.

"Good luck, Your Grace," Carrasco said, clasping her hand. "Brynden and I will be minding Victory while you are away."

"Then the city is in good hands." She shook his hand, and Brynden's.

"We are ready for the worst, but I'm confident it won't come," Brynden said solemnly. "At their base, you have to believe they are good people, forced into hardship and rage, because that is what *they* believe."

"Agreed, but don't excuse them for their rage," Carrasco muttered. "They will not excuse ours."

Brynden bobbed his head. "Yes, I think that's just as important, perhaps more so. It may be a painful day in many ways, Your Grace, but the pain will be a release."

"Hopefully then the healing can begin." She took their hands again for a moment. "Look after the city."

"We will, Your Grace."

Eluco led the way up the boarding ramp onto the huge vessel, with two Royal Guards on either side of him. Allessandra followed, with Evandro beside her. The rest of the guards, as well as Jenifer, followed behind them. When they reached the deck, the ship's captain had all the crew arranged in rows. All knelt as Allessandra's foot touched the wooden planks.

They were a mixture of Haamans, Caelish, even a few Mokkans and stocky, pale Noorani who were a head taller than everyone else. The majority were men, with a few in their early teens and others perhaps even their seventies. All wore a light blue uniformed shirt over black trousers, loose fitting and comfortable.

The youngest among them was a boy of eleven or twelve, staring at Allessandra while everyone else's heads were bowed in deference. She grinned at him, and the man next to him leaned over and whispered in his ear. The boy looked down quickly.

"Arise," Allessandra said warmly. "Thank you for the warm welcome, Captain, although the formality isn't necessary."

The ship's captain had a red collar and jacket over his uniform. He was a young Haaman man, handsome, with sandy blonde hair and a quick smile. He rose to his feet smoothly and confidently. "We wouldn't have welcomed you any other way, Your Grace. Welcome aboard *Mira's Favour*."

"Minister Carrasco and I were just complimenting the name."

The captain smiled. "I'm Tiberius, Your Grace, of the Cael/Haama Trade Association. I'm honoured that your talks will take place aboard our vessel."

"Thank you for hosting us, Captain Tiberius."

He bowed, and shifted his focus to Evandro. "First Minister, welcome aboard."

Evandro cleared his throat. "Thank you, Captain."

They shook hands warmly. Tiberius smiled. "Well, we had better get underway." He turned and raised his voice. "All crew to your stations!"

Almost as one entity, the crew stood and surged around the deck, moving down hatches into the bowels of the ship, climbing up onto the crow's nest, unfurling the sails.

"Clear all moorings and retract the ramp!" Tiberius ordered. He turned back again to the princess and her party. "Would you like a tour of the ship, Your Grace?"

"I would, once we're underway."

***

Mira's Favour was indeed an impressive craft. Its huge generator spanned four decks, and there was enough cargo space to transport everything in the Silver Throne Palace's stores, as well as all the furniture. The crew were deferential as they passed, well drilled in their decorum, although Allessandra had no doubt they were every bit the airman or sailor when she was out of earshot.

Captain Tiberius remained as courteous as their first meeting throughout the tour and beyond it. He offered Allessandra, Evandro, Jenifer and Eluco a breakfast in his cabin of his best provisions: grilled slivers of fresh beef and lamb, eggs boiled to perfection, delicate fruits from the farmland of Noor, Haama and Salketh, along with a herbal tea that Evandro had brought with him as a gift to the captain, as was tradition in the merchant navy.

The captain regaled them with tales of voyages across the world: encounters with brigands and mercenaries, great storms that they had navigated by sea and air. There was even an outlandish tale among the adventures: that of a great green hand that had risen from the sea to snatch at *Mira's Favour*. It had turned out to be the algae and seaweed covered hand of a great statue that had been covered by the oceans near to Valern, an island to the north of Old Esca. Perhaps a people even older than the Escans had walked the ocean floor in eons past, but when Tiberius had flown back over the area, there had been nothing but glittering, blue ocean below.

Eluco had snorted at this, and had told his own tales of law enforcement, and even some of his exploits as a close guard to the princess.

Not the most recent one, though, she thought to herself with a smile, a smile which her loyal protector caught with a grin of his own.

After the meal, they retired to their quarters, where they could prepare. At least one night would be spent aboard, even if the negotiations were swift. Allessandra hadn't packed more than one change of clothes, but Tiberius assured her that one of the Mages aboard could attend to more delicate clothing than their uniforms with magic, an offer extended to all in the princess's party.

Once their sleeping arrangements were established and their belongings stored, Evandro requested that they view the cabin aboard where the negotiations would take place. It seemed to be an officers' lounge of sorts, arranged for comfort mainly. With Captain Tiberius's permission, which he seemed bemused to give to the leader of Haama's governing council and the heir to Cael's throne, they began to rearrange the room for the talks.

The polished oak table was moved aside, and a lower one was placed in the centre of the room, one where refreshments could be placed.

"We want as little a wall as possible between the delegations," Evandro explained.

"A barrier, I understand," Allessandra muttered. "Why have a table at all in that case?"

"Because concessions must be make on all sides, Your Grace." Evandro thought for a moment. "Made on all sides."

Allessandra nodded with an encouraging smile. Evandro nodded to himself and continued. "With no barrier at all, one side will be overtake ... overtaken. We want the best outcome for Cael and Haama both."

Eluco and some of the crew moved the more comfortable chairs around the table in a circle, to project the image that there were not two sides in a conflict, but one side working on a resolution to a problem with equal say. The ship's cook was tasked with preparing food and drink from both Cael and Haama, and with what little knowledge they had, from Orlin and the Wyvern Bog. Drink was far easier, the wyvernborn aside. They had no time to prepare the fermented goat milk they drank in celebration. In fact, they didn't even have any milk aboard Mira's Favour, for it spoiled too quickly.

Around the table and chairs, the walls of the cabin were carefully adorned in what iconography they had for both Haama and Cael. Images of Queen Mira and the current Royal couple, with the child Allessandra between them. A tapestry of the old Melida City, a painting of the Four Guardians facing off against the black dragon of Cael. The Song Of The Four Guardians was also framed, the entirety of the epic poem that had been banned many times. One of the crew had been keeping a copy of it, and only turned it over to them with a barrage of anger and curses. Allessandra had personally convinced him that they would only have it for the negotiation, and assured him that she had no intention of confiscating it or worse. Evandro had balked at her with his eyes, but he deferred. The poem was, after all, one of the most important cultural creations in Haama's history.

Now, after fixing it into three separate frames and accepting Captain Tiberius's sincere apology for his crewman's words, Allessandra had picked out a place for it beside the tapestry, and began to read.

She had read through it twice before Evandro cleared his throat behind her. She turned around, to see him looking at the poem with disapproval.

"What is it, First Minister?"

"I am not agree with this being on display."

Allessandra raised an eyebrow at him. "I'm sorry ... what did you say?"

Evandro paused for a moment, considering whether he had stepped past his bounds, but rolled his eyes when he realised what he had said. "I am not agreed with this po-"

"Evandro ... you want the opposite of agree? Disagree."

"I am disagree with -"

"No, no ... not *am*. I disagree. Your name is Evandro, not Disagree."

Evandro threw up his hands and cursed in Caelish. Allessandra held up a hand. "It's alright ... you disagree with this poem being on display."

"Yes. It is a symbol of the Resistance, it has been used many times as a reason for crimes against us, it paints us as heartless, faceless invaders, as monsters, as ..."

Allessandra nodded, and held up a hand. "I know. It is ... certainly not an image we would want for ourselves, but it is the image we earned. It can be argued that it is exactly what we were."

"Next you'll bring up that damnable Castis Valar quote," he grumbled.

"That fits too well with us as well ... or rather it did. Have you read it?"

"The poem? Of course not, it wasn't just banned for the Haamans."

Allessandra guided him forwards with a hand. "Consider it practice."

Evandro grumbled to himself, and read the first lines to himself. He

The Empire Of Fire
clenched his jaw and glanced at her, before clearing his throat.
He began reading aloud:

"'The rumblings came from across the sea,
Lands of sand and Kings and Queens,
The sharp'ning of blades, gnashing of teeth,
And the roar of a beast that no soul had seen.

Great friends we were in long decades past.
Before the sands swept over grass
Before starving voices screamed their last
Before the slow drum of rage beat too fast.

Gradually words lost mirth and laughter,
Voices of anger rose loudly,
Friendships forgotten, ever after,
Armour and blades would sing far more proudly.

Six decades passed of bitter bloodshed,
Thrice did the Caelish cross the waves,
Smash'd through ports, farms, towns, and Haama bled
But Melida City beat back the knaves.

Melida City, her walls hardy
No army could breach her defense
Siege-fires and soldiers seemed foolhardy
And were destroyed by each counter-offense

Stopped at all turns, eyes looked to the East
Songs of warning in every tome
Told tales of lands devoid of all peace

Matt Waterhouse
Where monstrous evil was rumoured to roam

'Twas the Magi in their high tower
Hungry eyes on glitt'ring thrones
Plotting despite the peace that flowered
'Tween Haama and Cael, built on past war's bones..."'

Evandro stopped and sighed. "It's true. We were once allies, close allies, until the Great Drought."

Allessandra bobbed her head in a quick nod. "And these Magi, are they supposed to be the Arch Mages?"

"Yes. It was rumoured even before my time that they had long held influence over the Royal Family and the military. Logical, considering that their advancements are part of what has made us so formidable for so long. Weaponry, arcane engineering, medicine ..."

"Do they still?"

Evandro paused. "Your mother certainly ... forgive me, Your Grace, but your mother seems to have Lord Marshal Vehnek on her shoulder, and he is definitely in league with the Arch Mages. Miranda and Lucian are held in high esteem."

"And opposing Miranda led to an almost immediate restriction of me, and my influence."

The First Minister pursed his lips. "They lean on us from time to time ... which is why we supported them ... and they can be very convincing."

"Any wrongs of that nature are long forgiven, First Minister."

Evandro bowed his head, and refocused on the poem.

"'Fingertips reached past Dividing Sea,
Brushing the ports and Scorpion's Tail,
Probing for gaps in the plate and steel,
To land the boats of the legions of Cael.

The Empire Of Fire

> Haama countered with men of legend,
> Ranging beyond the soldiery,
> A well-forged spear, and at the sharp end,
> The Warrior, Archer, Mage, and The Beast.
>
> Four great Guardians against the horde,
> Sure to return in greater force,
> Facing the foes at home and abroad,
> Bracing the great gates and barring the doors.'"

Evandro leaned forwards at this, and read slowly.

> "'The strong Warrior, leading the charge
> The fair Archer, graceful as the breeze
> The wise Mage, with the power of stars
> The selfless Beast, of blades and sharp teeth.'"

Allessandra swept a stray strand of hair back behind her ear. "The Four Guardians ... and to think, I may have met one of them."

Evandro raised an eyebrow at her.

"The man who infiltrated the palace. Kelad spoke of The Mage as Thomas ... the same name the spy gave me."

Evandro scowled. "Then how are we suppose to trust these people?"

"It must be built, though ... I can understand them."

Thomas was trustworthy, she was sure of it now that the Pil Valley incident had been concluded. The rest also, perhaps.

Her thoughts turned to Vehnek, and the departure of his fleet, and she backed away from the poem, wandering over to the couches and sitting down.

"Your Grace?" Evandro said over his shoulder.

"Things seemed so promising ... and now they are in jeopardy. The

Black Fleet are ... somewhere, and Kelad went with them, what does that say to you?"

"He is obviously on the move, and it tells me that we must make ground here clearly and quickly. As for Kelad ... who knows? He's always been willful, although the Vehnek line has considerable power over him. After the Pil Valley, though ... perhaps he is a safeguard against rash action. Vehnek will listen to him."

Allessandra grunted. "He seems to hold a more feminine council these days than our friend the general, who don't seem to want peace in any shape or form." She looked around at the space where the future of two nations would be decided. "Is there anything else we missed?"

Evandro sighed to himself. "No ... I think we are as prepared as we could be. Now, all we have to do is read and keep reading."

***

Night fell, the words in the books and reports began to blur, and Allessandra wandered up to the top deck, watching Breaker's Bay pass below them.

Eluco, ever at her side, pointed out the tavern he had spoken of the night before. Pretty, of course, overlooking the town and the sea on the peninsula. The lighthouse blinked a signal to *Mira's Favour* as she passed, and one of the Mages on deck pulsed a conjured light in one hand in return.

The coastline became sea, and behind the sounds of the night crew bustling around was the whisper of the waves.

The curve of Planar lay before them, with no land in sight to the West. Cael wasn't even visible to the North as of yet, they would need to go higher. Such a huge space, that made the problems of the two nations and their people seem small. But, they were plenty large enough to matter, not just in their perspective, but in the perspective of the greater consciousness itself, whatever form that took. Va'Kael, or Haama's Gods, or Alvalon, the elder in eons past, or even the pantheon of deities that existed in the hearts of the Noorani, Salkethian and Adrezstian people.

She had never been one to believe or disbelieve, although her parents were as devout as it was possible to be. She looked up at the stars peeking out between the tufts of cloud, and wondered if anyone was watching ... and if so, how she would be judged. Va'Kael was the Great Judge, although He was a compassionate judge, according to the stories in the holy scrolls.

Her life was doomed to be a short one, and for so long she had wasted it. She held her arms around her, keeping out a fresh chill that had taken in her skin. Eluco moved closer to her, and wrapped his cloak around her shoulders. She smiled around at him. "It's not that kind of cold, I'm afraid."

He coughed. "Still Haaman, eh?"

"You still need the practice."

"I'm willing to bet I speak more Haaman than you do, Your Grace."

She raised an eyebrow at him. "I think we're a little ways past 'Your Grace', don't you?"

Eluco cleared his throat. "Habits. I suppose it's Allessandra from now on."

"Ali."

He smiled, and gave small shake of his head. "I've never heard anyone call you Ali."

"No-one does ... not even my parents." Her smile died a little. "Someone may have, once upon a time, if I'd had friends, a normal life. I've always been Allessandra, or Your Majesty, or Your Grace."

He linked hands with her, and she glanced down at their entwined fingers, wondering if it was a good idea to be seen doing so, and then not caring in the least.

"If you're so sure you know more Haaman than I do, let's see," Eluco muttered. "Say this back to me in Haaman."

He spoke a short phrase, a couple of sentences in Caelish. Allessandra smiled and thought for a moment. "'When I look out at the sea, it reminds me of how you changed my life. You opened up a new world to me, sometimes uncertain, sometimes terrifying, but above all unceasingly beautiful.'"

She swallowed and glanced up at him. "Charmer, are you?"

"It was the first thing that came into my mind," he said with a smile warming his face. "And I thought you might have trouble with 'unceasingly'."

She answered him in Caelish, her voice whispered along with the sighing of the ocean below them.

"'I hope you realise that, given the Caelish laws of succession, that you'll be King if you and I last. That's quite the responsibility, so I also hope you're not an abolitionist.'" He smirked at her. "I'm not, although I hadn't considered that. I never paid the King and Queen much notice, I think they were coronated when I was three."

"I wonder if you would suit a crown..."

Eluco shrugged. "Would your parents have something to say about a future King who used to patrol the Old Town Streets?"

"They'd give you a title anyway, no doubt, for being a loyal protector of the Regent and the realm. This would just be a ... bigger title." She gave him a sidelong look. "Besides, better someone I care for than a Mokkan princeling whose parents want influence and Cael's gold more than a happy marriage."

"You want to marry for love, hmm?"

Allessandra smirked at him. The clouds seemed to be just above them now, as if they could reach out and brush a hand through them. The ocean had quietened to a murmur. "It's your turn."

Eluco spoke again in Caelish, this time for longer. Allessandra listened to him, almost transfixed.

"'For the longest time, for all my years in the City Guard and as a soldier, I thought I would never find anything close to love. I was sent out on tour after tour in the worst corners of Haama and beyond, saw things that still keep me awake on some bitter nights, the only company the soldiers in my regiment, many too broken to do anything but put on their armour and fight as hard as they were able. Too many had nothing to fight for, no-one to come home to but those who spat on them. You mean far more to me than words can say, than anyone could translate from any tongue.'"

Allessandra said nothing, just watched him as he turned to face her, his eyes almost reflecting the starlight.

"My turn," she said, and leaned forwards. Her hand stroked his jawline and held his cheek, her lips touched his ear as she whispered. His warm hand closed over hers as she pulled back, their lips brushed against each other as she gazed into his eyes.

"I can only translate that properly in your cabin," he murmured.

***

The two vessels met on the edge of the rest of the world, right on the cusp of the Meladrin Ocean and the Dividing Sea. *Mira's Favour* and the Alliance's vessel settled in the water, and sailed towards each other. While she was speedy in the air, Captain Tiberius's craft was slow and ungainly in the water, and a pair of booms were lowered on either side of the ship's aft to keep her stable.

The meeting point was an island called Watchman, a tiny rock with a smattering of greenery and resilient trees. At the centre of it was the ruin of a tower, that had once reached up to a near-unbelievable height, higher than even the tallest points of Victory's defensive city walls. It had been intended as a watchtower, most likely, according to Tiberius. Where it had gone, no-one knew for sure. Likely what remained of it was at the bottom of the ocean, long-since eroded away.

Only the foundations were left, covered by creeping vines and mosses and mushrooms in the shadow. Allessandra could have sworn she could see movement among the broken stones, glowing eyes watching her from beneath the ancient ramparts. The Alliance ship, thankfully, blocked her view of the old, dead place.

They had come on a military carrier, converted somewhat into a vast warship. They were flying a flag of truce, which didn't do anything to mask the dozens of cannon ports that lined the side, or the extra armoured plates that had been attached to the flanks, or the thick ramming spikes at the fore and aft. The hull was painted dark red and silver, with the image of a golden horse rearing up at the prow. Striking, formidable, and clearly stolen.

Evandro and Allessandra exchanged a glance. They were unarmed, but the Alliance were very capable of sinking them several times over with their behemoth vessel. They pulled alongside Mira's Favour and dropped anchor, and Tiberius gave the nod to extend the ramp slowly.

As the mooring ropes were lashed around each craft for stability, Allessandra's heart began hammering in her chest, so hard she thought she may crack a rib. She could see the crew of the other ship, their mismatched clothing, in some cases their rags, and over it their armour of leather and iron. There were fearsome winged creatures staring at the *Favour*, unblinking.

"We must have faith," she murmured to Evandro, and to herself as well. He gave her a nod.

The first one on the ramp was the man she recognised. Thomas wore his robes like a large, open coat, with a formal, thin doublet underneath. He stepped across and down onto the deck, striding to Allessandra, Evandro, and Captain Tiberius. Eluco was beside her, hand on the hilt of his sword.

Thomas bowed low before her, and spoke in Caelish. "*It is good to see you again, Your Grace.*"

Allessandra bobbed her head formally, and spoke in Haaman. "Indeed. Your delegation seems ready for a battle, not peace talks."

Thomas nodded solemnly, and switched his tongue accordingly. "I apologise for our manner, and for our means of arrival. I'm afraid it was insisted upon. We have no diplomatic craft, and there was some concern by our more cynical delegates that this would be a trap. The scars run rather deep, Your Grace, we have had little cause for friendship until recently."

"I suppose I can understand that point of view, although it saddens me."

Thomas gave a half-bow. "And I, Your Grace, but that is why we are here. To begin the healing process."

The Empire Of Fire

His eyes met Eluco's for a moment, and they exchanged a nod. Then he turned to Evandro. "First Minister, I am glad to formally meet you."

They shook hands. Evandro studied his face for a moment. "Indeed. You must be The Mage, of the Four Guardians."

Thomas swallowed. "Just Thomas, if you don't mind, sir. My companions and I are a little reluctant to be seen in such a way."

"Yet, you are seen in that way by many, including Cael."

"Hopefully as a force for good, henceforth." Thomas extended a hand to Captain Tiberius. "Captain, thank you for allowing your vessel to be the venue of these discussions."

"I hope you make good progress, sir, for all our sakes," Tiberius replied warmly.

"I have informed faith that we will." Thomas stepped aside, and gestured to the Alliance ship. The full delegation began crossing the ramp in small groups, and settling on the Favour's deck.

The first figure was a wyvernborn, although it had no wings. It was covered in a myriad of scars across every visible part of its hide. Two blades and a shield sat at its hips, and it moved with readiness and confidence, as if it were daring any potential threat to engage it in battle. However, its face was calm, almost serene, as it stepped onto the deck.

Behind it were another wyvernborn and a human woman, arms linked as they strode. The wyvernborn was a head taller than the first, with wings folded between its shoulder blades. Darker of scale, with almost a swaggering gait, clearly it was the figure of authority. The woman beside it walked with a quiet grace, but was lithe and athletic. The gown she wore was a simple light blue, baring arms that were toned and fit, muscles pronounced. She wore a band around her head at the line of her blonde hair, patterned with leaves and flowers. The manner of the pair was similar in a sense to the way her parents walked together, a unified position of power and a projection of their stability as a couple. This seemed far more genuine, though, something in their body language suggested love rather than strength.

As they approached, Thomas leaned over to Allessandra. "Thank you for using the Haaman language, Your Grace, and First Minister. I assure you it wasn't an expectation on our part."

"We wished to accommodate, and communicate as clearly as we could."

Thomas bowed his head, and turned to the delegates. "Princess Allessandra, First Minister Evandro, I present Barada, Alpha of clan Andros, and of the Wyvern Bog."

He gestured to the taller wyvernborn, who studied Allessandra with eyes of bright gold, and an expression of curiosity.

"Sandra Adenn, matriarch of clan Andros, and leader of the Orlin."

The woman smiled and bowed her head. Now that she was close, Allessandra could see that she was perhaps twice the princess's age, but there was barely a wrinkle or blemish on her face.

Thomas rested a hand on the shoulder of the wingless wyvernborn. "Bassai, of clan Reeva, although as you know me as The Mage, you would know him as The Beast, though the moniker is somewhat inaccurate."

Bassai took a single step forward and gave a half bow. His voice was gruff, but filled with the gravitas of a baritone singer. "Your Grace, First Minister."

Allessandra returned the bow. "I am glad to meet you all face to face. I have never met a wyvernborn, nor one of the Orlin Forest. I hope we have many more meetings."

Barada's wings slowly extended to their full width, enough to wrap around both delegations like a blanket. He bent forwards, but not in a bow. He pulled close to Allessandra, golden eyes locked on hers. Evandro glanced back at Eluco, who gave a subtle nod, tensing. Allessandra reached back and touched the hand that was now gripping his sword hilt.

She saw Thomas smile from the corner of her eye. Sandra watched carefully, and Bassai remained still, although his eyes were fixed on Eluco.

Barada's snout was half an inch from her when he inhaled. She didn't flinch, maintaining eye contact. His slit pupils widened slowly, and he inhaled again. At this, Sandra and Bassai both focused on the Alpha entirely, frowning.

Finally, Barada reared up again, and what sounded like a growl emerged from his throat. It wasn't threatening though, but softer, almost a sound of contemplation. He glanced at Bassai, and let out a series of growls, just as quiet, almost solemn. Bassai bowed his head and nodded, and Sandra's eyes turned to Allessandra, who by now was even more nervous.

Barada's eyes found hers again. "You hold my eyes like a warrior would, although you are barely beyond your twentieth year. You control your fear well, Princess ... and you come here with the strength of will that is rarely seen in generals. Worthy of respect."

He bowed, and Sandra and Bassai followed suit, this time bowing low.

Thomas nodded with a smile. "The first test is complete ... and not one you may have expected, Your Grace."

"But one I am happy to have passed," she replied.

They glanced back. The next group began crossing the ramp, and Allessandra stared at the procession coming towards them.

The first trio were all human. A middle aged man suppressing a furious scowl walked beside an older woman walking stiffly, wearing a robe that was woven with golden runic thread. Neither were armed, but the woman in particular radiated a nervous, and dangerous energy from her being. Allessandra suspected that she had no weapons because she herself was lethal enough, a Mage or Sorceress most likely.

Behind the pair swaggered a man in black, a wide brimmed hat pulled low over his eyes. A rapier was attached to his hip, a strange mechanical contraption adorned his wrist along with a small quiver of crossbow bolts.

Behind him, waiting until they cleared the ramp before boarding, were a lithe, red-haired woman in a green, simple summer dress, the familiar, warm face of Helen, Allessandra's former steward, and a giant.

The armoured man carefully crossed the ramp. It creaked beneath him with every step, and Allessandra feared for a moment that he would break through, fall into the ocean and sink. The armour covered him head to toe, the only gaps for his eyes, which glowed with a strange, purple light that shone with the same warmth as the runes on a Mage's cloak.

The woman stayed ahead of him, light-footed, as if she were stepping across a catwalk or along a wire. She was even more striking in her beauty than Sandra was, hair flowing in the wind, the figure of a dancer, the kind of woman that would have princelings falling over each other for her hand. Instead she had a sword strapped to her back in a black leather harness.

Even the hull of Mira's Favour creaked as the giant stepped aboard. As the six walked towards her, Thomas cleared his throat. "Princess Allessandra, First Minister Evandro, I now present Donnal, the leader of the Haaman Resistance in the West."

Donnal nodded to both Evandro and Allessandra, but nothing else. Most of the curtness was kept out of the gesture. While she felt Evandro bristle beside her, she returned the nod in the same manner.

"Seraphine, of the White Tower, formerly in Taeba District."

The older woman bowed her head respectfully. "Your Grace."

Helen wove around them and bowed, but Allessandra righted her with a smile, holding her hands. The steward beamed, and held her close. Allessandra's arms were tight about her shoulders. "I'm glad to see you well, Helen."

"And I to see you, Allessandra. When I saw the city burning, I feared … I didn't want to leave you there alone."

"I have been far from alone."

There was a whirl of smoke beside them, and the man in black appeared. There was a moment where everyone seemed to tense. Allessandra recognised him suddenly as the man who had been with Thomas in her chambers.

"Why do you people always insist on such dramatic uses of your power?"

The man smiled, his black eyes glinting. "It gets people talking at parties."

"This is Kassaeos," Thomas muttered stonily. "He is as he appears, and is here for security purposes."

The Empire Of Fire

"Indeed."

The final pair approached slowly. Tiberius said a quick, quiet word to one of the nearby crewmen, ordering him to check the integrity of the deck plates where the giant walked.

"Emeora Vonn, of the Orlin Forest, also known as The Archer."

Allessandra smiled. "I could have guessed. The poem does describe her as fair."

Emeora raised an eyebrow and bowed. "Didn't know there was a poem."

Thomas smirked. "Finally, I present Ironclad, formerly Tobias Calver of the Melida City Guard, also known as The Warrior."

"That, I could also have guessed," Allessandra remarked.

Ironclad chuckled, a deep rumble that resonated through his chest. "There has been an effort to lean me into that particular moniker, Your Grace."

Allessandra regarded them all. "Thank you for agreeing to meet with us. I assure you it means the world to me, and it will mean the same to both our nations, to put the last century behind us truly, and move forwards together."

"I wholeheartedly agree, Your Grace," Evandro added. Allessandra smiled at the corrected language he had used.

"I also wish to thank you for your actions in the Pil Valley, I understand that most, if not all of you were present."

There were a smattering of solemn nods from the group. Both of the wyvernborn closed a fist over their hearts.

"We united in a common goal, against a common enemy, and defended our collected people," rumbled the giant. "We share in victory and share in grief for those lost."

"And we share reverence at their memory," Allessandra added. She glanced at Thomas for a moment, whose head was bowed respectfully. "One of my former guards, Orso, fought beside you."

Thomas's eyes closed. A flicker passed over Emeora's face.

"He did," Bassai said. "A good man, whose courage saved many lives."

"Astrid too," Donnal muttered. Pain crossed Seraphine and Sandra's faces.

"They will both be in our hearts, and the success of our talks here will ensure they are never forgotten." Allessandra's eyes passed over the group once more.

"Shall we begin?"

The Empire Of Fire

19

Kelad paced slowly around the top deck of the skiff he had named *Shadowblade*, checking every possible thing he could. The business of the small crew, the rigging and sails, the armaments that were mounted on buffers and railings on either side of the stabilising sail at the fore, and the fleet surrounding him.

They had been moving at a quarter of the speed of which *Shadowblade* was capable in order to stay in formation with the squadron and the fleet. His own small force was in three groups. Shadow Group was his, with *Shadowblade* and two other skiffs behind him: *Shadow One* and *Shadow Two*. Rogue Group was much the same, three other skiffs, *Rogues One*, *Two* and *Three*. Paladin Group comprised his only battleship, the *Spearhead*, and the final skiff, named *Paladin One*.

He was becoming quickly accustomed to commanding a smaller craft, although the loss of the *Razorback* and her crew were a bitter, gangrenous scar across his soul. Every time he felt some pride at the actions of the crew of his current vessel, he felt the dead sting him.

Still, *Shadowblade* was a good craft, and the eight ships under his direct command had all been prepared for action and refitted at the Victory dockyard and shipwright. Five of the eight had served during the Battle Of The Pil Valley, and with distinction at that, so they had been pushed to the top of the list.

Rogue Group and *Paladin One* had been outfitted with stronger barriers, while *Paladin One* also boasted another pair of broadside cannons, in its fleet role as a shield in conjunction with *Spearhead*. The battleship had turret mounted double cannons at the fore and aft, bolstering her already impressive firepower.

Shadowblade and her squadron were the most changed. Two heavy cannons were fixed forwards, and the sails were all trimmed and sleek. The generators within were more powerful, to cope with the added armour plating and weaponry. The increased power also meant potential increased speed and strengthened barriers, vital for the battles to come.

She was a good ship, they all were, but with so few they would have to be used more carefully and precisely, regardless of the combined forces of the Black Fleet around them.

There were fifty ships in total, set to meet another three hundred and fifty above the Bay Of War, and another two hundred at Cael City. The hammer was truly about to fall.

Two squadrons of Black Fleet skiffs were on either side of Shadow and Rogue Group, ready for any potential treachery. Battleships with growling dragon heads fixed to the prow were either side of *Spearhead*. Again, Kelad's trust had been doubted, which carried significant meaning.

Vehnek and Mora had a plan so horrible that it required absolute loyalty. No-one could get in the way.

The fleet began crossing over the Cael coastline, and turned north-east towards the Bay Of War. Kelad crossed beside the main sail to the helm, and patted the young pilot on the shoulder. Saiyra was a hotshot he had been keeping an eye on in the Naval Academy at the Bay Of War, with excellent reaction times and decision making. She had the added bonus of riding him like he was a wild stallion when the mood took him, as it frequently did.

Saiyra reminded him of Ketesh too often for his liking, but also of Allessandra. His lechery had followed him across his entire career, but he had no desire to stop or settle. What would be the point? He would outlive any wife he took, love would be a bitter activity to take up. Ketesh had probably been the closest to him in his many decades, and even then, he had enjoyed hundreds of women at the same time as enjoying her.

"*Any orders?*"

"*Just to maintain course and speed,*" Saiyra said, glancing around at the cloud of airships around them.

"*And our ships?*"

"*No change. Captain Obrek is running combat readiness drills, he has response time at five seconds.*"

"*Very good. Tell him I want three and a half.*"

"*Aye, General.*"

There was a shout from the crow's nest. "*Ships!*"

Kelad turned. There they were, the might of the Black Fleet, ready for the operation that would make them legends.

The *Shadowblade's* communication stone began to glow. Kelad touched it, and listened.

Admiral Heztor's formal, officious voice echoed over the air. "*Annihilator to Shadowblade. You are to pull ninety degrees to port and make for the eastern edge of the Scorpion's Tail. Pest Control commencing.*"

Kelad nodded to Saiyra. She watched as the port squadron drifted away from them, and signalled Shadow Group to follow her lead. On a skiff, the pilot had more responsibilities than on a battleship, and were required to fly, signal, and sometimes spot for the enemy in combat. Communications were handled by the captain.

Ahead of them, a number of ships were breaking off to join them. The leviathan bulk of the *Annihilator* swung around slowly, sails billowing, its hundred cannons locked securely behind wide hatches in the hull.

All they would need to do is get that ship into position above the Wyvern Bog, and the battle would be over. There would be no mercy, no parley, simply a rain of conjured fire that would turn the marsh into an extension of the Orlin Dustbowl.

Kelad spoke into the stone. "*Rogue Group, Paladin Group, follow Shadow's lead. Ninety degrees port.*"

He folded his arms and glanced at Saiyra. "*I'd guess our course will take us around our defenses at the Haaman side of the Scorpion's Tail. Standing Army are garrisoned there, they would raise the alarm if a battle fleet was* spotted heading south."

"I agree, sir. Then over the Maldane Reach, and probably over the Orlin Dustbowl. Swift and decisive, especially as the wyvernborn don't have air defenses, as far as we know ... dragon aside."

"And the quicker the Wyvern Bog is burned, the quicker we can deal with that dragon."

Saiyra gave a single nod.

"Time?"

"At the Annihilator's airspeed, four hours."

Kelad stroked his chin, and signalled his ships. "*Battle readiness, immediately, but keep the barriers down until the word is given.*"

***

"We are pressed for farmland as it is," Evandro said with a rub of his head.

"Do you mean Haama, or Cael?" Donnal growled.

"For the moment we are one and the same. You need the food, and we need the food. This talk of a way to shift the sands back is only a theory, for the moment."

Thomas paused a sip of his tea to speak. "A sound theory, First Minister, that showed promising results in small scale tests."

Evandro waved his hand. "You're talk about applying that theory to a desert the size of a middle-to-large nation. It will take time to fine-tune these incantations so that they work in the way you intend. Arcane engineering can be a business of decades."

"It may well *be* decades before we need to expand," Sandra said to Evandro. "Our relationship with the farmers in the region is positive. As long as there is an agreement in place …"

"…and that agreement is honoured when the time comes," Barada added.

Sandra nodded. "In that circumstance, we will not have a problem.

The Empire Of Fire

Remember, Father will be working on the corruption of the Maldane Reach and The Orlin Forest."

Allessandra listened as the opinions and suggestions were knocked back and forth across the table, trying to get a reading on everyone's mood, on who would be the most difficult. Thomas aside, the Four Guardians had mostly been silent, watching the proceedings and looking at some of the art hanging around the room.

The Warrior was studying the Song Of The Four Guardians, and had been for twenty minutes of the negotiations. The Archer had drifted between him and Sandra, listening and occasionally nodding, but adding little. The Beast paced behind Barada and Sandra, grunting at some of what was said, holding his attention on every word and cutting in when he felt it necessary. They were fighters more than talkers, it seemed.

Allessandra refocused on the conversation as it was taking a turn.

Donnal was turning a dark shade of red. "You want to enslave our farmers as you enslave your own people. This is precisely what we were fighting against!"

"They will not stand for such pressures being put upon them," Seraphine urged hotly. "More discontent is not what any of us want."

"Meanwhile, our people starve?" Evandro snapped. "I think not. You dare attribute to slavery what is necessary to feed the hungry. Food and full bellies are what keep people from despair. You speak of discontent, I promise you have not seen discontent like you could."

Allessandra held up her hands quickly. "The issue of slavery is not what is on the table here. We are discussing the cessation of hostilities."

"How can we have a cessation of hostilities with people who buy and sell their own?" Donnal growled.

Thomas sighed. "As a former slave, I am forced to agree. We have all seen the reports. There are those who disappear from Victory and other places, only to end up cleaning a master's floor."

"Conjecture." Evandro spat. "Laws were passed to bar any Haaman from being sold or forced into slavery two decades ago. I was a member of the Council that passed them."

The Beast chuckled at that. "Which stops it happening, I'm sure."

"They are certainly not a part of the trade and nothing to do with us."

"Ha!" Donnal shook his head. "You have to be taking us for fools."

"Certainly not, although you are taking *us* for monsters."

Allessandra leaned forwards, with a hand on Evandro's forearm. "We may have to consider the slave trade ... especially considering the population crisis in Cael City. Too many are forced to live in and around the walls, and sandstorms make expansion of the city incredibly problematic."

"You talk of freeing them?" Evandro said incredulously.

The rest of the table fell silent. Thomas sat bolt upright. The Warrior turned from the poem and fixed his shining eyes on the delegates, speaking up for the first time. "Eventually, perhaps, but not now. We are not here to upend Cael as a nation. Drastic changes so quickly will simply lead to more of your *discontent* and more war, more support for Vehnek."

Donnal snorted through his teeth.

"He's right," Thomas murmured. "Bitter as it is."

Allessandra thought for a moment, sipping from her glass of water. "He is ... but perhaps all three of you are. There is a problem we have yet to consider: the problem of people."

Seraphine frowned. "People?"

"Farmers, specifically," Allessandra said. "In Cael there are few. In Haama, there are certainly fewer than there were. There are two nations worth of people to feed. We will need men and women to work the land to feed them ... and it presents an opportunity for thousands of slaves and thousands of the impoverished."

Evandro stroked his chin. "They could learn from the Haaman farmers ... assist your people here in farming, ease some of your burden."

"We don't want you to give us slaves," Donnal said stonily.

Allessandra shook her head. "Not slaves. Freemen."

The Empire Of Fire

Thomas looked up. Evandro considered her words with a hum. "Indeed … it … may not just be possible, but necessary. Once freed they will need a trade, and there are many roles to fulfill on a farm, large or small scale."

"Potential work, that doesn't involve soldiery," Thomas muttered. "It would be a radical change to a part of Cael's economy … but it would be a step in both our favours, in the direction we both desire."

Barada growled, drawing the attention of the room. Sandra took his hand quickly. "We have stepped away from the point. The land the wyvernborn need must be passed to us."

"Ultimately, it is not up to the Council Of Ministers or the crown," Allessandra said with a shrug. "Although First Minister Evandro is correct for the time being: farm land will be needed. We would need to open talks with those farmers who own that land … both you and I, Barada, and Sandra. As your matriarch has correctly said, it will take some time before it is truly needed. I would be happy for the land to pass to you, provided it could be leased to us for a period."

"With our oversight," Barada growled. "It would do no good if your people over-farmed the soil."

Allessandra looked to Sandra, who nodded. The princess smiled. "It wouldn't do anyone any good. I agree to your terms. The fine details can be straightened further with the landowners themselves, but as you say, your relationship with them is a positive one."

Barada's fierce eyes remained fixed on hers as he nodded. "Very good."

"Thank you for your understanding, and your effort," Sandra added. Barada grunted in agreement.

Allessandra bowed her head.

"There are more matters to consider before we call this a success," Seraphine said stonily. "Military, for example."

"When we have a representative of the Standing Army present, that can be discussed."

Seraphine pursed her lips, but bobbed her head in reluctant agreement. "I must say ... a lot of this proposed peace is based on wild theory and hope. How can we be sure that The Magus Towers will co-operate with us? Or a dragon, for that matter."

"Arcana is a precise, result-driven art," Thomas said. "They will not be able to resist such a opportunity. Don't tell me you're not curious about working with this 'Father'."

Seraphine grunted.

"I do not doubt that you have come here in good faith, or that your terms have been laid out in the same manner," Allessandra said. "I only hope you are extending myself and the First Minister that same allowance."

Seraphine sighed. "I don't doubt that Thomas has convinced you, and I don't doubt his enthusiasm, I am only skeptical that these things will go as smoothly as he thinks they will."

The Mage grinned. "I don't doubt it'll be a difficult process at first, but a child doesn't come out of the womb at a sprint. Again, it comes down to good faith, and transparency. We both want a solution to the same problem, that solution will benefit both nations."

Allessandra smiled to herself. "Is that what we are? Children?"

"There are some habits that never go away."

Evandro cleared his throat. "On the point of governance, a transition period should be set, to pass control to Haaman representatives, or perhaps an increase in Council seats should occur. Brynden should not be the sole representative."

Donnal snorted. "He shouldn't be there at all. All he does is sit back, watch impotently, and grow fatter."

"He wrote the law protecting Haamans from slavery and made sure it was passed," Allessandra snapped. "Working with us didn't make him an agent against your country, and he certainly isn't doing that now."

Donnal bared his teeth. "What was he doing while our people burned in Victory? What was he doing when they burned in Idris? What of our dead?"

"What of those your agents slaughtered in cold blood?" she hissed back.

The Empire Of Fire

"My people died when Victory burned, it was not us doing the burning."

"We are oppressed!"

Barada growled, a deep sound that shook the room. A large, iron hand gently set down on Donnal's shoulder.

"Remember why we are here, Donnal," The Warrior said, his great iron voice soft. "Remember the face of the true enemy. It is not the face of Princess Allessandra or First Minister Evandro. If we are truly to be independent, if we are truly to be free, we must be independent and free of our own past grievances."

Donnal held his breath, then let it out. He inhaled deeply again, and nodded. "You're right, of course. I apologise ... I have been a fighter for many years. I cannot remember a time when I wasn't fighting against your people, Allessandra."

"Nor I," Seraphine muttered. "Nor my grandfather."

The Warrior chuckled. "The world changes, and it is a struggle to keep up. All we can do is be vigilant that the change is for the better, and the winds of progressivism are not a blizzard, filled with ice as sharp as knives."

Donnal snorted again, but it became a quiet laugh. He shook his head and rubbed he face width both hands. "Truthfully ... this is terrifying for me. The idea of peace with you ... it makes me shudder, not because you're Caelish, but because I don't know what it means for me. What will I do with all that anger inside me, that energised me for so many years? The anger that made me?"

Allessandra leaned across the table, suppressing a grimace at the sudden pain in her stomach as she did so. Her hands took both of his and squeezed gently. "We will discover that together. I will be a princess without a throne, sooner or later. Haama will have no more need of me ... and that is a thought that keeps me awake on the quietest nights. Our purpose will be ... protection. For all our people."

"On the question of governance, First Minister, I suspect both a transitional period and an expansion of the Council will be warranted, within reason," The Warrior murmured, patting Donnal gently on the shoulder. "I think, in truth, the details will be decided over a period of years. All we must agree to now, for certain, is the cessation of hostilities, and the promise of cooperation, to be formally signed into law or decree."

Allessandra looked to Donnal and Seraphine, who both nodded. Sandra smiled, and nodded as well. Barada let out a single, quiet grunt.

"On that, we certainly agree." Allessandra sat back. She swallowed her pain with a forced smile. "Perhaps a brief recess would be a good idea, just to refresh ourselves. I'm sure more food and drink could be brought."

"A sound idea." The Warrior boomed. "I must extend my compliments to the captain of this vessel."

The rest nodded in agreement, apart from Sandra and Barada. She looked at him, and squeezed his hand, before turning back to Allessandra. "Can we speak to you privately, Allessandra?"

"I fear my protector will insist on remaining here," Allessandra said, quietly beginning to fret. Were they preparing to leave the negotiations? Had she made a mistake somewhere?

Barada looked at Eluco, who had moved a little closer, scrutinising him for a moment. His nostrils flared as he inhaled, then he gave a single nod. For a brief moment, Allessandra thought she saw a smile cross his face for the shadow of a second.

Evandro patted her on the back as he stood and joined the rest as they filed from the room. When only the four remained, silence hung for a moment, before Barada spoke.

"You are ill."

Allessandra swallowed, and nodded.

Barada glanced up at Eluco, then back to her. "It is not an accusation, nor a factor that will turn us away. My nose never lies to me."

Sandra stood and drifted around the table to sit beside her. "Can anything be done?"

"I ... do not know. My doctor tells me she is studying the problem."

"Our people will assist, if they can," Barada murmured. "This will remain private, should you wish it."

Allessandra wiped the sweat from the edge of her hairline with a handkerchief. "For now ... yes, I would prefer it remain as private as possible. I cannot be weak, in these times especially."

Barada smiled. "You are far from weak. I meant what I said when we arrived. You are courageous."

"Thank you. I hope I live up to those words."

Sandra smiled, and brushed a hand across her cheek. She leaned forwards and held Allessandra for a moment in a gentle embrace, before drawing back. "For Barada and I, it is a time of great joy, despite the uncertainty of certain matters. To see you coming together in the manner you are makes me believe that you can create a lasting peace. The right people found each other at the right time."

Allessandra smiled. "So much can come from such meetings ... great things, friendships that last decades ..."

"And love, of course," Sandra murmured, glancing up at Eluco.

Allessandra coughed. "I'm sorry?"

Barada chuckled. "I told you: my nose does not lie."

They spoke a little more, stories of the Wyvern Bog, the Orlin and wyvernborn in their first tentative steps to peace. That such bitter foes had come together in true harmony and friendship gave Allessandra more hope than any formal historical record could have. It also gave her a bolt of fear, settling in her gut. The image of the fleet departing Victory settled at the forefront of her mind, and when the rest of the delegates came back into the room, it was the first thing she spoke of.

The Warrior listened to her closely, and nodded. "This has been a concern for us. We feared Vehnek had accelerated his plans. If he is on the move he will not dither on his journey."

Evandro nodded in agreement. "But on the move where?"

"The White Sea," Seraphine said instantly. "We have a fairly educated guess as to what he wants there, but we should compare our knowledge on the matter."

"Yes…" Allessandra shuddered. "If he means to … no …"

Her eyes widened. She looked directly at Barada and Sandra. "If he is moving now, he is going to eliminate every threat to him he can."

Barada growled loudly, a twisted sound that made Bassai snarl and sit bolt upright.

***

General Kelad gazed down at the dust bowl below, that once was a vast, thick forest of trees that were so tall that they would have been interfering with the flight path of the fleet. The Orlin Forest had become a flat, blasted plain, as dead as Cael's desert.

He remembered the campaign well. He remembered the trees burning, catching so quickly that there had been almost no need for his army to firebomb the place with the catapults they had brought with them.

The memory of the great beast that had swooped over his head had filled him with a sense of awe and terror. Awe at its power. Terror at the screams it elicited, and that its dragonfire cut short.

His troops had barely needed to act at all, except in mercy. Orlin had come screaming from the burning trees, their bodies being swallowed whole by the fire covering them. They had been soldiers … and they had not been soldiers. Kelad's orders had been identical either way. By arrow or by blade, put them out of their misery as swiftly as possible. If it were a child, do it faster.

His army had not moved an inch for two dawns, waiting until the monster had completed its task, taking shifts to kill the burning stragglers. Orlin mad with terror had fled as well, scattering across the fields. At first, some of them had been cut down also as they screamed and wept, and Kelad put a stop to that with on-the-spot executions of the men under his command that did so.

When the dragon's screams of rage had fallen suddenly silent, Kelad had

The Empire Of Fire

run immediately to the gazebo where the Arch Mage controlling it had been in the meditative trance she required to enact the massacre. She was enraged, in an effort to cover her panic that the beast was loose. She screamed that it had been felled, that someone or something had broken her concentration, and as all Arch Mages like her seemed to, wanted to take immediate charge of the armed forces. She began crying orders at Kelad, to take his men into the inferno to retrieve the dragon, destroy those that had brought it down, or kill it if it was wild once more.

Perhaps the Dragon's Arrogance had infected her like a virus, closing her ears, intoxicating her in her own ego and lust for power. Nothing Kelad said in counter to her got through her fury. Most of his men would cook in their armour or burn before they even reached the dragon, and even if they did, what were they supposed to do about it?

The rudimentary siege engines of the time couldn't move between the trees, and they wouldn't make it far in the heat either. It was a dragon, a beast of myth and fury and war, and they would have nought but swords and bows. The Arch Mage, in return, had decided that she magically had the authority to relieve him of command. Before she could burst from the tent, and start screeching orders, Kelad had grabbed a fistful of her cloak and yanked her back.

The single thrust of his blade severed her spine and burst through her lungs. She had simultaneously sprayed blood from her lips and collapsed as her legs stopped working in an instant, as abruptly as if he had blown out a candle.

Face down in the mud, drowning in her own blood, Kelad had almost given her the same mercy he was giving the Orlin. If he hadn't been slaughtering the terrified for two days, without sleep, he probably would have. Instead, he poured lantern oil on her, and set her alight.

Then he had set the gazebo alight, and strode out without a word, some uncomfortable part of him relishing, even delighting in her strangled screams. Not a single soldier under his command had questioned him, or even batted an eye in shock.

He couldn't remember in that moment what excuse he had given to the Lord Marshal for that particular murder. Spontaneous combustion, perhaps. The dragon had backfired, or something like that. By that time, Kallus Vehnek had been too drunk on his own victories to give it much thought.

It had been another dawn before he finally pulled his troops back to the ruins of Melida City. In those three days, he had watched, listened to, and contributed to the extinction of a culture, or so he had thought.

Was it then that his heart had been embittered, or was it after his death? He had been a loyal man of Cael, unquestioning to the last. Burning Melida City hadn't shaken him even slightly. It had been different, it had felt different. The citadel had been the old fortress of his enemies, the place that they had lorded over them as impregnable. With the Black Dragon, they had taken great, cathartic pleasure in thoroughly impregnating it.

Destroying the Orlin and their forest had been more than just another campaign. The Orlin weren't an enemy ... they had been a *potential* enemy, one that Kallus Vehnek and the Arch Mages had not allowed to fester.

A culture eradicated. A stunning example of nature, unrivalled across the world even in Adrezsti's deep jungles or the Salkethian palms, or South Mokku's thick swamplands, incinerated. In many ways a needless display of ruthless terror.

And with the erasure of the Taeba clans, Kelad had now committed such an atrocity twice.

"*Sir?*"

He swallowed the bile that had risen in his throat, and beat back the shudder it sent up his back.

"*General Kelad, sir?*"

He turned from the starboard rail. Saiyra glanced at him from the helm. "*What is it?*"

"*Orders from Admiral Hezstor, sir.*"

Kelad strode to the communication stones and touched one, listening to the fleet commander's clipped orders. He confirmed, then looked back at

The Empire Of Fire

Saiyra. *"Decrease elevation by three hundred feet."*

He signalled Paladin and Rogue groups as Saiyra signalled the rest of Shadow group. The airships around them were beginning to descend. Kelad nodded to himself.

As he suspected, the Admiral was conscious of aerial sentries. The lower the fleet were, the less visible they would be until the attack began. They would have to pull up, of course, before the bombardment could commence. The skiffs were to stay low and engage the wyvernborn as they tried to counter-attack, delay and harass until the larger vessels and the *Annihilator* were in position. If the dragon appeared, then the battleships would engage it, and leave the siege to the *Annihilator*.

At the prow of the *Shadowblade*, he could see the band of green and fog just coming into view, before the horizon concealed it.

"General?" Saiyra muttered as she manipulated the controls of the craft, putting them into formation.

"*Yes?*"

"*Permission to speak freely?*"

Kelad raised an eyebrow and nodded.

"*If we live through this ... you'd better marry me.*"

Kelad grinned and chuckled. "*If we live through this, my dear, I'll make you a queen.*" He looked up. There was a Black Fleet skiff above them, near-directly. "*I assume you can get us around that.*"

Saiyra grinned. "*Of course, sir.*"

"*How far out are we?*"

Saiyra glanced up at the horizon. The Wyvern Bog was visible now, on the other side of a glittering river, catching the dappled sunlight like a beacon. "*Maybe six miles. Three minutes.*"

Kelad touched three communication stones on the plinth: one for each of his three fleet groups. "*This is General Kelad. All ships, brace for manoeuvres. The word is imminent.*"

He touched another and repeated the order to the *Shadowblade's* crew. He glanced at Saiyra. She wiped the sweat from her top lip, and nodded to him.

Every nerve in his old body fired at once. He checked his pistol, and loaded a lightning stone into the breech. His hand gripped the railing beside the helm so tightly that he heard the wood creak.

Holstering his pistol once more, he reached for the stone that would connect *Shadowblade* to the *Spearhead*.

"*Captain Obrek.*"

Obrek's voice came back immediately. "*General.*"

"*Razorback.*"

No other word was needed. Two seconds later, the dragon-head Construct at the *Spearhead's* prow opened its iron mouth and roared so loudly that it could have been heard in Breaker's Bay.

A second after that, a bright beam of conjured flame blasted from its mouth and disintegrated the entire aft of the Black Fleet battleship in front of it. The cracking and splintering of wood and iron was followed by a boom as the generator inside was destroyed, flinging flaming debris in all directions. The dead hulk dropped like a stone, and splatted across the dustbowl in a smoking ruin.

At the same time, every cannon on the *Spearhead* emerged from their hatches, and sent two dozen blasts of energy into the battleships on either side, smashing through their hulls before they could raise their barriers.

Paladin One banked over another Black Fleet ship and opened fire with its eight cannons directly onto the top deck, killing the captain, helmsman and most of the crew, as well as setting the sails on fire. The skiff nimbly banked around and began to climb with the Spearhead.

Kelad felt the rush of battle flash through him, and for the first time since his death nearly a century ago, felt truly alive.

20

Zeta folded her powerful arms and glared at Olimar. "A sheep, and not one of those young ones with soft meat."

Olimar shook his head and smiled. The shanks of meat hanging up on the branch behind behind him were wrapped in wide, waxen Zub leaf, to keep it fresh, and Zeta was scrutinising them closely, even leaning forwards to sniff a couple of them. "I thought you might want a change," he chuckled. "I hear cityfolk prefer the softer meat."

Zeta growled. "That's because cityfolk have weak chins and infant teeth. I like to chew my meat ... as you well know."

Olimar laughed. "Maybe I just wanted an excuse to have a longer conversation with you..."

Zeta gave a loud bark of laughter. "A bolder strategy would be to walk up to me and start having one."

The Orlin shepherd spread his hands. He was indeed bold, and perhaps a charmer, or so he thought. A widower, whose wife had been one of the unlucky few lost giving birth to his wyvernborn daughter. To handle a wyvernborn female of any age, a male had to have some gumption about him."Would that I could catch a moment with you, but I couldn't hope to fly after you without wings of my own. I have enough trouble keeping up with Meikya."

"Now that she's found her wings, she won't stop using them," Zeta chuckled.

"Yeah, I noticed ..." he grinned. "I have the perfect sheep for you, anyway. Nice and tough, how you like it."

"Good."

"Trouble is, it's in my cabin, not here. Let's eat together, a little later."

Zeta snorted. "That's certainly more bold."

"The way to a woman's heart is through her stomach."

"Ah, it's my heart you're after, is it?"

Olimar opened his mouth to respond, but a deafening sound stopped him dead, a booming shriek that came from the depths of some mechanical hell.

The roar shook the willows of the Wyvern Bog like a tremor in the rocks. It made Zeta's scales tighten in agitation. It was a roar of fury and agony, like a dragon's, but ... wrong. Twisted and warped. Immediately following it was a sound like rolling, cloud-bursting thunder. A storm? No, it was too close: Zeta would have heard it hours ago.

"That wasn't Father," Olimar muttered, eyes fixed on the canopy above him. "Was it a dragon?"

Zeta took in a deep breath, and immediately smelled flame and death on the wind.

"Sound the alarm!" she shouted, and flared her wings to take off. Before she did, though, she shot out an arm and pulled Olimar close to her. She gently touched her forehead to his, then swept into the air.

***

General Kelad held on tightly as Saiyra pulled *Shadowblade* into a steep, swift climb. The skiff above them had no time to react as Kelad's nimble flagship shot past and raked it with her broadside cannons.

He glanced back over the ship's aft. Shadow Group were in close formation behind them, hitting as many of the skiffs around them as they could with blasts of magical energy. Rogue Group were engaging with the skiffs around them. They had destroyed two, their wrecks tumbling to the dead ground, and were dancing around the rest.

Above *Shadowblade*, a number of the battleships were turning inwards, bringing cannons to bear on Paladin Group. *Spearhead* was pulling above them as they sluggishly turned to where it should have been. One of the Black Fleet commanders had anticipated the move, and let loose a barrage of cannonfire that crashed against *Spearhead's* barriers.

Paladin One quickly dived forwards and fired its own cannons, including the portable, shoulder mounted ones on the top deck.

"*Take us through them,*" Kelad ordered. Saiyra nodded, her face set, and signalled. Shadow Group fell into formation, bringing a quartet of skiffs in behind them, firing on them with what little they were able to field head-on.

Despite the careful eye they had kept on Kelad's forces, most of the battleships in particular were configured for a siege, but that would change in less than a minute, most likely, as the captains and crews worked out what was going on.

The skiffs were there to cover them in air-to-air combat, and they were on their game, as far as Kelad could tell. Shaking them would be the biggest challenge, and would require a minor tweak in the plan.

Shadowblade and her squadron were coming up on the battleships above quickly. One was dead ahead, the lower hatches beginning to open, perhaps having spotted them. By now, their barriers would be up.

Kelad tapped the communication stone to Shadow Group. "Heavy cannons to bear on our target. Fire at will. *Shadowblade*, hold."

On either side of them. *Shadow One* and *Two* opened up with a deafening boom from the heavy cannons attached to their prows. Lightning bolts smashed against the battleship's barriers. Another volley had them significantly weakened, and a third breached them.

"*Shadowblade, fire at will!*"

The lightning projectiles left a pair of jagged, burning holes in the ventral hull, and showered Shadow Group's barriers with small chunks of wood and iron.

When all three fired, the Black Fleet's stricken vessel listed and dipped to port, before diving nose first. Saiyra dodged it as it fell past them and speared one of the pursuing skiffs. Both wrecks shattered upon the dustbowl like a vase on a stone floor.

"Broadsides, fire as we pass those battleships!"

Shadow Group twisted in the climb and let loose a volley from port and starboard. Only eighteen shots between them, but it was enough to pull a battleship's attention away from Paladin Group for a moment.

"Shadow Group, this is Kelad. *One*, hard to port, assist Paladin Group. *Two*, hard to starboard, assist Rogue." He let go of the stone and glanced back as the squadron split simultaneously, like synchronised dancers. One of each pursuer followed them, leaving *Shadowblade* with one dogged Black Fleet skiff following them as they headed for the *Annihilator*.

"*One pass should do it, Saiyra.*"

She nodded again, hands tight on the helm.

"*Heavy cannons, fire at will. Ready broadsides.*"

Ahead, the four skiffs directly escorting the *Annihilator* had turned, and were diving towards them. Saiyra leaned forwards, and Kelad ordered as much strength as possible be channelled into the fore-facing barriers with a gesture to his well-drilled crew.

Saiyra pointed *Shadowblade* towards the quartet ahead, and signalled the heavy cannons to fire. The lead Black Fleet skiff took one hit that breached its barriers, setting fire to the sail. The two on the flanks pulled wide, and Kelad saw the ripple of the cannons on their broadsides.

Saiyra pulled up sharply, but now they were in a near vertical climb. The crew, who had lashed themselves to the deck, yelped as they were left hanging over a near thousand foot drop to the dusty ground below.

Four of the dozen flaming projectiles struck them on their side barriers. Kelad caught his helmsman's glance, and touched the communication stone again. "*All hands, brace!*"

As the skiffs closed in, and their deck-mounted light cannons began firing, Saiyra pulled *Shadowblade* into a dive, trimming the side sails so they were falling like a rock. Two of the skiffs followed them down.

Kelad held on as best he could, watching as the ground rushed up to meet them. Saiyra glanced around behind her and spun the wheel, turning and rolling the ship towards the Wyvern Bog. Their sails flared. The men on deck with light cannons jumped to their feet and began firing at the pursuing skiffs. The *Shadowblade* came around again, whipping to port to bring their broadsides to bear.

All six shots struck the nearest skiff. Its barriers collapsed and it pulled away sluggishly, making for the river where they could land and make repairs. Saiyra grinned and pulled up again.

"*Head straight for the Annihilator,*" Kelad growled. "*All costs. We're running out of time.*"

She nodded grimly, and *Shadowblade* climbed once more.

Above them, the leviathan weapon of war was two miles away from firing range. There had been no response as of yet from the wyvernborn or Orlin.

"*What are you waiting for, lizard men?*" Kelad muttered under his breath. He looked around at the air battle.

The dustbowl was littered with burning wrecks. In among the capital ships, *Paladin One* and *Shadow One* swept past a Black Fleet battleship firing on the *Spearhead*. Kelad's only battleship had taken a beating, but it was still fighting ferociously. Its hull was breached, its sails had burned and been put out.

Every cannon on the ship was still blasting pulses of death at the fleet surrounding it. Rogue Group, despite the assistance of Shadow Two, were faring worse. One of the skiffs was spinning, ablaze, to the ground. The others were damaged, but still fighting.

Kelad was pulled from his thoughts by the mad flying of his pilot, who was throwing *Shadowblade* to the left and right, dodging fire from the two skiffs above them that swept past. Again, around half the shots hit, weakening the barriers on both sides.

The skiff behind them was curving around in its course and preparing to dive towards their flank. Once they had slipped past all of the escorting skiffs, their way was clear, but it was also clear for *Annihilator*.

Kelad saw the rippling of dozens of cannons on the side blazing towards them.

"*Evasive!*" he barked at Saiyra. "*All weapons, target the Annihilator's port hull, lower decks, and fire at will!*"

The heavy cannons boomed first, and Saiyra began to spin *Shadowblade* in a spiral course. The gunners on deck piled forwards and joined in the barrage, their shoulder mounted light cannons barking at the gargantuan dreadnought like a pack of furious guard dogs.

As Saiyra presented the *Shadowblade's* flanks one at a time, the side cannons fired towards the behemoth as well. Despite the assault, the *Annhilator* was more than responding in kind.

No pilot could have hoped to dodge the sheer volume of cannonfire relentlessly battering them. The forward barriers absorbed strike after strike, sometimes two at once, and the closer they got, the more hit. A hundred yards away from their target, they collapsed, and a blast put a hole in the front armour.

"*Hard to port, and keep firing!*" Kelad shouted over the punishment inflicted upon his ship. "*Can you get us above them, Saiyra?*"

"*Hold on!*" she cried, and yanked the controls to take them higher.

"*When we're fifty feet above, dive. Take us as close as you dare.*"

Even through the fear, rage, and adrenaline of battle, Saiyra raised an eyebrow and grinned. *Shadowblade* corkscrewed upwards, firing everything they had. *Annihilator's* cannons peppered their belly and flanks, and the topsail caught fire, only to be quickly extinguished by the Mage in the crow's nest.

Swiftly, though, they were out of their field of fire, and at the mercy of the Mages on the leviathan's deck. Conjured fire and ice rained upwards at their weakened barriers. Saiyra yelled: "*Brace!*" and balletically flipped *Shadowblade* end over end. On deck the crew were thrown to the limit of their bracing ropes, and a third of them vomited as their stomachs performed the same acrobatics as the skiff. Kelad grabbed hold of Saiyra to keep them both from falling.

The Empire Of Fire

He looked up to see that the heavy cannons were in the perfect position and bellowed a laugh. *"Heavy cannons! Fire!"*

The two blasts, at point blank range, blew straight through the *Annihilator's* barriers and smashed into the top deck. Kelad crouched on the railing, and drew his sword and pistol. *"DIVE!"*

The *Shadowblade* plummeted, barely ten feet from the dreadnought, and Kelad leaped through the hole in the *Annihilator's* barrier. More than a thousand feet up, now, staring at his target, he called upon the power his arcane rebirth had bestowed upon him. In a whirl of black smoke, he shifted through a cannon hatch and onto the gun deck, coming face to face with a Mage aiming one of the cannons.

He beheaded the woman before her brain processed that he was even a threat. Blasts of lighting from his pistol took another three gunners, before he leaped from the room. Incantations splintered the wooden inner hull and melted the iron supports of the dreadnought behind him.

Kelad quickly got his bearings. The fore of the ship would be to his right, the aft to his left. The *Annihilator* had to use two generators to keep it in the air, one in each of its split hulls. Dead ahead and to his right, one of them lay behind two feet of steel armour, right in the middle for the most protection.

Kelad moved down the wooden corridor swiftly, checking the rooms on either side. They were storage bays for the cannons, with spares and repair tools hanging in racks. At the sound of booted footsteps barrelling down a side corridor ahead, he shifted into one of the bays, melting back into the shadows.

"Check them all. He's an Aether, so watch yourselves. He could appear out of any shadow, any wall. Kill on sight."

Kelad raised an eyebrow. So, they knew it was him. Of course they did, he had made enough of an entrance.

Getting past the marines would take time his fleet and the Wyvern Bog didn't have. Engaging them would take longer. He leaned over and grabbed a long pick from the rack. On the count of three he drove it into the space between two of the wooden planks, making a gap only a tenth of an inch wide.

Matt Waterhouse

The door into his bay flew open, and three marines rushed in as Kelad shifted again, through the gap he had made in the bulkhead behind him and into the next room. Shifting through solid objects was possible, but very ill-advised, he needed ideally to have at least a small space for the smoke to move through. When his sight returned he saw the three marines searching the room wheel around, and shot one immediately.

As he flew back and sank to the deck, shaking and smoking, Kelad was already moving in on the other two. He stepped to his right, keeping one of his opponents behind the other at all times. He parried the first and cut his throat, and shot the other with his pistol's last charge as he began to raise the alarm.

Kelad spun and tipped the closest rack against the door. Marines immediately began hammering on the door, trying to shove it open or beat it down. Opening the breach of his pistol and dropping another lighting stone inside, he glanced around the bay. His eyes fell on a spare cannon barrel and he grinned.

"*Oh really, gentlemen, you shouldn't have...*"

It wasn't in a mount, but that didn't matter so much.

Accuracy wasn't exactly his priority, more ... volume. The amplifier attached to the back was just waiting for the right pop, to turn into a boom.

"*Now ... how do they do this again?*" He mused. He touched the barrel of his pistol against the little sphere on its mount, and put one finger in his ear.

When he squeezed the trigger, the cannon jumped, and his ears popped. The hatch and bulkhead turned into splinters, melted armour and boiling blood. He had no time to be disoriented or marvel at his destructive handiwork. He jumped past the gory wreckage and past what remained of the marine contingent. He even left the wounded and disoriented to their groaning without finishing them off.

Doubtless, more marines would be waiting for him further in. Any Admiral worth their salt knew that an incursion aboard your ship required marines around the sensitive areas. The mistake Admiral Hezstor had made was in not anticipating that the incursion would come from a source other than the wyvernborn.

At the sound of more footfalls ahead, Kelad ducked into another bay. This one held much the same as the rest of them, although it also had a number of shoulder-mounted light cannons in racks, as well as a number of swords, amplifiers like his pistol and crossbows. He grabbed one of the cannons and slipped back out into the corridor as the marine contingent passed by.

If the Annihilator was arranged in a similar way to a standard battleship, there would be a crew deck above the gun deck, which at this time would have far less foot traffic.

The deck access ladder was just ahead of him and to the left. He waited at the bottom for a moment, training his ears for any sign of trouble. When he heard none, he shifted to the next level up. As he suspected, it was indeed a crew deck. The bunk rooms were empty, as was the galley and mess hall. The patrolling marines and repairmen were easy to slip past, and Kelad made quick progress across the leviathan craft.

He could hear the battle raging outside, so his ships were still fighting. In fact, there seemed to have been a shift in intensity. There were a lot more shouts coming from the upper decks, and the amount of cannonfire had doubled.

The wyvernborn must have joined the fray, and as the question drifted across his mind: *"Where's that damned dragon?"*, a deafening roar shook the deck plate beneath him.

He smirked and doubled his pace. The air began to tremble around him at he drew closer to the generator. He knew there would be no access from the crew deck, he would have to go back down another two levels.

He punched a hole in the deck plate with his pick, and shifted down one level. The voices of crewmen and Mages were audible through the bulkheads around him, and as he punched down again into the deck plate, he heard their voices raise in alarm. He had a hand on his pistol in an instant, but it quickly became clear that it wasn't him they were worried about.

The roar of fury was so close the Annihilator almost creaked in response.

The cannons began firing, and the temperature inside suddenly doubled. Dragonfire, but being absorbed by the barriers. Kelad exhaled and shifted down to the arcaneum.

Most of the deck was armour, and resting areas for the Mages that powered the generator. He had put himself right where he needed to be, in the corridor leading to the generator. However, he was not alone.

A dozen marines were waiting between him and the steel-armoured, reinforced door, armed with crossbows. They raised them in unison.

Kelad smirked and gave them a slight bow.

"*Gentlemen.*"

"*Loose!*" one of them yelled, and the bolts flew with a thrum and a snapping sound.

Kelad shifted as they sped towards him, and re-materialised at a crouch. The light cannon was off his shoulder in an instant, and his pistol against the amplifier.

With a boom, nine of the dozen were incinerated or smashed against the doorway in an instant. The other three dove out of the way. Kelad closed the distance swiftly and finished them before they could get up and collect their senses. The door to the generator was locked and bolted, so Kelad backed off, and fired the cannon again.

The door buckled, the metal rending and melting. There were dozens of shouts behind him as he fired one more time, and the door flew inwards in two pieces. Instantly, the cacophonous hum of the generator filled the corridor.

Kelad ran for the opening, firing the last two shots in his pistol behind him without looking. The Mages attending to the generator were seemingly in two minds. With their ship under attack from a dragon, the generator needed to be running and the barriers high, but Kelad was certainly a more immediate threat, as he proved by cutting the first one down.

He shifted and beheaded another before a bolt of conjured lighting struck the deck an inch from his feet. The catwalks above were filling with Mages and marines, firing down at him. No time for that. He threw the cannon at another

Mage and reloaded his pistol. With one more shift to throw off the shots coming at him, he spun and fired all of his shots into the generator.

It fizzed and sparked, the arcane runes covering it flickered. The roar outside seemed to grow louder.

BOOM! CRACKKKK!

Kelad's ears popped, and he was thrown to the ground alongside all the rest of the Annihilator's crew. There were wet thuds all around him as Mages were thrown from the catwalks. He turned and looked up.

The ceiling of the generator chamber high above was glowing red hot. Kelad rolled under the cover of the catwalks as gobs of molten iron began dropping. With his head still spinning, the screams of those that the iron struck were dulled, but no less horrifying.

The heat flared and rose again, and the roar screeched though Kelad's head even though he could barely hear. In fact it seemed to clear his head, the urgency of it made him look up, and spot the fireball surging down and engulfing the generator.

He shifted immediately, among and past the marines. He half-sprinted, half-stumbled towards the hatch to the gun deck. Screams of horror and agony seemed to follow him along the corridor, closing in until they were almost whispering in his deafened ears.

He shifted as many times as he could to stay ahead of them. He realised he had no time to get to the hatch. Instead he jumped and shifted up into the gap he had made with his pick.

A Mage gaped as Kelad appeared in front of him out of nowhere, and Kelad shoved past without a word. He bolted past the armouries and the workshops, staggering as the *Annihilator* thrashed again. He burst through the door to the cannons, as a huge claw burst through the hull ahead of him.

It tore and rent the wood and iron, ripping bulkhead and deck plate and cannon and crew away, and throwing them to their doom. Kelad dodged to his left, feeling the huge weapon of war tipping and leaning.

He went with it, bolting along the sloping deck, and dived past one of the cannons, straight through the gun-hatch.

The smoky air whipped past him as he fell, his eyes stung and filled with tears from the assault, but the sight around him was glorious.

Hundreds of wyvernborn swooped and dived across the Black Fleet, dropping firebombs, landing and engaging their crew and marines hand to hand. As he watched, a skiff tumbled, blazing, to smash into the ground. One of the battleships clung to life, although it was little more than a fireball, somehow floating still, like a ghost.

His own ships had followed their orders to the letter. All had raised green flags on their highest masts, emblazoned with a dragon in white and gold. The symbol seemed to have been recognised. The wyvernborn and his fleet were fighting side by side.

The *Spearhead* was half-wrecked, but it remained fighting and flying, despite losing half her cannons. *Paladin One* and *Shadow One* flew in formation, spiralling around the stricken battleship to protect it. Rogue Group had lost another of their number, but the rest were engaging and keeping the Black Fleet skiffs off the wyvernborn.

As he turned back to the battleships, he saw *Spearhead* begin to list to port, tipping as if she were about to capsize. Two battleships swung around to bring their broadsides to bear on it, and Paladin One broke formation, jumping between the cannonfire and her ally.

The skiff caught most of the shots, and her barriers were immediately breached. Shadow One dipped and blasted one with its heavy cannons and broadsides. A second volley struck Paladin One, and the skiff shattered in the air, sending hull fragments and crew spinning in every direction.

Spearhead threw a volley towards the battleships as a cloud of wyvernborn dove down and firebombed them as well, and when the barriers were breached, the flying warriors dived and boarded, slicing through the deck crew.

For a moment, Kelad couldn't see *Shadowblade*, and as his heart began to sink in grief, she swept around from behind the raging battleships. With a sharp turn, her heavy cannons blasted two burning holes in the side of the other Black Fleet vessel attacking *Spearhead*, while her broadside cannons let out a burst that made a flanking skiff pull away in alarm.

Kelad grinned as he turned and tumbled in the air. *Give them all the hell they deserve.*

Above him, the bulk of the *Annihilator* was completely dwarfed by the ancient beast that was systematically ripping it apart. Both of the false dragon heads on the prow were roaring in fury and confusion, before the jaws of the real thing crushed one in a single bite, and tore it away with a triumphant roar. The twisted mess of steel tumbled away.

The *Annihilator's* crew were sending crossbow bolts and waves of magical energy at the dragon, to no avail. The cannons, perhaps, would have dissuaded it from its assault. Their attempts to beat it back were met with swift streams of dragonfire, consuming them and their craft as if they were nothing more than annoying kindling.

Then Kelad tumbled around the other way, and lost sight of the battle, although he could still hear the dragon over the cannonfire. He was about three hundred feet above the ground and closing on it fast. Shifting wouldn't do him much good, he would simply either splatter into the ground faster, or a fraction of a second slower. Even grabbing on to a skiff...

He held the communication stone to his mouth, shouting into it with a throat that was immediately dried out by the dustbowl air. *"This is General Kelad! I'm in freefall beneath the Annihilator! I need pickup!"*

The stone slipped from his fingers and spun out of his reach. Three hundred feet to the ground became two hundred in a flash, or so it seemed. A blink or two later it had become a hundred and thirty.

He closed his eyes and prepared to meet his death, his final act one of some redemption, or so he hoped.

He felt the impact across his ribs, and then there was a nauseating jerk. The wind around him died, then became a breeze. He could still hear the battle above him, but there was another sound inches away from him. The beating of leathery wings, exhalations of breath snorting from powerful lungs.

Kelad opened his eyes, catching his own breath. A scaly, clawed hand and arm were wrapped around his chest, under his arms. He craned his head around, and saw the jaw and narrowed eyes of a wyvernborn, wings spread wide. It was in formation with two others, carrying Kelad closer and closer to the ground gently.

Their wings flared a yard up from the dust, and they dropped. Kelad grunted as they hit the ground, and grunted again as the wyvernborn let him go. He managed to land on his feet, and turned to look at them. All three glared at him.

"I appreciate the catch, gentlemen. Thank you."

The one that had caught him stepped forwards with a growl. "I am Kanku, of clan Reeva. You wear the colours of Cael, and the stones and medals of a General. You are, therefore, my prisoner."

Kelad smiled, and raised his hands. "I am General Sel Kelad, Standing Army. I command the vessels assisting you. I assume you fought at the Pil Valley?"

Kanku growled.

"I thought so. We made a deal after that, a deal of non-aggression, did we not? I intended to honour that deal. The Lord Marshal did not. My soldiers are fighting and dying to defend your home, and our peace."

A triumphant roar blasted out across the dustbowl, drawing Kelad and the wyvernborns' eye.

The dragon swept up and flared its wings, flapping and roaring, breathing huge jets of flame into the air and onto the *Annihilator*. It had sensed the kill.

With a creak and a groan, that could have erupted from the dying throat of a great beast, the *Annihilator* began to fall. Slowly at first, but then faster and faster as its bulk dragged it towards the blasted ground.

When it struck like a meteorite, almost half a mile away, there was a tremor that made the ground leap. The burning dreadnought wreck was curling and flaking like a stack of paper. There were no screams from Admiral Hesztor or any of his crew.

With the siege craft now a smouldering pile of slag, Kelad's eyes turned to the fleet above. The remaining battleships and skiffs slowly began to come about. They were limping northwards, sending a few parting shots towards *Spearhead* and Kelad's remaining skiffs.

He counted five green flags remaining of his eight-strong fleet. Three of the Black Fleet's battleships lingered, however, and Kelad noted with a raised eyebrow that their insignia had been lowered from the mast. Surrender or capture? Possibly both.

Shadowblade regrouped with the remaining ships. Rogue Three formed up with Shadow One and Two, and the quartet set off in pursuit of the fleeing ships at full sail. A contingent of wyvernborn went with them, more than two hundred of them. High above, the dragon began to climb up above the clouds, as dragons did when they were about to dive at speed, and lay waste.

They closed in quickly, right at the edge of his vision and hearing. He heard the rumble of cannonfire, saw the smoke forming. He saw the dragon drop from the clouds and arrow downwards, and a boom rumbled over the ground, shaking the dustbowl almost as much as the impact of the *Annihilator*.

Spearhead slowly drifted to the ground close by. Around a hundred wyvernborn glided down with her, wings opened wide, some landing on the deck, some guiding her in. The crippled battleship stopped at a hover, six feet above the ground, but she was still listing to port.

This close, Kelad could see the extent of the damage. Dents, holes, and melted scorches lined the hull. The main sail was half-incinerated. Smoke rose from the deck. It was a miracle, coupled with the skill of her captain and crew, that she was even able to float.

The ramp lowered, as Kelad approached with his wyvernborn 'captors'. Captain Obrek stood at the top, and saluted. Kelad returned it, and beckoned him downwards.

"I trust I am your only captive, Kanku?" Kelad muttered.

The wyvernborn growled. "We will see."

Obrek sent an order to one of his officers, and walked down the ramp. He was heavily favouring his left leg, and there were bloody marks on his uniform. He was stained with soot and smoke.

Kelad grasped his hand and clapped him gently on the shoulder. "*Good to see you alive, my friend. The Spearhead?*"

"*Flying. That's all I can ask for from my crew. We have ninety dead or wounded ... I hope our ... allies here can assist with that.*"

Kelad glanced around at Kanku and grinned. "*I'm told it remains to be seen.*"

Kanku snarled in return, but quickly fell silent. There was a swoosh of air, and a heavy thud beside them. A familiar tall, female wyvernborn straightened her back, and folded her wings behind her.

Zeta snorted, and smoke curled from her nostrils. "General Kelad."

"Zeta, if I remember correctly. In my old age, names tend to escape me, but actions do not."

"They do not escape us either." Her face remained stern, but she leaned forwards and took his hand and forearm. Kelad smiled and clapped her on the shoulder.

She bared her teeth in a grin, and chuckled. She extended the same hand to Obrek, who took it with a bow of his head. "You and your crew fight like wyvernborn, Captain. The shamen are ready to receive your wounded."

Obrek nodded, and replied with his own heavily accented Haaman. "Thank you."

"And we have prizes," she muttered, looking up at the three battleships. "And prisoners." She barked at Kanku, who nodded and took to the air with his fellows. Her large, yellow eyes narrowed as they focused on Kelad. "You and your men saved us, General. There were some who questioned it ... but you are a man of honour, as are you, Captain."

Kelad took a moment before he replied. He found himself having to swallow bile again, feeling singularly unworthy of her words. Victory or no, he was currently standing in the dust of a massacre of his own making. "I have been on the wrong end of enough pain."

Captain Obrek raised an eyebrow at him. Zeta growled again, a more thoughtful sound. "It cannot have been easy. We understand. We have made difficult decisions in the past, decisions that many only understand later ... because we believed them to be right."

"Did history prove you right?"

"At first, no, not even close. However, we put things right eventually. The road was difficult." Zeta laid a hand on his shoulder. "You are, perhaps, now men without a nation, without a flag. There are those who will understand better than I how hard it can be to turn away from your people."

"Men without a nation?" Kelad smiled. "No. We are men of Cael, as you are a warrior of the Wyvern Bog. It is not Obrek and I who have betrayed our nation."

He grasped Zeta's clawed hand. "Cael does not betray its allies. Cael, Haama, the Wyvern Bog ... we are allies, are we not?"

Zeta smiled. "Yes we are."

21

Allessandra's steepled fingers framed the Black Fleet attaché perfectly. It was as if the officious, towering woman was in front of a cannon's sights.

She had the wisdom, it seemed, to sense the danger she was in. The attaché's back had not relaxed a single fibre of muscle since she had walked into the throne room, and stood in front of Allessandra and the Council Of Ministers.

The princess was sitting back on the Silver Throne, regarding the military official with the eyes of a savage predator. Helen was back where she was supposed to be, where she was always supposed to have been, by her side, on a high-backed armchair to her right, placed at the foot of the five steps which led to the seat of the Regent. The Council sat on Allessandra's left hand side, watching proceedings in a row of large, wooden seats.

Despite the scrutiny, the attache's voice was strong. *"Intelligence was received that the wyvernborn were planning an attack on Victory, as well as the settlements between here and the Wyvern Bog, utilising their dragon in the assault. The loss of life was projected to be devastating."*

"*Spare me,*" Allessandra spat. Along the edge of the room, the Council of Ministers stiffened, more in alarm than anything else. Helen turned to her in surprise, a smile slowly forming on her lips.

The attache frowned. "*Your Grace...*"

"*In the middle of peace negotiations, which have a chance of succeeding for the first time in a century, do you think the wyvernborn would be foolish enough to mount an assault on the capital?*"

"*Our intelligence...*"

"*After decades of holding back from going on the offensive with that same dragon? Decades where they seemed to decide that it was in their best interests to remain in the Wyvern Bog and defend it from us? Decades where they made peace with their closest neighbours, whom they had been at war with for almost three centuries?"

The attaché was gradually turning brighter and brighter shades of red, while Helen's smile was widening. "*I ... Your Grace, I assure you...*"

"*When was this attack supposed to have taken place?*"

"*It was ... our intelligence suggested it was imminent ... and that the peace negotiations were a way to lull us into a false sense of...*"

Allessandra threw up a hand, and the attache's voice fell silent, as if she had cast a spell. "*Why are First Minister Evandro and I still alive?*"

Out of the corner of her eye, she saw Evandro stroke his beard, perhaps to suppress a smile or a chuckle. Helen frowned for a moment, then caught on.

"*I... don't understand, Your Grace.*"

"*The Caelish delegation arrived at the peace talks aboard a trading barge. The Haaman delegation arrived on a dreadnought. They had us ice cold. Why miss that chance, to remove the head from the sand snake?*"

"*I ... do not know.*"

"*Why would the wyvernborn plan to raze and poison lands that they are negotiating for? That they already have a positive relationship with in trade and defense?*"

The attaché's voice was little more than a whisper. "*I do not know, Your Grace.*"

"*Do you take me for a fool, attaché?*"

The woman's back became even straighter as she shook her head quickly and vigorously. "*No, Your Grace.*"

"*Does Lord Marshal Vehnek take me for a fool?*"

Evandro was no longer hiding his smile. The attaché swallowed. "*No, Your Grace.*"

Allessandra lowered her hands to rest them on the arms of the throne, and crossed one leg over the other. "*You are merely the messenger, I suspect. It is not you that came up with the cock-and-bull report you were about to give. I suspect you never planned to report to the Council and I at all. In fact, I suspect Lord Marshal Vehnek expected to raze the Wyvern Bog with his fleet before we even knew they were conducting an operation in the area. Remove an enemy, weaken the Haaman Alliance, and leave us picking up the pieces while he and the rest of his forces range abroad with less scrutiny, or none."*

Allessandra looked to the Council of Ministers, specifically to Commander Codesh Ulan, the acting Minister Of Defence. Kelad had lent him the position while he had departed with the fleet. *"Who is the commanding officer of the Black Fleet contingent in Victory, Commander Ulan?"*

"Admiral Hurik, Your Grace."

"How many are currently under his command?"

"Fifteen hundred marines, and a hundred Mages."

Allessandra nodded. *"Mobilise the City Guard and Standing Army personnel. All Black Fleet personnel are to be escorted from Victory at once. I would like their barracks emptied and searched, and all of their ships and support craft impounded. The men will leave on foot."*

Ulan stood. *"At once, Your Grace."*

The Royal Guards left with him, leaving Eluco, who was slowly approaching the attaché. Allessandra looked at the woman closely, who was beginning to sag, her skin taking on the pallor of sour milk. *"You will not be harmed, attache, far from it, but I would like every scrap of information that has passed your hands since Lord Marshal Vehnek arrived in the city. The future of our nation depends on it. Eluco, please see to her accommodation and needs."*

Eluco nodded once, and guided the official, who had begun to tremble, from the room. First Minister Evandro coughed and gave Allessandra a look.

"She will be taken to a room, not the cells," Allessandra grunted. *"What do you take me for, First Minister?"*

"You've been reading your histories," Helen said approvingly.

"And practicing my Haaman," Allessandra told her with a grin. She

The Empire Of Fire

stood, and the rest of the room stood with her.

The procession left the throne room, and strode towards the council chambers. *"Has there been any more word from General Kelad?"*

Evandro nodded. *"He lost three of his ships, a fourth was crippled. However, the Black Fleet were repelled, with the assistance of the wyvernborn."*

"Did any of the attack fleet escape?"

Evandro paused. *"No, Your Grace. None have been seen by any of our watchtowers."*

Allessandra faltered half a step. *"None?"*

"Yes, Your Grace."

"How many were in the attack?"

"Fifty, including the Annihilator."

Allessandra swallowed. A bolt of terror shot through her body. If the wyvernborn ever felt betrayed by her, by Cael... *"Then, it is fortunate that Kelad took them off-guard. The rest of the Black Fleet?"*

"We do not know."

Brynden made a sound like a bubbling grumble. "Vehnek is a slippery one. He will have avoided any place where he does not have explicit support."

"Agreed," Carrasco added. *"I have commanded the Merchant Fleet to send word of them, should they be seen near to any of the shipping lanes or trade flight paths."*

"Excellent. Minister Brynden, please form a short-list of Haaman representatives who could serve on the Council, either now or in future. While conflict may be upon us, we must remain committed to our efforts for peace."

"Very good," Brynden rumbled, beaming. "I will do so immediately."

"Minister Carrasco, I'm sure you already have, but reiterate that the Black Fleet should not be approached or hailed. Your craft have armaments ..."

"But not enough to engage a battleship," Carrasco agreed. *"It will be done."*

***

The meeting between the remaining three lasted an hour, where reports were given of the engagement over the Orlin dustbowl. The movements of the remainder of the Black Fleet remained couched in the theory presented by the Alliance: that Vehnek had gone into the White Sea.

Two separate fleets had been spotted by military and civilian agents in Cael. One had set off on a northbound course from The Bay Of War, another headed due west from Cael City. Both could easily have changed course into the White Sea once they were out of sight. Allessandra drummed her fingertips on the table, and waited to hear news of an attack on a settlement, but none came.

The Alliance had fallen silent, as Allessandra had been afraid they might. All messages pledging support had thus far gone unanswered. She was worried that Vehnek's gambit, despite being obliterated, had still managed to sow enough of a seed of doubt to scupper every peace effort. There had also been no word from Kelad for several hours.

The Council quietened from their deliberations for a moment, exhausting all of their news. Only the drumming of Allessandra's fingers remained, until she cleared her throat.

"*Several concerns were raised during the peace talks concerning dragons. Outlandish as it is ... what are the odds of them becoming a threat, at Vehnek's command?*"

"*Records of the final battle where the beasts were used speak volumes, Your Grace,*" Evandro muttered. "*Once control was broken, they burned everything and everyone. The city of Uncur is uninhabitable to this day. The link that was used to control the beasts was tenuous at best, and Haama's Mages in Uncur were able to break it, albeit to their doom as well as ours. I don't know why Lord Marshal Vehnek would risk using them again, unless he is sure that his control cannot be broken.*"

The Empire Of Fire

"*It is immaterial, is it not?*" Carrasco said with a wave of his hand. "*The dragons are all gone, with the exception of the one in the Wyvern Bog.*"

"*They spoke of resurrection,*" Evandro added. "*If it is possible, then we may have cause for concern, but they would surely need something to resurrect. No-one knows where the corpses are, to my knowledge.*"

Allessandra stroked her chin. "*Would the Arch Mages know?*"

Evandro sighed. "*It is possible. Ack, it always comes back to the Arch Mages, doesn't it. They can never have enough power!*"

"*This remains speculation without concrete fact,*" Carrasco pointed out. "*They have very little oversight, as the council is well aware. The gold they spend is not under my purview, unfortunately.*"

"*'Government is a barrier to advancement' would be their argument, I'm sure,*" Evandro grunted.

Allessandra rubbed her head. "*For decades we have merely been pawns of them, pieces to move around their board. We cannot trust them unless they are regulated in some way. Otherwise, they can simply act against us whenever they wish, and do so effectively.*"

"*This is something I've long considered,*" Evandro mused, stroking his beard thoughtfully. "*Limits on power, checks and balances. Perhaps we must be the check on the Mages and the military, while the citizens are a check on us.*"

"*As a finance man, a well-balanced scale is something I approve of,*" Carrasco said with a smirk. "*However, I fear we have escaped the point. Where could the corpses of these dragons be? With the Arch Mages?*"

Evandro nodded. "*Possibly. The bones of the Black Dragon were removed from the palace. The Magus Towers were the most likely destination.*"

The opening and closing of the chamber door drew their attention. Booted footsteps quickly ascended the chamber stairs, and at the top Eluco bowed. His face was set in a grim line. "*I apologise for the interruption, but there is an urgent message for you, Your Grace. It is from His Majesty The King. He requests to speak with you and The Council immediately.*"

Allessandra glanced at Carrasco and Evandro, before all three stood.

They walked brusquely and silently to the long range communications chamber, tension rising the entire way. The King rarely used magical means to contact his daughter, preferring letters under the royal seal, and as for the urgency...

When the three reached the chamber, they saw that it was fully operational once again, and had been cleaned of the massacre that had befallen those inside on the night of the fire. They stood in front of the amplifier dish pointed at Cael City, and sat down in the area where the King would be able to see them. After a moment, his haggard and tired face appeared before them.

Allessandra frowned at her father. He seemed thinner, his eyes bloodshot. He was reclining on a chair with an attendant close by, as well as old Doctor Ostruk, who had been an ancient man even when Allessandra was a girl. He had always seemed old, and had likely come out of the womb a shrivelled, shrunken octogenarian.

"Can you hear me?" King Alesio's voice was weak and strained, more whisper than spoken word, and Allessandra frowned.

"Father, what has happened?"

"I bear ... ill tidings, my dear. I am sorry ... the Queen ... she made an attempt ... on my life ..."

Allessandra frowned and sat up straight. Eluco moved closer to her. She couldn't believe it, and based on the reactions of Evandro and Carrasco, neither could they. *"What ... an attempt ... what happened?"*

His eyes drooped, it seemed he could barely hear her. The doctor put an old arm around his shoulder in comfort and strength. *"Yes ... it was a very effective attempt ... but merely an attempt nonetheless."*

Allessandra gaped at him, and her chest clenched like an angry fist. She couldn't breathe. Evandro placed a hand on her shoulder and gently squeezed. *"What is your condition, Your Majesty, and where is the Queen?"*

King Alesio closed his eyes, and with a voice that wavered between strangled and hoarse, he began to tell the tale.

The Empire Of Fire

***

Alesio watched the Black Fleet ships through his spyglass. There were a hundred and forty two of them, he had counted twice to be sure, just at the edge of the city, never straying closer. They had arrived the day before in dribs and drabs, clusters of three or four, and he had thought little of it until they had numbered in the three dozen.

The spyglass had been a gift from a Mokkan land lord, and it was quite good. It was likely one of several coming gifts that would precede a marriage proposal for Allessandra. They always were.

Mokku were a persistent nation, more persistent than any other. Dignitaries and oligarchs had sent potential suitors for his daughter since she had turned thirteen, hoping for a pact, hoping for a stake in Cael, perhaps. The advancing sands did little to dissuade them, what Cael had to offer wasn't farmland or crops. Haama had plenty of those, and royal control over Cael meant control over Haama as well. Allessandra was merely the potential pawn in a lordling's game.

Their offers were good, very good, but not for his daughter or his country. There were many in the Caelish Government who were likely bought off, telling him that the marriage would be a boon for the economy of the nation, usher in a partnership with Mokku that would breed prosperity and new horizons. There were so many of them and so vocal, that their persuasive, snake-like words hissed through his ears even when his mind tried to block them out.

As distasteful as it was, the Queen's racism was the largest and most impenetrable barrier to Mokku's cultural conquest of Cael ... and he was oddly thankful for it.

Mokku and Mirell had that particular set of views in common, although they were directed at different groups of people. Mokku had been long obsessed with the pigment of skin. Despite the endless confidence in triumph at the breaking of their chains, their uprising from bondage had never ended, at least in their minds. They were at the head of the world, the most powerful nation on Planar, and yet, of course, it was not enough. It was never enough.

"It is time, Alesio," they would always say. "It is time for us to join together, for we both have quarrels with the rest of the world. The snow-skins of Noor, the olive-skins of Adrezsti, the pink-skins of Haama, who have ever been a thorn in your side. We can bring them all to our heels together."

The King wanted his daughter to be more than a piece on a game board played by knaves, he always had, and she certainly had little interest in the boys and men who had attempted to win her as a prize. He knew the price of marrying for power rather than love, and he knew it well. Mirell was the daughter of Arch Mage Yinnorin, the former head of the Magus Towers. His marriage to her had been one of convenience and drive to further her father's goals.

She had been a beauty, she still was, and in his youth the beauty had been all he saw. It was only as they had grown into middle age that he had seen what often lurked beneath it. Both he and Allessandra had paid a heavy price for his youthful foolishness. Now that his daughter was such a wonderful part of his life, and the Queen had begun to mellow, he had made a degree of peace with his difficulties with both of them.

The effect of it, however, remained. He wanted his daughter to marry a man she loved, and who loved her. He didn't care if it was a farmhand or a sailor or a soldier or an emperor, as long as he loved her, and did right by her ... as long as that man was not named Sel Kelad.

Still, the princelings' gifts were a silver lining to the black stormcloud. The spyglass was an excellent piece, which he used frequently to watch the birds and ships overhead, or the people in the streets and markets below. Now, he was watching a battle fleet, heading westward under full sail.

When they were out of sight he descended from the roof garden and back down into the Golden Throne palace. The sun was setting and soon he would be able to see little through the glass anyway. His eight Royal Guards followed him, their steps perfectly synchronised with his. Through the halls they walked, the attendants and slaves parting before them as if they were a boat in a sea of people, all bowing as low as they could, like the dipping of the waves.

They stepped onto the lifting platform at the base of the Royal Tower, and waited as it quickly ascended the thousand feet to the top.

"*Keep outside the room, but please come in if there are any undue noises,*" The King muttered to Jannoth, the head of his guards.

"*As you command, Your Majesty.*"

It was the same order he had given every time he had gone to the chambers since Haama's Council Of Ministers had agreed to the ceasefire. He had been anticipating the usual inferno of rage, but so far Mirell had only shown him the coldness of a Noorani winter blizzard. Not even a word had passed her lips in his direction, and he found the anticipation of the squall more uncomfortable than weathering it.

A cowardly part of him wanted the platform to slow to a crawl, or for the tower to grow and keep growing so he never reached the top. This time, more than any other, could feel the energy of Mirell's rage shaking the palace.

But reach the top it did, and Alesio stepped from it with his retinue. The doors stood before him, with more Royal Guards on either side. The entryway was meant to be large and imposing, but not to him, the man who lived there.

The Royal Guards bowed. Alesio raised his hands for them to rise, and listened for any sound beyond the huge, ornate double doors. The sigil of Cael was emblazoned upon each, carved in the thick white wood by an artisan's hand. Painted with unerring smoothness, flawless, set with jewels and real, melted gold, the eyes of the snakes atop their pyramids stared at Alesio accusingly.

There was only silence in the Royal chambers. He gestured, and the guards on either side pulled the doors open. They didn't even creak. Mirell seemed to have banished sound itself from her presence.

He walked in, holding up a hand to his retinue. They waited outside, and the doors closed between them. More silence greeted him, and only silence. He took careful steps forwards, watching all of the doors carefully. The foyer was gargantuan, with stairs spiralling up to two more floors. The vast lounge lay ahead, with its balcony overlooking Cael City and the Esperrten River. Studies were on either side of it, and the library, and another lounge, and even a banquet hall that was large enough for thirty people.

Alesio strained his ears. Nothing, at least nothing down here. He climbed the spiral stairs to the next floor. The bedrooms, even more studies, the nursery, the privy, all too were quiet.

When he listened again, he thought there may have been a whisper, a small sound above him.

He ascended again, for some reason wanting to keep his steps as silent as possible. His own nerves, maybe. He even kept his breathing slow and calm, through his nose and out of his mouth.

The whispered voice was coming from Mirell's study, certainly hers. But as he approached, he thought he could hear something else. A second voice, even quieter, distorted somehow.

He closed the distance to the study, and wrapped a hand around the handle. He held there for a moment, eyes closed, trying to listen.

What counsel Mirell and the stranger were keeping: Alesio couldn't tell. He could make out no words, although the tone was sharp, urgent. Whose tone?

Both seemed unhappy with something, although the voices began to quickly fade. She was walking out onto the balcony.

Alesio glanced down at his hand. His knuckles were white. He swallowed and opened the door.

The armchair had been dragged back from her mahogany desk. The drapes fluttered beside the open balcony door. He crossed the room, the carpet masking his footsteps.

He saw her then through the open glass door. She was leaning over the marble railing, her dress fluttering, black hair dancing around her neck and shoulders. He frowned as his eye caught a quick movement, a flash almost. Something fell from her hand, dropping out of sight, small, dark and round.

The Empire Of Fire

Straight off the edge of the balcony it went, falling out of sight quickly, and with no change in her posture at all, he dismissed it as something planted by his paranoia, a side-effect of his heightened nerves.

Alesio walked onto the balcony, lingering by the door.

"*Mirell.*"

She turned her head an inch in his direction.

"*Love ... we are one. We are united in Cael's traditions and her future both. We are united in the raising and the love of our daughter. Let us not be apart now.*"

It was a speech he had given many times, variations of words and terms, but it was concise enough to make his point. Sometimes it worked, sometimes not. He was curious which would be the case now.

"*Perhaps you're right,*" Mirell said calmly, her voice drifting on the wind. "*When did our little girl become a woman?*"

"*When, indeed ...*" Despite the words, he drew no closer to her. The chill of the high winds, thinner up here on their high tower ... perhaps that was all it was that was making the hairs on the back of his neck stand on end. It had to be, for there was no sign of the coming storm that had always struck when there was potential for a quarrel. Mirell's upper back was tense, as was her neck. Her breathing was quick, but not audible, she was not huffing like a charging bull.

When she turned to face him, her face was lined with worry, but not rage. She studied him, studied his face.

"*Come inside, Mirell. The night is drawing in. Let us light the fire ... perhaps take a night cruise on the river or the sea, get away from the palace for a day or two.*"

Mirell turned away once again. "*While our daughter and our enemies decide the fate of our nation?*"

"*Nothing will be decided in two days. The Council Of Ministers will have much to negotiate, especially after a hundred years. If anything goes seriously wrong, we will be informed, and we will be able to veto whatever it is with a word.*" He could have drawn close to her then, but still the uneasiness at the back of his mind wouldn't let him go. Normally he would have, to attempt to quell her rage, but without the rage now, he didn't exactly know what to do.

"If it will ease your worry, we can remain here. In fact, it certainly is a wiser course than mine, although less relaxing."

Mirell's shoulders moved a fraction of an inch. Perhaps a laugh. *"Remaining here doesn't have to be stressful, Alesio."*

She turned to him then, drifting towards him with one hand on the balcony rail. Her eyes were fixed on his, holding him there in place. She leaned forwards and touched her lips to his. Her hand stroked his beard, then his neck, teasing beneath the collar of his doublet.

"What's that for?" he asked.

"For raising a daughter with a strong will, and a kind heart," she whispered. *"Let's go inside."*

He joined her, letting her lead him towards their bedchamber, his uneasiness being drowned out by foolish carnal desire for her. Mirell was still a beauty, her age had not dulled any of it in his eyes. It was only her mood that did that, and her mood now was something outside the norm, some of the affection he desired from her that had become more rare as the years had passed.

They had lost much of whatever love had been present in their marriage, which had been little. Any affection had been doled out as a reward, as transactional as the relationship between a tavern keeper and a drunk.

As she turned into him and wrapped her arms around him, it felt different. Her kiss was hungrier, more tender, more passionate. She allowed his hands to move the straps of her dress from her shoulders, run his fingers through her hair, down her bare back. She skilfully unfastened his doublet, guided his hands to her breasts.

It was enough for foolish desire and nostalgia to override sense, and he fell with her onto the bed. They struggled out of their clothes, and began the dance that they so rarely had the desire to dance.

It was far from the cold experience it often was. Their steps were

The Empire Of Fire

synchronised. They twirled and leaped like young lovers. Breathlessly they were entwined, lit by the sunset, then by the stars.

They held each other in the aftermath, curled up in the sheets. He could feel her heart beating swiftly as she reclined against his chest.

"*I would make a vow to you,*" Alesio murmured, intoxicated in the ecstasy that they had made between them. "*To stand by your side in loyalty and protection, to share in your burdens however I can, to continue to raise and counsel our daughter together. To do so when eyes are upon us, and when they are not.*"

Mirell made a sound, an exhalation of air, a laugh to Alesio's ears. "*She seems to close her ears to our counsel.*"

"*She does. She inherited that from both of us, I think. It has certainly been a trait in my family.*"

"*Mine, also.*"

"*I am ... very proud of you, Mirell.*"

She turned to face him, and he brushed the hair from her face. Her brown eyes were searching his face for some sign of ... deceit? She only found sincerity. "*For what?*"

"*Allessandra has a fire to her, an edge. It will make her a formidable queen, and a formidable woman. It is an edge you sharpened, but tempered with love. You raised her to fight, and never give in, and I cannot imagine a better mother for a Queen.*"

Mirell stared at him for a moment, and chewed her lip. She turned her face down to kiss his chest, and then rolled onto her back, face turned away from him again. Her hand guided his to her belly as she arched her back, and the dance began again.

"*I'll ring for the servants,*" she muttered in the aftermath. "*I haven't eaten, have you?*"

Alesio shook his head drowsily.

"*Food and wine, then ... and perhaps something else...*" Mirell kissed him, and donned a flowing robe to descend to the lower levels of their personal chambers.

Alesio lay beneath the sheets, dismissing his earlier unease. Perhaps this was what Mirell had needed, proof that Allessandra was no fool, that she was ready for the responsibilities of the throne, that she would be no pushover. There had certainly been many times that Alesio has worried for his daughter's manner, worries that she had put to rest in his mind.

He mused on his wife and daughter as he put on his own robe. Allessandra had been shown warmth and cold, a caring touch and the back of a hand. Her birth had been difficult, Mirell had suffered in pain for days, and had not fully recovered for the first year of Allessandra's life. She had vowed to Alesio that she would not bear another child, which had been the cause of a long-lasting quarrel between them. He understood and respected her wishes, but the perspective of heirs and the strength of a bond between Allessandra and a sibling fell on deaf ears.

He had often considered that he was wrong to ask her to go through whole process again, and when it came to it, he didn't want to lose her. Loveless marriage or no loveless marriage, he didn't want his daughter to grow up without her mother.

He descended the stairs, to find servants arranging the dining table in their banquet room. Food was already being brought out on trays for the pair of them: flanks of pink, lemon and salt spiced fish, fruit that was fresh from the protected gardens within the palace walls, thin slices of beef and lamb that had been dipped in seasoned broth, and flagons of wine and mountain water.

It smelled intoxicating. He smiled at Mirell, who sat down at the table with a sigh. *"You all may go."*

The servants bowed and departed. Alesio circled the table and kissed Mirell on the cheek, before sitting down to eat.

They laughed as they dined, reminiscing about their early years, their marriage, their journeys to Adrezsti and Salketh, for diplomacy and otherwise. After an hour, the King was well on his way to happily drunk.

"You made the Governor soil his robes," Alesio said with a laugh.

The Empire Of Fire

"*He mistook me for his own weak councillors, to his error.*" Mirell took a mouthful of wine, and savoured it.

"*Imagine considering you weak...*" Alesio drained his glass. "*Nights like this make me remember ... how much time we have. How much can be so easily wasted.*"

Mirell put down her glass. "*How much of it we have wasted, you mean.*"

Alesio sighed. "*Perhaps. But more nights like tonight, a chance to simply eat together and talk ... and the rest ...*"

The queen rolled her eyes, and sighed. "*Perhaps you're correct... although you will have to earn that kind of lovemaking on a regular basis.*"

She stood and strode to the cabinet, taking out two glasses. They were tumblers, small and crystal, enough only for a mouthful of liquor.

"*Those are lovely,*" Alesio mused.

"*A gift, from some lordling or another,*" Mirell muttered.

"*Probably to butter us up to offer them Allessandra.*"

She pulled a bottle from the top shelf of the cabinet, a twenty year old fire-whiskey, bought on the day of Allessandra's birth. "*This seems appropriate, now that she's standing up to us, hmm?*"

Alesio chuckled. "*I think it just might be.*"

"*Next time, we can take her dresses and her palace as well as her ship.*"

He stood up, and massaged her shoulders gently. She stepped away as she turned to face him, handing him one of the glasses.

He studied the fluid inside it for a moment. The fire whiskey was the colour of golden honey, leaving a faint trace of itself as it swirled around the bottom. There was a pattern carved into the base of the glass, weaving and twisting.

"*To our daughter,*" Alesio said.

"*To the future of Cael,*" Mirell returned.

They clinked glasses together, and Mirell downed the whiskey in a single gulp. She gave a small cough and rubbed her throat. "*I'd quite forgotten the burn it leaves.*"

He smiled and raised the glass to his lips. The fire whiskey was chilled, the cold and the heat of the spices within mixing together on his tongue.

Two things stopped him from swallowing. The first was a subtle glow of light at the bottom of the crystal glass. It was a rune, the shape of a swirl and a musical note entwined together. It was red, at the centre of the patterns on the base on the inside. He frowned at it, and looked up at Mirell.

The second thing that stopped him was her expression. Her eyes were wide, her mouth twisted into the snarl of a gargoyle, but turned up at the edges in a savage grin.

Alesio's skin began to itch, and his throat tightened. Something dripped onto his top lip, then onto his robe. Specks of red, moving from his nose.

He spat out the whiskey, and tried to call for his guards, but his voice was completely silenced, choked as if hands were around his throat and squeezing.

"*Drink deeply, my love,*" Mirell hissed. She surged forwards, pushing him to the marble floor. The back of his head clonked against the floor, and he gasped for air.

She was on top of him, pouring more of the whiskey into his glass. She filled it right to the brim, and grabbed Alesio by the neck. He already couldn't breathe, and could barely feel the fingers digging into his throat. As she picked up the glass again, tipping it towards him, his dying brain made a final connection to buy him a few more seconds of life.

He clamped his mouth and eyes shut, and wrenched his head to the side as the liquid fell towards him. It splashed into his hair and down his neck. Mirell's fingers began squeezing his face, trying to open his mouth.

Alesio's hands opened. His right wildly swung at her, and she pinned it to the floor beneath her knee. The cartilage and bone focused under her weight into a pressure that almost made him cry out in pain, if not for the certainty of death as soon as his mouth opened.

Before she could pin his left hand as well, he swung it outwards, and grabbed a fist-full of the cloth covering the vast dinner table. With the last of his strength, he yanked on it hard, sending the empty wine flagons and the plate of fish clattering to the floor, where they shattered on the marble with a loud crash. Barely a moment later, he heard the door into their chambers flying open, and the pressure on him immediately released. The Royal Guards and servants pounded into the dining room, where Mirell began to wail.

"*The King! Help the King!*"

A voice commanded that the palace doctor be fetched immediately. Alesio was rolled onto his side, where he could stare directly at Mirell.

Tears were falling down her face, and the act in her expression was worthy of the highest paid mummers in Cael. He grabbed at the guards arm weakly, and mouthed the words he couldn't say through his tightened throat.

"*Glass ... Poison...*"

Mirell still held the crystal tumbler in her hand. The guard beside him looked up at the Queen with narrowed eyes.

"*Your Majesty ... hand the glass over, please.*"

Her mummer's grief turned to a poisoner's rage in an instant. "*The impudence! The King is ill, tend to him!*"

The guard nodded to a subordinate, who began to approach. "*Your Majesty, please ... the glass.*"

Mirell backed away, turning red, a demonic creature rather than the woman he had lain with, the mother of his daughter.

"*He will lead you to ruin. Allessandra to worse. Everything we are will be eroded, destroyed.*"

She stepped out onto the balcony, continuing until she was backed against the railing.

"*Your Majesty, come inside. We can get everything straightened, you will not be harmed.*"

"*Oh, I will. I will be raped, as this land will be. If you have the blood of the serpent, you will let the poison take him before it takes Cael!*"

And with that, she grasped onto the railing and jumped. It was the last thing Alesio saw before he was overcome, but not the last thing he heard.

Mirell didn't scream as she fell the thousand feet to her death. Madly, and hysterically, she laughed.

***

"*She was still holding the glass,*" Alesio rasped. "*The arcanists in the palace examined it. The rune etched into the base was the rune of corrosion. It would have killed me within a minute, had I swallowed the whiskey.*"

Allessandra wept into Eluco's shoulder, and Evandro let her do so. Despite the news, she had refused to be taken away to grieve, and he trusted that she was taking in as much information as she could.

"*You said she was speaking to someone before you met her on the balcony, Your Majesty,*" Evandro said. "*Did you recognise the voice?*"

"*I barely recognised Mirell's voice, First Minister.*"

Eluco looked up from Allessandra to the King. "*Your Majesty, if I may, you mentioned that the relationship between yourself and the Queen was difficult at times, but has she ever attempted anything like this before, or any violence of any nature?*"

"*Some violence ... an object thrown, or an attempt to strike me. Usually I would grasp her wrist, or restrain her until she calmed.*"

"*The poison would have been found in an autopsy,*" Evandro muttered, stroking his bearded chin.

"*I've seen those runes used, First Minister,*" Eluco said, shaking his head. "*The poison is imparted into the liquid in the container by the rune. The rune transforms the liquid into something deadly, then it changes back after a few minutes. It is virtually undetectable if you do not have the container. This is why the staff check your glasses and plates thoroughly, even your cutlery. It is a popular method of assassination, particularly among the Mokkan aristocracy.*"

"*Therefore, all she would have had to do is dispose of the glass, and no-one would have known.*" Evandro hummed as he mused on Eluco's words. "*If it had been anyone but the queen, Mokku would be suspect, but she has no love for them."*

"She could have been tricked into it," Alesio groaned.

"The final words she gave are telling, First Minister, You Majesty, Your Grace," Carrasco said thoughtfully. *"The death of the nation ... there can only be one culprit, given recent events."*

Evandro nodded. *"Attack the Wyvern Bog to destabilise us. Assassinate the King to destabilise Cael, leaving Queen Mirell on the Golden Throne alone."*

Allessandra leaned up and wiped her eyes. *"She would have pinned it on the Alliance, were it discovered that Father had been murdered. An excuse to cast aside the ceasefire."*

"His Majesty's support was key, it stopped the Royal veto." Carrasco folded his arms. *"Vehnek must be close."*

Allessandra's jaw set. *"Minister Carrasco, recall the Merchant Fleet and track every loose gold elif that has been going to the Black Fleet and the Magus Towers."*

"At once, Your Grace."

"First Minister Evandro, contact the Alliance. I would like the peace delegation to come here by tomorrow afternoon at the latest ... and tell them to prepare their armed forces to mobilise."

Evandro squeezed her shoulder, and nodded.

"Eluco ... contact Acting Defence Minister Ulan, and General Kelad if you can. Mobilise the Standing Army and deploy the fleet. Call every banner from Montu Fortu to our allies in Salketh."

Eluco took a hold of her hand. *"What do I tell them, that we're going to war?"*

"That we're going to stop one before it starts."

***

The White Sea stretched out like one of its watery namesakes: dry sand in all directions, as far as the eye could see, as if there was not a drop of moisture left in the world.

The realm was arid, cracked plain, and that damnable sand, lined with the scars of what once was. The wounds left by long-dried streams and riverbeds. Unnatural shapes and shadows, perhaps signs that there was something there before, some civilisation or citadel, driven away or murdered by the hostile environment. Rocks and mountain ranges rose up like jagged teeth, with dusty winds sweeping around them. Dust devils and swirls of sand roared across the flats. Above it all, five hundred ships flew, steadily travelling north.

Vehnek paced across the *Inquisitor's* top deck, inspecting the formation of his ships, scrutinising his crew. He had heard no news of the Wyvern Bog attack fleet, but it made no matter to him. Whether they had succeeded or failed was immaterial. The Black Fleet were far away now, they couldn't be caught. If his enemies had taken one small victory, so be it. They would be in for quite the shock when he returned.

Arch Mage Miranda lingered near the prow, and caught his eye as he patrolled between the masts. She was leaning heavily on her cane, her hair rippling in the wind.

Vehnek joined her, straightening his uniform. *"Have you had any news from the capital?"*

She shook her head. *"None. We should have heard by now."*

"Word will reach us naturally soon enough." Whenever a member of the Royal Family passed away, all of the citizens of the realm were informed with a wide-spreading message to all those with communication stones. Thus the word would be spread even further, to everyone else.

"Yes... I suppose it will." Miranda's eyes went back to the lone figure standing at the prow.

Mora was still, her robe dancing madly in the breeze. Her eyes were fixed on the desert ahead of them.

"She hasn't moved an inch," Miranda muttered.

"She has her way."

The Empire Of Fire

Miranda looked at him, and chewed her lip nervously. *"She? It's not a she in there anymore, Morad."*

"I'm well aware of that."

Miranda breathed, and licked her lips. They were dry and cracked, as if the White Sea was reaching up to draw every scrap of moisture it could find. *"This whole damned desert stinks. I thought it was just the smell of Cael City ... but it's ... all of it."*

Vehnek knew the smell. He knew it very well. It was the scent of bones, dried and dessicated, melded with the dust of a million years. How many wars had been fought in this dry hell? How many armies had entered the desert and never returned? For all he knew, a billion men had been eroded away into sand, along with their armour, along with their steeds and siege weapons, along with the mountains and the rivers and whatever life had ever been there in the eons gone by. Lives from civilisations that passed into memory, and then out of it.

"Pay it no mind, and pay her no mind. Focus on your own work with The Colonel."

Miranda sniffed. *"I understand ... however ... we maybe dealing with forces far beyond our power to comprehend."*

Vehnek fixed his gaze on her fully. *"Ah ... having doubts, are we?"*

"I am concerned ... that is all."

"We made a deal, Miranda. It knows we can honour that deal. Besides ... your work will be considerable insurance, will it not?"

Miranda sighed. *"Yes ... perhaps it will."*

Vehnek turned back to Mora, standing on the deck. *"If it is a threat, as you think it may be, it is trapped in a mortal body. You kept that body still with ether, I suspect a blade will be more than sufficient to snuff it out."*

Miranda's lip curled, and she chewed it again. *"I hope so. You will find out before I will."*

There was a cry from the watchman in the *Inquisitor's* crow's nest. Vehnek walked to the prow, and scanned the horizon. Off the starboard side, in the distance, there lay a vast gash in the desert, a canyon that stretched farther than his eye could see.

He turned back, and nodded to his first officer, pointing to the canyon. A cry went up, an order to the helm, and the *Inquisitor* slowly turned towards the ancient echo of a river.

Vehnek watched the flotilla behind him turn and follow, as if the *Inquisitor* was the head of a great creature, or a hive of great creatures winging through the air. When he turned back to the prow, and Mora, she was smiling.

For the first time, Vehnek noticed that the figurehead on the *Inquisitor's* prow, the replica of the Great Black Dragon, was silent.

He peered over the railing and down at it. It snorted, and turned its head towards him for a moment. The glass and ruby eye regarded him dispassionately, before focusing again on the canyon ahead.

"You have a strange obsession with these creatures."

Vehnek turned to Mora, who still wasn't looking at him.

"Obsession?"

"You dress your men to look like them. Your battleships have facsimiles of them on the front. Your serpent is close in resemblance to them. You used them to conquer Haama. Even your plan now hinges on using them and bending them to your will."

Vehnek clasped his hands behind his back. "Why are you obsessed with the spiral?"

Mora's smile widened. "You think of it as a simple shape. How amusing."

"You think of a dragon as simply a creature."

"Oh no," she said as she looked him in the eye. "Oh no, not at all. I think of them as the logical part of you thinks of them: as a tool. A tool like your airship is a tool, like your sword and your armour are tools. Like the powers in this body are tools."

"They are more than a tool, they're a symbol." Vehnek couldn't help but bristle, and swallow the nausea elicited by the description of Mora. "They have a historical and cultural significance. They are power, and fear. They are intelligence beyond measure ... more intelligent than us, I have no doubt."

"More intelligent than *you*."

Vehnek frowned at her maddening smile. He looked into her eyes, finding something swirling in the colour of her irises.

She turned back to the view beyond her. "Can you imagine it, Vehnek? What lies beyond the edge?"

Vehnek frowned, and looked. "The edge of the horizon? Our goal."

She laughed out loud. "Beyond that?"

"Salketh."

"Beyond that?"

"The ice lands."

"Beyond that?"

"I ... Planar is round, if you go far enough you will reach the north of Mokku."

"Hmm." She looked up. "Beyond that, Vehnek?"

He looked upwards. The moon was visible against the blue sky. "The Heavens. Va'Kael, somewhere."

She chuckled. "Beyond The Heavens, and your Va'Kael?"

He looked down at her with a frown. She continued looking upwards.

"What are you talking about?"

She laughed again. "Let's try this. From here at the prow, to the railing at the aft of your ship, how far is it?"

"Three hundred feet, give or take."

"If you want to travel to the aft, you would simply walk. If you walked halfway to the aft now ..."

She strode, and he found himself following her. She stopped beside the main mast. "One hundred and fifty feet," she murmured.

"Yes."

"We are halfway to the aft railing. If you go half the distance again ..." She walked again, and he followed. Near the sixth sail, she stopped. "Now?"

"We're three quarters of the way to the aft railing."

"And if we went half the distance again?"

"We'd be seven eighths of the way."

"And again?"

"Fifteen sixteenths of the way."

"And again?"

Vehnek frowned. "What's the purpose of this?"

Mora cocked her head. "If you continued to do exactly this, travel half the distance every time ... you will never reach the aft of your mighty ship, Lord Marshal Vehnek. You will be walking until the day you die, and you will still never reach it. If you could live forever, never age, and your world lasted forever ... you would never reach the end of that three hundred feet. Can you comprehend that, Lord Marshal? Can you begin to? Can you wrap your tiny mind around infinity?"

Vehnek tried. He didn't know why he tried ... but he did ... and he began to feel ill. His head began to feel heavy, then throb gently, then less gently.

He swallowed bile that rushed suddenly up his throat. He reached out a blind hand, and touched the nearby mast. It was enough to ground him, just for a moment, and he blinked. He breathed the desert stink, and found that his hands were trembling.

He looked around, but Mora was gone. His vision cleared itself, and he saw her back at the prow, looking onward, seeing things that Vehnek could neither imagine, or begin to comprehend.

22

Fresh scars littered what had once been the Orlin Forest. Bassai looked over the wreckage strewn all across the dusty ground and long-dead tree stumps. Some of it was singed and blasted to glass all over again. Scraps of airship deck plate and bulkhead surrounded twisted wrecks of skiffs and battleships. The dragon figureheads sometimes reached up, jaws wide, inert like the skulls of their real counterparts. Some of the craft were mostly intact, laying on their sides, beached. Nothing moved around or among them that wasn't influenced by the breeze.

Bassai paced across the deck to Sandra, who was standing on the prow, statuesque. Barada and his wyvernborn retinue had gone on ahead, swooping and diving across the dust and tearing towards the Wyvern Bog.

"No smoke," Sandra murmured as he drew close.

"None from the Bog, at least."

She nodded. "Were we fools to think this could be possible? That our defenses couldn't be breached? That peace could really work?"

"We will see what awaits us when we land."

The misty green jewel lay before them, the smell of nature tingled Bassai's nostrils through the acrid stench of dragonfire. Four fat specks sat on the river.

A cry of alert went up behind him, and the *Dreadnought* set to readiness. Cannons slid from their hatches, and warriors ascended to the deck. Ironclad, Ember, Thomas and Kassaeos joined them, and made their way to the prow.

"What have you seen?" Ironclad asked. His grip was tight on his shield.

"Battleships in the river. Perhaps some in the air," Sandra murmured.

Bassai could see a few smaller shapes moving within the mist. As they drew closer, the shapes banked towards them. Military skiffs, but refitted.

"The ones in the river aren't flying their colours," Ember muttered. "Anyone have a telescope?"

"Scope to the fore!" Ironclad bellowed back at the crew. Someone rushed up and held one out, and the Construct gestured to Ember.

She took the telescope with a nod and studied the ships. "They're all damaged, one heavily. The one in the worst shape is flying a green flag from the top mast."

Sandra nodded to the skiffs. "What about them?"

Ember peered at them through the scope. "More greens ... and we're being signalled by the lead ship. Parley."

"Hmm ..." Ironclad looked around. "Are they Black Fleet ships?"

"I don't think so," Ember muttered. "Three of the ones on the river are, though, by their insignia."

"Hmm..." Ironclad hummed again, before he raised his voice. "Stand down the cannons!"

Now that they were close, wyvernborn were visible, flitting through the trees and gliding through the mist. Some were taking off and landing on the skiffs.

"Put us down in the river," Sandra murmured to a nearby airman. "We must take stock of our losses."

***

After they landed and disembarked, pushing through the cloak of mist, they found the Wyvern Bog was bustling with activity. The four battleships on the river were undergoing repairs, with Orlin, wyvernborn and Caelish crewmen heading back and forth, fixing up the holes in the hull and replacing melted iron plates. The sails were patched, the masts raised to their full height once more.

The three Black Fleet ships were in the process of being completely repainted. Their black hulls were hovering off the water, and rowboats bore the painters beneath them. There were Orlin hanging on to ropes at the sides, running wide brushes over the vessels' flanks.

Some of the wyvernborn had taken a grim fascination with the living figureheads at the prow of each one. They stared at the mechanical dragon heads, growling at them in dragontongue, and humming at the lack of a response. The facsimiles seemed to try and speak, but only unintelligible growls came out of their mouths, the sounds of metal grinding.

It seemed they were more than just replicas of the real thing, imbued with some kind of life. Bassai and Ironclad watched them closely, wondering. The limit of the Magus Towers seemed to be far beyond their own.

The mists swirled, and Father landed with a boom, the ground trembling beneath him. The wyvernborn spread their wings wide and bowed, as did the Orlin. The Caelish soldiers and crewmen all backed off a little, at least one step, as the dragon leaned down and began to drink from the river.

The mechanical dragon-heads all watched Father intently. The one on the ship that remained in Caelish colours leaned down, trying to reach the river itself. It let out a groan, that made the real dragon look up with a snort.

Bassai and Ironclad watched as Father walked into the river. He was so large that most of his bulk remained above the water. He stopped only when he was nose to nose with the facsimile, and sniffed. The mechanical copy did the same but without any of the feeling or knowing.

Only Bassai and the rest of the wyvernborn could understand what the dragon said.

"You flew on my wing. I remember your scent. You remain, behind the metal and jewels they dressed you in."

Bassai saw the wyvernborn around him tense. He shot a glance at Ironclad, a look of warning.

The dragon-head groaned again, and bowed its head low.

"You died long ago ... the echo of you is now bound to this creation of wood and iron ... and bone ... your bone. The sand men put you here."

Father leaned forwards and pressed his forehead to the facsimile's. Then he looked up, and glowered at the soldiers on the deck. The wyvernborn watched him closely, waiting for him to act. The Caelish soldiers and crewmen were frozen in terror, looking between their wyvernborn allies and their god.

"Their sins are not the sins of their forebears," Father said to the wyvernborn. *"We have been learning that wisdom, as they are learning it now. Rage is a folly, even when it seems righteous, when words can achieve a greater purpose. For now, I choose to forgive this sin."*

The wyvernborn spread their wings and bowed, as did Bassai. Father retreated from the battleship and the river, shaking the water from his scales before taking to the air once more.

The wyvernborn nudged the Caelish and Orlin to resume their work, and they did so nervously. Words began passing between them, assurance and informing them of what had just passed.

"Problem?" Ironclad muttered.

"Hmm. Perhaps not," Bassai grunted. "Although it was ... a thing that needed to be addressed ... and I have wondered since we first saw these vessels about the figureheads on the prow."

"Tell me."

Bassai gestured for them to continue past the workers. As they walked, he spoke. "Some of them, or all of them, are real. The skulls of dragons long-dead. The bodies desecrated. Father has chosen to let the matter be for now."

"For now…" Ironclad muttered.

"For now. It could be a bone of contention later, but that will depend on Barada and Allessandra."

They passed by a large gazebo, filled with a medicinal smell and the tingle of healing magic. Shamen shifted from cot to cot alongside the medics both Orlin and Caelish, as they had in the Pil Valley. It was a far warmer sight. Their cooperation hadn't been a one-off, but it was capable of continuing far into the future.

"There are more than a hundred in there," Ironclad muttered. "Most

Caelish, some wyvernborn."

"Kelad's men."

"They must be. Isn't it strange, thinking of him as an ally?"

"Strange is not the word I would use," Bassai growled.

Ironclad nodded. "Of course, I ... your history with him has another layer than mine might."

"Like you and that black dragon, eh? Except you can't watch that creature smirk at you. Can't listen to its veiled barbs, and its self-satisfied back-patting."

They continued through the tree line, watching the Orlin swinging above and running past, bearing medicines and repair materials to the river. Wyvernborn were on guard, watching everyone from above, perched on the thicker branches.

The Alpha's burrow was surrounded by guards, Caelish, Orlin and wyvernborn. They kept wary eyes on each other, but there were a few that were beginning to idly chatter, offer liquor and ale to each other, even a little food. There were nods directed towards Ironclad and Bassai as they approached, and all parted to allow them to enter.

Inside the burrow, Barada was pacing restlessly, wings twitching. Sandra was standing beside Zeta, listening to the account of the failed attack on the bog. Ember had been standing by the doorway, watching everything closely, and now she joined Ironclad and Bassai, falling into step with them. Thomas was conferring with an older Caelish officer, with the ranking insignia of a Captain. General Kelad sat and observed everyone, smirking at Kassaeos in particular, who was watching him like a hawk.

"What's the damage?" Ironclad boomed, drawing every eye in the room.

"Luckily, to the Bog, none," Sandra remarked.

"Luck had nothing to do with it, I assure you," Kelad said smoothly, but with no mirth. "Ask our many dead."

"The luck, perhaps, comes from your presence, General," Ironclad cut in. He gestured to the other officer. "I will assume your compatriot here was a part of your fleet."

"He is. Captain Obrek, the only two you have yet to be acquainted with: Tobias Calver, and Bassai of the Reeva Clan."

"Is yours the battleship?" Ironclad asked. Obrek nodded.

"We lost warriors as well, General," Zeta growled.

"I am well aware," Kelad said with a nod. "And I must praise the training and intelligence of your warriors. They immediately recognised the flags we were flying, and there was no crossed fire. I also must complement your dragon, who seemed to dine quite heartily on the *Annihilator*."

Barada growled. "A traitorous blow, swung during negotiations for peace ... I will have your Lord Marshal's head."

"I won't shield his neck from the chop," Kelad remarked. "No, he has crossed a line here, and he knows it ... which means he is close to his victory. If I may, I suggest you close our peace deal sooner rather than later."

Barada turned to Kelad angrily. "I need to know that it will be honoured by your military. By your *entire* military. Not just your men."

"They will. You have my word."

Barada leaned down, looming over Kelad. He sniffed him with a growl.

"I haven't bathed since I was fighting for my life," Kelad muttered drily. Bassai growled at the disrespect.

"Alpha, he is a man of his word," Zeta grunted.

"Keep your place!" Barada snapped, smoke shooting from his nostrils. Zeta backed off a step. Sandra held out a hand to her.

"I trust the judgement of my best implicitly, General Kelad, but I must be certain. Not that you defended our home with your best, I know you did that, but men do many things to court favour. You smell like decades of death and shadow, but not of deceit."

Barada reared up to his full height, and Kelad held eye contact with him. "The question is: how can you stop them with four skiffs and one battleship?"

Kelad grinned. "Last I checked, there were four battleships in your river."

Barada snorted in response. "Three are ours now ... but together we are certainly more formidable."

"Where are the crews of those ships?" Bassai growled. "You don't have that many cells in your mountains."

"Those that surrendered are in the holds of their former ships," Zeta muttered with a grin. "Not sure what to do with them yet."

"How much clemency do you show war criminals?" Ember wondered with a savage eye.

"There are too many to feed and too many for our cells. We need the ships." Zeta let the prognosis hang in the air.

"Kill them then, if you wish," Kelad said with a casual wave of his hand. "You could question the officers, but they couldn't tell you much. Vehnek makes sure that information only crosses the people that need to know it. You can't let them go, or even integrate them into your community. There are too many. Your Bog would become their Bog swiftly enough."

Silence followed the statement. Kelad chuckled.

"Have you fooled yourselves into thinking that you're not that kind of army?"

"Victory has the facilities to hold them," Thomas said, glaring at the General. "And Princess Allessandra is our ally, is she not?"

"You'd be missing out on a lot of information, and a little cathartic bloodshed."

Ironclad's purple eyes began to glow brightly as he stepped closer to Kelad. "If their commanders didn't have the information they needed, these men were deceived into action. They have broken the laws of the land, as well as ours, but the fault still lies with the Lord Marshal."

"Besides, we don't need their information," Kassaeos said with a shadowy grin. "We know Vehnek is in the White Sea."

"Hmm …" Kelad leaned back and stroked his chin. "Why would he be going there? What does he need?"

"Whatever grants him power, no doubt." Ironclad sat opposite Kelad. "The Warlord in the White Sea. The one who made me."

"He would have plenty of reasons to go there, in that case. You've proved your worth. I would be more concerned about what he gained at the Watchtower, and I would be very concerned about Mora."

Thomas folded his arms, and Bassai saw bitter memories pass over his face at the mention of her name. Ember leaned on Ironclad and frowned. "Why?"

"Because she isn't Mora any more. She is different somehow, as if there is something hovering over her and puppeteering her body, speaking with her voice. It is not her. That much is certain."

Thomas nodded. "Like Ydra."

"Your necromancer?"

He nodded again.

"The last thing we need is another rogue necromancer," Barada growled. "How many more of your magic users are going to be eaten alive by their cursed powers?" He looked pointedly at Thomas.

"The boon, from my perspective, is that you dealt with that problem very well." Kelad sighed. "However, this will not be as easy, I have no doubt. You aren't ... excuse me ... *we* aren't dealing with a mindless horde of the walking dead. We are engaging a well-drilled and well-equipped fleet of the best airships in the Caelish aerial navy. Vehnek is a highly skilled tactician, although he can be fooled if the one fooling him gets close enough. Mora is the factor that worries me, and our view of his plan is mostly based on suspicions."

"Her part in this is a mystery, certainly." Thomas shuddered and shook his head. "The fact remains: we have little in the way of firepower."

"It's not the firepower that worries me," Kelad muttered, looking around at all of them. "What worries me is you, if you'll pardon the words."

Barada growled, as did Bassai and Zeta.

"Maybe not these three," the General said with a wide grin. "You don't seem to realise that you're at war. You don't seem to realise that there are no saints in war."

"We have learned that lesson well, as you are aware," Ironclad said stonily.

"Our war all those years ago didn't teach it to you in the way it could have. No, you were on the moral side, were you not? The invaded, bravely defending against the invader."

Bassai growled again. He saw Ember's shoulders tense, and saw Ironclad's huge armoured hand settle on her forearm gently, but pointedly.

"The conflicts today certainly have," Ironclad said firmly.

"And yet. Can you be trusted to put down a mad dog, even though you love your own family hound like a loyal friend? Can you make the really difficult choices when you need to?"

"I gave my life to kill your dragon," Ironclad snapped.

Kelad grinned. "And all it got you was killed. Your city fell, and your country fell under our control."

"Not completely," Kassaeos hissed.

"Completely enough to leave you scraping a life in a cavern, training Mages in the woods."

"People who remained a thorn in your side for a century," Bassai growled. "You may have killed us, but they rose again."

"And died in your name. Murdered in your name."

"And gave us a second chance to stop the bloodshed." Ironclad's amethyst eyes glowed brighter, lighting up the entire room in a purple glow. "Would you be here without us? Sitting in this room with no blade at your throat?"

Kelad tipped a hand. "I doubt it. Remember who you're dealing with, though. I know Morad Vehnek better than I knew his father and grandfather. He is absolutely ruthless. If anything, he is too good at making those decisions, too quick to make them. Had he not engaged the Taeba clans in the Pil Valley, we may have never had any kind of peace at all."

"A heavy price," Bassai murmured angrily.

"The price for peace is often higher that it should be. An outright rip-off, but before it is paid, people like us make far harsher bargains."

"Being at his side, you know better than we do," Bassai muttered.

"You're lucky you aren't dealing with his father." Kelad grinned bitterly. "He was far more measured with his resources, and far harsher. He had the temerity to die of old age, surrounded by his children, the bastard."

Thomas raised an eyebrow at him. "I read the histories. I thought you would have been viewed him more favourably, being at his side for as long as you were."

"From his birth to his death," Kelad muttered. "I told Kallus I'd keep an eye on him. Kallus was a soldier, Ulan was a tyrant. Why do you think we're still hated after a century, hmm? Because we beat you in a war? Burned your capital city?"

He snorted. "I've done far worse than killing the three of you, and unlike Kallus and Ulan Vehnek, I've lived long enough to see the scars I left."

Bassai inhaled the air, picking up a little of the General's scent. He seemed as genuine as ever, tainted with the same smoky scent as Kassaeos.

He had been the enemy for long enough that it was all Bassai saw, until then. He saw the same echoes of horror that he could see in his own reflection whenever he caught a glimpse of it in a pool or a mirror. Built for war though they seemed to be, the wyvernborn were not immune to it.

There was a commotion outside for a moment, before a woman ducked into the burrow. She was Caelish, and perhaps Mokkan. Her skin was darker than usual, but with the same desert-worn features. Her hair had more of a curl to it, and was as black as charcoal.

Her military uniform was battle-worn, and she glanced at the strange occupants of the Alpha's burrow with barely a raised eyebrow. She saluted both Captain Obrek, and General Kelad, before letting out a stream of Caelish, clipped and short, probably a military order.

Kelad listened, and raised an eyebrow. He responded to her, holding out a hand. Bassai glanced at Thomas, who had taken a deep breath. He wasn't on his heels any more, he was on his toes.

The officer handed Kelad a small piece of paper, and he scanned it

The Empire Of Fire

swiftly. Captain Obrek read it over his shoulder, and made a remark or two. The general finally nodded with a sigh.

Before the woman left, he called after her, and when she looked back a flirtatious smile crossed her lips.

"It seems that there has been a development, although I don't exactly know what it is," Kelad muttered. "Princess Allessandra had called the banners, and mobilised the Standing Army."

Ironclad leaned forwards. "Meaning war."

"Meaning that she is taking the threat offered by Vehnek seriously." Kelad stroked his chin. "This could be a deterring action ... make him think twice ... which of course he won't."

Ironclad looked around the room at the assembled warriors and leaders. "If our ally has called for aid ... we will answer that call."

Sandra nodded. "We can sign the ceasefire treaty into law, then get ourselves in a position to help the..."

The communication stones at Kelad and Obrek's belts suddenly spoke. The voice was deep and unnatural, conjured in some way, perhaps to resemble the voice of some long-dead king. Thomas frowned at it, and the two military officers exchanged a look of surprise and concern.

"The Queen of Cael is dead," Thomas muttered. "The Queen is dead, and the banners have been called. The two cannot be a coincidence."

Ironclad nodded. "Captain Obrek, how long before your ship is ready for combat?"

Thomas relayed the question in Caelish, and Obrek shook his head, speaking through his teeth. Thomas translated: "Another day at least."

"If she can fly true, we can conduct repairs on the way to Victory," Kelad said. "The shipwrights there can do more and more swiftly than we can in the river."

Ironclad looked to Barada and Sandra. The Alpha growled. "The three ships can bear six hundred wyvernborn between them. On the dreadnought, that number increases to perhaps nine hundred."

"Four hundred Orlin Rangers can be ready to fight aboard those ships as well," Sandra added. "They will need experienced crews, however."

"They can be crewed at Victory," Kelad nodded. "The dragon?"

"Remains here," Barada said bluntly.

Kelad raised an eyebrow incredulously. "What?"

"That dragon is our future."

Thomas sighed and nodded. "That's right. Not just for the wyvernborn, but for Haama and Cael. The desert, the corruption in the soil …"

"Oh … Va'Kael's flaming arse!" Kelad cursed. He pinched the bridge of his nose. "The dragon stays here … but if Vehnek moves and he gets past us, it won't matter."

"If he gets past us, nothing matters," Ironclad muttered. "Thomas, inform Donnal that we'll need whatever firepower he has. We can fly at your earliest convenience, General."

***

The alert came in from the south eastern watch. Nine airships on approach to Victory, some flying unknown heraldry, and some bearing the colours of the Aerial Navy. The cannons were prepared on the roof of the Silver Throne Palace. Allessandra wanted the precaution. With the silence that had followed the attack on the Wyvern Bog, she was nervous.

An hour after, the western watch reported two dozen airships of varying sizes and classes, a mismatched myriad of craft that flew in a loose formation. Their armaments were not at the ready, and shortly afterwards the south eastern group signalled a peaceful approach.

From the balcony, just below the roof, Allessandra watched the distant craft approaching, flying high to get over the walls. They were little more than specks closing in. She leaned on the railing, looking at each group in turn, then out at the city. Old Town swarmed with workers, erecting wooden scaffolding, rebuilding and repairing. The temple near the Market Square was a burned out shell, the stone was melted from the walls, and the residue from it had stained the cobblestones around it like blood. The smoke from the fire had reached out as far as the base of the hill that led up to the palace. Reached out, and not up, as smoke usually did and should have done.

Normality had yet to resume, but the mood was not as sombre as it could have been. There seemed to be a feeling of practical civility. The citizens had been helping each other pick up the pieces. Representatives had come and gone from the palace in droves, and Allessandra had provided whatever support she could from the treasury. She suspected that people were not asking for what they truly needed, maybe as a consequence of her own defense of the city on the night of the attack. She seemed to have helped give a sense of security, and the remnants of the City Guard were deployed in legions to assist and protect them as well. There had been little in the way of discontent, aside from a few flashes of grief or fury. They were coming together, and while it had taken too long and too much to reach that state, it wasn't their fault.

"Your writing is much better," Helen muttered behind her. She was sitting on a cushioned bench, peering close to the pieces of parchment in her hands. Allessandra had been working on the speech since she had been aboard Mira's Favour. "My eyes ... ugh. A word to the young, Allessandra, never grow old, it is a drag on the mood."

Allessandra swallowed at her steward's words.

Helen murmured to herself and put the papers down. "Yes ... very stirring, and honest, but ... are you sure about all of this? It could be a little inflammatory."

"It could be, but it may be the tone that's required."

"Hmm ... I suppose so." She put it down. "I can't find any mistakes in it, so on that regard you're fine."

Helen stood up with a grunt and strode over to the metal bucket, where their refreshments waited surrounded by cubes of conjured ice. "Noorani Ice Wine?"

Allessandra nodded absentmindedly, still focused on the approaching fleets.

"Never developed a taste for it. It's a bit too potent for me."

Allessandra chuckled. "Yes ... it is quite. Burns on the way down if it catches you off guard."

"We can get some port up here ... you are a princess after all."

"No, it's fine. Apparently it's good for me."

"I bet," Helen muttered drily. She joined Allessandra at the balcony, and leaned over with a handkerchief, brushing the princess's cheek. Allessandra frowned around at her.

"You're perspiring a little, and you're flushed."

"Don't worry about it, Helen."

"You could be pushing a fever. Rest."

"Our enemies are not resting, so neither can I."

Helen pursed her lips. "Well, your stubbornness didn't leave with your twentieth birthday, I see."

"Did you expect anything else?"

"I shouldn't have, I suppose."

Allessandra smiled. "You know better."

Helen grunted, and sipped a little Ice Wine from her glass. "Where will it be, this speech of yours? The Market Square?"

Allessandra hummed to herself thoughtfully. "I thought about it ... but no. There, at the temple ... alongside our allies."

Helen nodded, eyeing the smoke. "Is there danger?"

"Not according to the doctors in the palace. There are other Mages that can have a look ... Thomas being one."

"And Seraphine."

Allessandra nodded. "The area was made safe in the days following that awful night ... but it is best to be sure. Half of the people in the hospitals are there because of that smoke that you can still see everywhere in Old Town, look!"

She pointed to stains on every building for a mile and a half, in a near-perfect ring around the burned temple.

Helen nodded to herself. "It is time to clean those burns ... and time to rebuild that temple if we can."

"Together," Allessandra nodded. "To the Haaman Gods, as it was before. This culture ... is truly beautiful, when you learn what it means to people, when you learn what it gives, when you see the pictures it paints and the music it sings. It may not be what I believe, but that doesn't matter. The people of this country don't have to believe what I believe."

Helen held Allessandra's hand tightly. Her eyes shone, as the ships came into view over the walls. "That's all I ever wanted to show you, my sweet girl. That's all."

More airships were coming from the northern reaches, and possibly from the farthest southern outposts as well. They were dots on the horizon, as the first arrivals were drifting above the city.

She recognised the *Dreadnought*, vast and powerful, that had borne the Alliance to the peace talks. General Kelad's ships flew alongside it. One of the battleships made for the repair yard in the fisheries, but the other three continued on in formation.

It took a moment for Allessandra to recognise that they had been Black Fleet vessels, but no longer. They were each painted in dark green. The dragon heads on the front were mechanically and gaily roaring, announcing their arrival. The sails had the image of dragon wings on them, burned or etched in with charcoal.

The painted hulls seemed to glisten, as if they were still wet, but light danced across them in a scattering of rippling colour, like oil catching the sunlight on water. She made the mental note to ask what had been used to create the effect, as it would look just as striking on the *Sand Dancer*.

She saw her ship now, dwarfed by every other, leading what had to be the Alliance Fleet. The barges, skiffs and cruisers were all well armed, and she didn't doubt they had a few tricks hidden away here and there. She wondered how many had engaged in battles with Cael's fleets before. She could certainly tell which were the oldest: they were the ones with the most burns and scars across the hull.

The door behind them opened, and Eluco strode out in a suit of golden plate armour. It was a little lighter and better fitting than the armour of the rest of the Royal Guards, and seemed especially capable for combat. His sword rested at his hip, and his half-helm was tucked under his off-arm.

"*Good day to you, Helen,*" he said warmly. "*Your Grace, the commanders of both fleets have signalled the Palace. Dignitaries are ready to present themselves.*"

"*Thank you, Eluco,*" Allessandra raised an eyebrow. "*No cloak?*"

"*Easier to move, and there's no chance of it getting stuck in a door.*"

The princess grinned. "*How often does that happen?*"

"*More often than most admit. There are more ships arriving. The Kalenda defense forces will arrive within the hour. Fleets from The Port Of Plenty, Breakers Bay, and the Spears will rendezvous with us at the Mouth Of Life. The mountain outposts are able to send some vessels as well, but they are also contending with mountain tribes, and they require at least half of their forces to remain on station.*"

"*Are the south eastern and south western outposts aware of the ceasefire?*"

"*They are, they have deployed three quarters of their forces.*"

"*The Mountain Cities?*"

Eluco shook his head.

"*Send an immediate missive to Umber, using the long range equipment. I will speak to them myself, along with Donnal, Seraphine, Barada and Sandra. The Four Guardians as well, if they are respected in those circles. What are our current numbers projected to be?*"

"*One hundred and forty two ships. It will increase to a hundred and sixty shortly. Minister Carrasco has said that a number of ships in the Merchant Fleet have requested to join, and will be dragooned in.*"

"*And the Caelish Aerial Navy?*"

The Empire Of Fire

"*We are ... working on the Aerial Navy. With ... the Queen's death, there has been some civil unrest in Cael City. The fleet and the army may be required. At most we can perhaps expect two hundred and fifty ships.*"

Allessandra nodded, and wrung her hands. "*Meaning we will be outnumbered.*"

Eluco nodded.

"*Keep trying, love. Call in any favours you can. I will meet the delegates in the Throne Room.*"

He nodded, and departed. Helen sighed to herself, but darkness didn't quite descend over her face.

"Love?"

Allessandra found the energy to smirk. "That's a conversation that can wait."

Helen held up her hands with a grin. "As you wish, Your Grace."

23

General Kelad led the delegates into the Throne Room, and from there, everyone moved to the Council chamber. The negotiations were barely that, in fact they agreed unanimously and immediately that their peace treaty could wait for now, and focused their attention on other matters.

However they made very little ground otherwise. The Mountain Cities pledged no ships to their cause, even with Allessandra's personal assurances that the danger was real and immediate, and despite the pledges to repair the damaged relationships of the past. Likewise, the situation in Cael City was spiralling, although the Aerial Navy were at full attention and maintaining the threads of the barrier that kept the city from falling entirely into chaos. The Magus Towers had ceased all outside communication, even with the capital, moving their pieces across the board in the cover of shadow.

The best that the ramshackle allies could do, logistically, was to crew their fleet with the best they could and establish a search pattern over the White Sea, but even that was a measure that left them in the paralysis of choice. The desert was massive, with a million directions to fly in and enough horizon to hide even a large fleet. Even if Vehnek's forces were spotted, what then? Any search group would be chased down and destroyed by the Black Fleet's superior numbers, even if they did manage to sound the alarm.

After the frustration of the council, Allessandra paced anxiously, alone on the palace roof. Her throat was starting to tighten, and she was sweating again. She found her thoughts starting to muddy, and she had to sit down, rubbing her head.

Stress and lack of sleep was feeding the illness within her with a steady diet, helping it eat into her just as vigorously. They had come far, but the final hurdles were towering above them. Vehnek had them cold, and he knew it.

She sagged, slumping down on the cylindrical base of a cannon turret. Her breaths were becoming ragged, and her eyes were blurring, as if she was in the midst of heatstroke.

She was about to send for a cup of water from one of the guards, when she recognised a few familiar voices passing her by, though at a distance.

"I don't want to see it," a lilting Orlin voice muttered.

"Neither did I, but it hasn't changed so much." Thomas, that time.

"It has changed enough." The growl of a wyvernborn, and now she could place the voices.

The Archer, The Mage, The Beast, and likely the silent, heavy footsteps of The Warrior.

Allessandra stood, swaying on her feet. She followed their steps between the still deployed cannons.

They had stopped, all four of the Guardians of the city that had once been. Silently, they watched Victory from above, from a building taller than the defensive walls, taller than any other that had existed when the city was theirs. They watched the fresh wounds left by another Vehnek, the citizenry the tiny cogs spinning in the healing mechanism. There wasn't a single sound uttered by any of them.

Allessandra breathed steadily, until her head stopped spinning and her vision sharpened from a blur. "It is … on its way back, although it doesn't look like it from up here."

The Four Guardians turned to face her. Thomas was the only one who bowed in the way she was accustomed to, but Bassai lowered his head in the deferential way that the wyvernborn did toward those they respected. The Warrior and Archer did nothing. The Orlin woman's eyes were hard as chunks of ice, and the metal giant was entirely expressionless.

"I didn't mean to intrude."

"Not at all, Your Grace," Thomas said. "After seeing the fires begin, I must admit I feared it would look worse. It's a credit to your hard work that much of it still stands."

Allessandra strode forwards slowly, mulling over his words. "I did little, or nothing. The hard work was done by the City Guard, by the doctors and fishermen, by the store owners and builders and innkeepers, to the citizens who took into their homes those who had lost everything."

The Orlin woman raised an eyebrow at that.

"General Kelad told us the story, Your Grace," The Warrior said in a booming, yet softened voice. "We know that the arsenal still deployed on the palace roof was your doing. You had the courage to take up arms against a criminal act, from a vulnerable position."

Allessandra grinned wryly. "I'm heir to the throne of Cael. I knew there was a good chance he would stay his hand against the palace. It was about putting him in a difficult position. Now he has put us in one in return."

She joined them at the edge of the roof and looked out. "I know that the palace was not here in your time."

"No," Thomas sighed. "It was the seat of government, and the treasury. The guild offices, and the old high church to Alvalon, as well as the Window To The Gods."

Allessandra had heard of all but the latter. "The Window To The Gods?"

The four paused for a moment, and Allessandra realised then how significant it had likely been to Haaman culture of the day.

"An old amphitheatre," The Beast growled. "Built by ... who knows? Whoever dwelled in Haama before it was Haama. A ring of stone, a hundred yards across, carved with ancient runes, the floor inside marble only cracked by time. When the Gods were discovered, people would go there, to the city's highest point, and look up towards the Astral Plain. They would send prayers to the people they had lost, who had ascended into the divine. It was being used for little else. When the belief spread, it was where many people prayed together, particularly at night."

"It could have held thousands!" Allessandra sighed. "Thousands of people, united in a moment of divine peace ... looking up at the stars together.

The Empire Of Fire

Gone now. Gone, to make room for royal vanity."

She fell silent. The Silver Throne Palace was a complex that took up most of the hill. The vast building itself, along with the gardens and summer houses and guard barracks, had shoved culture and government aside so callously.

"There are more places like it in the south," The Archer muttered. "Been to one, in the mountains near the Wyvern Bog, a long time ago. Up near the top, or at the peaks. Probably some in Montu Fortu as well. The highest points in Haama."

"Maybe looking up was what they were always there for." Thomas shifted his weight onto his other foot. "I wanted to say ... I am sorry for your loss, Your Grace."

Allessandra blinked and turned to him. There was sincerity in his face. "Thank you. Although ... it is ... not the time for grief. Grief can paralyse like venom. The time will come, certainly ... and then how she will be remembered may be clearer."

Thomas considered her words, but chose not to press the matter. The circumstances surrounding the death of Queen Mirell had yet to be publicly revealed, and until the crisis had passed, it would remain so.

If the crisis passed, of course. Allessandra looked past him to the Warrior and Archer, who were gazing out over Old Town, and at the temple in particular.

"A speech will be given there later in the day, before the fleet deploys."

"A speech," The Archer murmured bitterly. "Aye, that'll re-shape the stone and get the blood out."

"For the moment, it is better than leaving it there as it is. It will be rebuilt in the coming weeks and months, no doubt."

"I'm sure it will," was the equally bitter reply.

Allessandra's temper momentarily batted past her nausea. "Many of the City Guard died there, defending it and the people outside who wanted to do the same. One of them was ... very well respected. A friend, perhaps, of which there are very few when you are of a certain bloodline. If you want to blame someone for its destruction, blame the Ghosts that hid and took hostages in the catacombs, and them blame Vehnek for burning the place to deal with them."

"We prayed there, all of us," The Warrior muttered, cutting into the potential argument. "We prayed at every temple that has been reduced to cinder by the Night Of Terror. It is a little ... close to home. Too close to a home that has moved past us."

The Archer blinked for a moment, and took his hand as he continued.

"It may not have changed so much on its face, but ... I feel as a foreigner would, looking down upon a land I don't recognise."

"It may yet change more," The Beast muttered. "In fact, that is a certainty. What has been unmade and obliterated will not come back as it was. There are temples to Va'Kael where people used to worship the Gods, or Alvalon the all-father. Caelish adorns signposts and shops, words I do not recognise."

"It will take time before our peoples stand on their own," Allessandra sighed. "I understand how you must feel to be back here, in a way ... although not completely, in a way that a Haaman would."

She looked to The Archer and Beast specifically. "Would your people ... want to live here? Or have embassies here?"

The Archer was quiet, but The Beast growled thoughtfully. "Embassies, perhaps. I suspect my people and the Orlin will simply wish to be left alone, largely, although their input will be required for matters of state. You share a country with them, after all. No doubt the suggestion will be made that someone sit on your Council of Ministers, to represent one or both the Orlin and wyvernborn."

The Archer nodded. "The one chosen might be a little reluctant. There aren't enough trees here. There never were, in truth."

"Perhaps something that can be remedied," Allessandra offered. "Trees are known to freshen and clean the air ... something that is sorely needed here among the smoke of industry."

The Empire Of Fire

The flame-haired beauty shrugged one shoulder. "Maybe so."

"I would like to see Old Town ... made less old," The Warrior murmured. "I can see some of the same buildings, the same dwellings as were there a century ago. Good people lived there."

"And still do," Allessandra said, remembering the doctor who had saved her life. "You could go and see it, before the speech."

"I could." The Warrior sighed. "But ... it would not be the Old Town I know. The streets, the people ... and that so much of it was burned. Again ... it is too close to home."

"It is old men like us that have the hardest time living in the new world."

General Kelad was behind them, standing with his hands clasped behind his back. The Beast growled quietly, almost to himself. The Archer's knuckles went from pink to white as she squeezed the Warrior's iron fingers.

Kelad knew well enough that his presence would cause some discomfort, but smiled sadly nonetheless. "It is not an allowance made by many of the young, unfortunately. They tend to simply demand we adapt, or die. Sometimes they even wish for our death, thinking that in their lack of wisdom, they can do better." He grinned at Allessandra, and bowed. "Present company excepted, of course, Your Grace."

"You'll be happy to hear that the phrase: 'adapt or die' did not make it into my speech this afternoon, General," Allessandra sighed. "I thought you would be drawing up deployment plans for the fleet."

Kelad waved a hand. "One does not simply fly aimlessly into the desert, Your Grace. I am aware of the urgency, but we need more information than we have. Luckily I may have a little."

Ironclad stepped forwards. "And you're telling us, of all people?"

"Well, I've already told my scouts, the Council Of Ministers, Seraphine, Donnal, the fleet commanders ... need I go on? I had a glance at a map of northern Cael and the White Sea that Mora ... or whatever she is, was pawing over. There was a mark on it, in the Ankhroah canyon, that wasn't there before, at least on any map I've seen of the area. Seraphine seemed to have an idea of what we might find there, as do I, considering the research that has been done." He fixed Ironclad with a pointed look and a grin. "It is definitely of interest to you."

Ironclad hummed to himself. "Where I was made."

"Correct, and where many others likely can be made."

"Re-made," Thomas muttered. He shook his head. "Hold on, now. That seems ... like only half the pieces of the puzzle. Vehnek's moving too quickly, and creating an army of Constructs would take time."

The Beast nodded with a grunt. "What of the dragons?"

"The dragons?" Kelad raised an eyebrow. "What of them?"

Allessandra folded her arms. "There are more than the one left?"

"No," Kelad snapped. "No, they're all dead. We buried them by the..."

Kelad closed his eyes. He let out a bitter laugh.

"What's funny?" The Archer grunted.

"It's not funny, really, it just doesn't happen very often."

"What?"

"Being outmanoeuvred." He looked at Allessandra, his face grim. "The bodies of those we found, and those we used, were taken to the Gravestone mountain ... at the centre of the desert. I was tasked with taking them there. Aside from the body of the black dragon, that stayed here. Kallus did have a fondness for trophies..."

Allessandra frowned. "No, wait ... the Gravestone ... the only thing there is a prison."

"Not the only thing, and certainly not at the peak. There was a laboratory of sorts, a branch of the Magus Towers. They were to study the dragons in secret, after Mokku caught wind of their use during the invasion and the war."

Thomas snorted. "They can't have been happy about it."

"They weren't. In fact, no-one was. Every nation threatened to sever diplomatic and trade ties afterwards, because of the destruction wrought. They even did, until the last of the beasts died over Uncur, or so we thought. Kallus Vehnek, and the Arch Mages, thought that something could be learned from studying the corpses. The dragon-heads on the prows of our battleships, for example. The destructive power of the *Annihilator's* weaponry."

Ironclad looked north, across the horizon. "And he's almost there now …"

Allessandra wrung her hands. "How many dragons?"

"Seventeen."

"Gods above us," The Warrior muttered.

As Kelad frowned, opening his mouth to respond, Allessandra cut in. "How soon can your fleets be ready?"

The General caught on to the urgency in her voice immediately. "The stragglers will arrive this afternoon."

Allessandra nodded. "Then I have time … time for one last word."

***

The temple square was a dirty, melted, desolate mess. It was dead, the most dead place in the entire city, but very slowly, it was returning to life.

The citizens streamed into the square, watching the podium in front of the ruin of the Temple To The Gods. They covered every inch of the smoke and blood stained paving. Vendors were selling food and drink at the edge and in the streets leading to the places of worship.

Minister Levez had died here, Allessandra knew. As such, it was a fitting place for what she needed to say. When the square was full, she stepped from the palanquin that had borne her from the palace. The Four Guardians and the Council of Ministers stepped from another pair. Barada, Sandra, Seraphine and Donnal stepped from a fourth. Allessandra walked slowly to the podium, feeling a tinge of fatigue as she walked across the tiles. There had been no ceremony, no decoration, only the scars that the great fire had left.

Cheers washed over her, despite the uncertainty that was coming from the fleet, and the events in Cael. The energy of the city had never been higher, the reception to her never warmer.

Matt Waterhouse

A pair of Royal Guards, including Eluco, helped her onto the podium, and the cheers grew in volume.

She took a deep breath, and touched a hand to the stone set into the table before her, where her speech lay waiting for her.

"People of Victory, from the bottom of my heart, I thank you."

The cheer that greeted her words was almost deafening. It was just shy of a minute before they quietened, and she made no move to silence them.

"The last few days have been filled with tragedy. We have lost many good men and women. Places of culture and business have been destroyed. Homes have been rendered uninhabitable, and yet ... our spirit is unbroken."

She breathed deeply and gripped the podium. "You have taken a city on the edge of death, and brought it to life again. You have given yourselves: your food, your homes, your time, your talent, to help your neighbours, Caelish and Haaman. It is a warming sight to see, especially here."

She half-turned, and raised a hand to the temple behind her. "This place was one of the oldest in the city. The Black Fleet may have melted the brick, and desecrated what made it a holy place ... but we can rebuild it together, piece by piece. I cannot promise that it will be the same, or that it will feel the same, but it will stand once more, and be a place where the Gods can be worshipped. The gods of Haama and Cael may be different, but we live together, and can respect each other's beliefs."

The cheers were not quite as loud, but the message was clear, and there were a number of vigorous nods of agreement.

"We stand together in this square, as we have stood together in celebration and mourning, because a time ... an inevitable time, has come: a time where we must decide, as the people of two nations, what our destiny will be. We are so close, across a narrow dividing sea, that it will be a destiny together ... perhaps not two separate destinies, but one."

She looked up. "Many airships have filled the air above our city in recent weeks. The fleet above us now comprises elements of the Caelish Aerial Navy, the border guards, the Merchant Fleet, Warriors of The Wyvernborn and Orlin, and the Haaman Alliance. The latter: formerly the Haaman Resistance. The beginnings of a formal ceasefire, and a formal peace treaty, are in progress as I speak to you here and now."

Murmurs spread through the crowd: curious, excited, concerned even.

"Why now? What has changed?" Allessandra shook her head defiantly. "I move that *nothing* changed in our hearts. Nothing. All that happened ... is that we saw each other, for the first time. We saw each other for what we are ... men and women that care about our nations, about our families, about the many intricate things that make up our daily lives, the friends we have made, the streets we walk, the shops we frequent, the taverns where we celebrate and meet after a long day. The Second Battle At The Pil Valley showed us what we can accomplish together. Forces led by General Kelad, and Barada and Sandra, Alpha Wyvernborn, and the matriarch of the Orlin, saved us all ... by working together."

She looked at the companions who had come to the square with her, blinking away the sweat of sickness running into her eyes. "I stand before you today with the Council Of Ministers, with leaders who represent the many cultures of Haama... and with the Four Guardians ... who have come home."

The Four stared at her, and at the crowd. Thomas straightened his back, The Beast bowed his head to the crowd. The Archer looked between Allessandra and the people of the city, and placed a hand over her heart. The Warrior's amethyst eyes glowed brightly, and he bowed slightly.

"They defended this city in decades past... and today they defend it again. They defend Haama ... and they defend Cael, from forces that would see us burn each other before we took each other's hands. We stand together against those that burned this city, and will see them brought to the justice they deserve."

The cheers and applause erupted fiercely. Pride in them swelled in Allessandra's chest. Tears formed in her eyes. This was the time.

"We stand together, because sooner or later, we must stand up. Cael and Haama, together, but apart, separated by the sea. Two, independent nations, not slave and master, not farmer and mule, two farmers together, trading crops, greeting each other with a friendly hand and a kind word, and a cup of strong spirits you brewed in the cellar. People might laugh at the idea, may say 'no, it's impossible!' but:"

Allessandra cleared her throat.

"'Great friends we were, in long decades past,

Before the sands swept over grass,

Before starving voices screamed their last,

Before the slow drum of rage beat too fast.'"

The words of the poem hung in silence. She saw recognition dawn on a few faces. She glanced around at the Council of Ministers, who were staring at her with wide eyes.

Thomas was smiling at her in surprise. The Warrior's eyes glowed brighter, and the Archer's eyes took on a warmth that wasn't there before. The Beast's teeth were bared in a grin.

"The Song Of The Four Guardians is a poem that speaks truly, and perhaps that is why some of our predecessors banned it. It will be banned no longer. Cael and Haama were true allies once, and we will be again. General Kelad and The Four Guardians fought against each other in bitter, bloody conflict, and yet fought alongside each other at the Pil Valley. General Kelad risked his life to defend the Wyvern Bog from a massacre that would have been performed by the Black Fleet. The Four Guardians, and the Haaman Alliance, gave their blood to defend Cael and Haama both, not just their own nation. You heard right when I told you before … that the wyvernborn and Orlin are alive. Former blood enemies, that now live together in peace."

A jolt of pain shot through her stomach, and she struggled to suppress a grunt. She leaned her weight forwards onto the podium, holding herself up.

The crowd murmured again. She looked up, and took a deep breath. She would finish, even if it would make her collapse. She held out a hand to halt Eluco, who had taken a step towards her.

"Rage can be a fuel, an energy, that drives empires. Mokku use their rage against everyone, to the success of their emperors and oligarchs ... but rage is also a chain, that shackles us to our own pain, making us rely on it and add to it rather than heal. We cannot grow, until we let go, and be honest about our own flaws. Cael allowed desperation to rule its sword-arm for too long, and allowed itself to become drunk on power. Haama in turn fed on the hatred of us, and a cycle began, a vicious loop of revenge for blood the two sides spilled. Peace means that those chains are broken. Peace means freedom for us all. Maybe not all at once, and not easily, maybe freedom will find some of us in time ... but we have been chained for too long."

Her voice was becoming strained. She swallowed.

"Our time has come. Haama and Cael have reached a point where we can get out of our own way, and truly prosper, together and apart. We will be enemies no longer ... nor, in time, will we be dependent on each other. Haama and Cael will be free, of our demons and our chains. A ... politician fishing for votes ... with all due respect to the hard work of the aldermen and Ministers present ... a politician would tell you now that it will be a transition difficult for some of us. I say, as someone who wants to tell you the truth ... that it will likely be difficult for everyone, in its own way, even for me. Freedom is terrifying. I understand. Free people stand and fall by their own actions, and when they fall, the people in control who had been there in perpetuity are no longer there to catch you. The point is that ... with freedom ... we can catch ourselves, and catch each other when we fall."

She took a breath. Sweat was streaming down her face. Her hand was shaking, and she concealed it behind her back quickly.

"You ... the people of this city, are what have made this city great, and will continue to do so. You have made it great together, regardless of those in your midst who have succumbed to their rage. The way you have ... accepted me into your hearts ... is forever humbling."

Her voice cracked ever so slightly, and the cheer that followed deafened her, louder than any other she had ever heard.

"Haama is a nation of beauty, as is Cael ... and today, we take our first step into the sunlight of a new dawn. The fleet above, of comrades in arms, from the searing sands to the cool long grasses, will soon depart ... and put an end to the tyranny that wishes to swallow us all. Together ... we will banish it. Together we will watch the sun rise anew, on a bright future of new possibilities. Long live this Alliance. Long live Victory. Long live Haama and Cael!"

"Long live Allessandra!" Came the response, scattered at first, but building to a chant that sent warmth through her body. It was enough to keep her on her feet, standing tall with them.

***

The Warlord In The White Sea ruled over a kingdom that encompassed almost an entire wall of the Ankhroah canyon.

The grand palace was carved into the rock face. An entrance hall had been tunnelled out, so tall and wide the *Inquisitor* could have flown inside. Twisting pillars reached up on either side, perfectly shaped at a distance, but lightly eroded by the desert winds when viewed more closely.

The canyon offered some shelter, but also funnelled the breezes and compressed them into squalls.

"*Keep the fleet a hundred yards above the lip, and spread out, a hundred yard gap between each vessel.*" Vehnek muttered to his helmsman. He turned to the communications officers beside the stones that hailed the fleet. There were so many stones and so many plinths that three men were required to operate them with enough speed. "*Signal the Colonel's group to hold. Have the second and third scout wings form on the Inquisitor. Cannons to stations, watch for movement. Have the perimeter groups keep watch.*"

Vehnek studied the complex carefully through a spyglass, trying to get a measure of the man who had built it.

Studying it further, he considered that what he thought was an entrance hall was more likely an interior dock, from the days when the river rushed

The Empire Of Fire

through the canyon. Ancient Salkethian ships were narrow, and depending on how deep the hall was, potentially dozens could have fitted inside.

Above the twisting pillars of the hall, walkways with ramparts had been carved and reinforced with steel, dirty and smudged with mud and dust. Triangular tunnels cut into darkness. Windows carved in strange shapes, curved and angular, also led into an abyss.

There were no frills to the place, it seemed. No balconies, no ramparts, no visible armaments, no guard-rails to stop anyone tumbling from the walkways.

Up at the top of the canyon, a round, angled wall curved in a half-moon shape around a cluster of squat, stone buildings, with a single exception in the centre: the tallest of them, which looked to be a pyramid.

It was unlike the old, long since destroyed stone pyramids that had become symbolic of Cael. This one had three sides rather than four, poking up over the walls. There were no windows and no visible erosion at this distance, despite the full exposure to the White Sea's wrath. The walls seemed to glisten, made of a stained black stone of some kind. The buildings surrounding it were dark, cloaked in the shadow of the angled walls. They seemed dilapidated, deserted.

Vehnek lowered the spyglass and frowned. Miranda limped up to the bridge and stood beside him. He handed her the spyglass, and turned to communications again.

"*Pull siege group one closer. Keep them two hundred yards above the pyramid and have their cannons stand by.*"

Miranda glanced at him with a frown. Vehnek stroked his chin, watching the fortress as a whole. Three separate architectures were battling with each other, it seemed.

Perhaps the warlord had evolved in his skill over the years, and his men too, learning as the decades had passed. He glanced down at the canyon. There was no trace whatsoever of the river that had forged it over tens of thousands of years or more. There was more sand in there than flat rock, no hint of vegetation or wildlife that had ever been anywhere near it. The pyramid pulled his gaze again, and he shook his head.

"*What a fascinating structure,*" Miranda murmured. She was looking though the spyglass directly at the black, smooth fang, uniform, perfect in dimension. "*I cannot identify the material from here, I would have to get closer. It could be obsidian.*"

"*Obsidian erodes,*" Vehnek muttered. "*What was the date of the Warlord's exodus from Salketh?*"

Miranda hummed to herself as she studied the pyramid. "*I don't think we have an exact date. It could either be from our conflict with them or their conflict with themselves, that's a fifty year period.*"

"*That's three hundred years ago at least. Does that look three hundred years old to you?*"

Miranda frowned. "*Well ... the pyramid ... I don't know. The buildings around it, yes. I suppose so. The carving in the canyon ... again, perhaps. I would need to get down there and examine the structure itself, but architecture is not my area of expertise.*"

"*If I were a gambler, I would bet you that it was older. I think the Warlord found these ruins in the canyon. I think he built his settlement around the pyramid, while initially sheltering in the dock and exploring further.*"

"*Meaning?*"

Vehnek sighed. "*Perhaps it means nothing ...*" Again, his eyes were drawn to the pyramid. He glanced around to the prow. Mora was watching the pyramid as well, smiling.

He narrowed his eyes, and turned back to the helm and communications officers. "*Ready one of the runabouts. Tell the Colonel to start his landings at his discretion. I'd like the air cover to remain in place while we're down there.*"

Miranda shook her head as the orders were sent. "*I cannot see anyone ... anywhere.*"

"*Nor could I. Perhaps these Constructs are not as ageless as they might have appeared. Head to the runabout, I'll ... collect Mora.*"

The Empire Of Fire

He walked to the front of the *Inquisitor*. The air seemed to shimmer the closer to Mora he got. She straightened her back as he joined her, not looking at him.

"The Warlord's lair," he muttered in Haaman, breaking the silence.

"Hmm," she replied with a smile. "Yes ... your 'salvage rights' apply, I suppose."

Vehnek glanced at her. "Ah ... so he wasn't the first here, as I suspected."

"On a world such as this one, large as it may be in your terms, very few people will have been the first ones anywhere."

Vehnek swallowed, as his throat had suddenly dried out. It must have been the desert. "Join us down there."

Mora smirked at him, amused. Without a word, she leaned over the railing and dived, head-first. There were scattered shouts from the deck, but Vehnek waved them off.

"*We'll join you, then,*" he muttered.

Two marines fell into step beside him as he climbed down to the lower decks of the ship, and to the hold, where the runabouts waited, sitting on the bottom.

The small craft were similar to the standard airship, but roughly a fifth the size of a skiff, too small for the standard core that kept them aloft. Instead, they used a canvas balloon, that a burner or Mage could fill with hot air to hold it aloft. They were good for short-range trips, but were incapable of holding the provisions or fuel to take them far. The hull was narrow, with a long rudder at the aft to manoeuvre. A crewman and Mage were already aboard, inflating the balloon and clearing the mooring ropes.

Miranda looked at him quizzically as he and the marines boarded. "*I thought ...*"

"*She decided on her own method of transportation.*"

Miranda pursed her lips. "*I don't blame ... her. Give it five years or so, these balloons won't be needed. We'll have small enough cores, I guarantee it."*

Vehnek nodded absent-mindedly. "*Good.*"

Miranda took hold of his forearm, and pulled him to the fore of the runabout.

"*Morad ... I want you to be very careful with that thing. She seems as keen on this place as you are, but not for the same reasons.*"

Vehnek had suspected the same when he had seen the way she watched the ruins. "*Oh, I agree. Feels like she knows something we don't, doesn't it?*"

"*To our benefit, or hers?*"

"*We have a mutual benefit. I have planned this for a long time, and every angle is covered. There will be no betrayal.*"

"*But how do you know that, Morad? How do you know for sure?*"

"*We had the power to uplift Mora, and feed it. It has been waiting for a long time to come to this world. It has tried before, and we are now at a level where it can. It will be our power ... sacrificing Mora as the vessel will be what brings the dragons under our control. Uncur will not happen again.*"

Miranda held her arms close to her as the runabout lifted from the hold and floated out into the canyon, falling slowly toward the ancient riverbed.

"*I cannot help but worry that there are forces working beyond our control,*" she murmured. "*Or understanding, for that matter. We've never gotten the kind of handle on magic we need to truly understand it ... yet we use it every day, even for mundane things like ... lighting a candle, or cleaning a cup. This level of magic is well beyond all of that.*" She shook her head. "*There are many times I considered ... we were never meant to use it. It burns us from the inside out, regardless of the skill of the user. We build amplifiers, but that only slows the process.*"

Vehnek smiled for a moment. "*Every pioneer wonders if the horizon leads off the edge of the world. Every soldier wonders if the next enemy will be the one to cut his throat. Those who operate on the forefront take the risks. Risks lead to reward. This may be a great risk ... but the reward is the kind of bounty that no-one in the world has ever seen.*"

24

The runabout settled on the dusty ground with a soft bump. The canyon walls loomed menacingly over them on either side. The cavernous opening yawned wide, dwarfing the small craft.

The two marines opened the arms trunk in the hull and brought out a pair of long magical amplifiers, similar in mechanism to the pistol. The barrel was as long as a person's arm, the firing mechanism attached to a cylinder that held four magical stones. Each stone carried enough charge to cast three or four incantations, and could be swapped easily by unlocking and twisting the cylinder to the next stone. The weapons were more accurate and powerful than the pistols, but only available to the elite for now while the design was refined and the materials were rare.

The marines led the way off the runabout, dropping to one knee and raising the amplifiers, sweeping the barrels in a wide arc up at the deserted walkways and around the interior of the dock, although the shadows within made the view entirely opaque. Vehnek stepped out after his men, followed by Miranda, limping behind him. The knocking of her cane on the ground was the only noise in the canyon.

There was no sign of Mora at all. Vehnek suspected that she had gone straight into the ruins without a moments hesitation.

The Lord Marshal turned back to the runabout. "*Signal Scout Group Three to drop their marines. Set up a perimeter around the complex at the top of the canyon and outside that dock. Another contingent is to hold the dock interior. If you see Mora ...*" he thought for a moment. "*If you see Mora, say nothing to her except that the Lord Marshal requests her presence. Otherwise leave her be.*"

The crewmen nodded. Vehnek turned back to the ruins, and clasped a hand over the handle of the pistol on his belt.

"*Do we wait before we go in?*" Miranda whispered.

Vehnek raised an eyebrow at her. "*Absolutely not.*"

She swallowed and nodded. Vehnek gestured to the marines, who ran forwards, flitting from the cover of boulders until they were pressed against the edge of the far right wall, where the rough natural crags of the wall gradually smoothed into the straight, flat surface hewed by centuries old tools.

Vehnek strode along with Miranda, keeping pace with her, close enough so she could shield the pair of them with a magical barrier. Not as much as a speck of dust reacted to their presence. The walls watched them with impassive indifference.

Regardless, Vehnek could sense someone or something waiting to greet them. His intuition never failed him.

"*Anything?*" he whispered to Miranda.

"*Something ... vague. At this distance, I can't be sure. It's ... in the walls. In the floors and ceilings, in the pillars ... in the ground and the rock.*"

Vehnek gritted his teeth. "*But what is it?*"

"*I'm not being cryptic on purpose, Morad. It's like nothing I've ever felt. It's ambient, unaware. Perhaps a power source.*"

"*We wouldn't be whispering over a power source,*" he hissed. "*Can you sense Mora?*"

Miranda nodded. "*She's above us.*"

Vehnek looked up towards the walkways. There was no sign of her. He wondered how big the complex was inside the rock.

The marines slowly moved inside the dock, and immediately seemed to vanish. The shadows surged around and consumed their bodies, leaving no trace of them whatsoever, even the echo of their footsteps. One of the twisting pillars was in front of Vehnek and Miranda. The structure of it was perfectly uniform, and thinner than it had first appeared from the air. The stonework was eroded a little, as Vehnek had suspected, pockmarked and chewed by the termites of time, yet it was not cracked or crumbling, not discoloured by the burning, stale air. The swirls of the spiral were no more than a foot thick, yet were capable somehow of supporting the weight of the ceiling, and the structure of the pillar itself.

"What is this stone? Do you recognise it?"

Miranda shook her head. *"Like I said, I'm no architect. It's a remarkable material. Perhaps one we can mine and use."*

Vehnek slowly drew his pistol as they crossed under the threshold, and into the inner dock.

His eyes slowly adjusted. The smooth stone floor led into a chamber that made Vehnek immediately draw back the hammer on his weapon.

He couldn't even see how far up and back it went. Past a mile, thick shadows protected the secrets within. More spiral pillars led back at intervals of a hundred yards, level with each of their identical counterparts on either side of the deep, wide canal. The base of the waterway was tiled with triangle-shaped slates, and stained by the water that no longer flowed through it. At the nearest wall, staircases led upwards into networks of tunnels, identical triangular shapes to the ones that swallowed the walkways on the canyon wall.

The two marines were standing still as statues, their amplifiers pointed directly at the same spot in front of them.

Miranda glanced at Vehnek with a frown. The Lord Marshal raised his pistol, and slowed his pace. He pushed Miranda behind him gently, and walked until he could see what his men could see.

A lone figure was sitting, slumped against the base of the nearest staircase. It was taller than them, almost twice as tall, in fact. Its body was slender and covered in armour plating. The hands and feet didn't appear human, there were too many fingers and toes, with a pointed heel that curved upwards.

The head sagged downwards, over a torso that was scarred by scoremarks and rippling magical burns, damage older than Vehnek could tell, like the markings on a castle wall. One of the marines knelt beside it, amplifier trained on the neck. He poked it with the end of the barrel, but there was no reaction.

Vehnek overtook the other marine and crouched down. The face was not quite human. The brow was smooth, the mouth a narrow slit with no lips, turned down in a grimace. Its eyes were dark stones, fused into shallow sockets.

"*Miranda, look at this.*"

"*I am looking at it ... from over here.*"

Vehnek glanced around at her with a smirk. "*The design is different to Calver. Taller and thinner ... no visible weapons.*"

"Look at the forearms," Miranda muttered.

On the left and right arms were a number of scrawled, curved markings, circles and swirls and twisting patterns. Vehnek didn't recognise them. "*What do you make of it?*"

"*It's an older form of Salkethian ... and something else. I can't recognise much of it, aside from the proper nouns. Place names, and the names of people. Hurrkesh was a small city on Salketh's coastline, before the storm seasons became more volatile. There are several names, Galgivar is a prominent one that is repeated. Perhaps the name this ... being ... went by.*"

Vehnek examined the body. There were no significant breaches in the armour, none of the oily black substance that had passed for blood inside Calver was pooling, leaking or staining the stone floor. "*Is it dead?*"

"*It seems to be ... it's showing no reaction to us.*"

"*Hmm...*" Vehnek stood up slowly.

"*There are more, Lord Marshal,*" one of the marines muttered.

Dozens of the Constructs were scattered across the ground and the walkways. There were slumped over, or curled up like babes in the womb, all inert.

Vehnek tensed. "*Slowly now ... Miranda, are they the same?*"

The Arch Mage worked her way around them. Her cane scraped across the ground as quietly as she could make it, but the sound bounced around the interior dock and down into the shadows out of sight. She leaned on the cane as she peered down at a few of the Constructs.

"*No signs of movement. The symbols on the arms are different ... still Old Salkethian.*"

"*They're dead?*" Vehnek pressed.

"*There is no magic within them. I doubt they would be able to move whether they are alive and aware of us or not.*"

Vehnek pointed to the nearest marine. "*Go back to the runabout and check on the Colonel. He and his men are to deploy on either side of the canal. A research team should be stationed here, going over the stonework and these bodies. I want samples, understood?*"

"*Understood, Lord Marshal.*" He turned and moved as quickly and as quietly as he could back towards the entrance.

Vehnek joined Miranda with the other marine. "*What happened to them? How did they ... die? For lack of a better term.*"

"*I cannot say. There seems no damage to any of them ... but at their core, these are machines. They may contain the souls of living people, but they are no different conceptually to your pistol. Machines break down if they do not have access to replacement parts or maintenance, no matter how sophisticated they seem to be. Look at where this fortress is: the middle of nowhere. They have no ships or access to trade. That's the most logical explanation.*"

"*Conjecture, but maybe.*"

"*Without a full range of testing we cannot be sure.*"

Vehnek stared at the nearest of the Constructs, curled in a ball, facing him and Miranda. "*You said they could be aware of us.*"

Miranda nodded. "*But as I said, without magic, they are unable to move. This was demonstrated in the Colonel's experimentation.*"

"*There are sure to be others in the complex, and they may not be in this condition.*"

"*True, but we're here to broker some sort of deal with them if we can, are we not? If they are alive that is.*"

Vehnek's eyes traced up along the walkways. More Constructs were sitting or laying on them, all the way up.

"*Look at this, Morad, it's fantastic!*" Eagerness had leaped into Miranda's voice, even though she was still whispering. She pointed a finger at the Construct in front of them. "*There isn't any rust along the exposed joints. No oxidisation on the armour. Some dirt and staining ... but that's surely from sand that has blown in from outside. They could have been like this for centuries ... and yet it is as if they have been here for barely any time at all.*" She held a glowing finger against the armour on the body's shin. A thin slice of it was sheared off, and she picked it up with a pair of tweezers from her pocket on the pouch around her waist. She placed it into a hollow glass cylinder, fixing it into a portable microscope that she unfolded from the pack.

Vehnek didn't disturb her, instead watching as the Colonel's men began creeping into the inner dock. The Colonel himself cared little for care or cover, simply striding around with wide eyed eagerness.

"*Yes ...*" Miranda muttered. "*... as I thought, there is a buildup of smaller particles of dust, the amount consistent with a dormancy of perhaps two hundred years. Your diplomacy appears to be unnecessary. Our task here is research and salvage.*"

"*Hmm.*" Vehnek was almost disappointed at that, given the Warlord's legendary reputation. Then again, taking what they needed was a far simpler task, and meant they would reach the Gravestone mountain sooner.

The Colonel smiled at Vehnek as he approached. Again, with no sense of the potential danger, his stride was entirely casual. "*Lord Marshal ... what a striking place. Wonderful architecture and design. The difference in form of the Constructs is similarly interesting. They are somewhat sleeker, are they not?*"

"*Do your men have their orders?*" Vehnek grunted, ignoring the man's enthusiasm.

"*They do, yes.*" He gestured back to the researchers who were already organising themselves into teams and beginning to take samples of the rock, dust and metal. "*I would like to see a little more of the complex, however, before I begin my own work.*"

Vehnek nodded and gestured to his two marines. "*Send a runner to the runabout. Tell them to meet us at the top of the canyon, beside the pyramid perhaps.*"

One of them split off and collared an underling, relaying the orders, as he ran over to the entrance, The Colonel raised an eyebrow. "*Why not simply use your communication stone to give the order?*"

"*Because there is latent magic in the area, and I would rather not ... trigger anything.*"

The Colonel's mouth turned up in amusement. "*I see... well, there seems to be very little danger.*"

"*We will be the first to find out either way.*" Vehnek gestured to the platoons of marines that were moving into the dock on either side of the canal. Each platoon consisted of two dozen men or women, armed with long-barreled amplifiers, and bayonets. Their armour was light but durable steel alloy, their helmets fixed in place to filter out smoke or poisons, and give them a degree of night vision.

He sent a series of hand gestures to each sergeant in each platoon, pointing them at the walkways and tunnels, or signaling them to remain in the dock. The nearest group stood to attention in front of Vehnek, Miranda and the Colonel.

"*Stay alert, and watch every shadow. Sergeant, take point with three of your men. We're going up.*"

The sergeant saluted, and the group began moving up the nearest walkway. Miranda's cane slowed them a little, but it would allow a greater study of the area.

They crossed into the tunnel and into blackness.

***

Matt Waterhouse

The Allied fleet drifted over the Dividing Sea, in full view of the Caelish coastline. Ironclad watched it coming from the prow of the *Sand Dancer*, musing to himself about the circumstances of the approach.

In days gone by, when he had gone by Tobias Calver rather than Ironclad, he had longed for the journey north in force, an offensive against the evil, faceless enemy in dark armour who had pillaged his home for as long as he had been alive. Now he was going up there to meet that enemy as a comrade in arms, to clash with a threat to both. The idea of getting into bed with Cael would have made him sweat, if his metal body could have.

It is old men like us that have the hardest time living in the new world.

What a new world it was, too. One potentially rife with possibility, a smaller world, with less secrets and less barriers. A world where the people of Planar could live and work together, taste each other's food, learn each other's stories, but also a world where each step had to be carefully considered. Cultures would be in danger of dying out or being swallowed or twisted by a powerful neighbour, a conquest without bloodshed, but a conquest nonetheless. The fires of progress all too easily burned those who ran instead of walked, choking on the black, billowing smoke.

He had never been to Cael in anger or otherwise. In fact, Montu Fortu aside, he had never left Haama. His homeland had been wild enough and diverse enough for him to gain some perspective, or so he may have thought. He watched, in the strange way his new eyes perceived the world, as the country became more detailed.

The sands of the shoreline stretched far back across craggy, dust-covered cliffs and arid plains. The grasses were dry and spiked, the only flourishing plants the hardy ones that relied on little water. The settlements he could see by the ocean were either derelict, or crowded and on their way to dereliction. He could see the essence and aura of life pressed together in desperation and waning hope. He could feel them on undersized, old boats in the sea, fishing for enough food to feed a fraction of the life on shore.

The Empire Of Fire

To the east lay the mouth of a brown and grey river, excreting into the Dividing Sea. A small city was clustered on the western and eastern shores, joined by a massive bridge across the estuary. The water level was fairly low for a river that size, and muddy. The greenery was much clearer in that direction, there were evenly spaced trees and some patches of water that glittered in the sunset.

He could feel Ember in the crows nest, watching everything along with him. Her aura glowed so brightly to him that he could see the emerald tint of it even though he wasn't even facing her. It flickered along with her emotions. Thomas came up on deck and folded his arms at the prow, standing beside Ironclad with a sigh.

"Has it changed much?" Ironclad asked.

"It's been a hundred years, my friend ..." Thomas replied sadly. "Those years have not been kind. These settlements all used to be one city, stretching along the coastline. You can only just see the marks where the foundations were now. There used to be farms across parts of this dust plain in front of us, but even when I was here they were dying."

"It can be green again, should we succeed."

"Can it?" Thomas shook his head. "The sight of it ... it makes me wonder."

"That's a bitter thing to hear."

"It's not a pleasant thing to say either. At the very least ... I'm sure I won't live to see it. It takes far more time to create and build than to destroy. Let's be honest ... so much work must be done. The strain on Haama will remain until things change ... when will they?"

"They already have. This change will be slower."

"Yes ... I suppose so ... it's just the sight of it, it takes you aback."

Ironclad chuckled. "Oh, I understand, believe me."

The White Sea lay on the horizon, a band of pale land where the air shimmered above. Ironclad could tell by the reactions of the crew that the air was getting hotter and drier. Cael City was a wide cylinder, appearing in and out of sight through the rippling air.

There was something on the horizon that shone in Ironclad's strange vision, to the east north east. It was glowing, pulsing and flickering, like a beacon-fire in a hurricane. "Ember, due east north east, do you see it?"

"I'm not sure what I can see that way," she called down. "Could be smoke ... but not from a fire."

"Hmm ... Thomas, what lies that way?"

Thomas followed his gaze. "The Magus Towers. Why? What can you see?"

Ironclad described the light. "If it's the Magus Towers ... I would have though the light would be bright and pulsing, like the White Tower's did. Not flickering like the dying embers in a fireplace. Could it be some form of concealment magic?"

Thomas shook his head. "They're well defended enough not to need it."

A great rumbling sound rolled across them, moving with the wind. Thomas frowned. "Even I heard that."

Ironclad nodded. "It came from those towers ... at least from that direction. Thomas, I don't like it at all. The Lord Marshal seems to have many facets to his plans."

He glanced back as Thomas leaned over the railing in the Magus Towers' direction. The crew on deck were looking that way as well. Captain Seret met his gaze, a question on her brow. Change course or carry on?

"We cannot afford the distraction," Ironclad said tightly. "We must carry on."

Thomas glanced at him. "The force of that blast ..."

Another rumbling sound crashed over them. Thomas swallowed. "*Those* blasts ... people could be dying."

"I know, but if he gets to those dragons, it'll be so much worse. Tell Seret..." If Ironclad could have swallowed, he would have. If he had a heart, it would have all but torn. "Tell her to maintain course to Cael City. All ships ... same order."

The Empire Of Fire

Thomas patted Ironclad's chestplate, and shouted back to Seret in Caelish. She paled, and shouted back at him furiously. He returned the shout just as furiously, and the captain's jaw set. She stared at the wheel for a moment, before she slapped one of the communication stones. She spoke into it tightly, before returning it to the small plinth beside her.

For a while, as Cael City came closer, and as the rumbling sounds carried on, making the air tremble in terror, no words passed between them. The sounds didn't let up, didn't stop, and Ironclad could have sworn that a deathly screech, a cry of terror or fury, was carried on the wind with the blasts. Eventually it was too much for him, and he had to break it.

"This heat is going to do us no favours," Ironclad grunted. "Vehnek is making us fight on his terms, in his territory. An intelligent move."

"We have enough water provisions," Thomas muttered. "Dehydration is a factor, cooling is another. Few ships fly over the White Sea because of the strain from the heat. We may lose elements of the fleet if we continue."

"We may be able to re-stock at Cael City, but ..."

The capital had tendrils of black, grey and white smoke trailing from its many districts. The curved wall was used as a makeshift dock for a vast fleet, almost the entire Aerial Navy. They were sitting in hastily constructed berths along the stretches where the ramparts were flat. Even more vessels were floating above the city. A group of them split off, and began flying towards the Allied forces.

Ironclad glanced across at General Kelad's flagship, *Shadowblade*, as she increased speed and pushed out to the point of the formation.

"My eyes aren't what they were, how does the city look?"

"There doesn't seem to be a huge amount of damage, relatively speaking." Thomas leaned over the railing. "It seems like there are a lot of people in the streets, whether they're soldiers or not, I can't tell from up here."

"Hmm..." Ironclad folded his arms. "So much for the extra ships. There look to be the number joining us that we agreed to, at least."

"That's good."

A hand tapped Thomas on the shoulder. Captain Seret held out a communication stone to him, and muttered something in Caelish. Thomas thanked her, and spoke into the stone. He touched Ironclad's shoulder, and nodded. "We can hear you, General."

"*Good,*" Kelad's voice smoothly appeared from the magical rock. "*Two hundred and seventy eight ships are joining the fleet, a couple more than we thought.*"

"Glad to hear it. Thank you for your hard work in mobilising them, General."

"*Oh, come now. They do what I tell them. Some interesting updates from the City as well: it seems the Lord Marshal took a leaf from the book your less reputable fellows were reading from. He had a number of commandos in the city who have been agitating, and decided to engineer a little chaos in the aftermath of the Queen's death.*"

Ironclad and Thomas exchanged a glance. "Have people been hurt?" Ironclad asked.

"*Several thousand, I'm afraid, including deaths. Many of these commandos have been captured or killed, but as you can imagine they are slippery bastards. Their training is based on not being found.*"

"Then how will they be?" Thomas asked.

"*With time and manpower. It will be a slow process of attrition, but they will be discovered and flushed out. Unfortunately for us, that limits our numbers, and makes resupply difficult. We'll have to do it on the move, can you see our solution? They should be at the middle of the formation.*"

Ten large carriers were floating along with the combat ships, defended by battleships, cruisers and skiffs. Along with their many sails they had docking arms fixed to their port, starboard and aft structures.

"I see them," Ironclad muttered. He hesitated before asking what he had to. "General ... is there any word on what's going on to the east?"

"*No. Educated guess, something is happening at the Magus Towers, but since they severed contact ...*"

"Do you think the two events are related?"

"*Perhaps distantly. We've long suspected cooperation between the Arch-Mages and The Black Fleet ... but as for the ... cacophony they seem to be creating ...*" Ironclad heard Kelad sigh loudly enough for the stone to pick it up. "*I fear we have very little time ... even less than we think we do. Are your ships ready to ... take the plunge into the White Sea, as it were?*"

Ironclad patted Thomas on the back. "Let's finish it."

***

The four marines on point illuminated clear, spherically-cut magical stones under the barrels of their amplifiers, tucked in beside the handle of the bayonet. Behind them the rest of the marines did the same. The triangular tunnel walls were made of dull, dark grey stone, covered in a mixture of old Salkethian scrawling and something else ... a runic, angular, twisted scripture in orderly clusters of two, three, five, seven and eleven. The strange markings were filled in with a smooth black substance, making them stand out even in the low light.

"*Do either of you recognise that writing?*"

Miranda shook her head. The Colonel walked closer and studied the walls as they passed. "*I haven't seen anything similar, to my knowledge.*"

Vehnek nodded. "*And the rest of it? The Old Salkethian?*"

Miranda didn't reply. Vehnek shone a light on her pale, sweating face. Her eyes drew down to the floor, and her lips drew back in a grimace.

"*Miranda, what does it say?*"

"*I ... I couldn't tell you ... it's madness. Pure madness ... unfiltered and ...*"

Vehnek followed her gaze downwards. The scrawling, scratching scripture covered the floor as well as the walls. Every inch was taken up by the writing.

"*Lights to the walls, marines, and the floor. Except for one rearguard and one pointguard.*"

The lights shone around. Every surface had been marked by hundreds or thousands of hands. Some of the characters overlapped others, some were scribbled out, stained with black oil.

"*It makes little sense,*" Miranda muttered. "*What seems to begin to be understandable is covered by more scratching, words that I can barely recognise.*"

"*Va'Kael's blood,*" The Colonel murmured, although not in fear. "*The time it would have taken! Although, considering that Constructs have no need of sleep or sustenance, it is entirely possible that ...*"

"You think the Constructs did this?" Vehnek hissed.

"With all due respect, Lord Marshal, who else is here?"

"*Not them, any longer.*" Vehnek glanced up and down the tunnel, still hidden by layer upon layer of shadow. "*At least ... as far as we know. Marines, check every shadow, every corner.*"

Vehnek looked down at the communication stone on his belt, and rested a hand on it. With the magic around them, and above them, he had been leery of using more, and yet it seemed the wisest course.

He plucked it off his belt. "*All marines, this is Lord Marshal Vehnek. Be very careful down here. Have your weapons ready at all times.*"

The marine groups sent confirmation to him. He paused, then held it up again.

"Mora."

There was no response at first. After a moment, though, her voice drifted through his mind. **"Yes, Lord Marshal?"**

"Where are you?"

"I'm examining these ruins, a few levels above you and the others you brought."

Vehnek tapped the stone against his chin. Miranda frowned. "*I can't hear her, is she speaking to you?*"

The Empire Of Fire

Vehnek nodded to her, then spoke again. "We're seeing signs of ... potential danger. Be careful. Remember that we still need each other."

He heard the laugh of surprise in his head. **"Thank you for your concern. Nothing will happen to me, don't worry yourself. I have yet to see anything that could truly be a threat."**

"Are you certain?"

"Keep your weapons and your soldiers with you if it will make you feel better."

He let go of the stone. "*Keep moving,*" he snapped.

They crossed into more passageways that rose up through the canyon wall. In the lights of his marines' weaponry, Vehnek could see that the scrawlings of insanity still covered everything, even as the number of yards they had walked went from hundreds to thousands. The only sounds were the booted footfalls of his men, the knocking of Miranda's cane, and the beating of his own heart.

The torchlight illuminated Constructs laying or sitting on the floor. They were always alone, one by one, fingertips stained with the dust from the walls.

"*How many men did this Warlord take with him into the desert?*" The Colonel asked. His voice wasn't even slightly hushed, and sounded to Vehnek like a shout, even though he was speaking at a normal volume.

"*Quiet!*" Vehnek snapped.

"*Apologies, Lord Marshal ... but I think we can see that there is no danger from these beings.*" Despite his words, the Colonel lowered his voice.

"*Miranda, answer his question,*" Vehnek grunted.

Miranda swallowed, sweating. "*The legends never gave a precise number. Some say ten thousand, some fifty thousand, some say as high as a million.*"

Vehnek glanced at her. "*Are you alright?*"

She shook her head. "*Be glad you can't read Old Salkethian, Morad.*"

"*Don't look at it. Try to focus on something else.*"

"*It's everywhere!*" she hissed. "*No matter where I look or what I look at.*"

Vehnek glanced around at the scribblings.

"*Speaking from the perspective of the person who is to be in charge of their manufacture and design, I believe it is important that we know what they wrote,*" The Colonel murmured.

Miranda swallowed.

"*He makes a good point,*" Vehnek said. "*If we know what went wrong, if something went wrong ...*"

"*Ha! 'If'...*" Miranda spat.

"*... then we must be wise to not repeat the mistake.*"

"*You will get no sense from any of this, Morad. No signs, no answers. This is the excretion from a broken mind, not a manual of instructions.*"

Vehnek matched her step and reached out a hand. "*It is my men, my most loyal men, who will undergo this change. We have to know. Read what ... makes the most sense.*"

Miranda's jaw set, and she clasped his hand tightly. She looked down at the floor, where a long trail of writing lay as they walked, and began reading. Her voice trembled.

"*'More dark. More dark. Dark in death, dark is death, dark brings death. More dark, close end. Voices. Same. Echo. Silence! Shut your mouths! No mouths to shut. No mouths, but screaming, always screaming. No more days, no more nights, one endless void of screaming. No death in darkness, only eternal, poisoned ...'*"

Miranda shook her head and trailed off. "*The rest is covered by more...*"

She took a breath and spoke again. "*'Damn the dead king. Damn the dead king. Damn the dead king. Dark mistress. Dark sister. Release. Prison. No escape. Never sleep. Poison dream of the Meladrin. Awaken. Steel coffin. Buried alive. Kill me. Kill me. Kill ...' Those two words ... repeat.*"

Vehnek heard one of the marines swallow, heard another begin to shake. "*Focus, marines. Seems they got their wish. Only us down here now.*"

The Colonel nodded solemnly. "*Please, continue.*"

Miranda glared up at him bitterly. Vehnek sighed, and nodded to her.

The Empire Of Fire

She shook her head, face pale. She read another part with a snarl.

"'*My mother's name is Shana. My son's name is Toli. My mother's name is Shana. My son's name is Toli. My mother ...' It repeats. It keeps repeating.*"

"*Any change at all?*"

"*The writing is becoming messier, less coherent, but it is the same.*"

The Colonel nodded. "*Memory. It began to fail. Most unfortunate. It cannot be helped. Our own memories fail, after all.*"

Vehnek grunted. "*We don't live for long enough to forget a lifetime of memories ... most of us at least. Who knows how many lifetimes these men led?*"

"*Who knows how many they led down here?*" Miranda muttered.

Vehnek glanced at her as she tightened her fist. "*The words have changed: 'My mother had hair, my son's name, My mother, Sara, my son ... my son was born, my son was born, my beautiful son.'*" Miranda trailed off again, reading the words. They continued walking in silence, until she spoke again, in a shaking whisper. "'*My son's name, my son's name, my son's name, my son's name. His face is gone. His name. He loved. I love. His name. His...*'"

"*Marines!*" The point man barked. The sound echoed up and down the tunnel.

Vehnek raised his pistol, and a ball of lightning appeared in Miranda's hand. The Colonel squinted forwards and hummed to himself. "*Fascinating.*"

The torchlight had fallen upon a Construct, standing in front of them.

Vehnek squinted. It had no weapons in its hands, no shield. It simply faced them, in the middle of the passageway.

Nobody moved. Vehnek glanced at Miranda. "*You can read Old Salkethian, can you speak it?*"

"*A little.*" She gritted her teeth.

"*Tell it we're here in peace.*"

Miranda took a deep breath and spoke, to no response.

Vehnek stared at the Construct as Miranda repeated her words. "*Colonel, what do you make of it?*"

"Good question. Perhaps it is as inert as the others, and if so, the balance of these creations is wonderful."

Vehnek shook his head. "*I don't care how wonderful the damned thing is, I care about it being a threat.*"

"*I can't say.*"

Vehnek walked forwards slowly. The two marines from the runabout followed, weapons raised.

He closed to within a yard of the figure, squinting at it. It had no reaction at all. He closed in again, and lay a hand on its chestplate. It was cold as a gravestone, entirely still. On the Construct they had captured, the gears and mechanisms had made the armour vibrate with energy, and warmed it.

Vehnek beckoned the Colonel forwards, and he joined him without hesitation. "*Your thoughts?*"

The Colonel walked around the figure, humming. He looked closely, gently touched it. "*Hmm ... yes ... it seems quite inert. I assume you concur.*"

Vehnek nodded. "*Although ... watch them, and keep watching them.*"

The tall, thin figure disappeared into the shadows behind them, and they continued walking onwards.

The passageways were a network that probably encompassed thousands of miles, twisting and turning in the dark. Following their orders, Vehnek's men took every path that led upwards.

Miranda turned to the rearguard marines. "*Could you fall back twenty yards, please.*"

The marines glanced at Vehnek. He could see that the sweat remained on Miranda's brow, soaking through her robes. He nodded to the marines, and they fell back.

Miranda dragged him back a little, so they were out of earshot of the Colonel and the rest of the men.

"*Morad ... are you sure about this?*"

Vehnek frowned. "*Absolutely. Aren't you?*"

The Empire Of Fire

She bit her tongue. "*The writing is no less clustered or mad than it was miles back. They went insane.*"

"*It took time. We can euthanise those that wish it.*"

Miranda took a step back. "*What if they wish it right away? What if they can't bear being locked inside one of those things?*"

Vehnek cocked his head to the side. "*They will be dealt with ... when Mokku is brought to heel, and not before. When we stand on the bones of those dark skinned curs that have kept a boot on our necks, demonised us to the world ... then they will be allowed to fall, should they wish it.*"

Miranda, despite her sweat, shivered. She held her arms around her waist. "*You'll have dragons...*"

"*There are ground engagements where dragons cannot strike. We will need an army, siege engines, warriors that can walk through fire and blood. An army that cannot be touched by mortal hands.*"

Miranda shook her head. "*We are ... playing with more than just fire and blood.*"

Vehnek stepped closer to her. "*You have an extraordinary lack of faith in your own work, and the Colonel's.*" He peered at her closely. "*Or is it mine?*"

"*Not every concern is an attack, Lord Marshal.*"

Similar words would have come from the mouth of Sel Kelad. Similar reassurances, concealing a coming betrayal. He would have her watched from here on out.

"*I hear those concerns. Should a problem arise in your work, inform me.*"

She gritted her teeth. "*I can see plenty of problems.*"

"*Past problems. Problems you would be incompetent to repeat, once their circumstances are clear. I believe that you are both skilled and intelligent enough to discover what occurred.*"

Miranda sniffed and bobbed her head. Her eyes turned downwards. "*I understand, Lord Marshal.*"

The communication stone warmed on his belt, and a voice emerged from it.

"*Lord Marshal Vehnek.*"

He plucked the stone from his belt, eyes locked on Miranda. "*Yes?*"

"*This is Major Irsu, Lord Marshal. We have spotted your sorceress. She was in a large chamber, moving upwards quickly on a floating platform.*"

Miranda glanced up at Vehnek, who raised an eyebrow. "*Where is this chamber? What is in it?*"

"*We will set out a beacon for your team, sir. The chamber is ... I am not sure, sir. The expertise of the Colonel and Arch Mage Miranda will be required.*"

Vehnek held out the stone to her. She took it hesitantly. "*This is Miranda, can you describe it?*"

There was a pause from the other side. "*I ... I'm not sure I can, ma'am. I wouldn't know where to begin.*"

She frowned at Vehnek, who was already turning to his men. "*Sergeant, you are about to pick up the signal of a navigator beacon, track it immediately.*"

"*It will be done, Lord Marshal.*"

They waited for a moment, before the Sergeant spoke again. "*This way.*"

They strode on ahead, and took the next right. The writing on the walls never stopped the entire way. Some Constructs were laying on the floor, some were standing and leaning on the wall, but all remained still, as if they were sculptures dedicated to great creations.

For almost an hour they continued through the passageways. Small chambers were branching off on either side of the tunnels, angular, geometric shapes, seven and eight and nine sided with that expanded outwards. Vehnek couldn't understand the structure of them, could see no supports or cracks that showed stress in the rock. The chambers were not empty, they contained eroded objects, covered in dust. Brittle fabrics on the angled walls, seats made of stone, blades and axes covered in light blue rust. In some, shards of ceramic and glass littered the floor, smashed and crushed by steel hands. In every chamber, madness covered the walls, as it did in the corridors.

The Empire Of Fire

Constructs sat on the chairs and benches in some of the rooms. They were almost serene, if not for the shadows, and the signs of the turmoil within all around them.

"*Why not just kill themselves?*" Vehnek wondered aloud.

"*The bodies must be incredibly durable,*" the Colonel said casually. "*They are likely able to damage themselves ... though on the examples we have seen, they are pristine. I wonder...*"

"*You wonder what?*" Miranda growled at him.

"*If they were brought back entirely the same ... or something was added. A barrier in the minds, that prevented them from harming themselves.*"

Miranda shook her head. "*Monstrous.*"

"*For all we know, they agreed to it,*" Vehnek grunted. "*Loyalty ran deep to the Desert King, according to the legends.*"

"*Or they didn't know what they were agreeing to.*"

They continued upwards, and before they knew it, the tunnel walls around them simply vanished. The lights shone by the marines were swallowed by the shadows.

"*This is the chamber, sir,*" the sergeant whispered.

"*Send up a flare.*"

Miranda nodded, and pointed upwards. She muttered an incantation, and a ball of light bright as the sun exploded into being on her palm. It floated upwards, and bathed some of the room in a soft, cold glow.

What it showed was entirely beyond Vehnek's comprehension.

Hundreds of thick, cylindrical columns reached up into the shadows, far beyond the limits of the flare. As the light fell, it illuminated vast, skeletal frameworks jutting out at obtuse angles, connected together like a spiders web made of metal. They didn't touch any of the columns, and again, Vehnek was struck by the structural strength of the metal, the fact that none of it seemed to have collapsed, and that there was no sound of creaking or the whine of stress.

There was, in fact, no sound at all, of any kind. The marines that were in here were silent, or too far away to hear.

Matt Waterhouse

The light fell past the scaffold. Hulking blocky objects lay in the team's path, their shape unknowable while cloaked in the darkness. They were so huge that they blocked out the light from the flare. The blocks were lined with strange windows that led to more blackness. Downward still, they were connected together by cylindrical and ... perhaps hexagonal connectors. It was difficult to make much more out about them, as Vehnek tried to get any idea of a detail in the environment, the light was gone before his mind could make any sense of it.

Before long, the flare touched the ground nearby, lighting up a passageway that led between the massive, oblong shapes.

"*Sir,*" one of the marines whispered. He pointed upwards. The ghostly light of another flare was slowly ebbing away above the unknowable objects.

"*Move out,*" Vehnek hissed. The flare returned to Miranda's outstretched hand, and the platoon slowly worked their way through the narrow spaces between the shadowy, bulky creations of the Desert King.

There was barely a foot of space on either side of them, forcing them to move through single file. The heat around them began to rise, a dry heat like in the desert outside, but closer, almost like a humidity. It didn't take them long to discover the cause.

"*These large constructions are still warm,*" The Colonel murmured. "*After all these years ... incredible.*"

"What are they?" Vehnek hissed.

"*I wish I knew for certain. If I were to speculate, we are in a chamber where a vast amount of energy was stored or passed though.*" The Colonel looked upwards. "*Marines, what can you see around us, with your darkvision?*"

"*Nothing beyond these ... things, Colonel,*" the sergeant muttered.

"*What details can you see on them?*"

He shook his head. "*There are small pipes on each side, leading up and across and ... at diagonals, it looks like. A few cutouts, but I can't see what's inside them exactly. I can see, perhaps a door or a hatch, coming up on our right hand side."*

The Colonel hummed to himself. *"I think ... we are inside a machine of some kind. A vast machine."*

"Inside?" Vehnek echoed.

"Oh yes. As to what the machine does ... I would need to be able to see it on a larger scale, study it for an extended period."

"It's how the Constructs are made." Miranda was looking down at the floor as they walked. More Old Salkethian scrawlings covered it, but at more irregular intervals. There was no writing at all on the obelisks on either side of them.

"Is that what the mad men are saying?" Vehnek muttered.

"They called it The Great Iron Mother."

The Colonel beamed. *"This is it. This is truly it. Lord Marshal, we can begin studying it immediately."*

"Then do so. Call up more of your researchers." Vehnek peered at Miranda. *"Curious that they didn't mark these ... machine parts, although if they revere it as a ... mother, why would they?"*

Miranda nodded.

"Send up another flare while I contact Major Irsu."

She nodded, and Vehnek spoke into his communication stone. *"Major Irsu, send up another flare and hold your position. We are coming to you."*

"Understood, Lord Marshal. We are at the platform your sorceress used to move upwards. Be advised ... there are bodies here. They aren't the Constructs, nor did they die ... peacefully."

The flare glowed somewhere above them and to their left. With the beacon as well, they would have no trouble finding the other platoon, but Mora was another matter entirely.

"Good work, Major. See you soon."

They wove through the massive structures that made up the machine, passing more twisting pillars spiralling around in helixes, and spinning into the darkness. They seemed to serve a different function than the other pillars and pipes, perhaps decorative, or a channel for something entirely different.

"*Do we have enough people to operate this ... machine?*" Miranda whispered. "*If we do not ...*"

"*We won't know until the initial study is completed,*" The Colonel whispered, cutting her off. "*If we do not, at least in our party, then more can be sent for from the Magus Towers.*"

"*Even if this will take time, the dragons will be enough of an element of shock and awe to allow us to maintain control over Cael and Haama while our task here is completed.*" Vehnek smiled. It was all coming together. The plan had been grand, some had called it impossible, and despite betrayal from some of his most loyal ... they were here. On the verge of unlocking the secrets that would propel his new empire to the summit of Planar.

The Empire Of Fire. Of winged death and iron.

A legacy that would make any challenger tremble in terror.

Around the next obelisk, Major Irsu stood with his platoon, facing outwards, watching as many of the shadows as they could, around and above them. "*Friendlies,*" one of the perimeter guards said. Vehnek nodded to him. Major Irsu saluted, which Vehnek returned.

"*Lord Marshal ...*"

He gestured. The platform sat on a small, raised, circular plinth, like a slightly larger than comfortable step up. It was covered with splashes of muddy brown and dark red. Around the base of the platform were bones, clad in and surrounded by sets of old Melidan armour that had been dented, rent and torn. All of it was stained with gore. The bodies were shriveled and drawn, and in pieces. Bones were broken, skulls crushed. The weapons, axes and swords, were bent and buckled.

Vehnek glanced at Miranda, who was staring at him with furious eyes.

"*We suspect there are at least eighteen bodies,*" Irsu muttered. "*Melidan armour and heraldry means they came here at least eighty years ago, and the armour is in reasonably good condition. No erosion in here.*"

The Empire Of Fire

"The bodies haven't decomposed to nearly the degree they should have for eighty years," The Colonel muttered. *"No contaminants either, I would guess, or very few of them."*

Vehnek grunted, and looked around at Miranda. *"The platform?"*

"It's very similar to the elevating platforms we use at the Magus Towers and in the palaces. I would guess it would respond to a Mage, if Mora has already used it."

Vehnek turned to the Colonel. *"Get to work down here with your men. Preliminary research will take how long?"*

"I'm afraid it could take days, with the number of researchers we have to hand ... and that's if we pulled all of them into the chamber to work here. There is much to be gained from the rest of the sweep of the complex."

Vehnek tried to keep the annoyance out of his face. *"Call in the rest of your teams, then. All of them, get to it. Major, cover them, sergeant, you too with your men."*

Both marines saluted. The Lord Marshal pointed to the two marines from the runabout. *"You two, come with us."*

He stepped onto the platform, and helped Miranda up. The marines followed.

"Don't do anything stupid, Colonel. Until you understand this machine, do not set it in motion, even to test."

"The only machinery tests will be done via scale models, don't worry, Lord Marshal."

Vehnek nodded, and looked at Miranda. She closed her eyes, and raised her hands. With a sudden jolt, the platform rose into the air. It floated upwards, remaining level.

Vehnek signaled the marines to point their lights upwards. He looked up as the platform deftly slipped through a gap in the tight web of metal pipes above them. Beyond the pipes were a series of massive gearwheels, tightly clustered together, completely still. They cast jaw-like shadows on each other as the light passed them. They continued onward and onward, and suddenly, the darkness was pierced by a blinding sliver of daylight.

Vehnek and the marines hissed. One cried out, and stumbled, arms windmilling at the edge of the platform. Both the other marine and Vehnek jumped forwards and grabbed his arms, pulling him back on. Vehnek looked up again. the circular doorway above them was sliding aside like an eclipse moon making way for the sun.

The light bathed the machine below them, or some of it. The gears and cogs, the columns, and something else. A cloud of something, fog or smoke or steam, floated above everything, merging with the shadows. Where it was coming from, he couldn't tell. Was it old, lingering from the days when the machine was running, or...?

Vehnek whipped the stone from his belt. "*Colonel, there are signs that the machine may still be active. I say again, be careful.*"

"*I will, Lord Marshal, but we will have to interfere with it in some aspects. We will be as careful as we can be ... but I assure you that it is not operating. From down here I can see no movement or sound.*"

Vehnek's hand tightened around the stone. "*I don't care what you can or can't see. Until you're sure how the damn thing works, feed it no power at all.*"

"*Of course, sir.*"

When Vehnek looked up and around again, the platform was reaching level ground.

The arid air filled his lungs. He looked around. It was warm out, but he was under the shade of the walls at the top of the canyon. The fierce desert sun was shielded behind the stone.

Around them were stone buildings, dozens of them. Sand brick had been stacked on sand brick, creating oblong, rectangular blocks. They were basic constructions, with dessicated, flaking tarpaulin draped across the rectangular doors and windows. They were the no-nonsense dwellings of military men.

They were well ordered, with more stone brick lain down for basic paving. Vehnek couldn't see a water hole or well, but it suddenly struck him.

The Empire Of Fire

Had they tried to dig one up here, it would have led to the machine. That had to be how they had found it.

Nothing moved, just as nothing had moved in the corridors and chambers below, aside from his soldiers and their charge of researchers. They were moving in and out of some of the smaller buildings, casting uneasy glances at and past Vehnek. When they realised it was him, they saluted quickly, which he returned, before taking a deep breath of the dry air.

Slowly, he turned around. The jet-black pyramid loomed over them, eating the sunlight. It was a hundred yards tall at least. The walls were completely smooth. A set of thin steps let to a triangular opening in the wall.

He began walking towards it.

"*Morad!*" Miranda hissed. "*Where are you going?*"

"*Where she went,*" he grunted in response. "*You don't seriously believe she went anywhere else, do you?*"

One of the marines overtook him, and took the lead, moving up the steps. He knelt in the entrance, amplifier pointing inside. He nodded back to Vehnek.

The air chilled immediately as he stepped across the threshold. The room inside stretched from wall to wall. Whether or not anything had been there before, Vehnek couldn't tell, but it was entirely empty save for one raised dais in the centre, with gently sloping sides. Upon it sat a black throne, inlaid with gold, and upon the throne sat what remained of a lone figure.

Mora was walking around the throne slowly. Her stride was unbroken as she spoke.

"Here sits Hakaan, son of Devros, The Warlord In The White Sea, The Desert King, and The Rightful King of Salketh. Or rather, what remains of him."

Vehnek kept walking, glancing up at the ceiling. It didn't reach out completely to the top of the pyramid, and it was round, like the ceiling of a dome. For a moment, the daylight caught a band of black somehow darker than the black stone that the pyramid was made of. He thought for a moment that it was a spiral, but it was gone before he could be sure.

The Desert King was a sorry sight. His bottom jaw was gone, his right cheekbone and eye socket had been shattered. Ribs were crushed, the sternum snapped in half, the calves broken. The Construct shell he had inhabited lay in pieces on the floor, neatly arranged at the foot of the throne. Dented chestplate, torn open to reveal the mechanised innards. Broken pauldrons and twisted greaves, still set with jewels and gold, stained blood red across the metal bands protecting the welds and seams. The helm, or rather, the Construct's head, was carved into the head of a shark, with sapphires for eyes, and golden teeth.

Vehnek stepped onto the dais. The Desert King's crown lay upon his broken head. It was a black stone and gold helix, a single band that stopped at his brow.

"I suppose that concludes your negotiations, doesn't it?" Mora said bluntly.

"I suppose it does." Vehnek leaned down over the corpse. "I take it he was like this when you found him."

"Hmm. It's not necessarily surprising. Your kings and queens are overthrown all the time. All it takes is the right set of circumstances."

Vehnek glanced up at her. "I'm sure. The circumstances being?"

"You're a smart man, compared to your peers. You can work it out."

Miranda looked up at the rounded ceiling. *"What is this meant to be? This pyramid is no mere construction of vanity."*

"No, it's not." Mora smiled at Vehnek. "Shall we depart?"

"Not so fast," Vehnek grunted. "What is this pyramid? Who made the machine below us? Hakaan found it and used it, but he didn't build it."

Mora frowned at him, but the smile remained. "What makes you think I know about the little civilisations that sprung up and wilted on this tiny world?"

"I think you know more about this tiny world than you let on."

"Morad, I think this could be an amplifier," Miranda said excitedly. *"This entire structure ... it's an amplifier!"*

Mora chuckled. Vehnek looked back at her.

The Empire Of Fire

"*Are you sure?*"

"*Not absolutely, but it looks to follow the same principle as our long range communication dishes. I think ... Morad, I think this powers the machine.*"

"*Even if it doesn't, it's worth studying for the materials alone.*" He turned back to Mora. "How long has it been here?"

"Oh ... a long time, in your terms. Far longer that your great Cael has existed, even."

Vehnek frowned. "*Miranda ... I think it may be time to leave.*"

"*Hmm?*" Miranda looked back at him from the ceiling. "*Oh, of course. Of course, but ... I'll need a team up here. This structure is simply...*"

"*You'll have your team. Arcane engineers and archaeologists both. I want to know how long this has been here, precisely. I also want people looking over those structures outside, the ones he built.*" He pointed at the broken skeleton on the throne. "*Signs of what befell him in particular are of great value to me. How it happened, why it happened.*"

"*How and why are obvious, Morad. He was torn apart and ripped out of his armour. The writing in the tunnels: Damn the Dead King. They hated him.*"

"*Yes, and how he went from loyally followed into the desert to being torn apart is what I want to know.*"

"*He locked them in undying bodies,*" Miranda snapped. "*Pain, their failing memory, the eons passing in the exile he pressed upon them.*"

"*Then the question is: why stay here? Why not march with his undying army? He had no reason to remain in exile, he could have taken back his land by crushing all in his path. He must have heard the concerns of his men, their demands. But... he stayed on this throne, in this pyramid ... why?*"

Vehnek took Mora's hand. She was gazing at The Desert King's bones, an expression on her face that he couldn't quite place. She raised an eyebrow at him as his skin touched hers.

"What is it?"

She looked back at the skeleton. "Oh ... nothing. Nothing at all, simply a reminder that things do not always go the way they are planned."

"How long before we can make Constructs of our own? I know what the Colonel told me, but you know far more than he does."

"Good question. It could be as little as a week. The machine doesn't seem that hard to operate." She smiled at him. "You and I have greater plans ahead, however."

"Indeed." He plucked the communication stone from his belt. "*Inquisitor, this is Lord Marshal Vehnek. Status?*"

There was some hesitation from his first officer. "*Fleet status is nominal, Lord Marshal.*"

"But something is wrong."

"*We have received word from our people in Cael City. A combined fleet has amassed above the Golden Throne. They have set course for The White Sea.*"

"*As expected,*" Vehnek stated.

"*Yes sir ... but there is more news, or rather rumour. The Magus Towers have been attacked.*"

Miranda looked over at him sharply. Vehnek frowned. "*Attacked?*"

"*From what scattered reports we are hearing, the West Tower has fallen, and The East Tower is ablaze.*"

"*The Haaman Fleet attacked them?*" Even as he asked, he knew that couldn't be the case. The Magus Towers could survive against an assault from two thousand ships, and force them to retreat.

"*No sir, the towers are well outside their flight path.*"

"Then what..."

"*The reports are scattered, but there was seemingly a single attacker. It emerged from the ground ... some are saying it was a dragon.*"

Vehnek's hand tightened around the stone. As soon as the ground had been mentioned, he had known. The Colonel did his best work in the subterranean laboratories beneath the Magus Towers.

The Empire Of Fire

"*Contact the Colonel and update him on the situation. Deploy Warlord Groups One and Two to cover the pyramid complex, Knight Groups Five and Six to cover the perimeter and the canyon, and send down all of the support personnel that The Colonel and Arch Mage Miranda require. Send the runabout down for myself and Mora. I want this place to be a fortress before the end of the day.*"

"*Right away, Lord Marshal.*"

Vehnek put the stone back on his belt.

"*Morad ... what in Va'Kael's name...*" Miranda started.

"*This pyramid is your priority, Miranda, and nothing else. My fleet and our own dragons can see to this threat, at the Gravestone. This new variable has no reason to come here. It is a minor hiccup, nothing more.*"

She pursed her lips, her eyes glistening. "*Morad...*"

"*Do not abandon our mission, Miranda, not now. We are so close to greatness. A matter of inches. This pyramid is a puzzle only you can solve. I need you. Cael needs you. We'll be back in a matter of days, with glory on our wing.*" He looked to his two marines. "*Remain here with her. Defend her.*"

He swept from the pyramid, with Mora in tow.

"I did tell you to wait..." Mora muttered to him.

"Good people are dying, Mora, this isn't the time."

Outside, the runabout was floating down towards them. Vehnek folded his arms.

"Can it be stopped?"

"With your weapons? Now? I suspect not. The dragons ..." She chuckled. "...the *other* dragons, they should be able to put it down. The combined forces of your fleet should be enough to damage it."

Vehnek ripped the stone from his belt again. "*Colonel.*"

The man's grave voice came back to him. "*Lord Marshal ... I ...*"

"*You told me that the damned thing wasn't ready. That it wouldn't be ready for another month at least.*"

"And it shouldn't be ready. It shouldn't be anywhere near flying. We had only just completed the armoured chassis, the inner workings hadn't even begun!"

"Should be and shouldn't be are immaterial at this point, Colonel. The thing is flying and killing people."

"It was a blasted corpse, a hundred years dead! I wish I could explain it."

A thought crossed Vehnek's mind. The map that Kelad had shown in the Council Meeting, after the Second Battle Of The Pil Valley. The dead sweeping across Haama and Cael, millions strong. If a million dead could be controlled, a single dragon...

"Well, now your priority is that machine ... and only that machine. I want a comprehensive understanding of how it functions, and I want it operable. By the time we fly back this way, I expect progress, is that understood?"

"I understand. Morad ... I'm sorry."

"I doubt you could have known the forces that were observing your work, my friend," Vehnek muttered.

He looked at Mora. Her face was impassive, neutral. She gave nothing away.

"It seems Kelad's entity was not as vanquished as he thought it was," she said bluntly.

25

The military skiff set down in a crescent shaped berth, a hundred yards from the coastline. The bustling settlement of the Port Of Plenty was normally a wealthy, vibrant trade town, up against the Dividing Sea, with wide, clear routes to the Meladrin.

Many of the town's citizenry had profited from the trade links. The owners of the warehouses, supply stores and repair yards had made enough gold elif to live in grand estates and penthouses. Their workers made a higher wage than any other place in Haama, and lived well, on wide cobbled streets and in houses with gardens that allowed them to grow some of their own food. In families, one parent typically worked at the docks, while the other tended the crop. Allessandra had fond memories of the weeks spent at the Royal properties here, a grand mansion and sprawling garden, a mile-long stretch of beach where she and other young friends had frolicked in the sand and waves, dined on freshly caught fish. The memory of her mother caught her off-guard, bringing tears to her eyes. The days on that estate had always been the days that Queen Mirell had smiled the most, laughed the most.

It had been three days since the Allied fleet had departed Victory, and two since they had crossed from Cael into the White Sea. It was a time of great tension and whispered rumour, but as yet, there had been no panic, for there had been no news to panic over … until now.

Eluco wiped the tear from her eye gently. She smiled at him sadly, and turned back to the town.

The Port Of Plenty was unrecognisable. The busy back and forth had taken on an edge of panic. People were streaming out to the coast, some armed, some carrying blankets and food. The seven great docks were being cleared of all ships, the water-bound galleons and barges, as well as the aircraft, split off. Some headed out to sea, some at diagonals, all to make room for the incoming boats.

Allessandra couldn't count them, there were so many. Hundreds at least, scattered on the horizon. Fishing boats, small rowers, old repurposed yachts, rafts, the odd frigate and galleon too. They floated towards the docks in no formation or order, but in panicked flight.

"According to my sources, there was no warning," Minister Carrasco muttered. *"There is still a lot of contradictory information. We aren't sure if the Magus Towers are still standing, even."*

Allessandra shook her head. *"Is there any news on who or what did it?"*

"No-one can say for sure. None from the Magus Towers have been in contact, we suspect they are unable to do so. We will find out from some of these survivors, no doubt. I doubt very much that any are Mages, however. Mages do not travel on trawlers."

"Meaning that a settlement or two were attacked as well," Acting Defence Minister Ulan muttered. *"One point of note, maybe some relief for Haama, is that whatever it is is likely heading north."*

Allessandra nodded. *"Agreed, these people wouldn't be fleeing south otherwise."*

Yaro, one of Ulan's compatriots and closest warriors, approached from the rear of the skiff. He saluted Ulan, and bowed to Allessandra. *"Sir, Your Grace, all four battalions have reached the southern gate."*

"Bring two of them down the main causeway, and the other two on the outskirts to the first and seventh docks. I want a perimeter, and I want those boats funneled into the three middle docks. The tighter the spread, the better the security. Direct all boats and airships at the port to establish a blockade, directing the incoming craft in."

Yaro saluted again, and stepped away.

"I'll say it again, you should remain on the skiff ... Your Grace." Eluco muttered.

The Empire Of Fire

Allessandra smirked to herself. *"That has never worked."*

"Ali, these are desperate people, and we don't know if they are all as they appear."

She turned to him. *"If they are desperate, we cannot turn them away."*

"I'm not saying turn them away, I'm saying we need to be careful."

"I must be here for them, Eluco. They are my people as much as the Haamans are. Words are nothing ... they might as well be bald-faced lies unless we act upon them, unless we practice what we preach."

"Admirable, and refreshing, Your Grace," Carrasco murmured. *"However, there are sharks in the water you bathe in. They will be waiting for an opportunity."*

"Then the four battalions were a wise move. They will protect me, as will the Royal Guards. They will protect Haama, as will the Royal Guards."

The skiff's ramp lowered. They strode towards it with the retinue of guardsmen in tow. Ulan had Yaro and another pair of soldiers, Elizia and Mule, at each shoulder and directly at his back.

The procession marched towards the sea across the cobblestones, and already the cries of the fleeing Caelish people were audible in their thousands.

"If anyone here can shed any light at all on what happened at the Magus Towers, or what attacked them, bring them forwards," Allessandra commanded. She glanced at the stiff expression on Eluco's face. *"Although, do not bring them forwards unguarded and un-searched."*

"At once, Your Grace," Ulan said. *"Elizia, Mule, take six men and deploy on the beach. Stick with the workers handing out food and blankets, and be careful."*

"Yes, sir." Elizia moved ahead with Mule, signalling to another group of Ulan's soldiers to follow her.

The first boats were landing, beaching themselves in the surf. The sailors within leaped out and onto the wet sand, crying out in relief, unloading children and whatever meagre possessions they could bring.

Workers from the port moved forwards to assist them, lifting and dragging the empty boats up onto the beach, wrapping blankets around their shoulders and offering water-skins. As they were led up the beach to medics and people offering tents and basic packs of food, Allessandra could see some had burns on their limbs, some were stained with soot and smoke.

She and the Ministers settled on the sea wall, on a semi-circular observation deck overlooking the beach and the docks. She shook her head in disbelief. *"If he can't have it, he'll burn it all."*

Eluco glanced at her. *"Vehnek?"*

She nodded. *"Who else? We know how closely he's been working with the Arch-Mages. We know how brutal he is."*

"I doubt he attacked his own allies on purpose, Your Grace," Carrasco said. *"It wouldn't surprise me to learn that he dipped his toes in a pool of acid, in the hope that it would clean his feet."*

"Fire means ... it could mean that our fears were well-founded. We needed more ships. We always needed more." Tears filled her eyes again. *"Our forces are going in outnumbered, and if whatever did this is going north, as you say ..."*

Ulan turned to Yaro sharply. *"Send warning to the fleet immediately. There is a long-range amplifier in the town hall."*

"Me personally, sir?" Yaro muttered.

"You personally. On the double."

Yaro nodded, although his face remained grim. Allessandra could tell he wanted to stay at the sea wall, but he followed his orders regardless, sprinting back down the causeway towards the town centre.

The larger vessels were mooring up at the third, fourth and fifth docks. Streams of people were rushing off, the dock guards struggling to keep order. Some were almost falling off the piers and into the sea, but were saved from doing so by their fellows. The beach was filling up quickly, the survivors of whatever tragedy had befallen them being led along the sea wall and towards the edges of the town. Several miles to the east and west had been hastily dedicated to temporary camping and basic shelter for the refugees, which would hopefully not be needed for long. Many eyes were cast towards Allessandra, goggling at her where she stood.

"*They will be jammed up at those three docks before long,*" Eluco muttered. "*We'll need to open more.*"

"*Only if we absolutely have to, guardsman,*" Ulan snapped. "*We don't have the men to protect every dock, and all of the town. If the situation truly becomes dire we can signal them to shift, and redeploy the men.*"

Allessandra barely listened to them, watching the Caelish people stumbling up the beach, led by workers and guards, being picked up and held up where necessary. Some Mages were with them too, tending the injured while they were trying to get off the sand and up the stairs to the top of the sea wall.

"*We'll be doing this all day and night,*" she muttered. "*So many.*"

"*Longer, if we're worth our salt,*" Ulan muttered. "*I've fought in Idris for long enough to be very wary of people that look helpless.*"

Allessandra glanced around at him. "*You may have been out there for too long.*"

"*With all due respect, Your Grace, Victory is replete with similar examples. Don't expect the enemy to not learn from each other's tactics.*"

Elizia and Mule were moving back towards them, guiding a young woman by the hand. The soldiers were around her, forming a perimeter of sorts. They moved through the rest of the refugees like they were fording a river of bodies. Allessandra's fingers twitched.

"*There must be more we can do than just ... stand here.*"

Carrasco folded his arms. "*That is entirely up to you, Your Grace. I can easily have a few ships from the Merchant Fleet on standby to bring more supplies or people. Even they could transport some of the Caelish people elsewhere.*"

"*I mean something we can do. Something practical. Hand out blankets and food, for example.*"

"*Not without the Royal Guard surrounding you,*" Eluco grunted.

She sighed. It was a sound precaution ... but it would give them a reason to mistrust her, project distance rather than care. She nodded, reluctant despite him being right.

Mule led the woman up the stairs to the top of the sea wall. Allessandra straightened up, and Eluco slowly moved in front of her.

They stopped a few feet away. The young woman was dusty and shivering, with a blanket wrapped around her shoulders. She was covered in a couple of days worth of grime, wearing the clothes of a aloe farmer, a hempen robe tied around her like a basic, grey and brown dress.

Her eyes were turned down, staring at the cobbles. She blinked furiously, tension in her shoulders, not looking any of them in the eye. A slave.

"*You may look at them,*" Mule said gently. "*I promise you will not be punished.*"

Slowly, the girl looked up, first at Ulan and Eluco in their armour, terror still written on her face. Her eyes fell on Carrasco, probably seeing his bearing as that of a master. Certainly, the wealthy clothes he and Allessandra wore, formal and perfectly fitted, would match with the rich tyrants in Cael City.

"*They only want information, then you will be free to rejoin your family.*" Mule patted her on the back of her hand.

Allessandra could tell that her eyes desperately wanted to look anywhere but at their faces, but she held firm. Her hands were shaking.

"*Where are you from?*" Allessandra asked.

"*Yu'Ket'Soth,*" she murmured.

Allessandra knew the town. It had grown from a collection of plantations and farms, connected up by roads, huts and shops. It was, or rather had been, one of the more prosperous settlements in Cael, and had served as a source of food for the nearby Magus Towers.

"*Is it still standing?*"

The girl's lip trembled, and she slowly shook her head.

"*You were attacked.*"

She nodded.

The Empire Of Fire

Allessandra stepped forwards and took both of her hands. "*I'm so sorry ... but we must know. Who attacked you?*"

The girl's head shook again. Tears filled her eyes. "*I don't know. It ... flew above us ... it screamed ... it burned everything. The fire burned blue, it melted stone, it turned people to dust.*"

Allessandra glanced up at Mule. "*Did you see it?*" he asked.

"*Only in shadow. It was huge ... and thin. The eyes glowed like suns, the body swirled and shifted with the darkness. The town guard tried to hurt it ... but they couldn't.*"

Allessandra nodded. "*And it went north ... so you came here.*"

She nodded.

"*Thank you,*" Allessandra said, squeezing her hands gently. "*That's all we need.*"

"*Head along the sea wall here to the first dock,*" Mule said. "*There will be people there waiting for you, your family included.*"

She nodded silently, and offered the princess and her retinue a clumsy bow. Then she was led away by a pair of soldiers, handing her a blanket and pack of food.

"*A dragon,*" Ulan muttered.

"*If it had been a dragon, she would have known what it was,*" Carrasco mused. "*She was lucky to escape with her life, Your Grace, if this ... thing is capable of crippling or destroying the Magus Towers.*"

"*Do you think the fleet could stop it?*" Allessandra asked tersely.

"*I can only speculate. I am not a military man, and I don't have any information about the attack aside from what we've been told.*"

"*Why would Vehnek release such a creature?*" Eluco murmured.

"*I don't think he did. The Magus Towers have been vital to his plans thus far, or so it seems ... now they are crippled, perhaps worse. Tactically nonesensical.*"

Allessandra gazed north, across the sea, towards her homeland and beyond it. "*And all of it is converging at the Gravestone Mountain.*"

She straightened. "*Minister Carrasco, please make your way back to Victory. We will remain here to assist with relief efforts.*"

Carrasco gave a half bow. "*Would you like my vessels to deploy?*"

"*I would, yes.*"

"*At once, Your Grace.*"

Allessandra glanced at Ulan. "*Update the fleet, and ... continue your efforts here. Care is to be taken at your discretion. You are correct ... we are at war.*"

Ulan saluted.

Eluco stood beside her, hand linking with hers, reinforcing her strength with his own. "*We will prevail. We have warriors of legend. We have powerful Mages. We have wyvernborn. General Kelad knows Vehnek better than most.*"

Allessandra gave a quiet sigh. "*And yet ... it doesn't feel like enough. We are moving against forces that ... shake me to my core, Eluco. Forces we aren't even able to make sense of. It feels ... like we are a dying animal, striking out at the hunter.*"

"*Then we had better go for the throat, and take it with us,*" he grunted. "*Everyone's time comes eventually ... but this is not ours. It must not be, no matter the cost. What may take hold in our place is worth fighting against. What we've built here is worth fighting for.*"

Allessandra squeezed his hand, and began to pray.

***

The Colonel strode along the dark, madness-covered corridor with Larisia, keeping one eye on the inert Constructs all around them. Four of Vehnek's marines were walking with them; one ahead, one behind and one on each flank.

He glanced at his assistant, his voice at a whisper. "*What distance have we walked so far?*"

"*Twelve hundred yards,*" Larisia whispered.

The Empire Of Fire

A doorway yawned open to their left, and the Colonel glanced inside. The thick jungle of oblong shapes, metal pipes and impenetrable darkness seemed to stare back at him. He couldn't make out any of the walls of the chamber that held the Machine.

"*Va'Kael,*" he whispered. "*We've walked twelve hundred yards, and we're nowhere near the edge!*"

Larisia shook her head in disbelief. "*Is it all one machine, or several different machines?*"

"*I wish I knew. Oh, if only I could speak to the builder, the...*" A Construct loomed out of the blackness cloaking the corridor ahead of them. The Colonel halted, startled. "*...designer.*"

Larisia stepped behind him quickly.

"*Oh, contain yourself,*" the Colonel chided. "*They're quite inert ... although they do somewhat ... pop up where you don't expect them, don't they?*"

"*That's one way of putting it.*"

The Colonel peered at the one in front of them. It was identical to the others, save for the faceplate. "*Oh ... this is fascinating.*"

The features of a human face had been painted and scratched onto the nearly-blank visage. Lips represented in fading, flaking black ink or oil framed the narrow, slitted mouth, pulled down in a sad grimace. There were eyebrows painted above the dark eyes, and the carefully etched image of a nose scratched in between them. Tears had been scratched onto the cheeks.

The Construct was standing still, facing them both, arms hanging loosely at its sides. Its hands were empty, and despite the scrawling echoes of insanity on the surrounding walls, floor and ceiling, it seemed to be completely calm.

The Colonel shook his head. "*An attempt to personalise itself, stand out from its uniform bretheren ... incredible.*"

"*Horrible,*" Larisia whispered.

"*Do you not personalise your living spaces? Your clothing? Your hair?*"

"*I don't think that's what I'm looking at.*"

The Colonel narrowed his eyes at her, sensing a teachable moment.

"*Consider the one we examined in Victory. You would consider it sane, yes?*"

"*Yes ... I would agree.*"

"*It had personalised its armour, hadn't it?*"

Larisia looked the Colonel dead in the eye. "*That isn't what I'm looking at. This one created a face it didn't have. It was desperate for a face, an identity.*"

"*Desperate? How do you know that?*"

She gestured to the walls. "*Did a sane mind do this?*"

"*How do you know that this Construct wrote any of the words here?*"

"*How do you know it didn't?*"

"*We don't,*" the Colonel admitted. "*We need more information, that's why we're here, and why we're here with marines.*" He turned back to the Construct, and gestured to it. "*What do you notice about the hands?*"

"*More fingers than the usual. Improved grip or dexterity, perhaps.*"

"*Perhaps. Logically sound. What is it carrying?*"

Larisia glanced at him and shook her head. "*Nothing.*"

"*None of them have been carrying anything. No weapons, no tools, no personal effects. It's fascinating, isn't it? These are meant to be soldiers ... yet they're unarmed.*"

"*Do they look like they need weapons?*"

The Colonel smirked. "*Formidable as they may appear, soldiers do not pass up extra protection. Perhaps their weaponry has long since rusted away...*"

"*I wouldn't-*"

Larisia was interrupted by a sudden, loud whooshing sound from the adjoining chamber, back through the door they had just passed. The Colonel spun around even faster than all four of the marines and bolted back down the corridor.

A jet of steam was blasting from one of the pipes at the base of the Machine, a cloud of white so thick it almost shone against the abyss of shadow. The Colonel tore the communication stone from his belt. "*All marines, all* personnel, the Lord Marshal and I gave explicit orders. If anyone has touched anything..."

An urgent voice came back. "*This is exploration team one. We touched nothing, Colonel, I promise you!*"

"*This is team two. We're mapping the perimeter of the Machine chamber on the opposite side to you, we aren't even in the room.*"

The Colonel watched the steam billowing upwards, and took a few steps into the room. "*Team three, confirm.*"

"*We haven't touched anything either, sir, but there's steam venting close to us.*"

The Colonel stroked his chin. Larisia wrung her hands behind him.

"Steam venting..." he mused. "*...the Machine was warm when we first discovered it ... this must happen periodically to stop it overheating, assuming it has a similar function to our magical generators.*"

"*Colonel ... does that mean it's active?*"

He tapped the communication stone against his lips for a moment, and sighed. "*Miranda?*"

Her clipped voice hit him like the whine of a faulty gear. "*Is there a reason for this interruption, Colonel?*"

"What are you doing up there?"

"*That's it? That's the reason?*"

"The Machine is starting to belch steam," the Colonel said, purposefully slowly and icily. "*Your ilk have a habit of sticking their fingers and spells where they don't belong, so I'll ask you again, what are you doing up there?*"

"*I resent the accusation. I am doing nothing of any note, especially not with any magic. If my theory holds: that the pyramid is an amplifier ... it would be idiotic to attempt to put any magic into it without knowing the mechanism.*"

"Because that has stopped you before, hasn't it."

"*Colonel ... I hope you aren't blaming the Arch Mages for the volatility of your creation. Your creation that they are likely fighting for their lives against, I might add.*"

The Colonel glanced up at Larisia and moved away, back towards the corridor. His voice dropped to a hiss. *"My 'creation', as you say, had absolutely no capability of as much as moving a toe, let alone blasting a crater into warded ground. Your Arch Mages and Lord Marshal Vehnek share the same insatiable greed for results, and you'll bend whatever rules you can to get it. Hang what anyone with any sense might say, hmm?"*

He steadied himself. *"Come down here at once. Your insight on matters of the arcane will be helpful. I want there to be no possibility of danger ... and if the Machine has been activated, you will be able to assist in stopping it."*

He heard Miranda sigh with annoyance. *"There is no way it could be activated, no magic has gone through the pyramid! I have too much work to do up here anyway."*

"The pyramid will be there when you return ... there is no way of knowing what will happen when this Machine starts, and I would prefer we do know before we start it."

"Argh ... fine!"

The Colonel put the stone back into the pouch on his belt, and grunted. *"Mages ..."*

As he steadied himself with a sigh, his analytical eye caught sight of a shadow that didn't belong.

He took a step forwards, towards the corridor. *"Marines."*

The men quickly filed in behind him.

"Lights ahead."

They pointed the illuminated stones on their amplifiers up towards the corridor. The light fell on the false face of the Construct they had observed before. Its painted expression was just as pained, just as sad, but it was a full six yards closer than it had been.

"Watch that thing. Don't take your eyes off it."

Larisia jogged up to them, and froze. The communication stone was already back in the Colonel's hand.

"All marine teams, watch the Constructs closely. They may be active."

The Empire Of Fire

He kept the stone in his hand, and walked forwards slowly. He held up his hands. "*We mean you no harm. I don't know if you can understand me, but I assure you, we only seek an alliance with you, one that is mutually beneficial.*"

The Construct remained as inert as a marble statue. The sad expression stayed upon its face. It seemed to be staring at nothing ... but also right at the Colonel, right into his very being.

The analytical side of him knew that it was conscious, and looking right at him.

He backed off slowly and held up the communication stone. "*All teams, check in.*"

A shaky voice of one of the researchers whispered out of the stone. "*Colonel ... there are two of them standing very close to us ... and I don't think they were there before.*"

"*This is Sergeant Erzan ... my squad are at the north west entrance to the Machine chamber. This corridor was empty ... now there are nine of them just standing there, watching us.*"

"*This is Clea, I can confirm that these things are moving, Colonel. We've been cataloguing them on the upper levels, and ... as far as I can tell, when we have our backs turned, they move. They're looking at us now ... AH!*"

The Colonel flinched, waiting for another word from Clea. Her voice trembled as she spoke again. "*One of them just took a step away from the wall, but it's just stopped ... now I'm looking at it ... it's stopped.*"

He listened as more of the marines, scientists, engineers and researchers gave similar accounts of what was happening in the labyrinth of madness. He tapped two of the marines. "*You and you, stay here. One of you watch that Construct, the other watch the perimeter. The rest of you, with me.*"

One of the remaining marines took point, and led the way through the pipes and blocks that made up the Machine. They wove through the hulking maze of vast, unknowable components, a quartet of ants scurrying through the innards of a clock. A beacon had been set up beside the lifting platform that led up to the pyramid, and the Colonel could see the floating circular dais descending steadily, with the tiny figure of Miranda in the middle alone.

The Colonel held up his stone once more. *"All perimeter marine units, all airships, pull inwards. Pause fortifications for now, we need more eyes on these Constructs."*

The platform touched the base, and Miranda limped off it with her cane, glaring at the Colonel. *"You had better not have brought me down here purely due to your own jitters."*

"Have you been paying attention to any of the communications I just sent?"

Miranda rolled her eyes, and slowed her voice to a condescending crawl. *"I have been meditating to try and ascertain the status of the Machine, as you demanded I do."*

The Colonel folded his arms. *"And?"*

"It is as it was when we entered the chamber the first time ... inert."

"Good. Unfortunately, I cannot say the same for its custodians."

Miranda's frown deepened. *"The Constructs ...?"*

"Are moving."

Concentrated balls of lightning appeared in both her hands. *"I knew ... I knew that they were dangerous. I tried to warn Vehnek..."*

"As of yet they are not dangerous, although they do seem curious about us."

Miranda bared her teeth. The lightning stayed in her palms. The Colonel took a step towards her. *"What have you found above?"*

"Little. The pyramid has some familiarity in energy, but not in design. It is nothing like the ones that were uncovered in Cael, either internally or externally."

The Colonel raised an eyebrow. *"What energy is familiar?"*

"In the pyramid, woven into the walls ... its the kind of energy I felt when meditating with Mora."

The Colonel folded his arms and snorted. *"That explains some of her eagerness when we arrived, perhaps."*

The Empire Of Fire

Miranda shook her head. *"More than eagerness. The way she walked around the skeleton on that throne ... it was as if she knew him."*

"We know The Desert King by reputation."

"But not personally ... not like she seemed to."

The Colonel paced for a moment. *"You're sure about the Machine ... that it's dormant?"*

"Positive."

He sighed. *"Is the long range communication dish set up topside?"*

"Not yet, but I imagine it isn't far from completion."

"Let's prioritise that ... and Miranda, take a look at those Constructs. They aren't dangerous at the moment ... but that could change."

"Agreed." She squinted at him for a moment, before moving through the machinery towards the passageways.

The Colonel watched her until she was lost in the shadows, then looked around at the huge metal blocks pressing in around him. It was like a dark, silent city, where even the spirits of the dead didn't dare reside. His gaze turned upwards to the web of pipes, and the distant clouds of steam spinning above them.

No ... spiralling above them.

Larisia drew close to him. *"What do you think?"*

For a moment he didn't say anything. The pieces were slowly coming together in his head, even though many of them still seemed to be out of his sight.

"Colonel?"

"I think we are in unfamiliar territory, walking among the heart valves of a beast we don't have a full image of. What concerns me most is that someone in our party did have a full image of it, and knew exactly what it was. Once the dish is set up... we'll have to-"

He was cut off by a sudden roar and hiss, so loud it crashed straight through his ears and reached into his head. His vision blurred, and the heat around him sharply rose.

Wincing, he looked around blearily. Jets of steam were blasting out of every vent in sight. Larisia was screaming, holding the sides of her head, though he couldn't hear her at all.

Behind the dark hatches in the sides of the oblong blocks, a gentle glow began to grow fierce; the stoking of flame hot enough to melt steel.

The ground shook suddenly, a vibrating pulse that rocked the entire structure. Then came another, just as strong. The force of them drove the Colonel, Larisia and the marines to the ground.

The pulses kept coming, increasing in speed, faster and faster. It was completely disorienting, vibrating through the Colonel's body and making nausea threaten his stomach.

On his back, he could see the steam swirling and spiralling quickly above him. Voices were screaming in a panic from the communication stone, but he couldn't make out the words.

The Colonel lay there, willing himself to move his shocked arms and legs, as the Machine roared to life around him.

***

Vehnek stirred. He had been awoken by the whisper of a cold desert breeze, sneaking across his bare chest and beneath the sheets.

The window of his cabin was open. He turned over and sat up.

Mora was standing beside it, naked, silhouetted in the moonlight. She had her back to him. Her hair was dancing in the gusts that were reaching into the *Inquisitor*.

Vehnek watched her without making a sound. She was completely still. Despite the cold, her skin remained smooth, untainted by gooseflesh.

He stood up. When the bed creaked, she didn't even twitch. He pulled on a robe, and brought a second one with him as he approached her.

He reached out and stroked a hand down her back, from shoulder to waist. He frowned at the warmth of her skin.

The Empire Of Fire

She didn't look at him as he put the robe over her shoulders. With a glance through the window, he confirmed that none of his ships were directly behind the *Inquisitor*, meaning that no perverted watchman required disciplinary action.

When he looked back at Mora's face, her smile almost made him shiver.

It was far too wide, her teeth parted a little, her eyes fixed directly behind the fleet, right in the direction of the pyramid and the ships he had left behind. She almost looked like a skull, or a creature. Vehnek glanced down at her hands.

Both were tightly clenched into fists. Her knuckles were bulging so far that the bones were almost breaking through the skin.

"*What are you smiling about?*"

Mora's expression softened, and her eyes locked onto his. "*Smiling?*"

She laughed quietly, and her expression became quizzical. "*Laughter. It's quite the feeling. You don't laugh enough, Lord Marshal.*"

Vehnek raised an eyebrow. "*Maybe so. Maybe I need some of your mirth. What were you smiling about?*"

This time her smile seemed far more natural, but far less genuine. "*Progress. Plans coming to fruition. That's all.*" She glanced at the bed. "*Sleep, Lord Marshal. Days of glory lay before us.*"

26

For Ember more than almost everyone else, the White Sea was a dead, alien environment. From up in the crows nest of the *Sand Dancer*, she had a full view of everything in sight. It seemed that the soldiers and airmen in the fleet were the only living things for miles upon miles.

Below was cracked ground and fine sand, blasting the searing sunlight up to the underbelly of the ships flying above, as well as the top decks and sails. Ember had deployed a tarpaulin parasol above her, with water and aloe lotion on hand. She coated her exposed arms, neck and face with it, to stop her pale skin searing.

The fleet around her were flying onward in formation. The nearby wyvernborn craft signalled her, and she waved a hand in return. A wyvernborn scout glided back to the ship and landed on the top deck. Immediately another one set off, leaping into the air and spreading his wings wide. He swept down and forwards, the hot air catching him and propelling him upwards.

Ember glanced at the crow's nest on the other ship. A message came, a series of hand signals.

Clear ahead. Maintain course.

Since word had reached them about the attack on Cael's Mage stronghold, she had been waiting for the word that something was pursuing, or that the fleet they were pursuing had decided to stop and wait for them. Weapon emplacements in the sand, or some foreign magic deployed by Mora, or scout ships concealed in the craggy canyons and behind the great blistering rocks they were passing. She had never done well on long journeys to a fight, there had always been the need to distract herself.

Ember looked down at the prow, where Ironclad had been standing every

The Empire Of Fire

day, watching the path ahead of the *Sand Dancer*. For hours he stood silently, for he, like her, was above a new land for the first time in his life. In either of his lives.

One of Captain Seret's crew was climbing the mast to the crow's nest, shaking the platform. Ember grinned, relishing the practice at keeping her footing.

The crewman poked up his head. "Time for me," he said in broken Haaman.

She nodded, moving aside to let him up, then scrambling quickly down the rope ladder.

When her feet touched the deck, she strode over to Ironclad. She moved close to him and took his hand. Surprisingly, the metal was cool, almost as if something in his internal workings was keeping the temperature down.

"You see something the wyvernborn can't?"

He grunted. "I'm not sure what I see exactly, with these eyes."

She leaned against him. "Don't move for a minute, you're the only cool thing in this desert. It's so bloody hot."

"Hmm." He let out the sound of a sigh. "This is our first trip abroad, I suppose, isn't it."

"There's a little more company that I might have liked."

"Well, there's going to be quite the party."

She rested her head against his bicep. "I didn't know Cael would look like that. You hear the stories, read the books and hear what tales Thomas wants to tell ... but I'd never have imagined that it would be so ..."

"Desolate," he muttered. "Not so far from the desert we're flying over."

"They really do need us ... need Haama." Ember shook her head. "Wish they'd asked instead of taken."

"It's always the way. Words are the last resort instead of the first step."

He hummed again, and shook his head. "There is something about this desert that I can't place."

"What do you mean? I figured this was what deserts would look like."

"It's not how it looks, it's how it feels. Old, ancient ... and it feels like ..." he shook his head again. "Like I'm coming home. Like I've been away for years, and I'm walking a familiar lane that leads up to the house. Passing familiar neighbours, who recognise me and wave."

"Did you feel that way when we were back in Melida City?" She snorted. "Huh ... Victory. Victory, I mean."

"No. We were nowhere near where we should have been. Even in Old Town ... seeing it in ruins ... I don't know. It's not the place I knew."

"In the Wyvern Bog, I started to in places ... but it felt like ... I don't know. It isn't the Orlin Forest." She stroked his arm. "What is it about the desert?"

"I wish I knew. Seraphine said ... that they came here with me ... what remained of ..." His eyes glowed brighter, and he leaned forwards. "There."

She squinted. The wyvernborn scout was rushing back to the fleet, and landed on the deck of the nearby craft heavily. Ironclad didn't acknowledge him, staring ahead still.

"What do you see?" Ember whispered.

"The echo of something. A mirage ... an image in the sand. A shadow on the horizon ... where no light touches. A pit ... down below the rock and the hottest grains ... can you hear it, Ember?"

His voice was taking on an intensity that she had never heard. "No ... what can you hear?"

"The grinding of gears, the hiss of steam, lightning striking metal ... and voices ... Gods, they're mad. They're screaming. They're all mad!"

Ember took his hand in both of hers. "Come back to me, Tobias."

He looked down at her. His eyes dimmed back to a gentle glow, but the tremor in his voice remained. "You don't understand, Em' ... thousands of men and women ... thousands ... their minds are agony ... and they're *screaming* for help ... from anyone ... from anything."

Around them, the fleet were redeploying, and changing course. Thomas, Bassai, Seraphine and Kassaeos leaped up onto the *Sand Dancer's* top deck.

The Empire Of Fire

Thomas went back to chat to Seret in Caelish, before all four joined them at the prow.

"One of the scouts has spotted smoke on the horizon," Thomas muttered. "Two dozen ships are investigating, including us."

Ironclad looked around sharply. Seraphine was growing pale as she looked at the desert. Ember could see the recognition on her face.

"Stay in the air. Do not land, under any circumstances," Ironclad snapped.

Ember tightened her hold on his hands, but softened her voice as much as she could. "But you said they need help. We can help them, can't we?"

"If Vehnek is there ..." Seraphine started.

"Do not land!" Ironclad repeated, more slowly, more loudly.

"If Vehnek is where?" Bassai growled.

Eyes fell on Seraphine's pale face.

"The Machine," she whispered.

"What machine?" Ember demanded. A horn was sounded from one of the skiffs in their formation. She looked up and around. Cannons were sliding out of their hatches on every ship. The gunners assigned to the *Sand Dancer* were bringing light cannons up on deck and hoisting them up onto their shoulders.

The lookout shouted down in Caelish. Thomas frowned up at him.

"He says he's seen the smoke, and ... a storm."

Ember looked around. Ahead of them, there were columns of black, twisting threads of smoke reaching into the air. There was more than one fire burning. The smoke was dancing and swirling together.

"Raise the barriers!" Ironclad commanded.

Seret barked something from the helm. Thomas coughed. "I'll paraphrase: raise the barriers against what?"

Ironclad pointed at the smoky arms, swirling and turning together. "You can't see what I can see ... you can't hear them ... there's an energy ahead, right in the middle of that smoke, reaching up."

"What kind of energy?"

Ironclad shook his head. "I don't know, I'm not like you, I don't recognise these things, I just know it's dangerous!" His voice took on a razor's edge.

Thomas held up his hands. "I believe you. I can't sense anything yet, we're not close enough. Seraphine?"

She shook her head. "But Ironclad is right, we shouldn't linger around that infernal place."

"Take us a half-mile around the smoke, no closer!" Ironclad bellowed.

Seret again snapped from the helm.

"She doesn't want you giving ... hysterical orders on her ship," Thomas muttered. "Her words, not mine."

Ironclad pushed past everyone and marched to the wheel. Ember swore under her breath and followed swiftly, as did Thomas.

He stopped in front of Seret, whose anger had given way to the kind of fear that Ironclad instilled in his enemies. She swallowed, staring up at him.

"Easy," Ember muttered to him.

Ironclad ignored her. "Stay at least half a mile away, Captain. We don't have the ships to lose."

Thomas translated. Seret's eyes flicked to him, then backed to Ironclad. She swallowed again, and nodded.

"If I may," Seraphine said, ducking forwards. "We should perhaps reduce our altitude, and get into position where we can see what's going on. Vehnek may be there, if he isn't he has certainly been recently."

"He may also have ships there, on the ground," Bassai growled. "We may be able to reduce his forces before the main engagement."

"That's a mistake!" Ironclad shouted.

Ember put her hands on his chest immediately. Bassai took a half step back in surprise, but quickly stalked forwards. "We cannot pass up any chance to whittle down a superior force. You know that better than most."

Thomas relayed this to Seret, who sighed, and pulled a lever. She tossed a communication stone to Thomas, and jerked her head at the other ships in their

The Empire Of Fire

section.

As he relayed the orders, Ironclad returned to the prow. Ember stopped beside him. His eyes were glowing brightly again.

"You need to keep it together, big guy," she muttered. "We need you to keep it together, all of us. The whole fleet, the whole country. I know how much pressure it is, I feel it too, but ... please."

His head turned towards her slightly. "I'll ... try ... but Em' ... I don't know if I can."

She could feel the shaking in his hand, something she had never felt even when he was flesh and blood. Swiftly, she stepped into his eye line.

"We'll face it together, then, whatever it is, and we'll kick it into whatever oblivion it crawled from. Together we can face anything."

His eyes dimmed from dazzling to simply bright, as he nodded jerkily. "Together."

***

Miranda closed her eyes tightly, and shrunk back into the corner of the chamber. She pressed herself into the tight shadows and backed up against the obtusely angled walls.

Metallic screams echoed down the tunnels, bouncing around the weaving passageways. All too often, but growing increasingly rare, a human scream of horror found its way to her ears.

They were the only sounds that managed to reach over the indescribable cacophony of the machine, the hisses, the screeches, the grinding of foreign metal against foreign metal, and the sounds that her mind couldn't even begin to place.

She tentatively reached out with her senses. The corridor seemed empty. It was difficult to hear over the noise, but the traces of magic that kept the Constructs running were little beacons to track. Now, though, there was so much energy coursing along the corridors that it was almost impossible to discern the walking monstrosities from the background.

Miranda cursed. She limped forwards on her cane and whispered an incantation. Her left fingertip changed colour until it was reflective and mirror-like. She used it to see out into the corridor on either side. There was nothing out there.

She limped out, trying to get a sense of her bearings. The tunnels were labyrinthine, and the pulsing walls of noise were giving her no sense of which way led away from the machine.

The ships were up top around the pyramid, or in the canyon. The only way back to the pyramid that she knew of was the lifting platform, where the machine was. She cursed the Colonel for calling her down here with him.

She walked up the tunnel, trying to focus on her footsteps, narrowing her mind to stop herself losing it to the metal thunder battering her from all directions. One step at a time, one foot in front of the other.

She kept her focus as she stepped around still-wet puddles of blood. The armour of Vehnek's marines had been torn apart as easily as a toddler could eagerly rip apart the wrapping of a birthday gift. The amplifiers that they had carried, some of the most sophisticated infantry weapons in existence, were bent and broken.

As she rounded the corner, a huge, slim figure was hunched over on the ground, crouching in the middle of a cluster of body parts. It was painting symbols on the floor in blood, using someone's severed arm as a brush.

Miranda backed up immediately and took the nearest side passageway.

Her heart was hammering in rhythm with the machine. She glanced around for any other chamber she could duck into again. There were a few on the left and right. One had been spattered with an amount of gore that had once been a researcher and assistant, based on the scraps of bloody clothing that remained discarded on the floor. In another chamber, a marine was slumped against the wall, having pointed the barrel of his amplifier into his own mouth and flash frozen his own head. The chambers had been attempted places of refuge, and they had not worked. Pieces of scientists, runners and marines filled

The Empire Of Fire

them all. Miranda, feeling the panic in her heart rising, doubled back to the marine that had taken his own life.

She focused her energy, and conjured a bubble around her, one that would block out the noise. Even though it was dulled, some of the sound remained, pulsing and pounding in the background. She tucked the cane under her arm, and plucked a communication stone off her belt.

"*Colonel, can you hear me?*"

The voice that came back was unnervingly calm. "*Hello, Miranda. I can hear you well.*"

"*Where are you?*"

"*Where am I?*" He giggled. "*I don't quite know, Miranda. I am above you ... I know that much. I believe I will soon be at the pyramid you were examining.*"

Miranda cursed.

"*Language, Arch Mage. There are ladies present.*"

She wanted to scream. They had gotten separated. He had called her into the bowels, and now he was up in the safety of daylight where she had been. "*What are you talking about, Colonel? Who is with you?*"

"*My assistant, Larisia. Well, some of her.*" He giggled again. "*I liberated all the parts I could find.*"

Miranda held her breath, and pressed the stone to her forehead. There were no more allies here, or so it seemed. She turned to the corridor.

The incantation of silence had completely masked the approach of the Construct, standing in the tunnel. It was staring at her, head cocked to one side. It had painted itself a sad visage on its faceplate, complete with tears on its steel cheeks. She backed off and held up her hands in as calming a gesture as she could. It had seemingly no effect at all. The Construct took a shaky step forwards.

The hulking creature reached for her. Its forearm split open down the middle. A long blade extended out of the limb, and then began to spin, windmilling and spinning so fast that she could no longer see it.

Matt Waterhouse

She dispelled the silence around her, and was immediately overwhelmed by the maddening noise. The confusing cacophony of the machine, the screams of the dying and undying, and the whine of the spinning blade as the Construct staggered closer.

She gathered a bolt of lightning in her right hand, and sent it snapping forwards into the Construct's chest. It paused, then came at her again.

Miranda plucked the weapon from the dead marine's hands, and pointed it at the creature. A ball of ice erupted from the barrel, and crashed against the chestplate. It left a pale sheet of frost on it, but did not stop it.

Miranda could feel the stale air whipping from the force of the spinning blade, creeping closer to her. She frowned, and aimed at the blade itself. The first shot burst when the blade struck it, showering both her and the metal hulk with freezing air. The next two shots struck the mount of the blade, somewhere in the split forearm. The blade slowed to a halt and twitched.

Miranda wasted no more time. She ducked under the arm that swung towards her and dived for the corridor. She limped with her cane down the corridor. The thudding footsteps of the pursuing, undying, mad thing pounded the ground behind her.

How it had found her, she couldn't say. There were so many that it was possible, but the corridors had been more or less deserted, save for those the Constructs had murdered.

She thought as best she could, ideas being battered around by the noise. Those in the docking canal would have set up beacons, so that the marine teams wouldn't end up lost and going in circles in the tunnels.

She reached out with her mind. Some of the beacons were active, she could feel the pulse that gave her the reminder of home, but as she took the next passageway towards them, she felt one wink out.

She gritted her teeth and pushed forwards. Her leg was burning in white hot agony. She wasn't ready to be moving this quickly. As another beacon extinguished like a candle in a dark room, she was forced to increase her pace, screaming and grunting with every step.

The Empire Of Fire

There were shouts ahead of her, welcome shouts in Caelish, but as she turned the corner, her face fell.

A pair of marines were ahead, firing blasts of flame and lightning at a Construct pursuing them. The giant had a spinning blade coming from each forearm, closing in on them with purpose.

The volleys of magical energy did nothing to stop it. As Miranda limped onwards, one of the spinning blades chewed into one of the marines right through his armour. Blood showered the walls, pointed ceiling, and madness covered floor.

The other marine shrieked as Miranda ducked past. Something warm and wet sprayed across the side of her face. More of the beacons were going out ahead of her. She hoped it was because the scientists and marines on the dock were evacuating. There was no more reason to stay here. No one mortal could hope to control the machine, or master its creations.

There were three sets of thudding footsteps behind her now.

She turned to the left and right, almost falling, dragging her leg now, walking stick trembling. She was crying in a way that she hadn't cried since she was a child, when she had scraped her knee on jagged, sand brick paving and gravel.

Light ahead. Gently glowing daylight, orange with the setting sun. She could hear the Constructs behind her closing in, and could feel the last beacons winking out ahead of her. There was only one left as she crossed into blinding orange daylight.

Her eyes adjusted just in time to see the Construct's foot slam down on the beacon, crushing it, shattering it.

The canal and dock were soaked in fresh blood, pooling on the smooth tile. She almost skidded into a pile of heads that had been torn off at the neck, mouths agape in terror, skulls misshapen from being crushed.

She was pulled from her stupour by the advance of the bellowing metal warriors behind her. She conjured balls of ice in both hands and filled the tunnel with a thick frozen wall. Immediately there was a loud crack and a chunk of it flew out and shattered at her feet.

Miranda backed up so quickly that her cane slipped, and a lightning bolt of pain blasted up her injured leg. She cried out in pain, and her cry was met by a furious, mad roar of humanity lost behind iron and oil.

Miranda dragged herself up and staggered down the ramp towards the ground level. Constructs were closing in on her from all sides. There were several of them on both sides of the canal, streaming from the tunnels above. They were stomping through viscera, blades extending from their forearms. Miranda stumbled forwards and jumped into the dry canal. From one hand she cushioned the fall with a bolt of compressed air. Still, the pain in her leg was excruciating.

Miranda whined breaths in and out, dragging herself towards the daylight streaming into the canyon. She heard thudding behind her as Constructs dropped into the dry bed. Smoky air filled her lungs and she coughed, a hacking, desperate sound. The Constructs were groaning and snarling behind her, closing in swiftly. She tossed balls of ice out behind her, aiming for their feet, just to slow them down for a few precious seconds. She caught a few, snagging their feet, but they dragged themselves free to resume their relentless pursuit.

Salvation was close, so close. The setting sunlight blinded her, and the scorching desert air hit her like a wall of sandpaper.

***

The smoke continued to swirl and twist. Above the canyon, Ember narrowed her eyes at the strange structures ahead, barely visible through the obscuring clouds. She glanced upwards. A spiral shaped black cloud had formed above them, dwarfing the twenty five airships.

She unslung the bow from her back, and nocked an arrow. She didn't care about the impotence of the gesture. Whatever this was, there was no way an arrow could harm it. The weapon was little more than a comfort.

The Empire Of Fire

Bassai was at her back, sniffing the air pensively. Ironclad was standing behind her, shaking his head.

"What do you see?" she muttered.

Ironclad sighed raggedly. "I wish I knew. The smoke is getting in my way as much as it's getting in yours."

"But you can still feel danger, right?"

He nodded once. His voice was strained. "The voices are still a mess ... but they're no calmer. The feeling is so strong ... it's like I'm walking up to a bonfire."

Thomas drifted over to them. "We're with you, no matter what. There's a lot of energy moving and shifting ahead." He gave Ironclad a sidelong look. "You've been given command of this section of the fleet."

That made Ironclad turn around. "Command? I'm no expert in the aerial navy."

"I told them already you'd be humble about it," Thomas said with a grin.

Ironclad let out a grunt. "I don't think this is a laughing matter. You're one of the fools I'm meant to be commanding."

Thomas grinned wider.

"You know I could be compromised."

"I know that you're responsible enough not to risk our lives. If it does begin to affect you badly, we're here to support you, and if necessary, Ember or Seret can take command."

Ironclad turned to Ember, as he usually did when they were about to move into an area that wasn't familiar, potentially into combat. She nodded to him, and squeezed his hand, offering him what strength she could.

He gently squeezed her hands back. "Alright, in that case ... what's our terrain?"

Ember nodded. "The desert offers no cover. Can they see through the smoke? I don't know."

"And we don't know who *they* are," Bassai growled. "The smell is very strange ... although there's blood. Fire. Armour. Oil, the same oil inside you,

Ironclad."

Ironclad let out a low groan of pain. "Then perhaps they can see through the smoke, for all we know ... although I can't. I don't think we can take the chance." He steadied himself, and Ember heard the tremor in his voice become still. "Breathing it in won't be good for anyone on the ship ... and I don't want to be in it either."

"It's behaving like smoke ... at least in the sense that it's rising." Ember nodded at the canyon. "That's our best cover, although we'd be sitting ducks. Perfect place for an ambush, if you ask me."

Bassai grunted and nodded. Ironclad sighed and looked around at the airships flying with them. "Alright. Thomas, contact the ships in our section. Two skiffs are to pull into the canyon on either side of us, everyone else flies cover. Establish a perimeter around that ... around the edge of that cloud. Tell them not to get under it." He looked after he was done at the clouds again, and the hints at whatever lay beyond. "After those orders go through, contact Kelad and Barada. We may need everyone."

"For?"

"Long range bombardment."

Thomas swallowed and nodded. "Anything else?"

"Hmm ... yes, get Seraphine up here."

As Thomas walked back along the deck, Ember leaned over to Bassai. "You smell Constructs out there?"

"Perhaps. What I can mainly smell is the smoke."

Ember fixed the ship's spyglass into the tripod mount on the prow. The *Sand Dancer* began to descend into the canyon, with a pair of skiffs close behind. She peered through at the top of the canyon walls, along the desert.

She leaned forwards, twisting the lens to focus it. There were a number of burned out wrecks dotting the landscape, from skiff-size to cruisers. There remained little wood, just the blackened, iron bones of the superstructures, and even then, some of the thick bars and armour plates seemed half melted.

"Trouble here."

The Empire Of Fire

Ironclad nodded at her account of what she could see. "How many wrecks?"

"I can see six on this side."

"A battle," Bassai muttered. "Wreckage only from one side, however. A surprise attack, or an overwhelming one."

She continued watching as Seraphine joined them. Ember noted that her eyes were fixed on the spiral overhead.

"As I thought," Ironclad muttered, with a growl of anger beneath his voice. "You've got some idea as to what we're facing here."

"Maybe." She pointed. "That ... looks like what was projected in Ydra's mind. The spiral that ate worlds, that ate light itself."

Ember looked around at her. "Gods above us."

Ironclad's fists clenched. "Is the canyon clear?"

"Looks to be ... wait ..." Ember squinted into the vast cleft in the desert. There were more wrecks down there, shattered against the rocky, dried riverbed. These were not quite as badly burned or crippled as the ones up at the top. The canyon itself was completely still, apart from dust devils and streams of dust blowing along in dry desert breezes.

"Looks like a couple of crashes. No movement that I can see."

"Keep an eye on it."

She nodded.

"What do you think, Seraphine?" Ironclad murmured.

"The ... entity inside Ydra ... was incredibly powerful. We saw that for ourselves, all of us. What this is, if its similar ... it could be more than we or Vehnek could handle."

"Or he's found some way to handle it," Ember muttered, studying the canyon walls. "It doesn't seem like he'd plan anything that he wasn't sure he could pull off."

"Agreed," Bassai muttered.

Seraphine sighed. "Based on what we saw ... I don't think those entities ... those things ... care about our power struggles at all. I doubt they would pick sides, they have no reason to, no investment."

"One wanted to kill everyone in Haama," Bassai countered.

"That one ... wanted to consume the living. The dead were something it could use."

Ember snorted. "Use for what?"

"For its own designs and desires," Seraphine muttered. "An army, a workforce of slaves... we were never meant to know or comprehend it."

"Hmm ..." Ember sighed. "I can't see any signs of ambush at all on either side of the canyon. I don't want to say we're safe, but ... whatever downed those ships doesn't seem to be down here."

As the *Sand Dancer* drifted around the corner, she spotted more ships. These didn't seem to have crashed though, they had definitely landed of their own accord. They sat in front of a vast entryway, with twisting columns and platforms above, walkways leading between tunnels and balconies.

"Something here," Ember murmured. "Maybe a few live ones."

"Can't you all hear that?" Bassai snarled.

Ember looked up. Ironclad was nodding, eyes fixed on the wyvernborn. Bassai's eyes were wide with fury, and a hint of something rarer, a terror that was rarely present in his soul.

Ember shook her head. Seraphine too. "No, but I can feel it. I can feel it in the air, in the rocks."

Ironclad was frozen, like a statue, the sounds of fast, terrified breathing coming from him. Ember slapped him on the arm. He turned to her, head snapping around, and she gestured to the landed ships.

After a moment, he nodded. His voice regained its power. "Cannons forward!"

The gunners hefted the light cannons towards the prow, and fixed them to more tripod mounts. Ember watched the ships as they drew closer, listening as Ironclad tensed again beside her.

They were covered in gore. The crews were strewn around the top decks in pieces. Debris from the hull littered the ground and the flat stone paving, chunks of the hull and armour that had been torn off and tossed aside. The sails were torn, the masts snapped, as if a storm had passed through.

"What are we looking at?" Bassai growled.

"A ... rampage," Ironclad muttered. "I can't see any survivors."

"Neither can I," Ember said, shaking her head. "What is this place? What is this ... machine?"

"Movement!" one of the gunners shouted.

A lone figure was limping from the massive carved gateway, that led into darkness. Ironclad and Ember peered down at her.

She was wearing a robe, walking with a cane, covered in blood. She looked middle aged, moving as swiftly as she could.

"She's a Mage," Ember said. "Seraphine, have a look."

"I can see the ..." Ironclad trailed off.

Ember glanced at him as Seraphine peered through the spyglass. "Hey, are you alright? What is it?"

He didn't respond, staring at the shifting shadows behind the fleeing woman.

"I recognise her, I think," Seraphine muttered. "She's an Arch Mage, Miranda I believe. One of those that attempted to question me."

Ember grasped hold of Ironclad's forearm, but he didn't turn. "What's wrong?"

"She's not alone," Bassai growled.

Miranda's step faltered, and she screamed so loudly that they could hear it over the sounds of the crew on deck. She screamed again, and suddenly the sounds formed into words. She was waving up at the three ships frantically.

"What's she saying?" Bassai muttered, as Thomas walked alongside them.

"She's saying, 'help me'," Thomas murmured. "She probably has information we could use..."

"Do not land this ship, or any of our ships," Ironclad snapped, without looking around.

"Ironclad, wait a ..." Ember started.

The scream cut her off. Not the scream from the Arch Mage below, but something else.

A maddening, grinding roar, like an iron bar buckling and creaking under a heavy weight. More figures were emerging from the darkness beyond the carved gate. They were tall, gangling creations, bearing down on the lone figure swiftly.

"Oh Gods above ..." Thomas whispered. He stared around at Ironclad. "Are they...?"

The Constructs closed in on Miranda, who screamed at them in horror, and babbled up at the *Sand Dancer*. The metal men were spattered with blood, screeching with every step. Miranda sent bolts of lightning at them that had no effect, balls of ice that barely slowed them. They weren't going to stop.

Behind their audible footsteps and howls was a rumbling sound, a pulse, shaking the air itself.

Ember held her breath, and pushed past everyone. She stopped at the railing and gauged the distance and arc of a shot. The wind was focused in the canyon, blowing swiftly. The target was roughly a hundred and fifty yards away, almost straight down.

The arrow was already nocked. She drew it back and loosed it without hesitation.

The Constructs were ten feet away when the arrow hit Miranda. It entered her at the collarbone, and pierced her heart. As Ember watched, she shuddered, her muscles seized, and she dropped to her knees. She then pitched forwards, and her head struck the stone paving. The Constructs all stopped walking simultaneously, and looked up.

Ember backed up, and Ironclad wrapped an arm around her. She leaned back into him and closed her eyes.

"What do we do?" Seraphine whispered.

Ironclad shook his head, unable to speak.

Bassai glanced at him, and grunted. "Thomas, tell the skiffs to move down the canyon until they are clear of the cloud. Are the rest of the fleet in position?"

"They will be by now," he muttered.

"Tell our section to rendezvous with Kelad at barrage range."

Thomas nodded once, and moved back.

"Seraphine, can you shield the crew from this smoke?"

She gave a single nod as well.

"Do it. Captain Seret!"

The Caelish captain's pale face looked up at him in terror. He pointed a single finger upwards.

Ember gritted her teeth. "Are you sure about this?"

"We have to see. We have to know what we may be facing when we reach Mora."

A bubble began glowing around the *Sand Dancer*. Seraphine's arms were held wide as she cast it, sweat on her brow. Thomas came towards her and placed a hand on her shoulder, feeding his own power into her.

The small airship began to rise as the skiffs sped through the canyon. Up they went, passing beyond the dark gateway, looking over the platforms where Constructs were standing and watching them silently. The ship climbed and climbed until the lip of the canyon gave way.

A black pyramid stood in the centre of an angled wall, and a cluster of squat buildings. They were right in the middle of the smoke tendrils, and the spiralling black cloud sat directly above the pyramid's point. To Ember's eye, it looked like the walls of the strange structure were rippling and pulsing with an even deeper blackness.

A lone figure was sitting in front of the pyramid, covered in blood. Ironclad froze behind Ember.

"Halt elevation! Keep us here!"

Ember started at the sound of his voice, the rage that had filled it and ignited into a inferno. She stared at him in shock and terror as he leaned forwards, holding onto the railing.

The man on the ground looked straight at Ironclad, and after a moment, waved. The only response was a crack as Ironclad's fist tightened around the wooden beam before him.

"Who is that?" Ember whispered.

Ironclad didn't reply. Constructs were walking towards the man slowly. They had plenty of time before they reached him, though. Ember drew another arrow, but Ironclad's hand stopped her before she could nock it, closing around her wrist gently, but firmly.

"Should we pick him up?" Ember asked.

"No." Ironclad's voice was flat. "Leave him to those things that fascinate him so much."

She frowned at him, but Ironclad wasn't looking at the figure anymore. He was looking at the Constructs.

Some of them were singularly focused on the man, taking juddering steps towards him. The rest of them were kneeling in front of the pyramid. Some were walking aimlessly, holding their heads, screaming up at the cloud above. Nothing coherent came out of them, apart from pain.

"It's not right," she muttered. "Those things ... we should give him a mercy at least."

"He never gave me any."

She glared around at how cold his voice was. He had gone back to watching the Constructs approaching the man, unmoving.

Ember watched two of them wheel around and stagger towards the *Sand Dancer*. She shrugged off Ironclad's arm and nocked the arrow she had drawn. After a second, she saw that neither of them seemed a threat, though. They peeled away from the airship, barely aware that they were there. Both she and Ironclad watched as one of them held the other and threw it off the edge of the cliff. It watched the other one as it plummeted into the canyon.

There was a crash as it hit a walkway and spun, before it finally hit the canyon's rocky basin. Ember leaned over the railing. She could see it move and stand up, then heard the scream of anguish it let out.

The Empire Of Fire

The one at the top of the cliff sagged, and looked up at Ironclad directly. It reached out one massive hand, and Ironclad slowly did the same.

"Ironclad?" Ember muttered. "Talk to me."

"They cannot die," he muttered. "Trapped in a shell. A walking sarcophagus. They're in hell, Ember, and they cannot get out. All they can do is scream."

"Who is that man?" she demanded.

Ironclad's arm fell. "The man who took my eyes."

The man by the pyramid was watching them too, and Ember could see he was smiling, almost in pride. The Constructs were behind him, right behind him.

"So you want him to suffer like you did? That's who he made you into, is it?"

The railing snapped under Ironclad's grip. "If you knew half the things he did to me ... half the pain he caused ..."

Bassai looked at Ironclad and growled, a growl of anger. Thomas gently held the Construct's forearm. "This isn't our way, and you know it."

Ember's eye was sharp enough to catch sight of the projectile. It was a crossbow bolt, arcing through the air. It fell out of her sight, and the man by the pyramid jerked. He twitched and shuddered, staring down at a blooming patch of fresh blood on his chest.

The man looked up at the ship, at the crew on deck staring at him in horror. The madness left his smile as he slumped backwards, his eyes closed.

As they watched, the Constructs reached him, and ripped him apart.

They were far enough away that much of the visceral, nightmare fuelling reality was lost. Soon, all that remained of him was a dirty smear on the sand.

Ember's hands tightened around Ironclad's arm. She looked around at Kassaeos, who was folding his crossbow back up, fully businesslike. Thomas nodded to him, but the assassin didn't react.

No-one watching had a thing to say at first, until the *Sand Dancer* was well clear of the pyramid.

"Why would ... why would Vehnek ... do this?" Ember whispered. "Why wake these things up and unleash them on his own people?"

"He didn't," Bassai stated bluntly. "He's not that stupid. He overlooked something, or underestimated something."

"Is he down below somewhere?"

The wyvernborn let out a bitter bark of a laugh. "No. We've seen the wreckage of twenty ships at most. He has hundreds. No ... he is at the head of his fleet, flying to the mountain. He would never miss the chance to watch his glorious army of dragons take flight."

Ironclad turned to Seret and pointed north, up into the desert. The captain spun the wheel without a word.

Once they were clear of the cloud. Seraphine lowered her arms, and Thomas let go of her. He stepped around her and folded his arms.

"Contact the fleet," Ironclad muttered. "Once they are in range ... target the pyramid and everything around it ... and fire at will. Leave nothing here but a crater in the sand. If anything is moving after the barrage ... stop it moving."

Ember heard his voice crack at the end. Bassai grunted and nodded with approval. Thomas patted Ironclad's forearm and stepped away. Seraphine took a step forwards hesitantly. Ember could smell the terror radiating from her.

She didn't know what she expected from either of them. There were no words to say. Ironclad silently turned and waited, and Seraphine's eyes dropped to the deck.

"Rowan knew. You knew."

The sorceress shook her head. "I ... he never spoke of it. I asked him once ... but he wouldn't-"

Ironclad's voice loudly cut her off. "Is that the fate you and your grandfather gave to me, Seraphine? Is that the future I have to look forward to, when everyone I love is gone?"

Tears ran down Seraphine's face. She opened her mouth, but had no words for him.

A sound of thunder rumbled and rolled in the distance. The gathering darkness was illuminated by thousands of magical projectiles of lightning, flame and force.

It illuminated Ironclad as he crossed the deck and descended into the ship. Ember stood beside Seraphine as volley after volley hit, obscuring the pyramid and ruins in blasts of light and smoke.

***

The low rumble carried across the desert, and reached Vehnek's ears. He turned around on the *Inquisitor's* bridge, and folded his arms.

Perhaps something had hit the fleet pursuing them. Perhaps the escapee from the Magus Towers had caught up sooner than expected. They may have engaged the forces at the Machine, in which case they were doomed. That ancient place would be a stronghold by now, back to its full glory. No army had ever been able to conquer The Desert King's fortress.

Except his own, Vehnek's mind whispered.

There was a sudden presence off his shoulder, and a chill ran down his spine. Mora passed him silently. He wondered that her steps hadn't creaked the deckplates, only to spot that she wasn't even walking ... she was floating.

She gripped the railing at the aft, staring south. Vehnek walked until he was beside her, and carefully watched the neutral expression on her face.

"What is it?"

She didn't move. "Nothing at all. Your pursuit is delayed."

Vehnek frowned. There seemed more to it than that. He was starting to learn how to read the entity inhabiting Mora's body.

"*Tell the fleet to increase speed,*" he ordered the bridge crew. They nodded, and barked orders to the men on deck.

***

Ember opened the door to the royal cabin slowly. An hour had passed, and she could still hear the sections of Kelad's fleet bombarding the pyramid and Machine miles behind them.

Jack looked up at her from the desk in the corner, but couldn't muster a smile. He glanced back at the bed.

Ironclad was sitting there, his head down, hands in his lap. His eyes were still as bright as when he had first heard the echoes of madness from the pyramid.

Ember looked at Jack, who nodded and got up. He went out into the corridor and closed the door behind them.

Ironclad's voice was low, little more than a murmur. "I can still hear them."

Ember crossed the cabin, and sat on the bed beside him.

"When I was on the cusp becoming a man, my grandfather started to forget things. Simple things at first ... where he'd put something, or the name of an acquaintance he'd just made. But it got worse and worse. I can still remember the day I visited him to bring fresh eggs ... and when he answered the door, it was like he was looking at a stranger."

She took his hand.

"I was always afraid of that. I wanted to grow old with you, Em ... but I worried that I'd forget you, like grandfather forgot me."

He looked around slowly, careful to keep the bright glare of his eyes out of hers. "The way they're screaming, still screaming ... they're confused, enraged, afraid ... their minds are almost gone ... I know that feeling well. I recognise it from my grandfather, when he was near the end of his life. He couldn't remember anything ... hour after hour, it was like everything reset."

"Tobias..."

He reached out and touched her cheek. "I can't grow old with you anymore. What a thing to take for granted ... growing old ... with the woman I love."

He stopped for a moment, and listened to the barrage. His eyes glowed

The Empire Of Fire

brightly again. "If ... that ... happens to me ..."

"It looked like they were trapped there, Tobias, trapped in the middle of the desert. Where were they meant to go? You're not trapped. You're not alone. You're with people who love you, people who you matter to, and who matter to you."

He squeezed her hands, his eyes staying bright.

"What are they ... saying?"

Ironclad didn't move for a moment. "I can't understand the words ... but ... I do understand the gratitude. They've wanted to be released from their torment for longer than they can remember."

Ember moved onto his lap, and stroked his iron cheek. "Are you tormented?"

He looked at her, and his eyes dimmed to their normal brightness, and it seemed to cause him pain to do so.

"In a way ... but I'm also incredibly lucky, and I can't forget that. I'm surrounded by friends, what I do and what I've done matters to more people than I could have imagined it ever would. I'm the same man I was, just in a different form ... a form that locks aspects of living away."

"You've always had a good head on your shoulders. What happened to them ... it won't be your future. You aren't like them at all."

"Some of them would have been like me once, though. Good men, with a strong will ... now look at them."

Ember brought her arms up around his neck and shoulders. "Look at me, love."

His violet eyes met hers.

"You're the master of that future. No-one else is. You know that this is a possibility ... so don't let it be. Keep your head."

He rested his forehead against hers, and she leaned up to kiss him where his lips would have been. Her hand rested on his chest. "And keep me here. You won't be rid of me, ever. I'll be watching you after that time comes, from wherever I end up."

27

Thomas slowly walked along the top deck of the *Sand Dancer*. The dawn hadn't broken yet, but the night was far from dark. Strange lights wove and danced above the fleet, filling the sky between the stars. The sky was more elaborate and beautiful here than Thomas had ever seen, as if the heavens were looking down on the coming battle with baited breath.

As hot as the desert was, night always brought a chill that he had only felt among the deepest snows. The wind was sharp, cutting through his robe as deftly as a tailor's shears. It had thrown his body into a state of chaos. He changed clothes twice a day, making sure that the sweat the baking sun brought was as dry as possible before the thicker overcoats were donned. Now, he wore something slightly thinner over his standard robe, for he had to be ready for battle. The end of their journey was visible ahead, blotting out the stars.

The Gravestone Mountain reached up like a dragon's tooth. It was the largest in the region, larger even than any peak in Montu Fortu. In contrast to them, as far as he knew, not a soul lived there.

The nearest life occupied a prison, derelict now. It had been named Epitaph, and it was where criminals were sent to die.

There was little water and food, and even fewer guards. They weren't particularly needed at Epitaph, because where were the prisoners meant to run? On foot, the journey to either Salketh or Cael would take weeks, and there was certainly no respite on the way. They had flown over no oasis, no wildlife, and barely any shade.

Thomas could never sleep before a battle. Before the siege of Melida City had begun, he had alternated between praying and stretching, limbering up for combat. Now he was doing much of the same, although there was something else in his mind that occupied him, and kept sleep away.

The Empire Of Fire

There was a finality to this battle, one that there hadn't previously been. The threat of death had always been present in every scuffle or skirmish, let alone something on this scale. It wasn't fear that gripped him necessarily ... it was an uncertainty, an unwritten future, a blank page in a book that was still being written. The story of this war had been a part of his life for almost ten years. It had become something entirely different than he could have guessed, great unknowable powers had entered the fray, enemies had become allies, allies had shown some of the poison that flowed all too freely through their veins. If the tide swallowed them, it seemed it would be the end, truly the end, not just of him and his friends, but of all of the inhabitants of Planar, forever. If they prevailed ... well, that was a new library, let alone a new page in a book.

His feet took him to the helm, where Captain Seret was adjusting the *Sand Dancer's* course. Her eyes were fixed on the mountain ahead, but she held out a communication stone to him.

He took it, glancing up at the fleet. Three sections of airships were rejoining the main force, the sections that had been deployed to finish the job at the pyramid.

"*General Kelad?*"

"*Correct,*" the general said, some of his usual smoothness absent from his voice.

"*Are your sections all present?*"

"*They are.*"

Thomas tapped his foot. "*And?*"

"*They tell me there's nothing left but dust and sand. Anything that was still moving, is no longer moving. It is a glassed crater ... and next time you want something like that done, do your own dirty work.*"

Thomas raised an eyebrow. "*I apologise, General ... your ships are the most capable for that kind of engagement.*"

"*I'm aware. I have preparations to make with those ships now, excuse me.*"

Thomas handed the stone back to Seret with a sigh. He let his nerves return to a level of equilibrium, before turning to the helm.

"How's the ship, Captain?"

Seret glanced at him. "*She'll fly true. She always does. Although ... she's not been through anything like this.*"

"What was she used for before this?"

Seret snorted. "*She's a princess's toy. I barely ever flew over the Dividing Sea.*"

Thomas raised an eyebrow. "*I'm surprised she's lasted as long as she has.*"

Seret eyed him. "*She was built to carry a princess and her rich little friends, as well as foreign visiting dignitaries. The last thing she needs to be is flimsy.*" A grin crept over her face. "*For good or ill, I'm glad I had the chance to fly her properly ... the way a ship like this is meant to be flown.*"

There was a swirl of smoke beside them, and Kassaeos appeared, arms folded, looking at them stonily.

"You're keeping Seraphine awake."

Thomas looked at him in surprise. "Isn't that your job?"

The assassin scowled at him. "Yes, yes ... walk with me for a little bit, I'd like a word."

"I thought you might want one at some point." He glanced at Seret, and switched back to Caelish. "*I'd better arrest his bellyaching, but before I do I just wanted to say ... thank you. Everything you've done ... you put out your neck for us.*"

"*I put my neck out for Allessandra,*" Seret corrected. "*She's the one who put her neck out for you.*"

Thomas nodded. "*Then I owe you both thanks.*"

Seret winked at him. "*Go on. Go see to your smoky friend.*"

Thomas stepped away with a smile and fell into step beside Kassaeos, who was waiting with his arms folded at the railing.

"'Bellyaching' is it?" He grunted.

Thomas grinned. "Your Caelish is improving."

The Empire Of Fire

They padded slowly towards the prow. "You consider that I might have a reason to be 'bellyaching'?"

"Beyond keeping Seraphine awake, not that she'll be sleeping at a time like this, I suspect you do. Everyone has a reason to bellyache."

Kassaeos stopped walking and leaned over the railing, looking at seemingly everything: the stars, the sands of the dark desert, the looming mountain where the reckoning would happen. The *Dreadnought* was drifting over to them, trimming their sails and preparing to extend a gangplank.

"What's going on there?" Thomas wondered.

"Delivery for Calver. Something he'll enjoy."

"Ah ..." Thomas grinned. "A fishing rod."

Kassaeos snorted. "Aye, and some nice overalls, and mud boots, and a little raft."

Thomas chuckled, but as he looked at the oncoming mountain, he found his mirth wanting. "Kassaeos ... thank you for ... giving that man some mercy."

"The one at the pyramid?" Kassaeos tapped his fingers on the railing. "I'm surprised he didn't have Ember do it, but I understand."

"It's ... not usual. Ordinarily he would have, in lieu of doing it himself."

Kassaeos smiled bitterly. "He lived a moment in our shoes, Thomas. Pain stopped him doing what he would have, had it not been there. He finally found his own understanding, I think, a taste of what it had been like to live as one of us for all these years."

Thomas wrung his hands. "Maybe so."

"At any rate ... Ember, and Bassai, and yourself ... you all had a point. At a certain time, you have to rise above that demon that rests on your shoulder and whispers in your ear."

Their conversation paused for a moment. The only sounds were the rippling of sails, the quiet conversations between the soldiers in earshot.

"Vehnek will have a lookout on the peak, you know," Kassaeos murmured. "They'll know we're coming, and they'll know our numbers."

"Our Mages have managed to conceal about a third of the fleet with incantations, but a powerful enough counterpart would see through us. It was always a likelihood. That means that we both know what we'll be facing."

"Ha! Right…" Kassaeos shook his head. "Left with no choice but to charge across the bloody desert … on the back foot … with a fleet cobbled together. We're precisely where Vehnek wants us, and you should be under no delusion that we know all the forces at his disposal."

"This was our only chance," Thomas muttered. "And it's undoubtedly our best chance. We've tried the defensive before, hidden behind walls. This is where we stand … right on his doorstep. If it's our time, we'll take him with us."

The *Dreadnought's* chief yeoman signalled to Captain Seret, who signalled back to him. They matched speed, and the gangplank hooked on over the railing. A quartet of workmen picked their way across, carrying two long boxes between them, like a pair of thin coffins. Kassaeos jerked his head to the hatch down into the sub-deck, and they hefted the crates over.

"It'll be a lot of our times, I'm sure." Kassaeos turned to face Thomas, his eyes seemingly a part of the night itself. "If it is … I want it to have been worth it."

"Worth it?"

"Making nice, giving up the fight."

Thomas smiled and shook his head. "We never gave up the fight. This is the culmination of it. We revealed Haama's true enemy."

Kassaeos snorted and shook his head. "I hope so."

Thomas turned to him. "Hey, listen, because this is important. You are not defined by the fight."

Kassaeos frowned. "I'm an assassin, it's my line of work."

"Kassaeos …" Thomas put a hand on each of his shoulders. "For a lot of tyrants, the fight never stops, because it becomes a way to influence the people who idolise you. Look at Mokku … a nation that broke its shackles, and then used that act to snap more shackles onto people's wrists, to deafening,

The Empire Of Fire

thunderous applause. You've never been a tyrant ... you're a man who cares, just like Donnal, a man who wants to see people prosper, and live free."

Kassaeos grimaced, and shifted. The tip of his finger poked into Thomas's jugular vein from behind him.

"My skills will be wasted in peace."

Thomas pushed the finger away with a small magical barrier. "You'll manage, I'm sure."

"Haama and Cael will be weakened by this. Talking of Mokku, they might decide that they need a few more slaves, and come here to take them."

That was something that Thomas had definitely considered. He turned around. "In that case, if you can't be peaceful, be ready. Just in case."

Kassaeos grinned. "You and me both. If this fight's coming to an end ... just think twice before you get in bed with the Mokkans. I doubt their leaders are as easy on the eyes as your princess."

"Ha!" Thomas laughed. "I think Allessandra has an eye on someone else. So do I, for that matter."

"I bet." Kassaeos smirked. "It's Bassai, isn't it."

Thomas shook his head with a snort. "Don't let him hear you say that, unless you want to spend the rest of the trip answering very awkward and detailed questions about the mechanics of it."

Kassaeos laughed out loud. "Now, that's a tempting way to pass the time..."

"Just do it on the other side of the ship."

Kassaeos raised an eyebrow and disappeared in a puff of smoke.

Thomas sighed and paced along the foredeck. His fingertips buzzed with little bolts of lightning, his own inner power was anticipating what he would need. Lightning and fire, most likely. Barriers most of all.

His feet led him below decks. Past the staircase, and towards the aft, Bassai was training, performing slow moves with his blade and shield. He wore full, heat-treated chainmail, the rings light, over a leather jerkin and greaves. Mercifully, he was alone, and had yet to begin bombarding Kassaeos with questions of an intimate nature.

His eyes were closed, his movements flowed together like the patterns of a dance. As Thomas watched, he slid the shield down his arm and drew the offhand sabre in one graceful movement. He continued practicing blocks with his forearm, and sweeping, jabbing strikes to take care of any opening they created.

"How's the new armour?"

Bassai smiled as he continued his exercises. "Becoming as a second layer of scale, my friend."

Thomas nodded. "We're close. I thought I'd let you know."

"Good. Flying across the desert has been hot and dull, even with our detour to that pyramid."

"Kelad's ships have returned to the formation, and the report is in."

"And?"

"It's been dealt with."

Bassai grunted. "Now that we are close, we must leave it that way. The enemy we face now will not sit and allow itself to be obliterated."

Thomas nodded, drawing a Caelish short sword and practicing his own manoeuvres with it. "Has Ironclad said anything about it since?"

"Not to me. Ask Ember … or rather, ask her later."

Thomas glanced at the closed door to the bedchamber where the four of them usually slept. "Hmm, well, it's what they would usually do before a battle, isn't it?"

"There are many questions regarding the mechanics of such activity," Bassai muttered.

"Another thing to ask Ember later."

"I have. She does not answer, but she does smirk, so obviously it is not a sore subject."

"Immediately afterwards it might be," Thomas muttered with a smirk of his own. He sighed. "You can feel the change in the air, can't you? It feels like everything around us is holding its breath."

The Empire Of Fire

"It is a time of great change, and high stakes. A decisive time. We are moving through the rapids on a rocky river, trying to find the path that leads through, rather than shattering the boat. The way ahead froths and churns."

"Nervous?"

Bassai opened one yellow eye. The pupil narrowed at Thomas. "Only a fool wouldn't be. It is a different nerve that takes me, however. The wyvernborn live, and will live on. Our land has a chance to prosper. Our anger has a chance to calm. Our scars have a chance to heal. We face an enemy brutal enough to demand our lives to vanquish him. It is a price I am willing to pay. I do not fear death, but failure is a mistress a darn sight more bitter."

"An overly wanton and teasing mistress, and she should be treated as such."

Bassai grunted a laugh. "She is an especially dangerous when it seems you have a future."

Thomas smiled. "What does that future look like?"

"For me, discovering my people again. Discovering my home again. Learning their new ways, making friends with the young, teaching them. Acquainting myself with family once again, and hoping for their forgiveness. Earning it, one day. Finding a mate, bearing young of my own ... a choice I never had, in our time."

Thomas smiled at the thought. "Back to the Bog, then?"

"Yes. Be a part of what they are building. Watch it take form." The eye opened again. "What of your future, Thomas?"

"Mine?" Thomas considered for a moment. "I wish I knew. I suppose I will ultimately go where I am needed. Help with the research we need to do in our various ventures. The corrupted land, more newborns for your people, sending the White Sea into retreat."

"The princess will need you, as will Haama. You are in a unique position among us. You are of both nations, a hero to both as well. You have the future queen's ear and friends in high places. No doubt you will become quite the ally in political matters."

"Gods above us, anything but that," Thomas muttered.

Bassai chuckled to himself. "Well deserved, if I may say so. We would not be here, if not for you."

He turned to face the room where Ironclad and Ember were locked away. He lowered his voice.

"I worry for them."

Thomas nodded. "Why?"

"He will outlive her. He will outlive all of us, eventually. It is a factor that I have considered in my own potential future."

Thomas nodded. "You're thinking of a certain impressive farmer, I bet."

"I am. I will watch Kaitlyn grow old. I will watch Lance, Pia and Rory grow old. Their children as well, and so on. It will happen in the blink of an eye for me ... yet I am not immortal. One day I will die, and be buried in the Reeva mound. Unless I take a wyvernborn as a partner, the idea of growing old together will be lost on me. It is ... difficult enough knowing that one day ... I will bury you, and Ember."

Thomas nodded. "Ironclad will bury all of us."

Bassai sighed. "I hope that he carries us with him, in some way."

"Somehow, he will, I have no doubt. These are not the kind of days you forget. My worry is a little different."

Bassai focused on him.

Thomas sheathed his shortsword. "I know that they aren't comfortable with all this, not completely... the idea of peace between Haama and Cael. I hope that our friendship doesn't suffer because of it. I hope that they don't ... grow to resent me, for what I've done here."

Bassai growled. "There is no danger of that. Worry more about Haama and Cael's wine stores if we win, and worry about taverns closing for lack of business if we do not. In our day there were at least three smaller establishments that only stayed afloat because of Emeora Vonn."

There was a creak from inside the sleeping chamber, a long, whining sound of deck plates under the strain of a large, armoured foot.

The Empire Of Fire

"Give it five minutes," Bassai muttered.

"Only five?" Thomas grinned. "Right, show me a move or two with this blade. I'm not as adept with it as I might like."

They ran a drill or two in the corridor, a succession of blocks and parries. The shortsword was an effective weapon, well designed, well smithed. He had used it in anger, of course, but not in a situation like the one they would shortly be facing.

Seraphine came out of the other berth and watched them for a while. Kassaeos was behind her, arms folded. It was Bassai who spotted them first.

"Don't let us interrupt," Seraphine whispered. "I just ... I know we've fought together before, but this feels different. It feels like the stories my grandfather told to me, and to the students in the White Tower." She held out a bundle of cloth in her hand towards Thomas. "It's going to be a gruelling battle, I'm sure. Your energy will be sapped quickly without this."

Thomas unwrapped the bundle carefully. It was a pair of gauntlets, a perfect fit over his fingertips. The part over each palm was a bright green stone, with a metal ring in the centre, fused to it. The metal housings of the gauntlets were tight around his hands, but the fabric that cushioned them felt like velvet and leather, strong and comfortable.

"I appreciate it, thank you."

"No need."

Thomas smiled and bowed his head. "Has Kassaeos told you: we're close."

"Yes, he has. We don't have long." She wrung her hands, worry creasing her brow.

"What is it?" Thomas asked.

"Can you feel the same thing I can?"

Thomas grunted and nodded his head.

"Since we received news of the Magus Towers, I have ... sensed something familiar. A presence, a ... laughing voice, or something like a voice. More like vibrations, a dissonance."

Thomas raised an eyebrow. "Familiar, you said ... familiar in what way?"

Seraphine shook her head. "It is cloaked in shadow. I think ... it is being kept from me."

Thomas and Bassai exchanged a glance. "Is it ahead of us, or behind us?" Bassai grunted.

"Both, and getting closer. Fast."

"We should alert the fleet," Bassai muttered.

"Definitely ... but alert them against what?"

"A potential ambush, of course."

Seraphine narrowed her eyes. "But not to ambush *us*, I don't think that's its purpose. I can't explain it."

"What else could the purpose be? We threaten it all."

Seraphine shook her head. "I don't think it considers us a threat at all ... just something to be taken out of the way."

Thomas went cold. "Let's hope they're wrong."

The doors to the other cabin opened. Ironclad stepped out. His amethyst eyes regarded the four of them. The chest plate, bearing the shield and sigil of Melida City, had been polished and shined. The shield he had been given by the Silver Throne's quartermaster was a larger and wider tower shield than the one he had paid for in Maiden's Lock, all that time ago. Months, mere months. Thomas shook his head at the idea briefly.

The sigil of their old home was etched onto it, not in as much detail, but unmistakable.

Ember ducked out beneath his arm. Her armour was as it had ever been: light, thin leather across her chest, with a twisting pattern over her heart, a light blue flower. It was one native to the old Orlin Forest, growing from the vines that wrapped around the tops of the tallest boughs. Thomas raised an eyebrow at it.

"Sandra made it for me," she said. "A reminder of what they fight for. Of what *we* fight for."

The Empire Of Fire

Thomas nodded.

"It's time," Ironclad said.

"Not quite," Seraphine said quickly. She waved a hand over to her cabin, and stepped out of the way. The boxes the *Dreadnought* had delivered to them floated out through the doorway, and turned in the air, leaning against the wall beside Ironclad and Ember. "The bigger one's for you ... Tobias."

Ironclad glanced at her, and popped the lid off the box.

In among a bed of soft fabric was a greataxe, with two huge, thick and sharp blades at the head. Poking from the top was a jabbing spike for piercing armour and flesh like a spear. The grip was thick gripping leather, the shaft pure steel.

The head of the weapon, between the blades, was carved with a new sigil, elaborately woven and filled with liquid obsidian. It was a thin cross, with a different image in each of the four quadrants. In one was the rearing horse of Melida City. Beside it was the Caelish serpent and pyramid. Below it was a dragon with spread wings, the outline of a head and tail tiny in comparison. In the final segment was a twisting flower, that matched the one on Ember's chest precisely.

The weapon had an immediate energy to it that drew Thomas's eye. The shining metal of the blades rippled in the lamplight, waves seemingly stained in. It was more than that, though. The weapon was magical.

Ironclad took hold of the grip, and hefted the greataxe from the crate. His posture changed immediately. He stood straight and powerful, every bit the embodiment of the legendary Warrior he had become. He was no longer a metal imitation of Tobias Calver. He was standing like the man he had been, moving as he would have.

"You re-forged it," Ironclad murmured.

Seraphine nodded. "The axe belongs to you, it's only right you wield it again ... especially here and now. Astrid drew up the plans ... all it needed was a skilled arcane blacksmith."

Recognition dawned over Thomas. It was Tobias Calver's axe, an exact replica of it, but of a size to fit the hulking iron man. Proportionally it was near identical to the one he had used a century ago. As he swung the weapon back and forth, gently testing the weight and balance, it seemed to meld to his touch and movement instantly.

"It's ... perfect." Ironclad looked up at her. "Thank you."

"Wait until you hit something with it," Seraphine said wryly. "You'll thank me twice. Bassai, the other is yours."

The wyvernborn grunted, and snapped open the latches on the smaller box. Inside were a pair of sabres. They were both five feet long from tip to guard, and the off-hand had a shorter, more curved handle, allowing his damaged hand more grip. The blades were rippling in the same way that Ironclad's axe blades were, and again, Thomas felt that same echo of familiarity, and the same raw power flowing through them.

The handles were wrapped in cross stitched leather, and Thomas could see a familiar rune woven into the material and steel. Bassai frowned up at Seraphine. "I have swords already."

She grinned tightly. "Not like these."

"Giving me weapons I'm not used to before a battle ..."

Seraphine held up her hands. "You haven't used enchanted weapons before, have you?"

"I've never needed the help."

Thomas smirked, and Ember chuckled.

"These are attuned to you already," Seraphine said. "They know you. You will be able to use them as easily as your usual blades ... and considering what we're about to leap into..."

Bassai grunted and drew his own weapons, handing them to her. "I will try them, as a courtesy to you. Look after these, they have served me well."

"I will."

Bassai lifted the sabres from their crate, gripping the handles. He spun them for a moment, testing the weight and speed. A smile slowly spread across his face. "Exquisite."

The Empire Of Fire

"Those blades ... they were reforged from Ydra's rapier," Ironclad murmured.

Bassai glanced at him, then at Seraphine. He let out a growl.

She looked down for a moment. "I know ... but better the weapon be utilised for good than buried with her. She deserved a little peace."

Bassai grunted, examining the blades again. He peered at the runes, and touched his thumb to them.

Green flame surged up the steel, filling the compartment with a fierce emerald glow. The wyvernborn's eyes widened, and he slowly smiled again. He touched the runes again, and extinguished them. He slid them into the sheaths at his hips, and turned his head up to Seraphine. He met her eye to eye, then bowed his head.

"Wielding these weapons is a great honour for me. I will hold Ydra in my heart, and do her the justice she deserved."

She bowed her head in thanks at his words. Thomas flexed his hands in the gauntlets, getting himself more used to them. "We're getting close ... I can feel it."

Bassai sheathed his swords and said a prayer under his breath. Kassaeos plucked a crossbow bolt from his pouch, and flicked it between his fingers. Seraphine straightened her back and began climbing the stairs. Kassaeos grinned and shifted, swirling through the hatch.

The Four Guardians remained below decks, looking at each other.

"This is it, eh?" Ember murmured.

Thomas grinned and nodded to her. "The big one. The final night before a new day."

"Very poetic."

"I had no time to write a speech."

"Aye, but I bet you've been thinking of that one all evening."

Ironclad checked the straps of his shield, and the weight of his huge greataxe in his other hand. The savage, angular wyvernborn weapon he had been given sat on his hip. The savagery of it, alongside the elegant Royal shield and the re-made weapon of old was an image in and of itself.

"That's quite the carving on that weapon of yours," Ember murmured. "Like a family crest."

"Our Alliance …" Thomas said with a smile.

"Us," Bassai grunted softly. "One of the Bog, one of the forest, one of the sands, and one of Melida City."

The silence between them buzzed with an energy that Thomas couldn't describe, deeper and more powerful than any magic.

"Are you ready?" Ironclad asked.

The other three nodded. Bassai grunted. "I'm not one for … pretty words."

Ember's eyes widened at him, and her voice took on a hint of mirthful shock. "You're not?"

Bassai grunted again, he bared his teeth in a quick grin, before he became serious once again.

"I love you all."

Thomas paused, and turned to face the wyvernborn. Ironclad let go of his axe and shield, letting their weight fall against the straps on his hip and back. Ember blinked at him, losing some of her own amusement.

Bassai gave her the ghost of a grin. "Even you."

Ember managed a sad smirk.

"You are, and have been, the best. To me, and to our people. All of our people."

Ember took a deep breath, and walked forwards. Before Bassai could say anything else, she put her arms around him and held him tightly.

Bassai growled. "I told you, I don't hug."

"Tough."

Thomas stepped across to put his arms around both of them.

"You as well, hmm?" Bassai muttered.

Two large, metal arms gently wrapped around all of them. Ironclad was warm, as warm as Tobias Calver had been in life.

The Empire Of Fire

"No matter what happens, we'll find each other on the Astral Plain," Ironclad said quietly. "Whenever we may get there, whether now, or later."

Thomas reared up, and looked them all in the eye. "I suppose we should head up there and be legends."

Ember kissed Ironclad on the cheek. "Again?"

The Construct, The Warrior, climbed the stairs first. Ember followed, The Archer ever-present at his back. Bassai leaped up afterwards, taking the stairs three at a time. Thomas came last, closing his eyes for a moment.

"Gods protect us, and guide our hearts," he whispered. He took a deep breath, and strode to the upper deck. The final Guardian joined his three eternal companions.

The desert wind chilled him to the bone. The *Sand Dancer* was at the head of their section of the fleet, fifty ships including the Alliance vessels.

Nine sections of fifty made up their fleet. The flanking sections were to be two of the strongest, Kelad's group on the right, The Allies on the left, bolstered by elements of the Caelish Aerial Navy. The supply carriers were at the rear, pulling away from the fighting. They would be needed in the aftermath, regardless of who came out on top, but they were armed and ready to charge in regardless.

The Gravestone was close enough to make out details of the cracked rock face, the colours of the different veins of ore and fissures catching the shadows of night and the glow of the aurora above. There looked to be fortifications up at the peak, but they were long in ruin. There was a spire, a steep roof, weathered and prepared for the high winds and cold. The place hadn't been destroyed, but it was certainly abandoned, likely as it no longer had any use.

Thomas walked to Seret, and asked for a communication stone. She passed him the one that connected to Kelad.

"Can you hear me, General? It's Thomas."

"Yes, I can hear you. Are you ready to play the final tune in the show?"

"We're waiting for the applause to die down," Thomas muttered drily. "Can you see those buildings that are at the peak?"

Kelad chuckled. *"Of course. That was the laboratory I spoke of before. There were researchers there, examining the dragon corpses. They did some good work, but the station was impractical. Regardless of funding, it was too far away and too close to Salketh for political comfort. Some questions were asked about activity around the peak a few decades back."*

"Could it have been re-opened, re-staffed?"

"Not without me hearing about it. The majority of the research was moved to the Magus Towers, and I tend to keep a sharp ear around those arcanists in particular."

Thomas nodded to himself. A thought crossed his mind, troubling enough to voice. "Just how many dragons were they researching at the Magus Towers?"

"They had the remains of two, skeletons we found on our exploratory missions to the east, but recently including the Black. They were little more than bone."

Thomas pressed the stone against his chin in thought. "Have one section form a rearguard, and watch out for anything coming our way from the south."

Kelad chuckled in surprise. *"Since when were you giving orders like an Admiral?"*

"I'm no Admiral," Thomas muttered with a smirk. "Although apparently I'm a figure of legend, no thanks to you."

Kelad paused for a moment. *"Well put, and I won't deny the precaution. We can't spare the warships ... but I'll contact the carriers, and tell them to keep watch as well as keeping out of sight."*

"Thank you." Thomas tossed the stone back to Seret and walked over to the prow, where the rest waited.

He passed his gauntlet-clad hand over Ember's quiver of arrows, enchanting them. She glanced around at him.

"What's the flavour?"

"Force magic. Very difficult to resist, with a dramatic effect."

"Suits her perfectly," Ironclad muttered with a chuckle. Ember punched his forearm, and nocked one of them. Seraphine enchanted the bolts in Kassaeos's pouch as well with fire magic.

The fleet's course adjusted, pulling wide of the Gravestone mountain by a mile, then swinging around it. They climbed up higher by five hundred feet, slowly.

"I never asked you…" Thomas murmured. "When this is over, what are you two going to do?"

Ember glanced at him, then at Ironclad.

"More adventures, no doubt," Ironclad mused.

"An *expensive* airship," Ember said. "Expensive, luxurious, and fast."

Thomas chuckled. "Wouldn't expect any less, to be honest."

The fleet climbed faster, and more aggressively. Thomas felt his feet being pressed into the deck, and he bent his knees. They were sweeping around the mountain's western face.

Dark shapes appeared ahead of them from behind the rock, hundreds of them, floating high up on a cushion of air, glow stones lit, like an extra nebula of stars.

"All weapons to stations!" Seret ordered from behind them.

"They're higher than us, and climbing," Ember snapped, spyglass locked on the enemy fleet. "No dragons yet."

"They're moving up to bring their siege cannons to bear on the fleet," Kassaeos muttered. "And to stop us doing the same."

"Tactically sound," Ironclad said carefully. "Also very obvious."

Thomas nodded. "Agreed, this is a delaying tactic. They want to hold us here until the dragons are in the game … or until the thing coming from the Magus Towers hits us."

Below them, there was a cleft in the mountain. A wide fissure, almost large enough to divide the Gravestone into two peaks.

Ironclad leaned over the side, and his purple eyes glowed so brightly that the opposing fleet could probably see them.

Ember glanced at him, and pointed the spyglass down. "There's a small airship down there, looks like." She hesitated, and shook her head. "It's ... I'm not sure what I'm looking at. Thomas?"

She stepped back, and he leaned over, pressing his eyes to the lenses.

The small craft had landed on the edge of a flat plain on the northern edge of the fissure. On both sides of the vast cleft in the rock, there were a number of rectangular pillars, evenly spaced along each lip of the chasm. He counted twenty four, twelve on each side, directly opposite the identical counterpart. He could see the glyphs and runes on each face, protective incantations, concealment spells, ones to drain and nullify magic. All were dark, devoid of the energy that should have been coursing through them, and all were old enough to have been put there decades ago.

"I think that fissure is where the dragons are buried," he murmured. "Looks like a lot of precautions have been taken."

"There's something else down there," Ironclad muttered. "More than just bones. Something powerful ... spiraling."

Bassai growled. "Then that's where we go."

"We can't," Kassaeos hissed. He pointed at the fleet. "The moment we drop, those siege guns will open up on our ship. We won't get anywhere near the fissure."

Ironclad nodded. "He's right ... but we can't dither. We don't have time. The power down there is growing ... and it's growing quickly."

He walked back quickly, retrieving the communications stone that connected to every ship they had with them.

"*Sand Dancer* to fleet, this is Ironclad. This is The Warrior."

Thomas looked around at him with an eyebrow raised. Bassai grinned and chuckled. Ember turned back to the spyglass, but the adrenaline filled smile of defiance never left her face. She watched the opposing fleet closely for movement.

"Today, we walk a path we should have walked long ago. Today we cast a tyrant into the hell he would bring upon Cael, Haama, and all of Planar. We either stop him here and now, or we spit in his eye. Either way, he will know what he stood against in his final moments, feeling the wounds of this day, that will bleed him."

The crewmen of the airships on either side of them were against the railings, watching Ironclad on the *Sand Dancer's* top deck.

"Men of Cael's sands and great citadels, men of Haama's great plains and forests, wyvernborn warriors, Orlin bowmen, pilots, Mages, military men, we are allied together because we share a goal: that for the first time in a century, we will be able to shake hands in friendship. Vehnek would sooner see us at each other's throats."

His hands tightened into iron fists. "Now he has exposed his own. So ... for the new dawn we have ushered in, we fight! Not for hate's sake, not for the crimes against us, but for children we will return to ... who will bask in the sun we will drag above the horizon! Haama and Cael united ... we fly!"

Thousands of voices on either side of the *Sand Dancer* roared. A moment later, the Haaman voices were joined by those of the Caelish, the wyvernborn, men and women, beating weapons against shields and boots against the decks and masts of every vessel.

A chuckling voice came over the communication stone. Thomas recognised Kelad's laugh.

"No wonder you made Haama such a pain in the arse to fight, with speeches like that."

Ironclad snorted. "Wait until the one I give when we win."

"Ha! We're a minute or so to cannon range, still climbing. I don't think any airship has flown this high..."

Thomas glanced to right hand side of the fleet. The peak of the Gravestone mountain was still above them, but getting closer.

"Damn it all," he muttered. "The Black Fleet are drawing us too far away."

"It can't be helped," Ironclad muttered. "They'll have to wait for now." He held up the stone. "Well Kelad ... you're the General. On your signal."

***

Vehnek looked up through the fissure, the crack where the bones of monsters had been cast. He was walking among them, among the giant skulls, the smooth, heavy bones. Even the smaller ones in the wings were too heavy to lift.

The two fleets above were distant specks against the twisting patterns in the night sky. His forces were directly above the fissure, the insurgents and traitors were coming at them from the western side of the mountain. They hadn't been tempted to split their forces in a two-pronged attack, interesting. They were likely outnumbered by his people, and without the element of surprise, the result seemed a foregone conclusion.

He smiled to himself as he strode around a giant clawed foot, each digit as long as a skiff's mast. The claws themselves were still sharp.

The great terrors of legend were so impressive in death, he felt a pang of terror at what they would be in life.

Grand as their anatomy was, they were piled here on top of each other, in the kind of mass-grave saved for disposing of enemy soldiers. Terrible and formidable, but bested by old Cael, before the time of airships and the kind of magical weapons that could raze cities. With the improvements that would be made to them, they would be unstoppable in the modern age, invincible.

He looked up at Mora. She was kneeling before one of the skulls, staring into its eye sockets. The light from the glowstones around them was bending as it drew close to her, as if it was fleeing at her presence. It seemed to make her shimmer, like a desert mirage.

"How much longer?"

She didn't look at him. "Not long now."

Vehnek looked up again. The two fleets were close together now. A huge sound blasted down at them, nearly a thousand false dragon-heads on prows of ships friend and foe. They roared in fury, signaling the charge, and the light show began.

The Empire Of Fire

Pulses of energy crackled between them, thousands of them. His broadside firing lines unleashed blast after blast upon the traitors, who responded in kind, rushing towards them with abandon. He could seen the flare of the magical barriers as they blocked the incoming fire, saw the bursts of flame as shots began to get through. The night and the auroras above were illuminated in dancing colour and flashes. Thunderous sounds of war rumbled down the mountain and echoed across the sands.

"They are ready," Mora whispered. Even through the battle above, Vehnek heard her quiet voice, as if it had been spoken into his ear.

He looked back at her with a smile, and around at the bones. Triumph swelled in his chest. He could feel the spirits of his father and grandfather smiling at him from beyond the veil. He would deliver everything they had begun to bring, finish their work, birth the empire.

He waited, but nothing moved.

"What happens now?"

"The energy must be channeled through a vessel."

Vehnek glanced over at her. She floated upwards and gently lowered again, back on her feet. She turned around.

"That's what Mora's for," he grunted with a nod. "Channel through her."

Mora smiled. "This body? This body is dead. The only thing keeping it from rotting to bones is the spark of life I give it. The body must be ... living."

"What?" Vehnek frowned at Mora. Her eyes went black, and he knew.

"*Marines!*"

He drew his pistol and fired until the stone could give no more. The footsteps of his marines rushed closer.

The bolts of lightning snapped into Mora's chest, and she didn't even flinch with the force of the blasts. They left scorches, and the scent of burned flesh filled the air.

More shots began on either side of him as he snapped open the breech.

"No, no ... hold still," Mora said calmly.

One hand snapped forwards and pointed at Vehnek. Her fingers lengthened and turned black, thickening until they seemed like five huge snakes flying at him. Then they became ten, then twenty.

They wrapped around his arm tightly before he could close the breech. His fingers crunched against the metal and whalebone, but the tentacles didn't crush. They instead held him nearly inert, snaking around his shoulder and waist, then his thighs as he tried to back away.

The two marines with him leapt into action. One drew a serrated blade and began trying to saw though the tentacle, but the metal teeth found no purchase on the rubbery skin. The other set himself and kept firing at Mora, if only to distract her attention.

It worked. Her eyes darted to him, and to his amplifier. More tentacles sprouted from her other hand and wrapped around his neck. They strangled his scream as they tightened and crunched. The man's head was torn from his neck and tossed aside.

The other marine charged Mora directly, sprinting towards her with the blade high, in an effort to surprise her. When he got to within ten yards, he burst into flame. His shriek was deafening, the flames so intense that his metal armour was weeping.

The man only lived for two or three seconds, but for Vehnek, his screams seemed to burn into the mind, and rang constantly in his ears.

Mora walked forwards, her dress bouncing and flowing.

"Your bodies are so fragile, *Lord Marshal*."

Vehnek wanted to spit a retort, but the tentacles were wrapped around his neck, all that could come out were grunts.

"None could withstand the strain of possession, even with the power you gained from the Watchtower. Still, a life is a life ... even yours. Your life, such as it is, gives this all a sense of poetry, doesn't it?"

Vehnek grunted and struggled, finding a sliver of space that released some pressure on his windpipe. "*We had a deal!*" he grunted.

"And you thought that the population of Mokku would be enough to sway me? To *you*? Another insignificant waste of blood and oxygen on this little world?"

Vehnek worked his hand down towards the knife at his hip. He drew it swiftly and drove it into the tentacle around his neck, sawing the serrated blade into the cold, rubbery flesh. "*My fleet ... my army ... will stop you ...*"

"*My* fleet. *My* army." Mora's smile grew. "You haven't had any training in resisting this kind of energy, have you?"

Another of the cold, damp limbs reached out and snapped Vehnek's wrist with ease. His knife clattered to the rocky ground. His groan of pain was crushed in his throat as the tentacle there tightened.

"It will be interesting to see how long you last."

28

The air around the Gravestone mountain had become a squall so fierce that the storms on the Meladrin paled in comparison.

The sounds of cannons were only drowned out by the bellowing war cries of the dragon-head ornaments on the prow of almost every ship. It was as if they knew the stakes, knew that things had come to a head, and certainly that they knew something was coming.

Both fleets were shaking through the power of volleyed cannonfire. The constant recoil was starting to upset the flight patterns of the ships in the air higher up, thinner and more delicate. The heavy cannons fixed to the front of the battleships, cruisers and General Kelad's skiffs blasted into the vanguard of Black fleet vessels.

At least half of the five hundred enemy ships were in a three-row firing line, one atop the next. The rest were in reserve behind them, and Kelad knew a trap when he saw one.

"*We have a limited window of opportunity ...*" Kelad muttered. "*Communications, relay formation order. All central sections, form lines perpendicular to the Black Fleet, single or double file. Leave a gap of four hundred feet between the lines, match the Black Fleet's elevation. All flanking sections, make your move, now. All ships, all sections, accelerate to your best possible speed.*"

He nodded to Saiyra at the helm, the signal officer behind her relayed the order to their section: section number one. The Allied fleet had been split evenly into nine, fifty ship sections, for ease of organisation, deployment and maneuverability.

The *Shadowblade's* section was one of the flanking groups, and they dropped fifty feet immediately, swinging around to starboard beneath the rest of the fleet. They sped past the sections as they quickly formed single and double file lines. Kelad knew and had made sure that his forces were well drilled and well organised, and they were proving that training now. The former Resistance ships were a little more haphazard in formation, and chaotic, but they only made up two sections in the centre and two on the left flank.

He glanced across and raised a spyglass. The *Sand Dancer* and her section, number eight, were pulling hard to port. Section nine, comprising the *Dreadnought,* the wyvernborn ships, and other Resistance vessels, were heading that way as well. It was a classic tactic that Kelad enjoyed: mix up the formation before the close-in clash, while there was still room to maneuver.

The Black Fleet were reacting to them immediately, as Kelad knew they would. The firing lines were bending as the central ships drifted back, the rest were angling their cannons into a crossfire. From the front the Allied attacking lines were difficult to deal with, but from the sides they were vulnerable. If that was not enough, there were also elements of the reserve moving around to intercept the flanking groups.

"*What if the firing line start using the dragon heads against us?*" Saiyra muttered.

"*They won't risk it with our numbers. The power draw from the Mages and generators is too great.*" Kelad stroked his chin, observing the enemy's flight patterns. "*Pull us out a little wider, Saiyra. Communications: sections two and seven are to directly engage the firing line at close range, they are to be joined by the skiffs in sections three and six. All other vessels in the centre, full ahead.*"

Kelad watched the sections pull outwards and speed towards the firing line like a cavalry charge. Their cannons blazed, their barriers absorbed the incoming fire from the Black fleet. The skiffs that were joining them dipped and climbed, darting between the lines and engaging at point blank range. The cracks and booms were deafening. This was it, the true beginning of this clash of nations, clash of egos, clash of great powers. As Kelad watched, Black Fleet ships, and a few of his own began to drift and fall.

The reserve coming around the central groups towards Kelad seemed in two minds over whether to help the line, or attack his section. They were spreading out and splitting, sixty vessels of cruiser and skiff class. Kelad grinned.

"*Communications: Section One, pull in, hard to port, and fire at will!*"

***

"FIRE!" Ironclad bellowed at the front of the *Sand Dancer*.

"*Send to sections eight and nine: target vessels in clusters,*" Thomas shouted to Captain Seret. "*Volume of fire will overwhelm their barriers!*"

Ember watched the dark ships coming closer. The Black Fleet's reserve were flying at them fast, ready to meet them head on before they could hit the firing line. The sections behind them opened fire, but the light cannons they had weren't quite in range just yet.

The Black Fleet replied in kind with cannonfire, and the Allied sections spread out into packs of three or four ships. Seret whipped the *Sand Dancer* to port and starboard violently, and Seraphine knelt on the deck, her hands pressed to the wood. Ember felt the sorceress's magic course up from her feet to her stomach, holding her in place as if she was screwed to the deck plates. A bolt of lightning lit up the forward barrier in a bright, sudden flare, and the thunder from the strike rumbled across the ageless rocks all around them.

The lead Black Fleet ships were weakening, their barriers overwhelmed with cannonfire. One stuttered and plummeted as heavy shots blasted against the deck and prow. The false dragon-heads howled and snarled at each other as they drew close. As the two fleets began to pass, the Allies' broadside cannons battered the weakened vessels, forcing them to withdraw or crippling them. A few were destroyed outright.

"Firing range!" Bassai bellowed. He had a light cannon resting on each of his broad shoulders. One of the gunners was behind him, his hands glowing.

"Fire all!" Ironclad shouted.

Ember loosed an enchanted arrow. The projectile arced through the air, catching the wind. It burst in a pulse of force energy that warped and tore a skiff's weakened barriers.

She had another nocked in an instant. Bassai aimed both light cannons at the same ship, and the gunner grabbed the amplifiers. Both of them bucked violently, but Bassai held his ground. The shots smashed into the skiff's deck and flank, and were joined by an enchanted crossbow bolt from Kassaeos that set fire to the sails.

The swift attack of the fleet caused the Black Fleet to break formation. They pulled wide to limit targets for the Allies, and focused their fire on the straggling groups.

"Regroup the sections and drive those ships into their own firing line!" Ironclad yelled. "Box them in, and tell Barada to spread his wings!"

***

Zeta waited beside Barada and Sandra, watching the huge airships tearing chunks out of each other. She could never have imagined a battle like this. She had barely fought in anything close to the scale of it.

Thousands were fighting all at once, dying by the hundreds every minute. Her scales didn't feel like a part of her, they felt like a stifling second skin. Her body was itching. Her wings twitched. Battle had always been on wyvernborn terms. Always there had been a siege or an incursion from elite Caelish soldiers, always noticed and watched immediately, no matter how well they considered themselves concealed. The enemy had always been herded into boxes of dense foliage where they could easily be killed, or picked off one by one.

The attack on the Wyvern Bog, that had come so close to wiping them and the Orlin out, was easily the largest engagement she had fought in ... that perhaps any of the younger and even some of the older wyvernborn had fought in.

Barada growled at her. She looked at him and straightened. He could smell it on her: the terror.

"It has been a long time since you have given off that scent."

Zeta swallowed.

"I smell it on most of you warriors," he boomed in dragontongue. *"Fear!"*

The warriors let out a low, growling hum.

"Fear of them? Of weakling humans in their false, flying beasts? Of weak-willed fools following another fool?"

The three wyvernborn ships were flying in a row, bearing down on the firing line that were tangled with elements of the Standing Fleet. There was a blinding flash as one of General Kelad's ships burst into flame and exploded so violently that the debris collapsed the barriers of a cruiser and battleship in the Black Fleet, and set both on fire. The magic infused flames spread swiftly across the decks. Zeta winced at the sight, and the overwhelming smells of death and burning flesh.

Over those smells though, there was something else. Dry scales, cracked bones, the inert, dead magic that had once been borne through the blood of her forebears.

Dragons. Dead dragons. For the humans, it would be like walking among the corpses of their gods.

It filled her with a horror that couldn't be described. A coldness, a realisation of the dragon's vulnerability, despite their greatness and power.

If they had been slain and dumped in a hole in the desert, what of the wyvernborn? What of her?

"This is a battle greater than any we have fought, even in our long lives. A battle more treacherous than any we have fought. Do we fear death? Do we fear pain? No!"

The Empire Of Fire

Two fireballs the size of siege engines burst against the barriers of their ship. They rippled alarmingly, before the wyvernborn shamen on deck held up their claws to reinforce it. The force of the impacts was strong enough to shake the deck under their feet.

"Perhaps it is defeat you fear. Perhaps it is the uncertainty over the future. I say fear neither! We will not be defeated today! The fire in the blood of the dragon cannot be extinguished, and the soul of the dragon will burn itself onto the face of the world!"

But it was *extinguished,* Zeta thought. *It was extinguished in the dark, cold, dry sands of this dead place.*

"I see your faces, I look into your eyes, and I see that you smell the same thing I do, the ancient dead far below us, great dragons corrupted and turned to desperation and darkness. Our ancestors, perhaps. Lessons are learned from our ancestors, for good and ill. We have learned plenty of them. Father has taught us, shown us a truer path. We are not those bones below us, we are a far different challenge for the sand walkers to face."

Zeta felt the ship tremble again as the dragon head mounted on the front of it belched a pulse of lightning at the ships firing on them. All three of the wyvernborn chariots did the same, breaking the enemy battleship into two smouldering pieces.

"If our bodies are claimed today, then we take these fools with us! If we are to fall from the sky, we will drag their wood and iron creations down with us to smash into the rock. Our Father, our Orlin mothers, brothers, sisters, children, carry us in memory and power! No matter our fate today, we will live on in the glory of all time to come!"

Zeta glanced at Sandra. Her head was bowed, and tears were dripping onto the leather armour that covered her chest. Barada's hand was clasped around hers.

"For those enraptured in their fear ... have you forgotten who we are?"

The *Sand Dancer* pulled ahead of them and wove between the

wyvernborn ships. Light cannons and arrows fired and loosed from the top deck, battering against the Black Fleet craft ahead, offering a small distraction to allow Barada's warriors to do what they did best.

"WE ARE WYVERNBORN!" their Alpha roared, with the wrath of every dragon's flame, every wyvernborn cornered and slaughtered by the fearful. *"SONS AND DAUGHTERS OF OUR FATHER ... FLY TO GLORY, TO THE END OF TERROR, FOR OUR CHILDREN!"*

The wyvernborn, with one roaring voice, answered his call with a war cry that would have been heard by every ship in the fleet. Zeta's fear was shoved out of her mind, and a fire blazed into life in its place. She roared along with every other of her kin, and the time came.

The three wyvernborn ships punched into the firing line like a fist through a layer of wet mud. Barada rested his forehead against Sandra's for a moment. Her eyes were still filled with tears, but now her bow was in her hand, with an arrow nocked. She turned the rest of the Orlin archers at the railing.

"Loose!"

Her enchanted arrow, and fifty others, flew and burst against the already weakened barriers of the nearest Black Fleet vessels. As the walls of light tore and collapsed, Barada leaped from the deck. Zeta jumped after him and spread her wings. She heard the flapping and shaking of leather like a drumroll behind her as the army of wyvernborn screamed towards the enemy.

The crews of the Black Fleet's stricken vessels barely had time to look up before the firebombs began dropping onto their heads.

The enchanted fire chewed through iron, wood and flesh in moments, sending four vessels spiraling down to the rocks below. As the wyvernborn split into groups of ten and dipped around the enemy fleet, the *Sand Dancer* slipped beneath a battleship and then climbed aggressively. Zeta followed it with her cohort of warriors. The small ship sped towards a stricken cruiser. There was no mercy. Enchanted projectiles and powerful spells smashed into its barrier and through it, smashing the mast of the central sail into splinters.

Zeta sped along with the other nine of her group, and dropped firebombs on the bridge, sails, and through the hatch into the hold.

The cruiser drifted, its helmsman dead and burning. The *Sand Dancer* slipped behind it, pursued by a pair of Black Fleet skiffs, in turn pursued by twenty wyvernborn who had caught a swift breeze, bearing down on them with wings flared wide.

They drifted higher, then pointed their wings back, arrowing down. They shot past the skiffs and flared, their enchanted weapons raised. Each one sliced into the barrier and flipped into the gashes they had made, claws extending, latching onto the hull.

Zeta grinned and banked away, safe in the knowledge that the crews of those vessels wouldn't last long.

Her tasks were simple: kill the enemy, and defend the three wyvernborn ships. The rest of the Allied fleet were able to take care of themselves, and didn't have a sizeable chunk of their entire population in the conflict here.

The cloud of claws and fire had worn out their element of surprise. By now, she knew that Caelish marines would be swarming onto the decks of all their craft, ready to try and pick them off with volleys of arrows or magic. The skiffs were the enemy vessels to watch out for as well: they were quicker, more maneuverable, more capable of dealing with smaller targets.

Zeta signaled the cohort behind her to drop lower. Up ahead, two battleships from the Black Fleet firing line were closing on one of the wyvernborn ships, peppering them with cannonfire. Their ship's barrier was buckling under the strain, even as an Allied cruiser engaged them. The wyvernborn ship drifted around until the dragon-head was in position, and it unleashed a beam of bright, focused flame at one of the attackers. The enemy vessel's barrier collapsed, and the cruiser leapt in, pounding the armour with its cannons. The enemy's response crippled it as both battleships engaged with the full force of their cannons.

Zeta charged in with her warriors, gesturing to the two immediately at her back. Kanku and Morzok overtook her, their enchanted blades held beside them. As they closed in on the undamaged ship, the pair pulled up and slashed into the barrier.

Zeta zipped upwards through the gap they had made, which closed quickly behind her. Her claws latched her onto the battleship's hull with a maddening screech. She gored deep lines in the iron armour, before she found purchase.

Zeta crawled along the hull until she came to the cannon hatches. The lower levels were nearest to the spinning core that kept the contraptions in the air, and she knew that well from being aboard the three battleships the wyvernborn had liberated.

She could hear the crew inside through the hatch, calling out targets for the cannon they were operating. The air seared around her as a blast of fire shot forth and collided with the flank of an Allied ship. Zeta took the last firebomb from her sling, the Breacher. This one was packed tightly with three times the amount of black powder as the others, as well as its core of liquid flame enchanted by Father himself. She had yet to see one in action outside of the test bombs, that had been strong enough to make a ten foot, inferno filled crater in the Orlin Wasteland.

She lit the fuse, and waited until it was half burned down. With a grunt, she let go of the hull and took hold of the hatch, swinging towards the opening.

She landed with a crouch on the lip. The Caelish gunners leapt back in alarm, before forming battle incantations in their hands.

Zeta grinned at them and tossed the Breacher into the cannon deck behind them. The distraction of it was enough to allow her drop backwards and out of sight.

The shout of alarm was replaced with the din of battle, and then with the great fiery WHUMP as the Breacher ... breached.

The aft of the battleship exploded in a rain of burning wood and melted iron slag. Zeta twisted in the air and arrowed her wings so she was facing downwards. She dropped like a stone ahead of the debris, building up her momentum.

She was near to the ground when she flared her wings and sped along the

The Empire Of Fire

rockface. There was an almighty crash behind her as the battleship shattered itself into the ground. She grinned over her shoulder and began to climb again.

A strange feeling overcame her as she rose back towards the battle. She could see it all from down here. The broken, outmaneuvered Black Fleet firing line. The Allied ships dancing among them, smashing through their forces. The enemy's reserve ships, piling forward in a counterattack, that was already being met by the ships that had punched through the first rows. It seemed to be going well ... so why was she uneasy?

It was a feeling, more than anything she could see. Her scales were itching again, as they had before the battle had begun.

Barely a mile away was the great fissure, the black abyss, lined with totems, which had made her just as nervous from above. It wasn't as dark as it had been then. Now something in there was glowing faintly, somewhere far below the surface.

Zeta growled and flapped harder, pushing herself well beyond her limits. Freezing air whipped into her eyes, chilled her blood.

She would be no good up there if she was half dead from fatigue, but she had to get there as soon as she could regardless. Too much at stake. If an arrow or incantation took her life instead of someone else's, fine, as long as that other person ended two of the enemy in her stead.

She gritted her teeth as she continued upwards, her vision blurring and darkening at the edges. All that kept her going was blood rage, working its way through her veins under its own ancient power. Her breath panted in and out of her, she fixed her eyes on the fleet and focused her mind, blotting out the pain in her wings and her chest.

The dark spots swam across her vision still, but one in particular remained, completely motionless. It was past the fleets and upwards, atop the peak of the Gravestone, in among the ruins of the hubristic human construction long since abandoned. It was a shadow deeper than the depths of the deepest mountain caverns. Zeta mistook it at first for a cloud or a jet of smoke from the battle, but it stayed exactly where it was, poised but calm.

For a moment she thought that she could see stars through it, but then she realised, as they swept left and right, that they looked more like eyes, shining like the eyes of a predator peering out of a dark forest. Not just two, but six, moving in different directions, watching different clusters of the clashing fleets, as if getting a measure of them.

She thrashed her wings harder at the sight of the demon thing above, six eyes drinking in the chaos of battle, ready to strike.

***

It listened to Vehnek scream. His body was shaking uncontrollably, the skin turning red.

It paced around him, closing the eyes of the body It was inhabiting and pulling the mouth into a smile.

These two legged things were an amusing toy. As a vessel to control they left a lot to be desired, aside from their connection to the magic that wove through the fabric of realty. That was a curiosity, and It suspected that they only could maintain such a connection thanks to the meddling of Its eternal, cosmic counterparts and opposites.

The tether between It and the Lord Marshal was surging with power. Vehnek's screams increased in volume, and the final one was drawn out and long, rising in pitch.

His eyes burst into flame first, then the rest of him. The scream continued, and It felt something in the vessel, a surge of chemicals through the dead brain, sending a shiver down the spinal column.

The flames brightened and brightened, until Vehnek was an agonised, howling sun that illuminated the darkest shadows of the cavern.

The huge bones around them were shaking. The new light truly showed the process beginning. At each end they were pulled towards each other, locking into place, and then the connections began. Tiny tendons snapped between them. The muscles formed from light, surging around the bones, layer upon layer of them. Thick arteries and veins wrapped around them like jungle vines.

The long claws and claw bones began to curl and flex as scales grew from the muscles and blood vessels, soft and white at first, then thickening, darkening and hardening into natural armour harder than diamond. It rippled up the four legs and across the shoulders, along the chest and stomach, across the back. Giant bony spikes burst bloodily through the new scaly flesh, which immediately repaired, scarred and re-hardened.

It smiled at them all, and looked upwards. The eyes of the Black Creation, perched at the top of the mountain, met the vessel's from thousands of feet apart.

Not long now. Once Its beasts were remade, they would only need the spark of life.

It closed the vessel's eyes, but could still sense the energy of rebirth blasting through the screaming fool Vehnek, into the regenerating dragons. Closing off the sense sent shivers of pleasure tingling across the vessel's skin.

All that had the knowledge or power to resist were here, above, killing each other. Once they were gone, or had become the first of the thralls in Its army, the world they inhabited would be swallowed.

Not long now.

29

"*The Black Fleet have committed their full reserve,*" Saiyra cried from the Shadowblade's helm.

Kelad grinned. "*Good. In theory that means no more surprises.*" He scanned the ships around them, then down over the side of the railing. The fissure that served as the dragons' tomb was glowing fiercely, as if it had become the mouth of a volcano.

He gritted his teeth. "*Hmm... or not. Signal the Sand Dancer to begin their drop! We won't have long.*"

He turned to face forwards, and pointed at the cruiser ahead. *Shadowblade* and the skiffs on their wing blasted a cruiser and skiff ahead of them with their heavy cannons. The blast shook the air as they swept past. A moment later, the skiff on their starboard side burst into flame and began to drop.

"*Climb fifty yards and pull us hard to port!*"

Saiyra banked around and pointed the nose upwards. Kelad spotted two cruisers pulling out of formation to follow them, hunting for the glory of killing the famous general. The aft barriers bent inwards as a flurry of fireballs were tossed at them.

"*Can you shake them, my dear?*" He muttered to Saiyra tersely.

She grinned and wove to port and starboard. Their wingman did the same. Kelad signaled their captain to break formation and dive. It was both of their best chance.

"*If you spot a gap, feel free to exploit it,*" he said with a boyish smile. Saiyra immediately sent their skiff into a spiraling dive, between a pair of

The Empire Of Fire

battleships. The cruisers' cannonfire sailed past their aft harmlessly.

"*Fleet status,*" Kelad barked back to the communication officer.

"*The central sections have engaged the reserve. The Alliance sections have all but collapsed the left flank. We're in the thick of it, sir.*"

"*What of the Black Fleet?*" Kelad muttered.

"*The remains of the left flank and the central firing line are forming on the Inquisitor.*"

Kelad grinned. The word came out as more of a contemplative sigh. "*Ah ...*"

He scanned the skies. Vehnek's flagship would have likely been placed in the reserve, at the centre of the lines. Sure enough she was floating slowly higher, being joined by straggling skiffs, cruisers and battleships. From an elevated position the group would be able to deploy all of their cannons, including the siege batteries. It was a good defensive tactic. Limit enemy fire, while maximising your own.

The *Shadowblade* thrashed under the barrage of medium cannonfire from a vessel on their starboard bow. Saiyra pointed the heavy cannons at it, and signalled the gunners to fire as they swept past. The shots ripped a hole in the barrier, but the thing kept floating on its cushion of air.

"*Inform the Alliance sections immediately,*" Kelad ordered. "*Mop up those stragglers as best they can, the smaller that group up there is, the better.*"

***

Barada snarled in a rage, banking through the gap in the battleship's barrier. He and three other cohorts landed on the deck, weapons drawn and striking downwards.

Barada bisected the captain and beheaded the helmsman in two powerful strikes. Two of the communications officers sprinted away, the third frantically tried to contact the Black Fleet command ships. A slender warrior, Jion, swept past and cut him down, landing beside Barada with a snarl.

"Do we go below decks, Alpha?" she growled.

"No, they will simply fell their own ship if we do that. If we kill the crew, then there will be no barrier. We will be vulnerable. Drop two Breachers below decks at the midships, then we fly."

Jion bowed her head. Barada leaped off the bridge and into the fray on deck. Marines were streaming up through the hatches, brandishing amplifiers that were pressed against their shoulders.

They began firing immediately. Two wyvernborn were killed in the first volley, blasted apart. A third was set on fire. Jion lobbed a firebomb in among them, and the enchanted flames burst and drenched their armour. The flame and concussion gave them enough pause for Barada to act.

"Close in! Shields forward! No mercy!"

The wyvernborn jumped in, hacking at the marines, blades and axes clashing. The war cries met furious roars fuelled by dragon's blood. Jion wrestled a pair of amplifiers from dying marines, and studied them for a moment behind the shield wall the wyvernborn had formed. She took one in each claw and jumped, kicking off the main mast and spreading her wings. Both of her amplifiers erupted in lightning magic, blasting the marines. As their attention was jerked upwards, the rest of Barada's warriors charged, and before long, they had control of the central crew hatch.

"Cut the fuses, send both the Breachers down here. Blow this bitch in half!"

Two of his warriors bit the tops of the fuses off, and prepared to light them. More of the wyvernborn had picked up amplifiers and were exchanging fire with the crew at the rear hatch.

"Take off the moment they drop," Barada ordered. The shorter fuses sparked to life, and the warriors rolled them down the hatch and the corridor below. The moment they were released, the wyvernborn all took to the air.

The whoosh of hot air pushed the wyvernborn cohort higher, their wings spread wide, gliding upwards. Barada glanced back briefly at the wreck. The front of the battleship was plummeting, while the fireball that had become the aft remained where it was.

The smell of flame and glory filled his nostrils, and then another scent joined them. It was something he couldn't place, sulphur mixed with rotten flesh, obsidian and a blend of metals. Dragonfire, dust, the potions that the shamen struggled to mix in their caves.

He was yanked from the thought by the whistle of arrows zipping past him, and he spun in the air, darting from left to right. He led the wyvernborn behind him in a steep dive. They slipped beneath the clashing flotilla around them, heading towards their own trio of battleships. Barada could see them clustered together and battering the ships that tried to assault them.

The cohort split to avoid one of the cruisers that had flown with them, now a burning husk falling towards the rocks. A number of skiffs ducked down as well, three Black Fleet vessels pursuing two Allied ships. The Black Fleet's ships seemed faster, pulling out wide while still gaining on the other two. They caught the straggler in a pincer move, blasting it from either side with their cannons. The skiffs barriers were no match, and it quickly caught fire and began to drop, nose first.

One of the enemy skiffs climbed, pursuing their ally back into the main body of the fleet, but the other two arrowed inwards, speeding towards the wyvernborn. Barada grinned and signalled to his warriors. They broke formation and split completely, spreading out. Barada went low, his axe ready, not that it would do him much good. Ships that small and quick were difficult to engage, more so than the larger craft.

The fire from the deck marines and cannons struggled to pick out clean targets, and only a single warrior was hit. The rest sped through and continued on course without engaging.

"Reform, but stay loose on the wing!" Barada roared. The wyvernborn drew closer to him as they kept flying. One of the cohort roared a warning behind him. He glanced back.

The two skiffs were skidding around in the air, and were coming towards them quickly. This time they had no need to conjure their own wind, they had caught the same desert breezes that the wyvernborn had.

Barada snarled and signalled. The wyvernborn dropped a dozen feet. Their battleships were coming closer, but the skiffs would reach firing range first.

Barada roared an alarm, but they were still too far away. Behind them, a few tentative crossbow bolts were heading their way, falling well short of them. Barada could see them falling beneath him. Gauging distance, it seemed.

He roared again. The battleships continued fighting, oblivious to the danger. He growled and signalled the warriors to spread again. As incantations began flying at them, he thrust out a claw and flared his wings. The rest followed his lead.

They flipped in the air and doubled back, dropping again. This time, Barada brandished his enchanted axes and sliced into the lead skiff's barrier. Behind him, Jion tossed a firebomb through the gap. It bounced and burst off the side of the deck, catching some of the flames. The concussion of the blast shook the crew, giving the wyvernborn a little more room to breathe.

Barada purposefully led his warriors between the pair of ships, limiting some of their fire. He guessed that they wouldn't risk hitting each other, and he guessed half-right. A few of the marines still fired incantations at them from their amplifiers, but the cannons at least were quiet.

Barada dropped again as he made a swift left turn, passing along the other side of the skiff and slashing at the barrier again. Jion's firebomb landed amidships, and engulfed the cramped deck in flame. Barada roared again, and led the warriors back towards their lines. Another two were taken by incantations and sent spiralling to the rocky ground.

The remaining skiff had no motivation to help its stricken comrade, and pursued the wyvernborn. They were almost at the battleships now.

Barada roared again, and looped the cohort underneath their flying war chariots. They pulled up sharply on the other side and landed on the top deck. He looked back at the warriors as they landed, counting them. Of the thirty,

The Empire Of Fire

twenty two had returned. Half the survivors had superficial injuries, a slashed chest here, a hole in a wing there. A couple had burns, Jion had a crossbow bolt stuck in her thigh.

"Shamen!" Barada bellowed. Two of the twisted magic users came shuffling over, and began to treat some of the wounds.

Instinctively, Barada's eyes were searching for his wife. She wasn't at the railing with the rest of the archers.

He took a few steps inwards, around the Caelish and Haaman crew operating the ship itself. He picked up her scent over the stink of war, and pushed his way towards her.

Sandra was below decks, crouched beside the hatchway ladder that led up to the open air. Barada jumped down, recognising the slumped wyvernborn she was beside as Zeta.

His Beta was singed, but otherwise appeared unhurt. However, she was panting, her muscular chest rising and falling rapidly.

Sandra looked up at him with wide eyes, and grasped his arm, pulling him down with her. Quickly she kissed his bicep before turning her attention back to Zeta.

"She just got back aboard."

"What's wrong with her?"

"Exhaustion, and ... if I didn't know better, I'd say panic."

"Panic? She has never panicked. Ever."

Sandra sighed. "It's the only way I can describe it."

Zeta's eyes opened wide, and she reached forwards, grasping Barada's hand.

"Alpha ..." she hissed in dragontongue. *"The ... peak ..."*

Barada leaned back. The terror in her voice took him completely off guard.

"Demon!" She cried with the last of her energy, and collapsed. Her breathing was beginning to catch.

"Shaman!" Barada shouted. He jumped up to the deck and grabbed one as it shuffled past, carrying it down to Zeta. Sandra started swiftly leaping up the ladder, and Barada followed.

His eyes were drawn up to the Gravestone peak. The shadow hung there, amidst the ruins, watching them. He could almost feel his eyes meet … something's eyes. It was holy, yet entirely wrong. He bolted to the bridge, and the Caelish crew looked up at him in surprise, and even a little fear.

"Contact the section leaders!" Barada bellowed to the communication officer. "The peak!"

The captain glanced up and held a spyglass against his eyes. When he lowered them again, he was pale as a ghost. He shouted at the communications officers in terror.

***

There was a flash, and Lord Marshal Vehnek stopped screaming.

The great beasts lay still for a moment. It looked around at them with the vessel's eyes, seeing the shock of life trembling through their bones, through their bodies. Wings and claws began to twitch, scales began to ripple. Near to what remained of Vehnek, one of them let out a growl, low and rumbling, that made the bottom of the fissure tremble. Pebbles clattered from the edges of the gash along the walls, echoing through the air.

It pulled the vessels lips into a smile. Mora had thought It cold once, a feeling nestled in the back of her mind, but it was about to get far hotter in this particular realm.

One simple death was all It had needed to be reborn and grow. One dead boy, thrown into a battle by a fool with more bravado and libido than intelligence. One instance of grief to drive in a hook. One weakening of the morals and mind of a powerful enough vessel to feed it while it grew.

Lord Marshal Morad Vehnek would have his legacy, in a way. The legacy he had craved. His shortsightedness would certainly be whispered of,

The Empire Of Fire

cursed, and briefly laughed over by those that would let Cael burn for their own acquisition of precious metals, wasting them passing discs of it between insignificant people.

It drifted over to the largest of the dead beasts. Its scaled lips were twitching over its jagged teeth. Its ears were slowly raising until they were pointing straight upwards. Its nostrils flared as it gasped in a breath, that caused the stale air to surge around the vessel's robe.

The dragon's eye snapped open. Its pupil was wide. It breathed slowly, then more quickly, panting faster and faster. Claws scraped against the ground, its tail swished, then raised and crashed against the rock. A growl built up in its throat, louder and louder, until it was close to roaring.

The pupils narrowed, as if the sun was suddenly shining in its facade. It opened its salivating jaws and screamed.

Its scream was joined by another, from a dragon with rust red scales and thin spines in the place of spikes across its back. Two more joined in the cry. One had a pointed, elongated snout, made for squeezing into tight spaces like burrows or caves. The other's wingspan was far wider than the others, jaw wider as well, meant for hunting larger creatures.

The roar grew as more and more dragons began to scream at their new life. Smoke from their exhalations filled the fissure, blocking the beasts from the vessel's eyes. All It could see were the eyes, glowing with fiery yellow and orange light, and the flames they began blasting across the rocks.

Then there came another roar from above, a twisted screech of doom, one louder than the bellow of a hundred dragons.

The beasts around the vessel ceased their roaring and looked upwards. It sensed a feeling of terror cutting through their madness and pain, and latched on with the same hooks It had used to destroy Mora.

Every dragon looked down at It at once. One by one, their eyes went from yellow and orange to blood red. Their panting steadied. All were breathing at the same time, one entity.

"Burn them all."

***

The *Sand Dancer* wove between the battling airships. Captain Seret was moving the small craft so quickly and balletically that the Black Fleet's broadside cannons weren't able to track them. Only the light cannons and amplifiers were a threat.

They passed a cruiser, and the marines on deck began firing at them. The barrier around their belly and flank lit up, catching and deflecting the shots, far dimmer than it had been at the beginning of the battle.

Bassai growled and picked up both the light cannons. Trevor, the gunner behind him, grabbed the amplifiers. A pair of lightning projectiles smashed into the cruiser's barrier. further along the railing, Ember managed to loose two arrows that burst against the shield as well. A squadron of skiffs swept past them, and diverted the cruiser's attention with a barrage of cannonfire.

Ironclad wrapped his hand around the *Sand Dancer's* mast, calling out incoming ships and cannonfire. Seraphine's robes were soaked in sweat as she bolstered the barriers with her power.

Bassai's eyes scanned the battle, searching for a new target. The small craft squeezed through the narrow gaps between airships. The brightly coloured *Sand Dancer* was an eyesore, and they were damned lucky it was so quick.

A number of broadside potshots flew at them, but only two managed to hit. They were big hits though, and part of the rear barrier collapsed. Trevor jumped back to help Seraphine rebuild it, and Thomas sprinted to the aft with Ember. They loosed arrows and blasted powerful incantations at the skiffs pursuing them. One pulled away, another closed in to strike.

Captain Seret pulled the *Sand Dancer* into a dive, beneath the *Dreadnought*. Donnal's ship had taken a few hits to the thick armour plating, but the leviathan craft was still flying as if it were newly built. The heavy broadside cannons were ensuring that the Black Fleet were giving it a wide berth. The escorting skiffs, older models though they were, ensured that the smaller, more nimble enemy airships were dealt with or driven off before they could make too much of a mess.

As the *Sand Dancer* passed, the pursuing skiff was battered by cannonfire from above. As it banked away, Bassai bared his teeth.

"Trevor! Get over here!"

The small craft was presenting its belly to them, and he wasn't about to let it go. His eyes were wide, breath snorted in and out through his nostrils, leaving little plumes of black smoke to mix with the flames of battle.

His gunner ran across the deck and immediately grabbed the amplifiers. Bassai roared as the light cannons on his shoulders barked and sent a ball of fire and a bolt of lighting into the aft section. The wood in the armour caught fire quickly, and the lightning shorted out the generator keeping it in the air. It arrowed downwards quickly.

Bassai laughed out loud, each exhalation releasing a puff of smoke. Trevor leaned against him, and the dragon inside Bassai's blood almost recoiled at the inferior, dirty, clammy hands of a human.

Bassai growled to himself. Trevor was turning bright pink, leaning on the railings. "I can't ... I need to ... rest."

The blood fire calmed. "Aye, go below, then. Meditate. I'll catch Thomas's eye if I need to fire again."

Trevor stumbled away, and the scent came again, drifting across the battlefield. It was the smell that had filled Father's chamber. Magical energy, conjured fire, singed rock. It was the scent that had ignited the dragon's blood, heightened the rage that was a part of every wyvernborn who had ever lived.

His head swung around, trying with some difficulty to ignore the cacophony of war around him. He could hear the roaring of wyvernborn, lost somewhere in the chaos. They could smell it too, sense it, whatever it was. He could see the Black Fleet ships positioning themselves higher and higher, led by the *Inquisitor*, preparing their siege weaponry.

More than that, they were putting the Allied fleet between them and the fissure.

Seret barked at Thomas, who stumbled over to the helm as quickly as he could. Bassai growled and bounded over as well.

Thomas was listening at the communication stone, frowning. His eyes looked up and scanned across the mountain, up towards the peak.

"Something is here," Bassai muttered.

Thomas glanced up at him. "Barada, Bassai is here. He might understand more easily."

Bassai took hold of the stone and peered at it carefully. The wyvernborn Alpha's voice filled his mind as he followed Thomas again, this time towards Ironclad.

"You can sense the same thing I can, can't you?" Barada murmured. *"That feeling that speaks to the part of you that yearns to take flight and ... burn the whole world."*

"Never been my dream, Barada."

"But it was mine, for a time. A long time. The embodiment of it is up on the peak ... watching us all."

Bassai turned and looked up as the *Sand Dancer* cleared the battle, pulling up above the clashing fleets.

The shadow was moving, not sitting and watching as Barada had said, but hovering overhead, above them, blocking out the stars and twisting multicoloured blaze of light above them. Its six wings filled him with the kind of fear he had only felt once, when he had awoken as a hatchling, alone in a mountain pass to fend for himself. Not even when pursued by humans had he felt this kind of fear, that had been enraging in a deeper part of him, that lesser creatures had even dared to lay a hand on him.

Six wings, six eyes, but he could tell nothing else about its form. It was covered in shadow, drawing it from the night like it was drawing poison from a wound. It was practically formless, to the eye at least, but to the nose ... to a wyvernborn's nose, it was a dark, beautiful god.

Bassai backed up into a hard, metal wall. He looked around. It was

The Empire Of Fire

Ironclad, staring up at the creature. He was very still, his violet eyes glowing like a pair of suns. Thomas was trying to see what he was seeing, grimacing up at the thing above them.

"Do I want to know?" Thomas muttered.

"I do," Bassai growled.

Ironclad shook his head slowly. "It's an old acquaintance ... but not as exactly as it was when we last saw it."

Bassai growled. Any illusion of godhood left his brain immediately.

He'd seen it die. A mere human had killed it.

"I was hoping we would run into the black dragon again," he said quietly. He was smiling through his brow.

"The section leaders know," Thomas muttered. Ironclad didn't respond, and Thomas looked up and nudged him. "Ironclad ..."

"It's looking at me, Thomas. It's looking right at me, with two of its eyes. It knows who I am."

The *Sand Dancer* shuddered under abrasive cannonfire from a pair of skiffs. Thomas looked around as Ember loosed an arrow at one of them and sprinted back along the deck.

"What's got you three..." She trailed off when she saw Ironclad's eyes, and looked upwards. She paled and swallowed. Her voice trembled. "Well then ... what are we going to do about that?"

Bassai grunted. "Is that Mora's doing?"

"I wish I knew," Thomas hissed. "More likely it followed us, drawn here like we were. I think this is what attacked the Magus Towers ... and if so, it won't have any problem dealing with us."

Ember tapped Ironclad on the chest. He looked down at her. "One up there, more below us, you hear me?"

Ironclad nodded. "I agree. It's a pincer movement. The move will be made soon, we must make ours. Thomas, contact Kelad. Tell him we're making the drop, advise him to..."

A vicious screeching roar pierced the night. Bassai tensed immediately.

His scales tightened, his tail stuck straight out. He set himself and spun around to face the helm.

"Captain! Take us down! Now!"

Seret was looking around in a panic. Bassai roared again, as Thomas sprinted past him, translating and taking the communication stone from his hand. The battle around them seemed to hesitate for a moment, as if it was one entity, struck with terror at the sound.

The roar grew louder, as if more voices were joining in a chorus of horror. The sound was familiar to all of the Four Guardians, the deafening war cry of a dozen or more dragons.

Bassai could tell they weren't as they should be. There was nothing in the voices but rage and madness. There seemed no intelligence behind it. "They're being controlled!" Bassai bellowed back at Ironclad and Ember.

The roar stopped suddenly, and was answered by another, even louder, this one from directly above them. One voice, louder than anything that Bassai had ever heard, louder than the war taking place around them.

The cannonfire was silenced for a few precious seconds.

This roar was mad, just as mad as the others, but there was more than rage behind it. The feeling was far colder, far more sinister, far more conscious, and far more pained. It was full of an agony so visceral it sent a lance of grief through Bassai's chest, past the same godly fear for an instant.

"Seret!" Ironclad shouted, the moment it was silenced.

The captain was shaking, pale. Her hands were shaking. Her eyes were wide as bucklers when they fixed on him in terror.

"Take us down!"

Seret looked up at the giant creature above the fleets, and swallowed. She gave Ironclad a single nod, and cranked the lever beside the wheel.

The *Sand Dancer* dropped swiftly, pointing downwards. They picked up no trailing craft at first, in fact the volume of fire between the fleets was a fraction of what it had been a mere minute before. Every section leader was likely contacting each other, trying to work out what was happening.

The Empire Of Fire

The wind whipped over Bassai's head, whistling around his ears. He set himself low to the deck. Ember crouched close beside him. Thomas stopped beside Seraphine and placed a hand on her back, augmenting the power she was feeding into the barrier. Ironclad held on to the mast tightly, eyes aglow.

The black fissure in the rocky ground below was no longer black, it was burning with orange and red. Shadows danced in the magical light against the rock face, shadows of claws and spikes and teeth, winged demons of flame and fury.

Behind them, the fleets resumed their barrage. Behind the *Sand Dancer*, two squadrons of skiffs swept past the main body of the clashing ships, deployed directly from the *Inquisitor's* section hanging above them all. Magical projectiles and heavy harpoons whistled past the royal yacht's painted hull and delicate sails.

"Barriers aft!" Ironclad ordered.

Seraphine held her hand out behind her. A harpoon bounced off it immediately and spun away into the night. Seret bobbed and weaved the *Sand Dancer* to the left and right, up and down. She kept the manoeuvres quick and unpredictable, but the pursuing quartet were dogged. For every harpoon that shot past them, another two struck the barrier. One even forced its way through, clattering onto the deck, its momentum reduced to almost nothing.

Bassai grabbed it as it slid forwards towards the Mages, and looked up at Trevor sharply, who had staggered back up on deck. "Help them with the barrier!" he roared.

Trevor nodded and half ran, half crawled from the hatch. When he reached Seraphine and Thomas, he added his own power to theirs. The other gunner Mages joined them, planting their hands on her and Thomas's shoulders.

There was an explosion behind them, and burning debris clattered across the barrier. Bassai glared back. Another, larger skiff had joined the pursuit. Glowing points of light on the prow burst into two large lighting bolts, that cleaved into the rear of another of the pursuing craft. The wreckage of the already-obliterated skiff was drifting and spinning away.

Bassai recognised Kelad's ship with a growl, but a pang of gratitude went through his chest. It was begrudging, but he didn't attempt to deny it.

Another scattering of draconic roars drew his attention from ahead.

The fissure before them stopped glowing, but the shadows still thrashed and churned. More and more violently they twisted, until more could be made out below.

Bright, scarlet points of light burned from the shadows in pairs, smoke began to rise.

The shadows took form. Claws reached out and gouged into the stone on either side of the great crack, scaled and muscular forearms hauled the monsters' bulk through the gap.

The snouts appeared first, blowing out rippling air and smoke. The jagged teeth snapped, the huge, red reptilian eyes were fixed up at the *Sand Dancer* and the rest of the fleet.

"Barriers forward!" Ironclad shouted. "Seret, evade as best you can!"

The captain leaned over the wheel and set her stance.

Immediately, harpoons pierced the *Sand Dancer's* sails, and Thomas pointed up at them, weaving the broken fibres back together. Seret's hands were never still on the wheel and the elevation controls, twisting and turning, dipping and climbing.

Bassai could hear the thud of impacts on the hull, feel the shudder of the deck beneath his feet.

The dragons pulled themselves through the fissure, all eighteen of them. They glared upwards, huge beasts. Some were **Ovisrek**: slender, quick things, smooth, with streamlined wings and spines across its back. Second sets of wings were lower down the flanks, smaller, for tighter turns at speed. Others were **Felreev**: armoured scales, with massive wingspans and spikes across their spines and tails, wide jaws for larger prey. One was a **Trovska**, a dragon that hunted in the oceans, that flew and dived into the ocean to snatch up dolphins, sharks or small whales. Its scales were fine and smooth, with strong wings that doubled as fins for sweeping through the water, and a strong tail to propel it after its prey.

All were beautiful, intelligent creatures, reduced to war machines by a despot's dream of control and conquest.

The beasts leaped, their wings swooshed downwards with a rush of air so violent it sounded like the beating of a war drum. They struggled to heft themselves upwards at first, wings pumping, before some instinct took over, their flight smoothed out, and their ascent quickened.

The dragons roared again as they climbed, like the charging war cry of men on horseback. The cry was answered by the monstrosity hanging above them.

Bassai knew then: the Allies were not fighting Lord Marshal Vehnek. They were fighting something far worse.

"Thomas!" Bassai roared. "Signal the Black Fleet!"

Thomas's face was set in focused terror. His wide eyes flicked to Bassai. "What?"

"What did all the stories say, my friend? What did they say? The Witch And The Dragon…"

Thomas froze. "You can't control them … but their eyes are red. Something is … and they were controlled before!"

"One or two at a time … not eighteen … and not whatever that thing is above us!"

Thomas looked back at the fleets, at the beast above them. Ironclad and Ember were close enough to overhear, and they both nodded.

Thomas held up the communication stone, and spoke in Caelish.

***

Admiral Sorin wrung his hands, pacing across the *Inquisitor's* bridge. The communication officers were relaying urgent requests from each section of the fleet, requests for orders directly from Lord Marshal Vehnek. What Sorin couldn't tell them was that so was he.

The Lord Marshal had gone dark. As far as the Admiral was aware, everything was going to plan, with the exception of whatever the thing above them was. Some secret project, some weapon that had been deployed, maybe from that pyramid that had unsettled him so much.

He turned to the helm. "*Are we at optimal bombardment elevation?*"

"*Yes, Admiral.*"

"*And our two sections?*"

The helmsman chewed his lip. "*They are delayed, sir, given the presence of the dragons. There is considerable confusion...*"

Admiral Sorin's jaw set. "*I'm not interested in their confusion, I'm interested in them following my orders, and the Lord Marshal's orders!*"

The helmsman swallowed. "*Aye, sir.*"

Sorin walked to the railing and looked over. He could hear the dragons below, approaching quickly. There were a few scattered cannon shots between the fleets, but the majority seemed unsure.

The ships were now of roughly equal numbers, the so-called Alliance had struck with mixed tactics, throwing the Black Fleet off balance. With the rise of the dragons, even though it had been a part of the plan known by all the section leaders, the reality of them had been something none had been prepared for. Sorin cursed the old stories that had painted the beasts as simply that: beasts. They were more than that, they were nature's innovation, natural weapons, tools that could advance a civilisation beyond any that had ever graced Planar.

"*Ready bombardment batteries.*"

The Admiral smiled, searching the fleet for an optimal target. The largest Alliance vessel seemed the best choice. It was an ugly beast, an armoured mish-mash of cannons and close range spike weapons. The bulky thing and its escorts would be obliterated in the first salvo.

"*Who is this?*"

Admiral Sorin turned sharply at the communication officer's confused and tense voice. He marched over to her. The three officers immediately stood to attention.

"*What are you talking about, Lieutenant?*"

The officer swallowed. "*I'm sorry, Admiral, but we are being contacted by an ... unknown party. They are not part of the network.*"

Sorin smiled. "*Then it's the ... 'Alliance'. Hmph ... surrender, most likely. I'd surrender when faced with a flock of dragons. Give me the stone.*"

The officer gave him the stone quickly, and a Caelish voice filled his head, tainted by a Haaman accent.

"*Inquisitor, this is Sand Dancer, can you hear me?*"

"*Yes, this is Admiral Sorin of the Inquisitor. Stand down your forces and come to a hover. Prepare to be boar...*"

"*Admiral Sorin? Where's Lord Marshal Vehnek?*"

"*Never mind where he is, I'm in command of the fleet. You surrender to me.*"

The voice's anger and urgency grew. "*You bloody fool, do you realise what's happening?*"

"*What's happening is that we have you cold, traitor. Your cause is hopeless.*"

"*The dragons have all of us cold! Don't you understand? We're two lumps of soft iron in between a hammer and anvil, all of us! You think that thing hovering above your ship is your ally?*"

Sorin looked up. The creature's black wings had spread out wide, its eyes were watching every ship in both fleets, in exactly the same way Sorin had watched the enemy a moment ago. It was picking out targets ... and two of its eyes were locked onto the *Inquisitor*. Locked onto him.

"*Ready the dorsal barriers!*" He shouted. "*Mages to defense stations, quickly!*"

He turned to the communication officers, who were staring at him with wide eyes. "*Contact all section leaders, tell them to hold fi-*"

His orders were drowned out by a scream so loud and terrible that his eardrums shattered. Sorin cried out in pain, his vision blurring.

A shadow fell across them. Sorin could barely see it, but he saw the flash. Fierce and blue, sudden, burning through his eyelids as he closed his eyes against it. A wave of infernal heat blasted into him, and he was propelled backwards.

He fell, and kept falling.

Sorin's eyes snapped open. His vision was still blurry, but he knew immediately what had happened. He had been blown overboard.

Everything was so far away, it didn't seem like he was falling quickly, but he knew how doomed he was when he saw the *Inquisitor*.

He was racing away from the flagship. The craft was like a azure sun, consumed with blue fire, bursting apart, fragments of the dead airship showering like bright, flaming rain.

A shadow consumed the wreck. Six leathery, glistening wings closed around it. Three draconic heads dipped down, catching the light.

They were bony, scaly, lined with armour plating. The teeth were the length of an airship's ramming spikes. Blue flame coursed up their necks, visible through the scaled, armoured skin. All three heads blasted jets of flame into the skiffs and cruisers that had been escorting the *Inquisitor*, engulfing them in an inferno.

The only thing that glowed more brightly than the fire was the eyes of the creature. They burned with a light that was far beyond the arcane. Intelligence, power, an evil so raw and uncaring that it was entirely alien to Sorin's dying mind.

***

The burning blue light of the explosion cast all the way down, past the fleet, to the deck of the *Sand Dancer*. Bassai snarled, wincing against it.

Thomas's face fell, his hand dropped to his side. Ember stared up in horror. Ironclad's head turned away. At the helm, Seret even looked back.

Bassai gritted his teeth and roared. "Eyes forward!"

Thomas jerked and stared at him, and repeated the order in Caelish.

Ahead, the onrushing dragons had flame licking around their jaws. Seret leaned over the wheel, eyes focused. She issued orders, loud and clipped.

Thomas exhaled. "She's saying we should hold on."

Bassai grinned and dug his claws into the deck.

Seret cranked the lever beside her, and the *Sand Dancer* pulled into a steep climb. There was a blast of heat, and a splintering bang behind them. One of the pursuing skiffs had been hit with a blast of dragonfire, and the front of it was completely gone, swallowed in an inferno.

The *Sand Dancer* dipped again, and the eighteen dragons were so close that Bassai could make out the individual scales on the three that were leading the charge. There was no rage in their faces at all, no blood-lust, no emotion of any kind.

They were nothing but puppets. Even the Black Dragon, all those years ago, had growled and snarled in anger.

One of their heads turned towards them, fire filling its throat. All the Mages around Seraphine pointed their open palms towards the dragon, strengthening the barrier, focusing it at the point from which the blaze would spew. The burst of flame was caught by the barrier, but small fires erupted on deck from the heat.

Bassai leaped across to stamp them out as the *Sand Dancer* dipped and wove. The dragons were whipping past, buffeting the small airship with the rushes of air kicked out by the wings. Seret cried out in alarm as they began to tumble, losing control.

Cannonfire sounded behind them, the heavy shots of Kelad's *Shadowblade*. Dragonfire was the response, but the skiff nimbly dodged away. Another dragon broke off and sent a jet of flame into the vessel's fore-port quarter. A hole was left, punching through the barriers.

The *Sand Dancer* dodged around the legendary monstrosities. One of them, one of the swifter beasts, growled from up ahead, and a tail swung towards them. Seret cranked the lever again. The small ship climbed and dipped quickly. Bassai felt the rush of air as the spikes missed them by inches.

They were three hundred feet above the ground. Seret leveled them off, and barked an order at the gunners. They cast their eyes upwards, watching the dragons as they climbed towards the fleets quickly. Bassai growled as cannonfire began stuttering down towards them, from both the Alliance and the enemy.

The dragons twisted and turned in the air, dodging back and forth, splitting up in unison like a well drilled squadron. They were exactly like the wyvernborn when they attacked, the tactics had been passed down like an ancestral memory. Splitting limited the volume of cannonfire on the group, and many of the shots were missing.

Dragons were so much faster than airships, so much hardier. The magical projectiles that struck their scaly hides burst, leaving little more than scorch marks.

Seraphine looked up and shook her head. "They've been warded. That's Mora's doing."

Thomas shook his head. "One Mage can't ward eighteen dragons. It can't be her."

There was a shout from a gunner, and every eye turned upwards. The dragon that had been pursuing Kelad's ship spread its wings and dropped towards them.

Ironclad stood up straight. "Ground team, make ready. Thomas, tell Seret to take the ship as low as she dares, then run like hell is at her heels."

Thomas nodded and ran to the helm. Bassai slowly got to his feet, the Caelish skiff's harpoon clutched in his undamaged hand. Ember steadied her breathing and moved to the railing. Ironclad joined her, axe and shield in his massive hands.

Kassaeos ran to Seraphine, and turned her face towards him. Their lips locked together for a few seconds, before he shifted to the railing himself.

The Empire Of Fire

Once Thomas and Bassai were at the railing as well, the five of them stood and waited for the word to go.

"I suppose there isn't much of a chance we'll get that battalion of troops we were promised, eh?" Ember muttered.

"They're a little preoccupied," Kassaeos said as he checked his rapier and crossbow.

The dragon above them roared, arrowing towards them.

"I hope you have a plan ..." Bassai grunted to Ironclad.

Ironclad chuckled. "You won't like it."

Bassai growled. "Then I'm definitely taking the harpoon with me."

"Seret will have to wait before she gets out of here," Thomas said tersely. "Otherwise the dragon will chase the ship instead of chasing us."

Kassaeos stretched his neck. "Ember, Thomas, you'd better hold on to me. We're going to be need to be a bit more stable if we're going to shoot that thing."

Thomas raised an eyebrow. "Can you shift with both of us?"

The assassin nodded. "I've done it before."

Ember ran her tongue across her teeth. "Well ... if that's the best way."

"You didn't eat recently, did you?" Kassaeos muttered with a smirk.

"Nothing big." Ember narrowed her eyes. "Why?"

"No reason. It's probably fine. Mostly. Swallow whatever comes back up."

Ember scowled at him. "You can always be thrown."

Ironclad chuckled, and glanced at Bassai. "You good with jumping?"

"As long as it's not from a hundred feet up."

The closer they got, the more jagged the rocky ground became. Bassai growled at it, and looked back up. The dragon had fire in its throat, dropping like a boulder toward them.

The *Sand Dancer* was fifty feet from the ground, then forty, then thirty. The jagged jaws of the ground were reaching up around them, and Seret was weaving around the ones that were tall enough to damage the hull.

The night turned orange above them as a jet of flame came at them.

Seret banked the airship hard to starboard and accelerated. As the dragon began to turn, Ironclad's eyes flashed. "Now, Kassaeos!"

The assassin grabbed Thomas and Ember and shifted. A moment later, from among the rocks, an arrow and a bolt flew, as well as magical projectiles of lightning and ice. The enchantments burst against the dragon's flared wings and belly, and it roared in fury.

"Go, Seret!" Ironclad bellowed, and jumped.

With a roar, Bassai swung himself over the railing.

The Empire Of Fire

30

General Kelad held tightly onto the railing of the *Shadowblade*. The ship was flying upwards, nowhere near as fast as the dragons they were pursuing. The light cannon gunners were standing ready at the railings. One of the heavy batteries on the front had been destroyed by dragonfire, but the other was primed and prepared, as were the eight medium cannons on the broadsides.

Kelad listened to the chaos coming through the communication stones. The fleets above were scrambling into formations, and were attempting to counter the charging dragons. Cannonfire rained towards the swift-winged demons, but precious few projectiles struck. Before they could reposition, the monsters were upon them.

The swifter ones breathed intense flame on battleships and cruisers in their path, raking their claws straight through the barriers and armoured hull plating. The larger, bonier beasts simply crashed straight through the fleet above, not even bothering with fire.

Above them all, the shadowy bastard of creation chewed through what remained of the Black Fleet's command section.

Kelad's eyes were fixed on one particular dragon: the largest of the ones who had risen from their canyon grave. He knew that dragon well, had become quite taken with it. Kallus Vehnek had been obsessed with the Black Dragon, but Kelad had appreciated the raw power and terror of his. Nature sometimes built things that beggared belief, Va'Kael's will had a strange taint to it at times. Certainly, the dragon that the still-living Sel Kelad had named Razorback was a marvel of evolution.

Fast on the wing, armoured along the spine with bony plates and spikes.

The spikes were thin, but stronger that steel. The scales were tight, coloured a rusty red, like a sun peeking above the horizon. It was a smaller dragon than the others had been, but it was the fastest thing he had ever seen, even now a century later. Nothing compared.

He had watched Razorback devastate armies, and blast Kalendra into rubble when it had been a rebel stronghold. Fleets of warships on the Dividing Sea, trying to launch a counterattack against Cael City itself, had been reduced to nothing more than smoke and floating ash. Uncur had been incinerated under the force of its flame, and it had been so quick it had never been so much as scratched, until it had gone mad. Until the spell keeping it docile had been broken, it had been arguably the most powerful of the dragons ... one not felled by some upstart on a city wall with a harpoon.

It blasted a skiff in half with a fireball and latched onto the side of the Alliance's *Dreadnought*, snapping at the sails. Before it could incinerate the deck with a burst of flame, a cohort of wyvernborn swept around and jumped on its flank, burying axes and swords in its side. Razorback's head swept around and clamped its jaws down on one of the warriors, so small in comparison.

"*Heavy cannon to station!*"

Saiyra angled the *Shadowblade* towards the dragon, and a bolt of lighting blasted into Razorback's side. It screeched in pain, and let go of the *Dreadnought*, flipping back and flaring its wings. It swept beneath the huge airship, and Saiyra set off in pursuit.

Kelad placed his hand on the communication stone plinth beside the helm. He pulled a Mage towards him. "*Contact the fleet. All ships.*"

The Mage stared at him in confusion. "*We ... have a stone that contacts all sections, sir.*"

"*Including the Black Fleet.*"

The crewman nodded with wide eyes, and began focusing on the stones.

From above, a jet of blue flame engulfed one of the Black Fleet's battleships. The shadow creature descended upon one of the troop carriers and smashed wicked claws and jaws through its armoured hull. Two of the draconic heads pointed around and incinerated the top decks. The sails disintegrated instantly.

The Mage nodded and stepped back.

"*All ships, this is General Kelad, I'm taking command of the fleets.*"

Saiyra glanced around at him with a smirk.

"*Spread out into loose sections, gaps of a hundred yards at least. Staying so tight means the dragons can hit us far more easily. Coordinate fire. All skiffs, form into your squadrons and harass the larger ones. Stay fast, and make yourselves as small a target as possible.*"

Kelad peered up and around. "*Wyvernborn ... you know what to do. As for that thing above us ... sections three, four and five, engage by wave. Black Fleet vessels ... send up the reserve battleship wings. Keep it busy, kill it if you can. We are the barricade, our job is to hold them here so our people on the ground can end it.*"

He turned back to Saiyra. "*Follow Razorback.*"

She took a deep breath and swept the ship through the fleet. "*What makes you think we'll catch it?*"

"*He can't resist big game,*" Kelad muttered. "*There's plenty of it around.*"

She nodded, and took a deep breath as her eyes flicked to him again. "*Now that they're awake ... can our people on the ground do anything at all?*"

Kelad grinned tightly. "*Whether they can or not, our task remains the same ... and those Guardians down there have a habit of pulling off miracles.*"

***

Bassai rolled as he hit the rock, springing to his feet. He clutched the harpoon in his hand like a spear.

Both he and Ironclad skidded down the rise and sprinted towards the sounds of magical projectiles and draconic roars.

Jaws snapped, giant footsteps crashed against the rock and shook the ground. The sulphuric smell of dragonfire drew Bassai's nose, a pathway for him to follow. The beast screeched as two more bursts of arcane energy hit it. Both he and Ironclad could see the leathery wings and flashes of the monster's head above the jagged boulders ahead of them, glimpses of the bright, blood red eyes staring around in fury.

"It has to be here for us," Ironclad grunted. "It's protecting the fissure. Vehnek and Mora must be inside."

"It's stalling us while the rest obliterate the fleet ... both the fleets, it seems."

"Hmm. I'm starting to think that Vehnek seems to be the least of our worries."

Ahead of them, the dragon loomed. Only two or three rocks separated them now. Thomas slid down the nearby rise, and joined them. He clenched his fist, and a shield appeared around the three of them.

"Stay tight," Thomas muttered.

They moved around the rocks, and were confronted with a beast from the depths of all the hells. The snorting, enraged thing was tracking Kassaoes with its beady, red eyes, sending a blast of fire right on top of him.

Kassaeos reappeared on top of a nearby rise, having shifted away. He loosed a crossbow bolt at the dragon, which burst in a ball of flame against its shoulder. It left a glowing ghost of heat on its scales, but no blood.

The dragon looked up at Kassaeos, its throat glowing with flame, but Ember ducked from behind a boulder and loosed an arrow. The enchanted projectile arced into the beast's knee, making it stumble, and by the time it looked up again, to either of the two that were harassing it, they were gone.

"Stay close together, move as one," Ironclad ordered. "The barrier around us is stronger the closer we are. This will be a real test of our bond."

Bassai growled and grinned. "That creature doesn't stand a chance."

Thomas patted him on the back. "I'm ready."

The Empire Of Fire

Ironclad nodded, flexing his wrists.

"Charge!"

The trio broke from cover and tore across the ground. Thomas leaped up and grabbed onto the back of Ironclad's armour, letting them sprint faster than he could. One of the dragon's red eyes rolled around to look at them. It bared its teeth, fire built in its mouth.

Kassaeos's crossbow bolt struck its neck. Ember's arrow burst against the side of its head. It whipped itself around and roared in fury. By the time it refocused on Ironclad, Bassai and Thomas, they were right up against its left leg.

Bassai leaped and drove the harpoon into its ankle. Ironclad chopped his greataxe down into the clawed foot. On impact there was an immediate burst of bright blue light, warm against Bassai's flank, but searing and breaking through the dragon's flesh. In an instant, the foot raised into the air, and there were two huge gusts of wind on either side of them, knocking them onto their backs. Thomas pushed off Ironclad just before he was crushed, and rolled away.

As they started getting up, a blast of flame dropped right on top of them in a stream. It split and engulfed the barrier that Thomas cast above their heads. The runes on his gauntlet glowed as brightly as Ironclad's eyes. The fire suddenly stopped, and the dragon screeched. Smoke from one of Kassaeos's bolts lingered around one of its wings.

The vast creature turned in the air as nimbly as a bird of prey, and soared upwards. It flared its wings and flipped in the burning sky, dropping back down like an arrow.

"Up towards one of the rises, come on!" Ironclad ordered.

A blast of flame raked across them, battering Thomas's barrier. Bassai heard the crack of a burst of force magic above. The dragon grunted and growled. The ground began to slope upwards steeply, and Bassai was forced to clamber up using one hand as well as his clawed feet. He moved swiftly and delicately, while Ironclad brute forced his way up loudly, his heavy feet chipping off pebbles and fragments of rock.

The dragon swept around again, moving lower than before, claws raking forwards. Its fire had been deflected, but the sheer force of its weight would certainly stagger at least Thomas.

"Ready and brace!" Ironclad ordered.

Bassai glanced up, ready to dodge aside if need be. The dragon's red eyes were wide, its wings flared, its tail ready to sweep around to strike them if the claws missed.

Ember's force arrow burst against the creature's wing, and it screeched. It dropped a few yards, its flight disrupted, and it flapped to regain its balance.

From higher up the rise, Kassaeos jumped and shifted. There was a roar of fury from the beast, and the claw was still coming. Bassai jumped and rolled down the rise, the sharp bone slicing the air behind him. Ironclad wasn't as quick, but used his shield to deflect the claw and push his own bulk away.

The tail pushed towards them, whipping across the rock. Thomas cast his barrier wide and angled it like a ramp. The tail bounced and deflected over their heads.

Bassai turned and squinted up at the creature. Kassaeos was on its back, driving his rapier into the thin gaps between and beneath the scales. The creature twisted and thrashed in the air in a effort to shake him loose. It flipped upside down, and Kassaeos began to fall from its back.

The assassin shifted in the air, moving closer to the Guardians. Thomas's gauntlets glowed and he reached out. Kassaeos slowed in the air, and shifted downwards two more times. He dropped the final seven or eight feet and rolled into a sprint, tearing across the jagged rocks.

"We're about five hundred yards from the fissure," Ironclad grunted.

"Too far," Bassai snarled. "The fleet don't have time for this."

The dragon turned in the air again, coming back towards them.

"Then we have to fight on the move," Thomas said defiantly. "My barrier can protect us."

Ironclad nodded. "Send to Kassaeos and Ember, harass that thing as we go."

***

Shadowblade sent a heavy shot into Razorback as it raked its claws forward towards a battleship. It screeched and whipped its head around. The blood-red eyes narrowed at Kelad.

The dragon seemed to tumble in the air, but its flight was corrected instantly, wings spread wide to stabilise. It dipped beneath one of the Merchant Fleet's cargo ships.

"*Stay on him, Saiyra,*" Kelad muttered.

His helmsman tracked the dragon's flight path, adjusting the *Shadowblade's* course with tiny adjustments to the wheel and elevation levers. Every cannon was poised and ready to fire.

As they moved beneath the cargo ship, Kelad's eyes narrowed. There was no sign of Razorback on any vector.

His eyes widened. "*Aft barriers!*"

He wheeled around and drew his pistol. There was a rush of air as the dragon swept down behind them.

Razorback had fire flickering between its jaws. Kelad fired until the stone was spent, and slipped another into the breech, but his old friend was not deterred.

Dragonfire engulfed the aft barriers. Saiyra wrenched the wheel to starboard and cranked the elevation levers. *Shadowblade* turned sharply in the air, but Razorback was more than nimble enough to stay with them.

The rear of the ship was on fire, but still intact. Crewmen were scrambling towards the damage, regardless of the beast preparing to douse them with flame again.

"*Let him get closer,*" Kelad muttered.

"*Closer?!*" Saiyra yelled.

"*Closer. Ready a hard port turn and the broadside cannons.*"

Saiyra exhaled and trimmed the sails slightly, cutting their speed.

"*Take us higher,*" Kelad snapped.

As the ship rose, Razorback blasted them again. The weakened barriers collapsed, and the skiff shook violently. One of the sails on the port side burst into flame, and a deck Mage gunner leaned around to extinguish it with an incantation.

Saiyra was shaking her head, frustrated and tense. Kelad's eyes were fixed on the dragon. It growled and pushed forwards swiftly. The blood-stained jaws opened wide to chomp down on them. Razorback flared its wings and extended its claws.

"*Now! Broadsides, fire at will!*"

Saiyra deftly spun the wheel and increased the skiff's speed. *Shadowblade* turned in the air, and a series of rippling booms burst from their flank.

Lighting bolts slammed into Razorback's belly at point blank range. The dragon's jaws snapped closed and caught their aft starboard quarter. There was a crunch and a scream of metal. Some of the burning top deck and hull was ripped away.

Another volley of cannonfire left burns and bloody gashes on Razorback's flank and scales. A swift third volley of lightning and force made the dragon scream in pain, and there was an unmistakable snap of massive, thick bone.

A huge wing swept around and smashed into *Shadowblade*. Kelad was thrown from his feet. Saiyra tumbled through the air towards the railing, and the General shifted, grabbing her before she could fall into oblivion and throwing her onto the deck.

He could hear members of his crew screaming in terror and pain. Saiyra picked herself up and grabbed the wheel. After a moment, the skiff's mad, out of control spin began to slow and still.

"*Barriers as powerful as you can make them!*" Kelad ordered. "*Someone give me a damage report!*"

The Empire Of Fire

He looked around, searching for the communications officer. He was nowhere to be seen, likely falling to the rocks below.

A Mage staggered up to the helm. "*We've lost most of the cannons on the starboard side, as well as the port side sails!*"

"*I think the rudder's damaged, Sel!*" Saiyra shouted through her teeth. "*She's sluggish in the turn, and we're listing twenty degrees to starboard!*"

Kelad looked around at the combined fleet, struck by how much of it was on fire. He could see the surges of smoke and the rushes of air that were the only visible signs of the ancient beasts that were tearing through them.

One dragon appeared in the black smog surrounding them. Its flight path was erratic, but it moved straight towards them, singularly focused.

"*All barriers to the starboard side!*"

***

Ember hopped between the rocks, weaving between them. She could hear the dragon huffing and flying overhead.

Ironclad, Bassai and Thomas were sprinting across the ground below her. Out of the corner of her eye she saw them engulfed by a stream of white-hot flame. Her heart leaped into her throat, but when it ebbed away the three were still moving swiftly. The echo of a magical barrier ebbed away slowly.

She saw Thomas stumble, and almost fall to his knees, but Ironclad picked him up. He heaved himself up onto the Construct's back, and they continued across the blasted rock, steaming with the heat of dragonfire.

Ember nocked an arrow and waited, listening to the dragon sweeping around and flapping its wings. As it dived towards them again, she rose and loosed. The projectile whistled towards the dragon, but it dodged, twisting in the air. Its eyes were locked onto her, fire in its throat.

She swore in Orlin and jumped from the rise, a moment before a wave of heat blasted her in the back and singed her hair. She tumbled head over heels and slammed into a pile of stones and flat granite. The wind was kicked out of her, and she rolled until her hands could find purchase on the ground.

She hauled herself to her feet with a grunt of pain, and immediately glanced around for danger.

Thomas's concerned voice filled her head. *"We saw that, Ember, are you alright?"*

"Yeah ... just about. I can't see the dragon, any of you have eyes on it?"

"No, but those ears of Ironclad's put it somewhere to the south west, that's in your direction."

"Right ..." She took a breath. "Keep going. Don't worry about me, I'll catch up to you."

There was a pause. *"We've all heard that before."*

"Yeah, well ... we all get there, or we don't, it doesn't matter. We need every chance." Her hand trembled as she drew an arrow from her quiver. She'd had a steady supply of them on the *Sand Dancer,* but down here with only her own, she had expended half of them already.

She dived behind an outcropping and flattened herself down into a nook at the base. The furious snorts and beating wings of the dragon echoed overhead, only just above the sound of the infernal battle above them.

She heard an almighty crash as something, most likely an airship, smashed into the ground nearby. The creature roared and beat its wings again, and she caught sight of it heading towards the fissure again.

"You still there?" Thomas sent to her.

"Yeah. Be more worried about yourselves, it's coming your way. It's more worried about protecting the fissure than going after one of us."

"Hmm ... and it peeled around to come after us. They're being directed ... which means that the controller sees what they can see. It knows we're coming."

Ember picked herself up out of the fissure. She set off at a run between the rises, following the noise. The glow of falling debris lay to the south and west, casting an eerie blue and orange glow over the rocks. Chunks of molten

538

iron and wood, and smashed bodies, lay everywhere in her path. They were right under the battle now.

She had to keep an eye above her as she ran. "You said 'it'."

"Yes, I did. Hold on ... here it comes."

There was a roar ahead of Ember, and she bent down, doubling her pace. There was an ache in her back from where she had hit the ground, at least a bruise. She wove between wreckage, passing and ducking away from the burning skeleton of a battleship. Being anywhere near it was unbearable. The metal frame was curling and melting, like a cross between tissue paper and wax thrown in a fireplace.

Once Ember was past it, the desert wind froze her bones. Her whole body started to ache. She was panting like a racehorse thrown into a panic. As she bolted up a rise, fresh flame glowed from up ahead.

The dragon ignored the enchanted crossbow bolt that blasted against its wing, and breathed a jet of flame down onto Ironclad, Bassai and Thomas. The barrier protecting them was far weaker than it had been. Ember gritted her teeth and slid down the rise, feet pounding across the rock.

"Ironclad's asking if you're in arrow range," Thomas sent to her. His voice was more faint, tinged with exhaustion.

"Soon," she grunted.

"He wants you to aim for the head."

"Like that'll do anything."

"We only need it distracted for a second."

Ember took a breath, and kept moving. Her companions had slowed their pace, and she was catching up. She heard the furious screech come again, and the blast of fire against Thomas's weakened barrier. It swept over the rise she was beginning to climb, snorting ash.

She ducked, before bolting up to the top as quickly as she could, using every second of her climbing experience to stay on her feet and find the surest footing.

At the top, she lay flat on her back among the rocks. Her eyes tracked the dragon as it swept around, aiming back towards her friends.

The shot would be difficult to say the least. She would have to rise to her feet and loose the arrow within a second or less. If she didn't have to hit anything that wasn't a problem, but her target was fast-moving, and nimble despite its size. She'd have to wait until it had no chance to react to her presence also, because as well as being large and fast, it was the most dangerous creature to inhabit Planar.

Its eyes were wide and focused, glowing like two burning torches in the night. The glare grew in intensity as white fire licked between its jaws.

Kassaeos loosed a bolt at it, that exploded on one of its legs with a flash of conjured lightning. Ember tracked its speed and trajectory, trying to imagine that it was nothing more than a stalker or wolf. She counted down in her head, and then made her move.

She kicked the air and flipped to her feet, drawing back the arrow. Its jaws opened, and she loosed.

Its eye flicked to her. Its jaw closed. Its wings twitched towards her.

Then the arrow hit it in the side of the head.

The crack of force energy rang out across the mountainside. Thomas wheeled around, both of his gauntlets thrust out in front of him.

While it was briefly disoriented, white and cyan lashes of thick, whipping magic shot from his hands and wrapped around the dragon's neck and right leg. Thomas screamed with the exertion, his power filling his body to augment his strength. Ironclad and Bassai wrapped their arms around him, and dragged.

The dragon crashed to the ground with a piercing screech. Ironclad and Bassai were up and sprinting towards it in an instant, with Kassaeos shifting to join them.

Ember nocked another arrow, and loosed it towards the thrashing beast. The blast of force magic kept it on the ground, dazing the wing as it flapped to try and right the dragon.

It breathed white flame into the air, enraged. As Ember repositioned to take another shot, her friends leapt upon it.

The Empire Of Fire

Kassaeos shifted and reappeared on top of the beast's belly, driving his rapier down between the scales. Ironclad ran and clashed his axe against the dragon's claws as they swung towards the assassin, and with a flash of light, buried the blade in the base of its foot. A hind leg came around to kick at him, and he raised his shield, absorbing the blow that sent him sprawling.

He was back up on his feet immediately, and charged back in. Ember loosed another arrow, that struck the dragon in the foreleg and staggered it again.

It was all a distraction for Bassai. The wyvernborn leaped over Ironclad and landed on the dragon's chest. Ember drew and loosed again, striking it in the jaw, driving up the head.

Both of Bassai's sabres ignited in brilliant green flame, and he drove them into the monster's exposed throat, beneath the bony ridge that offered it protection.

The creature's roar was stifled, and the wyvernborn leaped back, taking his weapons with him. Liquid flame and thick blood shot from the wounds. Ironclad blocked and swung at the thrashing claw. Kassaeos shifted out of the way as one of the wings slammed into the ground almost on top of him.

Thomas was approaching, trudging slowly, his hands held out in front of him, gauntlets maintaining his incantation and holding the dragon down.

"Ironclad," he rasped. "I have to release it and meditate ... its not going to follow us now."

Ironclad nodded. "Get on my back. Let's move on, everyone."

Ember was taken by the beast in its death throes. Even controlled as it was, it fought death itself in a whole other battle. She had the perfect, brutal view of it as she crossed between the rises, following the path her friends were taking.

It was on its back, kicking at the air, trying to breathe fire, but only making the wounds in its throat catch and burn wider. It jerked and thrashed, its tail whipped back and forth, it wings tried to flap madly, like it was dreaming of the air in death.

Ember heard it stop moving, heard its huffing breaths stop. A pang of mourning for it pulsed through her chest. It was the forest girl in her, keeping the reality of the monster away. Even if it were not controlled, it was still a intelligent predator that would have never hesitated to kill all of them. She didn't look back, her adrenaline forbidding her from doing so.

***

Kelad hung on to *Shadowblade's* railing with a grunt of pain. Both shoulders felt as if they were coming loose. The Mages were unable to keep up with the fires on and below decks, and he was sure that half of them were dead.

Razorback was coming around again. One of his battleships attempted to cut it off, but the dragon dissuaded it with a jet of flame across the port side. The dragon-head on the prow howled in mechanical fury and agony, spewing its own beam of ice energy towards the beast. It glanced up Razorback's spike laden spine, half of its tail froze. The dragon tumbled in the air for a moment, before it curled up and breathed smog and embers on itself to thaw the ice.

Its wings spread wide two hundred feet below, and it roared in pain as its wounds caught.

Kelad ran to Saiyra, dodging the fires and breaches in the deck.

"*I don't suppose you have any idea how to put one of those things down?*" she hissed at him tersely.

Kelad knew where they were most vulnerable, but getting them into position was as likely to send them all spiralling down to the ground in flames. He had seen where Calver's harpoon had hit the Black Dragon to kill it, had lived long enough during the battle of Uncur to see what had put one of them down. "*Armour's weaker at the throat, but these are warded against our weaponry. Concentrated fire broke it, but we can't survive that kind of fight.*" He glanced at his burning ship, and stroked his chin. "*We still have the heavy cannon ... what manoeuvrability do we have left?*"

The Empire Of Fire

Saiyra snorted. *"With most of our sails gone we're at a crawl. We can only really turn to starboard, and barely list to port."*

Razorback screeched from below them. Kelad glanced over the railing. His old friend was engaging an Alliance cruiser, chomping into the hull and setting fire to the crew.

"What about elevation?"

Saiyra barked a laugh. *"Going lower won't be a problem, I'm barely keeping her in the air as it is."*

Kelad grinned, and turned around. *"Heavy cannon to station! All hands brace!"* He clapped a hand on his helmsman's shoulder. *"Take us down, point us at Razorback. You can adjust our trajectory, of course."*

She nodded. *"Pulling us out of the dive is another matter."*

Kelad smirked. *"Let's not be incinerated by a dragon first, hmm?"*

Saiyra steadied her breath, and cranked the lever beside the wheel.

It seemed as if *Shadowblade* went from something alive to dead weight in an instant. The airship dropped like a stone, still listing. Saiyra battled with the wheel, and clamped it as still as she could, her hands and arms shaking.

Razorback had the cruiser's main sail in its massive jaws. Saiyra gritted her teeth and grunted, struggling with the helm as she adjusted the course to point *Shadowblade's* nose at it.

"Heavy cannon, fire!" Kelad shouted.

The whole skiff jerked and creaked with the recoil of the shot. Saiyra cried out as the wheel tried to spin to the left and right. Kelad leaned over and grabbed the wheel as well. Even with both of them, the ship still struggled against their control.

Razorback took the heavy lightning shot in the armoured scales on its back. The dragon turned sharply, and its eyes widened at the skiff plummeting towards it.

"Again!" Kelad ordered.

He and Saiyra braced themselves as the heavy cannon boomed again. This one hit Razorback in the wing.

It let go of the cruiser, and its wings began to beat. It roared in rage and pain, climbing towards them.

"*Hold her steady,*" Kelad muttered through his teeth. He raised his voice. "*Ready ice in the heavy cannon!*"

The order was relayed forwards by the surviving crew. The distance between the skiff and the dragon was reducing by two dozen or more feet a second. Saiyra kept the nose up as much as she could, battling both with the helm and the elevation controls.

Shadowblade bobbed up and down, the lower power in the generator making them more vulnerable to the shockwaves from the battle and the high altitude winds. "*Keep that nose up, Saiyra.*"

"*I'm trying, Sel, it's not that easy ...*"

They were getting closer and closer. Dragonfire glowed in Razorback's throat, its furious eyes widened in anticipation of the kill.

The iron crosshair in front of the helm was dead on the creature's head. "*Fire on my mark,*" Kelad shouted. He stepped away from the helm and ran to the fore. He couldn't afford the delay from order to execution.

He stopped at the railing. He saw Razorback's chest expand.

"*Fire!*"

When the cannon boomed, they were practically at point blank range. Razorback's mouth opened, and the solid ice projectile struck the roof of its mouth. There was a short cry of alarm from the dragon. Kelad saw that the red light in its eyes was gone.

Saiyra dipped the skiff down, and the inert beast sailed past, trailing a stream of blood from its head. Its momentum was failing it, and it began dropping towards the ground.

Shadowblade remained in a dive.

Kelad held onto the railing and looked back at the helm. "*Saiyra! Pull up!*"

He could see her fighting with the controls, her eyes wide.

Kelad felt a sudden bout of vertigo as he looked back downwards. A number of ships rushed past, as did a huge, spiked dragon with armour as thick as a castle wall. Saiyra dodged most of the ships with what limited maneuverability she had, but still scraped the starboard side across a battleship's hull.

Kelad shifted back to the bridge and behind the wheel with her. "*Do we have any stones left?*"

Saiyra nodded to the plinth. One of the spares was in a compartment near the base, re-charged.

"*Shadowblade to Spearhead, can you hear me?*"

Captain Obrek's voice filled his head, tense but controlled. "*We're here, General. Holding our own.*

"*Take command of the fleet.*"

There was a pause. Obrek had understood immediately. "*It's been an honour, General.*"

"*Aye, you too. Go for the throat or the head.*"

"*Understood.*"

Saiyra breathed out, but her hands were still tense. "*Is that it, then?*"

"*Hopefully not.*" He spoke into the stone again. "*All Mages, get us power to the generator, as much as you can.*"

He held onto Saiyra's shoulder with one hand, and the wheel with the other. "*Try and get us level.*"

She nodded. He raised the stone to his mouth again. "*Kelad to carriers, ready one of you to take on injured.*"

"*Aye, General,*" came the reply.

"*Injured, eh?*" Saiyra's teeth remained gritted, but a mad grin spread across her face. "*Didn't know you could cure being splattered across a mountainside.*"

"*I have supreme confidence in you and the crew, my dear, so I'm banking on us not being splattered across a mountainside...*"

The nose of the skiff twitched up by half a degree. The slope of the Gravestone around the fissure seemed to be an inferno of twisted wreckage. He could make out two dragons laying inert on the rock, and grinned, although there were ships and debris all around them falling like burning rain.

Saiyra cranked the lever again. *Shadowblade* was still falling, but a little slower a little more angled. The ground was still hurtling towards them with abandon, although now they would hit belly-first instead of head-first.

"We're getting some lift .. but I'm having trouble steering, still." Saiyra shook her head. *"We're out of the fight, Sel, whether we survive the fall or not."*

The skiff was still slowing, making Kelad's stomach lurch. He peered over the railing. A hundred and fifty yards, maybe. The crash now wouldn't be fatal, he was sure. *"Crank it again."*

Like a leaf, *Shadowblade* slowly drifted to a stop, twenty yards from the rock face.

Kelad looked up at the fissure, which was black as the abyss once more. The *Sand Dancer* had landed, and a number of people were disembarking. He spotted a number of figures moving along the rocky ground at a sprint.

He smiled around at Saiyra, before raising his voice again. *"All Mages, put as much magic as you can into the generator. I want dorsal barriers and emergency sails readied. Helm, once they're ready, make for the fissure."*

31

Sandra watched the gigantic dragon coming at them with her heart lodged firmly in her throat. "Nock!"

The Orlin archers along the port side of their airship notched their enchanted arrows in the strings of their bows.

"Draw!"

The dragon roared, and glanced to its left. As it flew alongside a battleship, it beat its wings, and rammed into the vessel's flank. The spiked and armoured hide struck it like the mountainside. There was a smashing and shattering of wood that began raining downwards. While the battleship was still flying, its entire starboard side was little more than splinters, the glowing generator exposed to the air.

"Loose!"

Seventy five enchanted arrows flew, and burst against the dragon's face and wings. It growled and readied a pulse of white flame in its throat.

Wyvernborn warriors leaped over the archers and arrowed their wings, dropping towards it with weapons ready to swing. Several buried axes and great swords into the dragon's face, others focused on its wings. The white jet of flame missed the wyvernborn ship, but the blast of heat was still searing, and some of the vessel's iron armour glowed red-hot.

Sandra set her stance as their craft began climbing quickly. The ship trembled and jerked as the dragon passed beneath it. She could hear the snap and shudder of the hull as the spikes smashed into them.

The hulking creature swept along the other side of them. The shamen on deck began glowing as they cast a barrier to catch the dragon's spiky tail. They knew how this kind of dragon, the *Felreev*, attacked its prey.

The tail swept up and drove downwards like a hammer, the bony spikes and club on the end swinging towards them.

The impact drove many of the shamen to the deck, but the barrier remained strong above them.

Through it, Sandra could behold the hell beast above the fleet, tearing the sections trying to hold it to pieces. With every blast of infernal blue flame, some of the shadow was lifted from its form, revealing bone and metal, swirling smoke as thick as vast bundles of cloth bunched around it. All three heads were engaging the ships, misshapen claws were striking out at them. The entity was a vast whirling dervish of claws, teeth and fire.

They didn't have time to linger. The three wyvernborn craft turned in formation. Warriors landed on the deck and archers repositioned. Sandra counted them off as she ran, noticeably fewer than there had been before. Barada was among their number, as were some of his best. His eyes met hers with relief, before they hardened again.

He started coming over to her, walking across the deck between the throngs of warriors being treated by the shamen.

The *Felreev* was coming around again, and the Orlin on the ship off their port side were loosing volleys at it, partially a dissuasion, partially an attempt to find a tender spot.

"Port side archers, volley fire!" Sandra ordered. They had harpoons aboard, enchantable, but it wasn't obvious to her that they would do any more damage than the cannons. Bursts of lightning, ice and flame were clattering against the dragon's armour plating.

Barada joined her beside the third top mast. "How is Zeta?"

"The shamen are staving off the effects of exhaustion, but they can do little for her otherwise. She won't be ready for flight for days."

Barada growled. "In all the hells … I need her out here …" He shook his head. "But it can't be helped. A damned *Felreev* of all the beasts…"

"Loose!" Sandra screamed at the archers. She and Barada watched as the force incantations burst against the ***Felreev's*** armour. It ignored the cloud of force energy, and dove, releasing a stream of dragonfire over their sister ship's deck.

Their barriers caught a good portion of the flame, but a third of it licked through. Screams of horror and agony filled the air. The dragonfire was soon extinguished, but the bustle on the top deck told her that a number of the warriors, archers and crewmen on deck had been killed.

"Tell me your fliers are wounding it, at least," Sandra whispered.

"***Shamen, enchant the arrows with ice!***" Barada bellowed in dragontongue. He took her hand. "We have axes and swords. We're cutting him, not slowing him down … yet."

His eyes were determined, and she kissed him on the side of the snout. A shaman shuffled to her and touched her quiver of arrows, murmuring to itself.

"Then let's not wait around for him to take us down first."

Barada bared his teeth in a grin and a growl of satisfaction. When they parted, they were all business again, giving bellowed orders to their warriors, keeping their hands steady and their hearts defiant.

***

"Bring us to a hover on the other side of the fissure," Kelad ordered. Saiyra drifted *Shadowblade* around, still sluggish from the damage to the rudder. He had a far better view of what was happening here. Seraphine, and a number of other Mages, were approaching the nearest totem to the *Sand Dancer's* landing site.

"All Mages, disembark here," Kelad ordered. *"You're under Seraphine's command. Tell her I sent you with my compliments."*

All of them looked at each other in confusion as they came up on deck. Saiyra frowned at him. The boldest among them jogged to the bridge across the ruined deck.

"General ... we don't want to abandon the Shadowblade. You'll be vulnerable without the barriers, and the generators ..."

Kelad raised an eyebrow and held up a hand. "*You seem to be mistaking our military for a democracy.*"

The Mage's mouth shut quickly, and he took a breath before speaking again, defiantly and firmly.

"*We're not abandoning you, sir.*"

Kelad smiled tightly and stepped forwards. He glanced upwards to make sure they weren't attracting any unpleasant and fiery attention. "*Listen to me, Chief. If I order you and the rest of them to stay ... I would be ordering you to die, and die needlessly.*"

He pointed to the totems around the fissure. "*Those are important enough that Seraphine, their equivalent of an Arch Mage, is studying them. They matter. The more magic lent to that cause, the better.*"

He grabbed the Mage's forearm. "*You're my crew. I'm responsible for your lives. If it's necessary for you and I to give our lives on this ship, then so be it, but that's my decision to make.*"

The chief sighed. "*I understand, General.*"

He saluted Kelad, who returned the gesture and clapped him on the shoulder. The General watched his crewmen as the word spread and they began to reluctantly disembark.

Only a skeleton crew of technicians and deckhands were aboard now, even the doctor had disembarked. The only nurses left were two that had no magic, and dealt in medicine rather than incantation.

"*There goes all of our combat capability,*" Saiyra muttered.

"*Let's hope that Seraphine uses them well. They're good Mages.*" He glanced at her. "*Set course for the carriers.*"

Shadowblade came about slowly, making for the rim of the battle zone and creeping around the edge. Slowly, they gained altitude, and picked up speed as the air thinned.

Kelad looked across at the titanic engagement. The agility of the dragons

The Empire Of Fire

weaving between the fleet was unbelievable. Creatures that large moving so quickly and so delicately, it made no sense to the eye or the mind. They were flying in tight circles around the sections of the fleet, incinerating ships with wide jets of flame.

His people were fighting fiercely. He saw a half dozen skiffs peppering one of the smaller dragons with cannonfire, close up, and they had boxed it in. The dragon breathed a jet of flame on one of them, and bit into another. While the two above increased their volume of fire, the two below rolled almost onto their side, and riddled the beast's chest and throat. It stuttered in the air, and the rest of the squadron swung around to finish it, releasing another volley. The dragon dropped, limp.

The battleships were fighting bloody battles of attrition all across the sky. More armour, but far slower, and the dragons were far more able to inflict damage on them. His and the Black Fleet's captains were engaging them in staggered ranks, pulling back when damaged, only to be replaced by another vessel with cannons firing. Kelad nodded his approval, but he knew it was only a matter of time before they were all too heavily damaged to put up any resistance. Cruisers swung around to flank the beasts in two ship charges on either side, yanking the attention of the dragons when battleships were repositioning.

Above them, the night had become a dancing inferno of chaos, as if suns and stars were fighting a war. The shadow-beast was tearing vessel after vessel apart on its own. In contrast to the rest of the dragons (if a dragon was even what it was), it wasn't moving. It simply hovered, entirely still, swatting ships with claw and bullwhip tail, or chomping down at them, or blasting through their barriers with three simultaneous jets of flame. The ships up there were all but doomed, but fought on regardless. Kelad battled with himself silently, wanting to order them to regroup, but knowing that their efforts were keeping the entire fleet being struck by it.

None seemed to be able to even get close, much less wound or kill it. There had been a hundred ships up there, almost. Now there were far, far fewer.

The carriers were lingering close to the Gravestone's western face, staying out of sight. Saiyra gritted her teeth and shook her head.

"*Sel, we're losing altitude, the generator is almost inert.*"

Kelad nodded and held up the communication stone. "*Carriers, this is Shadowblade. We are heavily damaged and requesting assistance.*"

The lead carrier flashed a signalling flare at them, and they began drifting lower. A docking frame had already been extended to receive them.

The two ships met in the air. Saiyra settled *Shadowblade* into the frame. A gangplank extended towards them and crewmen immediately began streaming over to extinguish remaining fires and take stock of the damage. The injured were being taken the other way onto the carrier, a myriad of burns, severed limbs, blunt force trauma and a number of dead. Kassaeos watched them silently, before holding up the communication stone again. "*All crew, proceed onto the carrier for medical attention and resupply. No exceptions.*"

He nodded to Saiyra, who seemed to have real trouble letting go of the wheel. She trudged with him across the gangplank, the last two to disembark. They were met by the carrier's captain, who saluted. "*General Kelad, it's an honour to meet you in person.*"

Kelad glared at her, and she swallowed.

"*Apologies, General. This isn't the time.*"

"*Estimated time to functional repairs?*"

The captain glanced at *Shadowblade*. "*My chief engineer would know better, but it could take hours to patch the hull and replace the cannons. Where are your Mages?*"

"*Indisposed. Please check and charge the generator as much as is possible. That is the priority, understood?*"

The captain's jaw worked, and she bobbed her head. "*As you wish, General.*"

"*That, and the rudder,*" he added quickly. "*The emergency sails should propel the vessel acceptably.*"

The captain hesitated again, but saluted him regardless. She began issuing orders immediately.

The top deck of the carrier was larger than the top deck of the *Sovereign*. The space was full of repair sheds and containers, triage tents and benches for people to rest on. Light and medium cannons lined the railing, offering an impressive field of fire. Throngs of medics, soldiers, sailors and repairmen were all over the place.

Saiyra was leaning over the railing nearest to the *Shadowblade's* prow. Kelad picked through the deck crew to reach her.

"*I'm told we're only the ninth ship to make it back here,*" she murmured. "*The first since the dragons came to the party. Everyone else is either dead or still fighting.*"

Kelad bobbed his head. "*There's a ... there's always a feeling that nestles in the gut, a question of whether or not one could have done more.*"

"*This is feeling like the chain around a hellhound's neck. We killed one, we could get more ...*"

Kelad nodded, with a wry smile. "*On a crippled ship, that might be a problem.*"

"*We should be fighting them with everything we have. We've risked it all.*"

Kelad glanced at Saiyra. "*Let me worry about who's being risked.*"

She turned to him and folded her arms. "*We swear to give our lives for Cael, if that's the price demanded.*"

"*And I won't demand that of you.*"

"*You demand it of the thousands of men you've thrown at that monster.*"

Kelad tapped his fingers against the railing. "*What would you have me do, Saiyra? All of this is to buy time, and the stakes are higher than even our great nation. Lives aren't something to be thrown away casually ...*"

Saiyra turned away, and he shook his head.

"*There is a burden to command. When you do this job for longer than you should, it only grows. I am too old. Too old for many things.*" He waited maddening minutes in silence while *Shadowblade* was patched up. He watched the repairs to the rudder especially, the cables that turned the port and starboard emergency sails. He stepped away, looking for the quartermaster.

The officer was a short, wiry man, meant for crawling through ducts and into narrow spaces. He had the callused hands of an experienced workman and engineer. When he caught the General's eye, he saluted, but didn't straighten up. Kelad smiled to himself, taking an instant liking to the man.

"*Quartermaster, is the carrier equipped with portable generators and connectors?*"

"*Plenty of them, sir.*"

"*Could you please install two beside the helm, and connect them to the main generator?*"

The quartermaster nodded to himself. "*Three might be better. Better to have too many, than not enough, 'specially if you're going where I think you're going.*"

Kelad nodded with a grin. "*Good man. How long might that take?*"

"*If I do it, no time at all.*"

Kelad nodded his thanks and patted him on his narrow shoulder. "*Make sure you're last off. When you're done, retract the ramp and clear the moorings.*"

The quartermaster narrowed his eyes at Kelad, but nodded. He straightened a little, then saluted. Kelad patted his shoulder again, then stepped back with a salute of his own.

He wandered next over to the lead medic, who was presiding over his wounded crewmen. The doctors and Mages were clustered around the injured in pairs, the Mages stabilising and cleaning the wounds, the doctors binding them and cleaning them with salves.

The medic saluted him immediately. The hood of her robe was pulled up over her head, masking the majority of her greying hair, but not her soft features around her nose and eyes. Kelad returned the salute. "*How are they?*"

"*Many are out of immediate danger, General. Some will be ready to return to duty in a few minutes.*"

The Empire Of Fire

Kelad's eyes flashed. "*Oh ... better they remain here. They should rest. I was wondering ... in lieu of their presence, can you spare any Mages?*"

The medic raised an eyebrow. "*How many, sir?*"

"*As many as possible.*"

She nodded slowly. "*For your generators and your cannons?*"

"*Never you mind what they're for.*"

She swallowed. "*Well, I can certainly spare a dozen at least from the reserve crews. Perhaps two dozen.*"

"*Two dozen would be preferable. Have them inform the quartermaster that they are embarking Shadowblade on my order, and that his orders have not changed.*"

The medic saluted. "*Is there a message you want conveyed to your crew?*"

"*Live long and live well.*"

The medic nodded and saluted again.

Kelad watched the engineers working as he padded back across the carrier's deck to Saiyra.

"*All that 'Queen' talk was just words, wasn't it,*" she muttered.

"*What's brought that on?*"

She smiled bitterly. "*My impending death.*"

Kelad leaned over the railing, and edged over until he was a hair's breadth away from her. "*I wish it weren't so. Like I said ... I'm old.*"

"*I know how many you've bedded. I've never been under any delusions.*"

"*Nor should you be. You deserve far better than a lecherous old fool. Perhaps someone who has spent less time in death's company.*"

Technicians and Mages were coming back across from *Shadowblade*, being replaced by the quartermaster's men. The rudder was all but repaired, or so it seemed. The quartermaster himself was at the bridge, leaning over the equipment he had brought. Three large cubes, nearly three feet long and wide on all sides, were arrayed near the helm. His arcane technicians were laying and clamping steel and leather cables to the remainder of the top deck.

The ship was still a mess. Her pride had been hurt a little, but not obliterated.

He slipped an arm around Saiyra's waist in the silence, and she made no move to resist or deny him. They watched the repairs as they were conducted and checked.

"*I should like my regrets to be expressed to the Orlin,*" Kelad murmured. "*If any remain alive, to the Taeba clansmen also. I took large and unforgivable part in the destruction of both. I as good as wiped out a generation of both, or more. Apologies serve no purpose for that kind of crime.*"

Saiyra frowned at him. "*I can't really comment on that, Sel ... if you were looking for my opinion.*"

The quartermaster looked up at Kelad from the bridge, and patted the rest of his people on the back to dismiss them. He began checking the repairs that had been conducted.

Kelad turned his head to Saiyra. She was looking at him in a searching way, her beautiful, cocoa coloured eyes scrutinising his own.

He smiled at her. "*It was a request.*"

"*You ...*" Saiyra frowned at him. "*It was a different time, different circumstances. You were ...*"

"*... following orders,*" Kelad finished. "*Yes, we were at war. Certainly, I never set the rules of engagement. Perhaps, we needed the land in Taeba to farm, and the supply lines from Verna. There are a hundred military and political officials that could justify those actions until they were blue in the face. Both times, I should have had the strength to say no.*"

The quartermaster nodded and strode across the gangway and back onto the carrier. Immediately he hoisted the plank away. He had four other men untying the mooring ropes.

Kelad lightly kissed Saiyra on the lips, and shifted. He reappeared on *Shadowblade's* bridge, and cranked the elevation lever, whipping the wheel around to bank out of the docking web.

There were a number of cries and protests from the carrier, that were

The Empire Of Fire

quickly lost in the high winds and the distant sounds of cannonfire. Kelad took a deep breath, and pointed the ship's nose towards the fissure.

***

A chilling heat bled from the vast crack in the mountainside. The feeling it inspired within Seraphine was nothing less that a barely concealed menace, a coiled set of muscles on a wolf ready to pounce.

Seraphine nodded across to the Caelish Mages on the other side of the fissure. They were beginning to fan out, running as fast as they could towards the totems that had been erected on either side. She herself strode towards the nearest one.

There were half a dozen lining both edges of the fissure. They were taller than a four storey house, oblong, and made of a black stone that bore the shine of obsidian. Each caught and reflected the glow of the aerial battle above. In the intense fire coming from the scores of burning wrecks all around them, they seemed to be even blacker than the usual material, until the fire was directly behind. Then they seemed to be almost translucent, giving off a dark green glow that softly shone through the polished and sculpted rock.

The closer she came to it, the more resistance she felt. It was as if there was a fish hook in her back, tugging her backwards with every forward step, slowly but surely getting stronger.

Her eyes began to water.

Trevor, who was grunting in pain, held out a hand to her. She took it, and began to channel her power to a point in front of her, a drill bit to cut her way through the field ahead of them. Jack planted a hand on her back as well, channelling his own power to aid her.

While the fish hook remained, Seraphine found there was suddenly a lot more slack in the line. She took five more steps forwards, then another five, taking the approach a small chunk at a time. Behind them, Trevor was dragging a portable generator on a wheeled trolley, as well as a barrier amplifier. They would need it if they were to focus properly on the totem once they were close, yet the thing they still needed most was information. With all three feeding power into the incantation, they made good progress. Still, by the time they were within touching distance, all three were breaking out in a sweat, and their gauntlets were growing hot.

"Trevor ... the generator."

Trevor touched his hand to the top of the cube and sent a pulse of energy into it to get it going. The barrier amplifier, a spherical metal device with quarter-inch long indents evenly spaced along the surface, began to hum. The air rippled around the three Mages, and the resistance in the air slowly reduced. It remained there, just in the background, as if they were standing close to an oven.

"Everyone alright?" Jack said, getting his breath back.

Trevor wiped his brow and nodded. Seraphine was already peering closely at the totem. There were runes all over it, carved in large script on each face. She recognised the construction of the Caelish Magus Towers; they had definitely been put here by the Arch Mages. Concealment runes to keep the fissure from any prying eyes. Nullification runes to stop magic being used in the vicinity. Barrier runes in case someone found a way through. Curses if all else failed.

"Be very careful," Seraphine muttered.

"Yes, I see them," Jack said with a nod. He reached out with a small scalpel, with a long whalebone handle. He gently scraped it along the surface of the totem, and withdrew it.

"They're all warded," Trevor said as he wiped his face again. "That's the big issue we had getting close."

"Wards are breakable," Seraphine said defiantly. "We've come too far to be stopped by them."

"You say that, and I believe it, but we'll need more Mages down here." Trevor glanced upwards. "Before it's too late…"

The Empire Of Fire

Seraphine turned to one of the Mages on the periphery of the wards, and raised her voice. "Contact General Kelad, tell him we will need more support!"

As the others nodded in response, Jack hummed to himself. "Very interesting ... these totems are not made of obsidian."

Trevor folded his arms. "How do you know?"

Jack held up the scalpel blade. It was clean, but slightly bent. "Obsidian would have left a black residue on a blade this well crafted, and certainly wouldn't have bent it. No ... this is some form of latticed crystal, similar to diamond."

Seraphine stroked her chin. "But obsidian is the only material with this hue."

"Yes ... it's ... I suspect it's astralum. Very rare. I've never seen this much in one block, let alone in twelve of them."

Seraphine focused a barrier within herself and reached out a hand to touch it. It was so smooth it was almost like laying her hand on a pond's surface.

A boiling pond.

She whipped her hand away with a hiss. "Damn. Astralum, likely layered with diamond for structural strength from the elements."

Astralum was a stone that served as a natural store and conductor of magical energy. It was very rare, only found on the ocean floor, as far as Seraphine was aware. It was not black or dark green naturally, it typically glowed with a cyan hue. "Has it been corrupted somehow?"

"I suspect so," Jack muttered. "With brute force."

Seraphine folded her arms. "I suppose with a powerful enough incantation..."

"It would've burned out a Mage, even a powerful one, even with our most powerful amplifiers." Trevor shook his head. "It's not possible. It's not even conceivable," Jack said tersely, pacing across the rock. "But, of course, it happened."

"So how was it done?" Seraphine snapped. "We don't have time for this."

Jack considered for a moment. "The only thing with the power to do something on this scale ... was Ydra, your necromancer."

Seraphine stopped. "That wasn't her ... but I think you're right. It was the thing inside of her, feeding off her power, and controlling her, and her army. Its power was limited, though, based on every account of the engagement."

Jack paced again, this time more swiftly, tapping his fingers against his chin. "How much do you two know about necromancy?"

"Barely anything," Trevor muttered.

"Some things, I suppose, based on the conversations I had with Ydra, and based on research and accounts."

"How many corpses could she raise by herself?"

Seraphine thought back to Vash. "It must have been a thousand, but she was augmented by something else, an artifact."

Jack hummed to himself. "It raised at least twenty thousand in the Pil Valley, and that was a weakened version of the same power. It could still raise them again, but you and two others interfered. The thing is, I still don't think that's enough to corrupt and break through all of these totems. They're meant to be nigh on unbreakable."

"So how did it happen?"

Trevor looked around the totem, right at the edge of the barrier. "Let's move around this thing and get a better look."

The trio moved the generator around with them, studying all four sides of the totem. The side they had been studying had been unique. It was the only one missing a certain rune near the top.

"Can you see that?" Jack said, squinting upwards.

Trevor nodded. "It's a form of communication rune. Not woven in the usual way, it's similar to the ones we use on long-distance amplifiers."

Seraphine looked around at the other totems. They seemed to have matching runes at the top. "We need to see the ones at either end. I have a theory."

The Empire Of Fire

She squinted across at the other side of the fissure. The Caelish Mages were spread out along the totems, beginning to study them in groups of four. She focused on one at the totem on the western edge, and sent out a tether to speak to them.

"Can you hear me?"

The figure stopped walking.

"I am Seraphine, on the other side of the chasm. Do you speak Haaman?"

"Yes," came the hesitant reply. A man approaching middle age, judging by his voice.

"There are variations of a communications rune at the top of three sides of our totem. Are they on three sides of yours?"

"Wait a moment. I will look."

She waited, tapping her foot on the rock. The tether remained open between them.

The voice filled her head again. *"The rune is on two sides."*

Seraphine nodded to herself. "Facing other totems?"

"Yes."

"Thank you." She retracted the tether and turned to Trevor and Jack. "Those runes link these totems together. They combine their power to maintain the incantations."

Jack beamed. "A network, eh? Very innovative, especially for almost a century ago." He nodded to himself. "That also means that the network could have been used to break through, like jimmying open the back door, if you pardon the analogy."

Seraphine sighed. "One was corrupted, and the corruption spread through the rest of the totems."

"Exactly. What's more, this corruption doesn't have to be maintained. The astralum does it itself."

Seraphine tapped her chin. "Can we use the network to lift the corruption?"

Jack frowned. "Maybe. We need all of our people here. We may even need more Mages."

Seraphine glanced up at the war raging above their heads. "Get those Caelish Mages over here. We'll see what we can do."

***

Thomas could see the totems ahead of them, softly glowing. The fissure was a band of shadow cleaving the rock in two. He had a decent measure of his power back, meditation was coming to him a lot easier, but he still had to close his eyes to maintain it.

The rock face around them was littered with debris. He had felt the flame on his face the entire way across the barren ground beneath the battle. The clashing forces were still furiously throwing themselves against each other, and hadn't abated. The longer it went on, the more splintering booms of crashing airships there were, and no sounds at all of falling dragons.

They weren't invincible, though. One was dead, he and his friends had worked together to kill it. They were five warriors on the ground. The fleet were more than capable of doing damage with all that firepower. It was the thought that had fuelled his hope and maintained his focus.

Now they were almost at the end. He could feel it in his bones.

The *Sand Dancer* was nowhere to be seen, likely it had rejoined the fray. The small Caelish airship that had probably come from Vehnek's *Inquisitor* sat between two totems, empty. There were a cluster of Mages near one of the central totems, but giving it a wide berth.

He recognised Seraphine, Jack, Trevor, and the rest of the group that had been carried on the *Sand Dancer*. A group of airmen, wearing the uniforms of the Caelish Aerial Navy, were also conferring with them.

Seraphine jogged out to meet Ironclad and the others as they approached. Thomas hopped off Ironclad's back as she embraced Kassaeos tightly, and proffered swift hugs to the rest. "We're making progress here, we think."

The Empire Of Fire

Thomas looked over at the Caelish crewmen, then nodded to the runabout. "Did they come down on that?"

Seraphine shook her head with a grimace. "Kelad's ship dropped them off. That's a Black Fleet ship."

Thomas glanced at the fissure, and began channelling battle incantations into his hands.

"Any sign of the crew?" Ember muttered.

"A Mage and a pilot, both dead." Seraphine's face was even more grim than before. "They're little more than ... mush. Every bone in their bodies is broken beneath the skin."

Ember and Thomas stared at her, and then the small ship. Bassai growled, and Kassaeos raised an eyebrow.

"Where's the *Sand Dancer*?" the assassin asked calmly.

"Making a run to the carriers. We need more Mages ... a lot more. More generators too."

Ironclad nodded. "And the battle?"

"Two more dragons have been brought down, but far more of our fleet."

"I can stay and help if you need the extra hand," Thomas cut in.

Seraphine smirked. "And rob The Four Guardians of one of their number? No, you're better served with them. They'll need you."

"Vehnek's here, he must be," Ironclad muttered.

"Mora too," Thomas added. "I'd bet my house on her killing those crewmen ... if I had a house."

"What about these?" Bassai growled, jerking a blade around at the totems.

"They've been corrupted ... maybe by Mora, but she was never this powerful. The only thing that is, or rather was, is what possessed Ydra."

Thomas looked around at her in alarm. "We didn't destroy it, we just pushed it out of Ydra's head."

Seraphine nodded, and looked upwards, right at the shadowy monster above them, incinerating battleships with azure tongues of fire. "I've had that feeling since we crossed the desert, and it has grown and grown the closer we've gotten to the mountain, to the fissure."

Thomas could feel it too. It was filling his mind now they were beside the fissure. The scar on his neck was sore, and trying to strangle his voice. "What does it feel like to you?" he managed.

Seraphine shuddered. "It feels cold ... like ice down my spine."

"That's what I feel as well ... but through the scar. It's like an imprint Mora left on me ... or whatever is inside her left on me..."

Ember nocked an arrow. "She won't be happy to see us, you know."

Thomas stared at the fissure. The cold feeling in him was radiating from down there. "She doesn't need to see us. She knows we're here."

From behind them, a roar pierced the night. Two more answered it, roars of unemotional pain, like a long, drawn out groan.

They had a panoramic view of the slope of the Gravestone from where they stood. There were so many wrecks strewn over it that the mountain seemed to be catching fire. There were a few survivors from the crashes moving around the area, bolting for shelter or heading towards the fissure. All of them were running far faster than they had been.

Three dragon corpses were slumped among the rock and debris. They were far apart, miles apart ... and all three were moving.

They clawed themselves to their feet, their broken bodies snapping. All three let out another roar, and Thomas's heart stopped. It was the same timbre, the same blank agony, that came from the mouth of a ghoul.

"How did Vehnek and Mora get down into the fissure?" Ember snapped.

Thomas tore his eyes from the monsters ripping themselves from death's clutches. He scanned around the edge of the fissure, before Bassai grabbed his arm and pointed to the runabout.

"There. Climbing ropes."

Three coils were anchored onto the small ship, and disappeared down into the void. Thomas nodded. "Let's go."

He turned to the rest. All of them were focused on Ironclad, who was staring at the dragons.

"Come on, Tobias," Ember urged, pulling on his hand.

"What do you see?" Thomas asked, stepping in front of him.

Ironclad said nothing for a moment. "It's the same energy. The same."

"The same as what?"

"From the Pil Valley. Coming from the fissure. It's the same!"

The three dead dragons, as one, took to the air without a sound, aside from the swoosh of their wings.

Ironclad turned away from them swiftly. "Let's move!"

32

The Four Guardians and Kassaeos waited on the edge of the chasm, carefully scanning the shadows for any movement. Everything was still.

Ironclad took a hold of one of the Caelish climbing ropes for himself, after testing to make sure it would hold his weight, and not drag the runabout into the cavern. Bassai and Ember quickly planned to use another in tandem, and Thomas and Kassaeos took up the last one.

Bassai insisted on taking the lead in, and Kassaeos nodded. "I can shift down next to you when you touch the ground."

"We should be as quiet as possible," Ember muttered. "How's it coming, Thomas?"

His gauntlets were glowing, and he nodded. "We should be shielded from anyone's notice, but I wouldn't bet on us staying hidden for long when we get close."

"As long as it stops us being picked off on the rope," she muttered.

"In theory, it will reduce our profile enough not to be spotted, or Mora will just take no notice of us. I'm afraid I'm the thing that she's most likely to spot. If Seraphine and I can sense her, she can sense us." Thomas shuddered, and glanced down into the blackness. "She knows that we're up here, and she's likely waiting for us."

"Oh, good," Ember snorted. Ironclad watched her move her bow around so it was in reach, and flex her fingers. Thomas was channelling his energy and was ready for whatever may come. Bassai was, as he always was before a battle, a knot of coiled muscle waiting to snap. Kassaeos paced along the lip of the fissure, looking down.

The Empire Of Fire

Ironclad looked down into the darkness. He could see two huge sources of energy bleeding into the air, both equally strong. One was moving, the other wasn't. He could barely see them through a swirling black cloud of smoke spinning ten yards below the lip.

The warmth of his axe was a comfort, keeping him calm. The effect of it was nowhere near as intoxicating as it had been before. Clearly some work had been done on the enchantment, or perhaps the change was inside him somewhere. His hands felt like flesh and blood, it seemed all the better to help his grip, the way the weight shifted when he swung it. His fingertips brushed over the crest between the blades.

He looked up at his friends. They were all watching him now, waiting for the word to be given.

He tightened his grip on the rope, and nodded.

Bassai and Thomas began climbing downwards. A second later, Ember, Kassaeos and Ironclad set off.

The walls of the fissure were completely vertical and almost completely smooth from weathering. There were deep, rough claw marks all over the surface on either side, from the dragons digging their way to the surface. As they passed through the spiral covering, the fissure became visible to Ironclad's eyes.

Derelict scientific equipment was all over the wide, dusty pit. There were beakers and portable laboratories, cots and tents, crates full of books and testing equipment. The same grey and brown film of dirt covered all of it. The people studying the dragon bones had left in a hurry, and left long ago, probably due to some urgent political crisis between Cael and one of its neighbours. In among the flotsam, all over the bottom were rocks, pebbles and entire boulders kicked up by the ancient beasts that had been ripped back to life. A little cover for their approach, Ironclad thought.

They would land a few hundred yards from the energy sources at the bottom. As Ironclad studied them, the one still moving abruptly disappeared from his sight.

The climb downwards continued, the rest oblivious to what had happened. "Faster," Ironclad hissed to them. The urgency among them caused them all to double their pace.

They were around halfway down into the darkness when there was a flash of movement above Ironclad's head. It was a shadow moving within a shadow. All three ropes snapped.

There was a sickening lurch as Ironclad dropped like a rock. There was a popping sound from somewhere close by. Ember cried out, Bassai snarled in anger. Thomas and Kassaoes made no sound at all.

The ground began rushing up at them, and the two figures picking themselves up at the bottom. One of them thrust his glowing hands upwards, and a cushion of air blasted underneath Ironclad. His fall was slowed enough for him to land heavily on his feet.

Bassai and Ember landed deftly beside him. Thomas lowered his hands, and sighed with relief. He glanced around at Kassaeos. "Thanks for the catch."

The assassin held up a finger, and motioned them all to get lower. They all crouched behind the rocks, without making a sound.

Nothing moved in the dust and shadow. Ironclad could still not see the magic user, who he was now certain was Mora.

He saw Ember glance back at the ropes that had fallen to the ground behind them, and then squinted upwards through the darkness. "I need your eyes, big guy."

"No, you don't. They were cut."

"Those ropes were woven metal cable."

Ironclad nodded. "I know. Anyone picking anything up?"

Bassai was completely still, nostrils flared. "Burned flesh. Blood…" He shook his head slightly. "Old bones, dried scales … and a woman. Old perfume, wearing new silks. No sweat."

Thomas swallowed. "I can't sense anyone apart from the one, unmoving source a few hundred yards away."

"I could see her from the ropes, but she cut me off," Ironclad muttered.

The Empire Of Fire

"No movement," Kassaeos whispered.

Ironclad could verify that much. He couldn't see anything, apart from the magic up ahead bleeding from something he couldn't quite make out due to the force of it.

"I can't see much," Ember whispered. "Four sets of tracks, I think, but the dragons kicked up a lot of dirt and dust."

"Four sets of tracks and three ropes." Ironclad shook his head. He could still hear the battle far above, and new sound of droning death had joined the fray.

"Let's go, we can't afford to wait. Kassaeos, up front with me. Ember and Thomas behind me directly, Bassai as rearguard."

The five edged through the rocks and began crossing through the wreckage left by the scientists and researchers. Kassaeos stayed within ten yards of Ironclad, his weapons held loosely in his hands. They stepped over anything that could have made any noise: pebbles, broken glass or thin splinters of wood.

It was obvious where the dragons had been. Great clods of dust and compacted rock fragments had been displaced by claws and tails. Dark patches of old blood stained the flat stone patches that remained. The disturbed ground truly gave a comparison for how massive the monsters truly were.

The carcasses had been lined up alongside either wall of the fissure for study, not piled, but arranged with care. Even with the creatures on either side, there was a comfortable pathway for them to stride down. More worryingly, there was no cover anywhere.

"Hate this," Ember whispered.

Ironclad cast his eyes over as much of the space as he could, including behind them. "Thomas, anything?"

He shook his head. "Not a thing."

"Bassai?"

The wyvernborn growled. "Within a hundred feet. The scent is stronger."

Ironclad drew his shield in close to his body. "Where?"

"Difficult to say. The smell is all around us. There is ... something else. Rot, I think. The smell of what is ahead of us is overpowering it."

Ironclad turned his attention to the pathway ahead. Now that they were closer, he could make out some of the outline of the shape casting the incredible amount of magic. It seemed to be a figure, arms and legs stretched out, knees weak, head thrown back with the throat exposed.

Ironclad signalled to Kassaeos. "Can you make out anything about that?"

"I can get closer if you want." The assassin's footfalls were so quiet that even Ironclad's ears could barely register them. His mouth had only slightly moved when he spoke.

Ironclad almost took him up on the offer. "No. No, stay close. If Mora's down here, and close, splitting us up would benefit a surprise attack."

Kassaeos barely nodded.

"Spread out a little," Ironclad murmured. "Five yards apart. Ember, Bassai, switch positions."

The group repositioned, and continued on. Ironclad listened as Bassai sniffed the air behind him. Suddenly, he let out a very quiet growl. There was a pause, before Thomas's voice filled Ironclad's head.

"Bassai says she's behind us. I told Ember already."

Ironclad nodded, and kept his pace as unchanged as he could. The tension in his body was heightened, and almost human. The enchantment in the axe was giving him nerves that his mind could play with, puppeteer and play tricks on. The closer they walked to the figure in the middle of the fissure, the more it seemed to be wracked in agony, frozen in the middle of a death so violent that its limbs were twisted and stretched, the back broken and leaning backwards over its heels at an impossible angle.

"See that slag around the feet?" Kassaeos muttered.

Ironclad nodded. It looked like melted metal, alloys running together like a badly whisked egg. "It's no statue ... you recognise him or her?"

"The metal is Caelish steel, the marbling looks like gold and platinum. It's a Lord Marshal's armour."

The Empire Of Fire

They were ten feet away from him now. Vehnek was completely unrecognisable. His skin was black as coal, and tight around his shrunken skeleton. His eyes had been burned out, the sockets wide in horror. His mouth was fixed open in a scream. Some of his armour had fused to his skin, the rest was in the puddle around his feet.

"Gods above ..." Thomas whispered. Bassai and Ember turned back the way they came, and kept watch for Mora.

"What do you make of it?"

Thomas grimaced and coughed as he came close, his eyes watering. "The smell is ... acrid. Like burned hair and eichor, and sulphur."

"The smell is beside the point."

"I know ... but it's as if the body is being transfigured. Vehnek is being used as a channel, his soul, not his body. Its like a focusing lens ... or a prism, allowing light to become visible."

Ironclad nodded. "So Mora used Vehnek to focus the incantation that raised the dragons?"

"I think a better word is 'sacrificed'." Thomas shuddered.

"Can you do anything about it?"

Thomas circled Vehnek quickly, his face turning white.

"No. No ... there's nothing I can do. In order to dispel it ... we'd need to do what we did with Ydra ... but I don't know if there's any way I could get into Mora's head alone. The incantation running through Vehnek is too strong."

"Cutting it off at the source," Kassaeos muttered with an approving nod. "Now it's just a matter of finding the source ... or letting her find us. Hard to believe she betrayed him. Figured it would go the other way."

"It did."

Ember drew her arrow back, eyes searching the darkness. Bassai growled, and ignited his sabres, his head turning left and right. The voice had come from all around them.

"He betrayed Mora. He wanted to do it twice."

Thomas shook his head at Ironclad, still unable to sense anything.

Kasseaos was simply waiting, his senses attuned to everything around him, a still rock of calm. Ironclad's eyes could still see nothing but the near-blinding glow coming from Vehnek's corpse.

"When you build your grand palaces, the insects that infest the soil are in your way, and you care nothing for them. You sweep them away without a thought. Entire generations, gone in a moment."

Bassai sniffed the air and one of his fingers slowly gestured out to his left. As Ember turned an ear to face the same direction, Ironclad faced his shield towards whatever it was they were about to engage. Was it even something they could face?

"Your fleet burns. Your allies are dying. Your green fields are burning, your forests curling in the heat. All that will remain are the ashes, and out of those ashes of your world, mine will rise."

"Now!" Ironclad hissed.

Thomas sent out a wide wave of force from his hands. Ember loosed her arrow.

There was no reaction to the wave, but the arrow halted in the air, spun around, and flew back towards Ember. Bassai leaped forwards and blocked it with the shield on his forearm. The force enchantment burst, and blasted them both backwards, sprawling into the dust.

Kasssaeos sent a bolt towards her, and shifted away at an angle as it came back towards him. Once he reappeared he shot another, and this one slid through and burst apart in a flash of enchanted fire. In the flare, Mora was illuminated, cloaked in shadow, surrounded by jet black tendrils that were coming out of her fingers.

Thomas sent bolts of lightning towards her, as Ironclad advanced. The bolts slammed against the tendrils, that rose up to protect the figure at their core.

A blood red beam of unstable, chaotic energy sliced through the stale air towards Thomas, who brought up a shield to block it with both hands. Ironclad charged as the Mage was knocked backwards, but managed to stay on his feet.

The Empire Of Fire

Tendrils whipped towards Kassaeos, who shifted back away, but more of them were tracking his movements, as if they were anticipating him.

Another few whipped towards Ironclad. He batted one away with his shield, while another snaked around his wrist. He chopped down with the axe immediately. There was a flash of light, and the tentacle was severed.

Two more were moving in, but they seemed to hesitate, just for a moment. It didn't last long enough for him to capitalise. He dodged one, but the other grabbed for the axe, while a third found his weapon arm. He couldn't believe how strong they were, they could hold him near immobile no matter how much he strained.

With a flash of green flame and a snarl, one of Bassai's sabres passed through the tendril around his wrist. More closed in on them both, and they hacked through them with blade and axe. An arrow whistled past them, and burst against a few of the tendrils. They rippled, but barely moved otherwise. The response was another red beam from Mora's palm. Ironclad stretched out to block it, and it struck him with such force that he flipped in the air and crashed to the ground.

The ward on his shield held firm, but there was a singe on the metal, as if a blacksmith's poker had struck it. Bassai was a whirl of green flame and steel as he defended Ironclad. He managed to get back to his feet, and the wyvernborn repositioned back beside him.

Ironclad glanced around. Ember was in place beside Thomas, who was casting a barrier around them both. Black tendrils slapped against it, and a red pulse cast the light blue bubble into a scarlet and purple crackle. Kassaeos moved around the wide space, running, leaping and smoke-shifting, anything he could to open a little room for a crossbow shot. The tentacles were keeping up with him easily, swiftly cutting off paths and boxing him in. The bolts of fire did nothing to dissuade or damage them, and when he did find a gap to slip a shot through, it was fired right back at him.

"Kassaeos, over here!" Thomas shouted. The assassin began to shift over.

"We should give her something to think about," Bassai growled.

Ironclad nodded. "Forwards!"

The pair advanced through the tendrils, sweeping past them with strikes and slices. They chopped through them, their enchanted weapons making a huge dent in her defenses. Slowly, Mora's head turned towards them. Her eyes were shadows on a face already cast in darkness.

More tentacles came towards them like serpents. Some flash froze suddenly as Thomas's incantations struck them, though they quickly began to crack through the ice and thaw. Ironclad heard an arrow and a bolt whistle through the dust choked air and burst, coating several of them with more ice.

Ironclad and Bassai raced through the gap. They leapt over tentacles that tried to swing at their legs, and chopped through others closing in on them. As far as they seemed to get, there were always more of the twisting black bullwhips in their way. Mora was walking backwards, stepping away to allow for her hellish appendages to reposition and attack.

Ironclad could see her now. She seemed to be looking at him, and at Thomas's group at the same time. Her hair was wild, and the fabric of her robes was floating around her arms and legs. Her skin was almost glowing in the low light, her pallor almost light blue, catching the swimming auroras above them.

Suddenly, a wave of darkness burst from Mora's chest. It raced through the tendrils, right at them.

Ironclad stepped in front of Bassai and raised his shield. The wyvbernborn tucked himself in directly behind the shield and sheathed his blades.

It felt as if a tidal wave washed over them both. It was boiling hot and ice cold at the same time. The next thing they knew, they were being pounded into the ground, as if a giant stone hammer was crashing down upon them.

Ironclad looked around quickly. Thomas, Ember and Kassaeos were down. As he pushed himself to his feet, everything went black.

He was conscious still, and aware, and cold. He looked around and tried to move. The darkness was thick, like tar or treacle.

He could see none of his friends, and hear them only distantly. Wherever they had been kicked to, sound was all but sucked away. What cries and confusion escaped the smothering were nearly drowned out by the overwhelming ambience in the realm.

There were whispers from all around him, in a language he couldn't understand or even comprehend. They were near and far, in his ear and miles away. The twisted, alien words were punctuated by slurping sounds and eager hissing, as if billions of creatures were sprinting towards a dinner bell.

Ironclad's mind raced for some logic. He seemed to be floating, but he could feel solid ground beneath his feet. As he took a step forwards, testing the ground, he heard a hiss, and felt his greaves burn. There was a sour chemical smell, like his armour was being bleached or polished with something corrosive. The hot oil in his body was starting to freeze. The metal was acting as a thin barrier that the chill was penetrating easily.

His next slow step was even more of a struggle, and he felt slippery things dancing across his armour, leaving burning chemical lines along the metal.

The next step wouldn't come. He was rooted to the spot, his joints seizing. He let out a grunt, and dropped to one knee. The swarm closed in on him.

***

The first of the emergency generators coughed, and Kelad kicked the second one to life. He said nothing to any of the Mages on deck, even as *Shadowblade* dipped lower and stuttered. The crippled skiff stabilised her height, but remained listing to port by a few degrees.

She was heavy in the wheel, but kept going defiantly. Kelad was flying on a wide course, around the periphery of the battle overhead. Another dragon was falling, one of the big, armoured ones ... but as he watched, the limp body jerked and twitched. Kelad squinted at it through his spyglass.

It was struggling and thrashing with something ... with itself. There were chunks of flesh and bone, and rivulets of blood falling around it. It had been gravely wounded, perhaps mortally, yet it was moving as if it was enraged, full of life.

Kelad was almost fooled into thinking it was the beast's death throes, but then the wings spread wide and caught the air. It banked around and began to climb.

Kelad pulled back from the spyglass. When he did, he could see the three dragons below it. He could see Razorback, spiralling higher.

He beat his hand against the wheel. Hope was draining from him, what little had ever been there. He had allowed it in to poison his cold, hard reality, the reality in which he thrived.

He kicked the third generator to life, and *Shadowblade* straightened and quickened. The ship became lighter and caught the air more cleanly.

He had a clear view of the fissure, minutes away at the skiff's current speed. There were flashing bolts of light coming from the darkness. Mora had been engaged.

Ahead of him, the *Sand Dancer* was floating above the ground and dropping off Mages. He grinned. *"Great minds think alike, eh?"*

He glanced up. Of the two fleets, numbering nearly a thousand ships, he estimated between five and six hundred remained. The shadowy, undead leviathan floating above them had almost chewed through every ship he had sent up there to delay it.

He swallowed the knot of guilt in his throat, but it only settled in his heart. He grabbed the communication stone in his belt and squeezed it, gathering his nerve.

"Seraphine, this is Kelad."

"I can barely hear you, General." Her voice was quiet as a whisper.

"More Mages are coming your way. Where do you want them dropped off?"

"How many?" Seraphine asked urgently.

The Empire Of Fire

"*Twenty five, I believe.*"

"*Good, good. Given the situation above, it'll have to be enough.*"

"*Agreed.*"

"*Set down on our side of the fissure. The others you dropped have been ferried over. We have a plan, but it requires power and focus.*"

"*Understood. I'll be there in … two minutes. Fill me in once I arrive.*"

He held the stuttering *Shadowblade* steady as the totems and the dragons' graveyard drew closer.

***

Ember screamed as another burn lanced across her back. She couldn't open her eyes, whenever she did the pain was too much to bear, as if her eyeballs were freezing in their sockets. She moved as fast as she could, her light steps dancing across the ground beneath her.

She couldn't breathe, there was no air around her, and the stale air in her lungs was blown out every time she opened her mouth. Swift movement, and endurance, had kept her prosperous in the Orlin Forest and alive in every battle she had fought in. Even though the void around her was oppressive and cloying, she was pushing through it as nimbly as if she were leaping between tightly spaced tree trunks.

The warmth of sunlight was close to her. No light came with it, either the void was swallowing it or the entire experience was an illusion in the dark. But she could feel it was Thomas, his shield bleeding into the realm they had been banished to.

The hissing and slurping and maddening whispers got no quieter. Ember wasn't fleeing from anything, just moving through a crowd, reaching appendages out to brush her as she shoved by.

The cold was making her arms and legs numb. She could no longer feel her fingers. She could feel moisture being drawn from her cheeks and freezing, burning. Her saliva was freezing on her tongue with every attempt at an inward breath, that her panicking brain screamed for even though there was nothing to breathe.

Her mind was beginning to swim, the links that let her control her body with ease were beginning to shut down.

Ember stumbled. Her grace was being leeched from her. She took more steps, barely feeling the whipping, burning lashes the surrounding creatures were leaving on her body. Lights were madly dancing across the blackness in front of her.

She could no longer tell which way was up or down. It seemed like the ground had vanished from beneath her feet.

She realised suddenly that she was falling forwards. She was barely conscious as her cheek hit the dusty floor of the fissure.

The realisation dawned that air was brushing against her face, and she opened her mouth to suck it in. Her shrunken lungs inflated with a jab of pain.

She grunted and blinked around, her blurred vision getting clearer. She was in the chasm, where she and the others had been. The light hurt her eyes, even though it was night.

Ember looked behind her. Her eyes widened.

She was half in and half out of a jet black sphere. The circumference was a rippling line, curving and bending the world around it like she was looking at a curved mirror. The surface of the sphere was unblemished, like highly polished glass.

She crawled forwards, and felt something wrap around her ankle. It wrenched and dragged her backwards. She took a deep breath and held it as she was plunged back into the blackness.

The sudden cold kicked her in the chest, and the breath almost cascaded out of her. She kicked out with her other leg and stamped on the thing stuck to her ankle, muscular like an octopus's tentacle. It held its grip, and she stamped again and again until it finally loosened.

She drove her feet into the ground and sprang forwards.

The Empire Of Fire

Ember exploded out of the sphere and rolled. Her arms and legs were still numb, disconnected from her body. She fumbled with her bow, begging her fingers to obey. She had no hope with her arrows at all. She only had eight left, from a quiver of fifty.

Rolling behind a boulder, she took a look at the battlefield.

Mora's hands were wide, her tendrils waving around the sphere. The thing was huge, a hundred yards across. It made no sense to Ember's eyes. It had leeched into the ground, risen up into the air, a perfect, unblemished shape. Outside of it she could hear none of the horror within, and could see none of her friends.

She flexed her fingers, tingling as feeling started returning to her limbs. Along with it came the burning pain.

She gritted her teeth around a leather strap holding her quiver. On her forearms there were rippling red burns covered in weeping blisters. Breath snorted through her nose like she was a bull preparing for a charge, trying desperately to keep her pain silent.

From the quiver she snatched three of her eight arrows, and pinned them between her palm and the wood of her Orlin bow. The adrenaline of pain was buzzing through her body.

She sprang to her feet, and nocked the first arrow. As soon as the balls of her feet touched the dust she drew it back and loosed it.

Mora's deep black eyes snapped towards her. As the first arrow halted in the air, Ember nocked the other two and drew them back. The first spun around and whistled back towards her as she loosed the pair.

Ember dropped to the ground as the arrow passed over her. Mora stopped one of the two coming at her, but the other struck her in the stomach.

The incantation burst, and the enchantress froze solid.

Ember glanced to the side. The sphere disappeared in an instant, leaving her four friends in its place. Ironclad was sprawled on his front, groaning in agony, but beginning to move sluggishly. Thomas lowered the shield around him and stumbled over to Bassai, grabbing him and turning him over. His sabres were strewn beside him. Thomas's hands were glowing with a healing light, pressing against his chest.

As she began looking for Kassaeos, she realised that she had forgotten about the other arrow.

The kick in the chest was expected, and the adrenaline focused her mind enough to rip the arrow out of her and threw it as far away as she could. She could taste blood in her mouth.

The arrow went about ten feet before it burst. It felt as if Ember had been hit in the face by a blizzard. She flew backwards, and crashed into the ground.

***

Bassai's entire body was in agony. His scales were loosening now they were free of the sub-freezing temperatures in whatever horrific realm had enveloped him. In some ways it was a relief, but now the burns and lacerations on his body were stretching and opening, weeping blood onto the dust.

The warmth spreading from Thomas's hands into his chest was filling him, breathing life back into his body. His friend was unblemished, but his face was soaked in sweat and exhaustion.

Bassai tried to move his limbs, and found them heavy, but he was able to shift himself around to examine the threat.

Mora was coated in ice, unmoving. Dead?

He looked around. Ironclad was struggling to move, as he was. There was no immediate sign of Kassaeos, but smoke was slowly drawing together nearby into a column, forming into a figure of a man. Bassai could imagine that the realm had played havoc with his shifting ability.

He rolled his head around, and spotted the crumpled figure sprawled in the dust, with a shock of red hair.

Bassai grabbed Thomas's wrist. "Ember … go to Ember …"

Thomas followed his gaze and broke into a stumbling run.

The Empire Of Fire

Bassai pulled himself to his feet and picked up his sabres. He dug deep into his blood rage, focusing it to a point, letting the ancestral draconic scents and energies fuel it, and in turn let that fuel his body. He was torn between running to Ember, and watching Mora for any signs of movement or action.

The tendrils and tentacles were gone, dispelled from her body. While the sphere was gone, the dust and rock he was standing on had been stained dark grey, in a perfect circle. He squinted towards her limbs, which were still. Her face was also frozen in a sneer. The only movement came from eyes.

They were flicking between each of the enemies in front of her, assessing them.

Bassai growled. Ironclad's booming footsteps rushed past, moving towards Ember.

Bassai stepped toward Mora carefully. Both his sabres ignited in green flame. He crossed the chasm to the frozen figure, trying to ignore the sounds of his Commander's ... his friend's distress behind him, at another friend's injuries.

Mora's eyes fixed on him, focused her spiralling black pupil. Bassai growled, but a hand behind him patted his back, then his chest.

Kassaeos was thin and drawn, completely pale. He was slightly bent over, panting.

"Fire and ice mix in unfortunate ways, my friend," he said hoarsely. "Make it final."

Bassai nodded. He strode up to Mora, and met her eye. A chill came over him, and not from the ice. She was reaching inside his mind. He raised the sabre in his right hand, and chopped it across her neck.

The enchanted blade met little resistance as it passed through ice, flesh and bone. Her head dropped into the dust, and rolled. Kassaeos loosed a bolt that burst in an ice incantation, freezing it further.

There was a roar from above them, a united bellow of anger. Bassai looked up. The battle continued. The dragons were still flying.

Bassai looked back at the head. It was covered in so much ice he couldn't see if the eyes were still moving.

"Damn it all," he growled. "Back off. Watch her, Kassaeos."

The assassin nodded, not needing him to explain why.

They stopped when they were about thirty yards away, but Bassai kept going until he was next to Thomas, Ember and Ironclad.

Ember was on her back, eyes half open. Her skin was flushed red, burned by the ice and whatever they had been subjected to in the dark realm. Bassai could hear her breathing faintly, see her eyes half-open.

"How is she?"

Thomas had his hands against her chest on her blood-stained undershirt, having parted her leather armour to get at the wound. "I've repaired her lung, but she's in a bad way. The shock to her system from the burns, from the impact of the arrow, from hitting the ground hard ... there's not much more I can do. She needs an actual doctor, not me."

Bassai glanced up at Ironclad, who was holding her hand gently. For the first time, to Bassai's eyes, he did not take the form of the Construct, nor The Warrior. He was Tobias Calver, the compassionate man, the one who cared about every life under his command. The one who laughed and offered words of support and stood by them all in loyalty ... as he had always been, whether flesh and blood or iron and oil. He could see the man's pain.

"Calver."

Ironclad twitched. His glowing, amethyst eyes became brighter for a moment.

"It isn't over. The beasts still fly."

Kassaeos burst into being next to them, and lowered himself into a crouch. He cast his eyes over Ember, still pale.

"Our icy counterpart is stirring."

Bassai's eyes snapped around as his ears picked up the sounds of cracking.

Mora's body was shifting and changing beneath the ice, pushing outwards, turning black. The severed head was twitching and squirming. From the stump of a neck, a black tendril burst through the ice.

Ironclad's eyes were glowing so brightly that Bassai could barely stand to look at him. "Calver, we may be all that stands between that thing and oblivion. We stand together."

Ironclad's head bobbed slowly. His deep voice didn't waver. "Stabilise her as best you can, Thomas. We cannot engage her without magic."

Thomas's jaw set in a grimace. "I don't know if she'll make it if we're down here for much longer."

"Do the best you can."

Thomas took a shaking, deep breath, and pressed his hands to Ember's chest. Ironclad lay a hand on his shoulder, and lowered himself to speak into her ear.

"Hold on, love. Our airship's waiting for us to climb aboard."

He stood up, and turned. Bassai could see the damage on his armour plating, all across his body, rippling burns and scratches. He moved with the grace of the defiant wounded, held upright by his heart.

He hefted his double headed axe and shield into readiness. Bassai's breathing steadied.

"Stay close, all of you. Thomas, your barrier is the first line of defense, but we're going to need those tentacles frozen if they come at us. Bassai, Kassaeos, you know what to do. On me."

He began moving forwards, with Bassai and the others at his back. The ice around Mora cracked and chunks of it flew off and shattered on the rock. Tendrils and tentacles whipped out of the gaps and ripped more of the ice away.

Ironclad's pace quickened until he was in a barrelling run. Thomas jumped on his back and hung on to the shield strap. Bassai and Kassaeos were able to catch up easily, although the assassin was far grimmer and breathing more heavily than normal.

The tendrils from Mora's head snaked around the ones coming from her body. They swiftly passed the head between them, up to the neck where it had been. Tendrils whipped out and speared into the wounds, fusing the two parts back together.

There was a muted, but still loud, cracking bang, and the remaining ice fired out at them. Ironclad raised his shield, and the chunks hammered against it like the beating of a war drum.

The remaining four closed the gap between them and Mora swiftly. Bassai sprung around to attack her flank, both sabres burning with green flame.

Ironclad's axe came down towards her, and she dodged back. She raised an arm to catch the wide, heavy blade, and it chopped straight through. A tentacle immediately burst from the stump and swept around to crash into his left knee. Ironclad groaned in pain as his leg buckled.

Bassai drove both his sabres into her chest, making sure to target vital areas. Mora's head twisted around too far to be natural. Bassai heard the vertebrae in her neck cracking and snapping. Her deep black eyes locked onto his, and seemed to reach into his mind. Muddy pit walls seemed to rise around him, higher and higher. The blood of farmhands, the blood of the farmer's daughter, began to cover his hands. He roared, drew his sabres back and stabbed her again. The enchanted green flame was catching and licking at her robes. The expression on her face was something like annoyance, instead of the passive neutrality or sneer that had been there before.

"It won't be that easy for you, witch," he snarled.

While Kassaeos and Thomas were freezing the tentacles moving around to try and squeeze and strike them, the one that was attacking Ironclad wrapped around him and squeezed.

The sound of grinding metal filled Bassai's ears. As he moved his off-hand to slash at the tentacle, her eyes focused on his again, and widened.

In an instant he was gone from the chasm, but not in the shadowy void realm they had been exposed to before. He was confused, and terrified, and wracked with pain. He was freezing cold. The scales on his body were a softer membrane, not the hardened armour they should have been.

He let out a cry, high pitched, a mewl of desperation.

The Empire Of Fire

A gargantuan eye peered down at him, bright blue with a jet black, slitted pupil.

He felt warmth immediately, his blurry vision saw more of the huge shape above, illuminating in a hot, orange glow.

The warmth was fire, a narrow jet breathing from between vast sets of teeth. The head it belonged to was covered in scales, larger and harder than the ones on his tiny waving arms. Majestic, and it drew Bassai in.

Father.

The attachment he felt was clear, but it wasn't returned. What came back to him was resignation, disappointment, and a sorrow so thick and powerful that it made Bassai mewl even more plaintively.

But the fire filled his heart, and made it beat ever quicker. He, and his brothers and sisters, were not the cast-offs, the run-offs, the failures. They were the children of the dragons, they were their legacy, and they were strong, compassionate, capable of a greatness that the dragons had experienced at the height of their own empire. The scar of his birth was no longer there to be reopened.

The fissure, the battle, returned to Bassai's senses in an instant.

He grinned in Mora's face, and sliced down into the tentacle holding Ironclad in place.

The Construct had been raised into the air, and he came crashing down with a grunt. He shoved off the tentacle and struggled to his feet, favouring his right leg heavily.

On the backswing, Bassai drove the sabre up through her body from her groin to the top of her head. With the enchantment on the blade, the bisection was clean, the wound cauterised.

One half of her staggered back and fell backwards, while the other tipped to the dust.

"Pull back," Ironclad groaned. The four of them backed off a little. Ironclad was limping, and Bassai supported him as best he could. The tentacles were waving around, whipping towards them still. Thomas formed a barrier in a bubble around them. He glanced up and shook his head.

Bassai followed his gaze. Through the slight shimmer of the magical barricade, he could still see the dragons weaving and breathing fire on the ships. One of the fleet's vessels was near to the top of the fissure, heavily damaged, but circling. "What do we have to do to stop this?"

Ironclad shook his head. "If that's not Mora … then it isn't within our power. It's down to the Mages. We have to keep at her, buy them time."

"But it should be doing something, shouldn't it?" Bassai muttered. "Unless she isn't the source either."

"She is, in a way." Thomas said tersely. "With Vehnek's soul as the channel, she's been augmented. That power is probably limitless."

Kassaeos snorted. "Oh, good."

Ironclad chuckled, his voice defiant, even though it was lined with pain of the body and soul. "Hopeless causes seem to be our specialty."

Mora was pulling her broken body together again. The tendrils and tentacles were wrapping around the barrier Thomas was casting and squeezing it. Sweat was beginning to pour down the Mage's face.

"Ready to get rid of these?" Kassaeos muttered, gesturing around with his rapier.

Thomas had one hand against his chest, glowing fiercely. "Be fast."

He clapped his hands together, and an explosion of concussive force energy cascaded outwards and batted the tendrils back a few yards. Bassai jumped forwards and sliced through them, Ironclad's arms were pendulum and machine-like, pumping as he chopped and jabbed and slashed. They worked their way through the hellish, otherworldly appendages, keeping up the struggle against their own doom, hope and hopelessness be damned.

33

The impact into the side of the battleship jolted Zeta back to her senses. The smell of flame and melting iron let loose a wave of adrenaline that shot from the ends of her toes to the tips of her wings.

The panic remained as a thorny spike in her heart. She had no way to work it out, its barbs were digging in, anchored to her ribcage with flowering vines. Dragonfire in her soul began to burn those vines away. The ancestral terror of the dead gods who had now been raised to a falsity of life, and into the leviathan horror above them, charged her nerve endings. The monsters swooping around them were no longer dragons, no more than the false, mechanical heads on the prow of the Caelish airships.

The terror within her remained, but was ignited with a torrent of rage.

Zeta hauled herself to her feet, and then up onto the battleship's top deck. The sight before her almost caused the terror to bloom all over again.

One of the wyvernborn airships was ablaze but still flying. The other two were ahead of it as it pulled back away, cannons firing at a huge, spiked and armoured *Felreev* that was sweeping around to hit them again. Zeta knew that it had singled them out. It would have smelled the wyvernborn the moment it emerged from the fissure.

Sandra's archers loosed a volley as it came around for another pass at them. It breathed fire onto them, undeterred, coating her and her Orlin with flame. Zeta took a few steps forwards, before the smoke cleared. The six shamen beside them had cast a barrier against the fire. As Zeta drew close, she could see the Orlin grimacing in pain, their skin pink and scalded.

On their sister ship, another volley of arrows was met by a wave of flame.

Sandra caught sight of her, her grimace turning into a strained smile. "Zeta! Good to see you, you're needed."

Zeta nodded once. "I will be alright, although I've never heard tale of a **Felreev** felled by an arrow."

"What about a cannon?"

Zeta shrugged. "They don't seem to be doing much but singe the scales. The beam in that ... thing on the prow is too slow to charge and fire. We'll just end up shooting down our own allies."

"They're even armoured at the throat ..." Sandra steadied her breaths, ragged and pained.

Zeta grinned. "Do we have any Breachers left in the armoury?"

There was a screech above them. Debris from a battleship rained down and destroyed one of the merchant vessels that had been dragooned into the flotilla. The triple headed terror had chewed its way through almost all of the vessels that had been harassing them. The remaining craft, less than twenty in all, were regrouping and continuing to fire, the crews captured by the souls of the same dragons that fuelled the wyvernborn.

Sandra tore her eyes from it and grimaced. "I don't know. Maybe. *They will.*"

Zeta followed her gaze to a group of injured wyvernborn who were heavily landing on the deck. They were burned and cut. One was carrying another whose wings had been almost burned completely away, howling with madness and grief.

Zeta was sprinting towards them in an instant, her wings flaring as she sprang across the deck. She landed in front of them, and pressed her forehead against the crippled wyvernborn's, clasping his forearm.

"Do any of your cohort have a Breacher?"

The uninjured warrior nodded once, his eyes full of fury. He looked around to another wyvernborn, who was laying on the deck, with a shaman crouching above her.

It was Jion, her belly open in a jagged diagonal gash. The shaman wasn't attempting to heal her, it was praying.

Zeta touched her forehead as she unhooked the Breacher from the leather satchel on her belt. She said a quiet prayer, and forced herself to turn away, searching the skies around her for the *Felreev*.

It was swinging around the battleships engaging it in a wide arc, its eyes locked on their crippled sister ship.

Zeta ran and jumped off the deck, spreading her wings and catching the air. The *Felreev* was faster than any wyvernborn, but she had much less far to travel to intercept it.

She rose on the torrents of war-blasted air and arrowed her wings, speeding towards the crippled vessel. The *Felreev* was coming out of its turn and bearing down on the same target as she landed on the crow's nest, its huge wings flapping, breath and spittle snorting from its mouth.

There seemed to be many dead and burning, wyvernborn, Orlin and Caelish crewmen all. Shamen and mages were attempting to extinguish and control the blaze before it could start to damage the superstructure. Zeta thought of the warriors she knew that had been assigned to this vessel by Barada, wondering for a moment how many were turning to ash beneath her. The rage it ignited almost pushed her off the top mast, diving towards the dragon with abandon. Instead, she grasped the top of the mast and clutched the Breacher in her other hand.

The battleship began firing the cannons on the broadside, and Zeta lit the Breacher's fuse. The *Felreev* was speeding towards them, the weight of the behemoth adding to the momentum. She pushed off, and arrowed back her wings.

She made sure the Breacher was close to her chest, and she had a hand protecting the fuse from the rushing wind. She and the *Felreev* were on a direct course to hit each other. Its jaws were beginning to open and dragonfire was building in the throat.

Zeta twitched her wings and her tail, adjusting her course to pass over its shoulder. The same fear threatened to grip her: coming face to face with an ancestor, and the older fears from her first flights as a hatchling. She had always gotten vertigo, especially in the dive, and the bony spikes of the **Felreev** before her made her old memories think of the flight training grounds in the mountains.

The fuse disappeared into the Breacher, and Zeta flared her wings. Her right arm swung, and tossed the firebomb between the **Felreev's** jaws. Immediately she twisted her wings and her body. As she moved, the Breacher went off.

The shockwave hit her in the back and sent her tumbling into the dragons tail as it spasmed in the air.

Blood filled her mouth as her head struck one of the spikes. She beat her wings haphazardly, her mind and flight disconnected.

Strong arms grabbed hold of her on either side, and held her up as her head cleared. Both had soot stained and charred scales, and wild eyes, but they were smiling triumphantly. Zeta craned her head around.

The **Felreev** was falling limply from the air. Its bottom jaw had been blown off, and the top and sides of its skull was on fire, cracked and buckled. It was picking up speed, trailing vast rivulets of blood.

Zeta was certain it was dead. Absolutely certain.

Yet, as she watched, its wings beat once, then twice. Its body straightened.

She roared in fury and anguish. With a final beat of its wings, the **Felreev** began to rise again.

***

Thomas froze the tentacles bearing down on the four of them. Ironclad was continuing to lead them forwards, hacking through them with Bassai. Kassaeos was an overlap, shifting forwards and freezing the ones at the flanks with quick bolts from his crossbow. Thomas, in turn, was covering every flank

The Empire Of Fire

with incantations of ice and force.

Occasionally he caught a glimpse of Mora ahead of them. Her body was a ruin of corrupted and necrotic flesh. She still stood on two legs, still looked human enough, but the halves of her were misshapen and separated by a deep black, glossy-looking scar. Her robes had fallen away. She was naked, pale as the moon, skin squirming with sickening movement along every artery and vein.

Her eyes had expanded to fill the sockets. Her eyelids were completely gone, and the voids twisted and turned in her head.

"Thomas, can you hear me?"

Seraphine's voice was forcibly steady. Thomas cursed, his focus broken on his ice jets. He linked to the tether, and continued to freeze the tentacles as best he could. "Not a good time, Seraphine!"

"Sorry, I know, but things are getting desperate up here. We have a plan. Kelad will contact you."

Thomas switched focus as a tendril snaked around Bassai's leg. He froze it, and the wyvernborn smashed it with his clawed foot.

"Tell me. Short version."

Seraphine hesitated.

"Tell me, Seraphine!"

"Alright! The totems around the fissure are linked together. In short, we can use them as a channel, and nullify all the magic in the area. It will stop whatever rose, and is still raising, the dragons."

Thomas nodded. "Good! Do it!"

She hesitated again. *"All magic, Thomas. The traces of what raised you, and the others, are still there. It's still keeping you alive. If we nullify it ... you'll all die."*

Thomas knew exactly what the order was going to be when he told Ironclad, so he gave it now. "Same answer, Seraphine. Do it!"

She fell silent again. The three remaining Guardians and Kassaeos kept fighting, kept pushing. Finally her voice found his mind again.

"Thomas ... I'm sorry."

"Don't be sorry. Don't be. You can end it, don't waste that chance."

Ironclad glanced back at him. "Sorry? Sorry for what?"

Thomas let out a blast of force that knocked a tentacle in front of him and Bassai back before it could capitalise on the distraction. "Apparently we're all going to die."

Bassai grinned. "Ah, that same old tune, eh?"

The tentacles closed in again, and the two bladesmen leaped back and kept cutting. It was almost like they were cutting through an eldritch jungle. There seemed to be more of them, more and more coming over the top of the rest of them and even erupting up through the ground to nip at their heels. Thomas felt one grasp at his ankle and root him in place. He froze it, then shattered it with a force blast. It was quickly replaced with another, bursting up through the rock and bone dust, but Thomas was already past it. When he glanced back, he realised that they were being cut off. The space was becoming thick with tendrils more than ten feet tall.

"Ironclad!"

The Construct spotted the problem, and nodded to Kassaeos. The ice incantations on his bolts were as effective as Thomas's magic, freezing the ones at their back. They had gone from a field of danger to a frozen wall, equally as trapping.

They had been boxed in.

"We have to pull back," Thomas urged. "We'll be stuck in a meat grinder before long."

Bassai looked back and barked in dragontongue. Ironclad nodded to him, and he jumped back, his sabres blazing and slicing through them ... but all too slowly.

Another tendril rose up, behind and above the rest. It was made up of several of the thicker ones, wrapped around each other into a twisting, towering bludgeon. The top of it was like a fist or the head of a hammer, and Thomas could make an educated guess as to where it was going to strike.

The Empire Of Fire

Thomas fired an ice incantation in both hands up at it. Kassaeos loosed a bolt. The tentacle flexed to crack the ice and shook it away.

"Sustain the beam!" Ironclad bellowed. "I'll cover you!"

He limped into a two handed swing of his axe and chopped through more tendrils trying to harass them. Bassai joined him with a roar.

Thomas built up the energy in his chest, threw his hands forwards as the tentacle swung back and arced forwards. The freezing energy slowed it a little. Kassaeos's bolts flew as well, cracking against the side and adding more ice. Still it kept falling towards them.

An arrow whistled over them and burst against the tendril, adding even more ice.

Thomas looked around. Through a gap in the tentacles, he caught a glimpse of Ember. She was pale, on one knee, blood dribbling from the wound in her chest, and trickling from her mouth. She drew back another arrow, her back arching, her face lanced with pain but her eyes focused, She loosed it, and it arced against the heavy bludgeon falling towards them.

Thomas could feel his power dimming and waning, but he could see the thing slowing and slowing until it was at a stop.

A new voice filled his head, smug but terse. *"If you all wouldn't mind getting as far away from Mora as possible..."*

A moment later, he heard Ember's pained cry. "Get back! Get out of there!"

Thomas waved a hand over Kassaeos's quiver of bolts, only three now, imparting a force incantation on them. "Through the frozen ones!"

Thomas sent a blast of force backwards, shattering the frozen tendrils behind them. All three of Kassaoes's bolts aided in the endeavour. Bassai and Ironclad practically picked the two of them up as if they were difficult children and sprinted as fast as they could, chopping and slashing through the last of the tentacles.

Thomas had a view over Bassai's shoulder. More of the shadowy appendages were pursuing them around the frozen bludgeon, but his eyes were drawn away to the swirling bang of smoke ahead of them.

General Kelad was crouching behind a heavy cannon, with a portable magical generator beside him. He covered his head.

He looked over at Ember too. She was laying on the ground, facing away from Mora, curled up in a ball.

Thomas looked back, and then up as a shadow entered his peripheral vision.

The *Shadowblade,* nose down, fell like a meteor.

With a cracking, splintering boom, it crashed straight on top of where Mora was standing. Debris blasted outwards as the deckplates and bulkheads compacted down. The skiff split in half, the rear falling away and crashing, almost intact, into the dust.

The pursuing tendrils were dispelled in an instant. The shock of the blast kicked them all in the back.

Bassai landed on Thomas with a grunt, but they both quickly pushed themselves up to their feet. Kelad stood up, leaning over the cannon with a gasp. He looked exhausted, unable to stand up straight. *"Thomas, over here. I'm in need of a good fireball."*

Thomas ran over, muttering a flame incantation under his breath. He gripped the amplifier on the back, and the cannon rocked backwards on its mount. The fireball raced across the fissure, expanding all the way, and exploded against the remains of the *Shadowblade's* hull. Some of it was blasted away, but most of it ignited like a bonfire.

Thomas sighed and patted Kelad on the shoulder. "Immaculate timing, General. Are you alright?"

"Smoke-shifting with objects, especially heavy ones, takes a lot out of you," he gasped. He fumbled with the communication stone on his belt, and switched to Caelish. *"Seret, this is Kelad. Fly in on my mark."*

There was a cracking sound from the wreckage as parts of it caved inwards. Kelad put Thomas hand back on the amplifier. "Can you cast a barrier through one of these?"

The Empire Of Fire

Thomas shrugged. "I don't see why not."

Ember cried out in pain as Ironclad lifted her into his arms. Thomas wanted to go to her, but his attention was drawn back to the wreckage as another cracking sound and a groan of metal blasted across the walls, louder this time.

More of the ruined ship fell away, and a burning figure stumbled out onto the debris-strewn dust.

"Let's test the theory," Kelad grunted.

Thomas nodded, and focused the incantation through the cannon. A bright blue beam fired out and enveloped Mora in a bubble of light.

A moment later, he felt all the burden of the incantation leave him. He glanced at Kelad, who had connected the generator to the cannon's amplifier.

"There." He stood up, and held up the stone. *"Now, Seret."*

The *Sand Dancer* came into view and began descending downwards into the fissure.

"I assume Seraphine has told you the plan," Kelad muttered.

"She has, although I was under the impression we were all doomed."

"That was before I decided to join you down here. She's quite the pessimist, isn't she?" He grinned. His eyes were locked onto Mora. The interior of the bubble was no longer a figure. It was a deep black sphere, straining against her prison.

Ironclad came over to them, Ember leaning against him. Blood was staining her lips, running from the corner of her mouth. "She needs you, Thomas."

"I'll do what I can..."

Ember shook her head. "No ... don't bother. It's ... bad. I know ... it's bad."

Thomas hesitated, but held a glowing hand against her chest.

Broken ribs had pierced her liver, a kidney, her lung again. She was bleeding internally, he could feel her light dimming.

He knew that her injuries were beyond his power, beyond anyone's power, but he tried anyway, sending healing energy into her. He focused so hard that sweat broke out on his forehead. He gritted his teeth past the point where his jaw screeched in protest.

He only stopped when her hand lay on top of his and squeezed.

"Thomas ... it's alright ... just ... let me go. You don't have time."

It was as if every part of his being had been hollowed out of his chest. He looked up at her, with tears in his eyes.

"I'm afraid she's correct," Kelad muttered. "Our dark friend will break free eventually ... sooner than we think."

The *Sand Dancer* descended down to a hover, and Captain Seret had an airman lower the ramp.

"Jack can have a look at you," Ironclad said gently.

Ember put a hand on his cheek. "If you were the one hurt ... he could do something about it. Thomas ... can you just get me on my feet?"

"On ... your..."

"When she breaks out of there ... and she will ... I can keep her busy. Maybe just for another few seconds."

"If that's on the table, then I'm not leaving either," Bassai growled. "I will *not* leave you behind."

Kelad patted Thomas on the back. "Tell them."

Thomas sighed and swallowed. "Seraphine's plan will kill us if we stay down here."

"And?" Bassai asked pointedly.

Thomas nodded. "Right ... I agree. I can keep that generator going for as long as it needs to ... to keep her in there."

"Well, at least I'll have some company," Kelad muttered. Kassaoes snorted, drawing the flash of a glare. "I'm too old, assassin. I'd rather die for something good."

"I can get on board with that," Kassaeos sighed. "Never thought I'd die side by side with you, of all people."

Thomas's eyes fell on Ironclad. He was looking into Ember's eyes, and

The Empire Of Fire

she into his.

"Do as she says, Thomas. Get her on her feet."

Thomas sighed, struggling to focus his power. He sent a burst of energy into Ember's body, dulling her pain, letting her stand on her own.

"Now, get on the *Sand Dancer*."

Thomas stared at him. "What?"

"Get aboard, and get out of here. Allessandra needs you. Seraphine needs you. The new world needs you."

Thomas shook his head, almost frantic. "I'm ... I'm not leaving you down here."

"Consider it my last order to you." He looked at Bassai. "To both of you."

Bassai snarled. "You will not order *me* to flee from a battle ... or to leave you."

"You can go home. After years away, you can return to a place that your exile helped to build. They listened to you, in their own way. Now you can help it build further. You can be the bridge between human and wyvernborn. They need you."

"We left you behind once, not again!" Bassai's voice cracked with pain.

"You never left me behind in Melida City, or at the outpost. I chose to stay, so you could live, so you would have a chance ... and you were as brilliant as I knew you would be. You and Ember, Astrid and Kira heralded a new dawn. You must see it through. You aren't leaving me behind now, either."

"You *need* me here to keep that generator going!" Thomas shouted, his voice becoming desperate.

Ironclad shook his head and held up his axe. "This was forged from my old one, remember? It kept the White Tower going, it can power that cube."

He glanced at Kelad. "I can't order you to do anything, General."

Kelad grinned. "No, you can't."

"Nor me," Kassaeos murmured.

"No, *you* I'm very comfortable ordering to leave," Ironclad rumbled. "Seraphine would never forgive me, or *you* for that matter."

"She'd understand, believe me."

"She will need you, Kassaeos. They all will. You keep Thomas grounded, you'll keep everyone honest, and you'll keep Haama safe. You see danger before anyone else does, it's a valuable skill."

Kassaeos opened his mouth to argue again, but Ironclad held up a hand.

"More than that, you don't need to die here, today."

"Neither do you," Ember murmured. She had a strong grip on his hand.

Ironclad rested a hand on her cheek, and turned to the rest of them. "Go. Now."

Thomas glanced over at the barrier trapping Mora again. Parts of it were bulging outwards as she probed it for weaknesses.

He chewed his lip. "Tobias …"

Ember stumbled forwards and squeezed him, and he could hold the grief back no longer. His eyes streamed with tears. He buried his face in her shoulder, until her hands found his cheeks and pushed him up. "Go on, Thomas. I'll meet you at the taverns up there, okay?"

Thomas wiped his eyes, and nodded. Kassaeos's hand patted his shoulder.

"Come on," he murmured. The assassin clasped Ember's hand. "Give her hell if she makes you."

Ember grinned sadly and nodded.

Bassai pressed his forehead against Ironclad's, silent. Every word had been said, and no minds would be changed. As he repeated the gesture with Ember, Thomas wrapped his arms as far around Ironclad as he could.

"Sorry for leaving you with all the politics," Ironclad said with a sad chuckle.

Thomas's tears cascaded down his cheeks. "Be at my back in spirit, alright?"

"Always."

The Empire Of Fire

The Mage's eyes turned to Kelad. His hand came up in a salute. "It was an honour, General."

Kelad raised an eyebrow, and smiled. It was a genuine smile. He returned the salute. "You're warriors of legend. The honour was mine. If you wouldn't mind …"

Kelad popped open a pouch on his belt, and pulled out a small envelope, sealed with wax. "Give that to Allessandra for me."

Thomas took the envelope and nodded, as Kassaeos pulled on his forearm gently.

"Come on, both of you," the assassin muttered. "Now."

Every step up the *Sand Dancer's* ramp was heavy. Thomas wanted desperately to turn around and run back down to his friends. Once they were on deck, the ramp retracted behind him. Captain Seret looked from those on deck to Ironclad in the fissure below. Her eyes went from confusion, to realisation, to sadness. She saluted down at Ironclad, and cranked the elevation lever. The *Sand Dancer* began to rise. Thomas looked back as his friends grew smaller and smaller below them, fighting the urge to leap over the railing if it only meant spending a few more moments in their presence.

***

Ironclad watched the *Sand Dancer* pick up speed in the climb, his hand clutched in Ember's.

"You'd better not have stayed here for me," Ember murmured beside him.

In truth, that had been a part of it. A large part of it.

"Thomas or I could power that generator. If that's the choice, then I choose him to live, not me. I'm his commander, and his friend." He glanced at Kelad, who was pacing around the generator, looking at the warping bubble. "Besides, I hear the General is somewhat of a letch. Better I stay here so he doesn't get any ideas, eh?"

His humour elicited an eyeroll.

"Fair enough. You know you didn't have to stay."

He looked down at her. "I promised you a journey, didn't I?"

"You promised me an *airship*."

He stroked her cheek. "Where we're going, we can get an airship. Big, and plush, and quick, with a captain's cabin the size of a palace suite and no need for a crew."

She sniffed, and wiped her eyes. Her voice cracked. "Tell me more."

He put a hand on her back, and walked with her towards the heavy cannon. "Oceans and mountains and jungles and whatever you can imagine for thousands of miles. Villages and cottages with open doors. Tavernas with all the food and wine you could want, that make you no more than merrily drunk. Dancing into the night without getting tired, but when you do go to bed the sheets are soft, the pillows fluffed, the quilt warm."

He lay his axe down on the generator, and felt as well as saw the surge of power from the core of the weapon bleed into the cannon and strengthen the incantation. The barrier glowed brighter.

"What about the one I'm sharing that bed with, hmm?" Her voice was wavering, but her bow was in her hand. One of her two remaining arrows was nocked in the string.

"Oh, I imagine his love for you will never die. He knows that from experience."

Kelad drew close to them. He nodded down at the axe. "Impressive craftsmanship."

Ironclad nodded. "You fought well, General."

"Thank you for saying so." Kelad watched as the bubble warped again. "I suspect we'll be going to different places when this is all over."

"Oh? You don't think the Gods might look down on you with forgiveness?"

Kelad smirked. "Your Gods might. Mine won't. Va'Kael has a temper for those like me who cause the pain we do."

"You've healed wounds too, General. Deep ones."

A tentacle pierced the barrier, and Ember drew and loosed her arrow with a cry of pain. The ice incantation burst and froze the appendage, and the barrier closed in to shatter it.

Ember doubled over, and Ironclad extended a hand to her as she nocked her last arrow.

"I imagine it'll be no more than a minute," Kelad muttered, drawing a pistol from his belt.

Ironclad looked up, and willed Seraphine to hurry.

***

Seraphine watched the *Sand Dancer* clear the lip of the fissure and speed away at full sail. She caught no glimpse of who was on deck, but it didn't matter now. It was time.

She turned to Jack, Trevor and the rest of the Mages. They were all ready, waiting for the order.

"Prepare."

They all straightened up and closed their eyes. They were standing beside the totem Seraphine had chosen. They had created a bubble of safety from the wards on the corrupted pillars using portable generators and amplifiers, and were clustered close together. Seraphine built the energy within her and prepared the nullifying incantation.

It burned brighter and brighter in her chest, the threads of it flowing down her arms and feeding into the gauntlets on both hands. Her senses tingled and danced at the buildup of energy all around her. Her chest began to hurt.

"One ... two ... three ... now!"

Seraphine felt the immediate heat on her hands. The release of energy was like diving into a frozen lake from a scorching desert.

The more than a hundred Mages around her had brilliant white beams blasting from their hands, the light filling the totem rune by rune.

From above them all came a scream so blood-curdling and furious that it almost yanked Seraphine's attention where it wasn't needed.

"Maintain your focus!" Seraphine shouted. "We finish it here!"

***

Thomas looked back at the fissure. He wiped his eyes, standing at the aft railing. Bassai stood beside him, hand on his shoulder. Kassaeos was on his other side, arms folded. No words passed between them at all, they simply watched.

One of the totems was beginning to glow fiercely, every Mages' beam feeding into it. It was casting every other totem and the surrounding rock in shadow.

The screaming roar above them drew Thomas's eye. Bassai growled.

Every dragon, including the shadowy mishmash of broken dragon bones and death, was bellowing and howling. As one, all of them dropped into a dive, rushing past the remains of the fleet. Alive and reanimated dead, large and small, armoured and streamlined, they fell from the sky like rain.

Behind him, Seret shouted into a communication stone at the helm. *"Sand Dancer to fleet, full sail to the other side of the mountain!"*

The totem was lighting up from the base, glowing brighter and brighter. Above everything, the Allied and Black Fleets were banking towards the Gravestone, over the derelict outpost at the peak.

The runes at the top of the totem lit up, then the ones next to it lit up, then the ones next to that. Before long the ones on the other side of the fissure were glowing brightly as well.

The dragons were coming down swiftly, too swiftly. Thomas could see the fire glowing in their throats. They were almost halfway to the totems.

The Empire Of Fire

Thomas's knuckles went white on the railing. His jaw clenched. Helpless and fleeing ... in that moment, the new world could hang for all he cared.

***

Ironclad held firm as Kelad ducked out from behind him, balancing his pistol barrel on the Construct's massive tower shield. He released four shots into a tencacle that had pierced the barrier, grinning as it shattered. He grinned and popped another magical stone into the breach.

Ember was leaning against him, her strength waning, she had her last arrow nocked, but had been unable to loose it. There was blood on her lips, coming out of her mouth as red vapour when she coughed.

"How long do we have?" Kelad asked casually.

Ironclad looked up. The cloud of dragons were descending towards them directly, a winged terror.

"Not long."

Ember reared up with a cry of pain and loosed the arrow, freezing two of the tentacles as the incantation burst.

She dropped her bow and leaned down again, slumping against him, groaning.

Kelad fired again. There were many tentacles breaking through now, and Kelad was catching as many of them as possible.

Above them, the shadowy creature was starting to overtake the rest, its six wings arrowed back, a meteorite covered in smog. The roar continued in rage, a desperate war cry of charging cavalry.

All around the rim of the fissure, a band of bright light was slowly getting brighter. It build alongside a tone that Ironclad couldn't place, musical and rising.

Beams shot out above him. They had to be coming from the totems. They joined together at the centre of the fissure, forming a ball of light that was beginning to expand. First it grew slowly, then far, far more quickly.

Kelad exhaled, and grinned. "There we go."

"Yes," Ironclad murmured. He reached down, and clasped Ember's hand.

Her grip was weak, but she took great pains to stand up straight. "I guess this is it, huh?"

"Seems to be. Kelad?"

The General looked at him.

"Thank you. Thank you for everything you risked, and everything you did. I know it can't have been easy."

"But it will be worth it," Kelad replied. "Wherever you end up, however tumultuous the journey … I hope the destination is peaceful."

He extended a hand. Ironclad shook it, and it didn't feel strange to do so.

The ball of light above was expanding rapidly now. Ember was shaking.

"I love you, Em'."

"I love you too … Tobias."

He squeezed her hand gently. "Don't be afraid."

"I could never be afraid with you here."

She stumbled into him, holding him as tightly as she could.

The ball suddenly expanded exponentially, the edge of it like a tidal wave racing towards them. Kelad closed his eyes. Ironclad held Ember with both arms, and pressed his forehead against hers.

***

The dragons were in firing range, and their jaws were opening, when the wave of light blasted into view.

Thomas winced. It was like staring into the sun. The wave expanded in a sphere. It engulfed the totems and the fissure, and then came further. The dragons seemed to sense the danger, but nimble as they were, they couldn't escape. They were all engulfed by the light, and only the shadowy amalgamation of the Black Dragon showed any emotion at its fate. It roared in fury, until it was stifled by the sphere.

The sphere raced towards the *Sand Dancer*. Thomas's eyes widened. "*Faster, Seret!*"

"*I can't go much faster than this!*" she shouted back at him.

Thomas pressed his hands to the deck, and channeled his power into the incantation that lightened the yacht's mass. The wind kicked the *Sand Dancer* a little harder. He glanced up, and saw the leading edge of the wave nipping at their heels. Kassaeos and Bassai had stepped back from the railing, moving alongside him.

The wave touched the back of the ship, and Thomas felt the increase in mass as the incantations keeping it in the air weakened. He gritted his teeth and channeled every scrap of magic within him into the generator.

The *Sand Dancer* pulled away again with a shudder. The wave started gaining on them again, but then began to slow. The yacht kept flying even as the sphere's growth halted. It stayed where it was, massive, engulfing half of the entire side of the mountain and all of the cleft where the fissure had lain.

Thomas walked back to the aft railing with Bassai and Kassaeos. The night had become day, the auroras and stars were dulled by the arcane bloom. As it faded, the sky went from black to dark blue, with purple and pink tints on the horizon.

Around the totems were crumpled and sprawled forms, vast and ancient. None of the dragons moved, not so much as a twitch. The shadowy beast was strewn in a pile of molten metal and scattered bones.

Thomas breathed in the sudden silence, but his breath caught. The war had ceased, what he had wanted from the moment he had realised where peace could be found, and yet the fresh air was bitter on his tongue.

The *Sand Dancer's* crew were dumbstruck, gathering around the railing with them. Captain Seret leaned on it, breathing quickly, holding herself back from beginning to sob. Thomas took her hand as the crew behind them cheered in triumph and disbelief.

Bassai clasped Thomas's shoulder, unable to say a word or even make a sound. Kassaeos's head was bowed, brim of his hat pulled over his face.

The totems were no longer black, they were the translucent light blue of astralum stone. The runes were pulsing softly, the corruption gone.

Thomas instinctively looked around the totems for Seraphine. He couldn't pick her out, specifically, but he could see a number of figures sprawled out around one of the totems. Fear gripped him until he saw that they were moving, picking themselves up, helping each other to their feet.

A crewman rushed up to Captain Seret, but hesitated when he saw the emotion on her face. "*Captain ... we are being contacted by a number of ships, requesting orders and status updates.*"

Seret cleared her throat, and held out a hand for the stone. The crewman handed it to her.

"*This is Captain Seret of the Sand Dancer. We are still flying, and in fair shape. Call in the carriers and group by section for search and rescue operations. Stand by for further communication.*"

She dropped it from her mouth, holding it loosely at her side. Tears were beginning to run down her cheeks as she held it out to Thomas. "*They need a word from you, I think.*"

He took the stone from her, and pulled her into an embrace, patting her on the back. As he stepped back away to speak into the stone, Bassai moved across to her, clasping her hands in his.

"*This is Thomas ... The Mage ... aboard the Sand Dancer. Sending to all ships, Allied and Black Fleet both.*"

He tapped the stone against his cheek, suppressing his grief, and trying to find the words.

"*We both have airmen needing rescue on the ground, and working together, we will bring more of them home. Together, we defeated the true threat to our nations, and to this world. I propose we extend our makeshift ceasefire ... at least until the point we can sit down and fully come to an understanding as to what happened here ... and until the point our dead are at rest.*"

There was no response to his words.

"*We have accomplished much as allies. This is both of our victories. If we must be enemies again ... let it be later. Let us remain side by side for a few more days ... so our dead were not sacrificed in vain.*"

There was another pause. Thomas could say nothing more. He could think of nothing else. His mind was almost blank with everything that had happened.

A voice murmured over the stone. "*This is Rear Admiral Nyroshi of the Black Fleet cruiser Falcon. I am in de facto command of our ships. I agree to this ... temporary ceasefire.*"

Donnal's voice replied, gruff and pained. The man was injured. "*I concur.*"

Another voice joined them. "*Captain Obrek, Spearhead, Standing Aerial Navy. I also agree.*"

Thomas nodded, his grief beginning to swallow him.

"*Thank you,*" he whispered hoarsely. His hands dropped to his sides, and he attempted to hold the flood back no longer.

34

For the next two days, the remainder of the combined fleet descended onto the debris field, and picked up whoever they could. Around two thousand airmen and marines had survived the crashes of more than five hundred craft. Over half the Black Fleet and Alliance Fleet had been lost.

Still, the fact that anyone at all had survived the plummet from thousands of feet above was warming to Thomas's heart. Every time a survivor was pulled from the wreckage, he or another Mage and medic had been there to stabilise them. The huge carriers were being used as field hospitals, with a number of other battleships and the surviving merchant vessels serving as triage centres for whoever couldn't fit aboard. One, *Mira's Favour*, had cleared their entire top deck and one of their cargo bays, which was now filled with wounded.

The dead were being loaded onto two of the carriers and a number of Allied and Black Fleet ships, including the *Dreadnought*. Donnal's flagship was heavily damaged, and had been undergoing considerable repairs while corpsmen loaded the dead into the aft cargo bay, up the ramp.

Seraphine had assured the fleet captains that the area was safe to traverse. The nullification had faded away, the airship generators would not be in any danger of ceasing to function. No more would be added to the debris field.

The wreckage was a haunting sight, and an incredible one. It was a vast boneyard, but one that was no longer burning. If Thomas had to guess, he suspected that the nullification magic had extinguished the dragonfire. Perhaps it was another thing that could be salvaged from the tragedy, although the incantation would definitely need to be refined. If it were deployed in the

The Empire Of Fire

Maldane Reach, there was a chance it would damage the soil even further.

Melted iron frameworks jutted up from the rock, alongside blackened wood that was little more than soot, and bodies. Thousands upon thousands of bodies, slowly being dressed and wrapped to be taken home.

It took longer for the nullification in the fissure to fade. The concentration of dark magic down there was vast. Once it was safe, the *Sand Dancer* returned.

There was no sign of Kelad. It was said that when an Aether died, their physical bodies dissolved into smoke, releasing their soul for ascension or oblivion. Thomas couldn't say which of the two fates awaited the General, if his attempts at atonement had swayed the Gods at all. He hoped it had, and found the emotion sincere.

Vehnek's body had been obliterated. Little more than black soot remained in a neat pile, a fine powder that gave absolutely no indication that it had once been a man.

Mora's broken corpse lay exactly where it had been when Thomas, Bassai and Kassaeos had left, except not trapped within a barrier. She was at peace, in a way, but the state of her was a horror. Her eyes and eyelids were completely burned away. Her arms were broken. The stab wounds and slashes Bassai had struck her with left wicked, jagged scars over her pale skin, and up through her head, which had been misshapen by her bisection. Bassai covered her nakedness with a cloak, and it was decided that the body would be best burned.

Ironclad and Ember lay near the heavy cannon. He was sprawled out on his back, his eyes dark, shield discarded beside him, axe near the cannon, crest pointed at the sky. Ember was slumped over him, her red hair falling across her neck and Ironclad's bicep. Her eyes were closed, the only indication that she was dead was the pallor of her skin, and the silence of her form.

Seraphine broke down at the sight of them. Thomas and Bassai had known what they would see, but it made it no easier. While Kassaeos comforted Seraphine, Bassai chanted with Barada and Zeta in dragontongue, a funeral rite that hummed in a deep baritone, making the very air around them shake. Sandra knelt beside Ember and wept, cradling her head gently. Donnal gazed down at both of them, deep in thought, quietly mourning.

Thomas stayed back away from them all. Part of him naively hoped that if he ignored the reality of their deaths ... maybe they would just sit up, brush themselves off, and everyone would breathe a sigh of relief. Ember would make a dry joke, that made light of everything. Ironclad would chuckle and reassure everyone that it was over, that peace was all but certain now, that he knew exactly what to say to each individual general, ally, minister and royal.

Thomas may have been an architect of the potential peace, had made strides towards it, but the pressure on him was right on the heels of the grief that was dulled by shock. Captain Seret stood beside him, quiet while everyone mourned around them, before turning around and lowering her voice.

"*Go to them, to all of them.*"

Thomas glanced at her. "*It ... I don't think I can.*"

"*Why not? Would they want you to stand here and hide from the truth?*"

Thomas shook his head. "*I'm not hiding from any truth ... the truth is staring me in the face. I should be with them.*"

"*Then go.*"

He shook his head again. "*No ... I should be there instead of them. A ... a doctor could have seen to Ember ... and I could have-*"

"*Stop it,*" Seret snapped, her voice a nearly silent hiss. "*Don't re-litigate death. I was there, remember. I heard what you said to each other, most of it anyway. He had a responsibility as your commander, and that didn't include sacrificing your life. You tried healing Ember, she was too far gone.*"

"*Then I didn't try hard enough.*"

Seret lay a hand on his cheek, and turned his face towards her. "*No matter how hard people try ... sometimes you just can't win them all. When you first stepped aboard the Sand Dancer, I didn't believe in you at all. I was suspicious of you all from the outset ... and you all proved yourselves trustworthy to me, and a princess ... and maybe a king. You have worked so*

The Empire Of Fire

hard and sacrificed so much ... your own lives ... twice in Ironclad and Ember's case. You've given everything you can give, and maybe you feel you have to give more."

Seret's eyes were hard as diamonds, and just as vibrant. *"What more you have to give, give it in the future. Don't dwell on what you couldn't give in the past."*

He stepped out of her grasp, and his eyes returned to the mourners. Eventually Seret moved away, and he didn't make any attempt to see the expression on her face, one that could only have been disappointment.

***

Once Ironclad and Ember had been brought aboard, the *Sand Dancer* took off again. Seret floated the yacht above the debris field, where every scrap and every ship could be seen.

A Salkethian scout ship had buzzed the fleet, and was flagged down under a truce. A full explanation was provided to them, as well as many assurances that the hundreds of ships on their border did not constitute an invasion. A few hours later, a number of carriers and escorts joined them and assisted with injuries and salvage. Thomas had a sneaking suspicion that part of the reason was reconnaissance, but the humanitarian nature of it was appreciated. Likely, their leadership was in conversation with Allessandra as the pieces were still being picked up.

The sight was doing nothing for his mood, nor calming him. Usually watching some kind of process would, be it construction, or a herd of animals in the natural world, or insects on a tree, or the loading and unloading of ships on the docks. This process was something different, a triumph, but a bitter triumph. The cost had been half of their number, and many had died in the initial battle between the Allies and Black Fleet. Their former enemies had been led into the darkness by their commander, who seemed to have been led into the darkness himself. Tragic, in a way, but nevertheless, many would need to be held accountable for the crimes they had committed. The magnitude of that was overwhelming.

Thomas rubbed his head, running a hand through his hair. His mind was simultaneously racing and blank. Thinking about the implications of the battle, the future they would bring, was keeping him from thinking about anything else. Now they had won, all those theories and promises needed to be kept, and turned into realities. Cael and Haama would negotiate and a true Alliance would be formed. The mending and recovery of the land, of Montu Fortu ... of the relationships and bonds between people. Gods above, it would be difficult.

But it was possible. They had proved it ... although it of course had been a relationship forged to escape a dragon's jaws.

As Thomas continued leaning over the railing, he heard a smoke-shift at his back. Kassaeos leaned over the railing beside him.

"I've been told to check on you."

Thomas grunted. "Appreciated. I'm just thinking."

"Right." Kassaeos chuckled. "Salketh here as well, eh?"

"Hmm."

"Ironclad would like that. A bit of international relations, that type of thing really got him going."

Thomas said nothing at that, but before he could stop it, a laugh bubbled up from deep inside him. "You know ... he'd never even left Haama. Never in his life, until now. Well, except to the Mountain Cities."

"Good grief, you could've fooled me. He had the bleeding heart of a travelling missionary."

"That was from his work, I suppose. I don't know ... he was just a very accepting person. He accepted me, accepted Ember, accepted Bassai. You know Ember was a thief when they met?"

Kassaeos shook his head.

"Yeah, she was a cutpurse, and being Orlin, she was used to running and climbing and leaping. She was never caught. I mean ... what's a city but a forest with even less lines of sight? Man made, of course ... but still, there were millions of places to hide in Melida City's Old Town."

"Oh, I know, believe me," Kassaeos muttered with a grin.

"I bet you do ... you were around back then, eh?"

"I was a boy, loved a bit of hide and seek."

Thomas nodded. "Well, anyway, the first and only person to catch her was Tobias Calver."

"Caught her in more ways than one."

Thomas smiled. "Yes, I suppose so. Caught me, too. I was a vagrant and a stowaway and a thief. Made my way to the city from the Port Of Plenty, sneaking onto wagons trains and such. Used magic as misdirection to take food from the markets, until he spotted me."

"And I suppose you could say he caught Bassai, in a way."

"Oh yes, in a way. A lot of his Rangers were criminals in some way."

Kassaeos snorted. "Like I said, a bleeding heart."

"You know, maybe that's a part of it. That's not exactly what he did with me. He took me on a patrol with him, showed me the city as he saw it. People making their way, creating and labouring, feeding their neighbours, entertaining them so they forgot their troubles for a few hours, offering them prayers or other such comforts. He told me that I didn't have to take from them, that I shouldn't take from them. He told me I had potential to be better, to do better."

Thomas coughed to clear his throat. His voice was becoming thick. "He knew where I had come from. He knew what my life had been. He knew that ... there was some good in me. Part of why I stole was that I wasn't accepted by the Haamans. I was Caelish, the old enemy. It made me hate them, made me bitter. But ... he saw right through it. Right to my core. He offered me a bed in his barracks, offered combat and arcane training. He told me I had potential."

Kassaeos reached out and patted him on the back. Only then did Thomas realise the grief that had filled his voice.

"I've ... been trying to live up to that potential for as long as I've known him. Now I'm here ... and he's not. He thought ... I guess he thought ... that there was even more potential to come ... but I can't see it. I think on his last words to me, they're in my ears whenever silence falls around me. I wish I could see what he saw ... then it might make sense to me."

Kassaeos patted him on the back again. "Are you kidding? Look where you came from, and look where you are now. Look at what you've done. Look at what you could do in the future. You were a huge part of stopping a war. You convinced royalty to give you a chance. Your plan got us here, working side by side with the Black Fleet, and even if that's temporary ... we may well have saved the world. Whatever Mora had become, the dragons and that monster would have burned everything and everyone. Look at me, Mage."

Thomas wiped his eyes on his sleeve, and turned to him.

"You're not finished yet. You think your part in this is over? There so much work to do ... and you're the one to do it. You have the ear of our leadership and theirs. You have the ear of people in the armed forces. You think none of that matters? You know how you did that?"

"How?" Thomas murmured hoarsely.

"Off your own back, from your own mind. He taught you to see people for what they are, without bias or prejudice. This, all of this, was born of that. Ember and Bassai too, they got the Orlin and wyvernborn on side, following his example. All of that was accomplished while he was in the dungeon of the Silver Throne. You weren't following his orders, you were following his example."

Thomas bowed his head.

Kassaeos sighed. "You know, we'd already met."

Thomas wiped his eyes again and frowned.

"The White Tower wasn't our first meeting. You saved my mother and I in the Battle Of Melida City. I was a just a boy, eight years old and small for my age."

Thomas frowned. "He told you not to be a hero ... Cass. Your name was Cass."

The Empire Of Fire

Kassaeos nodded. "I may have taken him a little too literally in becoming an assassin."

"I'd call you a hero."

"No, no," Kassaeos snorted. "I told you, heroes make for poor assassins. Can't be accepting pints from strangers who recognise me while I'm tracking a target."

"I'm sure those skills can be put to more uses than just assassination."

Kassaoes grinned. "We'll see." He nodded to the hatch. "Now, get down there. It's not exactly a wake or funeral, that will come later ... but still. Say goodbye. Don't brood up here."

Thomas sighed. "I'm just ... not sure how I could go about it. I'm not ... ready to say goodbye to them."

Kassaeos nodded. "Take it from someone who has been around too much death: no-one ever is. But hiding from it makes it no easier. It just makes the wound bigger, and makes it fester. Be grateful you don't have to do it alone."

Thomas looked at the hatch, his heart beginning to beat in a way that he noticed more explicitly than he ever had. It was as if he was empty, and the sound was echoing through him.

He stepped away from the railing. That was the hardest one. His feet felt as if they had been welded to the deck, and strapped with weights, but he found himself getting used to the weight as he crossed the deck to the hatch.

Seret caught his eye as he began to climb down the stairway. She nodded at him, her eyes warm and assuring. He tried to smile at her, but he couldn't muster up the expression. He put his hand over his heart in a gesture of thanks to her, recognising her support, before descending out of the chilly mountain air.

The corridor was bare, as were the crew berths were Seraphine had recovered from her captivity. As Thomas had thought, everyone was in the princess's suite, where his friends lay in state.

Ironclad was as he had been when found, his arms crossed over his chest, shield fixed into his left hand. He was laying on his back, upon what was likely the slab upon which he had been tortured, and later rescued. A white sheet had been draped over it, concealing the horrifying history, woven with runes of preservation, peace and worship. Candles and incense were around him, symbols of rememberance, grief, but also joy. The joy of memory, of friendship, of ascendancy to the Astral Plain. The entire ensemble had transformed the slab from a instrument of terror into one of beauty. Considering it was probably all they had on hand, it was an impressive feat.

Ember lay upon the princess's bed, the same weavings on the sheets beneath her. She had been re-dressed, perhaps by Sandra and Seraphine. She wore a light green Orlin gown, with the floral pin she had worn over her heart placed there once again. Her pale hands were clasped together on her lower sternum. The same candles and incense were set out around her.

On a small stool between them was a single, wide candle, breathing a sweet, floral scent into the air. As it tickled Thomas's nostrils, his mind placed it as the scent of honey roses. The candle was a symbol of their love.

Jack Kilborn was sitting in the corner, reading a small book. The thin tome was aged, bound with twine that looked to have been replaced dozens of times. Wandering over, Thomas recognised it as the Song Of The Four Guardians, and other poems, written in full in bold, looping handwriting. The ink remained clear, even though the pages seemed fragile as late autumn leaves.

He patted Jack on the back gently, noticing that it was resting on top of all the notes he had taken on Ironclad's Construct form. Thomas wondered for a moment if Jack had scoured the notes for a way to bring him back to life.

"How are you?" Thomas kept his voice low, as if he were around sleeping children he didn't dare wake.

Jack shrugged with a sigh. "I suppose I'm … looking for answers. Answers outside of science, arcane and otherwise." He shook his head. "I can't answer that question that is always at the forefront of my mind: why? Why did all this happen? Who or whatever it was … they certainly weren't Caelish, Haaman, or otherwise. I'm most sure that they weren't human, wyvernborn, or of this world at all."

The Empire Of Fire

Thomas nodded. "Yes ... another thing we have to be vigilant for ... perhaps for the rest of time."

He turned back to the room. Barada and Sandra were by the door, holding each other tightly. Barada's eyes were locked on the two bodies, seemingly scrutinising them.

"Alpha," Thomas said formally.

Barada's eyes moved to him. "Thomas."

Sandra turned to Thomas and brushed a hand over his cheek. "How are you?"

Thomas swallowed. "I ... I don't think it has quite sunk in yet."

Sandra nodded sympathetically. "Sometimes it takes time. Especially when they're so close."

Thomas nodded. "Your warriors..."

Barada growled softly. "A hundred and fifty two wyvernborn were lost, and ninety five Orlin."

"All are heroes, and will be laid to rest as such ... we just aren't sure how." Sandra grimaced. "We haven't lost so many people since the Forest burned ..."

Barada growled again, thoughtful. "It takes bravery to stand up, to fight a battle you know you could lose, where the loss would be devastating. Tobias Calver and Emeora Vonn sacrificed their lives ... and did it for a second time. They looked death in the eye twice. I can only pray for such bravery, if called upon."

Sandra tightened her grip on his hand. "I hope this victory means we won't be called upon to do so. I hope it means that no one is."

"That's why all of this was done," Thomas murmured. "The price was very high."

Sandra squeezed his hand. "Go to them."

Thomas knew he was prolonging it, still, and Sandra knew it as well. She smiled at him encouragingly.

He turned.

Bassai and Seraphine were kneeling beside the two beds, deep in prayer, and each had their own figure of support. Kassaeos sat behind Seraphine on a hard-backed chair, his hand on her shoulder, gazing at Ironclad and Ember. His expression, as ever, was difficult to read. He was there as a rock, a stoic, calming presence for the grieving to centre themselves beside.

Behind Bassai, also with her hands on his shoulders, was Zeta. Thomas noted her closed eyes and bowed head, and the gentleness of her clawed, weapon-like fingers as they rested on him, almost tenderly. Both she and Kassaoes were helping the two focus in prayer, until Thomas approached. Seraphine stirred, and Bassai opened one eye to look at him as he settled onto his knees between them.

For a moment, none of them uttered a word. The scents of the candles and burning sticks danced around them in the silence.

"How long has it been since you've seen Ember in something other than her armour?" Thomas finally said, quietly.

"Not since we returned to the world, certainly," Bassai murmured. "Wait ... no. In Obsidian, after the Pil Valley. She was out of her armour then, the two of them were heading into the hills."

"I think for me it was the midsummer festival in Old Town, you remember?"

"Ha! I do. What was that thing you tried to get me to wear?"

"A doublet."

"Aye, a doublet." Bassai snorted. "She wore that white thing, didn't she?"

"That she did. Made even the monks blush."

Bassai chuckled, but the laugh quickly extinguished. "So many friends lost, in such a short time."

Thomas sighed. "I know. Any news from the Gods?"

"Only that they are at peace. I can feel that for sure. They are where they were always destined to be, among the ascended, walking the Astral Plain. They will be there for all time, for all existence." Bassai turned his full attention to Thomas. "Have you not sensed the same?"

"I ... haven't." Thomas scratched the back of his head. "I haven't found any comfort in prayer at all. I've been too ... preoccupied."

"With what?"

Thomas felt a pang of incredulity. "With *what?* With the implications of what we just accomplished ... and how we're going to manage it without them."

His eyes fell on Ironclad and Ember, and the reality of them being there, laying in state, wearing what they would be buried in, truly hit.

"What are we going to do without them, Bassai? She was our eyes and ears ... she was our heart. He was our rudder, he steered us. He was the one who spoke the words, who negotiated ..."

"Did you not walk into Victory undetected? Did you not make our case to the princess?"

Thomas sighed. "I did ... but ..."

"It was not he who began to turn our heads," Zeta growled behind them. "It was Emeora, and Bassai, Astrid and Kira. Were it not for them, we would never have flown with you to the Pil Valley."

Bassai's eyes were unwavering. "We all played our part. He was not present in our key conversations, yet we spoke with his words. In our talks with the Allessandra and Evandro, he barely spoke a word, because we were speaking with his voice. He has been our example, our lead to follow, and eventually to grow beyond. Eventually, we would have all had our own command. He knew that, and deep down, so did we. I suspect there is more to it than that."

Thomas chewed his lip for a moment. The grief within him was right at the tip of his tongue. "You ... are the only family I've ever known, only family I've ever had."

Seraphine opened her eyes, and her hand linked with his.

"He isn't just my commander, any more than you're just my friend, any more than Ember is just my drinking companion or our scout."

The pain was real, not just in his mind. It spread throughout his entire body like a burn, like all his bones were breaking.

"I've lost my sister ... and my big brother ... and I don't know what to do."

Bassai's hand clasped his shoulder. "Carry on, and carry them in your heart. Live by their example, as warriors, as people. Make sure they are never forgotten, that their story lives on."

Seraphine squeezed his hand gently. "From now, it will be difficult. More difficult than anything, it will seem, and it will feel as if it will never end. But we do not grieve alone. Always remember."

Thomas did his best to nod.

"In many ways, Tobias perhaps will be able to ... rest." Bassai's murmur was becoming a growl. "Since he awoke, he has never been able to sleep, to eat, to feel as we can. He has ... been in pain. Perhaps not in body, but in soul. Unable to be what he was before to the woman he loved, who felt that pain as keenly as he."

Seraphine's hand began to tremble. Thomas now was having to squeeze hers in comfort.

"He would have been spared the same madness as those who had followed the Desert King," Thomas muttered. "I'm sure of that. He was strong in soul, he would have remained a guardian for all time, until he decided his time came."

"Would he?" Seraphine whispered.

"I'm certain."

"I don't know. After hundreds of years ... or thousands, how would he not lose himself? After what we did to him."

Her voice was shaking. "We took his humanity away ... turned him into a weapon for our own use. We ripped you all from the Astral Plain ... but we put him in a prison with no escape. Someone who ... gave us so much ... and did it again, despite it all."

Kassaeos moved onto his knees behind her and held her tightly. She

The Empire Of Fire

leaned back into him with tears falling down her face.

"He was never the type to hold a grudge," Bassai grunted. "He, Ember and the two of us did not waste the second chance you gave."

Seraphine wiped her eyes, but the tears didn't stop. "I wish I could just ... say sorry to him. I can feel his presence up there, but communing with the Gods doesn't work that way. I've never known it to work that way, anyway."

Thomas bowed his head, and began to pray. He felt Bassai pat him on the back, and join him.

When Seraphine resumed her own prayers, Thomas felt something pulling him, like there was a string attached to his heart.

He couldn't see it, but it pulled gently again.

"Can you feel that?"

When he opened his eyes again, to check with the others, they were no longer in the *Sand Dancer's* state room.

Beneath him was a field of vibrant green grass. A gently flowing breeze made his robes sway gently. It was warm, a summer wind, spiced with the smells of nature and the ocean.

He could hear it, gently lapping a shoreline close by. When he stood up, he realised they were at the top of a cliff, with the edge and the ocean stretching out to the horizon to his left.

He didn't recognise the coast, and the ocean was certainly not the Meladrin. The colour was all wrong. There were purple bands mixed in with deep blues and swirls of cyan. The Meladrin was the same blue, but mixed with the green of vast clouds of seaweed.

Inland, there was no sign of civilisation, aside from a few distant cook-fires, tiny tendrils of smoke almost lost against the clear blue sky. What he could see were rolling hills and forests, huge distant mountains covered in snow.

Thomas looked around again. Seraphine, Kassaeos and Bassai were with him. Seraphine was studying the environment, equally as confused as Thomas. The other two were singularly focused ahead of them.

Thomas stared at Kassaeos. The assassin seemed far younger, just as built as he knew, but with a full head of chestnut brown hair, and vibrant green eyes instead of the black irises and pupils there had been. Seraphine took his hand in shock, and stroked his cheek. He smiled at her, bright and genuine, with no hint of the cold, sardonic lethality that he had become.

Bassai remained vigilant of what lay directly ahead of them, and Thomas followed his gaze. There was a cottage near the cliff edge. It was as if an architect had gone mad and only been given a pen and paper for company. The roof was a lean-to with windows fixed in, the glass glinting. There were three storeys below it, which seemed almost backwards. The third floor was the largest and widest, completely unsupported from below. A tree was growing through one corner, the canopy high above. Thomas realised suddenly that it was an Orlin oak, with a rope ladder tied to the lower branches. Those branches were still the equivalent of eleven or twelve storeys above the ground.

There were a few platforms built in the canopy. He could see glimpses of them through the leaves. His eyes fell back to the cottage and its peculiar construction. The second floor was about a third the width of the one above it, and cylindrical. The ground floor was still nowhere near as wide as the third, wider than it was long. The whole thing was made of different grains and kinds of wood, making the building appear almost multicoloured. Flat, thick planks made up the walls at every level, with wide glass windows facing every direction.

"Can you feel it?" Seraphine whispered. "All around us."

Thomas could. The vibration against his skin, the tingle of magic everywhere.

It suddenly became very clear where they were.

"Ahead of us," Bassai murmured.

There was a flash of movement from the tree canopy. Thomas spotted suddenly, as if it had appeared out of nowhere at all, a thin rope that had been pegged to the ground right in front of them.

Two figures were falling quickly towards them, using the rope as the

The Empire Of Fire

guide to a zip-line. They raced onward swiftly, their features becoming clearer as they drew closer. The lead figure's red hair blowing behind her in the ocean breeze. The powerful arms and shoulders of the man behind her. Her simple, comfortable clothes for climbing, his loose fitting athletic trousers and shirt for exercise.

Ember landed in a gentle crouch, walking towards them with a smile. A fresh Orlin lily was perched behind her ear, a beautiful blue twist against her copper hair. Tobias Calver landed a moment after and took a step to steady himself. He jogged up to them so the two groups converged at the same time.

"Ah," Tobias said warmly. "You came for a visit."

Thomas grinned. "Yes ... apparently so."

Bassai looked around them quickly. "Is this...?"

Ember nodded. "The Astral Plain, yeah."

"I never though it would look like this."

Tobias shrugged. "I don't know if this is what it really looks like. Maybe it is. Maybe your minds have painted a picture for you to see, so it makes sense to mortal eyes." He grinned. "Or maybe this is our heaven, or part of it."

Seraphine stepped forwards. "But you're ... you're alright, here, aren't you?"

Ember put her hands on the sorceress's shoulders. "It's heaven, of course we're alright."

"But ... I ... I just wanted to say ..."

Tobias shook his head, and held up a hand. "You don't have to. I understand, we both do." He looked at Thomas and grinned. "You too. In fact, you *twice*."

Thomas swallowed. "I don't ... know what to do."

Tobias clapped him on the shoulder, holding his gaze with those familiar, warm eyes. "Since when? You were always smarter than me. You're the one I listened to. You're the one who knew how to solve problems. How did we beat the odds all those times, eh?"

Bassai grinned. "Together."

Thomas felt a tear tickle his cheek. "But we're not together now."

Ember grasped his hand and hugged him tightly. "Yes, we are. We always will be."

"Don't you worry about us," Tobias said with a smile. "We're on our own adventure, but we're always in your heart. Every time you pray, and every time you don't."

"Speaking of which," Ember murmured. She was smiling out across the ocean.

Tobias nodded. "Our chariot awaits ... and that barrel of mead for Ydra and Vargas."

"Better take five or six barrels," Seraphine muttered.

"Only five or six?" Ember said with a chuckle. She nodded her head towards Kassaeos. "I'll always be a better shot than you, never forget it."

Kassaeos barked a laugh. "In your dreams, girl."

"We'll put a wager on that when we meet again." She shook his hand, and he stepped in to a hug, quick but warm.

Then she held Seraphine tightly. Thomas leaned forwards and wrapped his arms around Tobias, who returned it. Ember moved in behind him, patting him on the back and holding him tightly. Bassai too hugged them both without so much as a murmur.

"Be well," Tobias finally said. "And don't be in any rush to get here. You've got plenty of work to do."

He kissed Seraphine on the cheek, and with a glance at Ember and a cheeky wink, they both took off at a run.

They sprinted towards the edge of the cliff, straight towards the drop into the ocean. Without a pause, they both leaped off.

A split second later, an airship rose, the sails unfurled and billowing. Thomas could see them both standing on the deck behind the railing, waving at their friends.

As they began to pull away, out towards the horizon, Tobias brushed Ember's hair aside, and kissed her. Her arms wrapped around him immediately.

The Empire Of Fire

Warmth filled Thomas's chest as he watched her gaze into his eyes with a smile full of love.

Then they were back aboard the *Sand Dancer* in the blink of an eye.

Thomas almost fell over, but Bassai's hand kept him upright. Seraphine gasped. She closed her eyes, and fresh tears fell down her face.

Thomas gazed at the bodies of his friends. Now, like them, he was at peace. The sight of them was no longer one that brought him pain. Instead, they brought the memories of them into his mind on a wave of joy. Joy that he had known them, and loved them, and that they had loved him.

He barely noticed, and only after a moment, that the tension in the room had risen.

Two men waited at the threshold into the room. One was Captain Obrek, the other was in an even more formal naval uniform. The insignia of the Black Fleet was emblazoned on his chest.

Obrek directed his words at Thomas. *"This is Rear Admiral Nyroshi of the Black Fleet."*

Thomas nodded. *"Welcome aboard, Admiral, Captain. Do you need us for something?"*

Nyroshi shook his head. *"No. We are here to ... pay our respects."*

Thomas felt the warmth spread over him again, and felt Bassai exhale beside him. He beckoned them in welcomingly. *"Come in, join us."*

Obrek and Nyroshi nodded in thanks, and gestured behind them. A number of other Standing Navy and Black Fleet officers followed them in, dropping to one knee beside the bodies and closing their eyes. They began praying in Caelish.

"Va'Kael, we pray beside former foes, who became allies, and rescued us from our folly. Take care of them, Lord, as you take care of your most loyal children who have passed into legend, and we humbly ask you to watch over us, and our allies, to keep us on the path to a new day."

Thomas blinked at them in surprise. There were eight officers in there, including the Captain and Admiral, with more in the corridor. He spotted

Barada muttering to Kassaeos, who edged back over to them.

"You may have just started quite the procession, Mage."

"Really?" Thomas frowned. "How many are there?"

"Seret has had docking requests from eighty one ships, and counting. They all want to pray for Tobias and Ember. All of them."

The warmth became an overwhelming enormity. Thomas blinked, and found difficulty standing up. The tears that threatened were not ones of grief, but tears of hope finally perhaps turning to reality.

35

For the entirety of the fleet's return journey, officers and airmen from the Black Fleet and Standing Fleet, wyvernborn, Orlin and members of Donnal's Resistance docked with the *Sand Dancer* so they could pray and pay respects to the dead. Thomas and Bassai made the point to board the carriers, where many of the dead lay. They prayed, and shared words with the crew, hoping that the Gods were listening. The tingles of warmth in their souls told them that they were.

Donnal was one of the first aboard the yacht, and stayed for a day and a night, contemplating over the bodies of Ironclad and Ember. He barely said a word, barely ate, only prayed in silence.

Later, as they were fifty miles from the edge of the White Sea, and within sight of Cael, another group of airmen appeared in the hold, led by a dark skinned Caelish woman who cast her eyes around the room, over the bodies, only to avert her gaze downwards.

The woman was familiar to Bassai, he recognised her scent from a time before, from his interactions with Kelad. He stood.

"Yes?"

The woman spoke in Caelish, and Thomas stood up beside Bassai. "She's the helmsman of the *Shadowblade,* Saiyra."

"I speak a bit Haaman," she said, her accent a thick mix of Caelish and Mokkan.

"You are Kelad's crew," Bassai grunted.

Saiyra nodded. "He is no here."

"No ... we are not sure why. We did not find his body. As an Aether ... it may be better to ask Seraphine ... however, he was an integral part of our victory. He saved our lives, he ensured that Seraphine and the Mages had the time they needed to do what they did. He stayed behind with Tobias and Ember to ensure some us could survive."

Thomas translated for her, and she gave him a nod, her breathing heavy. The crew behind her were solemn, some of them were comforting each other, but some smiled at the recounting of their commander's actions.

"I owe you all thanks," Bassai said, walking towards them and stopping a foot away from the helmsman. "As his crew, you all had a hand in saving the Wyvern Bog from destruction. You are valiant warriors, and General Kelad proved himself to be an honourable man."

Saiyra nodded as Thomas translated, blinking, and looked up at Bassai with both an expression of grief and one of searching. "He was your enemy, long time ago."

"A long, long time ago. If times had been different, perhaps we would have been friends. Circumstances did not allow for that, but he was always a foe I respected, especially in battle."

"He had not many friends," Saiyra murmured. "Maybe many people scared of him. Should have more. He was a good man, in his way."

Thomas smiled. "I think maybe he was."

"Come," Bassai said. "We have some things to drink, and I would like to drink with you."

Thomas smiled. "I think that's a good idea. Swapping tales of Sel Kelad would be a fine way to honour his memory."

Saiyra grinned sadly and held up a ceramic bottle of dalivetra. Thomas chuckled. "Perfect."

***

Above Cael City, still smoking, several ships broke off from the

The Empire Of Fire

combined fleet. The word from below was that the commandos Vehnek had dropped, elite warriors, were still holding out. The news that Vehnek had been killed, and that Cael and Haama were under a state of full ceasefire, did not seem to dissuade them from their mission.

There were some fragments of news here and there regarding the rest of the nation. One of the Magus Towers still stood, but the other was melted and broken, all but unsalvageable. The King had declared the area a no-fly zone for the moment, until a time that they could ascertain that it wasn't a danger. There had been very little communication with the Arch Mages, and they had not requested assistance yet.

Scout ships had studied the area, and reported the vast rip in the ground in front of the ruin. The Arch Mages had offered no explanation for it, and considering the draconic monster that had attacked them at the Gravestone, more questions were there to be answered. The Towers would have to be held to account for their experimentation and their collaboration with the late Lord Marshal.

Thomas considered the way that would take place, the manner in which that accountability would be taken. A trial would be potentially too antagonistic, considering that the Arch Mages would be needed to hold back the desert. It also depended on how many, if any, of the Arch Mages were still alive.

They couldn't simply forgive and forget, not without considerable repentance. There were too many wounds inflicted, some of them likely not even known yet.

The king was still very ill, but was being taken care of by trusted physicians. Regardless of his health, he was eager to meet and hear the tale of their journey into the White Sea, and the seemingly climactic battle that had taken place. While the majority of the fleet assisted the peacekeeping force in treating the injured, proffering supplies to the worst affected, and hunting down the commandos, invitations were extended to a number of ships to dock at the Golden Throne Palace, and have an audience with King Alesio. He spoke to the senior captains, Rear Admiral Nyroshi, and the various Alliance leaders. The meetings were taken individually or in small groups, and no matter how long the conversations were, he seemed to will his ailing body to make the time.

Thomas and Bassai spoke to him together. King Alesio was laying on a bed, propped up on pillows. His skin was pale, and a warm, dark red solution was on a tray that had been placed beside him. He wore sleeping clothes, covered by an elegant robe, and a blanket up to his waist. Even in the heat of Cael City, the steam from his beverage was clear as it rose from the glass, and the sweet, medicinal smell of it was clear from the moment Thomas and Bassai crossed the threshold.

The bedchamber was an incredible sight. Having been a guest in Allessandra's own chambers, Thomas had an inkling of what to expect, but still found those expectations exceeded. The chambers were a palace in and of themselves, perched atop the rest of the complex. The bedchamber itself stood at the very top, as long and wide as the Silver throne room. The bed was massive, double the size of a double bed, with intricately woven quilts and fluffed pillows. Huge bay windows seemed to brush against the clouds, offering a panoramic view of the nation, not just the city. The coastline was clearly visible, the forests around the Magus towers, even the distant Three Hammers mountain range, where Cael's military industrial complex built and trained and prepared for war.

Despite the luxury, the chambers of the widowed King all felt empty, as if half of its decor was missing. Thomas could imagine that the Queen's passing had meant that Alesio had wished for her belongings, and reminders of her, to be put somewhere else for the time being, an aid to mourning and his own recovery. Of course, if the rumours of the origin of the King's ill health were true, they would also have served as a reminder of her treachery.

Many of the walls were bare, empty spaces remained on the floor where furniture and cabinets could have once stood. Some rooms that Thomas and Bassai had glimpsed as they had been escorted upwards were entirely bare, as if newly built. In the bedchamber itself, it seemed as if most of the room's contents had been swept away by a giant broom. There was no hint of a feminine touch in even an inch of the living space.

A woman sat on a chair at the foot of the bed, translating the King's words.

"I have been told many tales of you. I am told that you have had a considerable hand in the peace that has found our two nations."

Despite his ill health, King Alesio's voice remained powerful and deep. The translator expertly and accurately relayed the information. Thomas nodded to her with a smile. "*My compliments.*"

She blinked at him in surprise and blushed.

The King continued with a raised eyebrow at the exchange. "I hope that charm was not inflicted upon my daughter."

Thomas straightened up with a cough, and Bassai smirked. "No, Your Majesty. It never crossed my mind. Our conversations have had more of an intellectual and negotiation basis rather than any wooing."

"Indeed. No doubt Eluco was watching you like a hawk."

Thomas raised an eyebrow as Alesio's eyes moved over to Bassai. "From what little I have learned of your people from the conversations I have had today, you do not stand on ceremony in the same way that we do."

Bassai bowed his head. "Our ceremonies are simply different, Your Majesty. Princess Allessandra navigated them well in our negotiations. She is a credit to you as a father, and as a man."

"It warms my heart to hear it." Alesio sat up straighter, clearing his throat. "She will need you. She may have too much pride to admit it, but these things are not built by one person alone. I'm surprised she has managed to find some form of understanding with the Ministers."

"Politicians can be difficult to get on with." Thomas muttered.

"You do not need to tell *me*, young man. I served on that council for many years, in times as dark as ours have been recently." Alesio sipped from his glass and swallowed the liquid with a wince. "Although not as dark as yours were. I am told you were present during the invasion of Haama."

"We were," Thomas said.

Alesio focused on him. "And you were a slave in this very city."

"Yes."

Alesio clasped his hands together. "It was the reign of my great grandfather, Divos. I know little of his reign, however. He was elderly when he arose to the Golden Throne, and he had little of his wits remaining. I fear he was more puppet than man, and was, as many aged men and women of influence are, entirely corrupt. He did nothing of note, aside from being the one warming the chair when the drums of war began." Alesio sighed. "No doubt half the declaration was gibberish. The poor babbling fool was only awake for two hours at a time before he had to take a nap or be ushered to the nearest chamber pot. Cael was in a forced slumber, being shepherded to war by the devil's dogs. We will have to learn that lesson, and make sure it is not something we repeat."

"We each have our follies to learn from, Your Majesty," Thomas said.

"You and your friends, your Four Guardians, have given many people courage to stand up for their beliefs and their rights, for good and for ill."

Bassai growled in agreement.

"From across the sea, we look upon Haama as a defiant nation. Some are irritated by that, others admire it. Cael is a nation that has prioritised order, while Haama is more of a chaotic place. So many cultures in their own pockets of the land, like a continent in and of itself. Unlike us in so many ways ... yet we have somehow managed to find some kind of agreement. It is a source of great shame that it has taken so long, and cost so much blood."

"How do *you* feel about us?" Bassai asked, his back straight.

"I was the third Regent on the Silver Throne, after my grandmother and father. I found it difficult to adjust to how things were done in Haama, the balancing acts, the borders within borders, the military presence that still needed to be strong even seventy years after the war ended. The anger, the occasional assassination attempt, the ongoing military operations ... but the history too, the richness of the culture, the music, the green, rolling hills as far as the eye could see. I spent a long time trying to understand your people, but I never managed to. There were many distractions … including my late wife, and her particular attitudes to the world. She cared little for Victory, she preferred Cael City, and sometimes the Port Of Plenty in the summers. Then there was Ulan Vehnek …" The King shook his head. "A difficult man, a cold man, a brutal man. A hero to those who didn't know him, or never saw the effect he had on the places he touched."

Alesio grunted. "I hope now that a freer Haama, a more independent Haama, can flourish. That we can work side by side without unnecessary pressure … without unnecessary hatred."

Bassai nodded. "That will depend on us."

"Indeed it will. I would also like to extend my condolences to you both for your losses. I am aware that two of them were especially close to you."

Both Bassai and Thomas bowed. "Thank you, Your Majesty," Thomas said gravely. "And we extend the same to you."

King Alesio nodded to them. "Circumstances aside, I thank you. They have made the process of mourning more difficult, more bitter. With you both, I hope that is not the case."

"It is not," Bassai answered. "Although I know they are at peace … their absence is an emptiness within me."

"I heard, and read, a few tales of the four of you, in my time in Haama. Exaggerated perhaps, but you became immortal, larger than life itself."

He settled back and drank again, waving to the door. Attendants came into the room, bringing comfortable chairs and refreshments. A choice of wines, spirits and juices, as well as strips of meat and fish, lightly cooked and spiced.

"Please, sit. I would like to hear the truth of it, the origin of the legendary figures that have been written into the culture of our nations."

Bassai and Thomas looked at each other in surprise, then smiles broke out on each of their faces. "Where would you like to begin, Your Majesty?" Thomas asked as they sat down.

The King smiled. "You were each one individual, from opposite walks of life. Let us begin with how you came to be four."

***

Once the fleet, united, crossed over Victory's northern defensive walls, the cheers were loud enough for Bassai to hear it from the *Sand Dancer's* top deck.

The city seemed brighter and more vibrant than when they had left. The smoke that had been hovering between the buildings had been dispelled, and some of the stains had been painted over in dark red, blue and green paint. Construction had advanced considerably in the fortnight that the fleet had been away. The ruined buildings had become more as they once were, though still covered in wooden scaffolding. The Temple To The Gods in Old Town was almost entirely gone, the rubble cleared away. The Temple Square still bore the scars of the Night Of Terror, with melted, rippled tiles and blackened stains on everything.

Allessandra was waiting for them on the roof of the Silver Throne Palace, beside the docking frames, with the makeshift Council Of Ministers beside her, along with Helen and her guards. The *Sand Dancer* settled in its berth, and the ramp lowered. Thomas turned and beckoned to Captain Seret, who he found was already beside him, and had a foot on the gangway.

"Together," Thomas said.

She nodded. The group that descended comprised Thomas, Bassai, Seret, Seraphine and Kassaeos. Allessandra's eyes passed between them, taking in those that were missing, and she took a heavy breath. As they approached, the wyvernborn flagship slowed to a hover at the edge of the roof in order to allow Sandra, Barada and Zeta to disembark. Bassai saw the princess quickly scanning the skies, checking the approaching ships. She was looking for the *Shadowblade*. When she did not find it, her eyes slowly closed, and her head

The Empire Of Fire

bowed.

As they drew close, Bassai could see how exhausted she seemed. He breathed in, taking in her scent. Her illness had not progressed further, it was certainly fatigue, with the scent of the sea written into her skin. Some of the guards carried the same scent, as did two of the ministers. The elder minister, Evandro, held her shoulder gently.

The procession paused in front of Allessandra, who stepped forwards to meet them. "Are they aboard the ship?"

Bassai nodded. "We brought them home, all those we could bring anyway."

"I would like to see them, if I may."

"Of course," Thomas said, stepping aside to allow her to pass. She looked back and beckoned to the Ministers, who walked forwards to follow her, along with Eluco. Before she boarded, she grasped Seret's hands and held her tightly.

Bassai watched Seret's demeanour change. She seemed to shrink and draw in, and Allessandra moved in to hug her as she began to weep. The Captain's hands were trembling. Bassai had seen people, fresh soldiers in particular, succumb to the same release of their pent up terror and grief. He wondered how many battles Seret had fought in before, and found himself impressed that her piloting skills had helped her hold her nerve.

Aboard the *Sand Dancer,* in her former bedchamber, Allessandra paused above the bodies of Ironclad and Ember. She bowed her head. The rest of the ministers stood on either side, as if in formation. Carrasco held much of his emotion close to his chest, in contrast to Brynden, who held a hand over his heart, as if he was trying to hold it back from bursting open. He knew more than any one of the ministers what the two meant, what they had symbolised to Haama for a century. Ulan exchanged a curt nod with Thomas and Bassai, standing formally near to the princess. Evandro bowed his head solemnly and spoke a prayer under his breath.

"I am sorry," Allessandra said, her voice quiet. "I can ... only imagine how difficult this must be."

"There is a question of what to be done with the bodies," Carrasco murmured. "Meaning, where they are to be laid to rest."

"A moment, please, Minister," Evandro said, with an extended hand. "I understand the practical question, but the time for it will come later on."

Carrasco nodded.

"What became of General Kelad?" Allessandra asked quietly.

Bassai recounted the General's gambit to buy them time, and his sacrifice. Allessandra listened without a word. When he finished, Thomas took the envelope Kelad had given him from a pocket in his robes, and passed it to the princess. She held her composure as she recognised the seal, but her voice wavered as she sighed.

"I am ... I wish he were here. I wish he had found a place in the new state of affairs between our nations."

Eluco put a hand on her shoulder. "He has found peace."

"I had a feeling he would find a way to not return ... he was the type to give everything for a victory. His crew?"

"Most are alive," Bassai grunted. "He dropped them off on one of the carriers. His exploits in the battle were ... considerable, so they have told us."

"In that respect, he and Tobias weren't that different," Thomas said softly.

Allessandra looked at Ironclad, then at Ember. "Heroes. Heroes in two different eras ... in a time now where there have been precious few of them." She glanced across at Ulan with a sad smile. "The fates seem to bring them close to each other."

Ulan clasped his hands behind his back. "I never wanted to be a hero, Your Grace."

"It seems they never do." She turned back. "Minister Brynden, are you alright?"

Brynden sighed heavily. "Their deaths weigh heavily on me, Your Grace. While I have hardly been one to believe or ... revere the Four Guardians in the way many of my countrymen do ... it is still difficult. They have been, and are, very important people to Haama."

"I understand completely, Minister." Alessandra focused on Thomas and Bassai again. "There will be many discussions and disagreements over where your friends are laid to rest, a most unfortunate consequence of politics. Indeed, it may be our first bone of contention in the Alliance. But now is not that time. Now is the time to remember them, and mourn them, as people, rather than as symbols."

Bassai growled at that, but bowed as respectfully as he could. Thomas patted him on the shoulder.

Allessandra held her gaze. "I understand, believe me, as someone who recently lost a parent, who will no doubt be used for the same."

***

In the council chamber, the Ministers were joined by the leaders from the Wyvern Bog, Obsidian, The Aerial Navy alongside Rear Admiral Nyroshi, and three visiting dignitaries from the governorship of Cael. The terms of a formal ceasefire were drawn up and agreed to swiftly, with the agreement that Haama's defense would, for the time being, fall under the purview of a combined force of the Standing Army, Aerial Navy and Donnal's ships. The refugees from Cael were to be returned as soon as they were able to go, with segments of the nautical and aerial navies tasked with assisting the Caelish regional governors with support and aid in rebuilding and supplying the destroyed settlements. Allessandra had no intention of allowing them to rot in tents in the Port Of Plenty.

The terms for Haama's eventual independence was somewhat more contentious. The Caelish representatives were deeply concerned that the shipments of grain would stop, and Cael would be starved in revenge. Seraphine and Thomas assured them that the truth was nothing of the sort, as did Evandro and Allessandra. The rest of the council offered opinions here and there, and it became Allessandra's turn to silently wish that Ironclad were present, to argue the case in the way that would no doubt have made their intentions clearer, and more inarguable.

Still, the case was eventually left to be argued later, with Allessandra thankful for the ceasefire at least. The next conversation was more warmly received than she thought it might be, despite it coming up far sooner than any of them would have wanted.

The question of Ironclad and Ember, and where they were to be buried, was one that had several facets. Tobias Calver had been a child of Melida City, yet Ember one of the Orlin. The burial customs of the two peoples were completely different. The Orlin burned their dead, while the Haamans typically buried theirs in cemeteries, but it did not seem right for them to be separated. They had been apart in death before. In some ways, it would be fitting for them to lay in the Wyvern Bog or the city, or in Obsidian, or by Rowan near the ruins of the White Tower.

The two that would have been the makeweight in the decision, Bassai and Thomas, were quiet, until Allessandra called upon them.

Bassai growled to himself in contemplation. "As much as it would be an honour to have my friends lay in peace so close to the Bog, perhaps among our honoured dead ... it does not seem correct. It would be what *I* would want, but perhaps not what *they* would want."

Thomas smiled at the table, and his head bobbed in affirmation. "I feel the same way about them being buried here. While I know that times have changed, and our attitudes have changed with them ... Victory is not the city where they met, where they became friends, where they fell in love. Many of our friends died here ... and were not laid to rest in the manner where they should have been, such is war."

Allessandra was almost disheartened at that, but a realisation bloomed in her heart that brought a sudden tear to her eye. "They gave their lives ... for a future they knew would be difficult for them to live in. A peace that they may not have found their own peace in."

The Empire Of Fire

"It was his way, and her way," Bassai said quietly. "In many ways, they were made for each other."

"There are one or two places, perhaps," Thomas murmured thoughtfully. "The Temple To The Gods would have been such a place, however that is clearly no longer a possibility."

He exchanged a glance with Bassai, then turned to Barada. "We may require the assistance of your fliers to find the alternative."

"You shall have it," Barada growled.

"What is on your mind?" Allessandra asked.

"A place for them to rest together, and a monument in memorial. To those lost, and to the peace we found. Beside the Dividing Sea, that divides no longer. Overlooking a port, perhaps, where vessels of the sea and air depart on adventure and voyage."

Bassai closed his eyes, and smiled to himself. It was the swiftest discussion and warmest agreement that Allessandra had yet seen in politics.

***

The palace's banquet hall had never been noisier than it was two nights after the council meeting. The returning soldiers of all stripes were greeted with a vast dinner and dance. The palace grounds and gardens had been opened up and laid with long tables and chairs. The food delivered to each table was from each land the warriors hailed from. Caelish salt and freshwater fish, slow-roasted camel and fresh cactus berries, the finest roasted beef and vegetables from Haama's fields, with infused, merged chicken and rice dishes from Victory's street vendors, with honeyed lamb and potatoes from The Wyvern Bog, along with fresh flatbread and pies and fruit from the palace gardens. Jugs of juice, wine, and spring water, along with jars of fermented goat milk and dalivetra were placed next to every fifth chair. Dozens of barrels of mead in the hall alone were ready to be cracked open to replace the ones already cracked open at the head and foot of each table.

Banners and tapestries were hanging across all of the walls, ribbons in the colours of Haama and Cael were draped and winding around the pillars and beams. Fine tablecloths matched the rest of the decorations, and complimented the colour scheme. It was simple rather than lavish. The point was not to show off, the point was to come together and honour the living and the dead both.

Allessandra had been careful not to segregate the soldiers by origin, yet they had all begun the evening in their own groups, keeping to themselves. They were still full of mirth, but not together, until a wyvernborn named Kanku stood and stalked over to the Black Fleet. Allessandra noted that Bassai's gaze was sharp upon the young warrior, and worried for a moment. Her eye went to Eluco beside her, who was also watching, but with more interest than anxiety.

The Black Fleet soldiers were straightening up at the warrior's approach. All were armed with dirks, as was customary, and some hands crept towards them.

"Where is the crew of the *Charger?*" Kanku growled.

For a moment, no one spoke. A tall woman, hair pulled back into a bun, stood and cracked her neck. "I am the captain of the *Charger,* wyvernborn."

Kanku narrowed his eyes at her and prowled between the tables. "You sit with your crew?"

"The senior officers."

"Ha! Good enough. I will have to find the rest later on in the evening." He looked over his shoulder at the mead bearers, barrels sitting on trolleys, waiting until one was dry to replace it swiftly. "A fresh barrel over here!"

Kanku turned back. "We shall drink together, Captain, and your crew as well! I saw your vessel bring down a ***Trovska*** magnificently! You are true warriors, and skilled."

The mead barer cracked the barrel open, and Kanku immediately scooped up a pint-full into his tankard and the captain's.

The captain and her officers were dumbstruck for a moment, before they picked up their own tankards and stood. Kanku clasped the captain's forearm

The Empire Of Fire

with a growl and a grin and roared, upending his pint. The captain grinned and shouted "*cheers!*" in Caelish. The crew, and a number of the men and women nearby, echoed the call and drank.

When the captain was finished, having taken no pause from her drinking, Kanku grinned and clashed his empty tankard against hers. The sound rang out like a bell in the hall. "I like a strong woman who can hold her ale."

The captain grinned right back at him. "So do I."

Kanku let out a belly laugh at that. "Come, warriors, another! This time with the rest of my flight…"

He barked at the wyvernborn, some of whom hauled themselves to their feet and strolled over. One or two spread their wings and jumped over two or three tables in one leap. Zeta rolled her eyes beside Barada and stood up herself.

After that, the groups began to mingle. Some engaged in drinking contests, some ate the banquet side by side, recommending foods and strong drink from their own cultures for the rest to try, to positive, negative and amusing effect. Others simply laughed and compared tales of war. Some began to flirt and tease as the tables were moved aside, and the dancing began.

While inside the hall, things had begun somewhat cautiously, the troops in the palace gardens and grounds immediately began feasting, laughing and drinking together. Allessandra was told in whispers by the palace attendants that people were arm wrestling, running around, and engaging in song and dance, swapping stories and legends. The bards and bands who had been hired from the city and settlements were playing joyously and loudly.

The celebrations in the city were just as raucous as those among the soldiery. The streets were filled with people, aware of the festival of heroes happening at the palace. Every other bard was playing impromptu concerts in every space they could, the taverns and restaurants were serving food and drink, every facet and fragment of beauty in Victory was blooming to the fore.

***

Princess Allessandra was clearly taking some amusement in the stares of some of the celebrating soldiers as she was gathered into Eluco's arms and borne across the floor among the rest of the dancers. Her smile was warming to Thomas's heart. One so young should not be troubled with the matters of state and nation that she engaged with daily, regardless of the strength she had to do so. Seeing her full of the joy that love brought was rewarding, but also somewhat bitter. Love reminded him of Tobias and Ember, and of his own solitude.

He sipped his mead thoughtfully, pushing it from his mind. He, like Bassai beside him, had never been much of a dancer. However, even his wyvernborn friend was deeply engaged in conversation with Zeta. They laughed together in great bellows, clapped each other on the back, ribbed each other graciously and ungraciously.

"*Are you enjoying your victory, Thomas?*"

Thomas turned at the sound of Ulan's voice. Through habit, he almost saluted.

"*Well enough, Commander ... Minister ... I have no idea what to call you.*"

He chuckled. "*Just Ulan, even though having a 'warrior of legend' defer to me by rank is a fine tonic for the ego. This is hardly a military occasion.*"

Ulan sat down next to Thomas with a grunt. "*There's a rumour going around that there won't be a Lord Marshal any more. Seems there'll be a military council handling affairs of the armed forces. Good and bad sides to that...*"

"*On the one hand, there's less chance of the army being driven by one person's whim. On the other, they could be bickering when they need to take action.*"

Ulan nodded. "*Among other things, aye. Rumours are that I'm being put forwards for it.*"

Thomas chuckled. "*I don't envy you.*"

The Empire Of Fire

"*I wouldn't envy me either, but there you go. Before you know it, you'll be put on it as well, so watch that laughter.*"

Thomas's smile fell. "*Really?*"

Ulan cracked a smile. "*Just don't be surprised.*"

He leaned forwards and poured a little dalivetra into two glasses. He pushed one in front of Thomas. "*I hear it was quite the battle out there.*"

"*'Battle' almost doesn't adequately explain it.*"

"*I'm sorry I missed it ... but I don't think it was the kind of fight meant for me. I'm infantry, not navy ... although neither are you, eh?*"

Thomas raised his glass, and Ulan clinked his against it. "*To your friends' memory.*"

Thomas nodded with a sad smile, and drank. He reached out and poured another, this time a longer, far more dangerously generous helping. "*For Orso, Lazar, Pardek, Ilian, Virs, Aket, and Ori.*"

Ulan patted him on the back, and almost had to psych himself up for the drink. He poured one more.

"*For General Kelad.*"

Thomas nodded, and drank. It was the only of the three that didn't burn his throat.

"*I take it you were by the sea with the princess, eh?*"

Ulan nodded. "*Yes, marshalling the refugees, and getting them into shelter, making sure they're fed and the injured treated. It was long work, but it was ... rewarding to help.*"

"*It seems like what you've always tried to do.*"

Ulan nodded. "*Tried, aye.*"

Thomas went back to his mead, incredibly sweet after three shots of dalivetra. "*Are the rest of the squad around?*"

"*You mean, 'is Elizia around'. We all know you're a little sweet on her.*"

"*Not nearly as how sour as she seemed to be on me.*"

Ulan waved a hand. "*Ignore that. I'm serious. She was shocked as the rest of us when you appeared alongside the Resistance. You know what happened to her ... and I'm betting you're well connected enough to know who did it."*

Thomas sighed, thinking of Kira, who was no doubt at the end of her recovery in Obsidian.

Ulan patted his back again. *"Doesn't matter now, Thomas, although to her it almost certainly matters an awful lot."*

"The more distance between her and I the better, I fear. I ... only wish Elizia happiness, and comfort, and relief ... and love. Love, from someone good, and strong, and kind. She has a wicked sense of humour, you know ... I don't know if you've had a chance to see it."

Ulan smiled. *"Go on."*

"Before it all went wrong in the tavern downtown, Gods above, Ulan ... when she smiled it was like the room stopped. That smile was all there was in the whole world for a moment."

"Good job you weren't gawking at her for too long, or we'd all have been poisoned!"

The warm voice from behind him made Thomas freeze, then slowly get to his feet. Ulan's shoulders were slowly bobbing in laughter.

Thomas sighed. *"Well, Berek ... I take it you aren't alone back there."*

"Correct."

Thomas turned, smiling, yet very aware of the flush creeping up the side of his neck to his face. The same rosiness at the cheeks was mirrored on Elizia, as she tried to look at every possible object and person in the room that wasn't Thomas. Berek was beaming at him, Yaro was chuckling under his breath, with his arm around a gently swaying Mule. All of them were in dress uniforms.

He reached forwards and clasped Berek's hand, patting him on the back. *"Glad to see you up and healthy, my friend. I guess you've all been somewhere close to the sea?"*

"Oh aye, we took a beach holiday with the princess, and about five thousand refugees."

Thomas grinned at Mule. *"Little worse for wear? That didn't take long."*

The Empire Of Fire

Yaro patted him on the shoulder. *"Well he's celebrating twice. He's a freeman."*

"Freeman!" Mule bellowed, slurring the word.

Thomas laughed and hugged the former slave, taking a good amount of weight as he did so. *"Glad to hear it!"*

"Jus' need name, now ..." Mule said a little too loudly. *"Can't be Mule f' th' rest o' m' life..."*

"We'll work that out with him if he wants," Ulan said proudly, getting to his feet. *"Come on, you lot, let's get him another drink."* He looked pointedly at the lads, jerking his head away and giving Elizia and Thomas a sidelong look.

"One moment, sir." Thomas picked up the dalivetra jar and every glass he could find, pouring the rest of the bottle into them. He handed them out to the squad and looked right at Mule. He raised his glass. *"To freedom."*

"Freedom," Ulan echoed.

"Weheeeey!" Mule cheered, and knocked the shot back with a belch.

"Right ... now then ... let's get him a cup of water, maybe ..." Ulan patted Elizia on the back as he moved away with the others.

For a moment, she and Thomas said nothing, until he stepped forwards and took her hand. When she looked up at him, her eyes were searching his for something, perhaps deceit. Her face softened when she found none.

"Dance with me."

Elizia swallowed. *"You don't seem much of a dancer."*

"I've been waiting for the right partner."

She sighed to herself. *"Then, I had better lead. Wouldn't want you stepping on my foot."*

He led her out to the rest of the dancers, and slipped his hands around her waist. The singer, a bright red haired woman named Rose Thorn, began a soft ballad that was meant for the couples in the room.

"So ..." Elizia murmured. *"Before we were almost poisoned ... you were about to make a move."*

Thomas smiled. *"I was thinking about it."*

"*Something about a smile that stopped the room?*"

"*I think I implied it stopped the world.*"

The blushed crept over Elizia's cheeks again. "*You're easily impressed, I take it?*"

Thomas grinned. "*If that's the case, kissing you will probably give me a heart attack.*"

Elizia blinked, and the rosiness brightened. "*It's a kiss you're after, then.*"

"*For now, a dance will do ...*" He matched her steps, and brushed a hand from her waist up to her shoulder, and down her arm to her hand. He wove his fingers with hers, raised her hand, and took the lead in the dance, spinning her and then gathering her into his arms. "*I am hoping, however, to earn the kiss.*"

"*Perhaps you will earn it, but I'm not so easily impressed by dancing.*"

Thomas grinned. "*I look forward to impressing you in other ways.*"

"*None of that magic of yours, though. No hypnosis, or anything like that.*"

"*That isn't a power I employ, you'll be relieved to know. Before I earn that kiss, I want to give you an apology. Deceiving everyone in the squad, but you especially, isn't something I would have chosen to do, if it hadn't been necessary.*"

"*I think I understand why you did it ... and I probably would have done the same if it had been me ... and I would have regretted it as well.*"

She moved closer to him, re-taking the lead. "*I want to give you an apology as well, before I let you kiss me.*"

"*For what?*"

"*For being unfair to you ... even if you were a snake at the time.*" Her eyes flashed with a challenge to his sense of humour.

"*The good kind?*"

"*That remains to be seen. My own problems with magic got in the way. You saved people, a lot of them. You saved me.*"

"*Accepted.*" Thomas leaned around and kissed her on the cheek softly, keeping her close to him. He kept his cheek against hers as they slowly spun.

"*That wasn't the kiss I was expecting,*" Elizia murmured.

Thomas drew back, and as she turned her face up to his, he kissed her on the lips.

Her hand found his cheek and she drew him in further. The scent of her floral perfume filled his senses, and everything else in the room became nothing but complimenting harmonies to the music.

***

A full week after the banquet, Thomas and Bassai were brought to Obsidian on the *Dreadnought,* alongside the remainder of what had been the Resistance fleet. Fifteen of the original twenty four remained.

The two remaining Guardians stood upon the top deck, watching the repurposed mine approaching. The trip had largely been a calm one, but with few words between them.

It was Bassai who broke the silence. "You and I will have to part ways for a while."

Thomas turned to him. "We will?"

"I am taking Kaitlyn and the children to the Wyvern Bog, as soon as possible. It is her best chance at a new life … one where she will make a difference, and where the children will be protected."

Thomas raised an eyebrow. "They'll be protected in Obsidian, won't they?"

"Maybe," Bassai grunted. "But they would not flourish. I worry for them all. Apart from that … I barely know my own people."

Thomas patted him on the back. "I hear you. I have my own task to accomplish as well, and it hopefully won't be anywhere near as complicated as making a home."

Bassai grunted again. "This isn't a goodbye, my friend. Just a goodbye for now."

Thomas nodded, a pang of sadness still finding its way through. It seemed that they had barely had any time so sit down since he was sent away with Ulan's squad.

"Hopefully I'll meet you in Victory ... at which point, a quiet beer will be in order. Emphasis on the quiet."

Bassai grinned. "Agreed."

36

Bassai watched carefully as Lance swung from one platform to the next on a training rope. He was halfway up a pair of strong willow trees, the gap between them a solid thirty feet. The fronds were all gold now rather than green, the humidity of their summer truly departed and replaced with the refreshing, spiced breezes of the fall.

Lance let go of the rope at the apex of the swing, and flew through the air, landing with both feet solidly on the platform. The Orlin trainer patted him on the back and shook his hand. Lance looked down at Bassai, who was nodding his own approval with a smile. The boy pumped his fist in triumph, and listened as his instructor gave him his next task.

Maka chuckled beside Bassai. "He is a quick learner."

Bassai nodded. "He is. It is good to see him smile. It has been a rarity, but over the last few weeks he has started to ... be young again. He was forced to grow up far too quickly."

"All of the young grow up too quickly for me to keep up," Maka grumbled. He leaned on his cane. "By the dragon's flame, I remember when you yourself were a bald little hatchling, let alone Kanku and his generation."

Bassai patted the elder on his thick, armoured forearm. "Is that boy planning on settling down at all?"

"Kanku? Oh ... you know how the young are. He has got his eyes on the wyvernborn females, and needs a few more scars for them." Maka peered at Bassai for a moment. "There have been a few of them who have taken an interest in you, you know."

Bassai chuckled. "I am spoken for. Kaitlyn is quite enough woman for me."

"Practically a wyvernborn female herself, that one. When I met her I half expected her to have scales somewhere, hidden away."

"She has to be fierce, chasing those children of hers through the willows."

"I am glad they have found a home here ... and I am glad you have, young one." Maka patted Bassai's clawed hand with his own gnarled paw. "It means all of this world to me to have my son back here, and earning your respect back."

"Slaying a puppeteered dragon and saving Planar helped plenty."

Maka guffawed so loudly it shook the willow branches. "We are a stubborn bunch, lad. You would have to slay five and save the world twice!"

The pair watched Lance swing again, drop into a blade attack onto a training dummy, as well as practice with a bow. The spread of his arrows was the tightest so far, not quite in the bullseye yet, but getting there. During the second training volley, there was a swoosh of wings, and Zeta and Kanku landed beside them.

"Alpha," Kanku grunted respectfully, clasping a closed fist in his hand as a sign of respect to Reeva's elder. He nodded to Bassai as well, but without a word or gesture. Bassai nodded in return. Zeta grinned to herself.

"How is he getting along?" she asked.

"Well," Bassai said with a smile. He felt a swell of warm joy at seeing them both, Zeta especially. Her cohort had been ranging along the coast for a week, and the Beta had become a fast and valued friend. "What news from the north?"

"Two things," Kanku grunted. "The first refugee boats are starting back towards Cael. With the weather clement, it is the best time before Autumn truly descends."

"Good to hear," Maka rumbled.

Zeta straightened up and took Bassai's hands in hers. The gesture made him take in a deep breath. The news he had been waiting for since the end of the ceasefire had come.

"We have found the perfect place for them."

"Where?"

"On a cliff rise, seven miles from the Port Of Plenty. The docks are clearly visible, and should be even on a murky day. The ground is stable enough to support a structure and soft enough to work."

Bassai closed his eyes, and held his forehead against hers. Zeta growled in surprise, but it turned to a purr of warmth.

"I would like to see it, if possible."

"Yes ... I had an idea about that, but it may take a while. Word is being sent to Thomas and Seraphine as we speak." Zeta patted him on the chest. "We must meet with Barada, but the sparring platforms await us afterwards."

"I will see you there. Two handed axes this time."

Zeta grinned and took to the air with Kanku.

Maka chuckled knowingly as they disappeared above the canopy. Bassai glanced at him. "What amuses you?"

Maka eyed him with a chuckle. "Oh, nothing at all, lad."

"Something did."

The elder glanced up at the canopy where Zeta and Kanku had gone. "You made her purr. She *never* purrs..."

Bassai grunted with a shake of his head. "It is nothing of that sort. Zeta is a fine warrior, we share a mutual respect."

Maka just smiled at him like he was an infant. Bassai growled to himself. "Do not tell Kaitlyn."

This time, Maka's laugh shook the trunks of the trees.

***

Kaitlyn was planting a crop of cabbages when Bassai jogged up to the burrow. She had managed to pick one out that was next to a flat enough plot of land to set up a small farm. Their brace of young cows ambled around in the middle of the long grass, and the pen of chickens bobbled about clumsily. They clucked like a tiny chorus to announce Bassai's arrival, and Kaitlyn wiped her brow as she looked up at him with a smile.

There was a sheen of sweat across her neck and upper chest, and her biceps shone in the dappled sunlight. Her hair was pulled back into a damp ponytail. She was breathing heavily from the hard work she had been putting in all day, judging by how many vegetables seemed to have been planted.

Bassai gathered her up into his arms, and she gave a gasp of surprise as he lifted her out of the soil.

"I ... all right ..." Kaitlyn laughed and kissed the side of his snout. "I'm filthy ... I've been planting for hours."

"I know."

She raised an eyebrow. "I didn't realise sweaty farmers were so alluring to wyvernborn."

"You will fully realise it shortly ..."

"Luckily for you, Pia and Rory are at the school house ... so there's no need to be quick or quiet..."

He carried her down into the burrow with a grin. "Oh, we will not be..."

***

Zeta growled and tossed Bassai a two-handed training axe the moment he finished his climb up to the training platform. She grinned and stepped into a low stance. "First to three, or last to yield."

Bassai nodded. He tested the wooden weapon's weight in his hand. It had plenty of heft to it, and was top-heavy.

"Hope you are not too fatigued from throwing that farmer around the bedclothes of your burrow."

Bassai bared his teeth in a smirk. "Have a little more faith in your battle

The Empire Of Fire

capabilities, Zeta. Only lacklustre warriors rely on such distractions."

She growled. "We will see."

With a roar, she leaped. Her wings beat three times, giving her height, then spread to make her glide above him. He waited for her to drop, looking for the tells in her body language. She gave him none, suddenly arrowing her wings and dropping upon him. He rolled beneath her strike and swept his axe backwards as he jumped to his feet. Zeta easily deflected the blow.

She jumped again, he jumped with her. He dropped the axe and grabbed onto her ankle, dragging her down onto the platform. She swung the axe back towards him, but he was too close. He grasped her wrists and pinned her on her back, wings trapped beneath her muscular frame.

"Yield."

Zeta aimed a kick at him, and he twisted, pinning her thigh with his knee. She smirked up at him.

"You sure this is the position you want to be in?"

"Yield."

"I have you exactly where I want you."

Bassai grinned. "In your dreams, perhaps."

She barked up at him and laughed. "Argh, fine. I yield."

Bassai let her up and she stretched. Zeta eyed him. "Less of that dream talk. A human warms my burrow as yours does."

"You are distracted far too easily."

Zeta folded her arms. "You think I am distracted by something?"

"You rarely leave a trailing leg."

She chuckled and padded over to the weapon trunk with the training axes. She tossed them inside without a care. There was another trunk beside it, flatter and wider, with steel clasps.

"I have a question for you," she said. "How long has it been since you flew?"

Bassai frowned, trying not to think about how much pain the last memory of his flight brought.

"A long time."

"Do you remember how?"

Bassai's fists clenched. "You do not forget. It is a part of us. That is why the exile is so ... devastating. Why many of us give up on living."

Zeta paused before she unlatched the crate. "I had something made for you by the shamen and the smiths. Come here."

Bassai approached as she lifted the lid.

Inside was a leather and steel harness with room to fit beneath a set of armour. It seemed adjustable with buckles. The back of it was flat, with shoulder pads and supports, attached to two wings.

Instead of scaled skin there was a double layer of treated leather. Instead of the bones beneath, there were steel rods, one thick at the top and thinner ones lining the membrane. There were sleeves, with tubes like thick veins running down the arms, to two thin bone handles where the hands would be.

Bassai stared at the suit as Zeta carefully lifted it out. "Try it on. I need to see if it will fit you."

"How do I control the flight?"

Zeta pointed to the handles. "Hold those, and manipulate the wings with movements of your wrists. There are rods running up the sleeves, protected by hollow steel tubes." As she spoke, she lifted the device, and held it so Bassai could buckle himself in. He tightened the straps so it was as tight as he could bear. There were more buckles for his shoulders and ones for the base of his tail and his thighs.

"Comfortable?" Zeta said, letting the back of it go.

"No."

She grinned. "It may need refinement. Attempt to use the wings. Pull the handles down to spread them."

Bassai took a breath, and pulled the handles downwards. The wings extended on either side of him. The span between the tips was around twenty feet in length.

"Is this why we have been training on the highest platform?"

The Empire Of Fire

Zeta smiled. "These wings are meant to glide. We are not sure yet how to ... fly. Take off, anyway."

"From an airship, then."

"Any high place. I suspect it will be quite nimble in flight. You should be able to gain altitude and dodge, make sharp turns. Twisting the handles will trim the edges of the wings, and of course you would still be using your tail for manoeuvres."

Bassai glanced at her. "It has not been tested?"

"You will be the first to use it. How they are operated is different to how we would normally use our wings, but we are sure they will work. If they do not ... that is why we are not higher up."

Bassai barked a laugh.

Zeta patted his shoulder armour. "It may take some time to re-learn how to use the wings ... and refine the design, but it will be time well spent."

"I will let you know if that is the case after I inevitably fall."

"It could be worse. You could be negotiating with the humans in Victory."

Bassai smiled back at her. "Is everything in place?"

"Yes."

The moment she let him go, Bassai ran straight for the edge of the platform. He jumped six feet up and outwards, the same old rush of excitement and freedom blasting through his veins. As he began to fall, he pulled the handles down and flared the wings.

***

Thomas couldn't help but feel the same pang of sadness as the *Sand Dancer* floated above Taeba District. The forest was silent as the grave. There was no smoke from a cook-fire or camp, no beat of a drum alerting marauders to the airship's presence, no rumbling of hooves.

He folded his arms, and shook his head. General Kelad was no longer alive to answer for all this ... and he knew that someone would have to. He also knew that dwelling on the resentment the massacre had caused, however justifiable the ill-feeling was, was a barrier to the peace they needed.

They had almost all paid for the Pil Valley, every citizen of Haama, Cael and the Mountain Cities, of Salketh across the White Sea. The entity they had really been engaging, the hateful, twisted thing that had corrupted life and death for its own ends, had been a common enemy.

Likely it still was. Somewhere out there, in the dark realm it had attempted to banish them to.

"Try it ..." Thomas muttered under his breath. "We'll be ready for you."

Seraphine and Kassaeos were standing against the port side railing, close to each other, any words spoken entirely out of earshot. He didn't want to interrupt them. Where they were going would more difficult for her, as difficult as returning to what had been Melida City had been for him.

He was interrupted from his thoughts by a warm hand on his waist. He looked around with a smile as Elizia stood up beside him. She had donned a light leather, utility armour, segmented for mobility. Each plate was warded for magical protection.

"Your old stomping grounds, eh?" she muttered.

"Something like that. It wasn't this peaceful before ... and I don't know if I like it. We went through the hells in here."

"Then why the ill feeling?"

Thomas sighed and frowned. *"There could have been peace with the clans here. The ones we had a run in with, The Dragon Breakers and The Dead Men, were both different in many ways. Peace would have been possible eventually, had we gone about it the right way. Awful as they were ... as The Dragon Breakers were ... we never gave them the chance."*

Elizia shook her head. *"Did they earn that chance? You can't just give people things. We earned our chances together."*

Thomas nodded, thinking of Kalgan, then Ydra. *"Some more than earned it, some didn't."*

She squeezed his hand. *"The boys look like they're ready to go."*

He nodded. *"You're all clear about what you're looking for?"*

She kissed him on the cheek. *"Stop worrying."*

The ship passed over a thinning copse of trees, then a spaced out cluster of dilapidated wood and stone shacks. Thomas only recognised where they were when they passed over the familiar chapel spire.

Vash was abandoned, slowly being reclaimed by the forest. Mosses were creeping up the walls, the debris from the burned shacks was no longer recognisable. It seemed to have merged with the mud made by rainfall. Some of the huts were beginning to sink into the ground. There were no bodies anywhere from the engagement with the ghouls.

Thomas's eyes slowly moved up until he was looking at the edge of the ancient courtyard. Seraphine moved up to the prow, a hand over her chest. Kassaeos too was half turned away with his head bowed.

The White Tower was a wide pile of rubble, a mass of stone and powder that was completely unrecognisable from the grand structure it had been. Gone were the classrooms and tapestries, the library, the stairwell where Thomas had fought and bled beside his friends.

He reached out with his power, feeling for residual magic in the area. He came up against a wall in his mind, that could have fooled an unfamiliar Mage that they were detecting nothing.

"Are you ready?" he muttered to Elizia.

She nodded. *"Ready for anything."*

"The lads may need to be ready for combat. The burial site might have a strong reaction to our presence."

Her face hardened in an all too familiar way. he squeezed her hand. *"Just in case. Seraphine and I are the front line. We won't let anything happen to any of you."*

He padded back across the deck, and approached Captain Seret. *"Set us down at the southern edge of the courtyard. We have a stop to make before we locate and retrieve what we're here for. I'd stay at the edge and ... keep the generator warm."*

Seret raised an eyebrow. *"For what reason?"*

"Potential defenses."

Seret pursed her lips. *"I'll put us down, but staying at a hover. The barriers are going up and they're staying up."*

Thomas nodded.

"And the cannons," she added. Thomas grinned, but she didn't return the expression. *"This is my ship, and this isn't a battle."*

"I'm not trying to put you or the crew at risk."

"And I'm not allowing you to put them at risk, Thomas."

He let out a breath through his teeth, and nodded to her. *"I understand, Captain."*

As the *Sand Dancer* began to descend, Yaro led Berek, Goran, and a trio of younger soldiers up the ramp from the hold. Goran was the name that Mule had chosen, after extensive searching for his records revealed that it had been the birth name of his father. Elizia joined them, as Thomas approached.

He cast a quick eye over the three new additions, the first three in the rebuild of the squad. Taris was eighteen, from Nazraan, a small town on the banks of the Azure Serpent. She had the second highest scores in her classes and training at Three Hammers and had the confidence and assurance to match. Her light brown hair was in an immaculate braid at the back of her head, making her pointed features look even sharper.

Detaan was the one who had topped her in the same tests, the same age as Taris and half a head taller. His head was shaved, he was as muscular as Berek, but without the seasoning.

The third was a Haaman, a twenty year old lad from Kalendra called Niall. A farmer's son, who had joined the city guard at sixteen, he had a leaner physique than the others, his hair sandy blonde. His Caelish was near-fluent, having learned from some of the farmhands he had lived with when he was a boy.

The Empire Of Fire

"*Ladies and gentlemen, once we're down there, stay alert, and stay behind Seraphine and I.*"

"*Thought our armour was warded, boss,*" Niall muttered, folding his arms.

"*It is, but a barrier beats a ward in protection nine times out of ten. When we're down, keep an eye on the courtyard, but don't walk on any of the tiles until we know it's safe.*"

Yaro nodded. "*We'll keep an eye out for anything that looks off. Where are you going to be?*"

"*Perhaps a mile away, paying our respects to old friends ... and making sure of something.*"

Yaro nodded. "*Alright, we will be on the perimeter, in that case.*"

Thomas took a step back. "*Present arms, please.*"

The soldiers drew their weapons, long and short blades, as well as the arrows for their shortbows. Thomas touched each of them, imbuing them with some of his magic.

Seret brought the yacht to a hover and shouted an order to lower the ramp. Seraphine moved to the lip of it and held out a hand. Her eyes closed for a moment, then she looked around and nodded.

Yaro gave her a thumbs-up. "*Let's go. Ten yard spread. Stay between the ship and the tree line.*"

Thomas, Seraphine and Kassaeos jumped off, quickly followed by the soldiers. As the perimeter was set, Seraphine led the way into the trees.

The walk was silent, and dread had gripped Thomas's heart tightly. With Ydra's dark power taking her over, and the number of the dead that had been summoned to her aid, he was terrified of what awaited them in the meadow.

That fear was quelled as they reached the graves of the Dead Men, the ones that had given their lives defending the tower. The ground was undisturbed, the trees watching over the lost as tenderly as any mourner.

They waited there for a moment. Thomas said a prayer over the graves, wishing that the Dead Men and Ydra had found their way back to each other in the Astral Plane.

They're safe. They're home.

He looked up. The voice had startled him from his thoughts, but there were none around who could have spoken.

The voice had been familiar to him, but also not. Like Ydra's, but … more. It had more gravity to it, more energy, and none of the pain.

He closed his eyes and smiled. When he looked around at Seraphine, tears were running down her cheeks, but she was smiling. Kassaeos's arm was wrapped around her waist, an anchor for her strength.

Eventually they moved on, striding around the graves and deeper into the forest. The sounds of wildlife began building around them again. Birds called to each other in adjacent trees, and insects sang from the longer grasses and shrubs around the trunks. The leaves and twigs rustled as small mammals fled from the interlopers. Seraphine reached out a hand, and her fingertips glowed green. The panic around them calmed a little, the three humans were recognised as no threat.

The meadow opened out ahead of them, a sea of blue, orange and purple wildflowers. The centre, where Rowan lay, was covered by even more swirls and twists of colour.

The three of them walked through the wildflowers, taking care not to step on any. There were little islands of grass, like stepping stones, set close enough together to get them through the field. Thomas grinned at the seeming thoughtfulness of nature.

At the mound where Rowan was buried, they all prayed again. They had barely begun to clear their minds when they were hit by a wave of the purest euphoria that Thomas had ever felt. It was a swell of joy and fatherly pride, as rich as reading a library full of books and a walking through a gallery full of artwork, all focused into one emotion.

It seemed as if every flower bloomed wider, and even more of them sprouted and spread from the soil, not just on the mound but in the entire meadow.

The Empire Of Fire

The feeling painted a thousand pictures and spoke a million words. When the wave had passed, the feeling remained in Thomas's heart, swelling and warming his entire body.

None of them had anything to say. They simply basked in the meadow, laying down and staring at the sky, until the feeling turned into a nudge.

Remember why you're here.

They stood with renewed vigour, and made their way back to the courtyard.

Yaro glanced back at them from his position at the edge of the marble flagstones. His bow was drawn, an arrow nocked.

Thomas crouched beside him. *"Anything?"*

"No. Nothing that unusual either. Not much seems out of place."

"What's your bow out for, then?"

Yaro frowned. *"A feeling, right in my gut. There's danger here ... or there was. Since you three walked up, it doesn't seem to know what to think."*

Thomas nodded. *"It's the wards. Remember what I said on the ship?"*

"Stay behind you."

Thomas nodded. He looked around at Kassaoes and Seraphine. *"Kassaeos, stay behind Yaro's men and keep an eye on our backs."*

He nodded, and Seraphine stood. She and Thomas stayed a few yards apart as they stepped away from the marble.

The squad followed them back around the *Sand Dancer*, and deeper into the woods. The latent magic woven into the soil and the tree roots hummed beneath Thomas's feet. Despite the death that had come to the Taeba forest, part of it was very much alive.

There remained burned and ripped up branches and trunks. Splinters of wood from trees blown apart by siege engines covered the ground, shattered like broken glass. The soldiers behind the Mages tensed at the scars of the crusade that remained.

The forest had taken note of the presence of Caelish soldiers, and Thomas could feel an air of hostility beginning to rise. It was being filtered by the measure of the individuals, and by Seraphine, Kassaeos and Thomas's company. The anger remained, but had an element of hesitancy as well.

Thomas glanced around at Seraphine, and she nodded. She began projecting an aura of calm, but it didn't quell the feeling much. Thomas joined his power with hers, but still the only result was holding back, not a measure of relief.

"*Where's this thing we're looking for, anyway?*" Berek muttered.

Thomas held his focus. "*Just follow us, we know where we're going.*"

"*You said you buried the knowledge, didn't you?*" Elizia asked quietly.

"*Yes ... we're almost there.*"

They drew closer to the place where the magic went from natural to foreign. The smells of thick foliage and rich, freshly disturbed soil spiced the air. The trees pressed in tighter, winding and twisting together into misshapen formations. Thick roots and weeds had filled in stream beds where water had once bubbled and sloshed along.

Immediately in front of them was a thick knot of huge trees, clenched and winding together like the makings of a natural fortress. It seemed to be a massive ball, without a marked entrance or weakness. The canopy above thickened and strengthened the shadows.

They stopped ten feet from the twisted trees, but not of their own accord. It was as if Thomas's and Seraphine's feet had been welded to the ground.

Yaro grunted behind them. "*Here?*"

Thomas shook his head. "*Nearly, not quite.*"

"*Then why ...*"

"*Whatever happens next, stay your bows and blades until you absolutely have to.*"

The soldiers all dropped to one knee, and Kassaeos crouched behind them. Their eyes widened in amazement and fear as the trees shifted in front of them.

It started as the gentle rustling of leaves, like the whispering of a theatrical chorus. It gradually turned to a rumble and tear as giant roots and trunks fused together. Two mismatched columns of wood punched into the ground, then two more. Smaller trees wound together into a smaller ball to form the head. The torso was made up of soil, shrubbery and more trees, and four wooden legs cracked the ground as the giant golem stepped across the clearing that its forming had created. Fully upright, it was fifty feet tall.

"Back off," Seraphine hissed. The whole procession moved ten yards backwards, then ten more to the treeline. The blank, expressionless head followed their movements. It stepped forwards until it was clear of the rips it had made in the ground, and into the forest itself. By then, the salvage group were fifty yards back towards the ruins.

Seraphine stepped forwards and raised her voice. "You know who I am."

The golem had no reaction to her.

"I am Seraphine, daughter of Rowan. I stand here with The Mage, of the Four Guardians. You know we are here in peace. What we want … we want for the purposes of peace."

Thomas glanced back at the soldiers, wearing Caelish regalia, and stepped beside Seraphine. "We are not here under duress, as it may appear. The men and women of Cael beside us are here for the same purpose as us. You know this to be true."

The golem's head cocked to the side. Thomas glanced back. "Yaro! Come here. In Haaman, speak your case. Why are you here, and what have you done to prove your heart?"

Yaro stood hesitantly and held out a hand to hold the rest of the troops back. He stepped forwards until he was on the other side of Thomas. "In Haaman?"

Thomas nodded. "Have courage, my friend."

Yaro pursed his lips, and cleared his throat.

"I am Yaro, son of Torren, soldier of the Caelish Standing Army. I am here because I believe in Thomas. I am here to back up a friend, here so my wife and children will live in a place of peace and safety. I have stood beside the people of Haama for all of my time here. I have protected them to the best of my ability. I have helped those in need whose homes have been burned. I have helped those who have nothing find safety on Haama's shores. I will do so until I am no longer able to."

The golem stepped forwards and leaned down, daintily avoiding the trees, getting a measure of each of them in turn. It held on Yaro the longest, peering at him like a bird of prey would peer at a mouse.

"Open your mind to it, Yaro," Thomas whispered. "Let it see you, all of you."

"What do you mean? How?"

"Close your eyes, don't look at the golem. Clear every thought from your head as best you can."

Yaro gritted his teeth and closed his eyes. Slowly, his jaw started to relax.

The golem straightened up, and looked to Seraphine and Thomas again. Very slowly, it stepped back and bowed.

Everyone behind them, and Yaro, took a breath in relief. Thomas realised that a cold sweat was dripping around his spine. He glanced at Seraphine, who remained strong to everyone else. However, he could see the same anxiety melting away from her.

The golem settled back into the clearing, into the ground it had ripped up, and became another aspect of the forest once more. The trees were no longer in their protective formation, instead leaning away from each other, as if revealing a prize in their midst. No-one moved or spoke for a moment.

"*Any other surprises?*" Yaro muttered.

Thomas looked to Seraphine, who shook her head. "The only thing to do now is uncover the books."

***

The children sat beneath Maka, listening to another of his many stories. His kindly voice rumbled, wrapping around them like a blanket. He could be heard even above the revelry of the Festival Of The Moon, celebrating the first

The Empire Of Fire

full, glowing orb of autumn.

Pia and Rory were glued to every word the elder uttered. Lance sat with Barada and Sandra's son, as well as a couple of the other Orlin trainees.

Bassai watched Kaitlyn and Sandra talking across the clearing from where the Reeva clan were sitting and drinking. He was listening to Maka's tales as closely as the children were, with half an eye on Pia and Rory, and the other half of the eye on Lance. He had appointed himself the guardian role for them, as the Guardian role had been bestowed upon him for the entire nation.

Kaitlyn's eyes met his for a moment, and a smile bloomed across her face, the wonder of a Spring flower in the falling leaves. Sandra, beside her, followed her gaze and chuckled. Bassai felt the mirror of the expression on his own face.

It was enough to dull the pain in his back and hips for a moment. While he remembered exactly how to fly, he wasn't using the same muscles to do so. The new wings required an entirely new regimen of exercise and coordination. He had fallen a few times, hit a couple of trees, but he had also dodged between them, swooping and diving, gaining height until he had burst above the canopy with an intoxicating swell of joy.

A large wooden tankard thunked down on the table in front of him. The bench creaked as a large figure settled beside him.

Kanku barely looked at him as he slid one of two tankards over. The sour and sweet tingle of fermented milk tickled his nose.

"Didn't drink with you at that fancy festival we had in their stone nonsense," the young wyvernborn muttered.

Bassai growled to himself, and a huff of air escaped his nostrils. He gripped the tankard in his claws. "You still cannot look upon me, though."

Kanku's eyes stayed on Maka. "You know better now, as well as the hatchlings are learning: you will not fly when you first spread your wings."

Bassai snorted and nodded. "Indeed."

"But you are my kin. Whether I look you in the eye or not, your blood changes not. Your soul is Reeva, you fight as a Reeva fights ... and without you, perhaps all these Festivals of the Moon would never have happened. Children unborn, a future gone or poisoned by our crimes, directed by Rezara. Your mind built all of this ... and our future now is far brighter than it could have been."

Bassai reached out a hand to pat him on the shoulder, in the way he had when Kanku was a hatchling ... but he withdrew. Now he was a warrior, and deserved the respect that came with it. "You flew well in the battle, so I hear from Zeta."

Kanku grunted.

"It does not surprise me. You were the quickest learner."

"I was taught well. Another thing to thank you for."

Bassai tapped his bicep, and picked up his tankard. "How old's the milk?"

"Forty days."

Bassai growled approvingly with a nod. "If battle finds us again, I hope I fly on your wing, Kanku."

Kanku's head turned, and his eyes met Bassai's. For a moment, Bassai saw the young wyvernborn he had been, and the adult he had become, in the same moment.

The tankards clanked together, and the pair drank deeply. Once half Bassai's tankard was gone, he let out a satisfied, rumbling growl.

"Better than ale."

Kanku chuckled. "The Caelish stuff is not bad."

Familiar movement drew Bassai's eye. Kaitlyn was walking across the clearing, around the dancers and revellers and feasters. He straightened up, and Kanku patted him on the shoulder.

"Come and find me by the barrel when you are both ... ready."

He stood up with a toothy grin, and downed the rest of his tankard. He stretched his wings and strolled around behind Maka's chair, out towards the tables of food.

Kaitlyn settled down beside Bassai on the bench, squeezing in close. He

The Empire Of Fire

wrapped an arm around her, enjoying the warmth of her as she rested her head against his chest.

"Their wine is a bit too good..." she murmured.

Bassai chuckled. "You should try the milk."

She looked up at him with a quizzical grin. "The milk?"

He slid the tankard over to her, but paused for a moment. "How much wine?"

"Sandra kept filling it up ... I think maybe three cups."

"Hmm."

She held his head as she kissed his cheek. "I'm a farmer, love. Three cups is nothing."

Bassai chuckled. "Then go for it."

She hefted the tankard into her hands, and sniffed the contents. "Smells like ... cheese. Good cheese, though."

Bassai smirked as she sipped the milk, coughed, grimaced, then frowned.

"Did it taste like cheese?"

Kaitlyn hesitated. "Spicy cheese."

"It is forty day fermented. The warriors like it eighty days or more. The braver ones go past a hundred."

"How is it not just ... a block of cheese?"

Bassai chuckled, nuzzling her cheek gently. "We will be leaving on our trip once Thomas has reached Victory, and word has been sent to him. If possible, the *Sand Dancer* will come for me. It will save a few days travel."

Kaitlyn put the tankard down. "If the ship's coming ... I'd like to come with you. I think Lance will too. Olimar can watch Pia and Rory, if we won't be gone for long."

"You do not ... have to. The trip may be one of some ... sorrow."

"That's why I want to come, love. To be there, by your side." She took his hand, the one resting on her stomach. "You're every bit the warrior. You're strong, and you've had to be strong by yourself before, for a long time."

"But I am stronger with other warriors beside me." He nodded. "A different kind of conflict ... but still one that cannot be fought alone. It would be foolish to go to war by myself."

He rested his head against hers. "It is a mistake I have made many times. When I was exiled ... when I awoke at the White Tower. It would be a foolish one to repeat ... and I will not repeat it now."

A thought crossed his mind, a flash of what he thought was madness for a moment. However, it left a warm feeling in its wake, that filled his entire body.

It was something that Tobias Calver had told him once, from a story his grandfather had told him. A somewhat amusing, if macabre tale about the origin of the wyvernborn: *The Witch And The Dragon*. It was a part Tobias's grandfather had added himself.

"Marriage is for love that knows wisdom."

He looked down at her, and found her eyes were turned up to him. He held her gaze as she held his, its own intimate embrace.

"My kinsman wants to drink with us. More milk ... probably stronger milk."

She grinned. "As long as *you* are prepared to tuck Pia and Rory in."

"Lance and I can manage."

The music with the revellers suddenly swelled and jumped. Many of the Orlin laughed and leapt to their feet, beginning a swinging, cavorting dance in pairs. Some were dragging wyvernborn with them, who were making a good show of reluctance, its own kind of playful dance.

"Dance with me."

Kaitlyn smiled. "I thought you didn't dance. That's what you keep telling me." She narrowed her eyes playfully. "Have you been lying to me, Reeva warrior?"

"I do not dance ... but I would dance with you."

Her eyes shone for a moment. "Will your kinsman be too drunk by the time we're finished?"

"Considering how I may dance, I suspect he will watch in amusement."

He stood, lifting her into his arms. Kaitlyn held his shoulders with a

The Empire Of Fire

laugh as he deposited her on her feet. She took his hand as soon as she was down and led him to the revellers.

She jumped into his arms again once they were there, and he spun her in the air. The music surged around them, swirling like a ribbon in a dancers hand, like water being gently stirred in a glass.

The music seemed to have no ending, it simply went on and on, seamlessly transitioning from song to song. Bassai, with Kaitlyn close and laughing, wanted it never to stop.

***

"How much longer is this meant to take?"

Thomas could hear the shiver in Elizia's voice. He smiled and wrapped an arm around her waist.

"I doubt it'll be much longer," he said in Caelish. *"Dawn won't break, put it that way."*

She snuggled against him. *"I wish it would break a little sooner."*

Thomas grinned. The evening breeze had given way to a night time chill. The forest had become a corridor of swirling winds, cutting right through his robes. He had already wrapped a survival cloak around himself, warming it with an incantation. He could have simply set a small fire, but that would have spoiled the light.

Away from the settlements, the stars above him were full and bright. They were not quite as bright as they had been when the fleet had flown over the desert, but there was no sense of threat here in Taeba, either from above or from an enemy waiting in the distance.

They shone like a hoard of gold and jewels that the dragons of myth and legend collected. The beauty of the heavens was more than enough to captivate him, and stave off the monotony of waiting for Seraphine and Niall to finish uncovering the books that had been buried all those months ago.

Matt Waterhouse

Thomas and Elizia were meant to be asleep. The rest of the soldiers were on guard, but they were making the best of it. They had set up watches and digging shifts as best they could, covering most of the sight lines, joined by a few of Seret's crew. The watchers were passing the time by telling stories, playing word games, telling jokes.

"*Elizia ...*" Thomas murmured. "*Do you ever just ... look up at the stars, and wonder what's there?*"

"*Not really. I mean ... not anymore. I did when I was younger, on my father's boat.*"

Thomas smiled. "*On the coast ... I bet they were incredible.*"

"*Oh yeah ... they felt different back then. We were so poor ... they just ... felt like something hopeful. Something to escape to. Va'Kael's palace, where we could all live in peace. The feeling now ... they're beautiful. I don't know if I wonder what's there exactly.*"

"*Hmm...*"

"*What do you see?*"

Thomas hesitated for a moment. "*I'm not sure. Beauty, of course. I used to see the Heavens, much like Va'Kael's palace. Perhaps they're neighbours up there, who knows?*"

"*Yeah, maybe.*"

"*What we fought here, in Taeba ... and what nearly killed us all at the Gravestone ... they weren't of this world. That means ... they were from up there. Maybe in the dark between the stars, something's waiting.*"

Elizia was quiet for a while, leaving Thomas to take in eternity in silence. He sighed.

"*I don't know if I'll ever look up again without ... keeping watch. Now I know they're up there, I'll never forget it. Still, out here, away from the buildings and streetlights and pavements ... there's almost no darkness between those stars. They shine so brightly ... push the void away. They're like our guardians ... and there are two more up there now.*"

The silence drifted over them again.

The Empire Of Fire

"*Thomas?*"

"*Hmm?*"

"*Do you really think it will work? The knowledge in those books and scrolls you're looking for ... can it really help Cael?*"

"*I think it can.*" The confidence in his voice almost made his feeling of hubris rear up ... but he had seen the research with his own eyes. He had read the old notes decades ago, the experiments that had been failures. He knew that the ground had been tested, that the failures would lead to future success. That's how science, both arcane and traditional, had always worked. "*I'm not saying it will work tomorrow, or this year, or this decade, even ... but it will work.*"

Seraphine's voice overtook whatever reply Elizia may have given, calling from the trench. "I need you here, Thomas."

Thomas sat up, mentally switching his language faculties back to Haaman. "You've found it?"

"Yes."

Thomas stood up with a grunt, and jogged towards where Seraphine and Niall had been working. Elizia followed him, and the rest of the squad closed in as well on all sides.

The pit that the pair were standing beside was a perfect square. Thomas peered into the darkness, the starlight barely brushing the trunk that Niall was leaning on, waiting for them at the bottom. It seemed so simple, just sitting there like a normal chest of belongings that would be found in any house or hovel in any hamlet in the country.

"I'm guessing that if we lift it magically, the results will be a disaster," Thomas muttered.

"And if we tried to lift it without magic." Seraphine grinned over at him. "Up for a climb?"

"Always." Thomas looked around. The forest around them was full of watchful, wild eyes, but it remained quiet and still. "Everyone, keep your wits about you up here."

Thomas rubbed his hands together, and began his descent. The roots, soil and stone that remained made for effective handholds and places for his feet. Both he and Seraphine reached the bottom quickly and dusted themselves off.

The chest sat in front of them innocuously. Thomas could sense the runes and wards covering it, and the trapped lock. Seraphine took his hand.

"No amplifiers."

Thomas nodded, and removed his gauntlets. "What do we do? Break the wards?"

Seraphine shook her head. She knelt beside the chest, and pointed to the lock. "Breaking the wards will set it off. There's only one way to open the box. Join me."

Thomas knelt beside her.

"We must touch it at the same time. Focus your mind."

He nodded. "On three?"

"On three."

Thomas closed his eyes, and linked hands with her. He cleared every thought from his mind, reaching a place of calm serenity swiftly.

"One ... two ... three."

Their fingers brushed against the metal lock, and suddenly Thomas felt a surge of warmth that beat away the cold night air.

Thomas opened his eyes. He wasn't in the hidden dugout anymore. He was beside a huge marble fireplace, in a cushioned armchair he was practically sinking into.

He glanced around, and recognised the room immediately. The bookshelves following the curve of the walls were all full of tomes. The alchemical table was covered in bottles and vials, swimming with colours that were glowing and spinning.

Seraphine was beside him in another large chair, smiling at the man who was sitting opposite them.

Rowan appeared in his twenties, as Thomas had known him in Melida City. He leaned forwards, and took them both in, beaming.

The Empire Of Fire

"Good ... good. I'm glad to see you both safe."

"I ... don't understand," Thomas murmured. "We didn't ... trap you in a lock, did we?"

Rowan chuckled. "No. I'm ... an echo of the Rowan you knew. A guardian, who would recognise the soul of the person trying to take the knowledge you preserved."

He leaned forwards. "You are here with Caelish soldiers ... yet you aren't here against your will. Interesting." He stroked his chin. "Could it truly be peace?"

"That's how it looks," Seraphine muttered.

The echo of Rowan smiled at her quizzically. "Yet despite all you have seen, all you have experienced, you are resistant to that peace."

Seraphine's hands tightened on the armrests of the chair. "How can I not be? They killed you. They killed my parents ... they've been killing my students. I will not let that pass."

Rowan's smile dropped, and he sighed. "It was Lord Marshal Morad Vehnek who killed me. Ulan Vehnek's iron fist killed many, and was retired when he began to lose his faculties."

"It doesn't matter! The dead won't come back."

"No, they won't. There are crimes that cannot be forgiven or forgotten, nor should they be. There are those who will need to be held accountable, and only then can we heal, not only from the wounds of the past, but the potential wounds of the future. That being said ... you know that change is happening. You have met many good people from across the Dividing Sea. You know that peace will benefit Cael and Haama."

Thomas looked at her. "I think I know what it is."

Both Rowan and Seraphine looked at him. Rowan nodded. "I thought you might."

Thomas focused on Seraphine. "This wasn't your dream. It isn't what you wanted, when you began fighting. The end goal, for so many of the Resistance, was kicking the Caelish back across the sea, forcing them to retreat, taking back everything that they'd taken from you. Every death made that dream more powerful, more intoxicating, until that became the end goal: vengeance. Death, and pain. Not Haama's freedom. And every death will feel as if it has been for nothing, if total and brutal victory against the Caelish hadn't been the end result of all the fighting."

Seraphine's jaw clenched.

"They have hurt you," Rowan whispered.

When she looked up at Rowan, her eyes were glistening. She nodded.

"They will never hurt you again. They will never hurt any Haaman, as long as the bond you forge with Cael remains true, and strong." His eyes fell on Thomas. "And that is why I brought you back. I knew you would make them see ... and Seraphine knew it, the moment you stopped her burning the books."

Thomas felt his heart swell, as Rowan stood. He walked towards them, and stroked Seraphine's cheek, wiping her tears away. "You will be alright, my child ... and you will not be alone."

She held his hand, and closed her eyes tightly. Thomas stood up, and Rowan patted him on the back, turning him towards the library of tomes, scrolls and papers.

"Use them well."

The warmth remained as Thomas felt the ground harden and cool beneath his knees. The breeze brushed him gently as his eyes opened.

The lid of the chest quietly creaked open, and there they were. Thousands of books, decades of research on shelf after shelf, stretching further down than he could see without a light source.

"Bigger on the inside, eh?" he whispered.

Seraphine squeezed his hand. She was shaking.

"It's time, Seraphine."

She sighed. "The goal was always freedom. That's what they all died for. So we could be free."

Thomas held her tightly, and she rested her head on his shoulder. His eyes returned again to the library, tucked away in such an innocuous box, that

The Empire Of Fire

held their future. One book had closed, now. It was time to open the next.

37

Allessandra tapped the feather of her quill against her chin, reading over the scroll of law one last time. In six years, there would be an election to determine the new head of state, and the Council of Ministers. The length of time was for infrastructure and candidates to prepare. The candidates could be of Haaman or Caelish ethnicity, but had to have been born in Haama. The current Council members, if ousted in the elections, would move into advisory positions for a further four years, or until retirement in First Minister Evandro's case. They would hold no power over the Council itself, the point of the position was merely to assist with experience. The term limits were set at twenty years, with an election every five, although it was subject to amendment.

There was another scroll beside it, declaring that The Wyvern Bog would remain largely independent of the regulations of the country at large, although there were still one or two that they agreed to. Territorial matters were to be discussed with the neighbouring Districts, as would matters of cross-District crime, with the assistance of a mediator if needs be.

That six years would be well needed, and likely be incredibly busy. The mood she was picking up from meeting citizens was that they were ready to be free of as many governmental shackles as they could. What would likely await Haama when the time had passed was a very small government, a minarchy, with as much power devolved to the individual Districts as possible. What few laws there would be for the entirety of Haama, that every District would agree to ... well, those remained to be seen, but it was time for them to return to the governance that had worked for them for centuries before the Caelish had taken control.

Allessandra dipped the quill into the pot of black ink beside her right hand, and signed the bottom of both documents. She sat back, feeling two weights lift from her shoulders and be replaced with two more, entirely new ones, full of possible consequences.

"What's the next one?"

Helen looked up at her from her own stack of documents. "Nothing else for today, in terms of decree. Negotiations with Montu Fortu I think are the next item on the agenda."

Allessandra rubbed her eyes and nodded. "Those may take a while ... and they'll be based on promises alone."

"Thomas made promises, and judging by the initial reports of what's in those books, he kept them."

"Yes ... and he will be with me during the discussions, but there is a little resistance present on both sides. We caused the Mountains Cities a lot of problems in the past ... and they refused to help us against The Black Fleet. It's a bitterness, that's a little too recent."

Helen peered up at her, and took off her reading glasses. "Bitterness from yourself?"

Allessandra sighed to herself. "Many died. Sel Kelad among them, a flawed man, but a man who would be an asset now. Two of the Four Guardians died. Thousands of Haaman and Caelish airmen ... who have left people behind, who could have been the strong men and women Cael and Haama need to rebuild, and take us all forwards into this new day. They could have at least lived to *see* it."

Helen nodded. "And at the same time, Montu Fortu separated from Haama in order to secure their own freedom, stabilise their own economy, escape bureaucracy and the early Cael conflicts ... and were then crippled in the Caelish invasion. There is no love lost between us. You are aware that Morad Vehnek caused an ecological disaster around Uncur."

Allessandra picked up and waved the declassified reports of the Black

Fleets operations tiredly. "I certainly am now."

"I suspect they would have been a little more amenable to us if they had known then what we know now. Again … well, recently … we have all had a common enemy."

Allessandra brushed her hair back behind her ears, and took a sip of water. "All these barriers in our way …"

"They're there to be climbed."

That elicited a smile, and a little warmth. "You always know what to say, don't you."

"To you, perhaps, before you rope me into these negotiations too."

Allessandra laughed and held up her hands. "I didn't realise I was so transparent."

There was a rumbling knock at her office door. She had grown tired of doing the majority of her work in her bedchamber, and had moved it all into a new space. The chairs were all strong and comfortable, the desk made of beautifully polished oak, carved to look like two large, sleeping wolves, with the smooth surface balanced between them. One wall was painted to depict a huge map of Haama, with every settlement featured. The hills and mountains were raised slightly, the rivers and lakes and ocean embossed in. All of it had been painted and enchanted, so the image moved. The water flowed, the forests rustled with an imaginary breeze. When Allessandra reached out, she could feel the softness of the grass. Opposite it, the window offered the same view as her bedchamber, albeit from a lower angle. Victory was almost resplendent in its former glory. While major construction was still taking place to replace the destruction, the sounds of thriving humanity were music to her ears.

The door opened, and Eluco led Thomas in. Allessandra beamed at them both, although didn't try to keep the fatigue from her brow.

"Gentlemen … is it that time already?"

Thomas nodded. "Montu Fortu await you for negotiations."

Eluco brushed the hair from her eyes and grinned, although the silent question passed between them.

The Empire Of Fire

Are you alright?

Her smile gave him his answer as she stood and stretched. "Are the delegates in a good mood?"

"They're in the same mood as they usually are, looks like," Thomas muttered. He smiled at the map on the wall, tracing a finger along the coastline.

"Is there any word from the researchers working with ... our draconic ally?"

"There may be a way to get rid of the dragonfire corruption, although it will require a lot of fine-tuning of a few incantations. Dragonfire is purposefully difficult."

Allessandra nodded. "I would call that progress."

"So would I, tentatively. Hopefully it will be enough to give the Mountain Cities a little more faith in us."

Allessandra nodded, gesturing to the door. The four of them began their stride to the long-range communication chamber. "What of the White Sea?"

"More difficult, but using a similar principle, it could be possible to halt the sand's expansion. It seems the cause of it is not simply a changing of the weather. Perhaps a closer look at the Gravestone is needed, as the central point in the desert."

"No ideas on pushing the sands back?"

"The logic: stop it first, then worry about moving it."

Allessandra nodded. "And ... this afternoon? The ceremony?"

Thomas bowed his head. "Everything is ready. Our rehearsals went well. I imagine you have quite a stirring speech prepared."

Allessandra shrugged. "The speeches will be yours, I think. You knew them far better than I. Have the wyvernborn arrived?"

"They have set off, to my knowledge. They should arrive before midday, they like to tax the generators and fly at full sail. Airships are a little too slow for them, it seems."

"Did they name their airships yet?" Eluco said with a chuckle.

Thomas shook his head. "They don't understand why we bother naming inanimate objects. These are people who used to think that chairs were a waste of wood."

"Really?" Allessandra shook her head in disbelief.

"They're warriors. Would you rather have a chair, or ramparts and war bows?"

Allessandra laughed. "A chair."

Thomas gestured with a hand and nodded. "Fair enough, but you're Royalty, Your Grace. They've built a few chairs now, I think it's probably the Orlin rubbing off on them."

As they ascended to the upper levels, Allessandra swayed a little on her feet. Eluco caught her swiftly.

"I'm fine, Eluco. I'm fine."

"Ali…" he muttered.

"It's the medicine, that's all. When I exert myself, it makes my head swim a little. Once I sit down…"

"So you keep saying…" Eluco grunted.

"I'm told that there are refinements being made to that as well," Thomas muttered. "Nullification could end up being the basis for a lot of innovation moving forwards. It's a shame that it's so difficult to refine for specific problems. Everything is connected to magic in some way, and … collateral damage is a thing we have to be careful to avoid."

"Then feel free to take all the time you need," Allessandra said, her mind steadying itself again. She straightened up. "Don't rush anything on my account. Better to get it right than … not."

Thomas bowed his head, but Allessandra caught Eluco giving him a pointed look. She squeezed his hand, and straightened up before walking into the long range communications chamber.

***

The Empire Of Fire

Allessandra clutched her cold black tea and attempted to somehow regain a little more energy after her exhausting conversation with High Priest Gruzht. The nap that she hoped would give her a chance to recover had been in-and-out, not as refreshing as it could have been. It wasn't her body or illness keeping her from sleep, it was her anticipation of what was to come.

The chair was comfortable enough and firm enough to support her and help her relax, but that antsy feeling remained. The agitation did nothing for her fatigue, however.

The afternoon's event would be one that she hoped would be received well, but she knew there was a chance that some complicated feelings would arise in the populace. Hurt and death had held each of Haama's hands for so long that suggesting that certain people's death were more worthy of note was almost insulting … but Tobias Calver and Emeora Vonn were not just people, any more than Iara Levez and Sel Kelad had just been soldiers.

As her thoughts turned to Kelad, she opened one of the drawers in the desk, close to her left hand. His final message to her was the only thing in there. Her fingers brushed over the unfolded paper, next to the envelope it had come in, with its broken wax seal. She read it again, even though she had almost committed it to memory.

Allessandra,

Considering the magnitude of what we're about to do, I suspect I won't return from our expedition across the White Sea. This message, perhaps, will be lost with me, but if not, it is my last message to you.

While it is by far the longest, this is not the first of these letters that I have written. In fact, before every engagement I am sent on, before every battle I am about to fight, I write a new one, addressed to you. Previously I wrote to your father, and grandfather, and great grandmother. However, my messages to you have been somewhat different to my messages to them.

In messages to you, I have written many things. I once recommended that you wear shorter dresses, because of how much I enjoy seeing your thighs. I once bequeathed you an entire shipment of Tyranian port, and asked you to think of me with every sip. More than once, I apologised for the times my flirtation made you uncomfortable, as I know it did.

This time, I simply say this: should we succeed, know that you have been a light in whatever dark thing passes for my heart. I do not say that as a profession of unrequited, one-sided love, but as gratitude. For many years, I have been convinced that there would be no peace, no end to the bad blood between Cael and Haama. You have been a large part of that changing, as have The Four Guardians that I fought for so long. I do not know if they will return either, but I hope they do. If not, they will live on in song and memory, as is deserved.

In every letter to you, I have merely asked for two things. The first is that, for the love of all that is holy in the eyes of Va'Kael, <u>please do not give me a state funeral</u>. I neither wish for one, nor do I deserve one. History may disagree with me one day, when I am inevitably viewed through a rose-tinted haze, but it will be a white lie. I have wielded the blade that inflicted wounds upon Haama which will never truly heal. The Taeba Clans are all but gone, as are the Orlin. I can only hope that the scars will become unnoticeable with time, that good will be done that helps with the pain, and I am afraid that burden will rest upon you, Evandro, Carrasco, the Guardians, and all the rest who have worked so hard to bring us together. I have never been one to question an order, or my duty, and looking back, that is perhaps my biggest regret.

My only other request is this: find happiness, and find love. Romantic love, and the love between close friends, that will help guide you, and soothe the irritation that inevitably comes from politics.

I know you will rule Cael with the same compassion and zeal you have shown in Haama. I would have liked to have seen your coronation, met your children, lived in the Haama and Cael you will build.

Unfortunately, this was not to be, so I will finish with this. As much as it may be strange to read, coming from me, I am very proud of the fierce, intelligent, relentless woman you have become.

Long may you reign,

Sel

The Empire Of Fire

As much as it pained her, she had respected his wishes. There would be no state funeral for Sel Kelad.

He deserved more, in her eyes, but she had only ever known a fraction of the real man, a noble portrait of a brutal life. He knew better than her how much he deserved or didn't deserve to be honoured, but she couldn't have done any of what she had accomplished without his guidance, and his support. After everything he and the Standing Army had sacrificed for peace, it felt wrong for it all to be unacknowledged for the sake of optics.

A sharp, even knock jogged her from her thoughts. She cleared her throat.

"*Come in.*"

The newly promoted Colonel Ulan, Admiral Nyroshi, Captain Obrek, and Minister Carrasco marched into the office. All the military men wore their formal uniforms, with newly earned medals pinned with all the rest of the ones they had already earned.

With the exception of Carrasco, the men were overly formal, perhaps because of the vestiges of tension that remained between them, and also perhaps because they were in her presence, although Ulan in particular knew better. He was still in his role as Acting Defense Minister for the moment, drawing up potential candidates to replace him.

"*Sit down, gentlemen,*" Allessandra said. The three officers and minister sat opposite her. "*Captain Obrek, I wasn't expecting you. How are you?*"

"*Well, Your Grace, thank you. I hope the same for you.*"

She smiled and bowed her head to him. She focused on the group as a whole. "*What news do you have?*"

"*The next food convoys have been prepared, and will fly in the morning,*" Carrasco said formally.

"*We have employed a number of other airships from the Aerial Navy and reconfigured them for cargo hauling, as well as escort,*" Nyroshi added.

"*Thank you,*" Allessandra added. "*The taxes?*"

"*The discussion of the taxes should be secondary to the question of food production, for the moment at least,*" Carrasco muttered.

Ulan glanced at him. "*I do not agree. The sooner we act on the tax front, the better, although Minister Carrasco is correct in his assertion that food production is a vital factor to address.*"

Allessandra sat back. "*What do you both propose?*"

Carrasco raised an eyebrow. "*I believe the Acting Defense Minister is of noble intention, but not a practical one. As it stands, we have no more usable farmland than we had last year. We still need that food in Cael.*"

"*And while I concede that fact is true, the tax is the largest bone of contention that many of the independent farmers have.*" Ulan leaned forwards. "*On my patrols with the infantry, we interacted with many, and they all had the same complaint.*"

Allessandra stroked her chin. "*You both appear to be correct, so what is the solution?*"

"*Collective farms have served us well in the past,*" Nyroshi said gruffly.

"*Ugly things, and impersonal ... but practical,*" Ulan muttered.

Carrasco smiled tightly. "*Again, noble idealism.*"

Obrek looked over at the conversation silently, mulling it over. Allessandra gestured to him. "*Captain?*"

Obrek coughed. "*I'm a military man, I don't have much knowledge of these things, Your Grace.*"

"*Still, your input is appreciated. You are the three men who are directing a lot of practical resources.*"

Obrek tapped his fingers on the desk, then quickly withdrew his fingers at the sideways glances from the rest of his fellows. "*My thought is this: our own dedicated farms will be the ideal solution, without a doubt. I know that part of prior negotiations involved the indentured workers in Cael, and a path to freedom. You said at the time that they would need training in farming, those farms would be a good way to do that.*"

"*The problem being that they will take a long time to establish. At least a year."* Carrasco sat up straight, and clasped his hands together.

"Draw up those plans, and coordinate with the candidates for Minister of Agriculture." Allessandra sighed. *"Minister Carrasco ... by the time of the election, the tax should be highly reduced, if not gone entirely, would you agree?"*

Carrasco glanced at the others, and bobbed his head. *"In an ideal world."*

"In an ideal world it will be gone, not reduced. Reduction should begin sooner rather than later, because it's a promise we made."

"A promise you made, Your Grace."

Allessandra smiled through her teeth. *"And one I intend to keep, as long as it is practical. The moment those farms are set up, the tax is to be reduced by one fifth."*

"And if they aren't producing as projected?" Carrasco's face was frozen in the same smile hers was.

"Reduce it by less, but still reduce it. By then there will be more farms, and significant advances in the research being done to heal the Maldane Reach."

"And if they are not making any progress?"

Allessandra clasped her hands together. *"Then we will have to negotiate again, come to an understanding, and work out a path forwards that benefits all of us."*

"Including ... raising the taxes again? Breaking your coveted promises?"

An old anger bubbled in her chest, but she kept her voice even. *"We will cross that bridge when we reach it. If it does come to that, we will explain precisely why the choice has been made, and have a clear path forwards."*

"More promises."

She maintained her composure, just about. *"By then, perhaps you will have taught me the wisdom to make more realistic promises."*

"You've kept a lot of the big ones, Your Grace," Ulan muttered. *"I wouldn't allow naysaying to distract from the good work you have done."*

Carrasco turned with a slight frown. *"Nor would I."*

Allessandra leaned back in the chair, and clasped her hands together. *"For the moment, we have a path in sight. Set up our own farms, and relax the taxes on the Idris, Vissa and Verda farms as much as we can when they begin producing. Make it clear, through the town criers and printed news, that this is our plan. I would like as few secrets as possible between us and the people."*

"As you wish, Your Grace," Carrasco said smoothly.

They sat in silence for a moment, apart from the gentle tap of Allessandra's fingers.

She took a breath. *"You will no doubt be aware, knowing the plans for this afternoon, that General Kelad is not a part of the ceremony."*

They all nodded. She noticed that Captain Obrek's mood had begun to darken.

"I assure you ... I want to assure you ... it was not ..." she gathered her thoughts. *"It is not the path I would have chosen to take. It was, however, his own request."*

Obrek grunted, and allowed her a nod. *"I understand. Knowing him, he didn't seem like the type."*

Ulan sighed, and nodded in agreement. *"A pity, given how much he has done for both Haama and Cael, especially of late."*

"I would agree ... but he would not." Allessandra looked at them all gravely. *"I would have him honoured in some way, perhaps among the military. Captain Obrek, Admiral Nyroshi, you were two who knew him well, perhaps better than I. It would mean a lot to me ... if there were some kind of ceremony to honour him."*

Nyroshi narrowed his eyes. *"Wouldn't that go against his wishes, Your Grace?"*

"He specified that he didn't want a state funeral, but a military matter..."

Obrek's mouth turned up in a grin. *"I would be happy to make the arrangements."*

"Good." Allessandra exhaled, feeling a little relief. *"Flawed as he was ... he can rest now, in peace, honoured for the good he did."*

The Empire Of Fire

***

Along Victory's main causeway, throngs of the citizenry stood ten rows or more deep, waiting for the procession to pass. White bunting had been strung along the houses and street lamps along the way, from the statue of the Black dragon all the way up to the bottom of the rise that led up to the palace. Augmenting them were Haaman and Caelish flags, rippling reds and greens in the breeze. Many of the crowd had brought other flags in a multitude of colours, made from bedsheets and blankets, and were waving them at the back of the crowd tirelessly.

The band came first, blowing into trumpets and flutes, beating drums, brass glinting in the autumn sun. The tune they played was far from the tune that would be played at an occasion like this one. It was bright and joyful, rhythmic as a march would be, a blend of countryside lilt and military precision.

There were a hundred musicians at the front, and a hundred more at the back of the parade. Behind the musicians at the front were two large figurines, statues of a huge stallion and a snake. The horse was twenty feet tall, the serpent about forty feet long, moving up the causeway side by side in time with the drum beats. Neither made any sound aside from their footfalls, the animal symbols of Haama and Cael together. Both were made of marble, the stone enchanted to keep it fluid enough not to crack while they moved.

Behind them, a huge chariot bore the honoured dead, side by side. Ironclad and Ember lay beside each other, surrounded by flowers. The horses driving the chariot were as serene and calm as their stone counterpart, marching like a regiment.

The enchantments on the bodies had kept the fingertips of death from them for now. As they had in the *Sand Dancer*, they appeared to simply be asleep. As they passed, the crowds cheered, tossed flower petals and confetti into the air, even more colour adding to the mood. There was some grief, some tears, but many more roars of strength and solidarity, cheers of gratitude and love, and thunderous applause.

As the procession moved along the causeway, they passed large constructions, covered in tarpaulin draped around them like cloaks. A Mage stood at the foot of each, and as the carriage passed, they magically moved the tarpaulin away, letting it fall and then fold away into their arms.

Each one unveiled a statue, as tall as the pair that were preceding the carriage. The first was of Levez, tall and proud, wearing the armour of the City Guard. The next, a hundred yards ahead on the opposite side of the road, was of three City Guardsmen together, wearing their full regalia, representing those that had been lost in the Night of Terror, trying to defend the populace. The one after them was of a market seller, a fisher, a builder and a doctor, all standing together, representing the citizens of Victory that had been lost on the same night, and the solidarity they had shown to rebuild. The one after was a farmer, standing alone and defiant, a blade at his hip, for the Idris farmers and Resistance fighters who had stood up to the tyranny of Ulan Vehnek and Morad Vehnek's Black Fleet.

After that came the figures of a wyvernborn and Orlin together, opposite two military officers from both the Standing Navy and the Black Fleet, saluting each other. The wyvernborn's head was bowed in respect, the Orlin's hand over her heart. What had become known as the Battle Of The Gravestone had affected all of them, and all four groups had stood together eventually, and so far remained so.

Following them were statues of two members of a Taeba clan: Ydra and Vargas, as they had been in life, carefully crafted from images that Seraphine had created for them. She and Thomas had insisted upon their inclusion, and once they had explained why, Allessandra had quickly agreed.

The final two were side by side, hands linked together. Ember and Tobias Calver stood in their old armour, with their weapons sheathed. Opposite them were spaces for Bassai and Thomas. The statues would have been displayed, but the last two Guardians had shaken their heads at the idea.

"Wait until we have joined our friends in the Astral Plain," Bassai had told her. "Thomas and I have plenty to do, to make sure those statues are truly earned."

The procession came to a halt at the bottom of the palace hill, where Allessandra stood on a podium with Thomas and Bassai. The Council Of Ministers were present, as were a delegation from the Wyvern Bog and Obsidian, and King Alesio, with many attendants. His health had improved enough to travel, and he had insisted on being present in the city for the ceremony.

As the parade drew close to the podium, the music swelled. The stallion and serpent overtook the marching band, and stood on either side of the road, at the point where it sloped upwards, level with the podium. They turned back to the crowd, and bowed, then faced inwards. The stallion reared up, and the snake coiled and raised its head, meeting the horse eye to eye. Then they both froze, the poses held for all time, the symbols of Cael and Haama side by side.

The crowd cheered loudly, and moved into the road to get the best view they could of the princess.

An honour guard stepped forwards and surrounded the carriage, standing to attention in two ranks, the inner facing Ironclad and Ember, the outer facing the crowd.

Allessandra took a deep breath as the eyes of the crowd, tens of thousands of Caelish and Haaman people from all walks of life, settled on her.

"On today, of all days ... it means the world to me to see so many of you here."

She paused as the crowd cheered the statement.

"Our great city has been renewed by our determination and strength, and not the strength of one ... the strength of all. The strength of those in Old Town, who have weathered storm after storm, and rebuilt. For perhaps the first time, certainly in my memory, you have not rebuilt alone. Those from the Fisheries, who transported water to help fight fires across every part of Victory.

Those from New Town, who took in those whose homes had been destroyed. Those from The Overlook, who helped spot fires as they began. Those on the Main Street, who cleared debris from the road so convoys could get to the wounded faster. Those in the City Guard, who did their best to defend us all, to the cost of many lives, and helped with the rebuilding process. Those from the Silver Throne Palace, who took in the wounded and sent out food for the hungry. Victory's sandball team, The Victorious, who opened the stadium for triage of the wounded. Those who gave their food, their beds, their shelter, to help people in need."

The crowd applauded each other, cheered loudly when their area was mentioned.

"But it is not just the people of Victory who gather here today. The Aerial Navy, who defended us, and defended Haama. Those from the Wyvern Bog, wyvernborn and Orlin both, defended Haama, the nation we all have called home. The Resistance, who found peace with us to defend Haama. My father, the King of Cael, who is here in recognition of the importance of the new dawn that is approaching. Finally, but not least, those in the Black Fleet, who found the courage to stand up for what is right, stand against a true enemy, and defend Haama."

Another round of applause followed, less in cheer, but in recognition.

"We gather here for many reasons. To recognise the heroes ... all of the heroes ... who have rebuilt and are rebuilding our great nations. To mourn for the lost ... to honour the sacrifice they made, so we could live one more day. To celebrate the renewal of life, of friendships many thought doomed to be lost forever."

Allessandra looked down upon Ironclad and Ember, laying peacefully in the carriage. "The two people that lay before us ... have sacrificed their lives for us all. Once would make them worthy of song and story ... and did. The Song Of The Four Guardians inspired many for a hundred years ... but to do it twice ..."

Her voice wavered, and she paused as a deafening cheer, a release of emotion, washed across the city, shaking the air. It brought a rush of adrenaline and blood through her body, renewing her strength.

"To do it twice ... the courage may never be seen again, in the history of Planar, let alone our two countries. All I can do, all we can do as a people ... is try and hold a fraction of that courage within us."

Another blast of emotion shook her, ringing in her ears. She glanced at the Guardians on either side of her, making sure they were ready to speak. Bassai's eyes were closed, his body serene, his breathing steady. Thomas was swallowing, rapidly blinking, his nerves and some of his grief shining in his eyes.

"I could tell you all what Tobias Calver, The Warrior, and Emeora Vonn, The Archer, meant to me ... but my words would not do them justice. Better to hear from those that knew them better than anyone else. Better to hear from Bassai of Clan Reeva, known in legend as The Beast, and Thomas, The Mage."

She stepped back, and reached out a hand to each of them. She lay a hand on each of their shoulders, and stepped backwards.

Bassai opened his eyes, looked for a moment at Thomas, and stepped forwards, behind the podium. Allessandra moved around to take the place where he had been standing. She caught the eye of a woman, standing close by, looking up at the wyvernborn with pride. A teenage boy, face red with concealed grief, was standing in front of her, her hands on his shoulders, lending him some of her strength.

Bassai gazed out at the crowd calmly. "For a hundred years, I have been known as The Beast. Were it not for Tobias Calver, a beast is all I would have been."

He closed his eyes again, and took a breath. "Tobias Calver twice saved me from a pit of despair, and wild rage unbecoming of what the wyvernborn are. He demanded that I be allowed to join his elite force of Rangers."

Bassai hesitated for a moment. "He took me in when I needed him the most. When I had no family, no clan, he became my brother. Through him, the bright beacon of his soul, the Gods and I found each other. Through him, I found friendship with my companions, found a goal to fight for."

He breathed again. Allessandra could see the raw emotion bubbling beneath his outward strength.

"Emeora Vonn ... in days past ... and now it would be near inconceivable, the Orlin and wyvernborn were bitter enemies. When she first saw me, she almost shot me with an arrow. I was in an attack force, that burned her village, back when I still had my wings. She was ... fourteen or fifteen. When we met again, a decade later, she nearly shot me again. I don't know if she recognised me, if she ever recognised me. But she confirmed what I had grown to realise: that the Orlin and the wyvernborn could be more than enemies. She became a good friend, one I valued for her strength and compassion. I will ... forever be thankful that I was privileged enough to know her, because through her ... I found my home again."

His eyes tracked around to fix on Barada and Zeta, as well as their retinue of other wyvernborn warriors. He also looked at Sandra and the Orlin with her. "Both wyvernborn and Orlin are my people. Those who live in this city are my people. Without Tobias and Emeora, I would be alone."

He straightened up. "Our friendship reached beyond death, and into a new life ... and it will again. One day we will meet again, on the Astral Plain, but until then I will live according to their example. Their strength, their love, and the way they saw the world: full of people from all walks of life ... who could eat and drink together, laugh together, and stand together."

Bassai bowed his head to the crowd, and they cheered for him as loudly as they had cheered for Allessandra. She smiled at him as he turned, joining in the applause, and he bowed his head to her respectfully. His eyes turned to Thomas, and he patted the young man on his shoulder, lending him what power he could.

Allessandra moved around, so that Bassai could stand where he had stood before. She stood beside Thomas, and took his hand. He was staring at the podium, gathering himself, and when she touched him it seemed to rouse him from the moment.

The Empire Of Fire

He stepped forwards.

"Emeora ... Ember ... liked wine, a lot."

Bassai chuckled. Thomas smiled, and took a breath.

"I extend her apologies to the taverns and inns of Victory, that she won't be able now to drink you dry, spending all her money. I'll have to come in and drink for her, in her honour, in her memory."

There were a smattering of chuckles among the crowd, but far more cheers.

"I first met her, first spoke to her, when another trainee in the Rangers whacked her in the head with a training sword. I didn't let her forget it, which is probably why she got so fast. She gave every barb back to me with an extra thorn on it ... and soon we were doing that over an ale, then several ales ... and before either of us knew it, we were like a brother and sister. Like Bassai, I found a family with her, and with Tobias Calver. I never knew my own, I was sold to a Master before I could even talk."

Thomas looked down at his resting friends for a moment.

"As for Tobias Calver ... I have no idea the horror my life would have been without him. He pulled me off the street, and made me see something that should have been obvious. I was raised, barely, as a slave in Cael, around all the anger of those past decades directed at Haama. Even though I had no love for the nation that decreed I be bound in chains, that anger infected me. Tobias Calver showed me how futile and how wrong that anger was ... and all he had to do was show me you ... the people of this city."

Tens of thousands of voices rang out in reverence of each other, and of the speakers.

"Now, and a century ago ... you haven't changed so much. You showed me twice that what I had been told was not true. Tobias gave me faith, not just in the Gods, but in people. That lesson gave me faith in Princess Allessandra. It gave me faith in General Sel Kelad, a former foe. It gave me faith in Taeba clansmen who allied with us. It gave me faith that our warriors could stand together, and battle the darkness that threatened to infect us all. Bassai spoke true, for both of us. I will live by their example. Tobias and Ember were more than friends to me, more than fellow soldiers, more than people who I ... would have given my life for without a thought."

His head bowed, and his eyes closed tightly. Allessandra saw the pain on his face. His next breath was ragged.

"I will miss them every day that remains in my life ... but I will try my hardest not to grieve. Events such as this one can be somber ... can make us dwell on the absence that will remain in all our lives ... where they once stood. But today is not simply a day of mourning. It is a day of celebration. What they fought for, and died for, stand in front of me: the people of our nations. Their journey may have come to an end ... but that is not such a cause for sadness. I'll remember their laughter, their love for each other, the strength of their will, and how they looked past the body to speak to the soul of those they met. I am glad, and will always be, that I went on that journey with them."

He stepped back, to more applause from the crowd. As he stepped back, Allessandra held his hands for a moment, and leaned forwards.

"*Thank you for speaking of Kelad.*"

He nodded. "*His actions are more than worthy of note.*"

She faced the crowd once more, letting their applause for Bassai and Thomas calm.

"Soon, we will lay these two legends, these two who gave everything they had and more for all of us, to rest. Their legend will live on for all time ... as it should. I spoke to them for the first time on the roof of the palace, the first time they had returned to the city for a hundred years. I found them to be noble, and unafraid of those who hadn't earned their respect. I hope I earned it, in some way. The city they knew was known as Melida City ... and so shall it always be ... but the name Victory has never been more apt. It no longer means: Cael's Victory ... it means : Our Victory. Our victory against fear, against old anger, and against those forces that would have used both to destroy us. Soon, the news will reach the criers, and will reach you, the people, of what the future may hold. It will be a future that you will guide, free of chains, free

The Empire Of Fire

of oppression, free of the tyranny of men named Vehnek. We will write that future together, but today, we celebrate together. Celebrate the heroes of our nations. Now ... let all of our voices and applause ... and love ... reach the Astral Plain, where Tobias Calver and Emeora Vonn will hear us."

The force of sound from the people of Victory reverberated from the city walls. She felt the podium shudder. Energy coursed through her body like lightning.

More flower petals filled the air. Air bursts of magic filled the air with bright colours, not only the flag colours of Cael and Haama, but more besides, like every flower on Planar was blooming above them.

Something overwhelmed her suddenly, a feeling that she certainly was experiencing in the moment, but it grew so quickly it was almost as if it belonged to someone else.

Gratitude, and humility, the purest she had ever experienced. It brought tears to her eyes.

Instinctively, she stepped back from the podium, and in her peripheral vision she caught sight of Thomas and Bassai. Thomas's eyes were closed, and he was smiling, even laughing to himself. Bassai's hand was over his heart, and his eyes were shining. His gaze met hers, and he smiled.

"They heard."

***

Ironclad and Ember were brought into the palace, borne up the hill on their carriage. The band remained playing at the bottom of the rise, and the festival began. The people of Victory began dancing and eating and drinking together. The sounds of celebration rang out as all of the carriages taking the leaders climbed up the palace hill. Allessandra listened to them with a smile, holding Eluco's hand as he listened to more of Thomas and Bassai's stories.

They shared tales of their time in the city, for the Rangers had taken care of their home as readily as they had of the nation as a whole. As a result, they and Eluco had plenty in common. They had patrolled almost the exact same streets, drunk in the same taverns, eaten the same food but from different stalls. Listening to them had helped pass the time as the convoy climbed up the palace hill.

Once they arrived, everyone ascended to the Palace roof, and boarded the *Sand Dancer, Sovereign,* and one of the wyvernborn ships. Ironclad and Ember were placed on the *Sand Dancer,* the ship they had ridden into battle.

Cheers went up from below as the three ships passed over the city, and pulled north. The wyvernborn vessel took the lead, taking them towards the coast, where the place of true remembrance had been built.

The monument stood on a cliff beside the sea. It was forty feet tall, and fifteen across, a four sided, tall pyramid made of white marble. It was made to be visible on the approach to the Port Of Plenty. At night, the stone was enchanted to glow gently, not quite serving as a lighthouse, but enough to be a beacon of a different kind. It had been named The Beacon Of Peace.

At the base was a mausoleum, where the two Guardians would lay for all time.

The *Sovereign* and *Sand Dancer* slowed to a hover, and the dignitaries disembarked. The wyvernborn vessel stayed high in the air, in fact it seemed to pull higher. Allessandra and Thomas peered up at them as a group of figures lined up at the edge of the railing. With a flourish, they all jumped, and their wings spread wide.

Thirteen wyvernborn glided in in an arrow formation, with Barada at the point. All of them moved as one, in perfect, almost telepathic synchronicity. All of them landed a few yards away, except for one, that broke formation and smoothly turned towards Thomas and Allessandra.

Bassai drew close, a smile fixed to his face. Allessandra saw him flex his wrists, and his wings adjusted to drop him closer to the ground. Eight feet from the grass, he drew his arms closer to him, and adjusted his posture. He swept upwards a little, so his legs were pointing towards the ground, and his arms raised. The wings drew in a little, and he dropped into a crouch, landing perfectly cleanly. The breeze he kicked up brushed the grass, making it seem as if it was bowing in reverence to him.

Thomas was beaming, a laugh of joy escaped him. Bassai clapped hands with him and laughed with both he and Allessandra.

"Can you believe, Your Grace, that this is the first time I've seen my best friend fly?"

Allessandra examined the harness that Bassai was wearing, the simple mechanisms that seemed to control the wings. "The wyvernborn made this?"

"The wyvernborn and Orlin both." Bassai unfastened the supports around his wrists and arms, still smiling. "I wanted them to see it too, in their own way."

His eyes were drawn up to the casket that Tobias and Ember would both be buried in. Allessandra smiled sadly with a nod. "I sometimes ... wonder what my mother would think of me, now. How she would feel about everything we've done ... if Vehnek told her exactly what he was planning to do."

Bassai brushed a hand from her shoulder to her bicep, and gently squeezed. "Whatever had lain hidden within Mora, that had taken her over, deceived everyone, including Vehnek. Even those who operate in darkness cannot see into the void. Had she known what we know now, she would have been standing beside your father, as proud of you as he is."

A contingent of Orlin, including Sandra, approached them. Barada and his warriors closed in from the other side, and he linked hands with his wife. Their son moved close to them both, taking her other hand. He was almost as tall as his father, but not as broad, with smoother scales on his body. Alongside them, the woman and boy that Allessandra had seen beside the podium earlier in the day walked through the throng and stood next to Bassai. He let out a sound similar to the satisfied purr of a cat, and rested his forehead against hers. The boy clasped his forearm, and smiled up at him.

Everyone moved into step behind the casket as it was carried magically onwards, into the mausoleum. One of the soldiers walked alongside Thomas and took his hand, the one she had spied him kissing at the dance a few weeks prior. Warmth sent a vibration of joy through her grief. Both he and Bassai were finding a way to live, after such painful loss.

A long rectangle had been dug into the ground and lined with marble. Seraphine was at the front of the procession, her hands extended in front of her. She guided the casket through the wide doorway, and over the grave.

Music gently played from a pair of harpists inside, sitting in the two furthest corners. Allessandra glanced around at the walls of the mausoleum. A vast, enchanted mural wrapped around from both sides of the doorway. It told their stories apart, and then together. On the right hand side of the room, the young Emeora swung through trees taller than any building in Haama, covered in light blue flowers. In the next picture she sat with others on a platform above the forest floor, listening to a boy a little older than her playing a lute. The next showed her bolting and leaping along the walls of a city Allessandra knew well, although the buildings were a little newer, and the skyline was different. Domes and spires sat on top of the hill where the Silver Throne Palace stood now. The grace with which she moved took Allessandra's breath away.

She leaped off the roof of a building and into the arms of a tall man, who spun her in the air and kissed her. Glancing around at the opposite wall, Allessandra recognised the man as Tobias Calver.

His story began on a farm, mock sword fighting with a stick as a boy, sitting on the floor at his grandfather's feet as he read from a thick book of stories. He grew strong working the fields, before he left his home. There was a painting of him reaching the top of a hill, and looking out at old Melida City with a smile on his face. He trained as a city guardsman, rose through the ranks, married a beautiful woman with golden hair, who then fell into a grave.

There was a painting of despair, of him on his knees by a campfire, and Ember approached him, wrapping her arms around his shoulders. On both walls, they went on adventures with Thomas and Bassai and many other figures. Each wall depicted something different. One showed them battling privateers on a pair of corsair sloops, the ocean roiling around them. On another they were engaging a leaping tribe of horrifying fighters, their faces painted red, chests scarred, carrying curved knives, with skulls scattered around them.

The next one on Ember's side depicted her, Bassai and Thomas battling shadowy figures in a burning city. Behind them, people were fleeing through a gap in the city wall. Allessandra realised suddenly what she was looking at: their deaths. The beginning of the legend.

When she looked around, she saw Tobias atop the city ramparts, facing down a huge, black dragon.

She glanced at Thomas and Bassai, who were also looking at the pictures, tensing up more at Tobias's fate than their own. She followed their eyes to the ones following. On Ember's side, The Four Guardians, Seraphine, Kassaeos, Ydra and Vargas were battling on the twisting stairwell of a huge, white tower. On the opposite wall, they were engaging a Caelish skiff on foot, pulling it to the ground. On the farthest wall, they were atop the *Sand Dancer*, battling airships and dragons alike. They battled a dragon on foot among burning wrecks. Finally, in the middle but split in two parts, the four of them, Kassaeos and General Kelad battled a figure cloaked in shadow, with a dark spiral of tendrils coming from her back. Between the two halves of the picture, in line with the grave, Tobias and Emeora stood together, hands linked, gazing into each other's eyes with a smile. She wore a light blue dress, he wore a white shirt with the sleeves rolled up and cotton trousers.

The warriors, the heroes, finally at peace.

Seraphine lowered the casket down into the grave. She and Thomas extended a hand, and covered it with an ornate flagstone, the outline of the picture of them together etched into the marble, lines filled with gold.

The gathered companions, allies, and those there in respectful reverence, stood in silence for a few moments, silently praying to whatever God was listening to them. Allessandra spent the time looking at the painting of the two in love, and it made her dwell on Eluco, who was standing just behind her, his hand on the small of her back. She stepped back and leaned against him. His other arm wrapped around her.

In small throngs, the mourners left the mausoleum, and gathered on the grass, gazing out at the sea or sharing stories of Tobias and Ember, great deeds and small moments of joy.

Thomas, Bassai, Seraphine, a Mokkan girl named Kira, and those that stood beside them, were the last to leave. Barada, Sandra and Zeta lingered also, as did Donnal, waiting until all were ready to depart.

Once they did, their feet took them to the monument. Thomas smiled at what had been set into the marble at its base: an axe taller than he was, double blades shining, an etching carved into the head between them, boldly impressed with Obsidian.

It featured the rearing stallion of Haama, Cael's snake and pyramid, the dragon with huge spreading wings that symbolised the wyvernborn, and a small twisting flower for the Orlin. A weapon of war, uniting all those people, to be used for bloodshed no longer.

Thomas's fingers brushed against it. "Perfect."

Bassai grunted with a grin.

Allessandra's eyes were drawn up to the ocean, to the Dividing Sea that lay between Cael and here. The sun was beginning to set, the sky turning a light shade of purple.

For so long, that body of water had been a barrier that separated armies. Now it was a road that led them to each other in peace and friendship. The sun wasn't just setting on the day, it was setting on an era, one that had been shaped by violence.

Allessandra wondered if peace would truly be the thing that shaped this new one, or if their nations would slip into their old ways again.

"We earned this," she murmured. "All of us, together."

The rest looked at her, and followed her gaze to the sea.

"The earning does not stop here," Bassai grunted. "That is something we must not forget. But it is a beginning."

The sun blazed in its descent towards the horizon, and Allessandra smiled at the new world illuminated by the rays of orange and gold.

Seraphine held her hand out to Kassaeos. "There are many things not to forget. How it was earned ... and what we gave up to make it possible. There may be ... a few more obstacles in our path, ones we can't see yet."

Thomas nodded. "Then we will face them as allies, and as friends, as we should have always been."

There would be those who still lingered on the scars of the past. There would be those who looked upon a new alliance with fear or suspicion, from within and without. There would be growing pains in their tests to solve the problems caused by the more zealous of their forebears. But through it all, the first, most difficult barrier had already been crossed.

They had all agreed to sit down, and listen. From there, they had agreed to work together.

And if there was one thing the all silently agreed on, unanimously, it was that on that day, the sunset was beautiful.

"Make our new day more beautiful than this," Allessandra whispered. "It's quite the goal."

Bassai chuckled, and rested his free hand on Allessandra's shoulder. "Then we'd better get started."

Matt Waterhouse

The Empire Of Fire

The Main Players

The Four Guardians

Ironclad – The Warrior. Formerly **Tobias Calver**, leader of Calver's Rangers, stationed in Melida City before the Cael-Haama War. Killed in the Battle Of Melida City, later reborn as a Construct.

Emeora Vonn – The Archer. Known as 'Ember', former scout in the Orlin Forest and for Calver's Rangers. Killed in the Battle Of Melida City, later reborn at the White Tower.

Name Unknown – The Mage. Known as **'Thomas'**, former Caelish slave. Battle Mage and field medic in Calver's Rangers. Killed in the Battle Of Melida City, later reborn at the White Tower.

Bassai – The Beast. Wyvernborn, exiled from the Wyvern Bog a decade before the Cael-Haama War. Liberated from Caelish captivity, to become a warrior in Calver's Rangers. Killed in the Battle Of Melida City, later reborn at the White Tower.

Matt Waterhouse

The Resistance

Rowan – Former battle Mage stationed in Melida City. Later worked at The Watchtower in Uncur, and then supplied the Haaman Resistance from the White Tower in Taeba. Also pushed the myth of the Four Guardians. **Killed by Morad Vehnek during the Caelish incursion into the White Tower.** Survived by his granddaughter, Seraphine.

Seraphine – Granddaughter of Rowan. Grew up in the Haaman Resistance under Rowan's tutelage, later tutored students at the White Tower. Fought alongside the Four Guardians at the White Tower.

Kassaeos – Former resident of Melida City, later a member of the Haaman Resistance. Killed during the battle of Uncur, but re-born as an Aether. Has since served as a spy and assassin for the Resistance. Participated in the defence of the White Tower alongside The Four Guardians.

Donnal – Leader of the Haaman Resistance in Idris, stationed at Obsidian.

Astrid – Lead Mage under Donnal's command. Former student of Rowan and Seraphine at the White Tower.

Kira – Mokkan, daughter of travelling scholars. Trapped in Haama after her family were killed by wyvernborn. Member of the Haaman Resistance, leader of the Zarvanet cell.

Oliver – Younger brother of Kira.

Kaitlyn – Farmer in northern Idris. Married, mother of five. Farm destroyed in Caelish attack. Current member of the Haaman Resistance.

Lance – Twelve, son of Kaitlyn.

Pia – Six, daughter of Kaitlyn.

Rory – Seven, son of Kaitlyn.

Robb – Member of the Zarvanet Resistance cell under Kira's command.

Jonah – Member of the Zarvanet Resistance cell under Kira's command.

The Empire Of Fire

The Forces Of Cael

Morad Vehnek – Current Lord Marshal of the Caelish armed forces. Youngest General in the history of the Caelish armed forces. Inherited the Lord Marshal position at twenty five.

Ulan Vehnek – Former Lord Marshal of the Caelish armed forces and former First Minister of Haama, until his death. Known as the Defender Of Va'Kael. Writer of most of the tax laws in Haama and all of the security laws, that are still referred to today. **Died of natural causes**, succeeded by Morad Vehnek.

Kallus Vehnek – Former Lord Marshal of the Caelish armed forces. Known as the Liberator Of Haama. Chief strategist and general during the Cael-Haama war, personally led campaigns in The Maldane Reach, Idris, Melida City and The Mountain Cities. **Killed during the Battle Of Uncur**, succeeded by Ulan Vehnek.

Sel Kelad – General, commander of the Caelish armed forces in Haama. Killed during the Battle Of Uncur, later reborn as an Aether. Long serving veteran of the army, has a somewhat lecherous reputation. Member of the Haaman Council Of Ministers, Minister of Defence.

Mora – Former alchemist in The Dragon Breakers clan, later liberated by Morad Vehnek. Husband, Veloso, and son, William, both deceased. Is currently acting (officially) as personal advisor to Vehnek.

Arch Mage Lucian – Head of the Caelish Mages College, inherited position. Long serving member of the college. **Killed during exploratory incursion into the Mountain Cities.**

Arch Mage Miranda – High ranking member of the Caelish Mages College, head of the college in Haama. Also formerly a member of the Haaman Council Of Ministers.

Codesh Ulan – Squad Commander in the Caelish Thirteenth Infantry. Highly decorated and experienced, a veteran of seven tours of duty in Haama.

Yaro – Soldier in the Caelish Thirteenth Infantry, serving under Commander Ulan.

Elizia – Soldier in the Caelish Thirteenth Infantry, formerly assigned to the Black Fleet vessel *Annihilator*.

Berek – Soldier in the Caelish Thirteenth Infantry. Former member of Princess Allessandra's personal guard.

Orso – Soldier in the Caelish Thirteenth Infantry. Former member of Princess Allessandra's personal guard.

Lazar - Soldier in the Caelish Thirteenth Infantry, serving under Commander Ulan.

Mule - Soldier in the Caelish Thirteenth Infantry, serving under Commander Ulan. Slave, earning freedom through service.

Ophelia – Soldier in the Caelish Standing Army. Fought in the Battle Of The Pil Valley, and part of the subsequent rebuilding effort. **Killed during the undead siege of the Pil Valley.**

Moran – Captain in the Caelish Standing Army. Fought in the Battle Of The Pil Valley, and part of the subsequent rebuilding effort. **Killed during the undead siege of the Pil Valley.**

Obrek – Captain of the battleship *Spearhead*.

Nyroshi – Rear Admiral, de-facto leader of the Black Fleet in the aftermath of the Battle Of The Gravestone.

Heztor – Admiral, leader of three Black Fleet Squadrons. Third in command of the Black Fleet.

The Empire Of Fire

The Gold And Silver Thrones

King Alesio – Ruler of Cael, with power of veto over the Haaman Council Of Ministers. Inherited the throne from his mother, Queen Lana. Has reigned for twenty one years. Considered to be a decent ruler by the nobility, but the views of the general populace, particularly in Cael City, are less kind.

Queen Mirell – Chief Adviser to the King. Born to a noble Caelish family, married to Alesio for twenty five years, in an arranged marriage.

Princess Allessandra – Nineteen years old. Heir to the Caelish Throne, current Regent in Haama, officially the figurehead of the Haaman Council Of Ministers. Well regarded by the people of Victory, Maldane, Vissa and Verda for the most part. West of Victory, however, particularly in Idris, she is seen as just another oppressor. Her reputation is beginning to grow slightly in troubled areas.

First Minister Evandro – Chief advisor to Princess Allessandra, but is in reality the de facto head of the Haaman Council Of Ministers. Veteran of the council, also serving under Ulan Vehnek.

Minister Levez – Member of the Haaman Council Of Ministers, Minister of Internal Affairs and Defense. In control of law enforcement and peacekeeping forces in Victory. An inspirational figure in the Caelish armed forces, the first woman to reach the rank of general. **Killed during the Night Of Terror.**

Minister Brynden – Member of the Haaman Council Of Ministers, Minister of Haaman Cultural Affairs. Only Haaman on the ruling council, considered to be a shill.

Minister Carrasco – Member of the Haaman Council Of Ministers, Minister of Foreign Affairs.

Minister Janek – Member of the Haaman Council Of Ministers, Minister of the Treasury. **Missing, presumed dead, after the Night Of Terror.**

Minister Irina – Former member of the Haaman Council Of Ministers, specifically the Minister of Agriculture, before her dismissal by Royal Decree due to inaction regarding the crisis in the Maldane Reach.

Seret – Pilot of Princess Allessandra's personal airship, the *Sand Dancer*.

Helen – Princess Allessandra's steward and tutor. Half Haaman, half Caelish. Arrested and imprisoned by Royal Decree, due to suspected ties to the Haaman Resistance.

Vakesh – Member of the Silver Throne palace guard.

Jenifer – Attendant to Princess Allessandra.

Carla – Attendant to Princess Allessandra.

Eluco – Head of Princess Allessandra's personal guard, recently reassigned from his duties in the city.

The Dead Men (and other clans)

Ydra – Clan chief of the Dead Men. Former student at the White Tower, but left due to conflicts regarding her self-study of necromancy, and after an accident that claimed the life of another student. Formed the Dead Men from the remnants of clans that had been destroyed and settled in Vash. Fought alongside the Four Guardians at the White Tower. Responsible for the ghoul crisis in Vash.

Vargas – Right hand to Ydra, one of the founding members of the Dead Men. Fought alongside the Four Guardians at the White Tower. **Killed in the Pil Valley Massacre**

Rihd – Forward scout for the Dead Men, also responsible for the clan's stables. **Killed in the Pil Valley Massacre**

Kolnil – Forward scout for the Dead Men. Wife and child killed during the ghoul crisis in Vash. **Killed by the Blood Hawks in an incident between clans.**

Boras – Captain of the Maiden's Lock guardsmen. A long and loyal servant, he has defended the town from The Dragon Breakers clan and trained new recruits. Joined the Dead men in their excursion to the Pil Valley. **Killed**

in the Pil Valley Massacre

Darik – Chief of the Carvers clan, self-appointed leader of the clan army in the Pil Valley. **Killed in the Pil Valley Massacre**

Larisa – Chief of the Blood Hawks. **Killed in an engagement with the Caelish in Taeba District**

Matt Waterhouse

A Brief Afterword

Thank you for reading this book, and this series. It has been a ten year journey from the Battle Of Melida City to Cael and Haama standing together at a monument to peace.

The series has undergone many changes while it was being written. Elements have been added and taken away. War has given way to a chance for something better, something with more possibilities, something that we need a lot more of in our world as well as on Planar.

I have never wanted The Four Guardians to be a way to weave in any kind of political statement, as some writers do, and make a point to do. I disagree with the notion that everything is political, or that everything has to be political. All I have ever wanted The Four Guardians to be is a good story, and I hope it has ended up being that to you, the individual who took a chance on an independent author with dreams of airships and dragons.

For me, a story is a new world to explore, but not to get lost in. Building a world where a cast of characters, and indeed several casts of characters can inhabit, takes a lot of hard work outside of the novels, but it's work that needs to be done to add flavour. I hope that it has been a flavourful world for you, the reader, to get your teeth into. I hope that the characters have spoken for themselves, and told their own stories well. I hope they have told the story of the evolution of Cael and Haama well.

The Four Guardians has come to an end, but Planar remains. It's a big world, with many stories to tell.

I will return to Planar in the future, and many other worlds besides, and I hope you'll be there with me on the journey.

Artists before ideologues, always and forever.

Matt

The Empire Of Fire

Printed in Great Britain
by Amazon